"Several members [...]
killed in simulations have [...]

Something Orlando had long expected was now confirmed. He felt a cold lump in his stomach. "So what good will figuring out the gates do us?"

The stranger gave him a hard look, then turned his eyes back to his figures. "It will allow us perhaps to stay a step ahead of the worst destruction—to stay alive as long as possible. Because otherwise there is no hope at all. The Ceremony is coming, whatever it is. The Grail Brotherhood have launched their endgame, and we have nothing yet with which to counter it."

Orlando looked at the man, who seemed to have stepped through some mental gateway of his own and was already miles away. Little yellow monkeys stirred uneasily on Orlando's shoulder.

We're going to get herded like animals, he could not help thinking. *From world to world until there isn't anywhere else to run. Then the killing will really start.*

Praise for OTHERLAND

"On an epic scale and most impressive of all is *OTHERLAND*, a big colorful novel full of real-world conspiracy and virtual reality wonders, with characters worth caring about."
—*Locus*

"This is the best thing Williams has ever done, and it deserves attention, time, praise. More, it deserves to be read."
—*The Magazine of Fantasy and Science Fiction*

"Exciting . . . intricately plotted international adventure and suspense thriller set in the near future." —*Library Journal*

"Epic in scope and size, this near-future cyberspace adventure has likable characters, heinous villains, a plethora of classical references and a slew of powerful action sequences that propel its many-tiered plot forward. . . . Williams fills his pages with the sort of stories and characters that readers of epic fantasy are sure to love."
—*Publishers Weekly*

"The sheer breadth of Williams' knowledge and the richness of his imagination make this book, like its predecessors, a complex and slow-paced feast. Otherland still remains the state of the art in integrating virtual reality and folklore into a single comprehensive narrative."
—*Booklist*

"Once again, Williams displays remarkable talent in making the unbelievable seem more than plausible. The many virtual worlds he creates in Otherland offer entertainment, insights, and commentary on a near-future Earth that is often downright scary simply because it seems so familiar—in a bad sort of way. The author manages to portray a callous, uncaring society that still has concerned and unselfish citizens. Tad Williams is a master of description. Scenes seem to leap off the page, grab you by the collar, and then pull you into the story."
—*Science Fiction Weekly*—www.scifi.com/sfw

Praise for OTHERLAND

"The ultimate virtual-reality saga, borrowing motifs from cyberpunk, mythology, and world history."
—*San Francisco Chronicle*

"With *River of Blue Fire*, Tad Williams has done something amazing. Not only has he made the second volume of a vast SF epic enjoyable and exciting, he has also made the reviewer itch to read the third."
—*Interzone*

"OTHERLAND has true speculative grandeur . . . sticks in your head like Zen toffee."
—*Time Out*

"This sequel to *OTHERLAND: City of Golden Shadow* delivers a kaleidoscopic array of dreamscapes and nightmare worlds that form a setting for a complex tale of conspiracy and betrayal. Williams displays a prodigious talent for spinning multiple variations on a theme as he alternates between real and virtual worlds."
—*Library Journal*

"One has the powerful sense, reading this novel, of a writer at the peak of his craft, in absolute control of his material. There are no unlikely coincidences, implausible reversals, awkward juxtapositions, or obvious plot devices. There is only the story—smooth, organic, and completely enthralling. I suspect that in OTHERLAND we're witnessing the birth of a classic, one of the "must reads" for future generations of SF/fantasy fans."
—*SF Site*—www.sfsite.com

OTHERLAND

Volume Three

MOUNTAIN OF BLACK GLASS

TAD WILLIAMS

DAW BOOKS, INC.

DONALD A. WOLLHEIM, FOUNDER

375 Hudson Street, New York, NY 10014

ELIZABETH R. WOLLHEIM

SHEILA E. GILBERT

PUBLISHERS

www.dawbooks.com

This is still dedicated to you-know-who,
even if he doesn't.
Maybe we can keep this a secret
all the way to the final volume.

The list of the Kind, the Helpful, and the Patient who have contributed to the OTHERLAND books now includes the following excellent souls: Barbara Cannon, Aaron Castro, Nick Des Barres, Debra Euler, Arthur Ross Evans, Amy Fodera, Sean Fodera, Jo-Ann Goodwin, Deb Grabien, Nic Grabien, Jed Hartmann, Tim Holman, Nick Itsou, John Jarrold, Katharine Kerr, Ulrike Killer, M. J. Kramer, Jo and Phil Knowles, Mark Kreighbaum, LES.., Bruce Lieberman, Mark McCrum, Joshua Milligan, Hans-Ulrich Möhring, Eric Neuman, Peter Stampfel, Mitch Wagner, Michael Whelan, and my friends on the Tad Williams Listserve and the message boards of the Tad Williams Fan Page and the Memory, Sorrow and Thorn Interactive Thesis.

As always, I am especially grateful for the support and encouragement of my wife Deborah Beale, my agent Matt Bialer, and my editors Sheila Gilbert and Betsy Wollheim.

Confusion to our enemies!

For more information, visit the
Tad Williams website at:
http://www.tadwilliams.com

OTHERLAND: City of Golden Shadow Synopsis

Wet, terrified, with only the companionship of trench-mates *Finch* and *Mullet* to keep him sane, *Paul Jonas* seems no different than any of thousands of other foot soldiers in World War I. But when he abruptly finds himself alone on an empty battlefield except for a tree that grows up into the clouds, he begins to doubt that sanity. When he climbs the tree and discovers a castle in the clouds, a woman with wings like a bird, and her terrifying giant guardian, his insanity seems confirmed. But when he awakens back in the trenches, he finds he is clutching one of the bird-woman's feathers.

In South Africa, in the middle of the twenty-first century, *Irene "Renie" Sulaweyo* has problems of her own. Renie is an instructor of virtual engineering whose newest student, *!Xabbu,* is one of the desert Bushmen, a people to whom modern technology is very alien. At home she is a surrogate mother to her young brother, *Stephen,* who is obsessed with exploring the virtual parts of the world communication network—the "net"—and Renie spends what little spare time she has holding her family together. Her widowed father *Long Joseph* only seems interested in finding his next drink.

Like most children, Stephen is entranced by the forbidden, and although Renie has already saved him once from a disturbing virtual nightclub named Mister J's, Stephen returns to the net. By the time Renie discovers what he has done, Stephen has fallen into a coma. The doctors cannot explain it, but Renie is certain something has happened to him online.

American *Orlando Gardiner* is only a little older than Renie's brother, but he is a master of several online domains, and because of a serious medical condition, spends most of his time in the online identity of *Thargor,* a barbarian warrior. But when in the midst of one of his adventures Orlando is given a glimpse of a golden city unlike anything else he has ever seen on the net, he is so distracted that his Thargor character is killed. Despite this terrible loss, Orlando cannot shake his fascination with the golden city, and with the support of his software agent *Beezle Bug* and the reluctant help of his online friend *Fredericks,* he is determined to locate the golden city.

Meanwhile, on a military base in the United States, a little girl named *Christabel Sorensen* pays secret visits to her friend, *Mr. Sellars,* a strange, scarred old man. Her parents have forbidden her to see him, but she likes the old man and the stories he tells, and he seems much more pathetic than frightening. She does not know that he has very unusual plans for her.

As Renie gets to know !Xabbu the Bushman better, and to appreciate his calm good nature and his outsider's viewpoint on modern life, she comes to rely on him more and more in her quest to discover what has happened to her brother. She and Xabbu sneak into the online nightclub, Mr. J's. The place is as bad as she feared, with guests indulging themselves in all manner of virtual unpleasantness, but nothing seems like it could have actually physically harmed her brother until they are drawn into a terrifying encounter with a virtual version of the Hindu death-goddess Kali. !Xabbu is overcome, and Renie, too, is almost overwhelmed by Kali's subliminal hypnotics, but with the help of a mysterious figure whose simulated body (his "sim") is a blank, with no features at all, she manages to get herself and !Xabbu out of Mister J's. Before she goes offline, the figure gives her some data in the form of a golden gem.

Back (apparently) in World War I, Paul Jonas escapes from his squadron and makes a run for freedom through the dangerous no-man's-land between the lines. As rain falls and shells explode, Paul struggles through mud and corpses, only to find he has crossed over into some nether-region, stranger even than his castle dream— a flat, misty emptiness. A shimmering golden light appears, and Paul is drawn to it, but before he can step into its glow, his two friends from the trenches appear and demand that he return with them. Weary and confused, he is about to surrender, but as they come closer he sees that Finch and Mullet no longer appear even remotely human, and he flees into the golden light.

In the 21st Century, the oldest and perhaps richest man in the world is named *Felix Jongleur.* His physical body is all but dead, and he spends his days in a virtual Egypt he has built for himself, where he reigns over all as *Osiris,* the god of Life and Death. His chief servant, both in the virtual and real world, is a half-Aboriginal serial murderer who has named himself *Dread,* who combines a taste for hunting humans with a strange extrasensory ability to manipulate electronic circuitry that allows him to blank security cameras and otherwise avoid detection. Jongleur discovered Dread years before, and helped to nurture the young man's power, and has made him his chief assassin.

Jongleur/Osiris is also the leader of a group of some of the world's most powerful and wealthy people, the *Grail Brotherhood,* who have built for themselves a virtual universe unlike any other— the Grail Project, also called Otherland. (This latter name comes from an entity known as the "Other" which has some important involvement with the Grail Project network—an artificial intelligence or something even stranger. This powerful force is largely in the control of Jongleur, but it is the only thing in the world that the old man fears.)

The Grail Brotherhood are arguing among themselves, upset that the mysterious Grail Project is so slow to come to fruition. They have all invested billions in it, and waited a decade or more of their lives. Led by the American technology baron *Robert Wells,* they grow restive about Jongleur's leadership and his secrets, like the nature of the Other.

Jongleur fights off a mutiny, and orders his minion Dread to prepare a neutralization mission against one of the Grail members who has already left the Brotherhood.

Back in South Africa, Renie and her student !Xabbu are shaken by their narrow escape from the virtual nightclub known as Mister J's, and more certain than ever that there is some involvement between the club and her brother's coma. But when she examines the data-object the mysterious figure gave her, it opens into an amazingly realistic image of a golden city. Renie and !Xabbu seek the help of Renie's former professor, *Dr. Susan Van Bleeck,* but she is unable to solve the mystery of the city, or even tell for certain if it is an actual place. The doctor decides to contact someone else she knows for help, a researcher named *Martine Desroubins*. But even as Renie and the mysterious Martine make contact for the first time, Dr. Van Bleeck is attacked in her home and savagely beaten, and all her equipment destroyed. Renie rushes to the hospital, but after pointing Renie in the direction of a friend, Susan dies, leaving Renie both angry and terrified.

Meanwhile Orlando Gardiner, the ill teenager in America, is hot in pursuit of the golden city that he saw while online, so much so that his friend Fredericks begins to worry about him. Orlando has always been odd—he has a fascination with death-experience simulations that Fredericks can't understand—but his current behavior seems excessive. When Orlando announces they are going to the famous hacker-node known as TreeHouse, Fredericks' worst fears are confirmed.

TreeHouse is the last preserve of everything anarchic about the net, a place where no rules dictate what people can do or how they must appear. But although Orlando finds TreeHouse fascinating, and discovers some unlikely allies in the form of a group of hacker children named the *Wicked Tribe* (whose virtual guise is a troop of tiny winged yellow monkeys) his attempts to discover the origins of the golden-city vision arouse suspicion, and he and Fredericks are forced to flee.

Meanwhile Renie and !Xabbu, with the help of Martine Desroubins, have also come to TreeHouse, in pursuit of an old, retired hacker named *Singh,* Susan Van Bleeck's friend. When they find him, he tells them that he is the last of a group of specialist programmers who built the security system for a mysterious network nicknamed "Otherland," and that his companions have been dying in mysterious circumstances. He is the last one alive.

Renie, !Xabbu, Singh, and Martine decide they must break into the Otherland system to discover what secret is worth the lives of Singh's comrades and children like Renie's brother.

Paul Jonas has escaped from his World War I trench only to find himself seemingly unstuck in time and space. Largely amnesiac, he wanders into a world where a White Queen and a Red Queen are in conflict, and finds himself pursued again by the Finch and Mullet figures. With the help of a boy named *Gally* and a long-winded, egg-shaped bishop, Paul escapes them, but his pursuers murder Gally's children friends. A huge creature called a Jabberwock provides a diversion, and Paul and Gally dive into a river.

When they surface, the river is in a different world, a strange, almost comical version of Mars, full of monsters and English gentleman-soldiers. Paul again meets the bird-woman from his castle dream, now named *Vaala,* but this time she is the prisoner of a Martian overlord. With the help of mad adventurer *Hurley Brummond,* Paul saves the woman. She recognizes Paul, too, but does not know why. When the Finch and Mullet figures appear again, she flees. Attempting to catch up to her, Paul crashes a stolen flying ship, sending himself and Gally to what seems certain doom. After a strange dream in which he is back in the cloud-castle, menaced by Finch and Mullet in their strangest forms yet, he wakes without Gally in the midst of the Ice Age, surrounded by Neandertal hunters.

Meanwhile in South Africa, Renie and her companions are being hunted by mysterious strangers, and are forced to flee their home. With the help of Martine (whom they still know only as a voice) Renie, along with !Xabbu, her father, and Dr. Van Bleeck's assistant *Jeremiah,* find an old, mothballed robot-plane base in the Drakensberg Mountains. They renovate a pair of V-tanks (virtuality immersion vats) so Renie and !Xabbu can go online for an indefinite period, and prepare for their assault on Otherland.

Back on the army base in America, little Christabel is convinced to help the burned and crippled Mr. Sellars with a complex plan that is only revealed as an escape attempt when he disappears from his house, setting the whole base (including Christabel's security chief father) on alert. Christabel has cut what seems an escape hole in the base's perimeter fence (with the help of a homeless boy from outside), but only she knows that Mr. Sellars is actually hiding in a network of tunnels beneath the base, free now to continue his mysterious "task."

In the abandoned facility under the Drakensberg Mountains, Renie and her companions enter the tanks, go online, and break into Otherland. They survive a terrifying interaction with the Other which seems to be the network's security system, in which Singh dies of a heart attack, and find that the network is so incredibly realistic that at first they cannot believe it is a virtual environment. The experience is strange in many other ways. Martine has a body for the first time, !Xabbu has been given the form of a baboon, and most importantly, they can find no way to take themselves offline again. Renie and the others discover that they are in an artificial South American country. When they reach the golden city at the heart of it, the city they have been seeking so long, they are captured, and discover that they are the prisoners of *Bolivar Atasco,* a man involved with the Grail Brotherhood and with the building of the Otherland network from the start.

Back in America, Orlando's friendship with Fredericks has survived the twin revelations that Orlando is dying of a rare premature-aging disease, and that Fredericks is in fact a girl. They are unexpectedly linked to Renie's hacker friend Singh by the Wicked Tribe just as Singh is opening his connection to the Grail network, and drawn through into Otherland. After their own horrifying encounter with the Other, Orlando and Fredericks also become Atasco's prisoners. But when they are brought to the great man, along with Renie's company and others, they find that it is not Atasco who has gathered them, but Mr. Sellars—revealed now as the strange blank sim who helped Renie and !Xabbu escape from Mister J's.

Sellars explains that he has lured them all here with the image of the golden city—the most discreet method he could devise, because their enemies, the Grail Brotherhood, are so vastly powerful and remorseless. Sellars explains that Atasco and his wife were once members of the Brotherhood, but quit when their questions about the network were not answered. Sellars then tells how he discovered that the secret Otherland network has a mysterious but undeniable connection to the illness of thousands of children like Renie's brother Stephen. Before he can explain more, the sims of Atasco and his wife go rigid and Sellars' own sim disappears.

In the real world, Jongleur's murderous minion Dread has begun his attack on the Atascos' fortified Colombian island home, and after breaking through the defenses, has killed both Atascos. He then uses his strange abilities—his "twist"—to tap into their data lines, discovers Sellars' meeting, and orders his assistant *Dulcinea Anwin* to take over the incoming line of one of the Atascos' guests—the online group that includes Renie and her friends—so he can take on the identity of that usurped guest, leaving Dread hidden as a spy in the midst of Renie and friends.

Sellars reappears in the Atascos' virtual world and begs Renie and the others to flee into the network while he tries to hide their presence. They are to look for a man named Jonas, he tells them, a mysterious virtual prisoner Sellars has helped escape from the Brotherhood. Renie and company make their way onto the river and out of the Atascos' simulation, then through an electrical blue glow into the next simworld. Panicked and overwhelmed by too much input, Martine finally reveals her secret to Renie: she is blind.

Their boat has become a giant leaf. Overhead, a dragonfly the size of a fighter jet skims into view.

Back in the mountain fortress, in the real world, Jeremiah and Renie's father Long Joseph can only watch the silent V-tanks, wonder, and wait.

OTHERLAND: River of Blue Fire Synopsis

Paul Jonas still seems to be adrift in time and space. He has recovered most of his memory, but the last few years of his life remain a blank. He has no idea why he is being tossed from world to world, pursued by the two creatures he first knew as *Finch* and *Mullet,* and he still does not know the identity of the mysterious woman he keeps encountering, and who has appeared to him even in dreams.

He has survived a near-drowning only to find himself in the Ice Age, where he has fallen in with a tribe of Neandertals. The mystery woman appears to him in another dream, and tells him that to reach her he must find "a black mountain that reaches to the sky."

Not all of the cave dwellers welcome the unusual stranger; one picks a quarrel that results in Paul being abandoned in the frozen wilderness. He survives an attack by giant cave hyenas, but falls into the icy river once more.

Others are having just as difficult and painful a time as Paul, although they are better informed. *Renie Sulaweyo* originally had set out to solve the mystery of her brother *Stephen's* coma with her friend and former student *!Xabbu,* a Bushman from the Okavango Delta. With the help of a blind researcher named *Martine Desroubins,* they have found their way into Otherland, the world's biggest and strangest virtual reality network, constructed by a cabal of powerful men and women who call themselves *The Grail Brotherhood.* Summoned by the mysterious *Mr. Sellars,* Renie meets several others who have been affected by the Grail Brotherhood's machinations—*Orlando Gardiner,* a dying teenager, and his friend *Sam Fredericks* (who Orlando has only recently discovered is a girl), a woman named *Florimel,* a flamboyant character who calls himself *Sweet William,* a Chinese grandmother named *Quan Li,* and a sullen young man in futuristic armor who uses the handle *T4b.* But something has trapped them within the network, and the nine companions have been forced to flee from one virtual world to the next on a river of blue fire—a virtual path that leads through all the Otherland simulation worlds.

The newest simworld is much like the real world, except that Renie and her companions are less than a hundredth of their normal size. They are menaced by the local insects, as well as larger creatures like fish and birds, and the members of the group become separated. Renie and !Xabbu are rescued by scientists who are using the simulation to study insect life from an unusual perspective. The scientists soon discover that, like Renie and !Xabbu, they are trapped online. Renie and !Xabbu meet a strange man named *Kunohara,* who owns the bug world simulation, but claims he is not part of the Grail Brotherhood. Kunohara poses a pair of cryptic riddles to them, then vanishes. When a horde of (relatively gigantic) army ants attacks the research station, most of the scientists are killed and Renie and !Xabbu barely escape from a monstrous praying mantis.

As they flee back to the river in one of the researchers' aircraft, they see Orlando and Fredericks being swept down the river on a leaf. As they attempt to rescue them, Renie and !Xabbu are pulled through the river gateway with them, but the two groups wind up in different simulations.

Meanwhile, in the real world outside the network, other people are being drawn into the widening Otherland mystery. *Olga Pirofsky,* the host of a children's net show, begins to suffer from terrible headaches. She suspects that her online activities might have something to do with it, and in the course of investigating her problem, begins to learn of the apparently net-related illness that has struck so many children (including Renie's brother.) Olga's research also draws the attention of a lawyer named *Catur Ramsey,* who is investigating the illness on behalf of the parents both of Orlando and Fredericks, since in the real world both teenagers have been in a coma ever since their entrance into the Otherland network.

John Wulgaru, who calls himself *Dread,* and whose hobbies include serial murder, has been an effective if not one hundred percent loyal employee of the incredibly wealthy *Felix Jongleur,* the man who heads the Grail Brotherhood (and who spends most of his time in his Egyptian simulation, wearing the guise of the god Osiris.) But in the course of killing an ex-member of the Brotherhood at Jongleur's orders, Dread has discovered the existence of the Otherland network, and has even taken over one of the sims in Renie's marooned company. As his master Jongleur is caught up in the final arrangements for the Otherland network— whose true purpose is still known only to the Brotherhood—Dread busies himself with this new and fascinating puzzle. As a spy among Sellars' recruits, Dread is now traveling through the network and trying to discover its secrets. But unlike those in Sellars' ragtag group, Dread's life is not at risk: he can go offline whenever he wishes. He recruits a software specialist named *Dulcie Anwin* to help him run the puppet sim. Dulcie is fascinated by her boss, but unsettled by him, too, and begins to wonder if she is in deeper than she wants to be.

Meanwhile, a bit of Dread's past has surfaced. In Australia, a detective named *Calliope Skouros* is trying to solve a seemingly unexceptional murder. Some of the terrible things done to the victim's body are reminiscent of an Aboriginal myth-creature, the Woolagaroo. Detective Skouros becomes convinced that there is some strange relationship between Aboriginal myths and the young woman's death she is investigating.

Back in the Otherland network, Renie and !Xabbu find themselves in a weird, upside-down version of the Oz story, set in the dreary Kansas of the original tale's opening. The Otherland simulations seem to be breaking down, or at least growing increasingly chaotic. As Renie and !Xabbu try to escape the evil of Lion and Tinman—who seem to be two more versions of Paul Jonas' Finch and Mullet—they find a pair of unlikely allies, the young and naive *Emily 22813* and a laconic gypsy named *Azador.* Emily later reveals that she is pregnant, and says Azador is the father. Separated from Azador during one of the increasingly frequent "system spasms," they escape Kansas, but to their surprise, Emily (who they had thought was software) travels with them to the next simulation.

Orlando and Fredericks have landed in a very strange world, a kitchen out of an ancient cartoon, populated by creatures sprung from package labels and silverware drawers. They help a cartoon Indian brave search for his stolen child, and after battling cartoon pirates and meeting both a prophetic sleeping woman and an inexplicable force—entities that are really Paul Jonas' mystery woman and the network's apparently sentient operating system, known as *the Other*—they escape the Kitchen and land in a simulation that seems to be ancient Egypt.

Meanwhile, their former companions, the blind woman Martine and the rest of the Sellars' recruits, have hiked out of the bug world to discover themselves in a simulation where the river is made not of water but air, and where the primitive inhabitants fly on wind currents and live in caves along vertical cliffs. Martine and the others name the place Aerodromia, and although they are nervous about trying it at first, they soon discover that they can fly, too. A group of natives invite them to stay in the tribal camp.

Paul Jonas has passed from the Ice Age into something much different. At first, seeing familiar London sights, he believes he has finally found his way home, but soon comes to realize that he is instead traveling through an England almost completely destroyed by Martian attack—it is, in fact, the setting of H. G. Wells' *War of the Worlds*. Paul now realizes that he is traveling not just to worlds separate in time and space, but to some that are actually fictitious. He meets a strange husband and wife called *the Pankies*, who seem to be another guise of his pursuers Finch and Mullet, but offer him no harm. (Paul is also being pursued by a special software program called the *Nemesis* device, but he is not yet aware of it.) Then, when Paul and the Pankies stop at Hampton Court, Paul is led into the maze by a strange man and then shoved through a gateway of glowing light at the maze's center.

On the other side Paul finds himself in the setting of Coleridge's famous poem, *Xanadu*, and the man who brought him there introduces himself as *Nandi Paradivash*. Nandi is a member of a group named *The Circle*, who are working against the Grail Brotherhood. Paul finally learns that he is not insane, nor caught in some kind of dimensional warp, but is rather a prisoner in an incredibly realistic simulation network. But Nandi has no idea why the Brotherhood should be interested enough in Paul—who worked in a museum and remembers his other life as being very ordinary—to pursue him throughout Otherland. Nandi also reveals that all the simulations through which Paul has been traveling belong to one man—Felix Jongleur, the Grail Brotherhood's chairman. Before Nandi can tell him more, they are forced to separate, Nandi pursued by Kublai Khan's troops, Paul passing through another gateway into yet another simworld.

Things are no less complex and confusing in the real world. Renie's and !Xabbu's physical bodies are in special virtual reality tanks in an abandoned South African military base, watched over by *Jeremiah Dako* and Renie's father, *Long Joseph Sulaweyo*. Long Joseph, bored and depressed, sneaks out of the base to go see Renie's brother Stephen, who remains comatose in a Durban hospital, leaving Jeremiah alone inside the base. But when Joseph arrives at the hospital, he is kidnapped at gunpoint and forced into a car.

The mysterious Mr. Sellars lives on a military base, too, but his is in America. *Christabel Sorensen* is a little girl whose father is in charge of base security, and who despite her youth has helped her friend Sellars escape the house arrest her father and others have kept him in for years. Sellars is hiding in old tunnels under the base, his only companion the street urchin *Cho-Cho*. Christabel does not like the boy at all. She worries for the feeble Mr. Sellars' safety, and is torn by guilt for doing something she knows would make her mother and father angry. But when her mother discovers her talking with Sellars through specially modified sunglasses, Christabel is finally in real trouble.

Martine, Florimel, Quan Li, Sweet William, and T4b have been enjoying the flying world, Aerodromia, but things get uncomfortable when a young girl from the tribe is kidnapped. Martine and the rest don't know it, but the girl has been stolen, terrorized, and murdered by Dread, still pretending to be one of Martine's four companions. The people of Aerodromia blame the newcomers for the disappearance, and dump them all into a labyrinth of caverns they call the Place of the Lost, where they find themselves surrounded by mysterious, ghostly presences which Martine, with her heightened nonvisual senses, finds particularly upsetting. The phantoms speak in unison, telling of the "One who is Other," and how he has deserted them instead of taking them across the "White Ocean," as promised. The voices also identify the real names of all Martine's company. The group is fascinated and frightened, and only belatedly realizes that Sweet William has disappeared—evidently to protect the guilty secret of his true identity. Something large and strange—the Other—abruptly enters the darkened Place of the Lost, and Martine and the others flee the horrifying presence. Martine searches desperately for one of the gateways that will allow them to leave the simulation before either the Other or the renegade Sweet William catches them.

At the same time, Orlando and Fredericks discover that the Egyptian simulation is not a straightforward historical recreation, but a mythical version. They meet a wolf-headed god named *Upaut,* who tells them how he and the whole simworld have been mistreated by the chief god, Osiris. Unfortunately, Upaut is not a very bright or stable god, and he interprets Orlando mumbling in his sleep—the result of a dream-conversation Orlando is having with his software agent, *Beezle Bug,* who can only reach him from the real world when he dreams—as a divine directive for him to try to overthrow Osiris. Upaut steals their sword and boat, leaving Orlando and Fredericks stranded in the desert. After many days of hiking along the Nile, they come upon a strange temple filled with some terrible, compelling presence. They cannot escape it. In a dream, Orlando is visited by the mystery woman also seen by Paul Jonas, and she tells them she will give them assistance, but as the temple draws them closer and closer, they find only the *Wicked Tribe,* a group of very young children they had met outside the network, who wear the sim-forms of tiny yellow flying monkeys. Orlando is stunned that this is the help the mystery woman has brought them. The frightening temple continues to draw them nearer.

Paul Jonas has passed from Xanadu to late 16th Century Venice, and soon stumbles into *Gally,* a boy he had met in one of the earlier simulations, and who had traveled with him, but Gally does not remember Paul. Seeking help, the boy brings him to a woman named *Eleanora;* although she cannot explain Gally's missing memories, she reveals that she herself is the former real-world mistress of an organized crime figure who built her this virtual Venice as a gift. Her lover was a member of the Grail Brotherhood, but died too soon to benefit from the immortality machinery they are building, and survives now only as a set of flawed life-recordings. Before Paul can learn more, he discovers that the dreadful Finch and Mullet—*the Twins,* as Nandi named them—have tracked him to Venice: he must flee again, this time with Gally. But before they can reach the gateway that will allow them to escape, they are caught by the Twins. The Pankies also make an appearance, and for a moment the two mirror-pairs face each other, but the Pankies quickly depart, leaving Paul alone to fight the Twins. Gally is killed, and Paul barely escapes with his life. Still trying to fulfill the mystery woman's summons from his Ice Age dream, he travels to a simulation of ancient Ithaca to meet someone called "the weaver." Still shocked and saddened by Gally's death, he learns that in this new simulation he is the famous Greek hero Odysseus, and that the weaver is the hero's wife, Penelope—the mystery woman, again. But at least it seems he will finally get some answers.

Renie and !Xabbu and Emily find that they have escaped Kansas for something much more confusing—a world that does not seem entirely finished, a place with no sun, moon, or weather. They have also inadvertently taken an object from Azador that looks like an ordinary cigarette lighter, but is in fact an access device, a sort of key to the Otherland network, stolen from one of the Grail Brotherhood (*General Daniel Yacoubian,* one of Jongleur's rivals for leadership). While studying the device in the hopes of making it work, !Xabbu manages to open a transmission channel and discovers Martine on the other end, trapped in the Place of the Lost and desperately trying to open a gateway. Together they manage to create a passage for Martine and her party, but when they arrive, believing they are being pursued by a murderous Sweet William, they find that it is William himself who has been fatally injured, and grandmotherly Quan Li who is really the murderer Dread in virtual disguise. His secret revealed, Dread escapes with the access device, leaving Renie and the others stranded, perhaps forever, in this disturbing place.

OTHERLAND

Volume Three

MOUNTAIN OF
BLACK GLASS

Contents

Third

BROKEN GLASS

Fourth

SUNSET ON THE WALLS

Foreword

AS she spoke, the flame of the oil lamp repeatedly drew his eye, a wriggling brightness that in such a still room might have been the only real thing in all the universe. Even her eyes, the wide dark eyes he knew so well, seemed but a detail from a dream. It was almost impossible to believe, but this was unquestionably her, at last. He had found her.

But it couldn't be this simple, Paul Jonas thought. *Nothing else has been.*

And of course, he was right.

At first it did seem as though a door, long closed, had finally opened—or rather, with Paul still reeling from the horror of the boy Gally's death, it seemed he had reached the final round of some particularly drawn-out and incomprehensible contest.

The wife—and, most thought, widow—of long-lost Odysseus had stalled her suitors for some while with the excuse that before considering another marriage she must finish weaving her father-in-law's shroud. Each night, when the suitors had fallen into drunken sleep, she had then secretly unpicked her day's work. Thus, when Paul had come to her in the guise of her husband, he had found her weaving. When she turned from the loom he saw that the design was one of bird shapes—bright-eyed, flare-winged, each individual feather a little miracle of colored thread—

but he had not looked at it long. The mysterious creature who had
come to him in so many guises and in so many dreams, who in
this place wore the form of a tall, slender woman of mature years,
now stood waiting for him.

"There is so much that we must talk about, my long-lost husband—so very much!"

She beckoned him to her stool. When he had lowered himself
onto it, she knelt with careful grace on the stone flags at his feet.
Like everyone else in this place, she smelled of wool and olive
oil and woodsmoke, but she also had a scent that seemed to Paul
particularly her own, a whiff of something flowery and secretive.

Oddly, she did not embrace him, did not even call back the
slave-woman Eurycleia to bring wine or food for her long-lost
husband, but Paul was not disappointed: he was far more interested in answers to his many questions. The lamp flame flickered,
then stabilized, as though the world drew breath and held it. Everything about her called to him, spoke of a life he had lost and was
desperate to regain. He wanted to clutch her to him, but something, perhaps her cool, slightly fearful gaze, prevented it. He was
dizzied by events and did not know where to start.

"What . . . what is your name?"

"Why, Penelope, my lord," she said, a wrinkle of consterna-
tion appearing between her eyebrows. "Has your trip to death's
dusky kingdom robbed you even of your memories? That is sad
indeed."

Paul shook his head. He knew the name of Odysseus' wife already, but he had no interest in playing out a scenario. "But what
is your *real* name? Vaala?"

The look of worry was rapidly becoming something deeper.
She leaned away from him, as though from an animal that might
at any moment turn violent. "Please, my lord, my husband, tell
me what you wish me to say. I do not wish to anger you, for then
your spirit might find no rest at all."

"Spirit?" He reached his hand toward her but she shied away.
"Do you think I'm dead? Look, I'm not—touch me."

Even as she moved gracefully but decisively to avoid him, her
expression suddenly changed, a violent alteration from fear to confusion. A moment later a deep mournfulness came over her—a

look that seemed to have no relationship to the prior reactions. It
was startling to see.

"I have kept you with my womanish worries long enough,"
she said. "The ships strain at their anchor ropes. Bold Agamemnon and Menelaus and the others impatiently await, and you must
sail across the sea to distant Troy."

"What?" Paul could not make sense of what had just happened.
One moment she had been treating him as though he were her
husband's ghost, the next she was trying to hurry him off to the
Trojan War, which must be long over with—otherwise, why was
everyone so surprised to see him still alive? "But I have come
back to you. You said you had much to tell me."

For a moment Penelope's face froze, then thawed into yet another new and quite different expression, this one a mask of pained
bravery. What she said made almost no sense at all. "Please, good
beggar, although I feel certain that Odysseus my husband is dead,
if you can give me any tale at all of his last days, I will see that
you never go hungry again."

It felt as though he had stepped onto what he thought was a
sidewalk only to discover it was a whirling carousel. "Wait—I
don't understand any of this. Don't you know me? You said that
you did. I met you in the giant's castle. We met again on Mars,
when you had wings. Your name was Vaala there."

At first his sometime wife's face curdled into a look of anger,
but then her expression softened. "Poor man," she said tolerantly.
"Shouldering just a few of the many indignities that tormented
my resourceful husband has driven away your wits. I will have my
women find a bed for you, where my cruel suitors will not make
your life a misery. Perhaps in the morning you can offer me better sense." She clapped her hands; the aged Eurycleia appeared
in the doorway. "Find this old man a clean place to sleep, and
give him something to eat and drink."

"Don't do this to me!" Paul leaned forward and clutched at
the hem of her long dress. She jerked away with a momentary
blaze of real fury.

"You go too far! This house is full of armed men who would
be only too happy to kill you in hopes of impressing me."

He clambered to his feet, not certain what to do next. Everything seemed to have crashed down around him. "Do you really

not remember me? Just a few minutes ago you did. My real name is Paul Jonas. Doesn't that mean anything to you?"

Penelope relaxed, but her formal smile was so stiff as to look painful, and for a moment Paul thought he saw something terrified fluttering behind her eyes, a trapped creature struggling for escape. The hidden thing faded; she waved him away and turned back to her tapestry.

Outside the chamber he put his hand on the old woman. "Tell me—do *you* know me?"

"Of course, my lord Odysseus, even in those rags and with your beard so gray." She led him down the narrow stairs to the first floor.

"And how long have I been gone?"

"Twenty terrible years, my lord."

"Then why does my wife think I am someone else? Or think I'm just now leaving for Troy?"

Eurycleia shook her head. She did not seem overly perturbed. "Perhaps her long sorrow has sickened her wits. Or perhaps some god has clouded her vision, so she cannot see you truly."

"Or maybe I'm just doomed," Paul muttered. "Maybe I'm just meant to wander around forever."

The old woman clicked her tongue. "You should be careful of your words, my lord. The gods are always listening."

He lay curled on the packed earth of the kitchen floor. The sun had set and the cold night wind off the ocean crept through the huge, draughty house. The ash and dirt on the floor were more than offset by the welcome heat of the oven, which pulsed out at him through the stone, but even being warm when he might have been outside, chilled to the bone, was not much comfort.

Think it through, he told himself. *Somehow you knew it wouldn't be so easy. The serving woman said, "Maybe a god has clouded her vision." Could that be it? Some kind of spell or something?* There were so many possibilities within this world, and he had so little real information—only what Nandi Paradivash had told him, with many deliberate omissions. Paul had never been much good at solving puzzles or playing games as a child, far happier just daydreaming, but now he felt like cursing his childhood self for slackness.

No one else was going to do it for him, though.

As Paul thought about what he had become—a thinking game-piece, perhaps the only one, on this great Homeric Greece game board—a realization came to him, muffled and yet profound as distant thunder. *I'm doing this all wrong. I'm thinking about this simworld like it's real, even though it's just an invention, a toy. But I need to think about the invention itself. What are the rules of how things work? How does this network actually function? Why am I Odysseus, and what's supposed to happen to me here?*

He struggled to summon up his Greek lessons from school days. If this place, this simworld, revolved around the long journey of Homer's Odyssey, then the king's house on Ithaca could only come into it at the beginning of the tale, when the wanderer was about to leave, or at the end when the wanderer had returned. And as realistic as this place was—as all the simworlds he had visited were—it was still not real: perhaps every possible contingency could not be programmed in. Perhaps even the owners of the Otherland network had limits to their budgets. That meant there would have to be a finite number of responses, limited in part by what the Puppets could understand. Somehow, Paul's appearance here had triggered several contradictory reactions in the woman currently called Penelope.

But if he was triggering conflicting responses, why had the servingwoman Eurycleia immediately recognized him as Odysseus returned in disguise from his long exile, and then never deviated from that recognition? That was pretty much as it had been in the original, if his long-ago studies had served him properly, so why should the servant react correctly and the lady of the house not?

Because they're a different order of being, he realized. *There aren't just two types of people in these simulations, the real and the false—there's at least one more, a third sort, even if I don't yet know what it is. Gally was one of those third types. The bird-woman, Vaala or Penelope or whatever she's really called—she must be another.*

It made sense, as far as he could think it through. The Puppets, who were completely part of the simulations, never had any doubt about who they were or what was happening around them, and apparently never left the simulations for which they had been created. In fact, Puppets like the old serving woman behaved as though they and the simulations were both completely real. They were also well-programmed; like veteran actors, they would ignore any slip-ups or uncertainties on the part of the human participants.

At the other end of the spectrum, the true humans, the Citizens, would always know that they were inside a simulation.

But there was apparently a third type like Gally and the bird-woman who seemed to be able to move from one simworld to another, but retained differing amounts of memory and self-understanding in each environment. So what were they? Impaired Citizens? Or more advanced Puppets, some kind of new model that were not simulation-specific?

A thought struck him then, and even the smoldering warmth from the oven could not stop his skin pimpling with sudden chill.

God help me, that describes Paul Jonas as well as it describes them. What makes me so sure I'm a real person?

THE bright morning sun of Ithaca crept into almost every corner of the Wanderer's house, rousting the usurped king from his bed by the oven not long after dawn. Paul had little urge to linger, in any case—knowing the kitchen women were virtual did not much soften their harsh words about his raggedness and dirtiness.

Old Eurycleia, despite her workday already having reached full gallop as she saw to the demands of the suitors and the rest of the household, made sure that he received something to eat—she would have brought him far more than the chunk of bread and cup of heavily watered wine he accepted, but he saw no purpose in rousing envy or suspicion in the household. He found himself chewing the crusty bread with some pleasure, which made him wonder how his real body was being fed. Despite the frugal meal and his best efforts to be unobtrusive, several of the maids had already begun to whisper that they should have one or another of their favorites among Penelope's suitors drive this filthy old man out of the house. Paul did not want to fight with any of the interlopers—even assuming he had been given the strength and stamina to outduel one of those strapping warriors, he was tired and depressed and wanted no part of any more struggles. In an effort to avoid controversy entirely he took his heel of bread and went out to walk on the headlands and think.

*   *   *

Whatever else the creators of this simulation might have planned, Paul thought, they had done a very fine job of capturing the Mediterranean world's astonishingly clear, bright light. Even early on this hot morning the rocks along the cliff seemed as crisply pale as new paper, the reflected glare so fierce that he could not stand too close to them. Even with the sun behind him, he had to shade his eyes.

I've got to learn the rules of this thing, he thought as he watched the seagulls wheeling below him. *Not Greece, but the whole network. I have to make sense of it or I'll just wander forever. The other version of Vaala, the one that spoke first in my dream, then through the Neandertal child, said that I had to get to a black mountain.*

"It reaches to the sky," she had told him, "covers up the stars. . . . That is where all your answers are." But when he had asked her how he could find it, she had answered, "I don't know. But I might know, if you can find me." And then the dream-version of Vaala had sent him here, to search for what seemed herself in another guise—but that was where the whole thing fell apart completely. How could she know . . . but *not* know? What could such a thing mean? Unless, as he had guessed the night before, she was neither normal person nor simulation, but something else. Perhaps she had meant that in different simulations she had access to different memories?

But this Penelope version of her doesn't seem to know anything at all, he thought sourly. *She doesn't even know she's a version—doesn't know that she's the one who sent me here.*

He stooped and picked up a flat rock and skimmed it out into the stiff ocean breeze; it splashed long seconds later at the base of the rough cliffs. The wind shifted direction and jostled him a step nearer the precipice, still healthily distant from the edge but enough to make his groin tighten at the thought of the long fall.

There's so much I don't know. Can I really die from something that happens here in a simulation? The golden harp told me that even though nothing was real, things could hurt or kill me. If this is all a simulation network, the message was right about the first part, so I should assume it told the truth about the second part, too, even though it doesn't make much sense. Nandi certainly acted as though we were both in real danger in Xanadu. . . .

A skirl of primitive music came from somewhere behind him, breaking his concentration. He sighed. Questions and more questions, seemingly without end. What was that other Greek myth, a many-headed, dragonlike creature—the hydra? Cut off a head and two more would grow from the stump, wasn't that how it had gone? He would have thought that meeting Nandi and the Venetian woman Eleanora would erase all the mysteries that plagued him, but the more he chopped away at the questions, the more rapidly he created a dense bouquet of new hydra-heads. It was like some tangled modernist tale about conspiracy theories gone out of control, a fable about the danger of paranoid thinking.

The flute shrilled again like a child trying to attract his attention. He frowned at the distraction—but it was all distraction these days. Even the messages apparently meant to help him were dubious. A dream-version of Vaala had sent him here to meet another version of herself that did not know him. He had received assistance from the golden harp he had found in a giant's castle, but it had not actually spoken to him until he was in the Ice Age, where the harp had become a gem.

So was the castle a dream, or another simulation? And who sent me that harp-message in the first place? If it was Nandi's people—they're the only ones I've heard of who might try to warn someone like me—then why hadn't Nandi ever heard of me? And who is this bird-woman Vaala, and why am I so bloody, painfully certain I know her?

Paul took the last of his bread from a fold of his tattered robe, chewed and swallowed it, then continued along the hillside, wandering in the general direction of the insistent flute. As he followed the hill path down, the music was submerged in an angry baying which rapidly grew louder. It had only just begun to intrude itself on his distracted thoughts when a quartet of huge mastiffs burst into view, speeding up the trail toward him in full cry, red mouths wide, voices full of excitement and bloodlust. He halted in surprise and sudden fear and took a few steps backward, but the hill behind him was steep and without shelter and he knew he could not hope to outrun these four-legged monsters.

As he bent, clawing the ground for a branch to use as a weapon and slow down the inevitable for at least a few moments, a loud whistle shrilled across the hillside. The dogs pulled up a dozen meters from Paul, circling and barking angrily, but came no closer. A lean young man appeared from around a stone farther down the hill and examined Paul briefly, then whistled again. The dogs snarled as they retreated, unhappy at giving up a kill. When they reached the young man he gave the nearest a light smack on the flank and sent them all trotting back down the slope. He beckoned for Paul to follow, then lifted a flute to his lips, turned, and sauntered back down the path after the swiftly-vanishing dogs, tootling away merrily if not exactly musically.

Paul had no idea what any of this was about, but was not about to offend someone who was on good terms with such large, hostile animals. He followed.

A flat area between the hills came into view around the next bend, a great open space with a few buildings on it, but what Paul at first took for another large dwelling, a crude version of the palace upon the hill, turned out to be a compound for animals—specifically swine. A large walled area had been sectioned off into sties, and each open-roofed apartment had a contingent of several dozen pigs. Hundreds more lolled around outside the sties in the wide space between the compound's walls, as indolent as rich tourists on a Third World beach.

The young man with the dogs had disappeared somewhere, but an older man with a slight limp now appeared from the shade of one of the compound's higher walls, the sandal he was repairing still dangling from his broad hand. His beard was almost completely gray, but his heavy upper body and corded arms suggested he retained most of the vigor of his younger days.

"Come, old fellow," he called to Paul. "You were lucky that my boy was with the dogs when they went after you. I'm glad of it, too, of course—don't need any more problems around here, and it would have been a shame to see you chewed up and swallowed. Come have some wine with me, and you can give me any news you have."

This man and his speech rang a bell of some kind for Paul, but he could not tell what it reminded him of; once again he cursed himself for having paid so little attention to Homer when he'd had it, first at Cranleigh, then again at university.

Still, how was I supposed to know? I mean, yes, if someone had warned me, "Say, Jonas, one day you're going to get chucked into a live version of The Odyssey *and have to fight for your life there," I would probably have hit the books a bit harder. But who could have guessed?*

"You are kind," he said aloud to what he guessed must be the chief swineherd—the pork production foreman, as it were. "I didn't mean to upset your dogs. I'm afraid I'm a stranger here."

"A stranger? From that ship that landed at Phorcys' Cove, I'll be bound. Well come, then—all the more reason. Never let it be said that Eumaeus did not offer hospitality to a stranger."

Paul felt sure he had heard the name, but simply knowing he should recognize it was absolutely no help at all.

The swineherd's hut was modestly appointed, but it was still pleasant to get out of the sun, already quite hot long before noon, and to let the dry dust settle. The watered wine Eumaeus offered was also welcome. Paul took a long swallow, then a second, before he felt ready to make conversation.

"So tell me the truth, stranger," Eumaeus said. "You are from that Phaecian ship that stopped in the cove barely long enough to take on fresh water from the spring, are you not?"

Paul hesitated, then nodded. There had definitely been something in *The Odyssey* about the Phaecians—he remembered that much, at least.

"You come at a sad time, if this is your first visit to Ithaca." Eumaeus belched and rubbed at his stomach. "In other days I could have offered to dine you on fatted hog, but all I have to spare is suckling pig, and a lean, small one at that. The suitors who are encamped in my master's house are emptying his larders. Still, beggars and strangers come in Zeus' name, and you will not go away hungry."

The swineherd continued to ramble on in this vein for no little time, emphasizing the viciousness of Penelope's unwanted suitors and the shame of how the gods had treated his master, Odysseus. Paul dimly remembered that he was supposed to be disguised in some way—one of the gods had changed Odysseus' face so he could return to his home without his enemies realizing it was him—and wondered why the slave Eurycleia had been able to recognize him but the swineherd could not.

After perhaps an hour of preliminary chat his host slaughtered two young pigs and cut up their flesh to roast on sticks over the fire. Despite the swineherd's kindness, Paul found himself growing impatient and angry. *I could spend weeks wandering around here, with all the noble old servants rhapsodizing about their noble missing master, but meanwhile I'm going to be sleeping on the floor in my own house.* He caught himself and grinned tightly. *In the house of the character I'm playing. But the fact remains, I have to do something.*

Eumaeus served him barley meal and skewers of roasted pork. As he ate, Paul made desultory conversation, but he did not remember enough of the epic to be able to say much that interested the swineherd. After a while, assisted by the food, several generous bowls full of wine, and the afternoon heat, he and Eumaeus lapsed into a surfeited silence not much different than that of the animals outside. A dim memory tickled at Paul.

"Doesn't the king have a son? Tele . . . something?"

"Telemachus?" Eumaeus belched gently and scratched himself. "Yes, a fine lad, the very image of his father. He has gone to search for our poor Odysseus—I believe he has snuck away to see Menelaus, his father's comrade at Troy." As he went on to describe Telemachus' ill-treatment at the hands of the suitors, Paul could not help wondering if the son's absence was part of the simworld's scenario, or whether it might somehow be more personal. Was it supposed to have been Gally? The thought was painfully sobering, and for a moment Paul was looking at himself as though from outside—lolling in the reek of an imaginary swineherd's cottage, drunk on watered wine and unwatered self-pity. It was not a pleasant sight, even in his imagination.

Don't be stupid, he told himself. *The system wouldn't have any way of knowing Gally was traveling with me unless he came into this simulation with me, and he didn't. The bastards killed him in Venice.* Whatever his confusion about his own state, it was hard to doubt what had happened to Gally—the horrible, shocking finality of it had been too great.

But as he thought about the boy, he began to wonder again how the whole system worked. There were Citizens and Puppets, that was clear, but did everyone else, the Gallys and the Penelopes, fall into a single category? The bird-woman was here, but there was also a version of her on Mars. And what about the one that appeared to him in dreams? If there were somehow multiple versions of her, could they never coexist, never share their knowledge with each other? They must have some common thread, otherwise how could the Neandertal dream-spirit have known about her other self here in Ithaca?

And what about his pursuers, those two ghastly creatures that had hounded him from simulation to simulation. Were *they* real people?

The last moments in Venice came back to him, the bizarre confusion of events—Eleanora, a real woman, but appearing as a ghostly spirit in her own simulation, the Finch-thing and Mullet-thing, tracking him down again, heartless and inexorable as some kind of virus . . . and the Pankies.

My God, where do they fit in? Paul wondered. *They looked like Finch and Mullet, but they weren't—sort of like the different versions of my bird-woman. But there's only been one version of her in any simulation I've been in, either a real character, like Penelope, or sort of a dream version. The Pankies and their doubles both showed up at the same time in Venice. . . .*

It was hard to forget the strange expression that had crossed Undine Pankie's vast, flabby face—something almost automatic, so instinctive as to seem mechanical. Then she and her tiny husband had simply left—walked off, vanishing into the catacombs like two actors who had discovered themselves to be in the wrong play.

It was odd how often important things—especially having to do with the mystery woman—seemed to happen around the dying and the dead. The Venetian crypts, the dying Neandertal boy, the exhumed cemetery on the Western Front. Death and the dying. Although there had been the maze at Hampton Court, too. Mazes and cemeteries—what was it with these people, anyway?

An idea began to tickle at him. He sat up, suddenly more sober than he had been a few minutes earlier. "Tell me something, good Eumaeus," he began abruptly. If these things were machines, that was all the more reason why there should be rules, logic . . . answers. It was up to him to discover what they were. "Tell me how people in your country ask the gods for help."

*   *   *

Penelope rebuffed him again that evening, starting the audience as though Paul were the kindly beggar she had sent away the day before, but then veering rapidly into a wife's tragic leave-taking, bidding him farewell on his journey to Troy with many promises as to how she would keep his home and his possessions safe, and would raise his infant son to proper manhood.

I've definitely done something to catch her in a loop, he thought. It was hard to watch the woman he had chased for so long weeping bravely over something that bore no relationship to current reality, even the skewed reality of the simulation network, but it confirmed him in his intentions. *I could go on like this forever,* he decided, *and it wouldn't change anything.*

"Why can your spirit not rest, my lord and husband?" she asked suddenly, changing tack again. "Is it that your bones lie unmourned on some distant beach? That the gods who opposed you have tried to hide your name and your deeds? Do not fear—not all gods are your enemies, and there are those who will avenge you. There are others who will bring your memory and good name back from those foreign lands. A man waits to speak to me even now, to tell me of your life and deeds while you have been far from me, and someday your son, sensible Telemachus, will be able to avenge your wrongful death."

He felt a moment of interest until he realized that the man she spoke of was himself, that she had folded that version into this scenario where he was his own ghost.

I was right the first time, he thought miserably. *This could go on and on. I started this loop, somehow—I have to end it.* A chilling thought came to him: *But what if this is all there is to her? What if she's just a broken machine—nothing more than that?*

Paul shook it off—he simply couldn't afford to consider the possibility. The quest to find this woman was almost the only thing that gave his life meaning. He had to believe that his recognition of her meant something. He had to believe.

Two more days passed.

Gripped by a strange sort of loyalty, Paul gave Penelope one last chance to recognize the truth, such as it was, but again, after oscillating through Paul-as-ghost and Paul-as-beggar, she once more settled on the idea he was about to leave for Troy and would

not hear otherwise. Time after time she bade him a sadly loving
farewell, then moments later began her leavetaking all over again.
The only thing she did *not* seem to consider, he noted, was the
scenario that all the other Ithacans seemed to be performing—that
his character, Odysseus, had returned in secret, much aged, but
alive and well, from the Trojan War. He thought that was probably significant, but wasn't certain how. In any case, he was now
determined to smash the puzzle rather than to waste the rest of
his life trying to solve it.

The ancient slave Eurycleia, he was unhealthily gratified to
discover, still regarded him with the true belief of a faithful folk-
tale servant. When he had finished telling her what he wanted,
she recited his instructions back to prove she had them memorized.

Avoiding the brawl of suitors and the backstairs treachery of
the maids and house slaves, he spent the rest of his time walking the island, the dream-Ithaca. He visited Eumaeus again; then,
following the swineherd's directions, he took a long walk through
the bee-droning hills to a small rustic temple on the far side of
the island. The place gave every indication of having been ignored a long time: a faceless, time-rounded statue standing in a
niche dusted with the remains of long-dead narcissus flowers, surrounded by cypress branches so dry they had lost their scent.

As he stood praying before the forgotten shrine in the hollow
of the hillside, the air heavy and silent but for the constant breathing of sea, he prayed aloud for himself too, just to be on the safe
side. True, this was all a simulation, the painstaking creation of
people as human as himself, so for all intents and purposes he
was praying to some team of gear engineers and graphic designers, but his boss at the Tate had often warned him never to underestimate the sneakiness and self-obsession of artists.

HE woke disoriented from a dream about Gally, and for a moment could not remember where he was.

He groped around. Sand lay beneath him, and there was a faint,
dying light in the west where the sun had gone down behind the
hills. He had fallen asleep on the beach, waiting.

The lost child in his dream had worn the guise of the still-
unmet Telemachus, a handsome, dark-ringleted youth who never-

theless wore Gally's urchin squint. The boy had been rowing a small boat on a dark river through drifting mists, calling Paul's name. The urge to reach out to him had been powerful, but some dream-paralysis had prevented Paul from moving or even answering as the boy faded into a cloud of white nothingness.

Helpless tears were on his cheeks now, cool in the evening wind off the ocean, but through his misery he felt a kind of vindication: surely this dream of Gally on the river in the lands of Death must mean he was doing the right thing. Paul sat up, his wits returning with sleep's retreat. The beach was empty but for a few fishermen's boats, their owners long since gone to their evening meals. Sea and sky were quickly becoming a single dark thing, and the fire he had built with so much labor earlier in the afternoon was now guttering. Paul sprang forward and fed it with cypress twigs as he had been told, and then with larger pieces of driftwood until the flames began to mount high again. By the time he had finished, the sun was entirely gone, the stars blazing from a sky undulled by the pervasive ambient light of Paul's own age.

As if they had been waiting for everything to be correctly arranged, voices now came to him down the beach.

"There, where the fire is burning—see, mistress?"

"But this is most strange. Are you certain it is not bandits or pirates who have made a camp there?"

Paul stood. "This way, my lady," he called. "You don't have to worry about bandits."

Penelope came out of the darkness, shawl wrapped tightly around her, the firelight revealing her look of deep unease. Eurycleia, older and shorter of leg, nevertheless followed close behind.

"I have brought her, master," the slave announced. "As you asked."

"Thank you." He was certain there was something more poetic he should say, but he had no skill for this sort of thing. His personal translation of Homer would just have to be the utilitarian sort.

Penelope laughed nervously. "Is this some conspiracy? My oldest and dearest servant, have you betrayed me to this strange man?"

"So you still don't recognize me?" Paul shook his head. "It

doesn't matter. I won't hurt you, I promise. I swear it by all the
gods. Please, sit down." He took a breath. It had seemed so sensible when he had planned it—his decision to stop fighting the
simulation, to enter instead into its spirit and thus find a painless
way to jog this woman back into sanity, to make her useful to
him, as her own alter ego had clearly intended her to be. "In fact,"
he said, "I'm going to ask the gods for help."

Penelope gave one sharp glance to Eurycleia, then settled herself gracefully on the sand. Her dark shawl and darker hair, the
few strands of gray invisible in the starlight, surrounded the pale,
mistrustful face with a mantle of shadow. Her wide eyes seemed
holes cut directly into the night.

The slave woman handed Paul a bronze knife wrapped in a
cloth. He produced a bundle of his own and unwrapped the spindly
hindquarters of a butchered black sheep—the wage he had earned
from Eumaeus' brother-in-law for an afternoon's work fixing a
paddock. It seemed a paltry sacrifice to Paul, but Eumaeus—to
whom he had gone first in hope of pig flesh to sacrifice—had assured him that a black ram was the only correct choice, and Paul
had bowed to the man's clearly superior knowledge.

While Penelope watched in silent trepidation, Paul made a pyre
of sticks atop the fire, then did as Eumaeus had told him, cutting
the meat and fat away from the ram's thighs. He placed the bones
on the pyre and the flesh and fat on top of them. Within moments
the sacrifice was sending up plumes of greasy smoke, and as the
wind changed direction, he caught not only the alluring scent of
cooked meat, but something deeper, older, and altogether more
disturbing—the smell of burnt offerings, of ransom paid in fear,
the scent of human submission to a powerful and pitiless universe.

"I do not understand," Penelope said faintly. Her great eyes
followed his every move, as though he were a wild beast. "What
are you doing? Why am I here?"

"You think you don't know me," Paul replied. He tried to keep
his voice even but he was beginning to feel an odd elevation,
something he had not expected. The dream of poor, dead Gally,
the snapping flames on the windy beach, the woman whose face
had so long been his only talisman sitting across the fire from
him, all combined to make him feel as though he might at last

be on the brink of something real—something important. "You think you don't, but the gods will bring back your memory." He felt certain now that he was doing the right thing. The exhilarated rush in his head proved it. No more drifting—he was instead seizing the simulation by its own rules and making it work for him. "They will send someone who will help you remember!"

"You are frightening me." Penelope turned to Eurycleia, who Paul felt sure would reassure her, but the slave looked as unhappy as her mistress.

"Then just tell me what I need to know." Paul stepped back from the fire and spread his arms. The wind tugged at his thin garment, but he felt only the heat of the flames. "Who are you? How did we get here? And where is the black mountain you told me about?"

She stared at him like a cornered animal.

It was hard to be patient when he wanted to shout. He had waited so long—had been pushed and tugged and flung from place to place, always passive, always the one acted upon. He had stood by helplessly while the boy, his only real friend in this bizarre universe, was killed before his eyes. Now that helplessness was finally ending. "Then just tell me about the black mountain. How do I find it? Do you remember? That's why I came here. That's why *you* sent me here!"

She crouched lower. A strafing of sparks leaped out of the fire and swirled away on the wind.

"No? Then I have to ask the gods." He would use the logic of her own world against her. He would make something happen.

As he lowered himself to the sand, Eurycleia piped up nervously. "Surely that is sheep's flesh, my lord. A black ewe, my lord?"

He began to slap his hands against the ground in slow rhythm, striking the sand with his palms as old Eumaeus had instructed him. "It's a ram. Quiet—I have to remember the words."

The slave woman seemed restless and upset. "But such a thing is an offering to . . ."

"Sshhhh." He slowed his beat upon the ground, and then intoned in rhythm.

> *"Hail to thee, Invisible,*
> *Aedoneus, son of Chronos the Eldest,*
> *Brother of Zeus the Thunderer,*
> *Hail!*
> *Hail to thee, Lord of the Dark Pillars,*
> *Hades, Monarch of the Underworld,*
> *King of the Silent Realm,*
> *Hail!*
> *Take this flesh, Lord of the Fertile Depths,*
> *Take this offering.*
> *Hear my prayer. . . ."*

He paused. He had invoked the God of Death, which surely in this place was as good as any graveyard or dying Ice Age child.

"Send me the bird-woman!" he shouted, still drumming the tattoo on the sand. *"Tell her I want to speak to her—I want this woman Penelope to see her!"* The words seemed awkward, out of keeping with the poetry of the invocation, and he reached to summon the dream-woman's own words. *"Come to us! You must come to us!"*

Silence fell. Nothing happened.

Furious, Paul began to drum another tattoo on the sand. *"Come to us!"*

"M-My lord," Eurycleia stuttered, "I thought you meant to ask the help of Athena the Counselor, who has long looked favorably on your family, or of great Zeus—I thought perhaps even you meant to beg forgiveness of ocean-lord Poseidon, who many say you have somehow offended, and who thus murderously hindered your journey back to us. But this, master, this . . . !"

The last beat of his fingers upon the sand continued to reverberate—a noiseless echo that he could nevertheless feel pulsing away into the deeps. The bonfire flames seemed to have slowed, as though their light traveled to him through deep water, or along some kind of hindered and decaying transmission.

"What are you saying?" His impatience was tempered by a throb of worry—the slave's fear was powerful and genuine. Her mistress Penelope seemed beyond terror, her features slack and still except for her eyes, which stared feverishly from the winding-sheet white of her face. "What are you trying to tell me, old woman?"

"Master, you should not offer prayers for . . . such things as this to . . . to the Earthbound!" Eurycleia gasped, fighting for breath. "Have your years . . . in foreign lands robbed you of your . . . of your memory?"

"Why shouldn't I? Hades is a god, isn't he? People pray to him, don't they?" The feeling in his stomach was rapidly becoming a deep, nauseating chill.

The old slave flapped her hands, but she seemed to have lost the ability to speak. The earth beneath Paul's feet seemed taut as a drum, a breathing membrane pulsing to a slow, distant rhythm. But the pulse was growing stronger.

It's not a mistake—I know it's not a mistake . . . is it?

Even as he felt the clutch of doubt, she was there.

Her counterpart Penelope lurched to her feet, staggering backward on the suddenly unstable sands as the bird-woman's form took shape in the smoke, a monochrome angel in wispy gray, the vast wings trailing away into invisibility. The apparition's face was curiously formless, like the rain-eroded statue of the Earth Lord himself in its niche on the other side of the island. But still, from her expression of disbelieving shock, Penelope in some way recognized her own image, even in this insubstantial duplication.

The smoky face turned to him. *"Paul Jonas, what have you done?"*

He didn't know what to say. Everything he had planned, all he had thought might happen, was coming unstuck. The surface of the earth now seemed only a skin over some impossibly deep pit, and something moved there, something as vast and inescapable as regret.

The angel shivered, roiling the smoke. Even in this spectral form, he could clearly see the lines of the bird-woman from the giant's castle, and despite his terror, he ached for her. *"You have called out to the One who is Other,"* she said. *"He is searching for you now."*

"What are you talking about?"

"You have called to him. The one who dreams it all. Why did you do that—he is terrible!"

Through his confusion, Paul finally realized that he had been listening for long moments to Penelope moaning in terror. She had fallen to the ground and was throwing sand on her own head, as though she would bury herself. He pulled her upright, in part wanting to help, but also furious that her recalcitrance should have brought him to this. "Look! This is her!" he shouted at the smoke angel. "You sent me to her, but she couldn't tell me where to go. I wanted her to tell me how to reach the black mountain."

The apparition was no more willing than Penelope to meet her double's eyes: when Paul thrust his erstwhile wife toward her, the angel twitched away, a ripple passing through her entire body and deforming her wings. *"We do not . . ."* The face of smoke writhed. *"We should not . . ."*

"Just make her tell me. Or *you* tell me! I can't stand this anymore!" Paul could feel a growing presence, simultaneously beneath his feet and behind his eyes, a pressure building all around that made the very air seem about to burst. "Where is your bloody black mountain?" He shoved Penelope toward the apparition again, but it was like trying to force together two repelling magnets. Penelope tore free from him with animal strength and fell to the sand, weeping.

"Tell me!" Paul shouted. He turned to the angel. "Why won't she tell me?"

The specter was beginning to dissipate. *"She has told you. She has told you what she knows in the only way she can. That is why I sent you to her. She is the one who knows what you must do next."*

Paul grabbed at her, but the angel was truly smoke: she dissolved in his clawing fingers. "What does that mean?" He turned and seized Penelope instead. He shook her, his anger threatening to overspill, the bursting tension of the night like a great dark blood clot in his head. "Where am I supposed to go?"

Penelope screamed in pain and terror. "Why do you do this to me, my husband?"

"Where do I go?"

Penelope was weeping and shuddering. "To Troy! You must go to Troy! Your comrades await you there!"

Paul let go of her, staggering as though he had been struck with a great stone, the realization a searing pain in his heart.

Troy—the only thing she had said that did not speak of the end of the story, the only answer that did not fit with the rest of the simulation. Through the cloud of confusion caused by his presence, Penelope had been telling him what he needed to know all along . . . but he hadn't listened. Instead he had brought her here, the woman he had sought for so long, and then tortured her, after promising the gods he would not harm her. He had called up something none of them dared face, when she had already told him several times what her other self could not.

Whatever he had summoned from the dark regions below, it was he himself who was the monster.

His eyes blurry with tears, Paul turned from the fire and stumbled away across the drumhead sands. He tripped on the huddled form of Eurycleia, but did not stop to find out if she was alive or dead. The thing that had frightened even the winged woman seemed very near now, achingly so, as close as his own heartbeat.

Searching for me, she said. He tripped and fell, then wobbled to his feet again like a drunken man. *The Earthbound, they called him.* He could feel the breathing vitality of the soil beneath him. A part of him, a tiny, distant part, shrilled that it all had to be illusion, that he must remember he was in some kind of vast virtual game, but it was a pennywhistle in a hurricane. Every time his feet met the ground he felt the dark thing's presence, as alarming and painful as if he ran on a hot griddle.

A disjointed idea sent him hurrying along the beach to the fishermen's boats. He grabbed the nearest and shoved it down the slick strand, filling the air with panicky curses when it stuck, until at last it skimmed free into the shallow tide. He clambered up over the side and in.

Not touching the earth anymore. His thoughts were like a deck of cards knocked from a table. *Big thing. Dead thing. But it can't find me now.* It was impossibly strange, whatever it was—could a mere simulation do that?

He lifted the oar in the bottom of the boat and began to drive himself out onto the wine-dark sea. He looked back, but all he could see of the beach was the dying flame of his fire. If Penelope and Eurycleia were still there, they were lost in shadow.

The waves grew higher, lifting the front of the small boat with

every swell, setting it down again with a smack. Paul set aside
the oar so he could get a better grip on the sides of the boat.

Troy, he thought, clutching at prosaic things in the grip of great
horror. *A black mountain. Is there a mountain near Troy . . . ?*

Another swell almost knocked him overboard and he gripped
the boat even more tightly. Although there were no clouds above
him, nothing between him and the diamond-bright stars, the waves
were lashing the little craft harder and harder. One passed beneath
him and lifted the entire boat up, up, until he thought it would
spin him over and dump him out. As he pivoted slowly at the top
of his rise, he saw that a wave of unnatural shape was rising before him, higher than any others, a dark mass touched with lu-
minescence at its edges—a figure ten times his own height, the
ocean itself taking the form of a bearded man with a crown. For
a moment he thought that the thing the angel had called Other
had found him, and he gave himself up to despair.

A thunderous voice made the bones of his skull quiver. *"Wily
Odysseus,"* it boomed, *"mortal man, you know that I, Poseidon,
am sworn to destroy you. Yet you leave the safety of your island
home and return to my domain. You are a fool. Your death is deserved."*

The great sea-king lifted his hand. The waves now rushing toward Paul's boat were like mountains. Paul felt his frail craft lifted,
slowly at first, then jerked up into the air and tossed high.

He clung to the hull as he spun, and could hold no thought
except, *I am a fool, it's true—a bloody, miserable fool. . . .*

The ocean, when he fell from the heights and struck it again,
seemed hard as stone. His boat burst into fragments and Paul was
sucked down into crushing wet blackness.

First:

EXILES IN DREAM

"For the sake of persons of . . . different types,
scientific truth should be presented in different
forms, and should be regarded as equally
scientific, whether it appears in the robust form
and the vivid coloring of a physical illustration or
in the tenuity and paleness of a symbolic
expression."

—James Clerk Maxwell, address to the Mathematics
and Physics Section, Brit. Assoc. for the
Advancement of Science, 1870.

CHAPTER 1

A Circle of Strangers

IT was only a hand, fingers curled, protruding from the earth like a swollen pink-and-brown flower, but she knew it was her brother's hand.

As she bent and grasped it, she felt it move slowly, sleepily beneath her fingers, and was thrilled to know he lived. She pulled.

Stephen emerged from the clinging soil bit by bit—hand and wrist first, then the rest of his arm, like the root of a stubborn plant. At last his shoulder and head burst free in a shower of dirt. His eyes were closed, his lips curled in a tight, secretive smile. In a desperate hurry now to wrest him loose completely, she pulled harder, drawing out his torso and legs as well, but somehow his other arm, hidden from her view, still anchored him to the earth.

She yanked hard but could not pull the last inches of him out into the light. She planted her feet, bent her back, then put an even greater effort into another pull. The rest of Stephen abruptly jerked free of the ground, then stopped. Clutched in his trailing hand was another small hand whose owner still lay beneath the soil.

Increasingly aware that something was wrong, Renie kept pulling, frantic to dislodge Stephen, but now a chain of small dirty shapes lifted from the soil like the plastic pop-beads she had played with in her own childhood—a score of little children all connected hand to hand, the last still partially immured in the earth.

Renie could not see well—the sky was growing dark, or she had rubbed dirt into her own eyes. She made one last effort, the very hardest pull she could manage, so that for a moment it seemed she was in danger of tearing her own arms out at their roots. The last of the children came free of the soil. But this child's hand held another hand as well, only this last childish fist was the size of a small car, and the wrist loomed from the earth like a vast tree trunk. The very earth trembled as this last monstrous link in the chain, perhaps annoyed by Renie's insistent pulling, began ponderously to dig its way upward out of the dark, gelid soil toward the light of the surface.

"Stephen!" she screamed, "let go, boy! You must let go . . . !"

But his eyes remained tight shut and he continued to cling to the chain of other children, even as the earth heaved and the vast shape beneath it continued to rise. . . .

Renie sat up, gasping and shivering, to discover herself in the thin, unchanging gray light of the unfinished simworld, surrounded by the sleeping forms of her companions—!Xabbu, Florimel,

Emily 22813 from the crumbling Oz simworld, and the armored silhouette of T4b stretched on the ground beside them like a fallen hood ornament. Renie's movement woke !Xabbu; his eyes flicked open, alert and intelligent. It was a surprise, as always, to see that gaze housed in an almost comical baboon face. As he began to rise from where he lay curled near her side, she shook her head.

"I'm okay. Bad dream. Get some more sleep."

He looked at her uncertainly, sensing something in the ragged tone of her voice, but after a moment shrugged a sinuous monkey-shrug and lay down again. Renie took a deep breath, then rose and walked across the hillside to where Martine sat, blind face turned to the skies like a satellite dish.

"Do you want to take a turn sleeping, Martine?" Renie asked as she sat down. "I feel like I'm going to be awake for a while." The complete absence in the environment of wind and ambient sound made it seem as though a thunderstorm was imminent, but they had been here for what seemed several days now without any weather whatsoever, let alone a storm.

Martine turned toward her. "Are you all right?"

It was strange, but no matter how many times Renie saw her companion's bland sim face, when she turned away again she could hardly remember it. There had been plenty of similar-looking sims in Temilun whose faces were nevertheless full of life and individualism—Florimel had one, and even the false Quan Li had looked like a real person. Martine, though, seemed to have been given something out of a default file.

"Just a bad dream. About Stephen." Renie pawed at the oddly-textured ground. "Reminding myself how little I've done for him, perhaps. But it was a strange dream, too. I've had a few like it. It's hard to explain, but I feel like . . . like I'm really *there* when they're happening."

Martine nodded slowly. "I think I have had similar types of dreams since we have been on this network—some in which I felt I was seeing things that I have only experienced since I lost my sight. Perhaps it is to do with the change in our sensory input, or perhaps it is something even less explicable. This is a brave new world, Renie, in many ways. Very few humans have experienced such realistic input that was not actually real—very few who were not completely insane, that is."

Renie's smile was a sour one. "So we're all more or less having a continual schizophrenic episode."

"In a way, yes," Martine said thoughtfully. "The kind of thing usually reserved for madmen . . . or for prophets."

Like !Xabbu, Renie almost added, but was not sure what she meant. She looked back toward the rest of their comrades, and specifically to where !Xabbu lay curled, his slender tail pulled up near his muzzle. By his own standards, the Bushman was no more a mystic than he was a theoretical scientist or a philosopher: he was simply working with the laws of the universe as his people knew them.

And after all, Renie had to admit, *who's to say they're wrong and we're right?*

The silence stretched for a minute, then another. Although the strangeness of the dream still clung to her thoughts, especially the jangling terror of its last moments, she felt a kind of peace as well. "This backwater place we're in," she said at last. "What do you think it is, really?"

Martine frowned, considering. "You mean, do I think it's what it seems to be—something the Grail people haven't finished with yet? I don't know. That seems the most likely explanation, but there are . . . sensations I get from it, things I cannot describe, that make me wonder."

"Like what?"

"As I said, I cannot describe them. But whatever it might be, it is definitely the first place of its sort I have entered, so my speculations do not mean much. It could be that because of the system the Grail Brotherhood employs, any unfinished place would give off the kind of . . ." again she frowned, ". . . the kinds of . . . intimations of vitality this place has." Before Renie could ask her to explain further, Martine rose. "I will take you up on your kind offer, Renie, if it still holds. The last few days have been impossibly difficult, and I find I am much wearier than I thought. Whatever else this place is, at least we are able to rest."

"Of course, get some sleep. We still have a lot ahead of us—a lot to decide."

"So much had to be said simply to bring each other up to date." Martine's smile was wry. "I am certain Florimel and T4b were not entirely unhappy we did not have time for their personal histories."

"Yes. But that's what today's for, whether they like it or not." Renie noticed she had dug a little trench with her fingers into the strange, soapy ground. Remembering the dream, she shivered and filled it in. "They're going to have to tell us. I won't stand any more secrets like that. That might be what killed William."

"I know, Renie. But do not be too fierce. We are allies trapped in a hostile environment and must take care of each other."

She fought down a small twinge of impatience. "Yes, of course. But that's all the more reason we have to know who's watching our backs."

T4B and Florimel were the last to return. By the time they appeared around the curve of the hillside, trudging toward the otherworldly campfire across terrain whose surface hue shifted subtly from instant to instant like the colors on an oil slick, Renie was beginning to feel nervously suspicious about their long absence. Still, even though they were the last two maintaining a mystery about their identities, they also seemed a fairly unlikely pair of allies—a fact underscored as T4b clanked into camp and blurted out their news, clearly irritating Florimel.

"Saw some kinda animal, us," he said. "Got no shape, seen? Just, like . . . light. But all bendy."

At first glance, Florimel's sim appeared little different than the one Martine wore, a woman of the Atascos' Temilun simworld, with a strong nose and a dark, reddish-brown complexion not unlike the Maya; but just as two people might wear the same clothes to totally different effect, where Martine's guise gave an impression of blankness that belied her dry wit and careful empathy, Florimel's small sim seemed to have the coiled intensity of a Napoleon, and her face did not look unfinished or general in the same way Martine's did.

Just another mystery, Renie thought wearily, *and probably not one of the important ones.*

". . . It wasn't an animal in any normal sense of the word," Florimel was saying. "But it's the first phenomenon we've seen that wasn't obviously part of the geography. It was very fluid, but T4b is correct—it was made of light, or was only partially visible to us. It appeared almost out of nowhere and moved around as though it were looking for something. . . ."

"Then it just zanged out, like into an airhole," T4b finished.

"A what?" Renie turned to Florimel for clarification.

"He means it just . . . well, it *did* seem to step into a hole in the air. It didn't simply vanish, it . . ." She stopped and shrugged. "Whatever happened, it is gone."

!Xabbu had finished poking up the fire. "And what else did you see?" he asked.

"Saw too much zero, me," said T4b, levering himself down to a seat by the campfire. The reflected flames made unusual, almost textured patterns on his armor.

"We saw a lot more of this," Florimel elaborated, gesturing to the hillside on which they stood. "A thousand variations, but all much the same . . ."

"Don't touch me!" Emily stood up and moved away from T4b.

"Didn't. You're dupped and trans-upped," he growled. "Trying to bring friendly, me, all it is." If a warrior-robot could be said to sulk, he was clearly doing so.

Florimel let out a great sigh, as if to underscore what she had been forced to put up with all day. "Everywhere was like this— unfinished, disordered, silent. I do not like it, to tell you the truth." She made a dismissive gesture. "What was perhaps interesting, though, is that we found no sign of a river or anything similar, not even a river-of-air, as we had in the last place."

"William liked flying in that river so much," Martine said suddenly. "He was laughing and laughing. He said it was the first thing he'd found in the whole network that made him think the money was worth spending." Everyone fell silent for a moment. Sweet William's stiffened virtual body was only a short distance away, concealed in a sort of pit on the far side of a knoll swirling with evanescent colors. No one looked in that direction, but everyone was clearly thinking about it.

"So, no river," Renie said. "!Xabbu and I didn't find any trace of one either. Pretty much everything else we saw was as you said—more of the same. We didn't see anything I'd call an animal, though." She sighed. —Which means there isn't any obvious and easy way to travel through and out of this simworld."

"There is not even a way to know which direction we should

take," Florimel added. "There is no sun, no sunrise or sunset, no directions at all. We only found our way back because I left a trail of broken . . . sticks, I suppose you would call them . . . behind us."

Like bread crumbs, Renie thought. *Isn't that from "Hansel and Gretel"? We're living in a bloody fairy tale—except our story, like this world, hasn't been finished yet . . . and we might not be the folks who are going to be around at Happily Ever After time.* Out loud, she said, "We had !Xabbu's nose and sense of direction, although I have to admit I was a little nervous—it all just looks the same to me."

"Did you find food?" asked Emily. "I'm very hungry. I'm going to have a baby, you know."

"Oddly enough," said Florimel, saving Renie the trouble, "we realized that, yes."

ONCE she had decided to do it, Florimel appeared impatient to start. They had barely settled themselves around the fire pit before she declared, "I was born in Munich. In the early '30s, during the Lockdown. The part of the city where my mother lived was an industrial slum. We shared a small rebuilt warehouse with a dozen other families. Later, I would realize that it was not all bad—many of the families were political, some of the adults were even wanted by the police for things they had done at the beginning of the Guestworker Revolt, and I was taught a great deal about how the world truly works. Too much, perhaps."

She looked around as though someone might want to ask a question, but Renie and the others had been waiting too long to learn something of this companion-stranger to interrupt her.

Florimel shrugged and continued at a brisk pace. "For my mother, it was definitely too much. When her man, who may or may not have been my father, was killed in what the authorities called a riot, but was truly more of an attempt to round up and incarcerate large elements of the social fringe, she fled Munich entirely and moved to the Elz Valley in the Black Forest.

"You may or may not remember the name Marius Traugott— he has been a long time dead, now. He was a teacher, a holistic healer, I suppose a mystic. He rode the wave of superstition at the end of the last century to fame, bought one of the last stands of the old forest, which had been privatized by the Reutzler government, and founded a retreat he called Harmony Camp."

"Was that one of those, what is the name . . . ?" Renie tried to remember the news stories. "Is that the Social Harmony religion?"

Florimel shook her head. "No, not really. One of Traugott's very early disciples split from him and started the Social Harmonist Army in America, but we were nothing like them, believe me—although many people did call our Harmony Camp a religious cult. But whatever you call it, cult, commune, social experiment, it does not matter. My mother was one of the converts, and when I was just a few years old she became a member, giving away the few things she owned for a narrow bed in a bunkhouse and a seat at the foot of Doctor Traugott.

"Despite a diet made entirely of raw, living vegetables and plant material, Traugott died only a few years later at age eighty. Harmony Camp did not fold up or fall apart, though. Several of his lieutenants kept it going, and although it went through periodic shifts of philosophy, some fairly extreme—for a while when I was about twelve, people at the camp armed themselves against a feared crackdown by the government, and at one point some of the more mystical members were trying to beam messages to the stars—it remained more or less what it had been under Doctor Traugott. For me, it was simply home. We children ate together, slept together, sang together. Our parents did the same—lived communally, I mean—but the two groups were largely separate. The children were all taught together, with a rigorous stress on philosophy, health science, and religious thought. It is not entirely surprising that I became interested in medicine. What is more surprising is that when I was old enough, the Harmony Camp Foundation actually spent the money to send me to the university in Freiburg. It is less surprising if you know that the group mistrusted outside doctors and mainstream medicine, and that up until then we had only one nurse to minister to almost six hundred people.

"I will not bore you with how my years at university changed me. Meeting young people who did not call their mothers 'Sister-in-God,' and who had grown up sleeping in a bed of their own in a room of their own was like being introduced to creatures from another planet. Not surprisingly, I came to view my upbringing differently than before I left Harmony Camp, to be more critical of what I had learned, less accepting of the truths of Doctor Marius Traugott. What may surprise you, however, is that I still returned home when my schooling was finished. Even though I had no formal doctor's degree, I had learned enough to become the chief medical authority of Harmony Camp.

"I feel I must explain this, or you will all misunderstand, as people generally do. It is true that Traugott's ideas were largely nonsense, and that many of the people drawn to his doctrines, and thus to the commune, were those without the strength or resources to compete in the great commercial struggle outside the gates. But did this mean they had no right to live? If they were foolish, or credulous, or simply tired of trying to climb up a ladder that had many times already proved too slippery for them, did that mean they were without value?

"My mother was one such, you see. She had chosen to turn her back on the politics of the street, but she did not want simply to replace that with the values of the bourgeoisie, either. What she wanted was a bed, a safe place to raise her daughter, and the company of people who did not shout at her that she was ignorant or spineless because she was frightened to go out and throw bricks at police.

"My extended Harmony Camp family were mostly kind people. They were frightened of many things, but if fear makes people hateful, it had not yet risen to a sustained pitch with them. Not then. So after university I busied myself with helping them, and although I no longer blindly accepted Harmony Camp's guiding beliefs, I had no qualms about trying to make the lives of its people better. And I did make things better—very quickly, too. I was fortunate enough to have made a friend in school whose father was an executive in a large medical supply company, and at his urging—and much to my surprise—the company donated us some excellent equipment.

"Listen to me." She snorted. "I have already taken too long to get to the point. I started out to tell you of my life at Harmony Camp only because it explains much about me in a few words. But I also wanted you to know that my mother was taught, in part by her own experiences in Munich, in part by Doctor Traugott, to fear the modern life of instant communications and imaginary worlds—in short, the life of the net. I learned to partake freely of that life in my university days, but a part of me still feared it. It was the opposite of all we had been taught to revere, the raw, the tangible, that which *lived*. When I underwent my quiet rebellion against Marius Traugott's teachings, I undertook to face that which I feared, and I began to spend almost as much time connected to the information world as all but the most die-hard enthusiasts among my university friends. When I returned to Harmony Camp, I even had a showdown with the council, threatening to leave if they did not agree to allow me at least one line which could handle greater bandwidth than voice-only. I told them I could not be their doctor without one, which was only partially true. My blackmail worked.

"So I opened up Harmony Camp to the net. No one touched that system station but me, and after a while the council became less uneasy. Eventually, it was all but forgotten, although I would eventually pay for my pleasures, and pay very heavily. But at the time, once my own initial absorption with the novelty of it began to fade, even I used it only seldom. I kept in touch with a few friends from the university. I did my best to stay current with general medical information. On rare occasions I experimented with some of the other things the net had to offer, but my work at Harmony Camp kept me very busy. In many ways I was almost as disconnected from the modern world as you, !Xabbu, in your early life on the Okavango.

"What changed it was my child, and a man named Anicho Berg."

"My mother died in an accident—as yours did, Renie. It happened in the winter, twelve years ago. The heater in the cabin she shared with some of the older Harmony Camp women malfunctioned and they were asphyxiated. There are far worse ways to die. In any case, though, for the first time I began to feel that my fellow communards were perhaps not family enough—that with my mother dead, I lacked any deep personal connection to the world, even to my own life, if that makes sense.

"It was not very difficult for a woman in her forties to begin thinking about bearing a child. It was even less difficult for a woman with medical training and control over the health services of several hundred people to arrange an artificial insemination. I considered briefly just a parthenogenetic cloning of one of my own cells, but I did not want simply another version of myself. I took what I knew to be several healthy sperm samples from different donors, unfroze them, and mixed them together.

"Considering the clinical nature of her conception, you may be surprised to know that I bore my daughter Eirene full-term, and that she was beautiful to me beyond anything I can say. You may be less surprised to learn that someone who had spent her entire life in communal living found herself fiercely jealous and protective of her child.

"I could not continue living in Harmony Camp without allowing her to join the other children in their communal schooling, and I had no wish to leave—it was the only home I had ever really known. But I made sure that I taught her, too, and that I was not an essentially uninvolved figure like my own mother, who had been only a small degree more loving and intimate to me than any of the other Sisters-in-God. I was Eirene's *mother,* and she knew it. I told her every day. She felt it."

Florimel's clipped narrative came to a startlingly sudden halt. It took a moment before Renie realized that the woman was struggling with tears.

"Excuse me." She was clearly embarrassed. "We are coming to the things that are very hard for me to say, even to remember.

"Anicho Berg was not at first anything to fear. He was a thin, serious young man who had been part of Harmony Camp for a long time, since his youth. At one point he and I even had a short affair, but that meant little because none of us went outside the commune for our relationships, and although we were not one of those groups that emphasizes free love, neither had Doctor Traugott been anti-sex—he was much more concerned with people's dietary habits and bowel movements. We were normal, healthy people. Many of us had our flings over the years, and some married. But something in Anicho was ambitious, and could not bear things in the commune to be as they were and himself just one of many. He began to take more power on the council, which was not difficult—few at Harmony Camp wanted power of any kind. Had we not retreated from the world where such things were important? But perhaps by making ourselves a peaceful flock, we thus became an irresistible lure to a cunning predator. And that is what Anicho Berg was.

"I will not stretch out this portion of the story, because it is sad and unsurprising. Those of you, like Martine, who are familiar with the newsnets may have even heard of Harmony Camp's messy ending—a shoot-out with the authorities, several people dead, including Berg, and several others arrested. I was not there—Berg and his cohorts had driven me and Eirene away months before. Ironically, it was my possession of net gear that Anicho used to make me unpopular—what was I doing, he demanded to know, late at night when others of the commune were abed? Using electricity, talking with strangers and thus generally up to no good, was his insinuation. I am sad to say that in the climate he and his friends fostered, my fellow communards believed it.

"Again I have gone on longer than I intended. I suppose it is that I have kept this quiet for so long I had almost forgotten it, as though these events happened to a stranger. But now that I speak of it the wounds are once more fresh.

"What I was doing, of course, and what rapidly took over my entire life, was trying to find out what was wrong with my daughter. For like so many others, as we all now know, she had been struck down suddenly and terribly by a mystery disease. I had no idea at first it could have anything to do with the net, because at first I thought that she had only ever used my connection under my supervision. I was a fool, of course, and knowing that I was not the first busy parent to realize that does not make it any the less painful. Eirene was fascinated, and used every opportunity when I was out doing my rounds in Harmony Camp to explore the virtual world beyond the camp walls. I only discovered later, by tracing the records of my account, how far she had roamed. But at first I only knew that my daughter had succumbed to something as abrupt and brutal as a stroke, and that doctors far more knowledgeable than me could do nothing for her.

"But even as I was forced to have more and more dealings with hospitals and clinicians and neuromedical specialists, Berg and others had begun to make the people of our commune fear the outside world. These things happen, I suppose, with closed societies. Even large, open societies are prone to waves of paranoia, but because of their nature, the paranoia usually dissipates.

But in a tight community like Harmony Camp, especially when some among the group are fanning its embers, paranoia can smolder and smolder until it bursts into flame. Berg and his closest followers, many of them young men who had joined in only the last few months, began to target those with influence, trying to force them either to join Berg or to stay silent. In other circumstances, I might have resisted, might even have led the opposition to hold onto what was, after all, my home. But I could not care about anything except finding a cure for Eirene. Hours of every day, all through the night, I roamed the net—a path that eventually, after two years, led me to the Atascos' make-believe world.

"But long before that I found my home changing into something I did not recognize. When I actively began to fear for my safety—which I did not care about for my own sake, but rather because of Eirene—I left Harmony Camp.

"I make it sound easier than it was. I was frightened of Anicho Berg by then, and I went through quite vigorous steps to make sure no one knew I was leaving until I was gone, and I also did my best to cover my tracks. I was instantly denounced as a traitor, of course, the more so because I took much of the expensive medical equipment with me, but I had no choice, since I also took Eirene out of the local hospital so that I could care for her myself after we went into hiding. We moved to Freiburg, the only other place I knew, and where I felt there was a lessened chance of encountering any of the Harmony people. What I did not know was that as paranoia rose higher in Harmony Camp, Anicho Berg used my escape to denounce me as a proven spy. When Berg himself was killed by federal police, in what began as little more than a land-usage dispute but quickly became a small but violent war, several of his disciples escaped the camp's collapse, convinced that I had sold them out to the government.

"So I have been in hiding ever since, with very little contact with the outside world. I do not know whether Berg's disciples are still hunting for me, holding me responsible for their leader's death, but I would be surprised if they have given up—they are not very imaginative types and do not take in new ideas easily, especially if giving up their old ideas means facing up to the fact that they have been led astray.

"I can do nothing about that. I may still be able to do something about Eirene. And if not, then I have no reason to go on
living . . . but I will at least try to spit in the face of the people
who have done this to her before I die."

The dramatic ending of Florimel's recitation left everyone
stunned into silence. Renie found herself obscurely ashamed at
the German woman's ferocity, as though somehow her own sin-
cerity in trying to solve the riddle of her brother's illness had
been cast into doubt.

One thing had been nagging at her, though. "But if you're hiding," Renie asked at last, "if you're worried that those people are
still after you, why did you tell us your name?"

"I told you a first name only," Florimel said, then made an
odd face, half scowl, half smile. "And in any case, what makes
you think that is my real name? Did you go on the net to begin
this search using your own name? If so, then I have lost some
respect for you."

"No, of course I didn't," Renie said, nettled.

Little Emily leaned forward, eyes wide. She had paid far more
careful attention to Florimel's story than anyone would have expected, although Renie wondered how much someone who apparently had only experienced life within one simulation of the
network could make of such a tale. But the girl's question was a
sharp one. "What about your baby? How could you leave her behind?"

Florimel, who knew the girl's recent history from Renie's tales
of New Emerald City, looked at her as though she guessed what
caught at Emily's interest. "My daughter?" She hesitated. When
she finally spoke, some defensive barrier had dropped, and for a
moment the unhappiness and vulnerability were clear, even on her
sim face. "I have not left her behind. I told you that I brought
my equipment with me when I escaped Harmony Camp. It is very
fine equipment. She is connected to me, both of us sharing a
telematic circuit. We are yoked to a throughline onto this network.
So I know where she is, at least—that she lives. I can feel her in
her terrible sleep, and . . . and she is always with me. . . ." Florimel
drew a shaking hand across her face.

Martine broke the long, painful silence. "I sensed a second person," she said quietly, wonderingly. "I wondered how it could be, and to tell the truth, this was all so new to me I was not certain I was right, but I sensed another person with you from the very first."

"Where my real body lies, she lies beside me, in my arms." Florimel looked away, unwilling to meet the eyes of the others. "The machines keep our flesh healthy, our muscles functional. Eirene is with me, you see." She took a deep breath. "And when she leaves me . . . I will know. . . ."

It was T4b and Emily, oddly enough, who reached out to touch her. Florimel did not resist, but neither did she give any sign she was even aware of them. After perhaps half a minute unspeaking, she got up and walked away from the fire, out across the incomplete landscape, until she was little more than a small, dark figure against the eternal gray.

After Florimel's story, it was hard even to nudge T4b into speech. He answered Renie's questions at first only in sullen monosyllables. Yes, his name was Javier Rogers, as the voice of the Lost had announced, although he'd never liked it. Yes, he lived in the suburbs outside Phoenix, but he was actually from So-Phee—he pronounced it like the girl's name—from South Phoenix, Central Ave, the streets.

"Not no *sayee lo* 'burboy, me," he insisted.

Under further prodding, a rather strange and interesting story emerged, piece by garbled, Goggleboy-slanged piece. Despite his name he was half-Hopi, his mother a young reservation woman who had fallen in love with a truck driver. Her decision to run off with the man, Renie could see pretty clearly, had been the last romantic thing to happen to her: she and her lover had shortly thereafter begun a descent into drink and drugs, pausing only briefly along the way to bring several children into the world, of which Javier had been the first. After dozens of incidents, a sad list of drug-fueled batterings, petty crimes, and neighbors' complaints, social services had stepped in and taken the Rogers children away from their parents. Mama and Papa Rogers barely seemed to notice, so caught up were they in pursuing their own downward spiral. The younger children had been fostered to a family Javier had not liked, and after clashing several times with their new foster father, he had run away.

Several years on the South Phoenix streets had followed, running with Chicano and Amerind Goggleboy gangs, particularly one called *Los Hisatsinom"* or "Old Ones," named after an ancient Arizona tribe who predated even the Hohokam. The gang had a big old Krittapong Multiworx station in an abandoned apartment downtown, and they spent a lot of time on the net. *Los Hisatsinom* had a quasi-mystical bent, which T4b would only describe as "deep *fen*, man, deep and deepest," but they also kept themselves busy with the much more pragmatic occupation of buying discard or demo cartridges from Mexican charge factories and smuggling them across the border to sell in the black gear markets of Phoenix and Tucson.

Eventually, of course, and almost inevitably (although he clearly did not think of it that way) T4b was arrested, a "minor card" as he put it, stopped while driving a van full of stolen merchandise without even the mitigation of possessing a driver's license. Because of his age he spent some time in a juvenile insititution before being fostered, not to a family, but to a special halfway-house program for young offenders. When that had proved relatively successful, and he had been straight and more or less out of trouble for half a year, they released him to the custody of his father's parents, a couple in late middle age who had only seen their grandchild once in ten years. Grandma and Grandpa Rogers had belatedly tried to get custody of the younger children, but failed, and had received Javier instead as a sort of consolation prize. They were less than certain about inheriting a Goggleboy with a scalp-to-toe tracery of luminous subdermals, not to mention an arrest record, but they made the best of it. They put him back in school and bought him an inexpensive console, so he could put his Goggleboy tapping-and-napping skills to some use, perhaps even find a career someday.

It quickly became clear—and here for the first time T4b spoke expansively if, as always, somewhat opaquely—that he was a natural. ("Major hammerhead netboy," was how he described himself.) His grandparents began to feel that maybe their gamble was going to pay off. Things were not really that simple, of course—one of the main attractions of the net was that he could still run with his old Goggleboy crowd, even if only virtually—but it was true that young Javier had begun to feel a freedom and a sense of possibility he hadn't known before. "Magic big," he called the experience, providing a bit of poetry. But as he went on to explain, it was only when his friend Matti succumbed to a mysterious illness that he had made the net his full-time crusade.

"I have never heard of anyone your age being affected by the Grail Brotherhood's online virus, or whatever it is," said Florimel. "The illness that has taken my Eirene."

"So?" T4b glowered. "Calling me duppy?" His unchanging mask of Kabuki-warrior ferocity and his spiky, formfitting armor made it hard to think of him as someone named Javier, but it was not difficult to sense the insecure street kid underneath it all.

In fact, thought Renie, *that's what they all wear anyway. Whether they're on my street in Pinetown or wherever it is he comes from—"So-Phee"—most of them are so armored up that they can barely move. But here in VR you can actually see it.*

"No," Florimel told him calmly, "I am not calling you anything." Finally telling her own story seemed to have taken some of the edge off her approach; she sounded, Renie thought, almost human. "I'm just trying to get information which may be important to all of us. How old was this Matti when it happened?"

T4b stared at her, then abruptly turned away, going from frightening robot to spike-studded child in moments. Renie wondered whether they were asking for the right person's age.

"Please answer. It might help us, T4b," said Martine. "We are all here for the same reasons, or at least we are all in the same danger."

T4b mumbled something.

"What?" Renie resisted the urge to shake him, mostly because there were few spots on him that were safe to touch. She had never been good with people playing hard-to-get. "We can't hear you."

T4b spoke in a gust of anger and shame. "Nine. He nine. But wasn't nothing weird—not like that William. No babybouncer, me."

"William said he meant and did nothing wrong," Martine said, her voice so soothing Renie found herself nodding like a comic bystander. "I believed him. And I believe you, too."

Renie thought she saw Florimel mouth the words, *Speak for yourself,* but she was distracted by T4b's reaction.

"Don't understand nothin', you." He grabbed a handful of the not-earth and crushed it into translucent powder in his servo-motored fist. "Matti, he was crash—he knew all stuff nobody here know. All over the net, he going here, going there. For a micro, he was outmax. Whatever got him had to be far far dire. So got all matrixed and went lookin' for it, me." He proceeded to describe a search across the net that seemed to have taken him months, culminating in the discovery of one of Sellars' golden gems near a tribute wall in a VR park frequented by the youngest Goggleboys, like Matti.

Renie was wondering whether Javier Rogers' grandparents were rich, and if not, how he could afford to stay online so long; she was also growing curious as to who was taking care of T4b's physical body right now. Suddenly Emily spoke up with a question that Renie herself had occasionally been tempted to ask.

"So," the young woman asked, her tone half-contemptuous but ever so slightly flirty as well—a change, because she had been treating T4b like the plague since he had arrived—"what are you supposed to *be,* anyway? Some kind of spaceman?"

Florimel hid a snort of laughter, but poorly.

"Spaceman?" asked T4b in high dudgeon. It was an old-fashioned word, and he repeated it as though she had asked him whether he was a farmer or a janitor. "Not no *sayee-lo* spaceman. This a Manstroid D-9 Screamer Battlesuit, like outta *Boyz Go 2 Hell*!" He looked around, but no one responded. "*Boyz Go 2 Hell*?" he tried again. "Like with the Ballbuster Bugs and the Scorchmarkers . . ."

"If it's an interactive game," Renie said, "you've got the wrong crowd, I'm afraid. If Orlando and Fredericks were here, I'm sure they'd recognize it."

"Don't even know Manstroid Screamer . . ." he muttered, shaking his great metal head.

"I have a question, too," !Xabbu piped up. "Is that mask the only face you have in this place, or is there another underneath?"

T4b stared at him in stunned silence. "Underneath . . . ?"

"Underneath the mask," Florimel said. "Have you even tried to take it off?"

He had swiveled to face her now, but did not react to what she said, only stared as though in a dream. At last, slowly, his spike-gauntleted hands crept up to the flared sides of the battle-mask, sliding up and down the polished edges until one of his fingers slid into a slot below one of the finny protuberances. He found the corresponding slot, then pressed them both. A loud click was followed by the front of the mask swinging up out of the way like a medieval knight's face shield.

The face that peered out from beneath was simply that of a brown-skinned teenager with long black hair and startled eyes. Even the runic Goggleboy designs picked out on his cheeks, neck, and forehead in faintly luminous subdermals could not disguise how ordinarily homely and normal a face it was. Renie did not doubt that she was seeing a very convincing simulation of the true Javier Rogers.

Only a few seconds passed before T4b flinched beneath the weight of their collected gazes and clicked the mask back into place.

THE fire had burned down. They had talked and talked until they had fallen into a surreal timelessness unusual even for this place. ". . . So this is what it all comes down to," Renie said at last. "Do we try to explore this place and find a way out? Or do we search for the lighter that . . . I want to say Quan Li, but it wasn't Quan Li, of course. Do we search for that lighter instead, which could bring us some control over our environment?

"How we gonna hunt something like that?" T4b asked. Like Florimel, he seemed to have lost a little of his abrasiveness after confession. Even his rigorously unintelligible Goggleboy patois had shifted a little closer to normal speech. "Need one to find one."

"We may not." Renie turned to !Xabbu. "That's why I gave it to you to open a gateway for that monster—hoping that if you did it, it would make some impression on you. Do you think there's any way you could find that gateway again? By . . . dancing, or by doing anything at all?"

!Xabbu looked worried, an oddly natural expression for a fur-rowed baboon brow. "I found it difficult even when I had the lighter in my hand, Renie. And as I have told you, the dancing, the searching for answers, is not like ordering something in the mail. It is not a foolproof delivery system."

"Nothing is foolproof for us these days." She couldn't even smile.

"Perhaps I could help." Martine spoke slowly. "I have learned things myself since I have been in this place, and since !Xabbu and I . . . connected through the access device, I suppose you could say. Perhaps together we could find that gateway again and open it." She turned her blind eyes to Renie. "I think it would be a great gamble, but if you are all in a gambling mood, there are few enough opportunities left to us."

"Let's vote on it." Seeing the faces of her companions, Renie relented. "If you're not too tired, that is. I suppose we could wait until tomorrow."

"Could we not wait in any case?" Martine asked. "I mean, would it not be good to explore this unusual part of the network first, no matter what?"

"But if we wait, we give that bastard a greater chance to escape," Renie pointed out. "Not to mention the fact that you and !Xabbu may lose whatever insight you have—you may just forget, like trying to remember some stranger's name three days after they tell it to you."

"I am not certain that is a good analogy," said Martine, "but there is perhaps something in what you say."

"Very well, then, Renie," Florimel said, amused and disgusted. "We will have no peace until we give you your vote. I assume I know what you and !Xabbu will say. For me, I say we stay here until we know more about this place."

"But . . ." Renie began.

"Is it not enough we are voting?" Florimel asked. "Do you need to harangue those who disagree with you?"

Renie frowned. "You're right. I'm sorry. Let's go on."

"I want to vote, too," said Emily suddenly. "I know I'm not one of your friends, but I don't have anywhere else to go, and I want to vote." She said it as though it were a treat.

Renie was uncomfortable with the idea of putting someone who might not even be fully real on an equal footing with the rest of them. "But, Emily, you don't know all the things we know—you haven't been through everything . . ."

"Don't be mean!" the girl said. "I heard everything you've said since we've been here, and I'm not stupid."

"Let her," rumbled T4b, recovering from the embarrassment of showing his naked face. "Prejudiced, you, somethin'?"

Renie sighed. She didn't even want to begin discussing the ins and outs of Emily's possible status, since it would have to be done in front of the girl herself. "What do the rest of you think about Emily voting?"

Florimel and Martine nodded slowly. "You remember what I have said, Renie," !Xabbu reminded her quietly.

Which is that he thinks she's real, Renie thought. *Which should carry some weight, after all—he hasn't often been wrong about anything.* "All right, then," she said aloud. "What do you think we should do, Emily?"

"Get out of here," the girl said promptly. "I hate this place. It's not right. And there's nothing to eat."

Renie could not help but notice that she had been resisting a vote in her own favor, but was still not entirely comfortable about its source. "Okay. Who else?"

"I'm afraid I agree with Florimel, instead," said Martine. "I need rest—we have come through a very frightening time."

"We all have!" Renie caught herself. "Sorry. I'm out of line again."

"That was my thought, too," Florimel told Martine. "I don't want to go anywhere yet—if nothing else, I need to build up some strength. Remember that you were here for a day before we got here, Renie. Perhaps after the rest of us have had a chance to recover, and to get to know this place somewhat . . ."

"So we come down to you, T4b." Renie turned to the spiky, fire-glinting shape. "What will it be?"

"*Fen*—that dup tried to six us! Say we catch her, me, and vile her up good." T4b curled a mailed fist. "Don't let her get away, what it means."

"I'm not at all sure it's a 'her,'" Renie said, but inside she was pleased: that made it four to two to follow the spy—and, more importantly, Azador's lighter. "So that's it, then."

"No." !Xabbu raised one small hand. "I have not made my vote yet. Florimel said she assumed I would vote as you did, Renie. But I do not."

"You . . . you don't?" She felt nearly as astonished as if he instead of Quan Li had turned out to be a murderous stranger.

"When I look at our friends, I see that they are very tired, and I would like to see them rested before we run to danger again. But more importantly, Renie, whatever hid behind Quan Li's face, it frightens me."

"Of course it does," Renie said. "Don't you think I'm frightened, too?"

!Xabbu shook his head. "That is not what I mean. I . . . felt something, saw something. I do not have the words. But it was as though for a moment I felt the breath of Hyena, out of the old tales—or worse. There is a deep, hungry darkness in that one, whatever it is. I do not wish to rush toward it. Not yet, anyway, not until I can think about what I saw, what I felt. I vote we wait."

Renie was more than a little stunned. "So . . . so that makes it three to three. . . . What do we do, then?" She blinked. "Is that the same as if I were outvoted? That doesn't seem fair."

"Let us say instead that we will take the vote again soon." Martine patted Renie's hand. "Perhaps we will feel differently after we have had another night's sleep."

"Night?" Florimel laughed flatly. "You ask for too much, Martine. But just sleep will be enough."

Martine's smile was sad. "Of course, Florimel. I forget sometimes that for others it is not always night."

CHAPTER 2

An Old-Fashioned Sound

NETFEED/NEWS: Gruhov Denies He Implanted Russian Leader
(visual: Gruhov coming out of fast-food restaurant)
VO: Although he is avoiding the media, renowned behaviorist Doctor Konstantin Gruhov has flatly denied that he implanted a control chip in Russian President Nikolai Polyanin under orders from high officials in Polyanin's lame-duck Russian government, and that his being called suddenly to the Kremlin during the president's recent illness was merely a coincidence . . .
(visual: Gruhov in university garden, prerecorded statement)
GRUHOV: ". . . Really, it is preposterous. It's hard enough simply trying to keep someone from shoplifting—how could you hope to control a politician . . . ?"

WAITING to die, as Joseph Sulaweyo discovered, was surprisingly like waiting for anything else: after a long enough time, your mind began to wander.

Long Joseph had been lying in darkness on the floor of a car with his face covered by some kind of sack for what seemed at

least an hour as his kidnappers drove slowly through the streets
of Durban. The hard shin of the man who had snatched him from
in front of the hospital was pinning Joseph's arm against his side,
and the even harder barrel of the gun rested against the top of
his head like the beak of a murderous bird. The sack itself was
foul and close, with the ammonia-stink of old, sweaty clothes.

It was not the first time in his life that Joseph had been ab-
ducted by armed men. Twenty years earlier a rumor of cuckoldry
had led one of the neighborhood hard men and his cousins to
drag Joseph out of his house and bundle him into a truck, then
drive him to a shebeen one of the men owned on the far side of
Pinetown. Guns had been waved around and Joseph had been
slapped a few times, but at least a dozen witnesses had seen him
dragged from the streets and knew who had done it. The whole
thing was mostly a face-saving display by the husband of the
whispered-about wife. Joseph had been much more afraid of a
bad beating than of being killed.

Not this time, he thought to himself, and felt cold all over. *Not
these men. The kind of people Renie got onto, they don't bother
with no hitting and yelling. Take you out to the edge of the town-
ship and just put bullets into you.*

Beyond a swift, partially whispered conversation as he was
being forced into the car, his two captors had not spoken. The
man driving seemed in no hurry, or perhaps was trying to avoid
being noticed. Whatever the case, Joseph had at first been frightened rigid, but had found that he could not sustain such an extreme pitch of fear. After going round and round with the
imminence of his own death dozens of times, he began to slip
into a kind of waking dream.

This what Renie feel like, down in the dark? He shifted on the
car floor, his back arched uncomfortably. The man with the gun
shoved him, more in irritation than in threat. *Just wish I could
see her again, one more time. Tell her she's a good girl, even
though she drive me crazy with her nagging.*

He thought of Renie's mother, Miriam, who had nagged him,
too, but who had also loved him up sweet as honey. Once, when
they were first together, he had stripped naked and waited for her
on the front room couch. She had laughed when she came in and

saw him, saying, *What will I do with a crazy man like you? What if my mother had been with me?*

Sorry, he had said, *but you have to tell her I am just not interested.*

Miriam had laughed so hard. That night, as they lay together on top of the sheets, the old fan only barely pushing the hot air around the room, he had told her that she was going to marry him.

Might as well, she had said, and he could hear her smile, there in the dark beside him. *Otherwise you'll probably just keep bothering me.*

They had made Renie in that bed, and Stephen, too. And Miriam had slept with him there the last night she spent at home, the night before that terrible day when she did not come back from the department store. That had been the last night they lay together belly to belly, with her snoring in his ear the way she did—the way that sometimes when his head ached had made him crazy, but which he would now give anything to hear again. He would have slept beside her in her hospital bed in her last days, but she was too badly burned. Even a slight movement of the mattress, just setting down a magazine near her arm, had made her whimper.

Goddamn, it is not fair, he thought, then continued with an unusual leap of perspective. *Especially for poor Renie. First her mother, then her brother, now her foolish father gone and get himself killed, and she has nobody.* He entertained a brief fantasy of managing to escape when the car reached its destination, a sprint for freedom that would take the kidnappers by surprise, but the unlikeliness of it was too heavy a weight for his reverie to bear. *Not these men,* he told himself. *People burn down a whole flatblock just to tell someone like Renie to shut up and leave things alone, they not going to make any mistakes. . . .*

Without warning, the car slowed and then stopped. The driver switched off the engine. Long Joseph's body turned to ice in an instant—it was all he could do to keep from pissing himself.

"I don't go any farther," the driver said, the seat between them muffling his voice so that Long Joseph had to strain to make out his words. "You get me?"

It seemed a strange thing to say, but before Joseph could think about it, the man with the gun made a noise, almost a grunt, and pressed the barrel hard against his neck. "Get up," he told Joseph gruffly. "Don't do anything foolish."

Tripping and staggering, grudgingly assisted by his captors, Long Joseph at last managed to clamber out of the car and onto his own two feet again, lost in the dark sack covering his head. He heard a distant shout echoing as though down a long street. The car door slammed shut, the engine started, and it rumbled away.

Someone yanked the bag off, pulling at his hair in the process so that despite everything he yelped in anger and surprise. At first the dark street and its one flickering streetlight seemed shockingly bright. Tall, graffiti-tattooed walls loomed on either side. Half a hundred meters down the street a fire burned in a metal drum, surrounded by a small crowd of figures warming their hands, but before he could even contemplate calling out to them the gun jabbed his backbone.

"Turn around and walk. Through there." He was shoved toward a doorway in one of the walls. At the gunman's direction Joseph pulled the door open and stepped through into blackness. He flinched, positive that any second the bullet would slam into the back of his skull. When something clicked, he jumped. A moment later he realized he was still alive, but that controlling his bladder was no longer an option. He was ridiculously glad he hadn't had much to drink in the last few hours—at least he would die with only a small show of cowardice.

A fluorescent light spasmed on overhead. He had been brought to some kind of garage or storage room, empty but for a few cans of paint and some broken chairs, the kind of place someone whose small business had failed might rent to keep his equipment in until he could sell it off. Joseph saw his own shadow stretched against the floor with his kidnapper's flung alongside it.

"Turn around," the gunman said.

Long Joseph did, slowly. The dark-skinned black man who stood before him wore what surely had once been a nice overcoat, but which was stained, as was the white shirt he wore beneath. His hair had been expensively cut at some point, but had not been tended recently. Even Joseph, one of the world's less observant people, could see that the man was nervous and upset, but the gun in the fellow's hand kept him from saying anything about it. "Do you recognize me?" the kidnapper asked.

Joseph shook his head helplessly—although now that the man mentioned it, there was something vaguely familiar. . . .

"My name is Del Ray Chiume. Does that mean anything?" The gunman shifted from one foot to the other.

Long Joseph frowned, still frightened, but now puzzled, too. "Del Ray . . . ?" It came to him a moment later. "You used to see my daughter Renie?"

"That's right!" The man laughed explosively, as though Joseph had conceded a hard-fought point. "And do you know what your daughter has done to me? Can you even guess?"

Joseph watched the gun go up and down, up and down. "I don't know nothing that you are talking about."

"She's ruined my life, that's what she's done." Del Ray paused in his back-and-forthing to wipe the sleeve of his overcoat along his damp forehead. "I've lost everything because she couldn't leave well enough alone!"

"I don't know what you are talking about." Joseph gathered his courage. "Why you kidnap me? You going to kill me because my daughter break up with you or something?"

Del Ray laughed again. "Are you crazy? Are you crazy, old man? That was years ago. I'm a married man! But my marriage is over because of your daughter. I've lost my house, everything. And it's all her fault!"

Renie, Long Joseph decided, had clearly been keeping a lot to herself. And she had the nerve to criticize *his* behavior. He was beginning to feel that there was a good chance he was going to live after all, and he was torn between an urge to collapse and a desire to shout out his joy and fury. This was no hard man. Long Joseph knew this type. This Del Ray fellow was some kind of businessman, the kind who turned down your loan application with a sneer, but when push came to shove and he wasn't on top anymore, had no balls. "So are you going to shoot me, then? Because if you are not, then put your damn gun away, but don't keep waving it around like you some kind of Mafia hitman."

"Hitman!" Del Ray's laugh was theatrically bitter. "You don't know shit, old man. I've met the bloody hitmen. They came and had a talk with me—that was before they burned my house down.

One of them had fists as big as your head—biggest, ugliest Boer you ever saw. Face like a bag of rocks. You know what they said? Told me if I didn't do what they wanted, they were going to rape my wife and then kill her, right in front of me." Del Ray suddenly burst into tears.

Long Joseph was taken aback—how did you deal with a weeping man with a gun? In fact, how did you deal with a weeping man of any kind? "Why would they do a thing like that?" he asked, almost gently. "Why they so angry at you?"

Del Ray looked up suddenly, his eyes bright, madly intent. "Because of your daughter, that's why! Because Renie dragged me into something I didn't want to know about, and my wife's left me, and . . . and . . ." The tears returned. He sank to the floor and sat, legs stretched in front of him, like a toddler who had fallen down. The gun lay on the floor between his knees.

"So you going to shoot *me*?" Long Joseph asked. "You been waiting around in front of that hospital just to shoot me?" He considered for a moment. "Or you waiting to shoot Renie?"

"No, no." Del Ray wiped his sweat-shiny face with his sleeve again. "No, I have to talk to Renie. She has to tell these people what they need to know so I can stop hiding."

Joseph shook his head, unable to keep up with the man's logic. "I can't tell nothing to Renie. She is not here. I just come to see my son, and that's what I'm going to do. Unless you going to shoot me." He had allowed a sneer to creep onto his face—now that he thought back on it, he had never liked this high-talking fellow very much, and had been openly glad when Renie got shed of him.

Del Ray's hand suddenly snapped up, the gun clutched in it once more, the alarmingly large black hole pointing right at Long Joseph's face.

"You *are* crazy," Del Ray said. "You don't know how lucky you are it was me got you first. My brothers and I have been watching out for you or Renie for days and days, but if I can watch that place, so can the hitmen. Do you think for a second you can just walk in and see your son without them knowing? These people won't just kill you, old man, they'll torture you first to find your daughter—and then think what they'll do to her."

Joseph frowned. "I don't understand any of this talk. It all sound crazy to me—crazier than what Renie says, even." He blinked, trying to remember how it had been when he could talk to someone and make them understand him, and he could understand them in turn. It seemed like years. "Put that gun away, man. Just tell me what happened."

Del Ray stared at him for a moment, then looked at his own outstretched arm and the gun trembling in his fist. He tucked the pistol into his coat pocket.

"That is good," Joseph said. "Much better. Now tell me what happened to you." He looked around the dimly lit garage, then back to Del Ray Chiume's wide-eyed, sweaty face. "But can we go somewhere? I truly need a drink."

IT was not good to think too much about things, Jeremiah was discovering.

When there was no one to talk to but yourself and nowhere to visit but the same echoing rooms, when you saw no sun, and had listened to the radio voices babble about a world that had nothing to do with you until you wanted to scream, when you had heard little else except the breathing and amplified heartbeats of two people who for all intents and purposes had left you behind in another country, it was bad to spend too much time letting your mind wander.

There had been times during the years he had worked for the Van Bleecks, first for both of them, Doctor and Doctor, but most of the time for Susan alone in her long widowhood, that Jeremiah Dako had thought, *I would give everything I have for just a little time to rest and think.* Acting as secretary, housekeeper, cook, and chauffeur for a brilliant, cantankerous, absentminded old woman, he had done a job that two younger men would have found arduous, but Jeremiah had prided himself on his ability to take anything life (or Susan Van Bleeck's dubious skills of organization and personal punctuality) could throw at him and keep going, venting his frustration only in small steam-valve gusts of bad temper and irritable over-solicitousness. He had given up his own social life for it, had been out of the bars and club scene so long that on the few occasions he found himself with a night off and his mother otherwise engaged, he not only didn't recognize any of the people he met, but could not understand the music or

the clothing, as though an entire generational shift had happened
while he wasn't looking.

But even if he had little interest anymore in investing the hard
work of maintaining a social life, had weighed the pros and cons
and reconciled himself largely to celibacy and—much more frightening—perhaps a solitary old age, he had not entirely given up
his dreams. In all those years of fiercely hard work, he had never
regretted anything except the lack of rest, of time to think. The
worst thing about middle age, he had discovered, was that if you
weren't careful, your life sped past at such a breakneck pace that
an entire year could sneak by and leave no important memories.

So he had yearned through all the years with Susan for a little time to himself, real time and real leisure, not the annual week
of taking his mother to play the slot machines at Sun City (while
himself hoping for a brief and discreet romance, which had indeed happened a couple of times, a happy encounter at a casino
bar after Mama's bedtime, the memory of which would carry him
through the rest of the year.) Jeremiah had longed for time to
think, to read, to regain at least a little of the young man he had
been back in school, when he had felt that living in the world
should be synonymous with changing the world. What of all the
books he had used to read, the big thoughts, African history, sexual politics? He had been lucky in the Kloof years if he found
time to check the traffic reports and download an occasional recipe.

So here he was, after all these years and in this most unexpected way, with nothing to do but read and think, with no company but his own, with no demands on his time and attention that
could not have been fulfilled by a four-year-old child. He had exactly what he had wanted for so long. And he hated it.

Now that Long Joseph had—for lack of a better term—escaped, one of the things that Jeremiah found himself thinking
about far more often than he would have liked was the terrible
responsibility of being the only person looking out for Renie's
and !Xabbu's safety. There had been little need for worry thus
far: although their heart rates had spiked several times, nothing
had crested above the military's own warning system levels, so
he had to assume they were experiencing the normal ins and outs

of virtual existence. Not that there was anything actually normal about any of this.

It was nothing new, of course. Throughout his years as Doctor Van Bleeck's companion and protector the responsibility of her safety had weighed on him heavily. Durban had suffered several waves of carjackings and kidnappings, including a year-long reign of terror by one gang of young thugs who routinely murdered drivers just so they could steal a particular automotive opsys bubble chip that was then drawing a high price on the black market. Twice Jeremiah had escaped in high speed chases from threats that he felt were very serious indeed, and once he'd driven away from a crossroad with three hoodlums still clinging to the hood, trying to break the expensive, shatter-resistant glass with tire irons. When the last of the young criminals had tumbled to the pavement and Jeremiah had begun to turn the car back toward home, a shaken Susan had instead asked him to drive her to the hospital. Her heart was beating so swiftly, she later told him, that she had been positive she was going into cardiac arrest.

Even thinking back on that now, he felt cold. There were so many dangers in the world—so many crazy, desperate people!

A deeper and more subtle chill spread through him, a deep unhappiness that made him feel sick to his stomach. Here he stood in this vast underground fortress worrying about how someone had once almost hurt Susan, ignoring the fact that she *had* been hurt, and that in the end he had failed in his duty to her as completely as anyone could fail. Men had broken into the house and had beaten Susan Van Bleeck so badly that she died. All the things Jeremiah had done for her over the years, the dramatic and the domestic, had all come down to that. He had failed to protect her, and they had killed her.

And now he had been planted with ultimate responsibility for two more people—people he could not speak to, could not even see. But if something went wrong, if their hearts stopped, or if someone cut the power to the military base one night while Jeremiah slept, their deaths would still be his fault.

It made him want to follow Renie's father, to flee into the big world outside and leave the responsibility to someone else. But of course there wasn't anyone else, which made the duty even more miserable, more impossible to escape.

Jeremiah was thinking some variant of these thoughts—his mind had been traveling in rather unhappy circles in the days since Long Joseph's midnight departure—when the phone rang for the first time.

It was such an astonishingly unexpected noise that at first he did not even know what it was. The incredibly old-fashioned handset slung in its metal cradle on the huge concrete pillar beside the control panels had long ago lost even its initial novelty and become merely another object in his visual field, something that would have attracted his attention only if it had disappeared, and then perhaps not for days. When the insistent ringing began, a purringly metallic tone quite unlike anything he'd ever heard, it sounded five or six times before he even understood where it was coming from.

Decades of secretarial reflexes summoned into operation, for a moment he seriously contemplated answering it—he even had a brief vision of himself picking up the handset and saying *"Hello?"* like someone from a costume drama. Then the full magnitude of the thing came to him and he sat frozen in fear until the ringing stopped. His pulse was just beginning to return to normal rates when the ringing started once more.

The phone rang every five minutes for the next half hour, then stopped again, apparently for good.

After the worst of the surprise was over, he was able to put it aside, even smile at his own reactions. Obviously Martine and Singh had reconnected the telecom lines, otherwise Long Joseph wouldn't have been able to access the net, even in receive-only mode. So if there was a working line, phone calls could get through, too, even random ones. Someone had triggered a number that just happened to belong to Wasp's Nest—perhaps some autodialing machine, perhaps a simple mistake. It would be foolish to pick it up, of course, but even if he did, probably not fatal. Not that he would touch the phone if it happened again—Jeremiah was tired and worried, but not stupid.

It seemed much less academic when the phone rang again four hours later, then rang back every five minutes for another half hour, then stopped again. Even so, he did not panic. It meant nothing, and never would unless he himself answered it, and there was no reason to do that.

The phone continued to ring, sometimes after intervals as short as two hours, sometimes after a hiatus as long as eight hours, or once ten—always the same phone, always with the same, persistent pattern of five minute retries. If it was just gear, Jeremiah decided, just mechanical, then anything so aggressively upsetting must be Satan's own autodialer. But what if it wasn't?

Try as he might, he couldn't imagine anything good that the phone might represent—someone at Power or Communications trying to find out why an abandoned base was sucking from the grid at a greater rate than it had in years, perhaps? Or something even more sinister, the same mysterious people who had mauled Susan and burned down Renie's house and God knew what else? He could not think of anyone they knew who might even guess they were in this place, so there was no reason at all to answer, which should have made the whole thing easier. Still, the constant repetition was maddening. He tried to turn off the phone's ringer, but the ancient device had no external control. An attempt to remove the entire phone from the pillar was equally useless: he wrestled with the frozen bolts for the better part of an afternoon and managed nothing more than to scrape his knuckles bloody, until in a fit of frustrated fury he beat at the phone with the inadequate wrench, dimpling the several layers of bland graygreen paint but not even denting the heavy iron cover.

It went on. The phone rang every day, usually several times a day, and each time it did, he flinched. Sometimes he woke up from his sleep to the sound of the phone, even though he was now sleeping on the far side of the underground base, completely insulated from its noise. But by the end of the first week he heard it anyway, even in his dreams. It rang and rang and rang.

"MAN, you gone a long time. You just get one bottle of wine?" Joseph rolled down the sack and squinted at the label. At least Del Ray had gotten him Mountain Rose as he had asked, which might taste like cat-piss but had a reliable kick.

"It's all yours. I don't drink wine," Del Ray said. "At least I don't drink the kind of wine they sell around here. I got myself a beer." He brandished a bottle of Steenlager.

"You should get that Red Elephant." Joseph upended the squeeze bottle and took a generous swig. "That's a good beer." He settled on the garage floor with his back against the wall, unmindful of oil stains on his trousers. An hour ago he had been certain he was going to get a bullet in him, not wine, so he was in a very, very good mood. He had even forgiven Renie's old boyfriend for kidnapping him, although he had not entirely given up the idea of punching him a good one in the face, just on principle, to let him know that it wasn't smart to mess with Long Joseph Sulaweyo. But not as long as this Chiume fellow still had that gun tucked in his pocket. "So what is all this foolishness you getting up to?" Joseph asked, smacking his lips. "Why you running around all tooled up like some kind of Pinetown rude boy?"

Del Ray, who had only taken the first sip of his beer, scowled. "Because there are people trying to kill me. Where's Renie?"

"Oh, no." For once Joseph had right on his side, he felt quite sure. It was a novel feeling and he intended to enjoy it. "You don't come kidnapping and mistreating me and then expect me to answer all your questions."

"I've still got the gun, you know."

Long Joseph waved his hand airily. He had this young fellow's number. "Then shoot me. But if you not going to shoot me, then you better tell me what cause you to go snatching people off the street when they are minding their lawful business."

Del Ray rolled his eyes but did not pursue it. "It's your daughter's fault, and if you don't know about it, you ought to. She came to me, after all. I hadn't talked to her in years. I was married . . . I was married . . ." He fell silent for a long moment, his face morose. "My life was going very well. Then Renie called up with some crazy story about a virtual nightclub, and now it's all gone to hell."

After Del Ray's explanation of Renie's request and their meeting on the Golden Mile, the younger man fell silent, staring at his beer. "These three fellows came to talk to me," he said at last. "And everything started to get very, very bad."

Joseph noted with alarm that there were only a few swallows left in his bottle. He put the cap on and put it on the floor, tucking it just out his line of sight to make it last a bit longer. "Who come talk to you? You said some Boers?"

"Two of them were Afrikaaners. One of them was a black man. The main man, the big ugly white fellow, told me that I had been asking questions that didn't concern me—that I had made some important people very unhappy. They wanted to know who Renie was, and especially why she was talking to some French woman named Martine Desroubins. . . ."

"You are joking. All this about that French woman?"

"You had better believe it's true. I told them I didn't know anything about her or any of that, that Renie was just an old friend who'd asked me a favor. I shouldn't have told them anything, but they scared me.

"They came back a little later and told me Renie wasn't living in the shelter anymore—that you'd moved. They said they needed to speak to her, that they were going to explain to her she would be better off leaving this whole thing alone. So I . . ."

"Wait just one minute!" Long Joseph sat up and almost knocked over his squeeze bottle. Despite his rising anger, he snatched it up protectively. "You the one who tried to sell Renie out, I remember now. You traced her phone call . . . !"

"I . . . I did."

"I should knock off your head!" His words belied his secret pleasure. This proved exactly what Joseph had always believed about men like Del Ray, university-educated, fancy-suited. "You lucky you still have that gun."

"Damn it, I didn't want to! But they knew where *I* lived—they came to my front door! And they promised they weren't going to hurt her."

"Yeah. Believe an Afrikaaner policeman when he say that."

"These weren't police. These weren't anything *like* police. But they weren't just criminals either. They had to have found out about me from someone high up in UNComm, because they didn't just know I'd been talking to Renie, they knew what I had done for her, who else I'd spoken to, what files I'd accessed. And the phone-tracing gear—I came in to work one day and found someone had put it on my system. No, they weren't just some ordinary bonebreakers. They were connected."

"So you sold Renie out," said Joseph, unwilling to be lured from his moral high ground. "You made it so we had to run away."

Del Ray had lost the urge to fight back. "I made it worse for myself. They told me if I didn't find her, they'd kill my wife. And when I couldn't find her, they got me fired. Then they burned down our house."

Long Joseph nodded sagely. "They burn our house up, too. I barely pull Renie out in time."

The younger man was not even listening. "It was something about this Martine woman—they kept asking me why Renie was talking to her, whether I had hooked them up." He shook his head. "They burned my house down! If they hadn't started the dogs barking, Dolly and I would have both burned to death. It was so fast—some kind of incendiary grenades, the police said."

Long Joseph said nothing, but he was impressed. These were the kind of people you saw on the net shows. He felt more important just by dint of the fact that they were after him. He finished the wine, gave the bottle a make-sure squeeze; then, as though it were one of the grenades that had burned Del Ray Chiume out of his home, he lobbed it into the corner of the garage. Del Ray flinched at the clatter.

"Dolly left me. She went back to her family in Manguse. I've been staying at friends' places, this garage thing of my cousin's, wherever. They don't seem to be looking for me very hard right now, but I'm not stupid enough just to walk back into my old life and say, "Here I am! Come kill me!"

Long Joseph was judging whether he should stay seated and enjoy the heavy, satisfying warmth of the first bottle of Mountain Rose or try to use Del Ray's unquestionable guilt as a lever to make him get another bottle. "So why you come and grab me?" he asked. "Why you come down with your gun like some kind of Mafia man? Why not just let me see my boy?"

Del Ray snorted. "You must be crazy, old man. You weren't going to walk in and see your son without anyone noticing. You're lucky I saw you first. You should thank me—if those thugs had gotten you, you'd be in a ditch right now, covered in petrol, and they'd be holding a lit match over you, asking if you had anything else you wanted to tell them."

Joseph shuddered at the image, which was not much different than what he himself had been thinking just a short hour earlier, but he was not going to admit it in front of this suit-and-tie fellow. "So now what?"

The younger man's eyes gleamed, as though he had been asked to describe the plot of a story he had long planned to write. "I need Renie to tell these people what they need to know. If she's been talking to this Martine woman, she needs to tell them she won't do it anymore. She has to leave this woman alone! That's what they're angry about. Then everything will be fine. Then I can have some kind of life again."

Even Long Joseph, whose comprehension of the scope of Renie's troubles was vague, had a feeling that Del Ray was being overly optimistic. Not that it mattered. "It is not so easy," he said aloud. "Not so easy at all. Renie is not around here. It is much more complicated, what she and I are doing, and we cannot just change things because some Afrikaaner hoodlums come and threaten you." He looked at Del Ray's worried face and shook his head with all the grave regret of a prophet regarding the sinfulness of mankind. "After I see my boy, we will think about what to do for you."

"After . . . ? What in hell are you talking about, old man?" Del Ray sat up straight and bumped his head against a shelf. "That hospital is under quarantine! And even if it wasn't, if you walk up to that front door again those bastards are going to tear your heart out!"

Joseph was calm, certain. "Then you going to have to think of some way to get us inside, boy."

"Us? *Us?*"

"That is right. Because I came to see my son, and if I don't get to see him somehow then I am not going to take you to Renie or that Martine woman. You spend the rest of your life hiding in a closet. So you better start thinking." He sat back, smiling the world-weary smile of a seasoned adventurer. "You can work on your idea while you go get me another bottle of wine."

CHAPTER 3

House of the Beast

THE desert evening was mild, the sands empty and still, yet Orlando Gardiner was being dragged forward by a compulsion as powerful as hurricane winds. His friend Fredericks had shown surprising strength and resourcefulness, but with the breaking of the great urn Fredericks' strength had gone, and now he too was being drawn helplessly toward the looming temple and the terrifying thing that slept inside it.

Whether or not they felt the same compulsion, the little yellow monkey-children of the Wicked Tribe clearly felt *something:* shrieking their dismay, they clung to Orlando like baby bats. He wore so little clothing in his Thargor guise that most of them clutched bare flesh, a living cloak of tiny pinching fingers that would have been excruciating if Orlando had not had far greater worries.

Something horrible is in that temple, and it's pulling us in. I asked that goddess for help, and all we got were these stupid monkeys. It doesn't make any sense! But nothing in Otherland ever made much sense.

Does it even matter? I'm dying, whether that . . . thing gets us or not.

He took a grudging step forward, then another. The monkeys scrambled around to his back in a leggy, tweezering mass, keeping the width of his body between them and the temple. They were terrified of the place, which was perfectly logical, but why on earth had the goddess thought these children could help?

"Run away now, 'Landogarner!" one of them squeaked in his ear. "Big Bad Nothing live there. All the gear is crazy. Run away!"

Orlando was already working so hard to resist he did not waste time explaining that at this moment he could no more run away than he could compose an opera in Turkish. Just as he realized that the yellow microsimian had used the word "gear," reminding him that there was actual machinery behind this madness, he stumbled on something half-buried in the sand. It was a piece of the broken pot which had imprisoned the Tribe, a section with only one visible carving on its surface—a feather in a rounded rectangle.

"Walk into the darkness," the goddess Ma'at had told him. *"You will see my sign."* But her sign so far had brought him only miniature monkeys, a dubious boon. He forced himself to stop anyway, bracing against a pull that felt like a window had been blown out of a jet in high-atmosphere flight, then managed to scoop the ceramic fragment into his numbed fingers before surrendering to the temple once more.

"What you do with that?" the monkey nearest his head demanded. "That from the Lady."

"You . . . know her?" Orlando was exerting a tremendous

amount of energy to slow himself, but that meant Fredericks had moved several paces ahead and the distance between them was widening.

"She talk to us in the dark. Tell us stories!" The monkey hand-over-handed up into the Thargor sim's dark hair. "You truly best turn 'round, 'Landogarner."

"Malocchio abbondanza!" shrilled another monkey fearfully. "Lady said stay away from that!"

"I'd . . . love . . . to stay away," Orlando grunted through clenched teeth. His head was hammering so badly it felt as though some artery might explode like a blocked pipe. "I . . . I can't. It's . . . pulling us toward it." He took a deep, shaky breath. All he could see of Fredericks now was his friend's back as he trudged forward, bowed and helpless. "You said . . . 'gear' . . . ?"

"Gear all crazy there," said the passenger in his hair. He suspected it was Zunni, but it was hard to think properly with all the noise in his head. "Like big what-is-a-callit—singalarity."

"Singularity?" If he had not been so close to screaming, he would have laughed. "Like a black locking hole? Is that what you mean? *This is virtual,* damn it!" His voice was so raggedly unpleasant that some of the monkeys fluttered free. It was bizarre to see them circling in the air—it felt so much like he was being sucked down a giant drain that he could not understand why they were not tugged straight toward the temple as well. *"Ohhhh,"* he groaned, finding it more and more difficult to speak. "Doesn't it . . . pull you, too?"

Zunni, if that was who it was, went on as though he hadn't spoken. "Singularity? All the arrows point one way? That not right?"

"Too inside out!" another one chirped. "Not get small like that."

Orlando could not make sense of anything and no longer had the strength to care. He realized he was clutching the piece of pottery so hard his fingers had turned white.

"You go there, but you don't want to go?" The little yellow shape was too close for him to focus on it. It flittered before his eyes, fuzzily insubstantial as an angelic vision. "Then you have to go through and bounce."

"Uh-uh, Zunni," one of the others said. "Not bounce." This one's voice was so high as to be almost inaudible, the lisping tones of a child too young even for school. "Wanna go 'round. Do Gavvy Well."

"She means 'Gravity Well,'" said Zunni confidingly. "That a game, okay?"

The facade of the red stone temple now loomed above Orlando like a cliff face, impossibly tall, impossibly harsh and imposing, and still the monkeys chittered among themselves. *Fredericks was right,* he thought despairingly. *It is like talking to breakfast cereal. . . .*

"Better run fast, 'Landogarner," one of the other little creatures told him at last. "That the best thing."

"Only thing," said another. "*Misterioso fabuloso.* Need the best tricks."

"I can't . . . run," he gritted. "I told you. It's . . . it's got me."

Zunni rappelled down his forehead on a strand of hair and poked at his cheek. "No, run *toward* thing. Run fast. Think fast thoughts, maybe."

"Zunni, you a big dumb *itipoti!*" another monkey squealed. "That never work. Tell him just run fast."

"Think fast stuff, too," Zunni whispered, a tiny, dangling co-conspirator. "Big Bad Nothing gone all asleep—maybe he fooled."

Orlando was almost weeping with the effort of slowing his forward march. The shadowed entrance to the temple stood before him, a wide black spot in the facade like the hole left by a missing tooth. Fredericks was a pale shape several meters ahead, almost absorbed by the darkness. "I don't understand," he panted. "Run toward it? Run?"

"We help," Zunni promised. She clambered onto his shoulder, then dropped onto his back, out of sight, but he could still hear her voice. "We help you come out fast, like Gravity Well. Here— we push!"

And suddenly the entire fluttering force of the tiny simians centered itself between his shoulder blades and gave him an astonishingly hard shove. He was propelled forward in a stumbling flurry of arms and legs, struggling just to keep his feet beneath him. Everything before him swirled, as though for the first time Otherland's latency could not approximate real life, but he quickly realized it was even stranger than that: the doorway, the huge sandstone blocks of the walls, even Fredericks turning in astonished slow motion, all were abruptly flattened and stretched, rolling themselves into a tunnel down which he plummeted. Orlando snatched at Fredericks as he sped past him—through him—beyond him. . . . For a moment he felt the hard piece of feather-scribed clay clutched in one of his hands like a shield, and his friend's fingers gripping his other hand, then all sense of his physical self dropped away and he was only an eye plummeting down an endless well, an ear that heard nothing but the rushing of endless wind.

I'm inside it, was all he had time to think, then an image burst upon him, sudden and vivid, a picture that drew itself on his mind rather than his sight. Hidden within the temple, he suddenly knew beyond doubt, but also encompassing that temple somehow, like a shadow bigger than the object which cast it, was the monstrous black pyramid of his desert dream. . . .

. . . The pyramid . . . the house of the beast . . .

Something struck him with an impact like a bomb—a great shuddering blow, as though he were a hammer that had just smashed down against a titanic anvil, a deep reverberating tone like the sound of a world being born . . . or ending. . . .

Doom . . . !

The tunnel around him shimmied and broke apart into opalescent smears.

First step, he dimly realized, his thoughts distant as the voices of migrating birds invisible in the night sky. *I've taken the first step into the temple . . . into the dark. . . .*

The thunderous concussion faded. The shivering, gleaming light reformed. He was a child again, following his mother home from the well, watching the sway of her hips and the jerry can balanced on her head. Something rustled in the dry grass and he saw the red-and-brown skin of a snake snap out onto the path before him. His mother turned in fear, her eyes wide, but the snake was between them. . . .

Now he was in the back seat of a car, driving along the coast, with his parents arguing in the front and his sister beside him, grinning and jabbing him with the neck of her headless doll. He kicked at her, but she stayed out of reach, and although he cried out to his parents, they were busy with their conflict. As the car rounded a bend in the highway the sun bounced its reflection off

the water, and for a moment he was dazzled by the light that silhouetted his parents' faces. . . .

His two younger brothers had crawled out of the tent. His
mother was yelling, which wasn't helping her soothe the sick baby
in her arms, but the bad thing was that his mother was really
frightened because it was night outside and dark and his father
still wasn't back yet. He pushed out of the flap and past the nervous goats, who rang their bells and bleated. The night sky was
huge and endless, running away in all directions, and the stars
were fierce, and he called his brothers' names over and over. . . .

But I don't have any brothers, he thought. *And those aren't my
parents, are they?*

Everything began happening all at once.

A shack high up in a valley between the hills, and his bicycle
lying in a ditch beside the front path, the wheel rusted to the forks
because he had left it there all winter, to win an argument with
his father that his father didn't even know they were having. . . .

The place in the long front hallway where his mother's and
older sister's pictures sat on a table, with a vase of flowers just
between them, and where sometimes, on holy days, his grandmother burned a candle. . . .

Playing in the river before the rainy season returned, with nothing but mud far down the banks. His cousin and one of the other
village children were wrestling, and they slipped down and for a
moment they disappeared into the sludge, frightening him, but
then they came up again laughing, with everything the same fecal
brown except their shining eyes and teeth. . . .

They were taking down his uncle's flag now that evening had
come, and he was rigidly at attention, hoping his uncle would notice how straight he was standing. . . .

Doom . . .

Second step. The smears of light fragmented into smaller, more
rigid pieces, shards of lives, thousands of bright, jagged insights
like broken windows—a high mountain trail, following the horses,
watching the brilliant tassel of a blanket . . . a sharp bark as his
dog heard something in the next apartment, where no one was
supposed to be home . . . his baby brother's crying face, fat and
red and completely without understanding why it had been pushed

down in the sandbox . . . a pair of new shoes set carefully on his folded communion suit. . . .

And all the time a great dark something was moving beneath these glinting bits, as though he, the observing eye, were a diver floating just beneath the surface while something impossibly large, something too big and traveling too deep to be fully comprehensible, passed slowly, slowly beneath him. It did not know he was there, and his fascination with it was almost as great as his naked terror, but nothing in the universe could have been more exposed than he was, a worm without even a hook, floating above the great shadow. . . .

Doom . . .

This third step brought the dark, as though the Big Nothing passing beneath him had risen and, without realizing it, accidentally swallowed him whole. Dark surrounded him now, permeated him, but it was a darkness that burned, the darkness inside the oven after the door has closed.

He screamed, but there were no words. He knew no words. There were flashes of light, but they had no more meaning than the burning darkness. He was not only bodiless but nameless. He had no brothers, no sisters, no fathers, no mothers, only pain and confusion. He was a singularity, one infinite point at the center of everything, and all that surrounded him was finite. He turned himself inside out over and over again.

The oscillations came faster now, hotter now, faster and hotter and he could not he tried but there was no sense or sound or sight or anything but fast and hot and

Faster hotter faster hotter broken-backed jerking scratch needle white heat can't stop strike out no no more no make it no faster hot stop make no it won't it too stop hurting not why understand no hot make faster inside stop inside hotter outside stop make faster no make hotter it stop . . .

Stopmakeitstopitwon'twhywon'titmakeit . . .

And then something finally did. Something blue, something quiet, something clingingly cool poured over and made everything slow down, slow down, blessed creeping syrupy slow frost that held him and covered him and let his deep black empty heart go slow, go so very slow, until it beat only once in an age, once in

an aeon, once when everything began and then again when everything would finally stop . . .

Doom . . . The fourth step.

And with that singular and potent reverberation came nothingness. And it was welcome.

He came up nameless, out of fundamental blankness into another, lesser blackness, a still place with no time except *now.* He
only knew it was a place because he had a sense of himself as
an individual thing, and thus a dim feeling that anything that existed must exist in a place, but he was in no hurry to know where
he was, or even who he was. With the acceptance of personal existence came a certain commitment, he knew, and he did not wish
anything so strenuous or permanent just yet.

The blackness, although it encompassed everything, nevertheless had a shape, a shape he had seen before, wide at the bottom,
narrow at the top—a mountain, a cup emptied and then turned
over, a pyramid . . . He was in the darkness—*of* the darkness—
but he could still feel the impossible geometry of the black form,
the vertices both converging and simultaneously extending upward
in parallel, forever.

And as he felt himself alive and tiny and for this moment unnoticed in the heart of the black pyramid, something began to siz-
zle in the emptiness. When he saw the torn place moving before
him, he realized that what had ripped the darkness was light, a
fizzing irregular glow like a Fourth of July sparkler. . . .

. . . *His parents' balcony, him with a cripplingly bad respira-
tory infection and too sick to go down to the fireworks, even those
on the compound's green, but his parents having their own show
just for him on the balcony, so he could watch it from his bed* . . .

The jagged place tore more widely, light spilling out now. For
a moment—only a moment—he was disappointed to see the beautiful darkness compromised so easily and so carelessly. But as he
floated in all that black he could not look away from the light,
which was spreading before him, becoming a field of regular
shapes, angled lines, a grid that turned inside out from white lines
on black to black lines on a white . . .

. . . *Ceiling* . . .

. . . And he came to realize he was lying on his back, looking up at the ceiling of some institutional room, all insulated tile and easy-clean surfaces.

Hospital. The word came to him after a moment, and with it the slowly dawning realization that he must have awakened—that he must somehow have been thrown out of the network and back into his body. Another thought came to him tardily, and he braced himself for the pain that . . . that . . . (the name finally came) that Fredericks had described, but after long moments of looking up at the acoustic tiles, it still had not arrived. He had, however, become aware of two other presences on either side of the bed, leaning over him, which could only be his mother and father. A quiet joy filled him as he opened his eyes.

The shape on his left side was hidden by shadow, so deeply hidden that he could not see it, only feel it. What he perceived was sentience, but also emptiness and the cold that came with it. It was not a pleasant feeling.

The shape on his right had a head that was nothing but light.

I've been here, he thought. *But it was an office, not a hospital. When I first . . . when I first came through . . .*

Hello, Orlando, said the thing with the face made invisible by its own brilliance. It spoke with his mother's voice, but it was not his mother, not by any stretch of imagination. *We have missed you. Although we have not been very far from you.*

Who is "we"? He struggled to rise but could not. The thing on his left side moved, the chilly shape he could not quite see; for a heart-stopping moment he was terrified that it would touch him. He turned away violently, but the light on the other side was blindingly bright, so he was forced to turn his face back toward the acoustic tiles. A small thing was crawling there, a tiny thing, perhaps a bug, and he pinned his attention to it.

"We," in the sense of "I," the not-his-mother continued. *"You," I suppose it could even be said. But of course that would not be strictly accurate either.*

He could make no sense of that. *Where am I? What is this place?*

The thing of light hesitated. *A dream, I suppose. Perhaps that would be the best explanation.*

So I'm talking to myself? So this is all in my head?

The cold fire rippled. He realized the shape was laughing. As if angered by this, the shadowy thing on his left periphery shifted. He thought he could hear it breathing, a slow, somnolent sound from a long way away. *No, no,* the shape on his right said. *Nothing so simplistic. You're talking to yourself, yes, but that's because that's where words come from.*

Am I dead?

That word doesn't mean much in this particular conversation. The glow rose a little, the fierce radiance bringing a tear to Orlando's right eye. He blinked as it continued. *You are between. You are near a boundary. You are halfway between Heaven and Hell—a place which, medieval theology aside, has nothing to do with Earth at all.*

Are you . . . God? Even in his distraction and disconnection, a part of him did not believe it. It all seemed too pat, too simple. The cold thing on the other side of him leaned closer, or seemed to—he felt a chill shadow inch across him, and he shut his eyes tight, terrified that he might see what stood there.

The voice that went with the radiant face was kind. *Here's the question, Orlando. It's kind of a Sunday School question. . . .*

Eyes tightly shut, he waited, but the silence went on. Just as he was about to risk everything and open his eyes, the soft voice spoke again.

If God is all-powerful, then the Devil must be nothing more than a darkness in the mind of God. But if the Devil is something real and separate, then perfection is impossible, and there can be no God . . . except for the aspirations of fallen angels. . . .

Orlando strained to hear as the voice, which had grown steadily fainter, whispered the last word. As if he might hear better with his vision restored, he opened his eyes to . . .

Blackness, complete and absolute and containing nothing but . . .

Doom . . .

FOR the second time in what seemed a very short span, he appeared to be back in a hospital. His eyes were tight shut, and the idea that those same odd bookend figures might still be sitting over him meant he was in no hurry to open them, but Orlando could tell that he was flat on his back, restrained by sheets or something equally binding, and someone was dabbing at his fore-head with a cold, damp cloth.

Also contributing to the hospital theory was the fact that he felt absolutely dreadful.

"He just blinked," said Fredericks in the excited tone of some-one who has been watching for something a long time.

"Oh, God," Orlando groaned. "I'm still . . . alive, then? God, that locks utterly."

"That's not funny, Gardiner."

As he opened his eyes a second sarcastic remark died on his lips. It was not Fredericks cooling his brow, but a round Egypt-ian woman with dark skin and an impatient expression. "Who are you?" Orlando asked.

"Just hush your mouth." She sounded far more Deep South than Nile Delta. "You were almost dead, boy, so I think you'd better keep still for a bit."

Orlando looked to Fredericks, hovering behind her, and mouthed, *Who is she?* His friend shrugged helplessly. The room decor gave no clues—the walls were whitewashed mud brick, the ceiling white plaster, and there was no furniture in the room other than whatever kind of lumpy, pillowless bed was beneath him.

The woman put a gentle but firm hand against his chest and pressed him back onto the rustling mattress. When he tried to re-sist, he realized that some kind of rough blanket had been tucked around him very tightly: his arms were virtually pinned against his sides.

"What's going on?" he blustered, frightened to be so helpless. "Are you planning to make me into a mummy or something?"

"Don't be stupid." She dabbed a last time and then stood up, fists on her full hips. Even with Fredericks wearing his slight-bodied Pithlit sim, she only came up to his shoulder. If Orlando had been vertical, the Thargor body would have towered over her. "You aren't a king, you're just an ordinary god like your friend here, and you're not even dead. You just don't rate mummifica-tion, boy. Now say your prayers and then get some sleep."

"What are you talking about? Who *are* you? What's going on here?"

"You were really sick again, Orlando." Fredericks looked to the woman as though asking permission to speak, but she did not look away from her patient. "When we came through . . . when we were out of that temple place . . . you were . . ."

"You were acting like a crazy person," the woman said matter-of-factly. "Hootin' and hollerin' and carrying on something terrible. You tried to kick your way through the wall of somebody's house, and then you tried to walk across the Nile."

"Oh, my God . . ." Orlando shuddered. "But how did I get here? And why won't you tell me who you are?"

The woman squinted at him as though judging whether he was worth the effort of serious conversation. "Watch that cursing, boy. My name is Bonita Mae Simpkins. My family call me Bonnie Mae, but you don't know me that well, so for now you can call me Mrs. Simpkins."

The headache which had been merely excruciating at first was getting worse every moment. Orlando could feel his eyelid twitching badly, but that was the least of his worries. "I . . . I want to get some answers, but I feel pretty impacted," he conceded.

"You're not well, boy, that's why. You need more sleep." She frowned, but her touch was gentle on his forehead. "Here." She drew something from a fold of her baggy white cotton dress. "Swallow this. It'll make you feel a little better."

Under the pressure of that gaze, he did not argue, but dry-swallowed the powdery ball. "What is it?"

"Egyptian medicine," she said. "They make a lot of it from crocodile poop." For the first time she allowed herself a quick smile at Orlando's horrified expression. "But not this. Just willow bark. Another few thousand years, I 'spect they'll call it aspirin."

Orlando was not as amused as Mrs. Simpkins, but he had no strength left to tell her so. He lay back. Fredericks squatted beside him and took his hand. "You'll be okay, Gardiner."

Orlando wanted to remind his friend that okay was the one thing he would never, ever be, but already something was dragging him down, like river weeds tangling the legs of a drowning man.

He felt a little better the next time he woke, and after some bargaining was even allowed to sit up. All his nerves felt like they were coming back to life. Whatever was stuffed in his mattress felt as bristly as horsehair, and the light streaming in through the doorway of the room splashed with almost painful brightness against the white walls.

When Mrs. Simpkins wandered off briefly to another room, he called Fredericks over. "What's going on?" he whispered. "What happened with the temple and how did we get here? Where *is* here, anyway?"

"It's someone's house." Fredericks looked over his shoulder to make sure the formidable Mrs. S. was not in sight. "Pretty big, too. She was telling the truth, though—you were scanned out. A bunch of guys with, like, clubs were going to kill you, but she calmed you down."

"But where are we? It's still Egypt, right? How did we wind up here?"

Fredericks' face was unhappy. "Egypt, yeah, but I don't really know the rest. After we reached the temple place—I really thought some kind of monster was going to come out of there and just utterly devour us or something—I guess I blacked out, then I just kind of . . . woke up again. And you were gone. But we were near the edge of the river, and there was like this big city around us. And then I heard people shouting, and I went to look, and it was you, and you were standing in the river, scanning majorly, shouting something about God's offices."

"I don't remember any of that," said Orlando, shaking his head. "But I had some really weird . . . I don't know, dreams, experiences . . . about that temple place." He had a sudden, worried thought. "Where are the monkey kids?"

"They're here. They just won't come inside—that woman scares them. They were all climbing around on you when you were still sleeping, the first afternoon, and she chased 'em out with a broom. I think they're living in a tree in the open place out there—what's it called, a courtyard?"

"I don't get any of this . . ." Orlando said. "I mean, what's someone named Bonnie Mae doing in ancient Egypt . . . ?"

"There weren't a lot of folk named Orlando Gardiner laboring to build Pharaoh's pyramids either," said a sharp voice from the doorway. "Now were there?"

Fredericks started back guiltily. "He's feeling better," Orlando's friend asserted, "so he was asking some questions."

"Well he might," Mrs. Simpkins said. "Well he might. And I

s'pose I might have a couple myself. Like, where you got this, and why you were hanging onto it so tight there are still finger marks in the clay?" She held up the piece of broken pot, waving the feather design in front of Orlando's face. "Talk to me, boy. The good Lord don't care for liars—He cannot abide those who do not tell the truth."

"Look," Orlando said, "no offense, but why should I tell you anything? I don't know who you are. I mean, thanks for taking care of us and giving us a place to stay, but maybe we should just get going now, let you have your house back." He tried to climb to his feet, then had to try even harder to avoid falling down. His legs felt overcooked, and even the effort of steadying himself brought his breath fast and frequent.

Bonita Mae Simpkins' laugh was mirthless. "You don't know what you're talking about, boy. First off, you couldn't walk around the corner yet without your friend helping you. Second, in another hour it's going to be dark, and if you're outside, you'll get torn to pieces. You ain't the Daniel of *this* lion's den."

"Torn to pieces?"

"You tell him," she said to Fredericks. "I don't take well to being argued with these days." She folded her arms across her broad chest.

"There's . . . there's some kind of war going on," Fredericks said. "It's not very safe outside at night."

"Not very safe?" the woman snorted. "The Lord has given you a gift for understatement that is truly miraculous, youngster. The streets of Abydos are full of abominations, and that's the truth. Creatures with the heads of vultures and bees, men and women who throw lightning and ride in flying boats, scorpions with human hands, monsters you can't even imagine. It's like the Final Days out there, like the Book of Revelations, if the good Lord will forgive me saying so about a place that ain't no more than a poor copy of His universe in the first place, no more than the work of sinful men." She fixed Orlando with an agate eye. "And what's more, from what I understand, all this craziness is your fault, boy."

"What?" Orlando turned to Fredericks, who shrugged and looked sheepish. "What is she talking about?"

"Well," his friend said, "you remember Oompa-Loompa? The

guy with the wolf head? Apparently, he sort of started some kind of revolution."

"Osiris is gone at the moment, but his lieutenants Tefy and Mewat are wrathful creatures," said Mrs. Simpkins. "They are going to do their level best to get things back under control before their boss comes back, and to creatures like them, that means a lot of pain and a lot of killin'—and they've already done a goodly amount. So don't tell me what you're going to do or not do, boy."

Orlando could only sit for a moment in horrified silence, trying to make sense of it all. The angle of the light on the far wall had changed already, the shadows creeping up the whitewash, and with the woman's words still echoing in his thoughts he could almost feel the held breath of a community waiting fearfully for darkness to come. "So . . . so what are we supposed to do? What's all this mean to you . . . Ma'am?"

Mrs. Simpkins grunted, signifying her approval of a more respectful Orlando. "What it means to me is more than you're ready to hear yet, boy, but you came stomping through the tomb-builders' neighborhood with the feather of Ma'at clamped in your hand like it was your last friend, and I mean to know why."

"How do you know about . . . about her?"

"Who's asking the questions, boy?" She glared at him. Orlando felt certain she could crack a walnut between those eyebrows if she wanted to. "Not only do I know about her, my husband Terence died in Osiris' dungeons to protect her secrets, and eight more of my friends have died here, too. So you can understand I'm a little bit short-tempered about the whole thing. Now you better talk to me."

Orlando took a breath. Self-preservation screamed at him not even to think about asking another question, but he had been under sentence of death too long to be easily cowed. "Just tell me who your friends are, please. Why are you here?"

Bonita Mae Simpkins also took a breath. "I'm praying for patience, boy." She closed her eyes as though it were the literal truth. "We are the Circle, young man, and we are going to send every one of these sinners and false gods down to hell on the express elevator. Now, s'pose you start talking."

CHAPTER 4

A Problem With Geography

NETFEED/INTERACTIVES: IEN, Hr. 4 (Eu, NAm)—
"BACKSTAB"
(visual: Kennedy wrestling with crocodile)
VO: Stabbak (Carolus Kennedy) and Shi Na (Wendy
Yohira) must make their way to the Amazon rain forest in
pursuit of a chemical coveted by the evil Doctor
Methuselah (Moishe Reiner). 5 principal Yanomamo
aboriginals needed, plus extras. Flak to: IEN.BKSTB.CAST

"**N**O, that feels quite ordinary." Florimel opened her eyes. "Everything feels just as it does in real life. Sharp feels sharp, soft feels soft, hot feels hot, even when the fire is artificial. In fact, it is becoming a bit uncomfortable."

"Sorry." Renie moved the smoldering stick away from Florimel's bare shin. She tested it near her own hand; the heat did indeed feel quite realistic. "So even in this place, we're still getting almost perfect simulation."

"But we still do not know the whys and wherefores," said Martine, frowning. "We have quite different equipment, all of us. Renie, you and !Xabbu do not even have telematic implants. But we are all getting input that seems equally sophisticated."

"Not at first," Renie remembered. "!Xabbu used to say that his sense of smell was disappointingly limited, that he thought it was because they hadn't built much into the military VR system we were using. But I haven't heard him complain about it lately. Maybe he's just gotten used to it."

Martine seemed about to say something, but instead an odd expression crossed her face, what Renie thought of as her satellite-tracking look, as though information was being beamed to her from the black distances of space.

"There he is," said Florimel, climbing to her feet. "We can ask him."

Renie turned to see !Xabbu's familiar shape poised on the brow of a nearby hill, as though he had stopped to watch them. "They're back quickly. I wonder where Emily and T4b are."

"Fighting," said Florimel dryly. "Hitting each other with their school bags, perhaps. It is hard to tell sometimes if they are worst enemies or teenage lovers."

"Well, if Emily is looking for a stepfather for her baby, the choices are pretty limited in this group." She squinted. "Why is !Xabbu just standing there like that?" A breath of chill hurried through her, and she raised her arm to wave at the unmoving monkey shape. "!Xabbu?"

"It is not him," said Martine in an odd, choked voice.

"What?"

"It is not him." Martine was also squinting, her sightless eyes squeezed shut like someone suffering a bad headache. "I cannot tell who or what it is you are seeing, but I can tell you it is not !Xabbu."

Even as Renie scrambled to her feet, the baboon on the hill made a slight movement—whether backward or to the side was hard to tell—and was gone.

The spot where he had stood was quite empty, the unfinished land open and uninhabited around them as far as they could see, a rumpled crazy quilt with no folds or prominences substantial enough to hide anything.

"Where did he go?" Renie wondered. "There's nowhere to disappear to."

"Unless like the thing T4b and I saw the other day," Florimel suggested, "it merely stepped through the air and vanished."

"But what *was* it, then? What did you think it was, Martine?"

"I am sorry not to be more useful," the French woman said, "but I cannot guess. I know only that its pattern was not !Xabbu's. What I 'see' is too hard to describe. But I can tell you that it seemed both more complicated and less complicated than one of us."

"Was it like those ghost-children you described?" Renie asked. "One of those?"

"No. Those felt like people, whatever they were in fact. This seemed like an opening into something else, as though the thing you saw as !Xabbu were a kind of glove-puppet, and I was sensing the hand underneath."

Florimel made a harsh noise. "I cannot say I like the sound of that. Something from the Grail Brotherhood, come looking for us? Perhaps even the false Quan Li, come back again in a different shape?"

Martine shook her head, rubbing at her eyes as if she had tired herself out staring at something. "I think not. Perhaps it was just a strange quirk of this environment. A reflection, perhaps—a sort of echo of the real !Xabbu."

Renie suddenly needed to share the eerie thought that had gripped her. "Maybe it's something this . . . this *place* is doing. Watching us, analyzing us, making copies of us."

"Double-goers," said Florimel, pondering. "No, that is not right. Double-goers. Double-goers."

Renie was confused. "What do you mean?"

"I think you know the German word, but the software forces a translation."

"*I* can say it," Martine said with a small smile, "because I am speaking English. There is a paradox for you, no? The word Florimel is saying is *'doppelgangers.'* "

Renie nodded. "I've heard it, yes. But I don't like the idea." She shivered and looked around. "I know we already took a vote, and I'm not trying to reverse the outcome, but I never liked this place much and I feel even more that way now." What she didn't say, and perhaps didn't need to say now that her companions had come to know her, was that she was feeling intensely the pressure to *do something*—the need was thumping in her like a drumbeat.

"We know, Renie," said Martine kindly. "But we cannot do anything until the others return, in any case."

Renie started to say something, then had a sudden, vivid recollection of a ghost story she had been told by her grandmother in which the spirit of someone who was dying appeared at that same moment to his loved ones far away. For a moment her terror was so great she could not speak.

She felt such powerful relief when !Xabbu and the others eventually came trooping back that she could only give the man in the baboon sim a hug, then reach out to touch him from time to time as he and the others made their report.

". . . The truth," he said, "is that we have found nothing in any of four directions we have tried, except for some small strangenesses like the animal T4b and Florimel saw yesterday, and a few things I myself have discovered."

"Monkey-man tripped on some air," explained T4b, vastly entertained.

"That is not what happened," said !Xabbu, his dignity perhaps a bit bruised. "What I found is that just as there are places where the land does not feel right, or where we can reach through things that seem to be before us, there are also places where the air has grown solid. At least, it is thicker than air should be, as though it were . . . I cannot find a word. As though it were . . . becoming something."

"What does that mean?" Renie was so relieved !Xabbu and the others had returned safely that she was finding it difficult to concentrate.

"Some of this place is invisible to us, and some of it that we should be able to touch, we cannot touch." He lifted his hands to show he had no better answer.

"We cannot completely trust our senses, that seems to be the lesson," said Florimel briskly. "That has been true all over the network, although in different ways."

"But it's not the same here, and you know it." Renie found

Florimel easier to like after her confession, but there was still something in the woman's manner that occasionally rubbed her wrong. "We had an experience here that you should know about, !Xabbu." She quickly told him of the phantom baboon. He seemed more disturbed by it than she had expected, which made her remember her own fears.

"So you saw something with my shape," he said, nodding slowly. "But it would not speak to you."

"Speak? It didn't even move until just before it vanished." She didn't like his morose expression. Had she tripped him up with something that recalled one of his grimmer beliefs? "Martine thinks it might be a reflection of a sort."

"Like an echo, or a mirage," the blind woman said. "Perhaps a mirage is the better metaphor, because of the way it bends light."

"Perhaps." The man in the monkey sim was subdued.

"Maybe it's something like what happened to us on the boat with Azador," Renie said suddenly. "That disruption when everything seemed to be falling apart, going strange." That didn't really explain anything, she realized, just stated another instance of their ignorance.

"It isn't more monkeys, is it?" asked Emily, clearly apprehensive. The reference to Azador had caught her attention. "Maybe Lion sent more monkeys to get us."

Renie bit back a sharp reply. She very much doubted it had anything to do with New Emerald City, which was the only simulation Emily knew, but her idea wasn't any more farfetched than anyone else's.

This is truly like being in a children's story, she thought unhappily. *There doesn't seem to be any logic to it, no rules—literally anything could be true. How are we supposed to accomplish something under these conditions?*

It was another question—she was building quite a stack of them—without an answer.

"CODE Delphi. Start here.

"This is Martine Desroubins, resuming my journal. Considering how much more leisure we have had since entering what Renie refers to as 'The Backwater' or 'Patchwork Land,' it would seem I might have been more frequent in my entries, but other than the summation of two days ago, describing the events of our coming through to rejoin Renie and !Xabbu, things have been too hectic.

"We can make no sense of this place. The mysteries grow deeper with every day. Not only is the environment all but empty of anything resembling animal life, and very sparsely vegetated, the entire landscape seems to be undergoing processes of random change that have little to do with imitating real geography. Other than a general separation of ground and air, which mostly stay in their respective places, the flux is constant. In fact, I have ceased asking my companions to explain what they see, since it is so often different than what my senses tell me. They are living in an unstable but more or less comprehensible arrangement of hills and valleys, with things that resemble trees and boulders and other natural objects scattered about the landscape. For me, it often seems that my companions and I are in a place where the edges are always in transition—the ground swirls upward in plumes that they cannot see, the air is so thick in places that I would assume it blocks the light, except that they say it does not, and in any case, the light comes from every direction and no direction.

"Still, I cannot say it is upsetting to me—I do not feel panic, as I did so strongly in those final hours in the Place of the Lost. The changes are slow, and feel as though they are in keeping with the environment. I am learning to read the information that comes to me so that I am no more discommoded than the others.

"There are reasons for concern, however. Earlier today, Renie and Florimel saw what they thought was !Xabbu watching us from a distance. I saw nothing like the Bushman's 'shape'—what I think of as his insignia—but rather a strange, complex apparition that seemed oddly larger than the amount of virtual territory it displaced. My senses are still new, and I cannot describe it more clearly than that. Later, as we were all going to sleep beside the fire, T4b saw something he thought was Emily, some distance from our camp. Worried for her, he went toward it without noticing that the real Emily was sleeping only a few meters away on the far side of Florimel. The false Emily disappeared before our youngest companion reached it.

"What does all this mean? And how do this simulation and these phenomena relate to the bizarre dislocations where the entire network system seems to break down? I have no idea. In a way, though, it is perhaps a good thing we are in such an unusual spot. It minimizes our differences at a time when we are all tired, frightened, and short-tempered, and when there is genuine disagreement between us. Losing Orlando and Fredericks has been difficult enough, but although the hope is small, as long as they are merely missing there is always a chance we may see them again. But watching William die and discovering that Quan Li was not who she seemed have been terrible blows.

"Oddly, the changes in Renie have not been what I would have expected. She has always been volatile, and I would have guessed that our complete and utter failure so far to solve any of Otherland's riddles would have pushed her farther into anger and impatience. Instead she seems to have found a well of strength within herself, and has taken losing a vote on what we should do with good grace—even more surprising considering that the deciding vote cast against her came from her friend, !Xabbu.

"Something in her experiences has . . . I cannot think of the proper word. Broadened her? Deepened her, perhaps. She has always been a young woman of poise and sharp wits and courage, but with a certain brittleness as well. Now, although she is not by any means completely changed, she seems calmer in her spirit. Perhaps this is !Xabbu's influence. It would be tempting to suggest that as the representative of a simpler, more ancient way of life he has changed her with his simple, ancient wisdom, but that would be to grossly underestimate the man. His wisdom, what I have seen of it, is never simple, and although some of it comes from the thousand generations of his people's past, much of it has also come from being an intelligent young man raised on the extreme fringes of what the world calls 'civilization'—that is, knowing all his life that most of what the world considers important has nothing to do with him at all.

"In fact, I think !Xabbu by far walks the most difficult path of all of us, trying to reconcile a culture whose ways have been tested and settled a hundred centuries ago with a world of technological change that is almost cancerous in its constant growth and evolution. This place we are staying could be a metaphor for how what !Xabbu terms our 'city-world' must feel to him.

"He has had another effect on Renie as well, although I do not know whether she is entirely aware of it. I cannot tell whether he is in love with her—one of the things I undoubtedly miss because of my blindness is the way someone looks at someone else—but there is no question he is devoted to her. Neither can I tell for certain whether she loves him, but she is a different person when he is absent—much of what I perceive as her newfound inner peace is undercut. At times, hearing them speak of each other in the language of cheerful but casual companionship, I want to grab one of them—usually Renie—and give that person a shake. But must they not discover whatever is there in their own time? In any case, the differences between them are very great, so perhaps I am half-hoping for something that might turn out to be a tragic mistake. Nevertheless, there are certainly moments I wish for a fairy godmother's wand. I think if I had one, I would make a magical mirror, so both could see themselves as the other sees them.

"And what of me, in all this? As usual, I speak of others, think of others, observe or consider or—occasionally—manipulate others. Always I am outside. What does a fairy godmother do when she is not blessing babies or magicking up a coach and dress for Cinderella? Does she perhaps sit outside the ring of the campfire, watching over the others as they sleep, talking quietly to herself?

"If so, then it seems I am a natural.

"Someone is stirring, I hear. It is T4b, which means my time at the sentry post seems to have come to an end already. I will continue this soon, I hope . . .

"Code Delphi. End here."

THE shriek was clearly human, yet so strangely pitched that for the first instant of sudden consciousness Renie wanted nothing to do with it. As she sat up, bleary with sleep, the confusion of dream still clinging to her, she found herself wishing against all good sense that she had not heard it, that she could just drop away back into unconsciousness and let someone else deal with it.

After her eyes popped open, it took a long moment before she realized that something else was wrong, too.

"It's *dark!*" she shouted. "How did that happen? Where's the light?"

"Renie! There is a big hole here!" one of the others called. "Somebody fell in!"

She rolled onto her side and saw by the dim firelight that a huge black space now stretched on the far side of the fire, where previously there had been ground. "Who is it?"

"Martine!" Florimel said hoarsely. "I can't see her, but I can hear her!"

T4b was shouting, too, ragged cries in which Renie could make out no words. "Jesus Mercy," she snapped at him as she scrambled toward the edge of the hole, "that's not helping any!" Despite the sudden and unprecedented arrival of night, she thought she could see something moving in the depths, faint shadows of red and black: the weird transparency of the soil was allowing through a smear of firelight. "Martine?" she called. "Can you hear me?"

"I am here, Renie." The blind woman's voice was tightly controlled. "I am clinging, but the dirt is very loose. I am afraid to move."

Renie saw Florimel on the far side of the broad pit, but she knew more than the two of them would be needed. "Help us, !Xabbu, T4b!" Renie said. "She can't hang on long."

"My hand!" T4b sounded quite stunned, almost drugged.

Renie had no idea what he was talking about, but !Xabbu was now standing beside her. "Lower me in," he said. "I will hold her as we pull her out."

Florimel, a little wild-eyed, shook her head emphatically. "You are not strong enough!"

"I am strong," !Xabbu said. "Only my body is small."

Renie did not want to waste time arguing. She was inclined to trust !Xabbu, although the idea of lowering him into the dark was frightening. "If he says so, it's true. Come over here and help me, Florimel. T4b, are you going to help or not?"

The Goggleboy only made a strange gulping sound. He was crouched on the far side of the pit, a spiny shape like a large cactus.

With Renie and Florimel each holding one of his thin legs, !Xabbu walked himself over the edge on his hands, headfirst into the hole. When he had reached the limit of their armspan he still could not touch Martine, who despite her measured responses was clearly miserable. Renie and Florimel brought !Xabbu up again, then with great care lowered themselves to their knees and crawled toward the hole so they could lie flat on the ground, side-by-side with their shoulders protruding beyond the rim. "We really need you, T4b!" Renie called. Her voice seemed to go straight down into the dark, flat and dead. "We need someone to hold onto us!"

A moment later a hand closed on one of her ankles and Renie sighed in relief. !Xabbu climbed over her and Florimel, then clambered down their arms as though they were vines, allowing them at the last to clasp their hands around his ankles. Even his small weight felt as though it could drag them over the edge, and Renie's voice was breathless as she asked, "Can you reach her?"

"I am not . . ." He paused, then an instant later said, "I have her. Hold on, Martine. Take one of my hands, but do not let go with your other yet." When he spoke again, Renie could tell he had turned his head toward the surface. "But how can you two pull us out?"

With the strange, soapy earth of the place in her mouth and nose, her arms stretched until it felt as though they might tear loose at any moment, Renie was no longer merely frightened, but terrified. She and Florimel had no leverage at all, and every moment it was getting harder and harder to support !Xabbu's weight without adding Martine's as well.

"T4b!" she shouted. "Can you pull us back?" There was no response, so Renie gently moved her leg, afraid that if she kicked too hard he might let go. "Can't you pull us back?"

A small voice said, "I can't. It's already hard to hold on."

"Emily! That's *you* back there?" Renie had to push away her panicked fury at T4b—this was no time for it. She struggled to keep her voice firm, but she could feel her composure swiftly unraveling at the edges. "T4b, God damn it, if you don't help pull us back, Martine and !Xabbu are going to fall! Come help us!"

For a long moment nothing changed. Renie could almost feel her arms stretching like warm taffy, getting longer and thinner. She knew she could not hold any longer—something would have to give way. Then a large, painfully spiky hand closed on the back of her jumpsuit and began to pull. Renie barely had time for a gasp of relief before it turned to a hiss of anguish as Martine's full weight swung free.

For an instant her shoulders and elbows seemed full of burning rubber and she was certain she would lose her grip—as in her dream, it felt as though she were trying to pull the entire world inside out. Then the hand on her back tugged her far enough away from the rim that she could bend her knees and dig her elbows into the dirt. A few more moments and she could flex her spine and begin to apply leverage of her own.

Martine came over the top, scrambling, and actually crawled across Florimel in her desperate fight to get out of the pit. !Xabbu, who had swung to the side to let her climb out, followed a few seconds later. The four of them collapsed into a panting heap.

"Thank you. Oh, my God, thank you." Martine's voice, thickened by dirt, was little more than a choking murmur; Renie had never heard the blind woman so emotional.

"We must move away," said !Xabbu, rising on all fours. "We do not know there will not be more collapses here."

When they had stumbled and crawled back through the unfamiliar darkness to the embers of the campfire, Renie abruptly sat up. "T4b? What in hell happened to you? Why didn't you help us when I asked?"

"He's still by the hole," Emily said, more interested than disapproving. "I think he's crying."

"What?" Renie got to her feet, balance shaky. "T4b—Javier? What's going on?"

"He tried to help me . . ." Martine said, but Renie was already walking toward the huddled shape of the warrior-robot, mindful of the pit a few steps away.

"Javier?" He did not look up, but even in the half-light she saw his shoulders stiffen. "T4b, what is it?"

He turned the scowling battle-mask toward her, but his words were those of a shocked, frightened youth. "M-my hand . . . my lockin' *hand!*" He raised his left arm toward her. For a moment, she thought he had sustained some terrible fracture, that it had been bent away from her at a sickening angle; it took a few moments more before she realized that his hand was simply gone, neatly removed at the base of the wrist. The battle-gauntlet ended with a kind of gray flatness like a piece of lead, but with a faint suggestion of shimmer.

"What happened?"

"He was coming to replace me on sentry duty." Martine edged toward them, giving a wide berth to the place where the ground had opened. "All of a sudden, as I was walking away, the earth just . . . disappeared in front of me. No, that's too simple, it was more like an entire area of air and land just . . . changed. Like some kind of invisible field core-sampled the whole thing." She was breathing hard, still recovering from the shock of her ordeal. T4b pulled the affected arm in close to his body and rocked back and forth as though he held an injured child. "If I hadn't been blind," Martine continued, "I think I would have just walked into it in the dark, but because I sensed something was wrong I stopped on the edge and struggled for balance. T4b pulled me aside, but I think his other hand must have crossed the plane where the ground and air were still changing, because he let out a scream . . ."

"Yes! I heard him," Renie said, remembering the terrible cry that had woken her.

". . . And when I tried to go to him, I stumbled and rolled over the edge." Martine stopped, trying to calm herself.

Renie shook her head. They'd have to try to figure it out later. "Florimel!" she called. "You're our doctor. We need you right now!"

As with everything else in this bizarre and unique environment, T4b's injury and the unexpected nightfall followed no normal patterns.

Their Goggleboy companion had lost his hand, but as far as anyone could tell, only its virtual analogue: T4b still felt a hand at the end of his wrist (although he said it felt "*sayee lo* max," and described it as feeling "all electricity") even though no one else could feel it, and it did not seem to exist as far as the environment was concerned either. After the initial shock there was no pain, and the gray space at the end of his wrist where the amputation had occurred retained its faint gleam. Whatever the earth-hollowing effect had been, inspection proved that it had also removed a segment of Martine's baggy clothing as neatly as a swipe from a laser-scalpel.

Although they huddled long talking it over before they eventually went back to sleep, the darkness was still present when the last of them awakened, and Renie among others began to think that they were in for a night at least as long as the gray twilight of their first days in the place.

"And we cannot even guess how long this next part is going to last," Florimel pointed out, "because we might have missed the first six months of that gray light."

"I'm frightened!" Although she had played a surprisingly brave part in Martine's rescue, Emily had quickly reverted to her status as the group's official malcontent. "I want to go away from here *now*. I hate this place!"

"I don't want to seem to be taking advantage of a bad situation," Renie said, "but I think we should vote again. The dark is bad enough—we'll be out of this imitation firewood soon, and it won't be fun looking for more—but if pieces are just dropping out of the environment . . ."

Martine nodded. "I cannot help wondering what would have happened to me if I had walked into that space before it took poor T4b's hand. Would I still exist? Would my virtual body be gone, but my mind still be trapped online somehow, a kind of ghost?" The idea seemed to trouble her deeply.

"It does no good to think of it," Florimel said. "But there is no need for argument, Renie—not as far as I am concerned. This place has won your argument for you. We must leave."

"If we *can* leave," Martine pointed out. She seemed both smaller and less remote, as though the brush with possible oblivion had changed her. "Don't forget, it was never anything but an idea of Renie's, that we might find our way out of this place without the Grail Brotherhood's object."

Renie stared at the textured semitransparencies of the firelight. "If needing and wanting to get out will make it easier, then it definitely just got *much* easier."

"It is no use." !Xabbu sounded as dispirited as Renie had ever heard him. What must have been hours had passed, and he and Martine had tried everything they could imagine, even going so far as to make all the company link hands around the fire and concentrate on the idea of a golden-shining gateway—Florimel had scornfully called it a "seance"—all to no effect. "You have put your trust in me, Renie, you and the others, but I have failed you."

"Don't be silly, !Xabbu," Martine said. "No one has failed anyone."

He touched her arm with his long fingers, a gesture of appreciation for her kindness, then walked a short distance away and crouched with his back to the fire, a tiny, mournful figure.

"The problem is that there is no way for !Xabbu and me to explain to each other what we know," Martine quietly told Renie. "He and I . . . touched before, somehow, when we were all apart, but it was through the gateway the Brotherhood's object had already opened. Neither of us can use words to say what we felt, what we learned. We are like two scientists who do not have any common language—the barrier is too great to share our discoveries."

Florimel shook her head glumly. "We should sleep. In a while, if it is still dark, I will try to find more firewood."

Renie looked at T4b, who was sleeping now, exhaustion and shock having finally outworn the adrenaline; Emily also had taken refuge in unconsciousness. She tried to think of something optimistic to say but couldn't; she had not dared to consider what might happen if they could not reopen the gateway. A wave of unhappiness and fear swept through her. Even worse was the sight of her friend !Xabbu looking so defeated. She made her way across the untrustworthy ground toward him. When she reached his side she had still not thought of any useful words, so she sat beside him and took his small hand in hers.

After a long silence, !Xabbu abruptly said, "Many, many years ago there was another with my name. He was one of my people, and he was called Dream, the same as my parents named me, after the dream that is dreaming us." He paused as if Renie might respond, but she could feel nothing except a painful, heavy congestion around her heart and did not trust herself to speak.

"He was a prisoner, as my father became a prisoner," !Xabbu continued. "I know his words not because my own people remembered them, but because he came to know one of the few Europeans who studied my people's ways. One day this white scholar asked my namesake why he was so unhappy all the time, why he sat quiet, with his face in shadow. And the man called Dream told him, 'I am sitting, waiting for the moon to turn back, so that I might return to the place of my people and hear their stories.'

"At first the scholar thought Dream was speaking of going back to his family, and he asked him where they were, but Dream said, 'I am waiting for the stories that come from a distance, for a story is like the wind—it comes from far away, but we feel it. The people here do not possess my stories. They do not speak things that speak to me. I am waiting until I can turn around in my path, until the moon turns back, and I am hoping that some-one on the path behind me, someone who knows *my* stories, will speak a story I can hear on the wind—that listening I can turn around in the path . . . and that my heart will find a way home.

"That is how I feel, Renie—as that man also named Dream felt. It came to me when I did my dance that I should not try to be something I am not, but must do as my people do, think as my people think. But it has made me lonely. This world does not seem to me a place where I can understand the stories, Renie." He slowly shook his head, dark eyes lidded.

His words pierced her. Her eyes filled with tears. "You have friends in this world," she said, stumbling a little on the words. "People who care for you very much."

He squeezed her hand. "I know. But even the friends of my heart cannot always feed the Greater Hunger."

Another long silence crept by. Renie heard Martine and Florimel speaking softly a few meters away, but the words seemed mean-ingless, so much did she long for something to ease the small man's sorrow. "I . . . I love you, !Xabbu," she said at last. The words seemed quite stark, hanging in the darkness. She didn't know what she meant, and was suddenly frightened of something she could not entirely identify. "You are my best and closest friend."

He rested his furry head against her shoulder. "And I love you, Renie. Even the sharpest pains of my heart are less when you and I are together."

The moment seemed difficult to Renie. He had taken it so calmly, so matter-of-factly, that she almost felt insulted, even though she herself was not sure how she had meant that fateful word. *But I don't know what he means by it either,* she realized. *In a way, we're from so far apart, we still hardly know each other.*

Feeling awkward, she let go of his hand and touched the rough thing that had been rubbing at her wrist. "What's this?"

"My string." He laughed quietly as he unknotted it. "Your string, I mean, that you gave me from your boot. A precious gift." His mood had lightened, or else out of kindness to her he pretended that it had. "Would you like to see another story told with it? I can bring it back to the fire."

"Maybe later," she said, then hoped she hadn't offended him. "I'm tired, !Xabbu. But I loved the stories you made it tell earlier."

"It can do other things, too. Oh, such a clever piece of string! I can count with it, and even do more difficult things—in some ways, the string game can be like an abacus, you know, telling many complicated ideas . . ." He trailed off.

Renie was so absorbed in wondering what this latest, confusing interlude between the two of them might mean that she did not realize for a moment that !Xabbu was lost in thought; there was an even longer pause before she suddenly understood what it was he was considering. "Oh, !Xabbu, could you use it that way? Would it help?"

He was already moving on all fours back toward the fire, taking the easier, animal way of moving in his haste. She felt a twinge of worry at his growing facility with baboon-movement, but it was pushed away by a dangerous upwelling of hope.

"Martine," he said, "put out your hands. There, like that."

The blind woman, a little startled, allowed him to arrange her hands with palms facing each other and fingers extended. He quickly looped the string over them, then thrust his own fingers in and moved them rapidly. "This shape is called 'the sun'—the sun in the sky. Do you understand?"

Martine nodded slowly.

"And see, here is 'night.' Now, this means 'far,' and this . . . 'near.' Yes?"

Anyone else, Renie felt sure, would have asked him what the hell he was talking about, but Martine only sat quietly for a moment, her face distant and distracted, then asked him to do it again more slowly. He did, then showed her figure after figure, moving his hands through what seemed to Renie like a series of simple pictures, but she knew him well enough to know that this was only the beginning—the building blocks of the string game.

After perhaps two hours had passed, !Xabbu stopped talking. Martine had fallen silent some time earlier. Florimel and Renie took turns poking up the remains of the fire, more for their own cheer than any need of !Xabbu's or Martine's: except for occasional wiggles of her fingers when she did not understand something, or a gentle touch by !Xabbu when she had made a mistake, the two of them were now communicating entirely through the string.

Renie awoke from a light doze; dream-images of nets and fences that somehow let things out rather than kept them in were still running in her brain. She could not at first understand what caused the yellow light.

The sun came back . . . ? was the first coherent thought that crossed her mind, and then she realized what she was seeing. Heart speeding, she clambered to her feet and hurried to wake Florimel. Martine and !Xabbu sat facing each other on the ground, both with their eyes shut, totally still except for their fingers, which moved slowly now in the web of string, as though making only the most minute adjustments.

"Get up!" Renie shouted. "It's the gateway, the gateway!"

T4b and Emily both came clawing up from sleep, amazed and frightened. Renie did not bother to explain, just urged them to their feet; with Florimel's help she shoved them toward the shimmering rectangle of cold fire before going back for Martine and !Xabbu. For a moment she hesitated, as though getting their attention might somehow break the circuit and dismiss the glowing gate, but it could not be helped. Any escape that did not include !Xabbu and Martine was not an escape they could take. When she gently shook them, they seemed to awaken from a dream.

"Come on!" she said. "You did it! You brilliant, brilliant people!"

"Before you get too happy," Florimel growled from beside the gateway, "remember that they have opened a doorway so we can chase a murderer."

"Florimel," Renie said as she helped Martine toward the golden light, "you are absolutely right. You can be in charge of security on the other side. Now shut up." She watched as the others stepped through, disappearing one by one into the brilliant light. As Martine vanished, Renie reached down and took !Xabbu's hand.

"You did so well," she told him.

As she stepped into the gateway, she looked back at the odd country that had sheltered them, even stranger now in the glaring, flattening light. Something moved near the fire—for a moment she thought she saw a human shape, but then decided it was just the wind kicking up sparks.

But there is no wind here, she remembered, then the dazzle enfolded her.

NEMESIS.2 transitioned from the unstable appearance of flame to briefly inhabit something more like the shape of the creatures who had just vanished. As the icon representing the connection-point through which they had traveled shimmered and dwindled, Nemesis.2 prepared to give up shape altogether, but it still could find no coherent response to the organisms that had just departed.

It had observed them for a number of cycles, far longer than any observation it—or its more complete parent—had spent on any other anomaly, and although it had never found the right cues, the "XpauljonasX" cues that would trigger retrieval, still there had been something in their information-signature that had arrested its interest, kept it rolling through a kind of stasis loop. To the extent that Nemesis.2 could be spoken of as having feelings—which would at best be a grotesque form of anthropomorphism—it should have felt relief that they had released it from the unsatisfying, unresolved situation. But instead, a strong draw on its hunter-killer subroutines was urging it to follow them, to stay near them and study them until it had finally decided once and for all whether to ignore them or remove them from the matrix.

Nemesis.2 would already have followed the organisms and their strangely confusing signatures—and could at any time, since the way they had gone was as clear to it as footprints on new snow would be to a human—but this node itself was anomalous as well, and more than that, it was resonant of the greater anomaly that had so puzzled and intrigued (again, using human words to describe the needs of a sophisticated but unliving piece of code) the original Nemesis device, and which had led in part to it diminishing and multiplying itself, the better to serve multiple needs.

Nemesis.2, or at least the original version of the program, had not been created to hesitate. That it did so now, torn between immediate pursuit of the anomalous organisms and further investigation of the anomalous location in which it found itself, was perhaps indicative of why some programmers, even those who wrote code for the prestigious Jericho Team that had created Nemesis, liked to say of the products of their imagination and labor, "Just because you can tell it what to do doesn't mean you can tell it what to do."

Nemesis.2 analyzed, measured, and analyzed again. It considered, in its cold way. A drift of a few integers, and it decided. Because it did not think, even if it had been told that it had begun a course of action that would ripple out from this moment and change the universe forever, it could not have understood.

Even if it could have understood, it would not have cared.

CHAPTER 5

Tourist in Madrikhor

NETFEED/NEWS: Another House Collapse Blamed on Nanotech
(visual: Chimoy family camping in front yard)
VO: The Chimoy family of Bradford, England, are only the latest who are seeking damages against DDG, Ltd., manufacturers of Rid Carpet, a nanomachine-based carpet and furniture cleaner that they say destroyed their house.
(visual: foundations of Chimoy house)
In another blow to the stumbling nanotechnology industry, solicitors for the Chimoys allege that an imperfection in the Rid Carpet cleaning product allowed the dirt-eating nanomachines to continue far past the point at which they should have shut themselves off, and that the tiny eating machines went on to devour the carpet, the floor, the family cat, and most of the frame of their modest semidetached, which eventually collapsed. . . .

CHRISTABEL had discovered that if she held open the little door where the cleaning machine came out and vacuumed up all the dirt from the floor, she could hear what Mommy and Daddy were saying in the living room downstairs.

When she had been really little, not like now, she had been scared of the suckbot, which was her father's name for it (which always made her mother say, "Mike, that's icky.") The way it just popped out and crawled around the room on its little treads and lifter-legs, red lights blinking like eyes, had always made her think of the trapdoor spider she had seen at school. Many nights she had woken up crying after dreaming that it had come out and tried to suck the blankets off her bed. Her mother had explained many times that it was only a machine, that it only came out to clean, and that when it wasn't vacuuming, it wasn't waiting just on the other side of the little door but was at the far end of the duct downstairs, sitting on its base unit, charging.

The idea of the little square machine sitting quietly in the dark, drinking electricity, had not made her feel any happier, but sometimes you just had to let your parents think that they'd made things better.

Now that she was a big girl, she *knew* it was just a machine, and so when she had the idea of lifting the door to see if she could hear the fight her parents were having, she had hardly been scared at all. She had poked her head right into the dark place, then after a while she had even opened her eyes. Her parents' voices sounded far away and metal-y, like they were robots themselves, which she didn't like, but after she had listened for a while to what they were saying she almost completely forgot about the horrible little box.

". . . I don't care, Mike, she *had* to go back to school. It's the law!" Her mother had been shouting earlier, but now she just sounded tired.

"Fine, then. But she's not moving a step out of this house other than that, and she gets taken there and picked up afterward."

"Which means me, doesn't it?" Christabel's mommy sounded like she might start shouting again. "It's bad enough you're never home these days, but now I'm expected to become a jailer for our child as well . . ."

"I don't understand you," Daddy told her. "Don't you *care*? She's having some kind of . . . relationship with a grown man—

you heard it yourself! Some kind of bizarre softsex thing for all
we know. Our little girl!"

"We don't know any of that, Mike. She's got those funny
glasses, and I heard a voice coming out of them, saying her
name . . ."

"And I told you, these are *not* the standard issue Storybook
Sunglasses, Kaylene. Someone has modified them—somebody has
built some kind of short-range transponder into them."

"Go ahead and cut me off. Don't let me talk. That'll make sure
you win the argument, won't it?"

Something crashed and glass broke. Christabel was so startled
and frightened that she bumped her head on the hinged door, then
tried not to move in case they had heard her. Had Daddy thrown
something? Jumped out a window? She saw someone do that once
on the net—a big man who was being chased by police. She expected a lot more shouting, but when her father spoke he sounded
quiet and sad.

"Oh, Jesus, I'm sorry. I didn't even see it there."

"It's just a vase, Mike." It was a little while until her mother
said the next thing. "Do we have to fight about this? Of course
I'm worried, too, but we can't just . . . arrest her. We don't really
know for certain anything's wrong."

"Something's wrong, all right." He didn't sound angry anymore either, just tired. Christabel had to hold her breath to hear
what he was saying. "Everything's just gone to hell around here,
honey, and I'm taking it out on you. I'm sorry."

"I still can't believe it—this place is so *safe,* Mike. Like something out of an old book. Neighborhoods, kids playing in the
streets. If we were in Raleigh-Durham or Charlotte Metro, I
wouldn't ever have let her out of my sight, but . . . but *here!*"

"There's a reason it's like this, Kaylene. It's a backwater—all
the important action's Rim stuff, on the West Coast or the South-
west. This base would probably have been closed years ago, except that we had one old man we were supposed to keep an eye
on. And he got away. On my watch, too."

Christabel hated the way her daddy's voice sounded now, but
she could not stop listening. Listening to your parents like this
was like seeing a picture of someone naked, or watching a flick

you knew you weren't supposed to, with blood and heads being cut off.

"Honey, is it that bad? You never talk about your work, and I try not to bother you about it when you're home—anyway, I know it's all secret—but you've been so upset lately."

"You have no idea. My balls, not to put it too gently, are in a vise. Look, let's say your job, your *real* job, not just the day-to-day bullshit, was to make sure no one robbed a certain bank. And for years not only didn't anyone rob it, nobody even parked illegally in front of it, so that everyone thought you had the easiest job in the world. And then one day, when everything seemed just like any other day, someone not only robbed the bank, they took the whole damn building. Now, if you were that bank guard, how would *you* feel? And what do you think it would do to your career?"

"Oh, God, Mike." Her mother sounded scared, but she also had that whispery sound when she wanted to kiss Daddy, but he was busy doing something and wouldn't let her. "I didn't realize it was that bad. That strange old man . . . ?"

"That old bastard, yeah. But I can't tell you any more, honey— I really, really can't. But this stuff with Christabel is not happening at a good time, let's put it that way."

There was a long quiet.

"So what should we do about our little girl?"

"I don't know." There was a clink of glass. Daddy was picking up whatever he'd broken. "But I'm scared to death, and the fact that she won't tell us anything about it makes it worse. I've never thought of her as a liar, Kaylene—never thought she would keep a secret like that."

"It scares me too."

"Well, that's why the house arrest. She's not going anywhere without one of us around except to school until we get to the bottom of this. In fact, I'm going to go talk to her again now."

The last thing Christabel heard as she scrambled away from the cleaning machine's door was her mother say, "Go easy on her, Mike. She's just a little girl."

As she lay on the bed with her eyes closed, pretending she was still taking her nap, she could hear her daddy's footsteps com-

ing up the stairs, *clump, clump, clump.* Sometimes, when she was
waiting for him to come up and tuck her in and kiss her good
night, she felt almost like the princess in *Sleeping Beauty,* waiting for the handsome prince to get through all the scratchy thorns.
Other times it was like being in a haunted house, hearing a monster get closer and closer.

He opened the door quietly, then she felt him sit down on the
edge of the bed. "Christabel? Wake up, honey."

She pretended that she was mostly asleep. She could still feel
her heart beating fast, as though she had run a long way. "What?"

"You look very pink," he said, worried. "Are you coming down
with something?" He laid his big hand across her head. It felt
cool and hard and very, very heavy.

"I'm okay, I guess." She sat up. She didn't want to look at
him because she knew he was giving her a Serious Look.

"Look, Christabel, honey, I want you to understand something.
All of this about the Storybook Sunglasses—your mommy and I
aren't angry at you because we think you're bad, we're upset because we're worried. And it makes us very unhappy when you
won't tell us the truth."

"I know, Daddy." She still didn't want to look at him, not because she was scared, but because she knew if she saw his face
she would start crying.

"So why won't you just tell us what's going on? If you have
a friend your own age and you're just playing around, changing
your voices or something, we won't be angry. But if it's someone grown-up—well, then we need to know about it. Do you understand?"

She nodded. His fingers touched her chin and lifted her face
until she had to look at him, his big wide face, his tired eyes, the
bristly whiskers. It was the whiskers—Daddy *always* shaved every
morning, except on Saturday, and sometimes he shaved twice in
a day if he and Mommy were going out to dinner—that made
her stomach swim around and her face get hot all over again.

"Has someone touched you? Has anyone done anything to
you?"

"N-no." Christabel began to cry. "No, Daddy!"

"Just talk to me, kiddo. Just tell me what's going on with those
glasses."

She tried to answer, but at first could only make sucking noises like the vacuum. There was snot coming out of her nose, so she tried to wipe it away with her sleeve. Her daddy pulled a tissue out of the Zoomer Zizz box and gave it to her. When she could talk, she said, "I can't tell you. It's a secret, and . . ." She shook her head because she couldn't explain. Everything was so terrible, everything. Mister Sellars was with that bad, scary boy, and she couldn't get away even to explain to him that her parents had the sunglasses, and because she was lying she was making her mommy and daddy so sad, and her daddy looked so tired. . . . "I can't."

For a moment, she thought he was going to get angry again like he had the first night—that he might yell or break some of her toys, the way he'd thrown Prince Pikapik against a wall and smashed up his insides so now the otter would only walk in little limping circles. But the red in his cheeks was very bright, as bright as when he and Captain Ron had too many drinks and said things about the cheerleader girls on the wallscreen that made Christabel feel funny and nervous.

"All right." He stood up. "This isn't the Middle Ages, Christabel, or even thirty years ago—I'm not going to give you the kind of smacking my daddy used to give me when I wouldn't own up to the truth. But you *will* tell us where you got those, and you won't go out to play, or watch the wallscreen, or go to Seawall Center, or any of the things you like to do—we'll keep you home until high school, if we have to—until you stop playing these stupid games."

He went out and shut the door behind him. Christabel started crying again.

THE man who stood glowering before him was so large that he blocked most of the light in a tavern room that did not have much to spare. Tattoos covered his face and most of his visible skin, and small animal bones were knotted in his bushy beard. He raised a hand like a bear's paw and set it on the table, which creaked audibly.

"I am Grognug the Unlovable," he rumbled, "slayer of the ogre Vaxirax and several other monsters nearly as infamous. I make it my business to kill at least one man every day with my bare hands, just to stay in practice. I give preference to those who sit on my personal stool without asking." Teeth that had clearly never undergone any process as effeminate as brushing could not be said to flash; instead, they made a brief and mossy appearance. "And who are *you,* little man?"

"My . . . my name is Ka-turr of Rhamzee," the other stammered, "swordsman for hire. I am . . . a stranger here, and do not know . . ."

"It is good to hear your name before I yank off your head," Grognug interrupted, "so that the bards will be able to add today's victim to the long list. The bards keep very close track of my career, you see, and they are sticklers for detail." Grognug's breath was expertly rendered, and explained the rest of his fatalistic soubriquet: the VR scent-effect would have convinced almost anyone that they were standing downwind from sun-warmed roadkill.

"Heh." Ka-turr slid his stool back. "Actually, I was just leaving."

Ten seconds later Catur Ramsey was sitting splay-legged in the shadowy street outside, laughter still echoing from the door behind him. Even he had to admit that his swift exit, ending in a pratfall, had probably been worth a chuckle or two. "Jesus!" he said. "What is it with this place? That's the third bar I've been chucked out of!"

"First off," said the voice in his ear, *"it's a tavern, not a bar. You gotta get this stuff straight, that's part of the problem. Everyone always picks on the virgins."*

"I told you I should have been something else instead of a sword fighter—a thief, or a wizard, or something. A medieval accountant, maybe. Just because I'm pretty tall and I've got this jumbo can opener hanging off my belt, everyone keeps picking fights with me."

"Yeah, but this way if you find a fight you can't run away from, at least you got a chance of survivin' it," Beezle pointed out in his thick Brooklyn dialect. *"And at the rate you're goin', you'll find one of those pretty soon. . . ."*

Ramsey picked himself up and dusted off the knees and seat of his heavy wool breeks. His sword, which he had not yet dared to draw from its scabbard, thumped against his thigh. Not only had its dangling bulk already proved a problem when running away from bar fights, it had some bizarre name which he had already forgotten.

"What's this thing called again? Slamhanger or Hamslammer or something?"

Beezle sighed, a disembodied Jiminy Cricket floating in Ramsey's ear. *"It's called Slayhammer. It comes from the Temple of the Wailing God, in your home country of Rhamzee, beyond the borders of the Middle Country. How do you ever keep track of your legal stuff? You got a memory like a sieve, buddy."*

"I make notes. I sit at a desk and talk to my office system. I have paralegals. I don't usually have to crawl through the stinking gutters of the ancient city of Margarine to do my research."

"Madrikhor. You know, if you want me to laugh at your jokes, you should turn up my conversational sensitivity a little so I'd get 'em faster."

Ramsey scowled, but could not help being a tiny bit amused by what a complete and utter disaster this was turning out to be. "Nah. You might as well save your energy for finding me someplace new to get beat up."

Coming here had seemed an obvious idea at first, especially when most of the initial leads, all so promising, had proved themselves to be little better than mirages, receding and then fading as he approached. Beezle had made much information available about Orlando's last few months, but trying to follow up on any of it had been surprisingly difficult. The TreeHouse people, in part because of their own tragedy—several children of network users struck down at the same time, apparently with Tandagore's Syndrome—rebuffed all of Ramsey's quiet overtures. Smelling a lawsuit, perhaps, none of the engineers at Indigo Gear would admit even talking to an Orlando Gardiner, although one of the recruiting officers admitted having given him a scholarship. Ramsey had a feeling that were it not for the possible disastrous publicity of welshing on a deal with a kid in a coma, Indigo would already have withdrawn that scholarship and wiped all records off the books.

The last and best hope for information about Orlando's recent activities had been the Middle Country, but even here dead ends abounded. After requests to examine network records had been met with a polite but unmistakable go-slow policy, such that finding what he wanted the normal way would have taken a couple of years, he was forced to begin a search from the inside. But not only had his entry into the simworld made him feel at least as stupid as he had feared it would, it had made him feel stupid in some ways he hadn't even anticipated, as his sore tailbone now attested.

Beezle had first taken him to what had once been the site of Senbar Flay's magical tower, but the building was gone now, removed from what according to Beezle had been permanent nonstatus on the Middle Country's books. Testimony to the speed of virtual urban renewal, another wizard's castle already stood in its place, a small, jeweled fantasy of Moorish minarets. *Attractive starter chateau for sorcerers,* Ramsey had imagined the real estate listing. There were even rumors of a sentry-djinn guarding the premises, which the lawyer had no intention of trying to prove or disprove. It was clear there was nothing to learn from this particular site. The child who had once played the wizard's character was still in the same place—on life-support in a Florida hospital—but as far as the Middle Country was concerned, Senbar Flay was now history.

A ride into the distant Catspine Mountains that used almost a week of his pathetically sparse personal time furthered Ramsey's run of disasters. Xalisa Thol's mound, the place where Beezle said the whole thing had begun, was gone, too. The local inhabitants talked nervously about the night it had disappeared, of a blizzard of ice that had kept everyone indoors and the snow wolves that had made it seem a good idea not to hurry out right after the storm ended.

So Ramsey had returned to Madrikhor, hoping to turn up something the old-fashioned way. In real life he had walked into some of the ugliest neighborhoods of Washington and Baltimore seeking information in personal injury cases, so how bad could playing gumshoe in a virtual fairy tale be?

Worse than he had expected, as it turned out. Even the most unpleasant inhabitants of the Edwin Meese Gardens housing project had never tried to shove a basilisk into Ramsey's codpiece.

*   *   *

He was in a small, down-at-the-heels tavern named The Reaver's Posset, finishing his cup of mead (and counting his lucky stars that he had not invested more in the taste-simulation aspects of his gear) when a figure lurched up to his carefully chosen seat in one of the darker corners. It had been a long, frequently painful day, and the Posset was in one of the dingier neighborhoods of Madrikhor, so when the stranger stopped before him and then another unfamiliar figure stepped in beside the first, Ramsey sighed and braced himself for another thrashing.

"Ho!" said the taller of the two, a muscular, square-jawed fellow with a long mustache. "We hear that you seek information."

"And we have information to sell, forsooth," said his companion, a wiry little orange-haired man, a moment later. There was something oddly similar about their voices, although the little man's was a bit higher.

"Oh?" Ramsey tried not to show any interest. In a city full of people playing elaborate games, nothing would have surprised him less than someone wanting to take some of his money, but nothing would have surprised him more than getting something useful in return. "What makes you think this information of yours is something I want to pay for?"

"Gadzooks, and have you not been asking all over the Adventurer's Quarter for tidings of Thargor, the dark one?" said the large fellow. "Well, forsooth, it is Belmak the Buccaneer and his companion, the Red Weasel, who stand before you. We can help you."

There was a pause, then the little one piped up, "For gold, of course."

"Of course." Ramsey nodded gravely. "Give me an idea of what you know and I will give you an idea of what I might pay." He was feeling less worried about a thrashing now, although he was still fairly certain his time was being wasted. If the real people behind these comic-opera swashbucklers turned out to be even of driving age, he would be very surprised.

"We will take you to someone who can tell you where Thargor is," said the Red Weasel, winking roguishly. He appeared to hurt himself doing so, or perhaps a cinder from the fire blew into his eye, because he spent the next few moments alternately blinking and rubbing at it. When he had finished, his companion abruptly sprang into movement, as though he had been waiting for some cue.

"You must follow us, yea and verily," the mustached fellow announced. "Fear not that harm will come to you, because you have the word of Belmak, who has never yet played a man false."

"What do you think, Beezle?" Ramsey subvocalized. *"It's the first lead we've had since we've been here. You ever heard of either of these guys?"*

"Don't think so, but people change characters around here sometimes." The invisible bug seemed to be thinking it over. *"Might as well try it. I'll just cross-file the information on everything we've done so far today, so that if we have to drop off, we don't need to redo a bunch of stuff next time."*

"Very well," Ramsey said out loud. "Lead on. But no tricks." It was almost impossible not to fall into the b-flick melodrama of the place.

Either both Belmak and the Red Weasel were much the worse for drink or they came from some distant place where the ground was quite a different shape, because neither of them could walk particularly well. They were also completely silent, and as they led Ramsey through the slick, cobbled alleys of the Adventurer's Quarter beneath a light drizzle, he tried to figure out what was bothering him about the two of them.

"I confess that I do not recognize your names, noble heroes," he said. "Perhaps you could tell me something of yourselves. I fear I am a stranger here."

Belmak the Buccaneer walked three more steps, then turned back to Ramsey. His companion staggered on a few more paces before stopping, like a man carrying a bowling ball in each trouser leg. Oddly, he did not turn as Belmak spoke.

"We are famous not just in Madrikhor, but in Qest and Sulyaban as well, and all the cities that look upon the Great Ocean. Famous." He fell abruptly silent.

"We have had many adventures, forsooth," the Red Weasel added, still facing in the other direction. He and Belmak then resumed their uneven progress.

"Beezle, what's with these guys?" Ramsey whispered.

"I don't think it's 'guys,' buddy," the bug answered. *"I think*

it's 'guy.' Like, one person trying to run two sims—and without very good gear."

"Is that why he's having so much trouble making them both walk?" Ramsey felt a laugh begin to bubble inside him.

"That ain't all—you notice they can't walk and talk at the same time either?"

It was too much. A great huff of amusement almost doubled him up, and he found himself struggling not to dissolve completely into giggles. Like mechanical figures on a medieval clock tower, Belmak and the Red Weasel turned slowly to face him.

"Why dost thou be laughing?" asked the Red Weasel.

"N-nothing," Ramsey said, wheezing. "I just remembered a joke."

"Gadzooks, then," said Belmak. "Verily," he added. With a last suspicious look, he turned back around. The Red Weasel followed suit, then they both set off once more, awkward as toddlers in snowsuits. Ramsey ambled after them, wiping at his eyes, still in danger of collapsing back into giggles, and so was not aware of the stone horse trough standing in the road until he smacked it with his knee.

As Ramsey hopped and swore, Belmak paused to observe. "It is a dangerous city, Madrikhor," he commented.

"Yes," the Red Weasel agreed a moment later. "Forsooth."

After following the two adventurers for over an hour, at an incredibly slow pace that Ramsey felt sure he could have improved on walking backward, their odd inability seemed nowhere near as charming. Catur Ramsey found himself fighting irritation with every plodding step.

Just my luck this Gardiner kid wasn't into science fiction. Why couldn't he have been obsessed with some scenario where everyone had little personal atomic rocket-cars or something?

As midnight approached, the city was no less lively than during the daylight hours, but had merely taken on a different kind of life. In a virtual world full of thieves, murderers, and practitioners of black magic, and with many of them the alter egos of people who were up past their bedtimes, it was no surprise if Madrikhor changed as darkness fell from faux-Medieval heartiness to febrile mock-Gothic. It was hard to find a shadowy spot without someone hiding in it, a dark corner where someone was not conducting a transaction or a betrayal just beyond the glow of the streetlamp. The shapes that hurried past along the windy streets wore billowing cloaks, but the outlines that could be seen were fantastical, and many of the eyes glinting from deep hoods shone with a light that did not seem particularly human.

It's more like Halloween than anything else, Ramsey thought. *Like Halloween every night of the year.* Although he was tired and beginning to get cranky, he could not entirely disapprove. One of the few consistent things about his childhood had been the holidays, which had a certain sameness no matter where his family had celebrated them. Sometimes they had been living in an actual neighborhood instead of on a military base, and those Halloweens had been the best of all.

A dark, cape-flapping figure leaped across the alley above his head, from one rooftop to another, and he suddenly missed those Halloweens, the happy terror of well-known streets gone dark and mysterious, of familar faces made strange by masks and makeup. He found himself wishing he had been more interested in things like role-playing when he was a kid, that he had found a place like the Middle Country when he had still had the trick of immersive belief. Now he could only be a tourist. Like Wendy and her siblings growing up and losing Never-Never Land, he had gone beyond the point where he could get back, but he could come close enough to feel something of loss.

If The Reaver's Posset had been in one of Madrikhor's less prepossessing neighborhoods, it was a beauty spot compared to the place Belmak and the Weasel now led him. They were not even truly in the city anymore, but had wandered out into a kind of extended poverty-village, miles long, whose houses appeared to be built of the flimsiest and least valuable materials, and which huddled against each other like the cells of a beehive someone had sat on.

"What the hell is this, Beezle?" he whispered. "Where are we now?"

"Hangtown. Orlando didn't come here much."

"It's a ghetto!"

"*That's what you get with laissez-faire economies, even the imaginary kind.*"

Ramsey blinked, wondering if he had discovered a socialist bias in Beezle's programming. "*It is dangerous?*"

"*As far as this gameworld goes,*" the bug replied, "*what isn't? But yeah, it's not real nice. Zombies, dark kobolds, lots of thieves and cutthroats down on their luck, of course. I think they have some kind of a werewolf problem out near the dump, too.*"

Ramsey made a face and quietly drew Slamheller or whatever it was called out of its scabbard.

Belmak paused long enough to deliver the message, "Fear not, we are almost there."

"Yea," added his companion, "and verily." They both sounded out of breath.

Beezle's remark about werewolves came back as it became more and more clear to Ramsey that he was being led to what could only be the aforementioned dump, a mountain of rubbish with several dependent foothills that covered the equivalent of several city blocks in the middle of Hangtown. Fires smoldered everywhere, most of them spontaneous ignitions in the rubbish. The medieval trash was genuinely dispiriting, even for a virtual environment, the preponderant articles being muck and bones and broken pots. Except for a few figures scavenging among the piles, barely visible even by the red light of the low flames, the area was deserted; Ramsey could see no reason he should be brought to such a place.

He lifted the sword whose name he could never remember. "Is this an ambush or something? If so, I wish you would have pulled it off a few miles back and saved us all this walking."

"No . . . ambush," said the Red Weasel, clearly even more winded than Ramsey. "The place . . . lies yonder." The red-haired man pointed to a dark clump at the base of one of the rubbish hills; from Ramsey's perspective it looked like just another pile of trash, but as he squinted he saw something moving in front of it, dimly outlined by fireglow. He lifted the sword before him and began marching across the spongy ground. Belmak and his small companion could not keep up the pace and fell behind; within moments they were barely visible.

The clump turned out to be a cottage, if a word so often used in fairy tales could be applied to a structure that was little more than a shed made of old boards and chunks of broken stone. Rags stuffed in the cracks to keep out the wind, or perhaps the ubiquitous dirty smoke, gave it the appearance of a doll losing its stuffing. Standing in the opening (which would have been the doorframe if there had been a door) was a tall figure wearing, as did so many in this city, a long black cloak with a hood.

Ramsey strode determinedly toward this apparition. He'd been online about two hours longer than he'd planned already, his feet were hurting, and if he waited much longer he was going to miss even the chance to get take-out food from the place downstairs. It was time to get some answers and then, if this new venture was as pointless as he suspected, get out of the simworld.

"So here I am," he said to the silent shape. "Tweedle-dum and Tweedle-dee are back there a ways, but they'll be coming up before long. I've walked a damn long way for this, so who are you and what information have you got to sell?"

For a long moment the dark figure was statue-still. "You forget yourself," it said then, the voice deep and impressive. "No one speaks thusly to the great enchanter . . . *Dreyra Jarh!*" The stranger threw his arms up in the air; as the sleeves billowed around long, pale hands, lightning turned the entire Hangtown dump into a flash-photograph. Thunder exploded overhead, making Catur Ramsey's ears pop.

In the pinwheeling dark after the bright light, Ramsey made a dizzy try at finding his balance, managing it finally by using the sword in his hand as the third leg of the tripod. His initial alarm was ebbing swiftly. "Yeah, that's pretty good," he said aloud. He could not see well enough yet to make out his adversary, so he hoped he was facing in the right direction. "And that was probably a pretty expensive trick—probably cost you a month's allowance, or a few weeks' worth of running around here collecting bonus points or whatever. But if you had more than one or two tricks like that, I don't think you'd be out here in the middle of nowhere, now would you? You'd have a place like that big old wizard's castle I saw the other day."

Dreyra Jarh paused, then slowly pulled back his hood, exposing a shaved head and a long thin face of corpselike whiteness. "Okay, Gardiner, you win. Let's talk."

Gardiner? Ramsey was about to explain, then thought better of it. "Yeah, let's talk."

The house of Dreyra Jarh, Ramsey decided, was probably one of the few realistic examples of actual Medieval Living to be found in all of the Middle Country. The ambience was not improved by the dried, flattened cakes of manure which the enchanter used to keep his fire stoked, but under the circumstances such fuel made sense: this was not a society which would have paper or even wood to throw away. He hoped it was not also an omen about the quality of Dreyra Jarh's information.

Perhaps in a last effort at one-upsmanship, the enchanter had settled onto the only seat in the one-room shanty, a tall but rickety stool, leaving Ramsey to settle on the floor—or more precisely, on the flat, pounded earth. The firelight revealed a tiny, spade-shaped beard of sky-blue on the end of Dreyra Jarh's chin, a foppish detail that suggested he had once seen better days, or at least that the person behind the character lavished more time on his grooming than his home furnishings.

"Beezle," Ramsey murmured without moving his lips, *"have you ever heard of this guy? Why does he think I'm Orlando?"*

"Heard of him? Hell, yeah, I've heard of him. He and Thargor have had more run-ins than you could count, but he used to be doin' a lot better than this. He used to have a whole country, y'know? Like, he owned it. That's when he was the Wizard-King of Andarwen. But he lost that to some demon in a dice game. The last time Thargor bumped into him, he still had a big old estate, and everything on it—servants, pack of hounds, you name it—was made out of living glass." Beezle considered for a moment. *"I'd say he's had some hard times since then."*

Ramsey could not suppress a snort. *"I guess so."*

"You *are* Orlando Gardiner, aren't you?" The enchanter, for all his bony, hardened look, sounded almost plaintive. He had a slight accent, something Catur Ramsey couldn't quite put his finger on. "I'll put a Table of Judgment seal on everything that happens in this room if you want. Dupping not, swear I won't tell. But I need to know."

Ramsey hesitated, but he knew that even after weeks of investigation, he could not lie convincingly enough about this environment to pull off the deception. "No, I'm not. I've just been asking around about his character, Thargor."

"Damn!" Dreyra Jarh stood up and stamped in frustration. "Locking mother of uttermost damn it all!"

"So that's why you brought me out here?" Ramsey asked when the other had calmed a little. "Just because you thought I was Orlando Gardiner?"

"Yes," said the wizard sullenly. "Sorry." The apology didn't sound very convincing.

After walking a half-dozen virtual miles through some of the least charming sights that Madrikhor had to offer, Ramsey was not going to be put off so easily. "What did you want to say to him?"

The thin face turned suspicious. "Nothing."

"Look, I'm not just interested in Thargor, I'm interested in Orlando Gardiner, too. I'm working for his family—doing some investigating."

"Working for his family? Why?"

"First off, I'm the one asking questions—and here's why." Ramsey took a clinking purse out of his tunic. He had only planned to make it stretch through another couple of fact-finding missions, anyway. "I'll give you this if you help me out. All of it—twenty gold emperors."

"Imperials." But the wizard who had once ruled an entire nation was obviously interested. "Just to talk to you?"

"As long as you're reasonably interesting." Ramsey set the money-sack beside his knee. *"Tell me if he says anything obviously false, Beezle, will you?"* he murmured. Aloud, he asked, "Why did you want to talk to Orlando Gardiner?"

Dreyra Jarh settled back onto his stool, long hands draped in his lap. "Well, he's been around a long time, like me. We've been enemies, kind of . . ."

"Enemies?" Catur raised an eyebrow.

"Not in real life! Just here. In the Middle Country. We've had some big contests, seen? I've tried to destroy him, he's tried to destroy me. We've never sixed each other, but we've gone back and forth, each won a few . . ."

"That's a lie right there, buddy," Beezle said loyally. *"Orlando never lost to this guy at anything."*

". . . But then he got toasted by some low-grade sport demon, and the Table denied his appeal, and he was gone."

Ramsey nodded. Accurate so far, to the extent it mattered. "And?"

"And there were all kinds of rumors that before he left, he was asking about some golden city—something nobody in MC had ever heard of before. But then he was gone, seen? So I never found out for posdef what the ups were."

At mention of the golden city Ramsey grew very still. The sullen noises of the fire seemed unnaturally loud, the rundown hovel even smaller than it had been.

"Then I found this jewel thing," Dreyra Jarh continued. "One of my zombie minions brought it to me from where they were excavating for me at the site of the lost Catacombs of Perinyum. Zombie minions don't care about jewels or that kind of thing— they make pretty good workers. Then, when I examined it, it kind of . . . I don't know, opened up . . ."

"Yes?" It was hard to keep the excitement out of his voice. "So . . . ?"

Before the enchanter could resume, Ramsey was jolted by Beezle's voice in his ear again. *"Hey, buddy, there's someone coming . . . !"*

Ramsey climbed to one knee, trying to drag his sword free of the scabbard, a far trickier procedure than was apparent in adventure stories. He was still struggling to disentangle the hilt from the folds of his tunic when Belmak the Buccaneer and his companion the Red Weasel appeared in the doorway, wheezing in perfect unison.

"Gadzooks!" Belmak appeared to feel this was enough to state their case; he resumed struggling to catch his breath. After long moments had passed, the Red Weasel looked up beside him.

"The stranger moves . . . like the wind!" The Weasel made a broad gesture, trying to show how windily Ramsey had outpaced them, and how manfully they had struggled to keep up.

The corpse-skinned enchanter wiggled his fingers impatiently. "That's fine. We're talking. Lock it and rocket, okay?"

Belmak stared. "What?"

"You heard me, go on. Why don't you go down to Ye Tavern and wait for me."

"We just got here!"

"It won't kill you. Go on."

Belmak and the Red Weasel looked like it might indeed kill them. In a sudden fit of sympathy, Ramsey took a coin from his purse that he was pretty sure was smaller than an Imperial and flipped it to the Red Weasel, who almost caught it. Somewhat mollified, the adventurers recovered the coin and went clumping back out into a night lit by garbage-fueled fires.

"You can't use zombie minions for *everything,*" an embarrassed Dreyra Jarh said by way of explanation. "And I'm a bit short of resources lately. . . ."

"Just finish the story. You found a gem."

The enchanter wove a tale much like what Ramsey knew of Orlando's. He had been obsessed by the golden city, so different had it been from anything else he had ever seen in the Middle Country, and so positive was he that it signified some quest that only the elite players would have a hope of successfully pursuing. But the quest had been fruitless, and he had exhausted every option both within the simworld and outside, in RL, trying to track the place down. He had used his position as one of the Middle Country's paramount enchanters to turn the simworld upside down, searching everywhere, questioning everyone, mounting expeditions to every dimly-remembered bit of virtual archaeology in the entire game environment.

"It broke me," he explained sadly. "After a while I was spending Imperials I didn't even have. But I didn't find it. I kept thinking that maybe Orlando did, that that's how come he went off the system, but I couldn't get in touch with him." The wizard tried to make his voice casual, and failed. "So . . . so did he?"

Ramsey was half-lost in thought, trying to put pieces into a recognizable shape. "Hmmm? Did he what?"

"Did he find the city, man?"

"I don't know." After a few more questions, Ramsey stood up, irritated to discover that even sitting down for too long in a virtual environment could prove just as uncomfortable as in real life. He tossed the pouch into Dreyra Jarh's lap. "You must have information on some of the resources you used," he suggested. "Research trails, like that?"

"Huh?"

"Just . . . records of things you did, trying to find the city."

"I guess." The enchanter was counting his earnings. It was clear that while he was happy to have the money, he wasn't going to be able to buy his country back with it, or even hire too many more zombie minions.

"Tell you what," Ramsey said. "If you let me have access to all your records, strictly privately, I'll arrange to get you a lot more than that bag of funny-money." He tried to figure out the true age of Dreyra Jarh's role-player. "How about a thousand credits? Real-world money. That ought to buy you a lot of spells. And maybe you could even get some decent gear for that poor guy running those Belmak and Weasel sims."

"You want to give me . . . money? To see what's on my system?"

"I'm a lawyer. You can work it however you want to—a contract, anything. But yes, I want access to everything you did. And do you still have the golden city or the gem?"

Dreyra Jarh snorted. "Chance not. Whole thing went *pffftt*. Gone. Ate a little hole in my storage, too, like it had never been there at all. You'll see."

Before he remembered that he could simply drop offline, Catur Ramsey had walked a fair distance back along the edge of the vast rubbish mounds. He was caught up in his thoughts, aware of little except the possible significance of what he'd just learned.

Whatever had happened to Orlando had happened to others, too. But for some reason it hadn't gone as far with all of them. The kid playing Dreyra Jarh was flat broke and not very happy about it, but he sure wasn't comatose.

Ramsey found himself standing a few hundred yards from a shack only slightly larger and more inviting than the enchanter's hovel. The sign swinging above the entrance proclaimed it Ye Tavern at the Dump. Two familiar faces stood in the doorway.

When he recognized Ka-turr of Rhamzee, Belmak the Buccaneer shouted for him to come join them.

"No thanks," Ramsey called. "I've got to go. You two take it easy."

Just before the dump, Madrikhor, and the entirety of the Mid-

dle Country vanished, Catur Ramsey saw first Belmak, then the
Red Weasel, wave good-bye in sequence.

DREAD parked the Quan Li sim in a dark, quiet place and left
it sitting there like a marionette with slack strings. Although there
was much, much more of this newest simulation world to investigate, he had explored enough already to know that there was no
shortage of places of concealment—knowledge that warmed his
predator's heart. Also, with Sellars' troop of misfits left behind,
there was no longer a need to pretend that the sim was always
occupied.

   Thinking of them and the way they had jumped on him, like
jackals on a lion, he felt a brief and salty pang of hatred, but he
quickly pushed it away. He was after a bigger enemy, and the
idea that had kindled inside him was far more important than those
small people and the small irritation they had caused.

   With a single command he was offline, stretched on a comfortable massage-couch in his Cartagena office. He thumbed a
couple of Adrenex tablets from his dispenser and swallowed them,
then downed the contents of the squeeze bottle of water he had
set beside the couch before beginning this most recent session.
He switched the music in his head from the Baroque strings and
phase-shifted bonebass that had seemed appropriate for exploring
the new simworld to something quieter and more contemplative,
more appropriate for the scenes of the hero beginning his great
work—*magnum opus* music.

   It would all be so, so sublime. He would execute a stroke so
bold and audacious that even the Old Man would be stunned.
Dread did not know the *how* yet, but he could feel himself drawing closer, as he felt the presence of his quarry when he was
hunting.

   He checked to see if Dulcie Anwin had returned his reminder
call. She had. When he rang her again she picked up quickly.

   "Hello." He kept his smile small and cheerful, but the dark
something inside him, fed by the adrenals, wanted to grin like a
jack-o'-lantern . . . like a skull. "Did you enjoy the days off?"

   "God, did I!" She was dressed all in white, a conservative but
stylish slant-suit that emphasized the new, golden gleam a day's
sunbathing had lent to her pale skin. "I'd forgotten what it was

like just to do things around the apartment—read my mail, listen to some music . . ."

"Good, good." He kept the smile, but he was tired of the small talk already. It was one of the few things he liked about men— some of them actually kept their mouths shut unless there was something to say. "Ready for work?"

"Absolutely." Her return smile was bright, and for a moment he felt a twinge of suspicion. Was she playing some game of her own? He had not been paying very much attention to her in the last few days before he put her on hiatus. She was a dangerous, weak link, after all. He added some slow pinging tones to his internal music, like water dripping on rocks, and smoothed the momentary wrinkle out of his calm, confident mood.

"Good. Well, there have been some changes. I'll bring you up to date on them later on, but I've got something important for you to do first. I need you in your gear-master mode for this, Dulcie."

"I'm listening."

"I'm working on something, so for the moment I don't want you using the sim, but I've built a box routine within the simulation and there's something there I'd like you to look at. It looks like a plain old lighter—you know, the old-fashioned kind for cigarettes and things—but it's more. A *lot* more. So I want you to study it. Do everything you can to figure out how it works and what it does."

"I'm not sure I understand," she said. "What is it?"

"It's a device to manipulate gateways in the Otherland network. But I'm pretty sure it has other uses, too. I need you to find out."

"But I can't get into the sim and try it out that way?"

"Not yet." He kept his voice level, but he did not like having his directives questioned. He took an unobtrusive deep breath and listened to his music. "And there's one other thing. It'll have some kind of tags for its home system, but even if it doesn't, I want you to figure out where it comes from."

She looked doubtful. "I'll try. Then what?"

"We'll signal it destroyed, or lost, or whatever. If it acts as a discrete object, it might be that it will continue to operate."

She frowned. "If it's working now, wouldn't it just be easier

to keep using it until someone notices, instead of taking the chance
of turning it off for good?"

He took another deep breath. "Dulcie, this thing belongs to one
of the Old Man's cronies. If somehow those Grail bastards realize someone has it, they may be able to figure out *who*. And if
they figure out who, then within about ten minutes an urban combat team will come through your door with bang-hammers and
you'll be gone so quickly and so thoroughly your neighbors will
think you spontaneously combusted. This will happen in the real
world, not in some VR network. Do you understand what I'm
saying?"

"I do, yes." This time, she was properly quiet and respectful.

"Good. Check in with me every three hours, or if you find
anything interesting." He broke the connection.

He sat back on the couch, lit himself a thin black Corriegas
cigar, and thought about the time when he could hunt in RL once
more. He found himself considering what it would be like when
red-haired, backtalking Dulcinea Anwin was no longer useful. He
could be in New York in a few hours. . . .

But even this familiar and entertaining sort of speculation could
not long keep his mind off his new plans. *And when I'm a god,*
he thought, *what will I hunt then? Other gods?*

The idea was deliciously amusing.

CHAPTER 6

A Rock and a Hard Place

NETFEED/ENTERTAINMENT: Psychopathically Violent?
You Bet!
(Review of interactive game "Poison Heart Mother IV—
Mother Knows Best!")
VO: "... But thank God the people at U Suk Gear have
gotten over that brain bubble they went through with PHM
III, where players actually lost points for maiming, raping,
or slaughtering innocent civilians. Box that! Ultravile IS
ultravile, seen? You start differentiating kills and pretty
soon characters are having to stop and think all the time—
and that's fun? Chance not ..."

PAUL Jonas clung to a spar of his ruined boat and tried to keep his head above the surface of the violent sea. He barely knew where the sky was, let alone how to find distant Troy, and he still knew nothing of the black mountain. His enemies now included gods, and he had failed the few friends he had.

If misery were money, he thought, trying to cough out the brine before the next wave hit, *I would be the richest man in this whole bloody imaginary universe.*

*   *   *

The night seemed to stretch on forever, a thing not of minutes and hours but of thousands of half-breaths snatched between the battering of waves. He had neither the strength nor leisure to indulge in a review of his failures—the one thin blessing of his predicament. At best, when he found strength enough to lift his face a little higher above the waterline than usual, he slipped into microsleeps, brief moments of darkness, fragments of dream. In one, his father leaned down, giant-high as he towered over his son, and said in a tone of muted disgust, *"If you just write in any letters you want, you're not really solving the puzzle, are you?"* His father's glasses threw back the light, so that Paul could see no eyes, only fluorescent bars reflected from overhead.

In another, Paul held something shiny in his hand. When he saw it was a feather, he felt a brief moment of happiness and hope, although he had no idea why that should be, but the feather proved to be more insubstantial than a butterfly wing; even as he tried to keep his dream-hand steady, the bright blue-green thing crumbled into iridescent powder.

What have I done? he thought as consciousness returned and waves slapped him. *Even if this place is just a simulation, why am I in it? Where's my body? Why am I being trotted through a bizarre quest I can't even understand, like some trained dog being made to act out Shakespeare?*

There was no answer, of course, and even his desperate review of questions was beginning to become an exercise in horror. Perhaps there was no *because* at all, only an endless catalog of *whys*. Perhaps his suffering was just an accident.

No. Eyes closed against the stinging salt, jounced by the waves like a highwayman's hostage tied across a horse's saddle, he reached for belief. *No, that's me floating again. I made a mistake, but I tried to do something. Better than floating, drifting. Better.*

Tortured the woman, another part of him pointed out in unanswerable rebuttal. *Made Penelope fear for her life. That's better? Maybe you should just go back to being useless again.*

It was no use arguing with yourself, he learned as the night crawled along, waves splashing him over and over like some endless slapstick sketch from Hell's own music hall. Misery always knew all the weak spots. Misery always won.

*　　*　　*

Things looked a little better when the dawn came, at least in a spiritual sense: Paul had come to terms with his inner voices and achieved a sort of *détente*. He had agreed with himself that he was the scum of the universe, but had pleaded special circumstances of amnesia, terror, and confusion. No final decision would be reached, it seemed. Not yet.

How things actually looked, to his actual brine-smarting eyes, was a different story. The empty ocean stretched in all directions. His arms were so cramped that he did not think he could let go of the boat-timber now even if he wanted to, but he assumed that state of affairs wouldn't last forever. Eventually he would drop away and accept the full embrace of the waters he had spurned for so long.

He had grown quite familiar, even comfortable, with his coming death by drowning when he saw the first sign of land.

At first it appeared to be only another tiny white point on the horizon, one of a million wave crests, but it came to loom clearly and plainly even above the highest of swells, growing slowly upward toward the almost cloudless blue sky. Paul stared at it with the absorption of an idiot or an artist for most of an hour before he finally realized he was looking at the top of an island mountain.

Detaching one arm from its death grip on the spar took a long painful time, but at last he was able to start paddling.

The island grew nearer far faster than it should have, and the part of him that had not completely surrendered to the moment guessed it was the system speeding up parts of the experience to get to what its designers likely thought of as the good stuff. If that was true, Paul did not mind the dilution of reality at all, and would have been happy if there was even more of it.

He could see now that the crest of the mountain was only the highest point of a range of spiky hills above a natural harbor. The city was a proud thing, all stone battlements and white clay houses along the hillside, but the current was drawing him past the harbor and its broad causeway to another landing spot, an area of flat, pale beach and rock pools. The ocean's slow, smooth pull made him feel for the first time in a while that the designers, or others, were actually looking out for him. What he could see of the olive-clad hillsides and the distant city, the quiet peace of it all, made his eyes fill with helpless tears. He cursed himself for being soft—it had been only a day since he had left Ithaca—but could not ignore the mighty wash of relief.

The tide skimmed him safely past a large stone standing a few hundred meters off the gentle coast, and when the obstruction was gone Paul was surprised and delighted to see human forms on the nearest beach—young women by the look of them, slim and small, with masses of black hair, their pale clothes fluttering as they went through the steps of some kind of game or dance. He was just about to hail them, so as not to wash up in their midst and startle them into running away, when suddenly a cloud rolled in front of the sun and mountain, beach, and ocean all grew dark. The girls stopped their play and looked up, then a brutal crash of thunder rolled across the sky and sent them scrambling for the shelter of caves above the rock pools.

Paul had only an instant for astonishment—only a minute earlier the sky had been completely clear—then black thunderheads swept over him, turning the world a seething gray and throwing down rain that felt as hard as gravel. A wind blew up out of nowhere, battering the wave tops into froth. Paul and his spar were jerked sideways by a change in the current, sliding parallel to the beach for a moment, then away from it, and no amount of paddling or screaming his frustration at the rumbling sky made any difference as he was tugged back toward the open sea. Soon the island had vanished behind him. Beneath the thunder, like the deepest bass pedal of a church organ, he could hear the laughter of Poseidon.

When the storm died down he was surrounded by open sea once more. The moment of hope and its snatching away seemed so obvious in retrospect and so much in keeping with everything else that had happened to him that it was hard even to feel outrage. In any case, he had little strength left for anything but clinging to the spar, which seemed more than ever to be a mere postponement of the inevitable.

I don't know what I've done, but there can't be any crime dreadful enough for me to be punished this way.

His fingers were cramping badly, and even changing position

every few moments did not make the pain less. With each successive crash of cold, salty water, each rise and plummet between waves, he felt his grip growing weaker.

"Help me!" he shouted at the sky, spitting mouthfuls of ocean. "I don't know what I've done but I'm sorry! Help me! I don't want to die!"

As his numb fingers slipped from the wood, the sea around him suddenly calmed. A figure shimmered into view, insubstantial but unmistakable, the suggestion of wings a cloud of flickering light that haloed her entire form as she hovered above the now-gentle swell. He stared, helpless, not entirely sure that he had not in fact let go, that this was not just a last confusing vision granted to a drowning man.

"Paul Jonas." Her voice was quiet and sad. *"I do not belong here. It . . . hurts me to be in this place. Why do you not come to us?"*

"I don't know what any of this means!" he spluttered, fighting angry tears. Despite the gentling of the waves, his hands were still knotted in cramp. "Who *are* you? Who's 'us'? How can I come to you if I don't know where you are?"

She shook her head. A shaft of sunlight pierced her, as though she were a glass vase. *"I do not know the answers to these questions, and I do not know why I do not know them. All I know is that I feel you in the darkness. All I know is that I need you, that what I am cries out to you. Ideas, words, broken visions—there is little more."*

"I'm going to die here," he said with weary bitterness. He slipped and tasted brine, then dragged himself back until the spar was under his chin again. "So don't get your hopes up . . . too high."

"Where is the feather, Paul?" She asked it as she might question a child who had lost his shoes or his coat. *"I have given it to you twice. It was meant to help you find your way, to keep you safe—perhaps even lead you through the shadows of the One who is Other."*

"The *feather?*" He was stunned. It was as though he had been told that locating the pencil given to him on the first day of primary school would determine his university degree. He racked his brain. He barely remembered the first feather—it was as distant

as an object in a dream. He guessed it had disappeared somewhere on Mars, or perhaps even earlier. The second, pressed into
his hand by the sick Neandertal child, he thought he had left behind in the cave of the People. "I didn't know . . . how was I to
know . . . ?"

"*You must know I can only give it to you three times,*" she
said solemnly. "*You must know that, Paul.*"

"Know that *how*? I don't understand any of this! You talk like
this was a fairy tale . . ."

She did not reply, but unwrapped something from the vapors
of her ghostly being. The sea breeze snatched it from her fingers,
but Paul closed his fist on it as it flashed past. It was a scarf or
veil, light as gossamer, glimmering with its own faint light. Woven
into the fabric was a stylized feather in shining greens and blues
and other colors so faint that they seemed to come and go as the
light changed. He stared at it stupidly.

"*It may help you,*" she said. "*But you must come to us soon,
Paul. I cannot stay here—it hurts. Come soon. It grows harder to
see you through the gathering shadows and I am afraid.*"

Hearing that forlorn tone he looked up and met her dark eyes,
the only things in her entire smoky form that seemed entirely real.
The sky darkened again. A moment later he saw someone else in
her place—the same woman, but younger, and dressed in clothes
that, although they still seemed somehow old-fashioned, were
clearly millennia advanced on Homeric Greece. As she stared back
at him, her curly hair merging into the jacket and long dark skirt,
the simple white blouse setting off her mournful gaze, he felt a
shock so profound he almost slipped from the floating spar again.
This vision of her was so different, so unreal, and yet real in a
way none of the others had been, that for a moment he could not
remember how to breathe.

Half a dozen swift heartbeats hurried through his chest as she
stared at him, this achingly familiar stranger, her expression one
of deep, helpless longing. Then she was gone, leaving him alone
on the open sea once more.

In a last moment of clarity before fatigue and misery and confusion again overtook him, Paul used the scarf to secure himself
to the spar, looping it beneath his arms and tying it in a clumsy

knot. Whatever else it might be or represent, it was substantial enough to save his life. The muscles of his arms writhing, he let go of the timber at last.

As he bobbed on the ocean he slid in and out of sleep, but the dreams that came to him this time were far more focused, and at first painfully familiar—a forest of dusty plants, the clanking rage of a mechanical giant, the endless, heartbreaking song of a caged bird. But this time other ominous threads ran through the tapestry, things that he did not remember ever dreaming before which set him twitching in his half-slumber. The giant's castle surrounded him like a living thing, and in every wall there was an unblinking eye. A cloud of beating wings enveloped him, as though the air itself had come to explosive life. The final noise, which startled him up out of darkness, was the explosive crash of breaking glass.

Paul shook himself awake, still up to his chin in cold seawater, in time to hear the distant concussion of thunder fading away. The setting sun was in his eyes, a broad, dazzling smear of gold on the face of the waves. He was still condemned to the ocean. His disappointment only lasted moments: as his eyes became used to the glare, he saw the island.

It was a new land—not the jutting, wide country from which the storm had swept him, but a small, forested rock, lonely in the expanse of darkening sea. He paddled toward it, awkwardly at first because of the long scarf binding him to the spar, but then with increasing facility. He had a moment of panic when he saw the rough shore, the rocks jutting from the coastal waters like Gorgon-struck ships, but luck or something more complicated caught him with a shoreward tide and pulled him harmlessly past them. Soon he felt rough sand beneath his feet and was able to drag himself onto the beach. Shivering, his fingers so numb and cold that he might have been using animal paws, he picked loose the knot and looped the feather-veil around his neck, then crawled to a spot where the sand was white and dry before collapsing into deepest and most dreamless sleep.

It was the nymph Calypso who awakened him.

At first, as she stood with the morning light behind her, black hair moving as slowly in the wind as kelp in a sea current, he thought that the bird-woman had returned. When he saw Calypso's startling, coldly perfect beauty and realized that this was not the creature of his dreams, he was both disappointed and relieved.

He rose to his feet, the pale sand of the beach covering him all over in a fine crust, and followed when she beckoned. She sang as she led him through meadows full of irises—a song of almost impossible sweetness, a thing of flawlessly contrived unreality.

Her cave was nestled in a grove of alders and cypresses, its mouth bearded with grapevines. The sound of running water joined her song, and the two melodies twined, the crystalline chiming of sweet springs and her soft, clear voice lulling him into a waking sleep, so that for long moments he could not help wondering if he had finally drowned and was being gifted with some last vision of paradise.

When she offered him ambrosia and sweet nectar, the sustenance of immortals, he ate and drank, although her singing alone seemed almost enough to feed him. When she touched him with long cool fingers and led him to the springs to bathe the salt from his skin, then led him into the deeper shadows of the cavern to her bed of soft rushes, he did not resist. A part of him knew he was being unfaithful, although to what or whom he had no idea, but he had been lonely for a long, long time, lonely in a way no human creature should be, and his spirit was starving. And when in that long cool time of whispers and beading sweat, as the distant noise of the sea played counterpoint to their urgent sounds, Paul cried out and felt himself falling away, he would not let himself wonder into what sort of void he had spent himself, what kind of illusion.

He could not turn away from comfort, whatever might lie behind it.

"YOU are mournful, clever Odysseus. What ails you?"

He turned to see her gliding across the sand, hair streaming. He turned back to his contemplation of the endlessly rolling afternoon sea. "Nothing. I'm fine."

"Nevertheless, you are heavy of heart. Come back to the cavern and give me love, O sweet mortal—or even, if you wish, we will stay here and make the soft, fragrant sands our bed." She ran a cool hand across his sunburned shoulders, then let her fingers trail downward to the small of his back.

Paul found himself suppressing a flinch. It was not that there was anything *wrong* with being stranded on a paradise island with a beautiful goddess who wanted to serve his every need and make love half a dozen times a day, but although he had welcomed the opportunity to rest and be comforted, his heart was still hurting, and other parts of him were beginning to smart a little as well. Whoever had designed this part of the virtual *Odyssey*—which had covered something like half a dozen years of the fictional character's life, if Paul remembered correctly—was either a simpleminded, inexhaustible lecher or had not given the whole thing much thought.

"I think I'd like to be alone for a while," was what he said out loud.

Her charming pout could have caused cardiac arrest in someone whose sexual interest was a little less numbed. "Of course, my beloved. But do not stay long away from me. I ache for your touch."

Calypso turned and almost floated back up the beach, moving as smoothly as if she slid on oiled glass. Whoever had created this exemplar had given her the long-legged figure of a netshow hypergirl and the voice and presence of a Shakespearean actress, the kind of fantasy female that should have satisfied any heterosexual man for an eternity.

Paul was bored and depressed.

The thing of it was, he realized, he was . . . nowhere. He wasn't home, not what *he* thought of as home, anyway—half-decent job, some half-decent friends, a quiet Friday night on his own from time to time when he could just vegetate in front of the wallscreen and didn't have to pretend to be witty. He wasn't getting any closer to finding home, either, or to answering any of the riddles of his current existence.

But there had been that last moment with the bird-woman, that flash of another existence. He had heard a name drift through his head, or almost had, but it had left little trace in his memory, and was mixed up with other names he had heard—Vaala, Viola. Something kept bringing *Avila* up to the surface, but he knew that couldn't be right—wasn't that a saint, Saint Theresa of Avila? She had been, as best Paul could remember, a medieval hysteric who inspired more than a few pictures and statues. But he knew that his own vision, the girl in her old-fashioned clothes, was just as important to him as Saint Theresa's vision of The Lord. He just didn't know what it meant.

The distant moan of Calypso's song came floating to him through the sandalwood-scented air. He felt a weirdly twinned shudder of longing and revulsion. No wonder visionaries like Theresa had to lock themselves away in convents. Sex was so . . . distracting.

He had to get away, that was clear. He had experienced all the benefit that rest and virtual companionship could give, and if he had to live for years on this island, as the real Odysseus had, he would be worn away like a child's coloring crayon long before it was over, not to mention brain-dead on top of it. But the question was, how? His single timber had been swept back out to sea. There was no boat on the island, or any wood that was not attached to a heartbreakingly beautiful tree of some kind. He supposed he could try to build a raft, but he was completely unqualified to do so, not to mention the fact that the nymph Calypso watched him with the proprietorial care of a tabby guarding a catnip mouse.

But I have to keep moving, he realized. *I said I wouldn't drift anymore, and I can't. I'll die if I do.* It wasn't an exaggeration, he knew: if he did not actually keel over dead, a part of him, a vital part, would certainly wither and perish.

The nymph's song grew louder, and for all his disinterest and weariness, he felt a certain stirring. Better to go now, he decided, so that for once she might let him sleep through the night.

Wincing, he stumbled back across the sands.

The morning sun had only just begun to filter through the cypress branches when the strange thing happened.

Paul was sitting on a stone in front of the cave's entrance, having just finished choking down yet another nectar-and-ambrosia breakfast—which he now suspected Calypso was giving him as a sort of performance enhancer—and wondering if he had the strength to walk across the island in search of some fruit or anything else that even distantly resembled real food, when the air before him began to glare and pulse. He could only stare stupidly as the harsh white light spread; it remained strangely contained at first, then abruptly took on a roughly human, but featureless, shape.

The apparition hung in the air before him, wriggling. The childish voice that came through it was so unexpected that for a few moments he could make no sense of what it was saying: "Mira! Man, op this! Like *Shumama's Shipwreck Show*!" It swiveled and then seemed to see him, although it was impossible to tell which way the blank whiteness of its head was facing. "Hey, you Paul Jonas?" It made his last name sound like it started with "Ch."

"Who . . . who are you . . . ?"

"No time, man. *El Viejo,* he got words for you. *Mierda,* who that?" It turned to look at Calypso, who had appeared in the entrance to the cavern, an oddly blank look on her beautiful face. "You shoeboxin' with that? Ay, man, you lucky." It shook its shapeless head. "*Pues,* the old guy, he wants to know why you ain't movin', man? You found them others?"

"Others? What others?"

The apparition hesitated, tilting its head like a dog listening to a distant sound. "He said you found the jewel, *vato,* so you must know." He made it sound like four words or one long one, *joo-el-vah-toe,* and it took Paul a moment to catch up.

"The golden thing? The gem?"

"Yeah, 'course. He said you gotta fly, man. No clock to stay in one place—all the big stuff's going down."

"*Who* said this? And how am I supposed to get out of here . . . ?"

The shining thing either did not hear him or did not care about his questions. It flickered, flared brightly, then evaporated. The island's spirit-haunted air was still.

"The gods have taken pity on you at last, faithful Odysseus," said Calypso suddenly. He had forgotten her, and now her voice made him jump. "It makes me sad, though—they are hard-hearted and jealous. Why should Zeus interfere when one of the immortal number takes a human lover? He who wears the aegis has taken dozens, and given them all children. But he has sent the divine messenger, and thus his will must be done. I am frightened to resist him, for fear I may incur the Thunderer's wrath."

"Divine messenger?" Paul turned to face her. "What are you talking about?"

"Hermes—he of the golden wand," she said. "I knew, as we immortals know the shape of things ahead, that someday he must come, bearing an Olympian order to end our love-tryst. I did not think it would be so soon."

She looked so sorrowful that for a moment Paul felt something like real affection for her, but he reminded himself—not for the first time—that she was a collection of code, no more, no less, and that she would be saying and doing the same things no matter who wore the guise of lost Odysseus. "So . . . so that's what he was saying?" he asked. "That Zeus wants you to let me go?"

"You heard shining Hermes, messenger of the gods," she said. "The immortals of Olympus have given you enough trouble—it will do you no good to set yourself against the Thunderer's will in this."

Inwardly he was rejoicing. It had been some kind of messenger, certainly (and a decidedly odd one at that), but from the person who had sent Paul the earlier gem-message, who he strongly doubted had anything to do with Mount Olympus. Calypso, however, had simply incorporated it into her world, as Penelope had tried to reconcile Paul's confusing presence within hers. He had experienced an attempt by someone—someone outside the system?—to communicate; Calypso had seen a decree from the Lord of the Gods.

"I am sad if I must leave you," he said with what he thought was necessary hypocrisy, "but how can I do it? I don't have a boat. It's miles and miles to anywhere—I can't swim that far."

"Do you think I would send you away without gifts?" she asked him, smiling bravely. "Do you think that immortal Calypso would let her lover drown in the wine-dark sea, unhelped? Come. I will take you to the grove and give you an ax of fine bronze. You will build yourself a raft that may carry you across Poseidon's domain and on your way, so that the gods can lead you to your destiny."

Paul shrugged. "Okay. I guess that sounds reasonable."

Calypso produced the promised ax—a huge, double-headed thing that nevertheless felt as light and well-balanced in Paul's hand as a tennis racket—and other bronze tools, then led him to a grove of alders, poplars, and tall firs. She paused as though she would say something to him, but instead shook her head wistfully and glided back up the path toward her cave.

Paul stood in the grove for a moment and listened to the sea wind breathing in the treetops. He had little idea how to go about building a raft, but there was no use worrying about it. He would do the best he could—he could certainly start by cutting down a few trees.

It was surprisingly easy work. Despite his lack of experience, the ax bit deep with every stroke; it seemed only moments before the first tree began to shudder, and its fall came so suddenly that Paul was almost caught by the wider branches. He paid better attention next time, and soon had brought down over a dozen of the straightest and most slender trees. As he stood contemplating them, pleasantly out of breath but uncertain as to what to do next, something rustled in the undergrowth. A quail hopped out of the leaves and onto a stone. The little bird stared at him with one eye, then turned its head, topknot bobbing, so it could fix him with the other.

"Strip off the branches and make the logs smooth," the quail said in the voice of a mischievous girl-child. "Didn't your mother and father teach you anything?"

Paul stared. It was not the strangest thing he had encountered, but it was still a bit surprising. "Who are you?"

She made a little chirping sound of amusement. "A quail! What do I look like?"

He nodded his head, conceding the point. "And you know how to build a raft?"

"Better than you do, it seems. It's a good thing Calypso herself brought you here, because you didn't even ask permission from the dryads before you chopped down their trees, and they'll all have to find new homes now." She flicked her tail. "After you strip off the branches, you need to make all the trunks the same length."

Deciding that it was a poor idea to look a gift-quail in the mouth, he bent to work. With the olive-wood handle that felt as though it had been carved for his hand alone, he found the work went as quickly as felling the trees, and soon he had a nearly identical row of logs.

"Not bad," his new companion said. "But I'm not sure I'd let you make a nest for me. Now let's get back to work or you're going to lose the light."

Paul snorted at the idea of taking orders from a small brown-and-white bird, but under the quail's patient instruction the raft came together in short order, a sturdy little craft with a mast and a half-deck and a rudder, and with a sort of wall of plaited branches all around the side to keep the sea from washing unimpeded across the deck.

Calypso appeared later in the day with a great roll of heavy, shiny cloth to use as a sail, but otherwise Paul worked alone, with only the little bird for company. Between her clever suggestions and the almost magical tools, the work proceeded at an amazingly swift pace. By late afternoon there was only the rigging left to do, and as he lashed the various bits into place with the quail hopping back and forth to stay out of his way, lending advice interspersed with mild avian insults, he became aware of an unfamiliar sensation, the warmth of accomplishment.

Let's not kid ourselves, though. This whole thing has been set up to help useless sods like me do what they need to do without violating the simulation's rules—I'm pretty sure there wasn't any magical quail in the original, because the real Odysseus probably could have thrown together the ancient Greek equivalent of an aircraft carrier out of a couple of feathers and a stick. . . .

Thinking of feathers, he checked to make sure the scarf was still tied about his waist. If he knew anything about these kinds of things, he was pretty sure he shouldn't lose this last version of the bird-woman's gift.

Bird-woman . . . I'm going to have to think of some better name for her. Sounds like a comic-book heroine.

After the quail's suggestion of chopping down a few more small trees to use as rollers proved a good one, he was at last able to ease his raft down to the white beach, where Calypso appeared again.

"Come, Odysseus," she said. "Come, my mortal lover. The sun is almost touching the waves—this is no time to set out on a dangerous journey by sea. Spend one last night with me, then you can leave on the morning tide."

Without realizing it, he waited to hear from the quail, who had followed him down to the sand. "She is kind, but sometimes she is headstrong," the bird said in a voice he alone seemed able to hear. "If you stay the night, she will cover you with such kisses that you may forget tomorrow you mean to leave. Then the gods will be even angrier with you."

Paul was amused in spite of himself. "And what do you know about kisses?"

She stared at him for a moment, then with an irritated waggle of her tail she scurried behind a rock. For a moment he was sorry he had not thanked her properly, then remembered he was responding to an amalgam of code, however charming. This led him to think about what Calypso offered, and what the goddess herself almost certainly was as well.

"No, my lady," he said. "I thank you, and I will never forget my time here upon your fair island." Paul wanted to smack himself—bad as he was at it, it was still hard not to fall into flowery, epic language. "Anyway, I need to go."

Sorrowfully, Calypso bade him good-bye, giving him skins of wine and water and food she had prepared for him. Just before he could push the raft out into the water, the little quail came pottling back around the rock and hopped up onto the timbers. "And where are you going?" she asked.

"Troy."

The bird cocked her head to one side. "You have gone all topsy-turvy, noble Odysseus—perhaps you have hit your head. I'm certain your wife expects you home to help her look after your fledgling, not clumping around fighting with Trojans again. But if you insist, you must remember to keep the setting sun on your right hand." She hopped down. He thanked her for all her help, then slid the raft off the rollers into the water, climbed on, and began to push away from shore with the long pole he had made.

"Farewell, mortal!" called Calypso, a tear gleaming prettily in her eye, her hair billowing like storm clouds around her too-perfect face. "I shall never forget you!"

"Watch out for Scylla and Charybdis!" piped the quail, nam-ing what Paul's dim, spotty memories of Homer suggested were some dangerous rocks. "Otherwise, they will take you as a serpent takes an egg!"

He waved and slid out into the open sea, everything around him now turned to beaten copper by the setting sun.

Night at sea in the Age of Heroes was a much different thing on a boat than floundering in the water, clinging to a piece of flotsam. The sky was black as tar and the moon merely a sliver, but the stars seemed ten times as bright as anything he had ever seen. He understood how the ancients might have thought them gods and heroes looking down on the deeds of men.

Toward the night's longest, darkest hour he found himself full of doubt once more. It was hard to remember the boy Gally and his terrible death without thinking that everything else, even his own hopes and fears, were rendered meaningless by it, but even at his lowest ebb, Paul had understood that it was pointless to think that way for long; he was even less willing to do so now. The ship responded to his fumbling control—the sails and rigging seemed as magical as the boat-building ax—the night air was tangy with salt, the waves actually gleamed in the starlight, and three times now he had been briefly surrounded and paced by dolphins, whose swift beauty seemed a kind of blessing. Paul could not lose his unhappiness and guilt, but he could at least put them to one side. He was rested, and he was on his way again, in search of Troy and whatever destiny held.

Destiny? Paul laughed out loud. *Good God, mate, listen to yourself. It's a gameworld. You've got about as much destiny as a bleeding pinball—ping, there goes Jonas again. Oops, now he's gone that way! Ping!*

Still, it couldn't hurt to feel good, at least for a little while.

The first hint that perhaps he had been a little too quick to trust his fragmented memory of the classics came with the gray light of dawn, presaged by a slow but steady increase in the current—a current that he had not even noticed until now, but which was clearly tugging his boat astray despite the bellying sail pulling in a slightly different direction.

He had been so busy steering the raft between the occasional tiny, rocky islands, and trying to think through the confusing things he had been told by the bird-woman—his angel, as he was now beginning to think of her—that he had given scarcely any thought to the little quail's warning, but as the current began to assert itself and a low but definite roar made itself heard, he suddenly felt sick to his stomach.

Hang on for a bit, he thought, *that Scylla and Charybdis—were they just rocks? Wasn't one of them actually a whirlpool—something that sucked down boats and ground them up like a waste disposal swallowing kitchen debris?* And, he suddenly realized as the deep roar mounted, wouldn't something like that sound just like this?

He let go of the tiller and made his way forward, hanging onto the mast with one hand as he strained to see what was ahead. Releasing the rudder allowed the little craft to give in to the pull entirely, and its lurch to the west almost pitched him off the deck. In the morning mist ahead lay two rocky islands with only a few hundred meters between them, the one on the left a tall, jagged spike of mountain jutting up from the sea, its top shrouded in black clouds. Where the waves crashed against its somber flanks, it looked rough enough to peel the sides off a modern battleship, and Paul was definitely not sailing in a modern battleship. But frightening as that was, it was toward the other, lower island that the raft was bearing. The side facing on the strait curved in a rough semicircle, like a sunken ampitheater; at the center of the curving bay the waters swirled around and around with incredible violence and then funneled downward, creating a spinning cylindrical hole in the ocean wide enough to gulp an office building.

The wind was rising. Suddenly dotted with fear-sweat despite the chill morning, each drop a cold pinpoint against his skin, Paul lunged back along the sloping deck toward the tiller. He yanked back on it until the raft was on a course that would take it closer to the sharp-pointed rocks on the left: there was at least a chance of missing those, but once he came within the compass of the maelstrom, nothing could save him. The wood of the rudder groaned as the current continued to pull the raft sideways, and as he clung to the tiller, he prayed that the quail had known as much about shipbuilding as it had seemed to.

One of the braces snapped with a disheartening *twang* as the

raft entered the strait; the unsecured yard began to flip from side
to side and the sail popped in and out. No longer aided by the
wind, the raft began to slide toward the whirlpool side. After a
moment of helpless panic, Paul thought of the feather veil at his
waist. He quickly untied it, then knotted it to hold the tiller as
straight as he could before rushing to the mast. The yard was
swiveling as the winds changed, and he caught more than a few
hard blows to the arms and ribs, but at last managed to pull it
back to its proper position, then drag the brace around the yard
and secure it, tying the best knot he could under the circumstances.
It would not have impressed most sailors, he felt sure, but he
couldn't care less. The swirling black waters of Charybdis were
getting closer by the second.

He scrambled back to the stern. The veil had already been
stretched and loosened by the pull of the current, and he had to
lean hard on the tiller to bring the front of the raft back toward
the spiky rocks on the eastern side, then hold on with all his might
as his beleaguered craft touched on the outermost ring of the
whirlpool, which was agony on his battered ribs. Paul closed his
eyes tight, gritted his teeth, then screamed as hard as he could, a
noise that vanished without trace in the roar of the waters. The
tiller jerked, then slowly began to turn against his grip, as though
some massive hand were twisting the rudder. Paul bellowed his
anger and fear again and hung on.

It was impossible to tell how much time had passed when he
first felt the whirlpool's grip begin to lessen.

Exhausted and so weak in the knees he could barely stand, he
opened his eyes to see the battlement cliffs of the mountain-island
leaning out above his head, so near he could almost have touched
them from the edge of the raft. He barely had time to make sure
that his course would keep him off its rugged flank when something swung down from above—impossibly long, with fangs flashing in its business end. Paul did not even have time to shriek as
the serpentine shape struck at him, but his legs buckled and dropped
him to the deck so that the attack missed him, but the thing—a
sort of tentacle made of rough, cracked leather—hit the mast and
snapped the stout log as though it were a piece of uncooked
spaghetti. The mouth at the tentacle's end snatched up the sail
from the flinders of the mast and shook it viciously; in a second

little bits of cloth were filtering down all around, swirling in the wind; Paul might have been fighting to keep his balance in a particularly unpleasant snow-globe.

He barely had time to reach down for his ax before the great snaky thing was grabbing for him again. If it was a tentacle, the rest of the body was somewhere high above on the rock face, in the dark cavern from which this limb extended; if it was not a leg but a neck, the face at the end of it was eyeless and noseless. Whatever it was, dripping jaws large and toothy as a great white shark's clacked at the end of that huge rope of scaly muscle. Paul stumbled back and swung the ax as hard as he could. A brief moment of joy as it sunk deep into flesh was shattered as the thing jerked back, the ax still lodged in its hide, and lifted him three meters off the deck. Pinkish slime frothed from the deep wound and spattered his face. For an instant he was paralyzed, trying to decide whether to cling to his only weapon or drop away from the snapping teeth, then the ax-blade ripped free and he fell hard onto the logs he had so carefully cut and shaped.

The thing twisted away, whipping from side to side in obvious pain, banging against the rocky cliffs and spraying froth everywhere, its jawed end half-severed from its long stem. Through the burning pain of his injuries he felt a fierce, mindless joy at seeing it crippled and suffering. Then five more identical mouths, each on its own serpentine neck, slithered down from the cavern above.

The next moments passed in a kind of roaring, turbulent dream. The eyeless heads darted at him. He managed to duck the first, then the second stabbing strike. He sliced scaly hide from one of them, but a third snapped at him from behind and almost caught him. The sail was gone and the broken mast offered little shelter, but he slid across the froth-slicked deck and planted his back against it anyway, swiping continuously back and forth with the ax as the heads paused and then lunged, searching for a way through the whirl of razor-sharp bronze. He chopped into a jaw and the mouth drew away, hissing through the sudden fount of bubbling pink, but it did not retreat very far.

He was growing tired rapidly, despite the magical lightness of his weapon, and the heads were no longer striking rashly. They swayed like cobras, waiting for a chink in his defense.

The roar of Charybdis had been growing louder for some time. Paul's only fleeting thought had been that he was probably now being drawn into the whirlpool, too, just so the gods could make certain that he was doomed, but he could not help noticing that the sound had changed to a deep, gurgling bellow, like nothing so much as the world's biggest ogre slurping soup. Then, as Scylla's heads bobbed, waiting for the ax in his weary hands to slow just a little, the crashing noise of the whirlpool abruptly stopped and the seas became still.

Paul had only a few heartbeats to experience the immense, eerie silence—he could actually hear the wet wheeze of Scylla's multiplied breath and the splash of waves against the rocks—then with a roar easily as loud as before, Charybdis suddenly vomited up the ocean she had been swallowing, a great geyser of seawater that burst through the surface and fountained hundreds of meters in the air. The blind, fanged heads hesitated as the first sheets of white-and-green water began to splash down, then the underwater force of the whirlpool's reversal heaved Paul's raft up into the air as violently as if it had been flung from a catapult. Scylla's mouths snapped in vain before the waters covered them, but he was already gone. The great wave carried the raft rushing down the strait; as the little craft spun, Paul had only an instant to grasp for the tiller. His hand closed on the veil.

Black rocks appeared to whirl around him, and the sea was first above, then below, then above him again. White foam flew past as he rose into the air above even the cliffs of the strait, so that for a long moment he could see the ocean and islands twirling below him as he floated at the end of the veil, no longer tethered by gravity. Then the wave threw him down again and he smashed against the ocean's back once, twice, skipping like a stone before a last impact dashed all the thoughts out of his head.

CHAPTER 7

The Battle for Heaven

NETFEED/NEWS: "Armored" Toddler Survives Dangerous Plunge
(visual: Jimmy with father and stepmother)
VO: Three-year-old Jimmy Jacobson, already the focus of a well-known "tug-of-love" custody battle two years ago between his mother and father, apparently survived a fall from a fourth-floor window due to biological modifications. His father, Rinus Jacobson, who has custody of the child, claims that he has strengthened the boy's skeleton and hardened his skin by the application of "simple biological science."
(visual: Rinus Jacobson at press conference)
JACOBSON: "I have done it myself. This invention will be a great help to parents everywhere. All can do what I have done to protect the little ones, now that I have perfected the method."
VO: Jacobson plans to sell the engineered bioorganisms, which he claims work in conjunction with a standard ultraviolet sun lamp to strengthen developing skin and bones.
JACOBSON: "It creates a, how would you call it, a rind. Like the skin of a rhinoceros. This child will never scratch his knees or scrape his face."

*VO: Staffers from the Child Protection Agency, not to
mention neighbors, are skeptical, and an investigation is
underway.*
(visual: anonymated neighbor)
*NEIGHBOR: "Let's put it this way—even if he did make it
work, and the kid's certainly looking kind of stiff, then we
wouldn't be surprised if Jacobson threw him out the
window to test it. . . ."*

IT had been a while since Orlando had spoken for such a long
time, and he was not in very good condition. By the time he
had reached the part of his recent history where he and Fredericks had first entered the harbor at Temilún, he was feeling much
as he had been feeling then—tired and sick.

Bonita Mae Simpkins said very little, interrupting only to get
an occasional clarification on some piece of netboy slang or to
grouse at him for spending too much time on details interesting
only to teenagers. She had offered nothing yet of her own, but
her very reticence was making Orlando feel more trusting. Whoever she was, she was certainly not trying to sweet-talk him into
betraying confidences.

A flaming wick in a bowl of oil colored the room with flickering yellow light and long shadows. Outside, the imaginary Egypt
had grown dark, and from time to time strange sounds drifted to
them through the hot desert night. As Orlando told of the Atascos' death and the flight from their throne room, a terrible, sobbing wail from somewhere nearby made him stop and fall silent,
heart beating. Fredericks, sitting on the foot of the bed, was also
pale and nervous.

"Don't worry, boy," Mrs. Simpkins told him. "Before he went,
Mr. Al-Sayyid made sure that this house was protected. You could
say it has charms on it, but that's heathenish, and what he did's
more scientific. But nothing's coming in—not tonight, anyway."

"Who's Mr. Al-Sayyid?"

"You're not done talkin' yet, and I haven't started. Keep going."
Orlando shrugged and tried to pick up the tale. He moved

quickly through the escape from Temilún and their travels in the miniature world, grimacing when Fredericks insisted he explain how he had fought with a giant, homicidal millipede. It wasn't so much that Orlando was embarrassed—he had acquitted himself fairly well, he thought—but it was clearly the sort of swash-buckling detail this stern woman did not want to hear. He hurried on to their sojourn in the cartoon world, then was forced to re-peat the tale of what had happened to them in the Freezer sev-eral times while Mrs. Simpkins asked a number of shrewd questions.

"So that was her, too—the feather-goddess? You're sure?"

Orlando nodded. "It . . . it feels like the same person. Looked like her, too, sort of. Who is she?"

His questioner only shook her head. "And the other thing, the thing you only felt—what your friend here called 'the actual fac-tual Devil'? Tell me about that again."

He did, or tried to, but it was hard to put the experience into words, as difficult as describing really intense pain—something he had done enough times for people who wanted to understand but couldn't to know it never really worked. "So, was it the devil?" he asked when he had finished, although he felt pretty sure he knew what this woman with her frequent talk of the Lord and Jesus would say.

She surprised him. "No, I don't think it was. But it may be something almost worse. I think it's a kind of devil that mortal men have made, men so full of pride they think they are God Himself."

"What do you mean?"

Again she would only shake her head. "It's too much to talk about all at once. Anyway, you're tired, boy—just look at the state of you. You need some sleep."

Orlando and Fredericks both flinched as something that was not a dog whined and barked in the street just outside the win-dow. "I'm not going to sleep for a while," Orlando said truthfully. "Tell us where you're from. You promised."

"I did no such thing." She stared at him hard, but he had seen enough of her to know she was not angry, only considering. She turned to Fredericks. "I suppose you want to hear, too."

Orlando's friend nodded his head. "It would be nice to know *something* for a change."

"All right. But I don't want any questions until I'm done, and if you open your yaps before then, you can just watch me walk away." She scowled to show she meant business. "And I'm not going to say anything twice.

"My husband Terence and I belong to the Revelation Church of Christ, down in Porterville, Mississippi, and we are proud to do the Lord's work. You have to understand that first of all. We're what you might call muscular Christians—that's what our pastor says, anyway. We work hard for Jesus and we're not much on that airy-fairy nonsense like church picnics and car washes. We come to church and we sing and we pray, and sometimes we do get loud. Some people call us holy rollers, 'cause when the Lord lays His hand on one of us, we start to shout and talk about it a little."

Orlando found himself nodding, almost mesmerized by the rhythm of her voice, even though he had only the faintest idea what she was talking about. His parents had only taken him to church once, to a cousin's wedding, and didn't go much themselves except for chamber music, when one of the local places of worship was used as a concert hall.

"And we don't hold with judging people all the time either," she said in a tone that suggested Orlando might have been just about to suggest they did. "Our God is all-powerful, and He will show people the truth. What might be in their heart afterward is between them and the Lord. You understand me, you boys?"

Both Orlando and Fredericks hastened to indicate that they did.

"Now, the Lord never gifted me or Terence with children—it just wasn't His plan for us, but I'd be lyin' if I told you I never wondered or questioned why. But we both had a chance to work with plenty of 'em, Terence teaching shop at the local middle school, me working in the emergency room at the hospital in De Kalb. It's sad, but a whole lot of the children I saw were in bad shape. If you don't think you need the Lord in your heart and your life, you never saw a bunch of children been in a school bus crash start coming into the ER by twos and threes. That'll test you.

"Anyway, that's none of it to the point. What I'm trying to

say is that we had plenty of things in our lives. God had already given us our work to do, and we had nieces and nephews, too, so if we wondered sometimes why the Lord never gave us our own baby to raise, we didn't wonder long. Then Mr. Al-Sayyid came to First Revelation.

"He was this little dark-colored man, and when Pastor Winsallen first brought him up to introduce him, I thought he might be collecting for one of those backward foreign countries you only hear about when they have an earthquake or something. He had a nice voice, though—very proper, like that English gentleman you see on the net in all those imitation beef commercials, you know the one? Anyway, this Mr. Al-Sayyid told us that he was a Copt. I didn't know what that was—at first, I thought he meant he was a policeman, which was kind of funny because he wasn't much higher than my shoulder and I'm not all that big. But he explained that he was from Egypt, and the Copts were a Christian religion, even if we hadn't heard of 'em. He gave a little talk about the group he belonged to, called Circle of Fellowship, which did all kinds of charitable work in poor countries, and then Pastor Winsallen collected some money, just like I figured.

"But it was afterward that we found out the whole truth. Pastor Winsallen asked Terence and me if we would stay and talk after the rest of the congregation went home, so of course we stayed. We were thinking he would ask us to put this little man up at our place, and I was in a fret because I had all my mother's things still packed in boxes in the guest room and it hadn't been aired out or anything. I suppose I was also a little worried because I'd never had a foreign person in my house and I didn't know what kind of food he'd eat or anything. But that wasn't what the pastor wanted at all."

Mrs. Simpkins paused, considering. For a moment she almost smiled, a twist of the mouth that might have been embarrassment. "That was the strangest night of my life, I can tell you. See, turned out that not only was this Mr. Al-Sayyid's group a lot bigger and more . . . unusual than he'd let on before, but Pastor Winsallen knew some of them from his days at the university and was looking to help them out. But that wasn't what was strange, no, not by a long yard. Mr. Al-Sayyid began telling his story, and I swear it sounded like something out of the worst kinds of science-fiction nonsense. It got dark outside, he talked so long, and I thought I was in some kind of dream, the things he said were so unbelievable. But there was Pastor Winsallen—Andy Winsallen, who I've known since he came in to have his broken leg fixed when he was thirteen—just nodding his head at all of it. He'd heard it before and he believed it, you could tell.

"You know some of what Mr. Al-Sayyid said to us, because it was said to you, too—these Grail people, and all the harm being done to innocent children—but there was more. Mr. Al-Sayyid told us that his Circle group, which was made up of people from all kinds of faiths working together, thought that the Grail folk were using children somehow to make their immortality-machines work, and that they would have to keep using more and more of them, because even though the project had only gone on for a few years, some of the children had died already, and these people planned on living forever and ever."

"Does that mean that Sellars was one of those guys, Orlando?" Fredericks asked suddenly. "One of these Circle of Fellowship or whatever they're called?"

Orlando could only shrug.

"I never heard of your Sellars before now, if that means anything," Mrs. Simpkins said. "But what was even stranger still, Mr. Al-Sayyid told us that night, was that one of the people in the Circle—the real group doesn't have any "Fellowship" in its name, that was just one of their charities—was a Russian fellow, a scientist, I guess, and he had told the other Circle folk that he thought these Grail Brotherhood people . . . that they were drilling a hole in God."

Orlando waited a moment to make sure he'd heard correctly. He glanced over at Fredericks, who looked as though he'd just been struck on the head with a good-sized rock. "Drilling a hole in . . . ? What kind of scanbark is *that*? I mean, no offense, but . . ."

Bonita Mae Simpkins laughed, a quick slap of sound. "That's what *I* said, boy! Not quite those words, but that's pretty much exactly what I said! I was surprised Pastor Winsallen didn't call it blasphemy, but he just sat there looking serious. I don't know what that young man got up to while he was away at college, but it wasn't like any preacher-teaching *I've* ever heard of." She laughed again. "Mr. Al-Sayyid tried to explain it to us. He had such a nice smile! He said that even with all the differences between our faiths—he and his Coptic friends, we Revelation Baptists, the Buddhists and Moslems and whatnot, all the other kinds of religions they had in their Circle group—there was one thing we all had in common. He said we all believed that we could get in the right state of mind, I guess, and touch God. I'm probably saying it wrong, because he was a very good speaker and I'm not, but that's more or less the size of it. We reach out for God, or the infinite, or whatever people want to call it. Well, he said, some of the people in the Circle had been feeling that something was . . . wrong. When they prayed, or meditated, or whatever it was they all did, they could feel something was different in the . . . in the place they went to, or the feeling that they got. In the Holy Spirit, we Revelation folk would say. Like if you walk into a room you know real well, you can feel sometimes if someone else's been in it?"

Orlando shook his head. "I don't think I'm getting any of this. My head hurts. Not from what you're saying," he hastened to explain. "Just because I'm sick."

The woman's smile was almost gentle this time. "Of course you are, boy. And I'm just talking and talking. There's really not much more to explain about that, anyway, because I don't truly understand what they're saying myself. But you get some sleep now, and we'll think about where we're going to go tomorrow."

"Where we're going to go?"

"I told you, this is a war zone. Those miserable creatures, Tefy and Mewat—the ones who work for Osiris—are pretty busy putting down this uprising. But after they do, I can promise you they're gonna be going house to house, rounding up whoever they want to call sympathizers, scaring everyone as bad as they can so it doesn't happen again. And you boys stick out like two real sore thumbs. Now get some sleep."

Orlando slept, but it was not very restful. He found himself floating in a black sea of troubled, feverish dreams which washed across him in waves, as though he were once again trapped in the temple. Images of various childhoods, none of them his own, followed one after the other, interspersed with cryptic visions of the

black pyramid, a vast and silent observer looming over everything.

Oddest of all, though, were dreams that were not of children
or pyramids, but of things he could not remember seeing when
either awake or dreaming—a castle surrounded by clouds, a jungle full of heavy, flowered branches, the shrieking of a bird. He
even dreamed of Ma'at, the goddess of Justice, but not as she
had appeared to him before, with feather and Egyptian garb: the
dream-version was something kept in a cage, a winged creature
that seemed more bird than human, with only feathers to cover
her nakedness. The only thing the same was sadness, the deep,
mourning look in her eyes.

He woke to flat morning light on the white walls. His head
still hurt, but it felt a little clearer than the night before. The
dreams had not completely left him: for the first moments of consciousness he was both in a bed in Egypt and pitching and rocking on rough seas. When he groaned and swung his legs off the
pallet, he almost expected to feel cold water.

Bonita Mae Simpkins poked her small, black-haired head
around the doorframe. "Are you sure you're ready to be up and
around, boy? Do you want a pot?"

A first attempt had convinced him he was not yet ready to sit
up. "A what?"

"A pot. You know, to do your business in."

Orlando shuddered. "No, thanks!" He considered for a moment. "We don't need to do that here, anyway."

"Well, some folks prefer to do things the normal way when
they're having a long stay in VR, even if it doesn't make any
real difference." She had put down whatever she had been doing,
and now walked into the room. "Mr. Jehani—he was one of the
other fellows—said it was easier on the mind if you just pretended you were still in the real world, and kept drinking, and
eating, and even . . ."

"I get it," said Orlando hurriedly. "Where's Fredericks?"

"Sleeping. He sat up half the night with you. You made a powerful fuss." She flattened her hand on his forehead, then straightened. "You were talking about Ma'at in your sleep. The goddess
with the feather."

Orlando's decision to ask Mrs. Simpkins what she made of his dreams was interrupted by a cloud of small yellow flying things that whirled in through the doorway and settled on his arms and legs and on various other surfaces in the sparsely-decorated room.

"Awake! 'Landogarner awake!" Zunni cried happily, and rose from his knee to turn a little somersault in the air. "Now we set off big fun-bomb!"

"Kabooom!" shouted another monkey and pretended to explode, flinging itself into some of its companions and setting off a wrestling match that rolled down Orlando's stomach, tickling horribly.

"You get off him, you creatures," said Mrs. Simpkins irritably. "The boy is sick. Just because this is ancient Egypt doesn't mean they don't have brooms, and if you don't want me to take one to the whole lot of you, you'll go perch on that chair and mind your manners."

Watching the Wicked Tribe immediately do as they were told was one of the most astonishing things Orlando had ever seen. His fearful respect for the little round woman went up another notch.

Fredericks came in, rubbing puffy-lidded eyes as he delivered his news. "There's a bunch of people shouting outside."

"Freddicks!" called the monkeys. "Pith-pith the mighty thief! Play with us!"

"There is indeed," said Mrs. Simpkins. "If Orlando feels strong enough, we're going up to have a look."

After getting slowly to his feet, Orlando was pleased to discover he felt reasonably able. He followed her out into the hallway with Fredericks and the monkeys close behind. The house was bigger than Orlando had guessed—the hallway alone stretched almost fifteen meters—and the beautiful wall paintings of flowers and trees and a marsh full of ducks suggested it must belong to someone important.

"Yes, it does," his guide said when he asked. "Or it did. To Mr. Al-Sayyid, who was an undersecretary in the palace—a royal scribe."

"I don't understand."

"Because I never finished explaining. All in due time."

She led them down the hall, through a set of family apartments, and finally to an airy, pillared room which seemed to have been the master bedroom, but showed no signs of recent habitation. A door off this room opened into a pretty walled garden with trellises of flowers and a pond; Orlando was quite surprised at how much like a modern garden it seemed. They did not linger, but followed Mrs. Simpkins as she stumped up a series of ramps that led to the roof, which was flat and surfaced with dried mud spread like plaster. An awning had been erected at one end, and cushions and stools and a neat small table made of painted wood arranged in its shade showed that this was probably a favorite spot on warm days.

Orlando noted these details in passing, but was more immediately arrested by the sight of the city itself spreading away on all sides. Beyond the gardens and walls of the villa—which was even larger than he had suspected—lay other, similar properties, surrounded by a broad belt of smaller houses on narrower streets, extending outward right to the river's edge. Even from so far away he could see naked people clambering in the mud along the riverbanks, perhaps making bricks to build other villas. Although hundreds of boats and ships still plied its waters, the Nile was clearly at very low ebb and the mud flats were wide.

But the most interesting views were in the direction away from the river. In the extreme western distance, set neatly atop the spine of the mountains that ran parallel to the broad Nile, was what appeared to be a beautiful city of temples and palaces, so starkly white that it shimmered like a mirage even in the mild morning sunlight.

"Abydos," said Mrs. Simpkins. "But not like in the real Egypt. That's the home of Osiris. *He's* as close to an 'actual, factual devil' as I hope any of us are likely to see."

Closer, clinging to the foothills like barnacles on the upturned hull of a boat, were many more temples in many different styles; between the temple hills and Orlando's balcony viewpoint lay more of the city and its houses, box after box of pale mud brick like an overambitious display of rectangular crockery.

The mild afternoon breeze changed direction and a roar of voices suddenly drifted to the rooftop, the more impressive because it came from such a distance. A vast crowd of people were gathered around a particular building on the outskirts of the temple hills, a huge pyramidal shape made of piled slabs; it looked older than almost any of the structures with which it shared the hilltops. Orlando could not make out the reason they were surrounding the building, or even how many people there were, but it was not a quiet or peaceful crowd; he could see it surge and then fall back in waves, as though something held it loosely bound.

"What's going on?" Fredericks asked. "Is it something to do with all the trouble in the streets when we got here?"

"It is," Mrs. Simpkins agreed, then shouted so suddenly that Orlando and Fredericks both jumped, "You monkeys, get back on this roof!" The yellow miscreants fluttered back to the shadow of the awning, protesting. "That's the temple of Ra there in the middle of that crowd," she explained, ignoring the Tribe, "—see, that thing that looks like two sets of stairs pushed together? Your friend is in there."

"Our friend?" Orlando couldn't make sense of any of it. The light bouncing from the numberless rooftops of the mud brick city was making his headache worse.

"You mean the wolf-head guy?" asked Fredericks. "Upsy-Daisy, or whatever his name is?"

"Upaut, yes," said Mrs. Simpkins a little sourly. She didn't like jokes much, except for her own. "His rebellion hasn't worked out, but he's taken sanctuary in Ra's temple. Tefy and Mewat can't defile the temple of such an important god by just snatching him out of there—certainly not without their master's permission, and Osiris isn't back yet. But just in case, a lot of the working people and some of the lesser gods who are on Upaut's side have joined up into sort of a human wall to keep the soldiers away from the temple. So it's a standoff, for now."

Orlando was definitely feeling the effects of too much bright light. "So that's where he wound up. That's . . . um . . . that's interesting. But you said we had to get out of here in a hurry, and I don't feel too good anyway, so why are we standing here staring at some temple?"

"Because," said Mrs. Simpkins as she took his elbow and turned him toward the ramp, "that's where you're going."

DESPITE the fact that it was his own form that looked back at him from the mirror-window—the hard planes of his face as they had looked a century earlier, the silvery hair a little long but immaculately styled—Felix Jongleur felt as humiliated as he ever had in the dark days of his childhood, when he would kneel on the floor listening to the senior boys discuss his imminent punishment. He was unused to wearing any body but that of Osiris the God, even less accustomed to leaving his own virtual domains, and he did not like changes in his routine.

But there was nothing to be done about it. One did not become the oldest and arguably most powerful man on Earth without learning some of life's harsher lessons, and one of them was that there were times when pride must be put aside. He took a deep breath, or rather a series of cybernetically-controlled pumps did it for him, but just before he stepped through, a flash in the corner of his vision signaled a call on one of the emergency lines.

"What is it?" he demanded of the priest-engineer who appeared in the window. "I'm about to have a crucial meeting."

"The . . . system," stammered the bald acolyte, unprepared for his master's particularly snappish tone. "Set, I mean. He . . . it . . . there is a problem."

"Again?" Jongleur's irritation was mixed with a healthy dose of fear, but he would not show that to one of his minions. "Tell me."

"Set has been in K-cycle now for forty hours. We've never had one go much beyond half that long before."

"How are the other indicators?"

The priest tried to find a respectful way to shrug, and ended up looking as though he were having a small seizure. "They are . . . mostly normal, O Lord. Things are running smoothly. There have been some small perturbations, but nothing beyond what we've been experiencing the past few months. But this K-cycle, Lord . . ."

Jongleur had a sudden moment of almost irrational terror that this low-level functionary might be seeing the temporary sim of mortal man in white tailored suit, but a quick check reassured him that the priest was experiencing the full glory that was Osiris. "Yes, yes, the length of the cycle is unusual. But we are approaching the Ceremony and making many unusual demands on the system. Watch the indicators—let me know if anything changes dramatically. But unless we have some kind of complete meltdown, I don't want to be bothered in any way for the next hour. Is that *absolutely clear?*"

The priest-engineer's eyes grew wide. "Yes, my Lord. Thank you, O He Who Makes the Grain Spring from the Earth . . ."

Jongleur ended the connection as the man broke into the first bars of the Grateful Leavetaking.

One thing Jongleur had to grant to his Grail Brother—Jiun Bhao had undeniable style. His virtual home showed none of the ostentation of others in the Brotherhood, no Gothic-fortress-perched-on-impossible-cliffs or Caligulean excesses of decor (usually accompanied by an equally Caligulean want of decorum.) Neither was it falsely modest: the financier's node presented itself as a graceful agglomeration of broad pale walls and subtle tiling, with dark accent lines so uncommon as to arrest the eye when they appeared. Here and there a work of art was set with seemingly casual offhandedness—a delicately painted Tou-ts'ai porcelain of a water-bearer, a droll bronze of a muzzled bear trying to eat a piece of fruit—but the overall effect was of clean lines and space. Even light and shadow had been artfully arranged, so that the height of the ceilings or the length of the cross-corridors could not easily be gauged.

In keeping with the lack of ostentation in his house, Jiun Bhao wore a gray-suited sim that reflected the truth of his well-preserved ninety years; as he appeared in the central courtyard and came toward Jongleur, they might have been two dapper grandfathers meeting in the park. Neither extended a hand. There was no bow. The intricacy of the relationship obviated the need for such things.

"You do me great honor, my friend." Jiun Bhao gestured to where two chairs waited beside a whispering fountain. "Please, let us sit and talk."

Jongleur smiled and nodded. "It is I who am honored—it is too long since I have visited your home." He hoped the tacit admission of the change in their relative status would start the meeting off on the right foot. It was arguable as to which of the men was richer or wielded greater power in the real world—Jiun Bhao held entire Asian economies in the palm of his hand. The only rival to either of them was Robert Wells, but the American had never tried to build an empire of the sort both Jongleur and Jiun had constructed. But until now, Jongleur's position as the chairman of the Brotherhood had given him an undeniable edge, at least in anything to do with the Grail. Until now.

For some moments, both men merely sat and listened to the water. A small brown sparrow appeared from the indeterminate upper spaces of the courtyard, alighting on the branch of an ornamental plum tree. Jiun regarded the bird, who stared back at him in turn with the boldness of well-simulated innocence.

"I am reminded," Jiun said as he turned back to Jongleur. "I hope you are finding time lately for peaceful contemplation, my friend. These are hectic days." The financier spread his upturned hands in a gesture of surrender. "Life is a wonderful thing—it is only when we are too busy living it that we sometimes forget this."

Jongleur smiled again. Jiun might be only a little more than half his own age, but he was certainly no fool. Jiun was wondering whether Jongleur was up to the job, here at the most critical point, and was both making a quiet inquiry and perhaps suggesting that he did not find the grasping Americans particularly sympathetic. "It is during times like this that I remember why we began this project, so long ago, old friend," Jongleur replied carefully. "Quiet moments, when what we have and what we have made can truly be appreciated."

"It is a good thing to share such a moment with you. As I said, this visit is a great honor." Jiun spoke as if he himself had not all but demanded it, however well-disguised the suggestion might have been. "May I offer you any refreshment?"

Jongleur waved his hand. "You are too kind. No, thank you. I thought that you might like to know that I will announce a date for the Ceremony tomorrow, when we meet with the rest of the Brotherhood. The final step—or the first true moment, one might equally say—is only days away."

"Ah." Jiun Bhao's eyes were misleadingly mild, but even this simulation of his face was a marvel of subtle expression. Rumor suggested that in the early days he had ordered the deaths of competitors without ever speaking a word, signing the warrants by nothing more than a look of tired indulgence. "Splendid news. Then I take it the . . . inconsistencies of the operating system are now a thing of the past?"

Jongleur flicked nonexistent lint from his virtual suit to cover a moment of consideration. "There are one or two details still being pursued, but I promise they will have no bearing on the success of the Ceremony."

"That is good to hear." Jiun nodded slowly. "I am sure the rest of the Brotherhood will be pleased by your announcement. Even Mr. Wells."

"Yes, of course. He and I have had our disagreements," said Jongleur, amused at how the company and surroundings led one almost automatically to decorous understatement, "but we still share a single goal. Now we are ready to achieve that goal."

His host nodded again. After a moment of silence during which Jongleur watched several small fish in blurry movement beneath the rippling surface of the fountain, Jiun said, "I have a small favor to ask of you, old friend. An imposition, I am sure, but I pray that you will consider it."

"Anything."

"I am deeply interested in the Grail process itself, as you know. I have been so ever since the first day you told me of your researches—do you remember? It is astonishing to contemplate how quickly the time has passed."

Jongleur remembered only too well—Jiun Bhao and his Asian consortium had been a crucial bloc in the initial financing; behind the screen of polite discussion, the bargaining had been even more vicious than usual. "Of course."

"Then you will understand my wish. Since the Ceremony is such a splendid occasion—unprecedented, really—I would ask you for the boon of perspective."

"I'm afraid I don't understand."

"I would like to be last. So that I may observe the splendor of our accomplishment before being caught up in it myself. Otherwise, the excitement will doubtless be so great that I will regret afterward all the details I have missed."

For a moment Jongleur was off-balance. Did Jiun suspect some kind of double cross? Or—and here was a truly disturbing thought—did the Chinese magnate, with his vast resources, know something that even Jongleur did not know? But to hesitate could only fuel suspicion, if Jiun was feeling such a thing. "Of course. I had planned that we would all partake of the Ceremony together, but no favor is too great for one who has given me . . . *and* the project, of course . . . so much timely support."

Jiun inclined his head. "You are a true friend."

Jongleur wasn't quite sure what exactly he had bargained away, but he did know what he had received in return—an all but iron-clad promise of Jiun's backing in any contest with Wells. He had come prepared to give away much more, and not certain that he would gain what he wanted even so.

They made small talk for the rest of the hour, speaking of grandchildren and great- and great-great-grandchildren in the benevolently vague manner of hunters evaluating different generations of foxhounds. There was no more talk of business, as everything important had been settled. Several more sparrows took up places on the branch beside the first, finding it comfortable to sit and even to sleep in a room where the only noise was the murmur of water and the equally soft conversation of two aged men.

"**W**HAT are you talking about?" Orlando demanded as Bonita Mae Simpkins led him, Fredericks, and the cloud of tiny, sulphur-colored primates down the stairs again. "We're not going there—into the middle of a bunch of soldiers! That scans, lady!"

"You best not get too snippy with me, boy," she said. "Or you'll find yourself without any friends in this town at all."

"Look, it just doesn't make any sense—you said we can't let those Osiris-guys catch us, so why should we go right to them?" He turned to Fredericks, who shrugged, clearly just as confused.

"If you'd learn a little patience, you'd be better off." Mrs. Simpkins tilted her head. "He's here."

"Who's here?" Orlando asked, but she was already bustling off down the main hallway. He and Fredericks followed her, the cloud of monkeys trailing behind like a visual representation of an embarrassing noise. They all stopped in the doorway. Limping up the long ramp that led from the front gate to the elevated main floor of the house was one of the oddest looking people Orlando had ever seen, a tiny man barely three feet tall with thick, mis-shapen limbs. His face was even stranger, broad fishy mouth and bulging eyes so grotesque he seemed to be wearing a mask, but despite all this deformity even a brief glimpse of him revealed a quick intelligence and a strange, mocking glint in the exaggerated stare.

"It's kind of you to come," said Mrs. Simpkins, then astonished both Orlando and Fredericks by bowing to the bizarre dwarf. "We are in your debt."

"Not yet," he replied, then revealed his huge, horselike teeth in a grin. "But I'll let you know when you are!"

"This," she said to the youths beside her, "is Bes. He's an important god—and a kind one."

"A household god," he demurred, "—a minor deity of hearth and home."

"These are Thargor and Pithlit," she said, with a warning look at each. "They are warrior gods from a small island in the Great Green."

"Warrior gods?" Bes turned his goggling stare on Fredericks. "Must have been a small island indeed—this skinny one looks as though he would fight to get to the *back* of a battle, not the front. Now are you going to invite me in, or keep me out here in the midday sun until I am as scaly as Sobek?"

She ushered him into the hallway and down to the largest room of the private apartments. "It's generous of you to help us," she said.

"I have only said I would consider it, little mother." The dwarf continued to examine Orlando and Fredericks, but seemed almost not to notice the monkeys, who had clustered on Orlando's shoulder and were watching the new arrival with unhidden fascination. "First this pair must answer at least one of my riddles." He whirled in place, surprisingly graceful, then stopped. "Now tell me—who am I?" Bes dropped to all fours and lifted his rump in the air, then began to crawl around the room backward, emitting busy, farty little noises. The monkeys laughed so hard several of them tumbled down Orlando's front and had to hang onto his belt to keep from falling. Even Orlando had to smile. Mrs. Simpkins merely rolled her eyes.

The dwarf stopped and looked up. "Do you not recognize Khepera the dung beetle, the only deity in the heavens who is brown at both nose and nethers?" He shook his head. "What do they teach young gods these days?" Bes rolled onto his back and let his limbs go limp, then arranged his hands decorously across his chest and closed his eyes. "Tell me this one, then. Who am I?" After a long moment, one pudgy hand crept free and finger-walked down to his crotch, where it grabbed and squeezed.

Embarrassed, but still amused, Orlando could only shake his head.

"By the swinging udders of Hathor, do you not recognize our lord Osiris? Who else could be dead and yet still lust?" The disgust in his voice made Orlando realize suddenly that this riddle-game was in deadly earnest—that their salvation might hinge on it. Before he could ponder the meaning of the dwarf's riddle about Osiris, the tiny man had bounced up onto his feet. "I will give you one last chance. Tell me who I am."

He lifted his hands to his curly hair and spread the fingers like ragged ears, then screwed up his face into a broad, toothy gape before throwing back his head to bay like a sick dog. The Wicked Tribe, vastly amused, began to do the same, so that the room echoed with shrill yips. "Ah, me!" the dwarf moaned. "Although it is daylight, my head is muddled, so I will howl at the sun instead of the moon!"

Fredericks suddenly laughed. "It's Oompa-Loompa!"

"Upaut," said Orlando gratefully. "That's Upaut."

"Well," Mrs. Simpkins began, "if we've had enough of these games . . ."

Bes raised a bushy eyebrow. "That one was too easy, I think. Let us try one more." He paused for a moment, waiting for the Tribe to fall silent, which they at last reluctantly did, then lifted his hands and covered both eyes. Through some ventriloquial trick, his voice seemed to come from everywhere in the room except his own broad mouth.

"I am lost in darkness," he sighed. "I am sealed in a coffin, wandering in darkness and cold forever . . ."

"I know that one, too," Orlando said. "And it's not funny."

The dwarf dropped his hands. "Ah, so you were correct, little mother. They *do* know something." He turned back to Orlando. "You speak the truth. It is not much of a joke." He spread his arms as if in a gesture of welcome, then abruptly did a backward flip, landing solidly on his bandy legs near the doorway of the chamber. "Let us go, then. The temple of Grandfather Ra awaits us."

"Just a minute," Orlando growled. The energy which had allowed him to get out of bed and walk to the roof was beginning to flag, and he was having trouble keeping his temper. "How are we going to get through all those soldiers? And why do we want to go there in the first place?"

"You have to get out of here," Mrs. Simpkins said in the sudden quiet. "I told you—this place isn't safe for you or anyone who's helping you."

"But why don't we just go down the river to the next gateway, or whatever they're called. Why won't anyone tell us anything? We still don't know what *you're* doing here, let alone why we have to go join some stupid revolution."

She nodded her head. "You're right, boy. I owe you the rest of my story. I'll tell you what I can when we're on the way. But Tefy and Mewat have boats full of soldiers all over the Nile during the daytime, and at night you'd never be able to get down there in the first place before something ate you—if you were lucky."

Fredericks spoke up. "But why go *there?*"

"Because it's the only gateway you can reach," she said quietly. "And Bes is the only one who can get you there."

"Not if we stand here all day like old, constipated Taueret, waiting in the water lilies for her bowels to move," observed Bes.

Mrs. Simpkins fetched a thick white robe which she threw over Orlando's shoulders. "That'll keep the sun off you, boy. You're still not well." At her direction, but not without a few muffled squeals of protest, the squadron of monkeys climbed underneath the robe. "Let's not turn this into any more of a circus than we have to," she said.

But that, Orlando reflected sourly as he followed the surprisingly nimble dwarf out the door and across the villa garden, was exactly what they most resembled.

"Hey, if we have to go to this temple and see Wolf Boy," Fredericks said brightly, "maybe we can at least get your sword back, huh?"

Orlando was already feeling tired as he watched Bes climbing the garden wall, apparently with the idea of taking them out some less obvious way. "I can hardly wait," he said.

                    *   *   *

IT was at times like this, reflected the man who was both Felix Jongleur and Osiris, Lord of Life and Death, that the life of a supreme being felt more than a little lonely.

The meeting with Jiun Bhao had been heartening, but the effects had not lasted long. Now, as he lay in the eternal blue nothing of his system's base level, he was already beginning to wonder what kind of Mephistophelian bargain the Chinese financier had secured. Jongleur was not used to making deals whose fine print he had not read.

More worrisome, though, was the latest news on the Other, which continued to run deep in K-cycle and showed no signs of changing any time soon. No one else in the Brotherhood had any idea how unstable the system beneath the Grail Network truly was, and as the days approaching the Ceremony dwindled away, Jongleur was coming to feel he might have made a terrible mistake.

Was there a way to detach the network from the Other and substitute another system, even at this late date? There were things Robert Wells and his Jericho people at Telemorphix had developed that might work, although some functionality would certainly be lost in the changeover—slower response times, at the very least, and perhaps a price to pay in the dumping of some of the less important bits of memory as well, not to mention that the Ceremony itself would have to be postponed still further—but the essential functions of the network would surely be saved and the completion of the Grail Project could go forward. But did he dare? Wells was as desperate for the Grail's success as Jongleur was himself, but that still did not mean he would sit back and allow the chairman of the Brotherhood to admit defeat quietly. No, the American would rescue the project then make all the political capital of it he could. The prospect was galling. But not to do so would be to risk everything, absolutely everything, on a system that was daily proving itself to be unpredictably, unknowably strange.

He moved uneasily, or would have, had his body not been restrained in a porous microfilament webbing, drifting in the viscous fluids of his life-preserving chamber. For well over a hundred years he had kept his own counsel, but it was hard at times like this not to wish that things were different.

Jongleur's brain again sent a signal for movement to dispel nervous energy, and again the signal arced into nothingness. He longed for bodily freedom, but more specifically, he longed for the soothing environs of his favorite simulation. Still, there was business to take care of first.

With a thought, he opened a communication window. It was only short moments until Finney's face appeared in it, or rather the vulture head of its Egyptian incarnation, Tefy. "Yes, O Lord?"

Jongleur paused, taken aback. "Where is the priest? What are you doing there?"

"Seeing to your interests, O Lord of Life and Death."

"You have interests of mine to see to, certainly, but I don't . . ." A sudden suspicion clutched him, and with it a shiver of anticipation. "Is it Jonas? Have you got him?" A more reasonable, but still hopeful interpretation occurred to him. "Or have you simply tracked him into my Egypt?"

The vulture head dipped. "I regret to say that we do not know his present whereabouts at all, master."

"Damnation! Then why aren't you out looking for him? Have you forgotten what I can do to you any time I wish?"

A vigorous shake of the beak. "We forget nothing, Lord. We are just . . . seeing to some details, then we will be on the trail again. Will you grace us with your presence soon?"

Jongleur shook his head. "Later. Perhaps . . ." he consulted the time readout, the numbers showing GMT, still the marker of global imperium long after the English sea empire had shrunk to a single dreaming island, ". . . perhaps not today, though. It would be too distracting with all these meetings."

"Very good, Lord."

Felix Jongleur hesitated. Was that relief he saw in his servant's inhuman expression? But such concerns could not be as significant as the decision he had to make, and time for that decision was running short. He cut the connection.

So . . . was it time to give up on the Other? Time to trigger the Apep Sequence? He could do nothing, of course, unless he received assurances from Wells, and that would mean throwing his entire system open to the Telemorphix engineers. Jongleur shud-

dered at the thought. Tomb robbers. Desecrators. But was there
an alternative?

Again he found himself wishing for one person, just one, whose
counsel he trusted. Long ago he had held a hope that the half-
Aboriginal boy Johnny Wulgaru might become such—his intelligence and complete lack of sentiment had been obvious from the
first time Jongleur had seen him in the so-called Private Youth
Authority in Sydney, a warehouse for damaged children. But young
Dread had proved too wild to be completely tamed, and too much
a creature of his own predatory appetites ever truly to be trusted.
He was a useful tool, and at times like now, when he seemed to
be behaving himself, Jongleur even considered that he might be
given a little more responsibility. Except for the worrisome matter of the air hostess, a homicide which Jongleur's agents suggested had been filed by the Colombian police and Interpol as
unsolved and unlikely to change, there had been no signs of bad
behavior. But an attack dog, it was now clear to him, could never
become a trusted companion.

He had also once thought Finney might be someone worthy
of the gift of Jongleur's confidence, despite his strange relationship with the nearly subhuman Mudd. But the night of broken
glass had changed that—had changed everything.

Jongleur sighed. In the tower stronghold high above Lake
Borgne the web of systems adjusted, flashing messages of imaginary muscular movement to his brain, gently shifting the O_2/CO_2
ratios, imitating to near perfection the experience of embodiment,
but still, somehow, falling just ineffably short.

CHAPTER 8

House

THE gateway did not stay open long. Within seconds after Renie
had stepped through with !Xabbu's hand still clutched tightly
in her own, the pane of light flared and then vanished, leaving
them dazzled into darkness.

Emily cried, "I can't see!"

"We are in a large room." Martine sounded exhausted—Renie
could only guess what the effort of opening the passage had done

to her and !Xabbu. "It is very high and very long, and I sense many obstacles on the floor at our level, so I suggest none of you move until I have time to map things out."

"There's a little light," Renie said, "but not much." The initial dazzle was fading. She could make out the edges of otherwise formless things and vague gray splotches high overhead. "There are windows up there, I think, but it's hard to tell. They're either partially curtained or they're just a really strange shape."

"Martine, is there anything else we need to know about?" Florimel asked sharply. It seemed she was taking Renie's half-in-jest commissioning of her as security officer seriously.

"Not that I can tell. I cannot sense whether the floor is solid all the way to the walls, so I suggest we stay in one place." The French woman was obviously thinking of her own recent fall, and Renie heartily agreed.

"Let's just sit down, then. Are we all here? T4b?" When he responded with a preoccupied grunt, she lowered herself onto what felt like a carpet. "Well, it's certainly something different than the last place, but it would be nice to know more."

"I am going to break something," !Xabbu suddenly announced from a short distance away.

"What are you talking about?"

"There is furniture here—many of the shapes are chairs and tables. I am going to break up one of them and see if I can make a fire." The little man seemed to take a long time, perhaps looking for the right sort of wood, but at last everyone heard splintering. !Xabbu returned, saying, "Much of it is broken already, it seems." He set at the lengthy task of spinning one piece against another.

Mindful of the fact that she had more or less accepted—or perhaps demanded—the responsibilities of leadership, Renie made a quick, crawling tour around her troop. Martine was busy trying to make sense of the new environment. Florimel was waiting for something unpleasant to happen and did not want her concentration disturbed. Renie thought of something she wanted to ask Emily, but before she went to the girl, she stopped to exchange quiet words with T4b.

"It's back," he said wonderingly, and held up his left hand so she could see it silhouetted against one of the gray windows. It seemed a little translucent, although it was hard to be sure in such dim light, but he was right: it was undeniably back. She reached out to touch it, then snatched her fingers back.

"It . . . *tingles.* Like electricity."

"Pure tasty, huh?"

"I guess." She left him admiring his restored digits and crawled to where the girl sat by herself. "Emily?" The girl did not reply. "Emily? Are you all right?"

She turned slowly. "It's funny," she said at last. "For a moment, I didn't think that was my name."

"What do you mean?"

"I don't know. It just didn't seem like my name. It didn't . . . feel right."

Renie had no idea where to go with that, so she left it. "I wanted to ask you if you still have the gem Azador gave you."

Emily hesitated. "My pretty thing? That my sweet pudding gave me?"

It was hard to hear that self-absorbed bastard Azador described as a "sweet pudding" and not laugh out loud, but Renie managed. "Yes. I'd like to look at it, if I could."

"Too dark."

"Well, I'd like to hold it, then. I promise I'll give it back."

The girl reluctantly passed her the stone. Emily was right—it was indeed too dark to see much. Renie rolled it in her fingers, feeling the hard, many-faceted weight of it. "Did it ever do anything?"

"Like what?"

"I don't know—change. Talk to you. Show you pictures."

Emily giggled. "That's silly! How would it do that?"

"I don't know." She handed it back. "Can I look at it again when we have some light?"

"Okay." Emily was still amused by the idea of a talking gem. Renie crawled back toward the others just as a small flame began to grow beneath !Xabbu's ministering hands.

The Bushman took three broken table legs and held their splintered ends in the fire until they caught, then handed one to Renie and one to Florimel, keeping one for himself. As the flames multiplied, yellow light reached out to the walls, revealing the room around them. It was as large as Martine had suggested, a huge, high-ceilinged hall like something from a manor house—Renie could almost picture the bejeweled nobility from some costumed net extravaganza waving their fans and gossiping beneath the now-dusty candelabra. Large pictures hung on the walls, but either the torchlight was too dim or the pictures too old: only vague shapes were visible within the cumbersome frames. Bits of furniture stood here and there around the carpeted floor, as though the place had once been a reading room, or an oversized salon, but as !Xabbu had reported, much of the furniture was broken, although the villains seemed to be extreme age and neglect rather than violence.

Florimel stared up at the distant ceiling. "It is monstrously big. Like a train station! I do not think I have ever been in a room so large. What sort of palace must this be?"

"Some kinda scan-ass Dracula house," opined T4b. "Saw this in *Vampire Sorority: Utter Suction,* me."

"T4b's right about one thing," Renie said. "It's not the cheeriest place I've ever seen. Do you think the whole thing's a ruin? More important, is it deserted?"

Emily suddenly got up and moved closer to the rest of the group. "I know what kind of place this is." Her voice was tight. "There are eyes in the walls."

"Martine, is there anyone around?" Renie asked. "Someone watching us?"

"Not that I can tell." The blind woman shook her head. "The information is very static here. It seems to have been deserted for a while, just as it appears."

"Right." Renie stood up, holding her torch high. "Then I think we might as well start exploring. We're never going to find Quan Li—the spy, I mean—if we just sit here."

No one was thrilled by the idea, but no one raised any useful objections either. !Xabbu broke legs off a few more collapsed chairs to use as spare torches, then put out the campfire, leaving a small burned spot in the ancient carpet that made Renie feel obscurely shamed. They headed out across the shadowy room.

"Stay close together," Renie warned. "We have no idea what this simulation's supposed to be—T4b could be right. There could be vampires or anything."

"Eyes," Emily repeated quietly. Renie asked her what she meant, but the girl only shook her head.

It took them perhaps a quarter of an hour of cautious exploration to cross the great hall. They stopped to examine many of the crumbling artifacts on the way without adding much to their understanding. The furniture and ornamentation seemed like something out of the Baroque era in Europe, but there were other elements that seemed likely to be of an earlier time, and some—like a plaque bearing an unconvincingly-rendered carving of a railroad train—definitely from later. Renie also spotted what looked like a row of dusty electric lights along the top of one of the walls, but it was too dark to be sure.

They stepped through the tall, wide doors at the room's far end, Florimel walking point with T4b flexing his new hand at her side, Martine and Emily behind them. Renie and !Xabbu brought up the rear, and so were the last to learn that the room on the far side, except for the shapes of its high windows—more and smaller—and its furniture—less of it, and with a vast wooden floor instead of the thick carpeting—was much like the first.

"Whoever used to live here," Renie noted, "must not have liked being crowded."

The three pictures in this room were hung closer to the floor, only a few meters above the parquet, and Renie paused to examine them. Two of them contained what looked like hunting scenes, highly stylized. The hunters appeared human, if oddly archaic, but the animals they were riding did not quite look like horses, as though painted from hearsay by someone who had never actually seen one.

The picture in the middle was a vast portrait study of a person who might have been either male or female: it was hard to tell because the subject was wrapped head to foot in a dark robe which blended into the blackening background. The hood was pulled so low over the sitter's face that only a pair of sharp, glittering eyes, a prominent nose, and an unsmiling mouth were visible in its shadowy folds.

Renie wished she had not stopped to look.

This second vast room had doors on all four sides. After walking all the way across to the farthest door and finding what appeared to be another hangar-sized chamber beyond it, Renie and the others trooped back across to one of the side entrances. The corridor outside ran parallel to the great halls, and although it, too, was lined with pictures and busts in shadowy niches, it was of more human dimensions, only a few meters wide and the same distance high; no vote was needed to settle which route the company preferred.

"Any suggestions on a direction?" Renie asked Martine.

The blind woman shrugged. "No difference that I can perceive."

"Then let's follow this hallway back in the direction we came from. That way, if we don't find anything, we'll at least be staying in the general area of the first room, since we know a gateway can manifest there."

It was a good plan, but after half an hour or so of tramping down the corridor, past locked door after locked door, and after a few entrances into and depressed exits from more huge, deserted rooms, Renie had begun to wonder if they would be able to remember which of these chambers had been their starting point. The decorations were no real help; most of the pictures were so faded and encrusted with dirt that they could have been anything. The busts uniformly portrayed old men, vaguely Caucasian, but with enough small variety in their features and enough dust caked in the crevices of the old dark stone that she would not even have sworn to that distinguishing fact.

After perhaps an hour, the monotonous trek was finally alleviated by Martine's announcement that she sensed a change in the information.

"What sort of change?" Renie asked. "People?"

"No. Just . . . force being applied. It is hard to explain, and anyway it is too far away to tell for certain. I will let you know when we get closer."

A few minutes later the blind woman stopped them and pointed to the corridor wall on the opposite side from the gigantic rooms they had first explored. "There. In that direction. I think it is the river."

"The *river?*" Florimel squinted at the wall; it seemed to pulsate gently, an illusion of the flickering torchlight. "You mean the *river* river? The one that runs through all the simulations?"

"I do not know, but that is how it feels. It is a torrent of change, that is all I can say for certain, and it is that way."

They began trying doors on that side of the corridor, but it was not until after at least a dozen attempts that they found one unlocked. They trooped through another large room, this one lined along the walls with gallery benches, as though it had once been used for some kind of performance. Most of the seats had collapsed. An empty space in the middle of the room where the dust was thick as icing sugar gave no indication of what the spectators might once have watched.

On the other side of a door at the room's far end they found a broad walkway, bounded on the near side by a wall not unlke the corridor they had been following, but on the far side by an ornate wooden railing. The passage was still roofed, but there was no wall behind the railing. Beyond they could see only darkness; the noise of moving water rose faintly from the void.

Renie tested the railing carefully before leaning her weight against it. The torchlight found nothing to bounce off, either across or below. "Jesus Mercy," Renie said. "It's a long way down to the river—must be at least ten floors below us."

"Don't be leaning out," T4b told her anxiously. "Just six that right now."

"I'm tired," said Emily. "I don't want to walk anymore."

!Xabbu fingered the railing. "I could climb down and see what is there."

"Don't you dare." Renie looked at the others. "Can we make it a little farther? If we turn right here we'll be heading pretty much back toward where we started."

The group agreed without much enthusiasm, although Emily continued to make her own feelings very clear. Renie did her best to be patient—the girl was pregnant, after all, or seemed to be, and they had made her walk for perhaps two hours—and concentrated instead on trying to make sense out of what they had seen so far.

"Could this be some version of Buckingham Palace or the Vatican?" she asked Martine quietly. "I mean, it's so huge!"

Martine shook her head. "It is like no place I have seen or heard of, but it seems to be bigger than either of those."

Their torches still illuminating nothing but darkness beyond the left-hand railing, their ears full of the urgent but muffled rush of water, they did not at first notice that the walkway was widening—that the wall on the right side and its row of doors had begun to curve away from the rail. When the difference had become something like a dozen meters, the companions suddenly reached a second railing that curved in from the wall side, then bent to run parallel to the first.

They stopped and looked around nervously. Although the wall that contained the doors and niches, now as familiar as a doddering uncle, continued to curve away from them to the right, the walkway beside it had run out, walled off by the second railing. Beyond, darkness lay on that side almost as deep as on the left, broken only by a few faint squares of light far in the distance. The twin railings stretched away in front of them along either side of a tongue of carpeted walkway, lonely as a trestle bridge over a gorge.

!Xabbu had already wandered past the security of the widest part, making his way cautiously out onto the carpeted spit, his torch held high despite his animal gait. "It is just as solid as it has been," he said. "And seems to be in good repair."

"Not going there," Emily said, shuddering. "Don't want to."

Renie was not particularly inclined to do so either, but she was struck by a sudden thought. "Hang on a moment. Those lights, out there." She pointed to the faintly glowing rectangles far along the right side of the great empty space.

"They are windows," said Florimel. "Why do you care?"

"They're *lit* windows," Renie replied. "The first lights other than our own we've seen."

"So? They are too far away even to make out properly. We did not bring binoculars."

"But there might be a crossing up ahead," Renie said. "Or this open space might only go on for a little while, then another hallway might curve out to meet it on the far side. Either way, it's the first sign of anything alive except ourselves."

The debate that followed was tense, and would have run longer except that everyone was tired. Although Martine and !Xabbu agreed with Renie, and even Florimel reluctantly admitted that it made sense to explore a little farther, Emily and T4b objected so desperately that they forced a compromise: if nothing important was discovered when Martine's undefined but so far quite reliable sense of time told her half an hour had passed, they would turn around and retrace their steps back to less nerve-racking parts.

As the little troop made its way out onto the walkway, which was of safe width and guarded by strong railings, T4b was so clearly miserable that Renie began to regret her own firmness of purpose. She remembered what Martine had said about the river-of-air—about how difficult it had been to get T4b to step out with the others and trust the wind currents—and wondered if he might be phobic.

Oh, well, she thought. *Better to find out now. Might be crucial up the line somewhere.*

The hulking battle-robot took a route directly down the middle of the three-meter pathway and would not walk even a step to either side, treading the rock-solid path as carefully as if on a trampoline. He shook off Renie's attempts at supportive conversation with animal sounds of discomfort.

They had gone scarcely a hundred paces when Martine abruptly clutched Renie's elbow. "I feel something," she whispered.

Renie waved the others to a stop. "Tell us."

"Something . . . some*one*. Maybe more. Up ahead of us."

"We're lucky to have you, Martine." Renie considered. The walkway was a bad spot to get into a fight, but the whole point of the exercise had been to find other people, perhaps learn something about this environment. In any case, why should it be someone hostile? Unless it was the Quan Li thing . . . That gave Renie another moment's pause—it would be horrible indeed, with all of them tired and dispirited, to have to deal with the lithe, cat-quick creature that half a dozen of them had struggled vainly to subdue back in the last simulation. But it seemed unlikely that given a two-day head start their enemy would be lurking here in the middle of nothing when he or she had the Grail's access device.

No, Renie felt certain that the thing they sought would either be gone entirely or would have at least found a more comfortable part of the simulation. It wouldn't be waiting for them because it could have no idea they were coming.

Florimel agreed, although not without some reservations. After a bit more whispered argument they started forward again, this time without conversation of any kind.

They had reached something like an island—a space where the railings curved outward on either side and the floor spread, a great oval widening of the walkway like the silhouette of a python with its dinner half-digested—when Martine touched Renie's arm again.

The island was clearly meant as a place for conversation and conviviality. The railings were higher here and lined everywhere except across the walkway by tall, dusty cabinets; the open, carpeted floor was cluttered with overstuffed sofas and chairs. Even as her heart sped with anxiety and anticipation, Renie could picture the lords and ladies of the ballrooms having something like formal picnics here—perhaps in daylight, when they could see the river running far below.

Martine pointed toward a cabinet along one rail, a huge affair covered with ornate carvings, its brass door handles now black with age. The company moved quietly toward it. When they had arranged themselves in a semicircle a few meters away, Renie said loudly, "We know you're in there. Come out—we won't hurt you."

There was a pause, then the doors banged open so swiftly that one splintered off its top hinges and sagged loose. Emily screamed. The figure that leaped out of the shadowy interior was brandishing something long and sharp, and Renie had a moment to curse her own stupid certainties before the stranger stopped, blinking in the torchlight, and raised the huge knife before him.

"I have little beside the clothes I wear," the young man declared breathlessly. "If you want them, you won't get them cheaply." The stranger was very thin, and it was hard to tell which was paler, his thatch of white-blond hair or his milky skin: if his eyes had not been dark, Renie would have thought him an albino. He waved the knife again, a wicked-looking thing as long as his forearm. "This is Gristleclip, whose fame you doubtless know, and I will not hesitate to use it!"

"Gristleclip?" Renie was almost startled into a laugh.

"We do not mean you any harm," said !Xabbu.

The young man's eyes widened briefly at the talking monkey, but he did not lower his knife—which, as Renie looked closer, appeared despite its impressive size to be something best used for chopping vegetables. "He's right," she said. "You can put your knife away."

He squinted at her, then surveyed her companions. "Where are your weapons?" he asked, a little surprised but still suspicious.

"Want weapons, you?" T4b, despite still moving like a high-wire artist in a stiff breeze, brandished a huge, spiked fist. "Op this, knife-boy."

"Stop it," Florimel told him. "We have no weapons and we want nothing from you," she told the stranger. "We are lost, that is all."

The pale young man's look of suspicion was not entirely gone, but he appeared to be considering their words. The knife sagged a little; Renie thought it must be quite heavy. "Are you from the Sunset Windows Wing?" he asked. "I do not recognize your clothes."

"Yes, we're from far away." Renie tried to sound like she was agreeing without committing herself and the others to anything. "We don't know where we are exactly, and we . . . we heard you in the cabinet. We'd appreciate any help you can give us—we'll do what we can for you in return."

His breathing now slowed, the youth stared at her hard for a moment, then carefully slid his knife into the sash at his waist. He was dressed in what Renie imagined a seventeenth century peasant would wear on his day out, all grays and browns, a blouse-like shirt with billowing sleeves over a pair of breeches, and shod in the kind of soft boots that she thought were called moccasins. "Do you swear you mean no harm?" he asked. "Swear by the Builders?"

She had no idea who the Builders might be, but she knew she and her companions had nothing against this skinny young man. "We swear."

He let out a last deep breath and deflated even farther, if such were possible. He was scarecrow thin; Renie found his willingness to stand up to a half-dozen strangers quite impressive. He surprised her then by turning to the cabinet and its sagging doors. He leaned into the shadowy interior and called, "Come out, Sidri," then turned a stern glance on Renie and her companions. "You gave your word."

The girl who stepped out was as thin and pale as her protector, wearing a long gray dress draped by a surplice figured with embroidered flowers. Renie guessed she must be the youth's sister, but he announced, "This is my betrothed, Sidri, a novice of the Linen Closet Sisters. I am Zekiel, an apprentice cutlerer—or rather I *was* an apprentice." There was quiet pride in his voice, and now that his beloved had appeared, he did not take his eyes from her, although she kept her own snow-lashed gaze downcast. "We are fugitives, you see, because our love was forbidden by our masters."

T4b groaned. "Not another *sayee-lo* fairy-story! Just want to get back on the ground, me."

"CODE *Delphi*. Start here.

"As usual, it seems, when we find ourselves in a new simulation, we also find ourselves thrown in among people and events as complicated as anything we might find in the real world. There are differences this time, however, both good and bad. We now have a goal, which is the recovery of Renie's access device, and as I mentioned in my last weary entry, !Xabbu and I have also discovered an ability to manipulate the system by ourselves, if only in the smallest of ways. I do not have words for it—the entire process was to find a way to communicate without such things—but it has given me ideas I must carefully consider. In any case, we have entered this simulation world in pursuit of a murderer, and what little we have learned has not improved our chances of overcoming this enemy, let alone the greater villains, the Grail Brotherhood.

"Still, it is useless to worry beyond the point of careful planning, and the simulation itself is not without interest. The single large and long-deserted room which was my only experience of it during my last journal entry has proved to be only one of many such rooms. We have walked for hours through corridors and other enormous chambers, and only at the very end did we find any other living creatures—a boy named Zekiel and his lover, the girl Sidri. We have camped with them, for lack of a better word, on a wide space in a walkway high above the river, and we have all talked for hours. They have run away from their own people, which is a relief because at least now we know there *are* people in this echoing ruin. In fact, Zekiel says that the two of them came to this part of the house, as he calls it—a bit of an understatement for such a mammoth structure—precisely because it was deserted. They feared Sidri's religious Order would try to reclaim her, since novices are given to the Sisterhood in a kind of bond-slavery, and may not marry or leave the Order. The pair are searching for a place where they believe they can live together freely, another part of the house called the Great Refectory, which as far as I can tell they know only by ancient rumor.

"Hearing them speak I cannot help wondering at how shot through with myth and story are all the parts of Otherland we have seen. It seems an odd obsession when one considers who built the place. I had never thought of billionaire industrialists and political tyrants as being interested in the structure of folktales, but I suppose I have not truly known many of either.

"Neither Sidri nor Zekiel can be much beyond fifteen or sixteen years old, but they are the products of a more or less medieval system, and clearly consider themselves to be of adult age. Sidri's Order, the Linen Closet Sisters, apparently have some kind of ceremonial duties caring for . . . well, linens. Zekiel's own guild, centered around a place called the Cutlery, maintains edged instruments from what seems by his description to have been an antique and very extensive kitchen complex. In order to protect himself and his ladylove from bandits and monsters, both of which he claims with great certainty haunt the corridors of this abandoned part of the house, he has stolen one of the ceremonial blades—a large chopping knife with the charming name of 'Gristleclip.' For this crime, he believes he is now a wanted criminal, and I cannot doubt he is right.

"As for us, the outsiders, we still have no idea of the true size of this building or what lies beyond it. Both Sidri and Zekiel seem slightly mystified by the question, so perhaps their sharply proscribed, feudal upbringing has kept them from traveling or even inquiring. For what it is worth, we have seen signs of technologies as modern as the late nineteenth or very early twentieth century, but from Zekiel's descriptions it seems most of the residents live like early settlers in the Americas, surviving off the bounty of the house and its grounds with the same innocent rapaciousness with which the European colonists exploited the endless natural resources of their new continent.

"Just in our short hours of conversation, we have heard Zekiel—who is more knowledgeable, because his existence has been less sheltered—casually mention at least a dozen different groups that share the house. Some he calls 'tribes,' which seems to mean that their significant characteristic is where they come from, rather

than what they do—Zekiel calls his Cutlery people a 'guild,' but
he has referred to others by names such as 'the Sunset Windows
Tribe' or 'the Upriver Pools Tribe.' The river does indeed seem
to run through this entire simulation, or at least through this immense building, which is apparently all Zekiel knows. It serves
to tie the various cultures together, although its flow seems to be
from the top of the house to the bottom, and thus it is convenient
only for downriver journeys. Most long river trips apparently end
in an even longer hike back.

"Fish live in the river, and there are fishermen who spend their
lives catching them. Other sources of meat are available as well,
cows and pigs and sheep, which as far as I can tell are pastured
in rooftop gardens, suggesting that Zekiel and Sidri are not the
only people in this house who have never left the property. Has
there been a plague here, I cannot help wondering? Are these folks
the descendants of survivors who barricaded themselves into this
great house, as in Poe's 'Masque of the Red Death,' and then
never went out again? It is a strange, Gothic place, of that there
can be little doubt. The idea of hunting for the person who pretended to be Quan Li through such a labyrinth fills me with unease. I cannot even guess what the mile after mile of shadowed
hallways must feel like to my companions, who are not as intimate with darkness as I am.

"The discussion is breaking up. I think everyone wants sleep,
although we can only guess at what the true time might be, even
by the standards of the network. T4b and Emily in particular have
found this a difficult day. We will continue our explorations tomorrow.

"But I cannot help wondering who made this bizarre place,
and for what purpose he or she meant it. Is it a pure diversion, a
Victorian folly writ large in virtual space, or was one of the Brotherhood preparing a suitably grandiose home in which to spend
eternity? If the second is true, the house's creator must be someone with whom I share more than a few similarities, for the only
real difference between entombing oneself in this vast ruined maze
and burying oneself as I have in my underground burrow—unar-
guably a cave, despite its amenities—is a difference of degree,
and of money. Otherwise, I would guess that the simulation's creator and I have much in common.

"I find that a very disturbing thought.

"*Code Delphi*. End here."

"**B**UT you think you have heard of such a person?" Renie asked. "A newcomer?"

Zekiel brushed his pale hair from his eyes. "I remember hearing something, Mistress, but I cannot be certain. A stranger, a woman, who said she came from one of the Attic tribes? I heard it in passing, while we were preparing for the Trooping of the Knives, and I paid little attention. People often come from far away, especially to the Library Market."

"Yes, some of the other Sisters mentioned a stranger," Sidri added quietly. Even after an evening and night spent in their company, she still had not looked anyone full in the face. "They said she must bring bad luck, because a young woman from the Upper Pantry Clerks ran away the night she arrived and has not been seen since."

The time had come to separate—Zekiel and Sidri to continue their journey away from all that they knew, Renie and the others to travel toward the place the young lovers had fled. Renie looked at the pair, colorless as creatures bred in a cavern, but so absorbed in each other and their plans that she knew she and her own companions were no more than an incident in these lovers' story.

"So if we find this Library Market," Florimel said to Zekiel, "we can ask questions there? No one will think us odd?"

He looked at her for a moment, then turned his gaze on T4b and !Xabbu. A smile creased his long face. "You will not be ignored, that is certain. Perhaps you should try to find some clothing in one of the big empty rooms—scavengers often do well in such old places, and I think these have not been searched before."

Renie could not understand how people could live full-time in a single house, however large, yet leave an entire wing unexplored for generations, but the ins and outs of the simworld were of less interest to her just now than the very real possibility that they might find the spy.

Zekiel and Sidri stood awkwardly for a moment at the edge of the walkway island, their path stretching before them. "Farewell," said the pale young man. "And thanks to you."

"We have done nothing," Martine told him. "You have helped us, though, and told us many useful things."

He shrugged. "It has been nice to spend time among people and to hear friendly voices. I do not think we shall be so lucky again for a while." As he spoke, Sidri reached for his hand and clutched it, like someone chilled by watching a funeral procession. Still holding hands, they turned and began to walk away.

"But where *is* this house?" Renie called after them.

Zekiel paused. "I was only a cutlerer," he said. "That is a question better asked of the Library Brothers, who understand the workings of the universe."

Frustrated, Renie let out a sharp breath. "No, where is it? Where in the world?"

Now Sidri, too, was looking at her in surprise, as though Renie had begun quizzing them about differential calculus. "We do not understand your questions," the young woman said shyly.

"Where . . . Let's put it this way. When you get to the end of the house, what is there? What do you find?"

Zekiel shrugged. "The sky, I suppose. The stars."

They waved and set off again, leaving Renie to try to work out where the conversation had gone off-track.

They found clothes two floors below, in a room that had obviously not been explored recently, since even the cobwebs were empty and clotted with dust. Chest after chest stood stacked in dangerously unstable piles that nevertheless had survived the years without tumbling. Renie and the rest of the company tried to be careful, but their first attempts set one such tower swaying, then the whole thing came down in a series of thunderous crashes.

"Well," Renie said, "everyone for miles is going to know someone's in here now."

Florimel pulled a heavy blanket from the wreckage of a sprung chest, unfolding it to expose an unreadable monogram interlaced with a stylized picture of a lantern. "From what the young man told us, no one would be much surprised to know someone was scavenging." She wadded the blanket and heaved it to one side.

Renie found a pile of foundation garments in one of the other trunks and lifted out a corset that was positively knobby with whalebone. "I know clubs in the Golden Mile back home where you would be the hit of the night in this, Florimel. Actually, there are lots of clubs where T4b would be pretty popular wearing it, too." She found a long blue skirt with a pattern of golden leaves and held it up, taking a couple of steps to see how the fabric moved, then frowned. "This feels too much like a game of dress-up," she said. "But we're not just trying to fit in—we're trying to catch a murderer."

"I have not forgotten," said Florimel.

"So what are we going to do if we find . . . her, him, whatever it is?"

Florimel was trying on a once-colorful cape, although from what Renie had seen of Zekiel's and Sidri's clothes, Florimel's Temilun peasant garb was not likely to raise any eyebrows in this world. "If we find the spy without him knowing we are here, we will try to take him by surprise," she said. "If not, plans will mean little. He is not the kind to surrender. We will have to overcome him by force."

Renie did not like the sound of that. "You seem very sure it's a 'he.'"

Florimel's lip curled. "It is a man, although I cannot pretend I guessed until we fought with him. That kind of hatefulness feels different when it comes from a woman."

"Whatever it is—he is—he scared me to death."

Florimel nodded somberly. "He would have killed us all if it suited him, without a second thought."

"Renie!" !Xabbu called from the other side of the mountain range of boxes and chests. "Come and see!"

She left the German woman unpacking a case full of what looked like opera gloves. !Xabbu was perched on the open lid of a huge steamer trunk, T4b standing stiffly before him in a huge gray robe, belted at the middle with a braided length of white and green strands. His robot helmet seemed ridiculously out of place, like a UFO perched on a mountaintop, but when she suggested he take it off, the young man balked.

"She is right," !Xabbu said quietly. "We must not attract too much attention. Our lives will be at stake."

T4b looked helplessly to Emily, but she only grinned, enjoying his discomfort. With a shrug that seemed to convey his surrender to an unfair universe, he carefully removed the masked helmet. His hair was pressed to his head in realistically sweaty ringlets around his long, sullen face. On either side, above his ears, a long streak of white ran through the black.

"Coyote stripes," was his defiant answer to Renie's question—apparently the current height of *Los Hisatsinom* fashion.

"Here, let me rub some dust on your face," she said.

T4b caught at her hand. "Whatcha doing, you?"

"Do you really want to walk around this old-fashioned place with those glowing subdermals shouting, 'I'm probably a warlock or something, so you better burn me at the stake'? No? I didn't think so."

He grudgingly allowed her to dirty his face and hide the Goggleboy designs. "So what about my helmet?" he demanded. "Chance not I'm leaving it here."

Florimel leaned around the nearest stack of boxes. "Turn it upside down and it will look like you are collecting for some charity. Perhaps people will throw money in it."

"Wild funny," he growled.

Martine, who wore peasant clothes like Florimel's, had not bothered to augment her wardrobe; as Renie pulled a skirt over the bottom half of her jumpsuit, the blind woman slid down from her seat on a box. "If you are all ready, we should move on. Half the day is gone, and people are always more suspicious of strangers who arrive by night."

"How can you even tell what time of day it is?" Renie asked.

"The place has rhythms," Martine replied. "And I am getting to know them. Now let us continue."

Zekiel's directions had been very general—half a day's walk in more or less one direction, and a dozen floors downward—but even before they reached the level of the river's passage through the house they began to see signs of human habitation. Flat stones had been placed in the middle of some of the wider corridors and used as fireplaces, although everything but the scorch marks had been removed from the sites; they could hear murmurings from some of the ornately screened ventilation ducts that might only have been wind, but could just as easily have been faint voices.

Renie also noticed something she could only distinguish because of its long absence from their lives: the growing scent of a human habitat, a scent both heartening and disturbing—heartening because it confirmed they were getting nearer to where the people were, disturbing because Renie suddenly realized she was reacting to her own full-blown sense of smell.

But when I was first in the network—when I still could feel my mask—we could barely smell anything. I was just talking the other day about how !Xabbu complained about it.

She asked him. He continued to pace on all fours beside her as he considered. "Yes, that is true," he said at last. "It was very frustrating, but I have not felt that way for some time. In fact, it seems as though now I learn much from what my nose tells me." He wrinkled his narrow forehead. "But perhaps it is an illusion. Have I not read during my courses at the Poly that after a long time in a virtual environment the brain begins to construct information for itself to make things seem more normal?"

"You were a good student," Renie said, smiling. "But that still doesn't seem enough to explain this." She shrugged. "But what do we know, really? There's never been an environment like this before. Still, we should have a better idea of how it works by now—how we can be kept online, and how things like neurocannulas, or even something as obvious as a mask, can be kept from us." She frowned, thinking it through. "In fact, that's the strangest thing about this environment. It could send information through a direct neural connection to tell the brain there *is* no neural hookup, no shunt. That makes sense. But you and I have a different, more basic kind of access which doesn't bypass our own senses, just adds to them. So how can *we* be fooled?"

They still had no answer for the question when the party descended the last bend of another exhaustive length of staircase to discover they had finally reached the river. The water, which had been a murmur in their ears for the last three floors of the descent, flowed past them along a mossy stone trough thirty meters across and flush with the floor, as though some ancient Roman aqueduct had been buried in the foundation. A lantern, the first light they had reached not of their own making, hung from a small dock that jutted from the hallway at the base of the stairs. The water was almost invisible in the weak light, rushing away into the shadows on their right.

"Upriver, then," Renie declared. "If the rest of what those two said is also true, we should have only about another hour's walk to reach the part of the house where people are." She stopped, aware of the incongruity. "Jesus Mercy, how big *is* this place?"

The architecture fronted by the hallway was more varied than the rooms which they had encountered above, as though more modification had been done to the parts of the building that lined the river. Doors opened off the hall as they had higher up, and were visible along the dim walkway on the river's far side as well, but there were also places where the walls had been knocked out, perhaps to improve the view, or elaborate additions had been built outward so that they jutted above the surface of the river, with the blocked hallway detouring along a catwalk that hung only a few meters over the gurgling waters.

As they made their way around one such obstruction, stopping to peer into the riverside windows at the room's empty interior, a boat with a lantern dangling from its bow slid past them on the far side of the river. Renie turned, startled by the movement, but the two shapes huddled in the small vessel only waved, then went back to paddling. Within moments the craft had slipped away into darkness.

Signs of habitation began to show more frequently now, and in places they could even see the lights of fires and lanterns burning on the far side of the river. More occupied fishing boats appeared; some simply drifted past, but others moved purposefully from one side of the river to the other as though searching for something. Renie could hear music and voices in some of the upper apartments, scratchy jigs played on stringed instruments, people shouting or laughing.

About a thousand meters past the first lantern, by which point they were walking through what was for all intents and purposes a small harbor town, albeit contained inside a larger structure like a ship in a bottle, Renie saw something she had not seen in several days.

"Daylight!" She pointed to windows high above them. The slanting sunlight spilled down across the clutter of jerry-built apartments which had been grafted onto the original halls, and which leaned so close above the river on both sides that it almost seemed the residents could reach across the water to borrow a cup of sugar. The huge windows and the wall in which they were situated were almost completely hidden by the crowding roofs of shanties. "I'm going to go have a look."

Only !Xabbu chose to join her, the others opting instead for a rest, seating themselves on barrels along a deserted wharf. Renie and the Bushman mounted a set of rickety stairs that wound in and out from one landing to the next, connecting perhaps two dozen shacks in its twenty-meter climb. People were obviously at home in some of the dwellings, and once as she passed an open door, a woman in a black bonnet and dress actually looked up from her sewing and met Renie's eyes. She did not seem surprised by strangers on the stairs, even though one of the strangers was a monkey.

The last landing still left them well below the nearest window, and Renie was about to content herself with just the glimpse of true daylight—she could see clouds drifting past, and the sky was a reassuringly normal blue—when !Xabbu said, "Over here!" He had found a ladder balanced against the back of the topmost apartment, a way to get up onto the roof, someone's refuge from the rest of the crowded shantytown. As she followed him up the rungs sagged alarmingly beneath her weight, but she was hungry now to see the world . . . or at least whatever world they had been given.

!Xabbu reached the top of the ladder and turned to the window, then frowned in puzzlement. Renie joined him, a couple of rungs below, eager to see the rest of the house and its grounds, or at least the part which lay below them.

Her first disconcerting realization was that they were not above much of the house at all, but only partway up one of the lower structures. The sky was real, but it was visible only between two other wings of the building, both of which rose far above their vantage point—higher even than the distance Renie and her companions had descended since leaving Zekiel and Sidri. The other disturbing thing was that there were no grounds to be seen whatsoever, except for a few glimpses lit by angling sunlight of roof gardens nestled between cupolas, or even one tucked into the wreckage of an ancient, broken dome. Instead, the house continued as far beyond the window as she could see, a stunning conglomeration of halls and towers and other structures for which she had no names, all connected in a labyrinthine whole, rooftops and chimneys spreading away and growing smaller and smaller with distance, an undifferentiated, choppy sea of gray and brown shapes that at last grew dim in the fading golden light.

"Jesus Mercy," Renie murmured. She could think of nothing else to say, so she said it again.

She was reluctant to share her discovery with the others, although her better sense told her that whether the house had an ending or not made little difference to either their hunt or their chances for escaping the simulation; it was only after Florimel had asked a series of increasingly irritated questions that she told them exactly what she had seen.

". . . And it looked like we could walk for months without reaching the outside," she finished. "Like a city, but all one building."

Florimel shrugged. "It makes little difference."

T4b, his sangfroid restored by a long time on level ground, said, "These *sayee lo* Grail-hoppers got too much time, too much money. I had something like this network, be making something bold tasty, me—no dupping."

Florimel rolled her eyes. "Let me guess . . . half-naked Gogglegirls with gigantic breasts, and plenty of loud music and guns and cars and charge, yes?"

T4b nodded vigorously, impressed by her perceptiveness and taste.

The byways along the river were beginning to fill with people abroad on errands both personal and commercial. Renie was relieved to see that she and her friends were not quite so unusual as she had feared: some of the locals were as pale as Zekiel and Sidri had been, but overall there was a fairly wide range of colors and sizes, although she had seen none yet she would call black. Of course, she remembered, her own current sim was not all that dark-skinned either. Even !Xabbu's current form did not seem to stretch convention too far, since Renie saw animals being driven to market, and even a few riding on their owners' shoulders, pigeons and a rat or two, that were clearly pets. In fact, as they followed the river shore which had widened out now into a boardwalk lined with makeshift peddlers' shops selling caps and rope and dried fish, Renie and her companions were quickly becoming just part of the crowd.

They stopped and asked an old man repairing a fishing net for directions to the Library Market, and although he seemed amused at the idea of someone not knowing where that was, he cheerfully instructed them. Wide hallways perpendicular to the boardwalk now opened into the main corridor at regular intervals, like the intersections of major streets, and when Renie and the others reached a particularly wide boulevard marked at the corner by a round-eyed bird carved on a wooden sign, they turned and headed away from the river, struggling through the thick crowd.

Black Owl Street was roofed with timbers, apparently a late addition, but was even broader than the boardwalk and more upscale as well, lined with shops and taverns and even restaurants. Some of the busy crowd wore clothes as antiquely idiosyncratic as those of Renie and her friends, but others, particularly men, were garbed in what to Renie seemed a nineteenth century style, black frock coats and trousers, or the same clothes in only slightly more imaginative hues of dark blue or dark brown, like counting-house employees in a Dickens novel. She half-expected to see Ebenezer Scrooge fingering his watch chain and cursing the rabble.

Lost in people-watching, Renie was brought up short by Martine's hand on her arm.

"Just a moment . . ." The blind woman cocked her head, then shook it. "No, nothing."

"What did you think you heard? Or felt?"

"Something familiar, but I cannot be sure—it was fleeting. There are so many people here that I am finding it hard to process the information."

Renie lowered her voice, leaning toward Martine's ear. "Do you think it was . . . you know who?"

Martine shrugged.

The company was beginning to spread a little in response to the Brownian movement of the wide, crowded corridor. Just to be on the safe side, Renie and Florimel pulled the companions back together. The crush was abetted by people entering from side channels, some pulling wagons piled high with goods, many the apparent product of extensive poaching: Renie doubted that peo-

ple in this squatter society would be building ornate candelabra
from scratch, and even if they were, she somehow doubted it
would be someone as shifty-eyed and dirty-fingered as the man
she was currently watching.

Almost without realizing it, they reached their destination. The
corridor widened so abruptly that the walls simply seemed to have
disappeared, and the ceiling retreated to a point that must have
been far higher than the top rung of the ladder Renie had climbed
earlier. The space they found themselves in was as large as four
of the huge upstairs ballrooms put together, and as crowded with
people as any of the hallway-streets outside. But it was the bookshelves that were truly impressive.

Shelves lined the Library from floor level all the way to the
ceiling, dozens and dozens of shelves mounting upward until, like
an art-class perspective exercise, they seemed to have no space
left between them. Every single one was jammed from one side
to another with books, so that the walls of the vast room had become abstract mosaics tiled in multicolored leather book spines.
Enormously long ladders stood in some places, stretching many
meters from the floor up the vertical facing of the book-cliffs;
other, smaller versions dangled between one row of higher shelves
and another, perhaps simplifying the journeys of scholars or clerks
who had to move back and forth between the same spots many
times. But in some spots along the immense shelves the only way
to get to certain locations appeared to be along frighteningly crude
rope bridges, one strand for the feet, the other chest high, the long,
sagging cables rooted on platforms built in the room's corners. It
was not the only use of rope: from the floor to a height of perhaps two stories the shelves were protected from theft and depre-
dation by nets of knotted silk, so that the books could be seen
but not touched or removed. The steep vertical shelves were acrawl
with people in gray robes—the Library-tending monks Zekiel had
mentioned. Quietly purposeful as bees on a honeycomb, these
dark-robed figures repaired the book net where a cord had frayed
or a knot had been cut, or moved carefully along the upper walkways. At least two dozen leaned out from ladders at various points
along the shelves, wielding long-handled dusters. Both the monks
and the Market-going throng appeared largely oblivious to each
other.

"It is amazing," Florimel said. "I cannot guess how many books are here."

"I believe seven million, three hundred four thousand and ninety-three is the most recent total," said an unfamiliar voice. "But most of those are stored in the lower catacombs. I doubt there are a fifth that many in this room."

The smiling man who stood beside them was young, plump, and bald. As he turned to gaze fondly at the shelves, Renie saw that all his hair except a single broad tuft on the back of his skull had been shaved. His gray robe and odd coiffure left little doubt of his profession.

"You're one of the monks?" Renie asked.

"Brother Epistulus Tertius," he replied. "This is your first time at the Market?"

"It is."

He nodded, looking them over, but she could see neither calculation nor suspicion in his open, pinkish face. "May I tell you something of its history, our Library? I am afraid I am very proud of it—I still cannot get over the idea that a boy like me from the Stovewood Scavengers should have come to such a wonderful place." He spotted !Xabbu and suddenly looked worried. "Or am I keeping you from your marketing?"

Renie wondered if he thought they were looking for a buyer for the baboon. She examined the monk carefully, trying to see whether the face of the thing that had pretended to be Quan Li might be hiding behind the benevolent exterior, but she could think of no reason why their enemy should bother to change his appearance if he had remained, nor could she find any evidence that this man was more than he seemed. Certainly, a friendly insider was the best thing to find in any unfamiliar place. "That's very kind," she said aloud. "We would love to learn more."

". . . And here are the greatest treasures of all." Brother Epistulus Tertius gestured reverently. "These are the books which our Order has translated. The wisdom of the ancients!"

In the context of the hundreds upon thousands of books ranged above them, tended by scores of gray-robed brothers, it seemed like the punchline to a joke. The crystal reliquary on the table before them contained scarcely two dozen volumes. One had been opened, as if for display. In beautifully-drawn letters, almost lost among the profusion of illuminations around capitals and in the margins, she could read the words, *". . . particular Care must be taken not to perforate the Liver during cleaning, or the flavours of the Bird will be spoyled. Seasonings, such as Shrew-Wort and autumn Carpet Buttons, may be Employed, but must be Added with a Cautious Hand . . ."*

"It's a recipe," Renie said. The Market crowd jostled past, kept from bumping the holy relics themselves only by a low wooden fence set directly in the carpeted floor. Engaged in haggling and gossip, none of them seemed particularly intent on leaping over the barrier to snag the holy cookbook.

"Perhaps, perhaps!" Their guide was cheerful. "There is so much we have left to discover. Now that we have learned the alphabet of the Solarium People, there are surely two or even three more volumes that will yield up their secrets."

"Do you mean that all of these books," Florimel waved her hand at the looming shelves, "are in unknown languages?"

"Certainly." The monk's smile did not lessen. "Oh, they were clever, the ancients! And so many of the languages are completely forgotten. And then there are codes—so many codes, some of them uniquely clever, some quite senseless and mad. And even though many of the codes are doubtless quite comprehensible, they are tied to other books which are somewhere in the Library— but of course we cannot know which books, because we do not understand the code in the first place." He shrugged, happy possessor of a job for life.

Florimel said, "That is very interesting, Brother Epistulus, but . . ."

"Please, I am only Epistulus Tertius—my master, God willing, will live many years more, and then there is yet another before me in line to shoulder his great burden."

". . . But can you tell us anything about the house itself? What is beyond it?"

"Ah, you will want to talk to one of my brethren with a greater specialty in matters philosophical," he said. "But first, I would like to show you my own specialty . . ."

"Op this!" called T4b, an unfamiliar tone in his voice. Renie turned to see him crouching on the floor a short distance away, surrounded by children. One of them had tugged back the sleeve of T4b's robe and discovered his gleaming hand; the teenager was cheerfully pretending to grab them, keeping the children squealing in excitement and mock fear. He looked so happy that although Renie did not like him attracting attention, she was reluctant to say anything. Emily stood behind him, watching the game, her narrow face lost in thought. Martine was closer to Renie than to Emily, T4b, and the children, but seemed even less connected to the group, head bowed, her mouth working silently, her eyes staring down at nothing. Renie wanted to go to her and see if she was all right—the blind woman seemed to be having a reaction like that which had first gripped her on their entry into the Otherland network—but !Xabbu was touching Renie's arm, silently asking for attention, and the monk was trying to get them all to follow him toward other treasures.

". . . And of course we are no farther in dealing with these missives than we are with the books themselves," Epistulus Tertius was saying to Florimel, "but we have had a breakthrough lately on the datal notations on some of the Far Eastern Porch Civilization lists. . . ."

A movement above her drew Renie's gaze. Several of the dusting monks were leaning out from the shelves above, eavesdropping on their brother's words and examining the newcomers. Like Epistulus Tertius they all had shaven heads, but in all other ways seemed a different species altogether, a younger, smaller, and livelier group, doubtless due to the demands of their task. They clung to the treacherous ropes seemingly without fear, and moved with the certainty of squirrels. Several of them wore the cowled necks of their robes over their mouths and noses as protection against dust, leaving only their eyes and the dome of their heads visible. One young man near the end was observing the newcomers particularly intently, and for a moment Renie almost felt she recognized him, but even as she watched he seemed to grow bored, and shinnied back up onto a higher shelf and out of sight.

Brother Epistulus Tertius was insistent, and after a few minutes they found themselves being led through the milling crowds toward the vault where the researching of antique correspondence was carried out. The monk talked in a nonstop rush of facts about the Library, most of them meaningless to Renie. She found her-

self instead watching the various denizens of the house as they
went about their business, the black-smudged Coal Scuttle Boys
larking on an afternoon's holiday, the various Kitchen guilds making arrangements with the itinerant sharpeners, the jugglers and
musicians that gave the whole thing the air of a Renaissance carnival. It was only as they reached a doorway out of the Market
Square and into the monastery halls—a section of the endless
bookshelves that swung outward to reveal a tiled hallway into
which Epistulus Tertius was beckoning them—that she realized
why the dusting monk looked familiar.

If you saw a monk you assumed it was a man, but if someone shaved off black hair, and pulled a robe up until it mostly
covered the face . . .

"It's him!" she said, almost shouting. "Oh, my God, it's him—
I mean her! That monk up on the bookshelf—it was Quan Li's
sim!"

Her companions turned from Brother Epistulus Tertius, startled into a flurry of questions, but !Xabbu's was by far the most
chilling.

"Where is Martine?" he asked.

They quickly retraced their path across the Market, but the
blind woman had vanished.

Second:

ANGELS AND ORPHANS

"The boundaries which divide Life from Death are at best shadowy and vague. Who shall say where the one ends, and where the other begins?"

—Edgar Allan Poe, "The Premature Burial"

CHAPTER 9

Eyes of Stone

NETFEED/INTERACTIVES: GCN, Hr. 5.5 (Eu, NAm)—
"HOW TO KILL YOUR TEACHER"
(visual: Looshus and Kantee hanging from wall in razor-lined room over vat of fire)
VO: Looshus (Ufour Halloran) and Kantee (Brandywine Garcia) have destroyed Jang the assassin, but are trapped now by Superintendent Skullflesh (Richard Raymond Balthazar) in the Detention Dungeon. Casting 2 dungeon attendants, 4 corpses.
Flak to: GCN.HOW2KL.CAST

DETECTIVE Calliope Skouros tilted the viewing lens away from her face and sighed. The display pinched the bridge of her nose. Her head was beginning to hurt. It was time to contemplate having another drink and saying the hell with it for the night, or possibly for good.

For the third straight evening she had spent hours of her own time using the department account to comb the vast data resources of the IPN, trying to find something that would take her another step forward on the Polly Merapanui case. She had run victim

Polly's own data every which way, all the mind-numbing trivia in the original case file and every useless bit she and Stan Chan had added to it with their own investigation. She had run the Woolagaroo angle through the informational meat grinder as well, hoping against hope it had come up in someone's M.O., been used as a nickname, anything, but with no luck.

Calliope's father had used to tell a joke, one she only dimly remembered. It had something to do with a wildly optimistic child who, when given a huge pile of horseshit as a cruel gift, had spent hours digging through it, reasoning, "There has to be a pony in here somewhere!"

Well, that's me, she thought. *And up to this point, I'm seriously short of ponies.*

Stan had a little pile of builder toys on his desk, cheap automata he had bought from a sidewalk vendor that would take any materials given them, like sand or sugar cubes or (in this instance) toothpicks, and turn them into odd little structures. His builders had gotten to a tricky point: he did not even say hello when Calliope swept into the room.

The door slamming shut behind her knocked the tiny structure apart. He looked up grumpily as the headless bug-things began the process all over. "Jeez, Skouros, what's your problem? You look happy—that can't be good."

"We've got it!" She dropped into her chair and slid in behind the desk like a cargo plane coming in for a landing. "Come and look!"

Her partner made a face, but sauntered over to stand behind her shoulder. "Are we going to explain what it is we've got, or do we just wait until symptoms develop?"

"Struggle to not be an asshole for just ten seconds, Stan. Look at this. I've been trying to get some kind of hit on 'Woolagaroo' for days, without luck. But it's the damn department search that's been locking me up!" She brushed her hand across the screen and a flurry of print danced behind, as though following her fingers.

"The search?"

"The gear, Stan, the gear! It doesn't do automatic phonetic matches—this stuff is from the Stone Age, I swear. I searched 'Woolagaroo,' and all I got back was hundreds of last names and town names with similar spellings, none of them right, and none of them anything to do with our case as far as I could see. But then I started wondering whether the searcher they make us use was as old and useless as everything else around here, and I put in a few soundalike variants of my own, figuring it might be in there but spelled wrong—that it had gone in originally as hearsay, or been misspelled by the arresting officer. Hell, *I* didn't know how to spell it properly until I got those articles from Professor Jigalong."

"You're taking an even longer time than usual to get to the point, Skouros." But she had him, she knew; Stan was trying hard to sound casual.

"So I threw in a bunch of variants—'Woolagaru,' 'Wullagaroo,' see? Like that. And look what came back."

"Wulgaru, John—aka 'Johnny,' 'Jonny Dark,' 'John Dread,'" he read aloud. "Okay, so you've found someone with an extensive juvenile record. Nasty little bastard, from the looks of him. But he's got no arrests in years—which, with his quick start in life, means he's probably dead. And that last known address is ridiculously old, too."

"Yes! And he fell off the map less than a year before Polly Merapanui was killed. The same year!" She couldn't believe he was trying so hard not to see it. Calliope felt a moment of worry—had she been after this too long? But in her heart she knew better.

"So you've got a similarity between this guy's name and something that Reverend What's-his-name's wife said about an Aboriginal fairy tale, and the guy disappeared, or at least stopped getting arrested under that name, within a few months of our murder." He pushed his glasses up his nose—like many other things about him, his look was decidedly old-fashioned. "Thin, Skouros. Real thin."

"Well, my doubting friend, how thin is this?" She waved her fingers and another window full of text drifted up like a carp rising to the surface of a pond. "Our young friend Wulgaru did time in the Feverbrook Hospital juvenile facility when he was seventeen, on the violent ward—'threat to himself and others' is the official catchall."

"So?"

"So did you actually read our case file? Polly Merapanui was there at the same time, a brief stay after a half-hearted suicide attempt."

Stan was silent for a long moment. "Damn," he said at last.

Her partner was unusually reserved on the drive out to Windsor, but he did point out that it would have been faster just getting the records sent to the office. "It's not like either of them are still living there, Skouros."

"I know. But I'm different than you, Stan. I need to *go* there, have a look at the place. Get a feeling for it. And if you give me any 'women's intuition' bullshit, you can walk back. This is my car."

"Touchy." His eyebrows rose briefly. Stan Chan was so deadpan that he made Calliope feel like some kind of circus freak—The Incredible Sweating, Shouting Woman. But he was a solid bloke, and his strengths meshed well with hers. Good Cop/Bad Cop was less important in most investigations than Excited Cop/Cautious Cop, and even though she occasionally got tired of playing her role—it would be nice to be the cool and collected one, just for once—she couldn't imagine working better with anyone else.

From the name, she had half-expected Feverbrook Hospital to be some castle monstrosity of turrets and cupolas, the kind of building best viewed under the lowering clouds of an electrical storm; instead, while it was indeed a remnant of an earlier architectural style, that style was from the earlier part of Calliope's own century, a look she tended to think of as "Strip-Mall Whimsical." The buildings were scattered about the grounds like a child's collection of blocks, except where they were piled high and awkwardly at the center of the complex to form what must be the administration buildings; most were painted in cheerful pastels, with ornamentation in bold primary colors—railings and awnings and annoying little decorations that served no obvious purpose. The effect was of something designed first to lure, then soothe and delight, the slow-witted. Calliope wondered how intentional that had been.

The hospital director, Dr. Theodosia Hazen, was a slim, tall, middle-aged woman whose graciousness seemed as practiced as yoga. She glided out of her office as soon as the detectives were announced, a smile of *noblesse oblige* tilting the corners of her mouth.

"Of course, we are happy to help," she said, as though Calliope or Stan had just asked. "I've had my assistant pull the records for you—we could have sent them!" She laughed at the silliness of it, as though the detectives had told a slightly naughty joke.

"Actually, we'd like to look around a bit." Calliope lit up a smile of her own and was pleased to see the other woman caught off-balance. "Has the hospital changed much in the last ten years?"

Dr. Hazen recovered quickly. "Do you mean structurally or operationally? I've only been the director for two years, and I like to think we've improved our management processes in that time."

"I don't know what I mean, exactly." Calliope turned to look at Stan Chan, who had clearly already decided that there were no bonus points for him in getting between his partner and the director. "Let's walk and talk, shall we?"

"Oh." Dr. Hazen smiled again, but it was reflex. "I hadn't . . . You see, I've got such a lot to do today. . . ."

"Of course. We understand. We'll just wander around on our own, then."

"No, I couldn't let you . . . that would be terribly rude of me." The director smoothed her gray silk pants. "Let me just have ever such a quick word with my assistant, then I'll be right with you."

The grounds were certainly nothing to complain about; even the most stiff-legged and disoriented of the patients did not, in the airy Sydney noontime, seem anything to be frightened of, but Calliope was still having trouble shaking her Gothic mood. As Dr. Hazen pointed out this or that fixture, her tone as bright as the day, they might have been touring the grounds of some particularly Bohemian private school. Still, Calliope reminded herself, most of these young people belonged in the category of dangerous-to-*somebody,* even if that somebody was only their own sad selves; it was a bit difficult to fall in with the director's breeziness.

As they passed through a long lavender courtyard surrounded by roofed walkways, Calliope found herself studying the inmates with a little more attention. After all, the murder victim Polly Merapanui had definitely been here, and every investigative cell in

Detective Skouros' body suggested that the girl had met her murderer here as well.

The hospital population, at least in this semirandom sample, seemed to contain only a few Aboriginal patients, but as she looked at the disaffected faces of all colors, at eyes tracking on any movement for lack of something better to do, Calliope could not help remembering pictures she had seen of cattle stations in the outback, portraits of the local Aboriginals who had lost their land and their culture—people with nothing left to do but stand in the dusty streets and wait for something that was never going to happen, without even an inkling of what that something might be.

The hospital also had rather a lot of armed guards, muscular young men talking to each other more often than to the inmates. Each wore a shirt with the Feverbrook corporate logo, as though they were roadies for a touring band; each had a stun-baton holstered on his hip.

Dr. Hazen noticed her staring. "They're hand-coded, of course."

"Sorry . . . ?"

"The batons. They're hand-coded, so that only the guards can use them." She smiled, but it was the tight sort that weather announcers wore when assuring viewers the hurricane wouldn't be as bad as expected, but that they should lock themselves in their cellars anyway. "We are a secure facility, Detective. We do need guards."

"I don't doubt it for a moment." Calliope squinted against the glare off a large pastel something-or-other that might have been a cement bench or a currently waterless fountain. "What's the building over there?"

"Our media center. Would you like to see it?"

The center was open-plan, a large space like an old-fashioned library with plenty of individual carrels, and with wallscreens placed at intervals around the perimeter on both levels. There were attendants here, or nurses, or whatever you called someone who worked in a secure hospital, but the guards seemed to outnumber them two to one. Calliope caught herself getting angry at being part of a society that put a higher priority on housing and stifling problem kids than on curing them, but pushed it aside: she herself was a link in the chain, and how much time did she usually spend worrying after the fact about the people she had arrested, or even their victims? Not that much, really. In any case, she had something more specific to do here than mourn the ills of human culture.

Many of the inmates were clearly linked into various media, some by remote connections, others by more old-fashioned means. They sat in chairs by themselves, some of them far from either console or wallscreen; they might have been sleeping, or thinking, but there was something about the way they shuddered, about the movement of their lips, that made Calliope ask.

"They're doing therapy-mods, most of them," Dr. Hazen explained, and then hurried to add, "We don't give them 'cans if they don't already have them, but if they've got them already—and almost all those who come in here with charge damage do—then we might as well put the holes to some use."

"Does it work?"

"Sometimes." Even the director couldn't muster much of a positive tone on that one.

Stan had wandered closer to one of the carrels to watch an Asian girl who looked about thirteen. She was clearly hooked into some kind of simulation: her hands were jerking back and forth as though she were trying to keep an angry dog away from her throat.

"Are they online?" Calliope asked. "Like, on the net?"

"Oh, my God, no," laughed the director nervously. "No, everything here is in-house. These are not young people who can be given free access to the outside world. For their own good, I mean. Too many dangerous influences, too many things that even healthy adults have trouble assimilating."

Calliope nodded. "We'd better see those files now."

The dark-skinned woman who met them on their return to the administration complex seemed almost youthful enough to be one of the hospital's inmates, but Dr. Hazen introduced her as her assistant. The young woman, who seemed to have adopted a nervous, downcast gaze as a counterpoint to her employer's crisp demeanor, murmured something to the director that Calliope could not hear.

"Well, if that's what we have, Miriam, then that's what we have." Dr. Hazen pointed them toward her office. "There's not much, apparently."

A quick survey of the wallscreen demonstrated the truth of this. Polly Merapanui had a reasonable file containing the minutiae of her stay—medicine and dosages, doctor's notes, a few comments about how she interacted in group therapy or how she responded to various work assignments. There were even a few words written about her "difficult" relationship with her mother. The last comments indicated she had been released to a halfway house in Sydney.

For Johnny Wulgaru, aka Jonny Dark, aka John Dread, there was only an admission date and the date on which he was returned to a standard juvenile correctional facility.

"What is this?" Calliope demanded. "Where's the rest?"

"That's all there is," said the director airily. "I can't manufacture information for you, Detective Skouros. Apparently he had a fairly quiet stay here—six months and out, no disciplinary problems." She was watching Stan Chan out of the corner of her eye as he rolled through the records on either side of Wulgaru's. "Please," she said to him suddenly. "We've given you what you came for, cooperated fully—that other information has nothing to do with your case. It's private."

Stan nodded but did not step away from the station.

"I'm finding it hard to believe that someone with a sheet in the police system as long as your leg came in here and waltzed out half a year later without attracting any attention at all." Calliope took a breath—it would do no good to antagonize this woman. "Surely you can understand our problem with that."

The doctor shrugged. "As I said, I can't manufacture information for you."

"Then is there anyone here who remembers him? One of the doctors—even one of the guards?"

The director shook her head emphatically. "There's been a complete staff turnover since this hospital was sold five years ago. To tell the truth, Lieutenant, there were some problems here before, and the new owners felt it was best to begin with a clean slate. You can do that with a private hospital—no unions." It was hard to tell whether she thought that was a good thing or not, but Calliope guessed the former.

Miriam leaned forward and whispered in the director's ear.

"Surely not?" said Dr. Hazen. Her assistant nodded. "Miriam

says there's one person here from that time—Sandifer, one of the gardeners." She looked a bit stone-faced. "Apparently I hired him without realizing he'd worked here a few years earlier."

"Let's talk to him," said Calliope.

"I'll have Miriam get him. Detective Chan, I've already asked you once—would you please get out of those people's files?"

Calliope had been expecting a whiskery old fellow in an ocker hat, but Sandifer turned out to be a husky, fairly nice-looking man in his late thirties who wore his hair in the dramatic fashion of a decade earlier. Calliope could visualize him playing in some kind of revival band and referring to his work at the hospital as "my day job." He was reticent until Calliope managed to persuade Dr. Hazen she wanted to interview him without the director's stifling presence.

In an unused office, Sandifer loosened up. "You working on a case?"

"No, of course not." Calliope was already tired of Feverbrook Hospital. "We're just driving all over talking to people because we get bored hanging around the police station. Did you know a patient who was here about five years ago named John Wulgaru?"

Sandifer stuck out his lower lip, thinking, and shook his head.

"Jonny Dark?" Stan chimed in. "John Dread?"

"Johnny Dread!" Sandifer barked a laugh. "Oh, yeah, I remember Johnny-boy."

"What can you tell us about him?"

Sandifer sat back, enjoying himself. "What can I say except that I'm glad I never met him outside. He was a doubtless psycho, tell you for free."

"What makes you say that?"

"His eyes, just for one thing. You know what fish eyes look like? How you can't even tell if they're alive or not unless they're moving? That was Johnny-boy. Scariest little sonofabitch I ever saw, and some of the kids that come through here are pretty lockin' scary, tell you for free."

Calliope felt a quickening in her pulse, and only barely resisted looking at her partner. "Do you have any idea what happened to him after he left here? More importantly, do you have any idea where he is now?"

"No, but it shouldn't be too hard to figure out."

"Why is that?"

Sandifer looked from her to Stan and back again, trying to figure out if he was being set up for some kind of trick. "Because he's *dead,* lady. He's dead."

THE voices in her head were silent now, but Olga was still having trouble pretending things were normal. *It's like I've been to another world,* she thought. *Nothing in my old life will ever feel the same again.*

The real world still looked much as it always had, of course, and corporate headquarters, a building she had visited many times for job reviews or company functions, was no exception. It had the same high ceilings as ever, the same employees scuttling like minor priests in a great cathedral, and here in this executive's corner office, the same face on the wallscreen that she had been living with, and living behind, for so many years.

The sound was off, but Uncle Jingle's dance filled the huge wallscreen behind the desk, Uncle moving through a silent sweep with baggy pants flapping, turn after turn so swift that even the animated birds, coded for flocking, were having trouble keeping up with him. Even with her old self almost gone, Olga Pirofsky could not help taking note of the character's skillful movements. That new girl was running him, the one in Mexico—or was it New Mexico? Wherever she was based, she was good. Roland had been right.

I'll never be the new girl, not anywhere, not ever again, Olga thought, and although it was not a very surprising realization—she was, after all, at an age when anyone would have at least begun to think about retirement—it still brought her up short. For a moment she could almost convince herself to ignore what had happened in the night, the voices that had come to her and changed everything. For a moment she felt herself worrying about the children she had entertained for so many years, and worrying about how much she would miss them. But the children that mattered most now were inside her, and if their voices were muted for the moment, there was still no ignoring them. Everything had changed. From the outside, it might seem like just another day in the world, Uncle Jingle spinning in his same circles and a hundred professionals behind the scenes working to make it so, but Olga knew that nothing would ever be the same.

The company vice president—Farnham, Fordham, she couldn't remember the name and would have no reason to care the moment she left the office—wound up his call, snapping a brisk farewell to an invisible someone. He grinned at Olga and nodded to show her that he was finished.

"I don't know why I'm smiling." He shook his head, bemused by his own madcap unpredictability, then rearranged his features into an imitation of concern. "We here at Obolos Entertainment are going to miss you, Olga. The show won't be the same without you, that's for sure." She was just old-fashioned enough to dislike hearing her first name in the mouth of a man almost twenty years her junior, but also old-fashioned enough not to make an issue of it, even today when she had nothing left to lose. But Olga didn't want to waste a lot of time with insincere pleasantries either—she had several things still to do, and some of them frightened her even more than accepting semipermanent medical leave from *Uncle Jingle's Jungle*.

"I'll miss the place," she said, and realized it was true. "But I don't think it's good for me to do live netfeeds any more—not with this problem." She felt more than a little treacherous calling it a problem, since it was now dazzlingly clear to her it was something much greater and stranger than that, but here in the normal world it was easier to speak a language the locals could understand.

"Of course, of course." On the screen behind Fordham or Farnham, Uncle Jingle had finished his dance and now was telling a story, with many broad hand gestures. "Needless to say, we are all wishing you a speedy recovery—not to hurry you back to work, however!" He laughed, then seemed a trifle irritated when Olga did not join him. "Well, I can't really think there's too much we need to do—these exit interviews are largely a formality, of course."

"Of course."

He scanned her file briefly on his shimmery desk, reiterating several facts about her medical leave package that she had already heard at several other interviews; after lobbing a few more homilies, he brought the audience to a merciful close. Olga could not help wondering what out-of-date concept this meeting served— would this once have been, in its original incarnation, a chance to pat-search the hired help as they left, to make sure no family silverware was going with them? Or did O.E. Corp. really believe its own marketing babble: *"Your friends for life!"*

Olga let the sourly amusing thought slide past. Was it always this way, no matter the power of the madness or glory visited on a person—the continual resurgence of the mundane, the petty? Had Joan of Arc wondered, on those occasions when her voices temporarily fell silent, if such and such a tower was as tall as another she had seen, or whether she looked fat in her armor?

It had happened only two nights before.

Olga had left both the Uncle Jingle character and the show half an hour early because her head was hurting so badly. It had been a while since she had experienced one of the headaches, but this one had been terrifying in its intensity, as though her skull were a hot, thin-shelled egg out of which something was trying to force itself. Even after a double dose of painblockers she had not fallen asleep for hours, and when sleep had come she had been beset by monstrous dreams full of images that she could not now remember, but which along with the continuing pain had several times shocked her into wakefulness.

She had awakened again sometime in that coldest, emptiest hour of the night, between three and four, but this time the pain was gone. She had found herself regarding the dark and quiet around her from an oddly dispassionate frame of mind, as though whatever had been causing the headaches had finally hatched from its egg, crawled out her ear, and vanished. She did not feel restored to her old self, however, but rather that as peace had returned, something else had been lost.

Without quite knowing why, she had walked across her house without switching on any lights, ignoring even the plaintive, questioning yips from Misha, and slipped into her deep station-chair. When the fiberlink was in place, she did not enter the Obolos system, or even the deeper levels of her own. She sat in darkness and felt the emptiness all around her, felt it fizzing on the other end of the fiberlink, so close it seemed that it could touch her any time it wished.

And then it *had* touched her.

The first moments had been a horrifying plunge into absence, into the empty dark, a cartwheeling fall without possibility of rescue. Fleetingly she had thought, *"Dying—this is death,"* before giving herself up to the black pull. But it had not been death, or else the afterlife was strange beyond the dreams of anyone's religion.

They had come to her slowly at first, the children—their lives separate and precious, each one a miracle as individual as a snowflake caught on a mittened palm. She had experienced each life—had *been* each child—so thoroughly that the part of her that had been Olga Pirofsky was barely present at all, a shadowy form clinging to a school fence, staring in as the little ones ran and laughed and danced at the center of everything. Then the trickle became a stream, lives washing through her so swiftly that she could no longer differentiate between them—a moment of family togetherness here, an object of intense wondering scrutiny there, each gone almost too swiftly to register.

The stream became a flood, and Olga had felt the last shreds of her own identity blasted away as the rush of youthful lives forced its way through her, faster and faster. In the last moment the inundation was so powerful that hundreds, perhaps thousands of individual moments became a single thing, a sensation of loss and desertion so powerful that it seemed to engage the very cells of her being. The flow of lives had combined to become a single, drawn-out, silent scream of misery.

Lost! Alone! Lost!

The voices had captured her completely, powerful and secret as a first kiss. She was to belong to them alone.

She had awakened on the floor, lying in an awkward tangle. Misha was barking fearfully beside her head, each sound sharp as a knife blow. The fiberlink lay coiled like a shriveled umbilicus beside her. Her face was still damp with tears, and her womb ached.

Unable to eat, unable to offer any real solace to terrified Misha, Olga had tried to convince herself that she had experienced some kind of nightmare—or, more plausibly, a nightmare coincident with one of the terrible headaches. If she had been trying to convince someone else she might have been able to make it sound reasonable, but every excuse met the transcendent power of the experience and dropped away.

Had someone dosed her with some kind of bad gear—what was it called? Charge? But she had accessed nothing. Olga could not bring herself to use the fiberlink again just yet, although she could somehow sense that there was more she needed to learn, that the children wanted to speak to her again. She brought her system records up on the wallscreen instead, and proved to her own satisfaction that she had not even moved past the maintenance level of her own system, let alone opened a line into the larger net.

So what had it been? She had found no obvious answer, but knew she could no more ignore it than she had been able to ignore the headaches. If those mysterious ailments had been the precursor to this experience, then at least they made more sense now. Perhaps there must always be pain when you touched something far larger than ordinary life.

Touched, she had thought, a cup of cooling tea undrunk in her hands. *That's what's happened. I've touched something. I've been touched.* And just as the prophets of old had left behind worldly things and especially worldly distractions, Olga had come to see on that gray morning that she, too, must make herself right. Could she go back to work with the children in Uncle Jingle's audience, selling them toys and clothes and breakfast cereals that screamed when you swallowed them? She could not. It was time to make some changes, she had decided. Then she would go back to listen to the voices again, to find out what the children wanted of her.

It was a call she had to make, but Olga had been dreading it far more than she had worried about leaving her job.

As soon as she returned home and put down Misha's food, she walked into the parlor and shut the door behind her. She paused, bemused—who was she trying to hide this from, anyway? Misha, gobbling so fast in the kitchen that little bits of dog food lay scattered all around the wide bowl? What was the shame in telling a man, even a nice man like this one, that she had made a mistake?

Because she *hadn't* made a mistake, of course. Because she was about to lie to him. Because she couldn't imagine any way she could explain what had happened to her, couldn't share the way it felt, how true and correct she knew it was. She also realized she might be losing her mind, but if so, she didn't particularly want to share that with the nice young man either.

Even as Catur Ramsey's office number was ringing, she realized that it was way past six; she was enjoying a moment of relief at the idea that she would only have to leave a message when his face appeared on her screen. It was not a recording.

"Ramsey." His eyes narrowed slightly: she had not opened a visual link from her end so he was facing a black screen. "Can I help you?"

"Mr. Ramsey? It's Olga Pirofsky."

"Ms. Pirofsky!" He sounded genuinely pleased. "I'm really glad you called—I was going to try you this afternoon, but things have been pretty hectic. I have some very interesting new developments to discuss with you." He hesitated. "Actually, I think I'd prefer to go over them with you in person—you never can tell these days who might be listening." As she opened her mouth to speak, he hurried on. "Don't worry, I'll come to you. Do me good to get out again—I've been living behind this desk. When would you be available?"

She wondered what his news was, and for a moment actually found herself hesitating.

Don't be weak, Olga. You've been through a lot, and one thing you know how to do is be strong.

"That . . . that won't be necessary." She took a breath. "I've . . . I'm going to be taking some time off." It wouldn't do any good to lie—lawyers, like police, could find things out easily enough, couldn't they? "I'm having some more medical problems and I need to get away from stress. So I don't think we should talk anymore." There. She felt as though she had finally dropped a large stone she had been carrying all afternoon.

Ramsey was clearly surprised. "But . . . I'm sorry, have you had bad news? About the medical condition?"

"I just don't want to talk about these things anymore." She felt

like a monster. He had been so kind, not at all what she had expected from a lawyer, but she knew that more important things
called her, even if she wasn't yet exactly sure what they were.
There was no sense involving anyone else, especially a decent,
rational man like Catur Ramsey.

While he was still struggling to find a polite way to ask what
was wrong with her, she told him, "I have nothing more to say,"
and broke the connection.

She disgusted herself by having a little cry afterward, something she had not done through even the worst pain of the
headaches. She was surprised at how lonely she felt, and how
frightened. She was saying good-bye, but she had no idea where
she was going.

Misha stood in her lap, bouncing on his tiny back feet, trying
desperately to reach her eyes and lick away the tears.

THE janitor Sandifer's information had come from a doctor who
had been on the Feverbrook staff before the hospital was sold.
The janitor had run into the doctor at a mall, and in the course
of a cursory discussion of old times the doctor had said that the
young man who called himself John Dread had died. Calliope got
the impression they had been talking about him in the way that
people talked about a famously dangerous dog in their old neighborhood.

Before she and Stan had even reached their car in the institution's parking garage, Calliope had tracked down the doctor, who
was now retired. He agreed to see them.

As they climbed the ramp onto the motorway, the little car
whining quietly, Stan reclined his seat a notch. "I hate to say this,
Skouros, but I think you're right. Don't get me wrong—it doesn't
mean anything, because this case is so old it stinks and all we're
doing is wasting our time—but someone in that hospital helped
Johnny-boy's records to disappear. I mean, they weren't even smart
about it. I couldn't find anyone but new arrivals with files as
empty as that."

"But why would someone bury his records? Because he killed
somebody after he got out?" Calliope scowled into her rearview
mirror. Several cars were stuck in the access lane behind her and
were clearly not enjoying it. "That makes no sense—half the peo-

ple in that place either killed somebody or tried to, and it's not like the hospital is claiming miracle cures."

"I'll bet you fifty we never find out." He leaned forward and began fiddling with the air controls.

Calliope took the bet, but mostly out of Stan-thwarting reflex: she wasn't feeling very lucky.

They met Doctor Jupiter Danney at his local Bondi Baby, a particularly garish chain of 24-hour coffee shops whose chief claim to fame was ultrabright decor and a huge ocean holograph, complete with surfers, which filled the middle of the restaurant. (You could dine waist-deep in the ocean if you wanted, but the roar of the breakers made it hard to have a conversation.)

Dr. Danney was a thin man in his middle seventies, and clearly aspired to nattiness, although his antiquated necktie pushed the whole look into eccentricity. He smiled as they approached the dayglo orange table. "I hope you don't mind meeting me here," he said. "My landlady would put the worst possible construction on a visit from the police. Besides, they do a very nice senior-price dinner, and it's getting to be that time of day."

Calliope introduced herself and Stan, then ordered an iced tea. Her attention was momentarily engaged by the attractively sullen waitress, who had a tattoo that covered one cheek from eye to mouth and looked like she might have spent some time living on the street. She returned Calliope's stare boldly. When the detective's attention had refocused, Dr. Danney was already finishing his *curriculum vitae*.

". . . So after I left Feverbrook, I spent a few years in private practice, but it was really too late for me to start over."

"But you knew John Wulgaru at Feverbrook, is that right?" She was distracted again, this time by a holographic surfer wiping out badly at the periphery of her vision. This was exactly the kind of place she hated—why were people so afraid to go somewhere and just talk?

"Oh, yes. He was my prize patient, I suppose."

"Really? There was nothing to show that—there was almost nothing on file about him there at all."

Dr. Danney waved a negligent hand. "You know how these corporate places are—they certainly aren't going to waste space with records they don't need. I'm sure they purged a lot of files when they took over."

"They might have, if they thought he was dead." The waitress appeared and clunked down drinks for everyone before sauntering off; Calliope heroically ignored her, eyeing Danney over the top of her glass. "According to you, he *is* dead."

The old man showed her his very good teeth. "Not according to me—I never examined the body or anything. Heavens, no. But when I tried to do some follow-up, that's what I was told. The juvenile authority records said he died—goodness, what was it, a year later, two years?—after he left the hospital."

Calliope made a mental note to find out exactly what records these were supposed to be. "Why were you interested in following up? Especially when you were already in private practice."

"Why?" He glanced at Stan Chan, as though Calliope's partner might want to answer the question for him. Stan looked back blankly. "Well, because he was such a rare thing, I suppose. I felt like someone who had discovered a new animal. You might turn it over to the zoological society, but you would still want to go see it every now and then."

"Explain, please." She poured half a packet of sugar in her tea, then decided to indulge herself and emptied the rest in, too.

Dr. Danney blinked his eyes. It took him a moment to respond. "It's just . . . I saw a lot of things in clinical practice, Detective. Most of the children that I dealt with—these were children who had severe problems, please remember—fell into two broad categories. Some had been so crushed by the cruelty of their upbringing that they would never think or act like a normal member of society—they were missing key components of personality. The others were different, either because their childhoods had been slightly less harrowing, or they were a bit smarter, or tougher, whatever it might be. These had a chance. These could at least theoretically lead normal lives, not that many of them ever would."

"And John Wulgaru fit into which category?"

"Neither. That was what was so interesting about him. He had the worst childhood you can imagine, Detective—mother a prostitute, mentally unbalanced and a serious abuser of drugs and alcohol. She had a series of brutal, violent partners who abused the boy. He got thrown into the institutional system early. He was beaten and raped there, too. Every element was in place to create a completely savage sociopath. But there was something more to him. He was smart, for one thing—God Almighty, he was smart." The doctor's dinner came, but for the moment he just let it sit. "He went through the standard intelligence tests I gave him with ease, and although there were holes in his understanding, he had a very good grasp of human behavior as well. Most of the time the sociopathic personality only understands others enough to manipulate them, but John had something that I would almost call empathy, except that you can't have an empathic sociopath—it's a contradiction in terms. I suppose it was just another expression of his intelligence."

"Sandifer, the custodian, said that he was frightening."

"He was! Even when he was demolishing the logic problems I gave him, it wasn't because he enjoyed them or because he wanted to impress me. He just had to do well at those things because he *could*. Do you see what I mean? It was like dealing with an artist or a mathematics *wunderkind*—he was driven to perform."

"And why was that frightening?" Calliope gave a stern glance to Stan Chan, who was beginning to make a little cabin of toothpicks on the table.

"Because he didn't care a jot about anyone or anything. Well, that's not entirely true, but I'll come back to that in a moment. But John Wulgaru certainly had no love in his heart for anyone. When he bothered with feelings about people at all, I would guess that what he felt was a sort of detached contempt. And he was physically quick, too—reflexes like an athlete, although he wasn't all that large. He'd look at me across the desk, and I could see that if it took his fancy, he could snap my neck before I could even move. The only thing stopping him was that it was a lot of trouble to go through—the punishment would be irritating, he would lose privileges—and I hadn't done anything to make him particularly angry. But to see that kind of brain sitting across from you, not only a quicker, sharper brain than your own, but knowing that he could kill you if the whim took him, and him knowing you knew, and being amused by it—well, it wasn't like working with a human, even the troubled ones I was used to, not really. It was like being the first scientist to study an alien predator."

Calliope felt her pulse quickening again. This had to be Polly's killer. Was he really dead? For the sake of society, she had to hope so, although it would make closing the case more difficult and less satisfying.

"And you kept records of all this?" she said.

"I did, but most of them were in his file on the hospital system. I might still have some of my own note files at home."

"It would be a huge favor if you could look for us." This felt like a break, although she could not say why. But someone had managed to lose Johnny Wulgaru's records, and even if it had been an accident, she couldn't think of any better reason for wanting to see them. "Just out of curiosity, did he seem interested in myths at all? Aboriginal myths?"

Dr. Danney narrowed his eyes, then chuckled, but it did not have much humor in it. "Funny you should ask that." The sullen waitress thumped the calculatedly old-fashioned little tray with the bill in it down on the table. In the moment's pause, the old man patted at his pockets, then laboriously drew out his wallet. "I suppose I should be getting back," he said. "I mean, if you want me to look for those files." He opened his wallet and examined its contents.

Calliope took the hint. "Let us buy the meal, Doctor. We're very grateful for your help." She would never get petty cash back for this case, so she was buying it herself. She flicked a glance at Stan, but his smile told her exactly how small the chances were that he was going to kick in.

"Kind, very kind." Dr. Danney flagged the waitress down and ordered dessert and coffee. When the server had finished rolling her eyes at the interruption of her journey to some other table, and had trundled on her way, the old man sat back and smiled expansively. "Very kind indeed. Now, where was I . . . ?"

"Aboriginal myths."

"Ah, yes. You said 'interested.' No, he wasn't interested in them. He thought they were a waste of time."

Calliope had to work to keep her disappointment from showing. She had been waiting for Danney to pull a last rabbit out of the hat, but instead the only thing inside had been the lining.

"The reason for that," Danney went on, "was because his mother went on about them all the time. That's what he told me, anyway. Her own mother—his grandmother, whom he never knew—was one of the respected elders, a storyteller. Even though Wulgaru's mother had run away from home to live in Cairns, she still harped on about the old stories—the Dreamtime and so on. It made him furious when I asked about them. He clearly associated them with his mother. I stopped asking after a while."

Calliope found she was leaning forward. It was there after all! She had known it, somehow, and there it was. At that moment she would have bet everything she had that they had identified Polly Merapanui's killer.

"I said that John didn't care about anyone or anything," the old man said. "That wasn't true, of course. Negative emotions are emotions, too, and he hated his mother. I think if she had survived he would have killed her one day, but she died when he was still quite young, while he was with one of his first foster families. Drug overdose. Not very surprising. He used to call her 'the Dreamtime bitch.'"

A holographic wave broke nearby, sending substanceless spray across the next table, and causing Stan Chan to jerk and tip over his toothpick structure. He made a face and swept the toothpicks into a pile where they lay like small discarded bones, the remnants of a miniature cannibal feast.

CHAPTER 10

God's Only Friends

NETFEED/NEWS: Squirt Goes Sour
(visual: first Dada Retrieval Collective "Sea Squirt"
broadcast)
VO: A group of information terrorists calling themselves the
"Sea Squirt Squad" unleashed their first action in their
campaign to "kill the net." The massive information dump
into one of the central networks did not work out quite as
its engineers planned. Instead of blanketing family-oriented
net channels with raw pornography and downing feed-
servers on other parts of the net, the data dump passed
largely unnoticed except for some accidental re-scrambling
of adult interactives, which drew user complaints.
(visual: anonymated Blue Gates customer)
Customer: "If they'd just been dumping more naked people
on the net, that would have been chizz. But the dim
bastards locked up the naked people we already paid
for. . . ."
VO: The unrepentant terrorists released a sound bite.
(visual: DRC member wearing Telemorphix tote bag as a
mask)

DRC: "Rome didn't crumble in a day, did it? Give us a chance."

"BES!" a child called. "Mother, look, it's him!"

The tiny, ugly fellow slowed so abruptly that Orlando almost tripped over him. As Bes grinned his grotesque grin and raised his hand as if to bestow a blessing, the little girl's mother lifted her up above the garden wall, angling the child toward the procession to intercept even more of the domestic god's radiant presence.

The company in which Orlando found himself was already fairly conspicuous, since besides the god Bes and Orlando's own massive barbarian sim, it featured Bonita Mae Simpkins, Fredericks, and a flock of tiny yellow monkeys—but Bes had chosen to lead them all boldly down the narrow streets of Abydos in the glaring sunlight.

"Shouldn't we be . . . hiding or something?" Orlando asked. Several more people leaned out of the houses to wave to Bes, who returned their greetings with the cheerful nonchalance of a returning hero. Orlando leaned closer to Mrs. Simpkins. "Going through back alleys? Instead of just utterly walking down the middle of the road?"

"Bes knows what he's doing, boy. They love him here—a lot more than they love Osiris and all his Western Palace lackeys. Besides, all the soldiers are busy surrounding the Temple of Ra, not wandering around in this part of town."

"Right. Surrounding the temple. Which is where we're going." Orlando turned to Fredericks, who at least had the good grace to share his confusion. "So because we want to avoid the soldiers, we're going where all the soldiers are . . . ?"

The woman snorted. "You have all the faith of a mud puppy, child. How do you get through life?"

For a moment, Orlando was stung. He wanted to lash out at her, to point out that she didn't have an illness like his, so she didn't have much right to be smug about how people got through their lives, but he knew she didn't really mean it that way. "Just

talk to me, Mrs. Simpkins," he said heavily. "I need some answers."

She darted a quick look at him, perhaps hearing something in
his tone. Her hard smile disappeared. "Call me Bonnie Mae, boy.
I think it's time."

"I'm listening . . . Bonnie Mae."

Fredericks was walking close beside them, anxious to hear
whatever was said. The monkeys had lost interest, and were following Bes like a fluttering yellow cape as the little god capered
for the children trotting out of the houses to line the impromptu
parade route.

"I told you how Mr. Al-Sayyid came to our church, didn't I?
And about Pastor Winsallen, how he had us come meet the man
afterward, and they explained about this Circle group of theirs?"

"Yeah," Fredericks said, "but you said something really strange
about God—that they were drilling a hole in Him, or something."

She smiled. "That's what I said, because that's what they told
me. More or less. And I can't really explain because I didn't completely understand it myself, but they said that people in religions
all over the world had been noticing something when they prayed—
or meditated I guess if they were those Eastern folk. Something
was breaking through into the part of them that touched God."

"Like it was a . . . a place?" asked Orlando, mystified. The sun
was beginning to tire him. They had moved into a less cheerful
part of town—the natives here were poorer, and while they still
greeted Bes respectfully, some covert glances were being cast at
the god's followers.

"Like it was a place. Or maybe not. Anyway, it doesn't matter, boy—if it's true or if it isn't, what you or I think isn't gonna
have a lot to do with it. A lot of very smart people believe it. But
all I needed to know was that these Grail people were using innocent children to make some kind of immortality machine, like
out of one of those science fiction things the kids rot their minds
with. Doesn't take any religion at all to know *that's* wrong.

"So we joined the Circle, and Pastor Winsallen helped us raise
some money to go stay with Mr. Al-Sayyid and his friends at one
of their special training centers. We told the congregation we were
going to do some missionary work with the Copts, which was
true in a way. Anyway, the Circle people got us fitted up and sent

us here, although I guess they didn't really send us anywhere. Hard to remember, sometimes—it *feels* like we're somewhere. Mr. Al-Sayyid and some of his friends like Mr. Jehani, who was a Moslem gentleman, were Egyptologists, so they had set themselves up here, but there are Circle people in lots of different Otherland worlds.

"It was pretty exciting in those first days—behind enemy lines, like something you dream about when you're a kid, but doing the Lord's true work. The Circle had the whole thing set up—the place you've been staying, that was one of our safe houses, I think you call it. We had a few, since Mr. Al-Sayyid had a good job in the palace. We had other Circle people coming through, updating us on what was going on outside—there's no way to communicate from one of these worlds to another, see, unless you're one of the so-called Grail folks."

She took a deep breath and wiped sweat from her brow—the sun was high now and the day was becoming uncomfortably hot. Orlando wondered what she looked like in real life. Her small, round, nondescript Egyptian sim fit her personality, but he of all people knew there was no judging people by what they looked like in VR.

"So there we were," she continued. "Doing research, I guess—the Circle's a big organization, and we were only foot soldiers, you might say. That's how I first heard about the woman with the feather, the one they call Ma'at here. She's in other worlds, too, as far as we can tell. Maybe she's one of the Grail folk, or maybe she's just something the engineers put in more than once—people tell me that these gear folk are big ones for jokes. But she's not the only one. Tefy and Mewat, those goons who work for Osiris? They're in lots of worlds, too. People call them the Twins because they always show up together. There are probably others as well—we never finished our research. The poop kind of hit the fan, as a matter of fact."

Bes had led them on a winding route through the town's close-quartered streets, but they had turned their backs on the river some time ago; because he was already fatigued, Orlando could not help noticing that they were now going uphill more often than not, heading toward the highlands—the gods' own turf. He would have been worried, but he had enough to do in this heat just walking and trying to pay attention to Bonnie Mae's story.

"You see, the biggest mystery of all is the Other. Do you know that name? I know you know what I'm talking about, boy, because you've had a closer look than most people. 'Set,' the Egyptians here call it, but it's got a lot of names in a lot of different simulation worlds. See, that thing is the key, somehow—at least, that's what all the big thinkers in the Circle believe. They think it's some kind of artificial intelligence, but it's also the system that operates the whole network. I won't try to explain, because you young people probably know more about this stuff than I do, but that's what they think. They guess that the Grail people may have tried to create some entirely new kind of life, y'see? And maybe that's the strange effect the people in the Circle felt—a blasphemy-wave, is what Mr. Jehani called it. He had a real nice sense of humor for an Islamic fellow. He was killed by some horrible thing with a hippopotamus head when Upaut's revolution went wrong.

"See, we made a mistake, and you young people would do well to pay attention. We made too many friends—we had to, because something changed a few weeks ago. No one could go offline anymore. So we were stuck, trying to get some answers.

"We figured any enemy of the Grail—and the Grail means Osiris here in this world, because if he's not Grail Brotherhood I don't know who is, he lives like some kind of Roman emperor up there—any enemy of them must be a friend of ours. So when your wolf-friend came along, we let ourselves get a little too familiar with him. But of course he was nutty as a bag of cashew brittle. We should never have gone near him.

"A group of our folk were meeting with him in one of our other houses when Tefy and Mewat and a mess of their devil-creatures crashed in. Mr. Jehani was killed. So was Mister Al-Sayyid, but they tore him up so badly that I don't think they even knew who they'd got. Wolfman escaped with some of his followers and a couple of other people from the Circle, but my poor Terence wasn't so lucky." She paused; Orlando expected to see tears, or hear a hitch in her voice, but when she continued, there was no sign of either. "It's just like the old Christian martyrs—my Terence knew what could happen when he came here. He put his faith in the Lord, just like I do every day. They took him to one of their cells, and I don't even want to know what happened to him. But he stayed strong. He *was* strong. If he'd given them anything more than name, rank, and serial number, I wouldn't be here today, and that safe house wouldn't have been safe for you.

"They dumped his body in one of the public squares. I couldn't go and take it, of course—didn't dare show any interest at all. It just lay there for days. Sims don't rot, but that didn't make it any better—worse . . . worse in some ways." Here she paused again, and now Orlando could begin to grasp the kind of control Bonita Mae Simpkins exercised over herself. When she resumed, she still sounded almost normal. "And I know he's dead, dead for real. Something's changed in this place. But I knew right away. It's like waking up and knowing you're somewhere different than you should be, even before you open your eyes. I lived with that man twenty-three years. I *knew* that he was gone."

She walked in silence for a while. Fredericks, who had been listening avidly, turned away with a miserable expression on his face. Orlando tried to watch the monkeys swirling around Bes, hoping for a bit of distraction.

Noticing him, a pair of yellow apes peeled off from the squadron and fluttered back, squeaking. " 'Landogarner! Why you walk slow, slow, slow?"

He wanted to hush them, but Mrs. Simpkins reached up her hand and the pair lit on her finger. "Goodness, children," she said, her voice a little ragged but otherwise strong, "you do go on. Aren't your mommas and daddies missing you?"

Zunni—Orlando had recognized her voice—looked up at Bonnie Mae, her tiny eyes wide. "Don't know. We go on fun trips lotsa time. They know we always come back."

Mrs. Simpkins nodded her head. "Of course they do."

The streets were emptier here, in what Orlando was coming to realize must be the mortuary district. The few residents, tomb caretakers and their families, also recognized Bes, but their reception of him was more muted, in keeping with the environs. The streets themselves were even narrower, little more than paths between the blocky stone buildings, the undistinguished resting places of civil servants and shop owners, as though there was even less room for the dead in Abydos than there was for the living.

But if this simulation is supposed to be the Egyptian afterlife, Orlando wondered, *then who's supposed to be in the tombs?* He couldn't think of an immediate answer, and was distracted by the little company turning off the street of sepulchres and into a tunnel.

As the tallest of the group, Orlando had to stoop a little to keep his head from brushing the unfinished granite ceiling, but otherwise there was no impediment. The tunnel was clean and the desert heat had baked it dry. The light became fainter as they got farther from the opening, but there was still quite enough to see, although most of the side corridors were pitch dark.

"Where are we?" he asked.

"Worker's tunnel," Bes called over his shoulder, his voice echoing faintly. "They run through the tomb and temple district like rat holes—each of these openings leads to another part of the complex."

"And we're going to get into the Temple of Ra this way?"

"If something large and unpleasant doesn't eat us first."

The little god had scored on him again: despite his weariness, Orlando was ashamed of how badly he'd let his Thargor repartee slip since he'd been in the Grail network.

As they turned into the first of what proved to be many branching corridors, Bes withdrew a lighted oil lamp from his loose but limited garments. Orlando and Fredericks had seen the cartoon Indian in the Kitchen do the same trick, and said nothing. The Wicked Tribe, who had achieved a level of Zen acceptance far beyond anything that Orlando could ever aspire to, pretended to be moths, enacting several tragicomic mock-immolations around the lamp flame.

What seemed almost an hour passed with corridor replacing corridor, each one as hot, dry, and empty but for a thin film of sand as the one before. Just as Orlando was beginning to feel certain he would never make it to the end of the journey, his breathing harsh and his legs so tired they felt rubbery, Bes led them through another entrance and stopped. He held the lamp out before him, a height only slightly above Orlando's knees, to reveal a small chamber. Most of the floor was missing, although the straight edges of the five-meter-square hole showed that this was not an accident.

"Down there," said Bes, grinning. "That's where we go. Straight down about twenty cubits, but into water. Problem is, there's no coming back that way—the walls are slick as polished amber. A protection against temple raiders and tomb thieves. So you'd better be certain you want to go."

"You mean we're supposed to . . . to jump?" asked Fredericks, who had been silent for some time.

"If you prefer, you can just sort of fall." The little god smirked. "The walls are this wide apart all the way down—that's to make sure people can't brace themselves and climb back up—so you don't have to worry much about scraping the sides."

Fredericks looked worried. "Can't you just . . . fly us down? Use your god powers or whatever?"

Bes laughed raucously. "God powers? I am a god of the hearth, patron of dung and whitewash and menstrual blood. *You* are the war god, aren't you—one of those deities who hurries to wherever the drums and trumpets are sounding? So why don't *you* fly us down?"

Orlando was too busy catching his breath. Fredericks was on his own.

"We . . . we have a flying chariot," he said at last. "That's what we have. Back home."

Mrs. Simpkins shot him a look. "They're not very important gods, Bes. Be nice to them."

The yellow monkeys, who had swooped into the hole the moment they saw it, now rose from the darkness like a cloud of burning sulphur.

"Long way down!" they whooped. "*Molto grosso* windy wind! Then wet wet splash splash!"

"Don't be 'fraid, 'Landogarner! Crocodiles be *muy pequeno* baby ones!"

"Crocodiles?" said Fredericks in alarm.

"They're making that up," said Bonnie Mae, swatting at the overexcited monkeys with her hand. "Let's get going."

Bes was amused by the whole thing. "They must fight unusual wars on those small islands in the Great Green," he said to Fredericks, leering. "Face-slapping, piss-your-loincloth, girly wars . . ."

"Hey!" Fredericks said, fluffing himself up to look bigger, not really necessary when his potential opponent was the size of a cocker spaniel.

"Stop it." Orlando was tired and had no strength to waste on such silliness. "Let's go. How far do we have to swim once we're in the water?"

Bes turned to him, still grinning. "Not far, not far. But you won't come back this way, as I said. You still interested?"

Orlando nodded wearily.

The leap, when it came, was a sort of relief—an escape from gravity, at least for a few moments. The water at the bottom was warm as blood. There was very little light. Fredericks splashed down beside him seconds later, and they floundered in place until Bes and Bonnie Mae Simpkins plunged in.

"Again!" squealed the monkeys, circling above the water.

"So," Orlando gasped some minutes later as Bes tugged him up onto a stone walkway, "if there's no way back, how are *you* going to get out after you take us there?"

"He's Bes, boy," said Mrs. Simpkins.

"What's that supposed to mean?" Orlando growled. The tiny man had a grip like a longshoreman; Orlando wiggled his hand to renew the circulation.

"It means that even Squinty and Bonebreaker will think twice about trying to keep me somewhere when I wish to leave." Bes shook himself like a dog, scattering water from his beard and matted hair. "They know that if they harm me or even try to hold me, they will bring the people down on them in a way that will make Upaut's little uprising look like a pleasure barge excursion."

"He's talking about Tefy and Mewat," said Bonnie Mae quietly.

Orlando nodded. He was saving his strength again. Even the few moments' hard swimming to stay afloat in the tepid water had tired him, and his muscles ached.

The little man produced another lamp from thin air, then led them through another series of corridors.

"What is he, anyway," Fredericks whispered, "—the god of hey-is-that-a-lantern-in-your-loincloth?"

Orlando grunted with laughter, although it hurt a little.

The corridors widened. The lamp's flame began to flutter in a thin breeze.

"The Breath of Ra," Bes said, scowling for a moment before choosing a direction.

"Which is . . . ?"

"Just the air that moves through the Temple of Ra. I suspect it has something to do with all these tunnels and the different air temperatures." He grinned at Orlando's expression. "I may be a mere household god, boy, but I'm not an idiot."

Orlando found himself almost liking the ugly little man. "So what do you do? I mean, how does a household god spend his time?"

"Mostly arguing with more important gods." Bes' homely face turned serious. "For instance, when one of the Hathors determines that it is time for a child to die, the mother will plead for me to intercede. Or sometimes I am pulled into a neighborhood dispute—if a man lets his animals trample his neighbor's yard, he just might wake up and discover that I have come in the night and made his animals sick."

"Sounds kind of petty."

The dwarf's glance was shrewd. "We can't all be war gods, now can we?"

They trudged on. Orlando could no longer remember what he had felt like earlier in the morning—that wonderful, if illusory, sensation of health that had seemed to run through him instead of blood. No one else appeared to be having a good time in these hot corridors either. Even the monkeys were drooping a bit, following a more or less straight course, fanned out in a tiny "v" behind Bes like geese flying south for the winter.

At last the little house god led them up a long incline that ended in what seemed to be a solid wall of stone incised with hieroglyphs. He made them all stand back from the wall, then touched a succession of characters so swiftly that it was impossible to follow what he'd done. After a moment of stillness the wall rumbled outward in a wide arc. Something huge and terrifying and pale blue stepped through into the lamplight, filling the doorway. Shrieking, the Wicked Tribe scattered in all directions.

For a moment, Orlando thought he was faced again with one of the monstrous gryphons of the Middle Country, but this creature was much bigger, and though it had the same leonine body, its head carried heavy-boned human features. It seated itself on its hindquarters, completely blocking the doorway, and lifted a paw the size of a truck tire. "Bes," the voice rumbled, making Orlando's bones jiggle. "You bring strangers."

The little god walked forward until he stood just beneath the vast foreleg like a chubby nail waiting to be hammered. "Yes, Dua. How goes the siege?"

The sphinx leaned forward to examine Orlando, Fredericks, and Bonnie Mae in turn. Although its size and deep, musky smell were terrifying, it was curiously beautiful, too: the vast features were those of a living person, but only barely—it had a strange, stony look, as though it had already become part statue. "The siege?" it growled. "Well enough, for an exercise in foolishness. But I am not here to promote wars in heaven—or to discourage them either. I am here to protect Ra's temple. And you, little Bes? Why are you here?"

The dwarf bowed. "To bring these guests together with friends of theirs. To see what I can see. You know, this and that."

The sphinx shook its massive head. "Of course. I should have known. I will let you pass, and the strangers, too, but they are none of them what they appear. I will hold you responsible for what they do here, little god." Dua's head swung forward like the jaws of a steam shovel, until it hung only inches from Fredericks' own pale, bug-eyed features. "Do not forget, care of this temple belongs to me and my brother Saf. We will not see it harmed either from the outside or the inside."

Dua stepped out of the way to let them pass.

"You have just met Tomorrow," said Bes cheerfully. "His brother Yesterday is just as friendly to visitors."

"I bet it's not worrying about defiling the temple that's keeping those bad guys outside," Fredericks said in a shaky whisper when they had put a few bends of the corridor behind them. "It's not wanting to get turned into pastrami by *that* bruiser."

"Don't underestimate Tefy and Mewat either, boys," said Bonnie Mae. "They got more than strength going for them, and even the sphinxes won't get into a tussle with them if they can help it." She shook her head. "But Dua and Saf won't let the temple be taken without a fight either. It's not going to be pretty when it comes."

"And this is what you led us into?" Anger brought back a little of Orlando's strength. "Thanks a lot!"

"You'll be gone before it happens," she said wearily. "It'll be the rest of us staying behind to clean up."

Feeling a little ashamed, Orlando fell silent. Moments later, they stepped through a brightly painted archway into the first strong light they had seen since entering the tunnels hours before.

The centerpiece of the Temple of Ra was a single beam of sunshine that knifed down from the ceiling scores of meters above, slicing through the smoky, dust-laden temple air like a searchlight through fog. Although the effect was starkly arresting, the rest of the titanic room was not in complete darkness—lamps burned in niches all along the walls, helping to illuminate the painted floor-to-ceiling scenes of Ra's heroic flight through the daytime sky on his solar barque, and his even more heroic journey through the underworld during the dark hours of night, where he battled the serpent Apep before his eventual dawn victory.

But, of course, this was not ancient Egypt—it was the Otherland network's version of ancient Egypt. There were many things stranger and more fascinating than even such an impressive building, and Orlando had already realized that the sphinx Dua was more representative than he was exceptional. Bonita Mae Simpkins had said earlier that at night the streets of Abydos were full of monsters. Orlando decided that if she thought the people in here were normal, she had probably been living in Abydos a bit too long.

There were ordinary Egyptians, of course, everything from children carried in their parents' arms to soldiers who seemed to have deserted from Osiris' army (many of whom had about them the faintly haunted air of people who still were not certain they'd backed the right horse.) These plain folk had spread bedrolls all around the edges of the temple's gigantic main chamber, turning the perimeter of the room into something like a campground, or one of the shantytowns Orlando was always seeing on the news. But this was a rebellion of gods as well as mortals, and those gods were strange and wonderful in their multiform designs— women with antlers growing from their curly black hair, or with the narrow heads of serpents or birds in place of normal human features. Some of the gods and goddesses were distinguishable as such only by their size or a certain golden glow to their skins, but others had gleaming thunderbolts hovering above their heads or wore curling ram's horns. Some had even taken on the full form of animals, like one large and particularly impressive cow, perhaps eight feel tall as she stood on her hind legs, with wide brown eyes of great sensitivity and understanding. Or at least that was what Orlando felt very strongly about her, even though she was over two dozen meters away and not even looking in his direction, which led him to suspect that inspiring empathy and trust might be part of her goddess-skills.

Their former traveling companion, the wolf-headed god Upaut, sat above it all on a high-backed chair on a platform near the center of the great chamber. The wolf's face was solemn, his long muzzle resting on his hand as he listened to three young women crouching by his feet who were singing him quiet hymns. Several other gods appeared to be trying to get his attention for reasons of their own, perhaps discussions of siege strategy, but with no visible luck. Orlando's sword, which the wolf-god had hijacked, was nowhere to be seen.

"Can you find your own way now, little mother?" Bes asked Bonnie Mae, jerking Orlando back to their present reality once more. "Or is there someone you'd like me to sniff out?"

"No. I've seen the others," she said. "Thank you."

"You are welcome, but you're not rid of me yet." The dwarf did a funny little step, spun, and started away. "I'm in no hurry to go home," he called over his shoulder. "Besides, there are enough people here that someone will probably be calling on me to bless a marital bed or a birth before too long. I'll come find you before I leave."

Mrs. Simpkins led them across the tiled floor—broadly skirting Upaut's chair, Orlando noticed with some relief: he wasn't quite ready to deal with the volatile god just yet. She led them unerringly through the squatter camp along one wall of the temple, as though it were a regular part of her morning commute, directing them at last to a group of people in the shadows near the corner of the room, a knot of mortals huddled beside the cyclopean blocks of the temple wall. The Wicked Tribe, revived now by the sights and sounds of the temple, flew ahead and circled lazily in the air above the little camp.

Bonnie Mae took Orlando and Fredericks each by an arm. "These are friends," she said. Bonnie Mae's other comrades, four in all, examined the two newcomers with weary interest. "I won't tell you their names just now," she continued, "because there are too many ears here, but I hope y'all will believe me."

No one seemed inclined not to, or perhaps they simply did not have the strength to question. A grim anticipation hung in the air, as though they were all prisoners waiting to become martyrs— which, Orlando reflected nervously, they just might be.

One of Mrs. Simpkins' friends, who wore the near-naked sim of a girl child, plucked at Bonnie Mae's sleeve. "Some of the godlings think the Twins won't wait any longer," she announced in a voice much older than her appearance. "The word is they'll wait until nightfall, then attack."

"This is Kimi," Bonnie Mae told Orlando. "She's from Japan, and I'm still not quite sure what her religion is—some cult, wasn't it, dear? As far as the Twins . . . well, if that's what they're going to do, then that's what they're going to do. But it doesn't give us long to get these two out." She sighed and turned back to Orlando and Fredericks. "I should introduce you to the others." She pointed to the two sitting beside Kimi, both wearing male Egyptian sims, one old, one young and smiling cheerily. "That's Mr. Pingalap there, and that's Vasily."

"So all these people are in the Circle?" Orlando had a horrible feeling that, siege and political intrigue aside, this was going to be like some weird religious camp.

Mrs. Simpkins nodded. "Yes. Mr. Pingalap is a Moslem, like Mr. Jehani was. Vasily is from Russia, and he . . . he has a very interesting background."

"She means I was a criminal," the youth said, smiling even more brightly. "Until I realized that the Final Days were upon us—that the Christos would be coming back. I did not want to face His terrible wrath. It would be horrible to burn forever."

Fredericks smiled weakly and moved back a step. Orlando stayed put, but made a mental note to keep distant from the Russian man—Vasily had the same feverish light in his eye as Upaut, and Orlando had learned the hard way what that meant.

"Now, I'm afraid I don't know this last gentleman's name," Bonnie Mae went on, drawing Orlando's attention to the man at the far edge of the little camp. The stranger looked up from a piece of tile of some sort, which he had covered with black marks with the stick of charcoal he held like a pencil. His sim was older than Vasily's but younger than Mr. Pingalap's, slender and anonymous.

"Nandi, Mrs. Simpkins," he said. "Nandi Paradivash. I have just arrived from one of the other simulations and your comrades have been kind enough to bring me up to date." He nodded kindly but briskly at Orlando and Fredericks. "Pleased to make your acquaintance. You will forgive me, but I am trying to make some calculations about the gateways."

Something drifted down into Orlando's hair, tugging at him like cobwebs: a few members of the Wicked Tribe were looking for a place to roost. Several more dropped and clung to Fredericks' shoulders. "So now what do we do?" asked Orlando.

Mrs. Simpkins settled herself beside the others. "At the moment, I just want to find out the news from my friends—we all haven't seen each other since this siege started. Then we'll try to figure out what y'all should do."

"Chizz." Orlando put his back against the wall and slid to the floor, extending his long Thargor-legs. A part of him bridled slightly at the idea that all these grown-ups were going to decide between them what he should do, but at the moment he did not have the strength to be too offended. He plucked a yellow monkey that was crawling ticklingly along his neck and held it up so he could see its tiny face.

"Which one are you?"

"Huko. You got hairs all up in your nose, *bra.*"

"Thanks for the report. Can you get Zunni for me? Or what's that other one's name—Kaspar?"

"Zunni right there." Little Huko pointed toward a spot on Orlando's own head that he couldn't see, somewhere just north of his left ear. Orlando gently moved his finger to the spot and called for her. When he felt her perch on the end of his finger, he brought her forward.

"Zunni, I need to ask you some questions."

Her eyes went wide. "Time to have big mister fun, 'Lando-garner?"

"Not quite yet. I want you to tell me what happened to you after . . . after the last time we were all together in my 'cot. Back in the real world—in RL? You were going to take us to someone named 'Dog,' remember?"

"Dog! Dog!" Huko, who was hovering maddeningly close to Orlando's ear, let out a little yelp of mourning. "Dog gone!"

"Doggie all dead, now," said Zunni. She sounded genuinely sad, the first time he had heard anything like it from any of the Wicked Tribe. "Big Bad Nothing got into him and made him scared so he went dead."

Orlando shook his head; a couple of Tribe monkeys fell off, grabbing handholds in his hair at the last moment and swinging back and forth before his gaze. "What does that mean? What exactly is the Big Bad Nothing?"

The children's communication skills still left something to be desired. It took the better part of an hour to piece together the Wicked Tribe's story. Fredericks came to sit cross-legged beside Orlando, which halved the amount of unwanted monkey-attention that Orlando had to endure and made questioning them easier.

The flightiness of the Tribe, metaphoric and actual, was not the only problem. They spoke a language of their own, and despite having spent most of his own young life online, Orlando found himself unable to make sense of half the things they said. These little ones, almost every one the product of a TreeHouse family—a near-certain guarantee of eccentricity to begin with—had been moving through the interstices of the world telecommunication grid since before they could even remember. They saw the world of virtuality quite differently than Orlando did. The Tribe did not worry much about what the virtual environment was supposed to represent, since they had developed a casually dismissive response to imitation reality before they had been old enough to talk. Instead, they were much more involved with what it was. Even the Otherland network, no matter how amazingly realistic it might seem to adults, was to them just a more complex than usual assembly of markers and props and subroutines—or, as the Wicked Tribe described these workings, according to their shared experiences and disinterest in real-world labels, *things that*

*were like (other things) which were themselves like (other things),
unless they were more like (those other things from that time before.)*

Orlando felt like he was trying to discuss philosophy in a foreign language when he had barely mastered, "Do you have a rest-
room?"

Still, with work he found himself getting at least a small sense
of their experiences in the network, although he was certain he
was missing important details that he could not recognize amidst
the babble that seemed almost the stream-of-consciousness of some
kind of group mind. The Tribe had gone through many of the
same things he and Fredericks had, at least at first—the feeling
of being pulled into a void, and of being examined, even stalked,
by some large and sinister intelligence, the entity they called the
Big Bad Nothing. After that, instead of waking up in a simulation as Orlando and Fredericks had found themselves in Temilún,
the Tribe children had experienced a long interval of sleepy darkness. Something had tried to communicate with them, apparently
in some way they either could not entirely understand or could
not explain to Orlando, but they retained images of oceans to be
crossed and others like themselves who were waiting for them.
After a while, a more comprehensible entity had come to them—
the one they called the Lady.

The goddess Ma'at had spoken to them soothingly, like a mother
would, and seemed to have promised she would do her best to
help them, that they should not be frightened, but she could tell
them nothing about where they were or what was happening.

But by this point some of the younger Tribe members had been
very frightened indeed. Things got worse when one of the littlest,
a girl called Shameena, had begun to shriek in terrible pain. The
screaming had stopped after a short time, but the little monkey
had gone still and silent and she never moved again. Orlando
guessed she had been pulled offline by concerned parents. Remembering Fredericks' experience, and thinking of that horror
being visited on a very young child, Orlando was coldly furious.

There was not much more to the Tribe's story. They had waited,
soothed by occasional visits from the Lady, drowsing like caged
animals, until Orlando and Fredericks had broken the urn and set

them free. How or why they had come to be inside it was impossible to discover.

"But how did you take us past the temple?" Orlando asked.

"That was major, major bad," said Fredericks, shuddering. "Never anything like that again. Never. I'd rather someone pulled my plug out than ever do that again."

Zunni made a face, clearly irritated by these older comrades' inability to understand even the simplest things. "Didn't go *past,* went *through.* Too strong to go away. Have to go at it, then through before things close again. But you went slow, slow, slow. Why you do that?"

"I don't know," Orlando admitted. "Something happened while I was . . . in there, I guess, but I'm not sure what it was." He turned to Fredericks. "It was like children were talking to me. No, like they were inside of me. Millions of 'em."

Fredericks frowned. "Scanny. Do you think it's the kids like Renie's brother—the ones that are in comas . . . ?"

"Can you boys come over and talk to us?" Bonnie Mae called. "Mr. Paradivash has some questions he'd like to ask you."

Orlando sighed. He'd been hoping to get a little rest—every muscle was throbbing and his head felt as heavy as the stone blocks of the temple—but he and Fredericks crawled over to join the others.

"Mrs. Simpkins has told me your story, or what she knows of it," the stranger said. "But I have some queries of my own, if you will indulge me."

Orlando couldn't help smiling at his overly precise way of talking, but instead of being asked about their experiences with the goddess Ma'at, or their first meeting with Sellars, the man called Nandi seemed primarily interested in how they'd entered and exited each simworld they visited. Some of it was vague in Orlando's memory—it was disturbing to realize how often he'd been sick—but Fredericks helped him over the rough places.

"What are you so interested in this stuff for?" Orlando asked at last. "Where are you from?"

"I have been in many parts of the network," Paradivash said without a trace of bravado. "Most recently I escaped from one of Felix Jongleur's simulations, although more by luck than my own skill, it must be said." He shrugged. "I was a prisoner in Xanadu,

but a sort of earthquake started an uprising among the more superstitious of Kublai Khan's guards, and since the Khan himself
was not present, things got rather out of hand." He shrugged. "But
this is not important. What matters is that we may have been
wrong about two, perhaps even three crucial things, and we in the
Circle cannot afford any more mistakes."

The young man named Vasily stirred. "You should put your
trust in God, friend. He is watching us. He is guiding us. He will
make sure that His enemies are brought low."

Nandi Paradivash smiled wearily. "That may well be, sir, but
He has never yet objected to His faithful servants trying to help
themselves, and it is equally certain that some who have waited
for God to save them have found themselves less central to His
plan than they thought they were."

"That is close to blasphemy," Vasily growled.

"Enough." Bonnie Mae Simpkins turned on the young man
like a grumpy mother bear. "You just keep your mouth shut for
a bit, then you'll get your turn. I want to hear what Mr. Paradivash has to say."

"It is this." Paradivash stared at the piece of tile, thick with
writing. "We had assumed that when the Grail Brotherhood sealed
the system a few weeks ago, that was their final step—that they
had finished what they planned and now meant to reap the re-
wards. It was a reasonable guess. They alone had freedom of the
system, while other users were banned, or—if they were already
on the system like our Circle members—they were somehow
trapped online. But the Grail Brotherhood have not finished, it
seems. One crucial aspect of their plan remains incomplete, although we know it only by the coded designation, 'the Ceremony.' "

"These Grail people must have spent like, centuries hanging
out in the Palace of Shadow," Fredericks whispered to Orlando,
citing a particularly melodramatic part of their old Middle Country simworld. "They just keep throwing utter creepy all around."

Orlando was fighting hard to overcome his fatigue. This seemed
like real information, the first he had been given in a long time.
"You said there were two crucial things. No, three. What are the
others?"

Paradivash nodded. "One is the involvement of this person Sellars. He is no one we know, nor have I ever heard of him before this, at least not by that name. It is curious—someone who claims to be opposed to the Brotherhood, and who has spent so much time and energy on this project, but has not contacted the Circle. I do not know what to think."

"Are you saying he's dupping?" Fredericks was angry, something Orlando hadn't heard for a while. "Just because he's not playing the game the way you think he's supposed to?"

The older man named Pingalap stirred. "Who are these young people, these strangers, to come and question us?"

Nandi Paradivash ignored his Circle comrade, but held Fredericks' stare for a long moment. "I do not know what to think, as I said. But it troubles me."

"Number three?" Orlando prompted. "Third mistake?"

"Ah. That is perhaps one we will be pleased to discover, if true." Paradivash held up his scribbled-upon tile. "Since the network has been sealed, we have believed the gateways between simulations, at least those which are not permanently linked to other worlds by the river, were operating at random. This has made it cruelly hard to plan, or even to communicate between Circle groups in different parts of the network. But I am no longer sure it is true—there may be an arrangement that is simply more subtle than we could grasp. With the information I myself have gathered, and that which you two have given me, it is possible I can finally discern the pattern which now controls the gates. That would be a major victory, if true."

Orlando considered. "And it if *is* true? What good will it do you?"

Paradivash looked up from his calculations. "You must have noticed that many of these simulations are breaking down in some way or other—collapsing into chaos, as though the system were going through some phase of instability. What you may not know is that the dangers here are real. The closing-off of the network from the outside did not happen all at once—it took the better part of two days. Before the last chinks were shut, it became clear from those who had been offline that the perils of this place were no longer just virtual. Several members of our organization who have been killed in simulations have also died in real life."

Something Orlando had long expected was now confirmed. He

felt a cold lump in his stomach, and avoided looking at Bonnie
Mae Simpkins. "So what good will figuring out the gates do us?"

The stranger gave him a hard look, then turned his eyes back
to his figures. "It will allow us perhaps to stay a step ahead of
the worst destruction—to stay alive as long as possible. Because
otherwise there is no hope at all. The Ceremony is coming, whatever it is. The Grail Brotherhood have launched their endgame,
and we have nothing yet with which to counter it."

Orlando looked at the man, who seemed to have stepped through
some mental gateway of his own and was already miles away. Little yellow monkeys stirred uneasily on Orlando's shoulder.

We're going to get herded like animals, he could not help thinking. *From world to world until there isn't anywhere else to run.
Then the killing will really start.*

CHAPTER 11

Quarantine

NETFEED/FASHION: Mbinda "Bored by the Street"
(visual: Mbinda's fall show—runway models)
*VO: Designer Hussein Mbinda says that changes in street
fashion will have little effect on his line. He continues to
emphasize flowing fabrics, as in his most recent "Chutes"
collection, but says that he's interested in color and shape,
not street cred.*
(visual: Mbinda backstage at Milan runway show)
*MBINDA: "I'm bored by the street—you can only spend so
much time thinking about people who don't even have the
sense to get out of the cold."*

FOR a moment Renie thought she had actually screamed—
caught in the tail end of a dream in which both Martine
and Stephen were sealed in some kind of barrel that was rapidly
sinking into the depths of a dark river, Renie herself unable
to reach them no matter how hard she swam—but when she
opened her eyes, the girl Emily was rocking back and forth
beside her and T4b was still sleeping, his head lolling on his

wide, armor-bulked chest. The angled light revealed acne scars on his dusty cheek; Renie wondered why any teenage boy would choose to have *that* feature made part of his virtual presence.

She was furious with herself for falling asleep, although since she and the two young people had returned first after hours of fruitless searching for Martine, there was nothing better to be done at present. Still, to have allowed weariness to tug her down while Martine remained lost seemed a form of betrayal.

So many people needing help, she thought with more than a little bitterness, *and we haven't helped one of them yet.*

Renie brushed reflexively at her eyelids and wondered about her real face under the bubble-mask in the V-tank. Was sleep crusting the corners of her eyes? Collecting around the inner edges of the mask like tailings from a mine? It was a disgusting thought, but oddly fascinating. It was hard not to think of her own body as something completely separate from her now, although it must be responding to her neural commands, flexing when she made her virtual joints flex to lift something, thrashing in its vat of plasmodial liquid when she felt herself to be running through the insect-jungles or freight yards of the Otherland network. It made her feel sorry for her body, as though it were something discarded—a toy with which a child had grown bored.

She shook off the gloomy thoughts and sat up, struggling to remember in which of the gigantic house's countless rooms she had landed. It came to her after only a moment's survey of the spare, functional furniture, the long table and several dozen chairs, and the icons propped in niches along the wall, each illuminated by its own candle.

The Library Brothers. Their executive dining room or whatever you'd call it.

Brother Epistulus Tertius had been horrified by their companion's disappearance, although he seemed a little doubtful that it had been a kidnapping—perhaps not a very common happenstance in this enclosed, semifeudal society. He had rounded up several of his fellows to help search the Library precinct, and had sent another to request an interview with Brother Custodis Major on the subject of the dusting monk Renie suspected had been their enemy in disguise. Epistulus Tertius had also kindly insisted that

Renie and the other newcomers use the Library Cloisters as their base of operations.

Renie struggled to focus on the problem. Every moment that Martine was in the monster's hands the risk increased. She looked at Emily and wondered why the Quan Li thing had not snatched her instead of Martine, as it had back in the unfinished simulation. Merely a case of opportunity, or for some purpose more complicated? Did that mean there was a chance the thing would keep Martine alive?

Steps clattered in the hallway outside. T4b stirred and made a drowsy questioning noise as Florimel and !Xabbu entered.

"Any news?" Renie was relieved to see them back safely, but she could tell already by their postures and expressions what Florimel's headshake confirmed. "Damn! There must be something we can do—they can't have just vanished."

"In a place like this?" Florimel asked heavily. "With thousands of rooms? I am afraid that is just what they *can* do."

"The young monk wants us all to come to the . . . what is the word?" !Xabbu wrinkled his brow. "Abbot's chambers. He seems very concerned."

"Brother Epistulus Tertius," Florimel said. "My God, what a mouthful. We could just call him 'E3'—our friend over there could make him an honorary Goggleboy."

Renie smiled politely and glanced at T4b, who was rubbing at his face sleepily. "We must take any help offered," Renie said as Emily sat up, looking as groggy as T4b. "Should we bring everyone?"

"Do we dare separate?" asked Florimel.

Despite the fact that it was a large room, the abbot of the Great Library seemed almost too big for it, a wide man with small sharp eyes and a charming smile that came with surprising swiftness to his heavy features. But however nice the smile, after greeting them and waving Renie and Florimel over to his vast desk—the others stayed behind on a bench near the door—the man the other monks respectfully addressed as Primoris had not had much opportunity to use it.

"A terrible thing," he told Renie and her companions. "We have labored hard to make our market a safe place for travelers.

Now two people are waylaid in a week! And by one of our own acolytes, if what you say is true."

"*Posing,* Primoris," said Brother E3 hurriedly—Florimel's joke would now not leave Renie's mind, and she silently cursed the German woman. "Someone posing as one of our acolytes."

"Well, we shall get to the truth of this. Here is Brother Custodis Major now." The abbot lifted a meaty hand and beckoned. "Come in, Brother, and lighten our gloom. Have you found the young villain?"

Custodis Major, who although he looked to be in his sixties at least, still had a beard that was primarily red, shook his head. "I wish it were so, Primoris. There is no trace of him except some clothing." He placed a small bundle on the abbot's desk. "Kwanli—that is his name—has been with us only two weeks, and none of the other acolytes know him well."

"I belive that," Renie said, "especially if they haven't noticed he's a woman."

"What?" The abbot frowned. "This criminal is a woman? I have never heard of such a thing."

"It's a long story." Renie had not taken her eyes off the pile of clothing. "May we look through those things?"

The abbot spread his hand, granting permission. Florimel stepped in front of Renie and began gently to unfold the cloth; Renie swallowed her pride and let her do it. There was little enough to examine, a rough tunic and a pair of woolen hose raddled with small snags. "Those aren't what she was wearing when I saw her," Renie said.

Brother Custodis Major lifted a bushy red eyebrow. "This is the Library, not the Gaol Halls, good lady, and these are not the dark days after the Upper Shelf Fire. My boys have a change of clothes so that when the fullers come, they can send their garments to be cleaned."

"What is this?" Florimel held up her finger with a tiny chip of something white on the end. "It was in the cuff of the sleeve."

Epistulus Tertius was the most nimble of the three monks. He leaned in, squinted, and said, "Plaster, isn't it?"

Brother Custodis Major was slower to speak. After examining the chip for a long moment, he said, "I do not think it comes from the Library. See, it is figured, and the only plaster we have here is on the flat walls in the Cloisters—the Library is wood and stone."

Renie could not help clapping her hands together in fierce joy. "Something! That's something anyway!" She turned to the abbot. "Is there any way we could find out where it comes from? I know it's a big house, but . . ."

The abbot again lifted his hand, this time to forestall more questions. "I'm sure we can." He lifted a fabric-covered tube from behind his desk and spoke into it. "Hello? Hello, Brother Vocus?" He lifted it to his ear; when no answer came, he shook the hose, then began the whole process over again. At last he said, "Someone has apparently left my speaking-tube disconnected downstairs. Epistulus Tertius, will you go and find Brother Factum Quintus? I believe he'll be cataloging in the Tile Halls today."

The abbot turned back to the outsiders as the young monk vanished through the door. "Factum Quintus is our expert on decorative building materials, although his knowledge is by no means limited so narrowly. He has done some wonderful work on crenellations, too—he enabled us, in fact, to identify what were then called The Semicircular Apse Documents as being from another source entirely. When they are translated someday, his name will be memorialized in them." His smile transformed his face like a fluffy cloud floating across the sky. "A good man."

Renie smiled back, but inside she could feel her engine racing. She wanted to *do* something, and only the knowledge that Martine's life was in their hands helped her calm the unhelpful internal voice that demanded immediate action, whether appropriate or not.

Factum Quintus appeared at last, silent and sepulchral as the Ghost of Christmas Yet To Come. Round-faced Brother E3 (Renie winced at the thought—it was starting to become automatic) stood huffing in the doorway behind him, as though he had been forced to carry the other monk all the way to the abbot's chambers on his back. Not that it looked like much of a job: Factum Quintus was quite the thinnest person Renie had seen in a long time, with a face like a fish staring head-on through the glass wall of a tank. He barely gave her and the others a glance, although she felt sure it was the first time he had seen a baboon in the same room with the abbot.

"You wanted me, Primoris?" His voice was as raw as a teenager's, although he looked to be in his early thirties.

"Just have a look at this, if you please." The abbot gestured at the fleck of plaster that Florimel had set on the refolded tunic.

The skinny monk stared at it for a moment, his face almost completely empty of expression, then reached into the neck of his robe and withdrew a rectangle of thin crystal on a length of chain. He settled this on his nose like a pair of spectacles—there was a niche cut in the center for the purpose—and tilted it back and forth as he leaned over the white spot making little lip-smacking noises. After a long perusal he straightened.

"It is a bit of ballflower. Yes, yes. A patch, I should imagine, something to fix a piece of exterior carving from one of the older turrets." He lifted the chip on his fingertip to examine it again. "Hmmmm—ah! Yes. Do you see the curve? Quite distinctive. Haven't seen one in a bit—fooled me for a moment. Thought it might be from one of those quoins they found when they stripped the Seashell Facade." Hugely magnified behind the crystal bar, his eyes appeared even more piscine than before. "May I keep it? Like to have a look at the plaster mix." He set it back on the folded clothes, then delicatedly licked the finger that had held it. "Mmmm. More gypsum than I would have expected."

"That's all fine," said Renie, speaking slowly to keep her impatience in check, "but can you tell us where it's *from*? We're looking for someone—that fragment was found in his clothes." The abbot and Epistulus Tertius gave her a strange look over the reswitched pronoun, but Renie did not bother to explain. "We're in a hurry—this person has kidnapped our friend."

Factum Quintus gazed at her musingly for a moment, his finger still pressed against his tongue, then abruptly turned and walked out of the abbot's chamber. Renie stared, aghast. "Where is he going . . . ?"

"Epistulus Tertius, will you follow him?" said the abbot. "He is a bit . . . distracted by nature," he explained to Renie and the others. "That is why he will never be Factum Major. But he is extremely clever, and I am sure he is thinking about your problem."

Moments later Epistulus Tertius was back at the chamber door, even more red-faced than before (and, Renie felt sure, growing increasingly sorry he'd befriended these strangers.) "He's gone to the crypts, Primoris."

"There." The large abbot sat back in his chair, like a piece of cargo in its stays. "He is looking for something to help you with your problem."

An awkward silence fell on the room. The abbot and brothers Custodis Major and Epistulus Tertius, who should have been used to stillness, fidgeted and looked at the walls. Renie and her companions were no more at ease, except for !Xabbu and Emily. !Xabbu was doing his best not to appear too human, since they had not encountered a single talking animal in this simulation, and was currently perched on the back of the bench beside T4b's head, picking imaginary nits from the Goggleboy's skunk-striped hair, much to T4b's annoyance and the girl's amusement.

"If we're waiting," Renie said, "can you at least tell us something about this place? How big is it? It seems huge."

The abbot looked up and smiled. "The Library? Ah, yes, I suppose it is big, although there are only two other Libraries within pilgrimage distance, so we have little to compare it to."

"No, I mean the house itself." Renie remembered the sea of rooftops. "It just goes on and on like a city, from what I've seen. How big is it?"

The abbot looked to Brother Custodis Major, then back at her. "City. I do not understand."

"Leave it alone, Renie," said Florimel. "It doesn't matter."

"How far from here until it ends?" Renie asked the abbot. God knew when they'd get a chance to have a normal conversation with anyone here again. "To the place where there isn't any more house?"

"Ah." The big man nodded slowly. "I understand. You have had some religious instruction, perhaps? Or there are legends of such things in the part of the House you come from? No one knows what lies beyond the House, of course, because no one has ever seen it and returned to tell about it, just as no one has come from beyond death to tell us of what they found. Those who believe in the Lady of the Windows would dispute me on both counts, of course, but the House is full of strange ideas and cults. We of the Library Brotherhood are only comfortable with facts."

"So it has no end? None at all? The . . . this house just goes on forever and ever?"

"There are those who say that the Builders are still out there somewhere, of course." The abbot spread his hands, as though admitting an unpleasant truth. "They believe that at some unimaginable distance there is a place that is . . . *not-House* would be the only way I can explain it. That out at the very edge of things, the Builders are still building. But the Builder cults have diminished during my lifetime—a long stretch of peace and prosperity will have that effect."

Before Renie could even begin to wrap her mind around the idea of a house that was an entire world—that literally had no edge, no ending—tall, skinny Brother Factum Quintus stalked back into the room, arms now full of rolled papers and parchments whose ends stuck out in all directions, so that he looked like a sea urchin on stilts.

". . . It's actually very interesting when you think about it," he was saying, as if he had never stopped the original conversation. "Most of our research in the Sanctum Factorum is about the original building of things—we have paid so little attention to the repairs, which have their own styles quite as fascinating and individual. Of course, there are records of some of the refurbishments, but far too few." Unable to see past the parchments, he bumped into the abbot's desk and stood there for a moment, a piece of flotsam balked by a seawall. "Yes, yes. There is a monograph there waiting to be composed, a genuine gift to learning that could be made," he went on, although everyone else in the room must have been invisible to him, but he had evidently started this monologue while by himself anyway.

"Brother Factum Quintus," the abbot said gently, "you are babbling. Please put those down—the table is just in front of you."

The scrolls cascaded to the tabletop like a pile of jackstraws. Factum Quintus' narrow, bug-eyed face was visible once more. He was frowning. "Ballflowers, though—those are also to be found in the Neo-Foundationist period ruins, and I worry whether we should consider those parts of the House as well. We would have no repair orders, though, since those early folk were evidently a people without letters or numbers."

"I think we can dismiss the Neo-Foundationists for now," the abbot told him. "Come, Brother, show these good people what you have found."

Factum Quintus began unfurling his collection of documents, spreading one yellowed, curling sheet atop another and directing various onlookers to hold down various corners until the abbot's desk had entirely disappeared beneath an autumnal mulch of what could now be seen as building plans, working orders, and hand-lettered invoices. They spanned what seemed centuries, from naive illustrations margined by mythical creatures, without a single truly straight line in the whole drawing, to quite modern-looking blue-prints with each duct and ornament carefully included.

The gawky monk was in his element, and kept up a running commentary as he leafed backward and forward through the layers. ". . . Of course that would be in the Sunrise Attics, several days away, and upstream at that, so it seems unlikely. But those repairs done to the Spire Forest could certainly qualify, and I'm sure . . . hmmm, yes, here, quite high gypsum content, so that's definitely possible."

Renie stared at the great pile of documents. "Aren't you worried about something happening to them?" She thought the monks seemed rather cavalier for an order of book-protectors. "What if one of them got torn?"

"It would be a tragedy, of course," said Epistulus Tertius, who had returned to his normal, albeit still pinkish, shade. He narrowed his eyes. "Goodness, you don't think these are the original documents, do you?" He and Brother Custodis Major shared a quiet chuckle, and even the abbot smiled. "Oh, no. These are copies of copies. Rather old, some of them, and still valuable, of course—even in this modern age it is difficult to make good copies of the original documents without risking damage."

Factum Quintus had quietly continued his own monologue, paying no attention to the conversation going on around him, and now lifted his finger as though he had reached a significant point. "If we imagine that this person has come within the last few days from the place this plaster fell—and it seems likely, or the plaster would have been dust by now—then I suppose we can narrow it down to two places," he said. "This bit has probably come from either the Spire Forest or the Campanile of the Six Pigs."

"That's wonderful." Renie turned to the abbot. "Do you have

a map so we can figure out how to get there?" She looked down
at the table, layers deep in plans of every type. "I suppose that's
a silly question."

Before the abbot could answer her, Factum Quintus suddenly
said, "Actually, *I* can show you both places. I am fired with the
idea of doing some useful work on facade repair." He shook his
head. His eyes were remote, but a light was in them. "It is almost entirely unexplored territory."

"Are these places so far away?" Florimel asked him.

"No one has even dreamed of doing a categorical survey of
repair work," he murmured, focused on glories only glimpsed by
others. "Yes. Yes, I will go and at least make a beginning."

The abbot cleared his throat. Brother Factum Quintus took a
moment to register it.

"Ah," he said. "If you, Primoris, and Brother Factum Major
will allow it." His face took on a slightly sullen look, a child denied a sweet before dinner. "I can't imagine what harm a quick
trip to look at some of the trefoils in the Spire Forest would do.
I am months ahead of schedule on that tile work—I have finished
Hipped Roofs entirely and have done most of the preliminary cataloging for Sloped Turrets as well."

The abbot looked at him sternly, but if Factum Quintus had
something of the child in him, his elders seemed to indulge that
child. "Very well," the abbot said at last. "If Brother Factum can
spare you, then I will give my permission. But you must do nothing to endanger yourself. You are a servant of the Library, not a
member of the Corridor Guards."

Factum Quintus rolled his large eyes, but nodded. "Yes, Primoris."

"Thank God," said Renie. It was like letting out a long-held
breath. "Then we can go. We can go look for Martine."

"CODE Delphi. Start here.

"I do not know if I am even speaking loud enough this time
to leave a record that can be found later. I dare not speak any
louder. He is gone, but I do not know when he will be back.

"He is the most terrifying person I have ever met.

"He took me so easily. I had only a moment to recognize that
something was wrong—dear God, despite my senses that should

have told me he was close by! But he found a combination of factors—noise and the heat of a brazier and the confusing movement of children laughing and running—and he was upon me before I knew it. I was knocked to the ground and his arm closed around my neck and within moments he had choked me unconscious. I'm sure the people around us only saw somebody fall and someone else try to help. He would have every excuse to pick me up and carry me. Maybe he even let someone else do it, a Good Samaritan bearing me away to doom without knowing it. He knocked me down and squeezed me silent in an instant, just with the pressure of his arm. He is shockingly strong.

"And it was Quan Li's arm across my neck. Somehow, that makes it even more dreadful. He inhabits the body of someone we thought we knew, like an evil spirit. Like a demon.

"I must stop and think. I do not know how long I can safely speak.

"I am in a room, deserted like some of those we explored earlier, but very small, hardly a half-dozen meters from side to side, and with only one obvious entrance, a door in the far wall. I do not know whether we are still in the great house—I woke up here, and remember nothing of how I came—but it feels much the same. Ancient furniture is stacked in the corner, except for one chair he moved into the center of the room, and in which he was sitting not ten minutes ago, telling me cheerfully about the terrible things he could do to me any time he wanted. My hands are tied above my head with some kind of cloth, and the cloth is knotted to something I cannot quite sense, a lamp fixture perhaps, or an empty water pipe. He has at least tied me so that I am seated on the floor—my arms hurt, but I could be in a worse position, especially if he leaves me here for a long time.

"I am frightened. It is all I can do . . . not to cry. All that keeps me from complete collapse is the knowledge that the others will be looking for me. But that makes me frightened for them—very frightened.

"He is a monster. The human kind, yes, but that is much more terrible than some creature built of code, programmed to act out but no more burdened with choice than an automatic door—step on the pad, break the beam, the door opens or closes. But this is a man. He thinks and then he acts. He enjoys the terror—oh, how he enjoys it. The quiet way he speaks proves it to me—he fears to let his own joy get the better of him.

"Oh, God, I am so frightened . . . !

"No. That will do me no good. If I am to live, I must keep thinking. I must think every moment. I must remember every detail. He could be back any time, and who knows what fancy will have taken him then? He spoke to me when I awakened here— he said many things. If this monster has a weakness, it is that he likes to talk. There is a great silence in his life, I suspect, around this most important thing to him, and so when he can speak to those who he knows will not live to violate his secrecy, his enforced silence, he can let himself go. And since he has opened himself to me, of course, that means . . . oh, God. No, I cannot think about such things—it will freeze me. I must think hard about where I am, what is happening, what I might do to escape. . . .

"But he is proud, this creature—proud like Lucifer, who wanted too much. Please let me make him pay for his pride, for his contempt. Please . . ."

"I will continue now. I am ashamed by my own tears, but I am not good at being helpless. What I *am* good at is remembering, and I will do my best to repeat what he said. The first thing he told me was, 'Don't bother to pretend. I know you're awake.' This was scarcely something I knew myself at that moment. 'I heard your breathing change. If you give me trouble, I won't kill you, but I'll make you wish I had. You know I can do that, don't you? This whole simulation network is very realistic, and that includes pain. I know—I've been experimenting.'

"I said that I heard him. I tried to keep my voice steady. I do not think I succeeded.

"'Good,' he said. 'That's a start. And if we're going to work together, it's important that we understand one another. No tricks. No bullshit.' He had abandoned the Quan Li voice entirely—whatever filters had been used were turned off. It was a masculine voice, with what I thought was a mild Australian accent, a cultured overlay on something that was stronger and earthier.

"'What do you mean,' I asked him. 'Work together?'

"He shook his head—at that moment, the only movement in the room. 'Sweetness,' he said, 'I'm disappointed in you. I'm not a stranger off the street. I *know* you. I've been traveling with you for days and days. I've slept next to you. I've held your hand. And if anyone knows the clever tricks you can do with your sonar or whatever it is, it's me.'

" 'So?' I asked him.

" 'So I've got a little problem to solve and I may not be able to do it myself. See, I'm not one of those old-fashioned blokes, too proud to get help from a woman.' He laughed, and the most ghastly thing was that if you had not heard the words on either side, you would have thought it the laugh of a charming, cheerful man. 'You aren't going to force me to explain all the tricks I can use to convince you, are you? I'm very good with sharp things.'

" 'I've noticed,' I said, half in anger, half hoping just to keep him talking.

" 'You mean Sweet William?' He smiled, reminded of a pleasant memory. 'I did rather spread his insides around, didn't I? That was the knife I took from the flying girl. Pity I couldn't bring it into the next simulation—you wouldn't any of you have laid a hand on me then. Or if you did, you wouldn't have got it back with all the fingers still on it.' He chuckled again. 'But don't worry. I've been knocking around this simulation long enough to take care of that problem.' He lifted a wicked-looking knife out of his belt. It had a finger guard, like the basket hilt of a saber, but the blade was short, thick, and heavy. 'Nice, this,' he told me. 'Cuts bones like they were breadsticks.'

"I took a breath, suddenly feeling that almost anything would be better than having him come near me with that ugly thing. 'What do you want from me?'

" 'Simple, Sweetness. I want you to help me figure out the lighter. Oh, and just to save us both time and trouble, don't think I'm so stupid that I'm going to let you handle it, or even get near it. But you're going to use some of those special perceptions of yours to make sure that I'm getting every last bit of good out of my little windfall.' His broad grin on Quan Li's face was like seeing the skull beneath the skin. 'I'm a greedy bloke, you see. I want it *all.*'

"Then, despite his professed reluctance of a moment before, he spent several minutes describing in loving detail a grotesque catalog of human body functions and how they each could be made to yield unbelievable pain, assuring me that all this and more could happen to me if I resisted him or tried any tricks—the complete master-villain's litany, as in a bad netshow. But the eager tilt of his shoulders as he talked, the slow curling and uncurling of his fingers, kept reminding me that this was real, that he was not another construct, but a psychopath set free in a world without penalties. Worse still, he promised me that first he would take Renie and the others and do all those things to them as I watched.

"I have never wanted someone dead before, but as I heard him speak in flat, conversational tones of how he would keep little Emily screaming until her larynx gave out, I had fantasies of my anger turned into some kind of energy, leaping out from me to burn him into dirty ash. But whatever new abilities this network has given me, they are passive ones. I could only listen as he talked on and on, heaping prospective cruelty on prospective cruelty until it all became a murmur and I lost the words.

"When he had finished—when, I suppose, he had exhausted his momentary passion—he told me he was going out, and . . .

"God help me, he is coming back. He is dragging something . . . or someone. God help us all!

"*Code Delphi*. End here."

"**T**HIS is the most foolish thing I can even imagine," Del Ray whispered. Long Joseph had invoked seniority, so Del Ray was wedged far back into the corner behind the dumpster while Joseph was near the outside edge.

"And you are the most cowardest man I ever see," Long Joseph replied, although he was more than a little nervous himself. He wasn't worried so much about Del Ray Chiume's Boer hitmen, who still had the faint air of make-believe about them—they sounded so much like something from an entertainment that Joseph couldn't help considering them in that light. But he knew that a hospital quarantine was enough of a serious situation that if they were caught they would go to jail, at least for a while, and he was beginning to feel he should get back to the place where Renie and the others were.

"I should have shot you when I had the chance," Del Ray muttered.

"But you didn't," Long Joseph pointed out. "Now shut that mouth."

They were huddled behind the trash containers in the Durban Outskirt Medical Facility's garage, a place only sparsely occupied with parked cars because of the quarantine. Del Ray, faced with Joseph's relentless lobbying, had called in a few family and neighborhood favors: if everything went just right, they would be able to get inside. Which as Del Ray kept pointing out, would be the least difficult part.

Long Joseph didn't care. The cabin fever that had spurred him to escape from the Wasp's Nest military base had subsided during his wanderings, and the thirst that had troubled him at least as badly had been slaked several times over. With his mind working a little more clearly now, he was beginning to suspect that if he went back without having accomplished anything besides drinking a lot of Mountain Rose, Renie and the others might think poorly of him.

Even that Jeremiah, he will look at me down his nose. The thought was hard to bear. It was bad enough to have your daughter think you were an irresponsible fool, but to have that womanish fellow thinking the same thing—somehow that made it worse.

But if he came back with news of Stephen, perhaps even news of an improvement in his condition, the whole thing would look much different.

"Oh, Papa," Renie would say. *"I was worried, but now I'm glad you went. That was so brave . . ."*

He was jolted from his imaginings by a sharp elbow in the rib cage. He started to protest, but Del Ray had his finger to his lips, begging Joseph for silence. The elevator was coming down.

The orderly emerged from the elevator doors pushing a heavy cart full of packaged medical waste—gauze, sharps, and emptied chemical ampoules. As he trundled it toward the disposal chute at the far side of the underground space, looking like a lost astronaut in his bulky Ensuit, Del Ray and Joseph slid out from behind the dumpster and hurried toward the elevator. With a burst of speed, Del Ray got his fingers in the door just before it closed;

the elevator dinged, but the orderly did not hear it through his heavy plastic mask.

When they were inside and the car was traveling back up, Del Ray fumbled the surgical scrubs out of the paper bag. "Hurry up," he hissed as Joseph laboriously transferred the contents of his pockets, including a squeeze bottle half-full of wine the color of cough syrup. "For God's sake, just put it on!"

By the time the door clanged open on the second floor, their own clothes were in the bag and they were both wearing institutional garments, although Long Joseph's showed an alarming amount of calf above his white socks. Del Ray led him quickly down the hallway, which by good luck was deserted, and into the orderlies' changing room. Ensuits hung on hooks all down one wall like the discarded cocoons of giant butterflies. A pair of men were talking and laughing in the shower, just out of sight around a tiled partition. Del Ray took Joseph by the elbow, ignoring the older man's mumble of irritated protest, and shoved him toward the wall of environment suits. Despite some fumbling with the closures, in less than a minute they had them on and were back out in the hallway again.

Del Ray was struggling to reach his pocket and had to stop and unseal the suit to get his hand into his surgical scrubs. He pulled out the folded map his cousin had drawn for them. It was not the most reliable-looking of documents: the cousin was no draftsman to begin with, and his tenure as a hospital custodian had been brief, ending with an argument with his supervisor over punctuality, something that Del Ray's cousin apparently hadn't been any better at than drawing.

"You see a man called Nation Uhimwe," the cousin had told them, "the head custodian, you feel free to stop and punch his head."

According to the map, Long-Term Care was on the fourth floor. After a whispered argument, Del Ray prevailed in his determination to stay out of elevators as much as possible, where their homemade badges might not survive close scrutiny. He led Joseph to the nearest stairwell.

At the top they peered around the door before stepping out into the corridor. A small group of doctors or nurses—everyone looked much the same in the slightly opaque Ensuits—crossed the hallway a few yards ahead, talking with their heads together, bound for another part of the floor. Del Ray led Joseph to a water fountain, then had a moment of panic when he realized it was impossible to drink through the plastic masks, so it made a very poor alibi. After a moment's agonized consideration he pulled the older man into a side corridor where there was likely to be less traffic; a few moments later another pair of hospital workers passed the spot where they had just stood.

As Del Ray held his cousin's map up to the off-white fluorescent lights, trying to orient himself, Joseph watched in irritation. The younger man was clearly not the kind of lion-heart that should undertake a job like this, he reflected. He was a businessman, and should never have started waving guns and driving kidnap cars around in the first place. Joseph thought he himself had handled the whole thing quite well. He was barely nervous at all, for one thing. Perhaps just a bit. And now that he thought about it, a drink would help steady his nerves, so that when Del Ray went to pieces Joseph would be ready to step in and take charge.

A moment's consideration told him that it would not be a good idea to take off his mask and have a swig right there in the hallway where anyone coming around the corner could see him. Del Ray was still turning the raggedy paper from side to side, squinting, so Joseph took a few steps down the hall, heading toward an open door. It was shadowy and silent inside, so he stepped in and tugged at the seal along the base of his mask, trying to find the bead Del Ray had shown him that would cause the top part to let go of the bottom. He found it at last and scrunched the mask up so that even though he could no longer see, he could reach his mouth. A mighty swallow nearly emptied the squeeze bottle, and he was just debating whether to finish it off or to keep it in reserve for further emergencies when someone moved on the bed at the far end of the room, startling Joseph so much that he dropped the bottle.

He kept his head admirably: despite his alarm, he managed to catch up to the bottle before it stopped spinning. As he grasped it, he stood to see a heavy Afrikaaner woman shoving herself away from her pillows, struggling to sit up.

"I've been ringing and ringing for ten minutes," she said, her scowling face full of pain and annoyance. She looked Joseph up and down. "You took your time, didn't you? I need help!"

Joseph stared at her for a moment and felt the wine turning to warm gold in his stomach. "You do, yes," he said, backing toward the door, "but there is no cure for ugly."

"Good God!" Del Ray said when he saw him, "where the hell have you been? What are you grinning about?"

"Why we standing around in this hall?" Long Joseph asked. "Time to get going."

Del Ray shook his head and led him back into the main corridor.

For a small local hospital, Durban Outskirt seemed to squeeze in a lot of rooms: it took them another ten minutes to find Long-Term Care. Despite how important it was they avoid embarrassing meetings, Joseph was outraged on behalf of his son and himself that there were so few staff.

"All shooting drugs and having sex," he muttered, "like on the net. No wonder they can't cure nobody."

Del Ray at last found the proper corridor. Three-quarters of the way down, past a dozen open doors, each one leading like the mouth of a tomb to a chamber full of dim, tented bodies, was the room with *Sulaweyo, Stephen* in the little name rack beside the door, beneath three others.

At first it was hard to tell which of the four beds was Stephen's, and for a grim moment Joseph almost did not want to know. He suddenly could not help feeling it would be better just to turn back. What would be accomplished? If the boy was still here then the doctors hadn't done anything to make him better, as Joseph had known in his heart of hearts that they wouldn't. He wanted very badly to have another drink, but Del Ray had already made his way down to the far bed on the left side and was waiting for Joseph there.

When he reached it, Long Joseph stood for several moments, looking down and trying to make sense of what he saw.

At first he felt a kind of relief. It was all a mistake, that was clear. This couldn't be Stephen, although his name was on the little screen at the end of the bed, so perhaps they had cured him after all, just forgotten to change the names and whatnot. But as Joseph stared at the emaciated figure in the oxygen tent, the arms curled on the chest, hands clenched in bony fists, knees drawn up beneath the covers so that the thing on the bed almost looked like a baby inside a pregnant woman's stomach that he had seen in a magazine photo, Joseph saw the familiar shape of the face—the curve of his mother's cheek, the broad nose that Joseph had often told Miriam was the only proof she had that she hadn't been stepping out on him. It was Stephen.

Del Ray, standing beside him, was wide-eyed behind the steamy mask.

"Oh, my poor boy," Joseph whispered. At that moment, all the wine in the world would not have quenched his thirst. "Oh, sweet Jesus, what have they done to you?"

Wires trailed from patches on Stephen's forehead like creeping vines; others were taped to his chest or tangled around his arms. Joseph thought he looked like he had fallen down in the jungle and the plants had begun to swallow him up. Or like the life was being bled out of him into all those machines. What had Renie said? That the people were using the net and all those wires and such to hurt the children? Joseph thought for a moment of tearing them all loose, of grabbing fists full of wires like dry grass and just yanking them free so that the quietly humming machines wouldn't suck out any more of his boy's life. But he could not move. As helpless as Stephen himself, Joseph could only stare down into the bed as he had stared into his wife's coffin.

That Mfaweze, he remembered, *that damn funeral director, he wanted to tell me I shouldn't see her. Like I hadn't seen her the whole time she was in this very same damn hospital, all burned up.* He had wanted to kill the funeral man, kill *somebody,* had only wrestled down the big black charge of hateful electricity inside himself by getting so drunk he had not been able to walk out of the church when the service was over and had just sat for an hour after everyone else had left. But now there wasn't even a Mfaweze to hate. There was nothing but the shell of his son, eyes closed, mouth slack, his whole body curling like a dying leaf.

Beside him, Del Ray looked up in alarm. A shape had appeared in the doorway, wide-hipped and dark-faced, the Ensuit not disguising the fact that it was a woman. She took a few steps forward and then stopped, staring at the two of them.

Joseph felt too empty to speak. A nurse, a doctor—she was nothing. She could do nothing. And nothing mattered.

"Can I help you?" she demanded, her voice distorted by the mask.

"We're . . . we're doctors," Del Ray said. "Everything's under control here. You just go on about your business."

The nurse surveyed them for a moment longer, then took a step back toward the door. "You are not doctors."

Long Joseph felt Del Ray stiffen, and somehow this was enough to start him moving. He took a step toward the woman, lifting his big hand and pointing a finger at her masked face.

"You just leave him alone," he said. "Don't you do that boy any more harm. Take those wires off him—let him breathe!"

The woman stepped backward until she was practically falling into the bed of the patient behind her. "I am calling security!" she declared.

Del Ray caught at Joseph's arm and yanked him away from the nurse and toward the door. "Everything is all right," Del Ray said idiotically, and almost ran into the doorjamb. "Don't worry. We're just going."

"Don't you touch him!" Joseph shouted at her, clutching at the doorframe as Del Ray tried to tug him through and into the corridor. Beyond her he could see the outline of Stephen's oxygen tent, like a sand dune, desolate, lifeless. "Just leave that child alone!"

Del Ray jerked him once again, even harder, and Joseph slid out into the corridor as his companion turned and sprinted toward the stairwell. Joseph walked after him in a kind of dull dream, only speeding to a trot when he was halfway down the corridor. His chest was heaving, and even he himself could not tell whether he was about to laugh or cry.

The nurse stepped over to examine the patient's tent and monitors even as she pulled the pad from her pocket. It was only after her first call was completed, to a black van with mirrored windows which had been stationed more or less permanently in the front parking lot for weeks waiting for just this call, and after she had allowed a good five minutes more to make sure that the intruders would escape the building, that she called hospital security to report a breach of quarantine.

CHAPTER 12

The Terrible Song

PAUL woke with an aching head, an even sharper pain in his
arm, and his mouth half full of brine.

He spat up a great deal of seawater, then groaned and tried to
stand, but something was twisting his arm behind his body. It took
him a few moments before he could make sense of his position.
The feather-veil was still looped around his wrist, a wet tangle

binding him to the tiller. The force of Charybdis' watery eruption, which had lifted his little boat on a great jet of tide, had also crashed him back against the ocean so powerfully that he was lucky his arm had not been torn out of the socket.

He released himself with small movements, trying to be delicate with elbow and shoulder, which both felt like they had been injected with something caustic. The ship was reassuringly stable, the only motion a slight rocking. The sun stood high overhead, hot and steady, and he was desperate to get back under his shelter.

But, as he realized when he could sit up straight, there was no shelter anymore. Only the mast still stood upright on the deck, and of that only the bottom half. The sail had snagged on the edge of the raft, but most of it was now floating in the water; the rest of the mast, still attached to the sail, trailed a few meters behind the raft. Of the remainder of Calypso's gifts, the jars of water and food, no sign remained except a pale shape that might have been one of the urns bobbing on a distant swell a hundred meters beyond his reach. Other than the twin silhouettes of Charybdis and Scylla's peak, now so far behind him they were only pastel shadows, he was surrounded by a featureless circular horizon of water.

Murmuring with weariness and pain, Paul tied the veil around his neck and set himself to the agonizing task of reeling in the heavy sail. He tugged the splintered mast on board as well, although the effort made his arm ache like a rotten tooth, then pulled up an edge of the sodden canvas and crawled beneath it. Within moments he fell into exhausted sleep.

When he crawled out from beneath the sail, he was not certain whether the sun being lower meant that he had slept for only a few hours or had slumbered the clock 'round and had lost a full day. Nor, he realized, did he care.

Knowing the drinkable water was gone made his mild thirst seem worse than it was, but it also set him thinking about his real body again. Who was taking care of it? Obviously they were feeding and hydrating him sufficiently—he was far less interested in eating or drinking than would have been the case otherwise. But what were they *doing* with him? Were nurses or other attendants watching over him with compassionate concern? Or was he stuck in some kind of automated life support, little more than a prisoner of the shadowy Grail Brotherhood that Nandi had mentioned? It was strange to think of his body as such a separate thing, something not really connected to him. But it was connected, of course, even though he could not feel it in any direct way. It had to be.

The whole muddle was a little like his only experience with hallucinogenic drugs—an ill-fated, ill-conceived attempt back in his schooldays to be like his friend Niles. Niles Peneddyn, of course, had taken to the world of consciousness-alteration with the same insouciance he approached everything else, from sex to Alpine skiing—as a series of lighthearted adventures that would someday make entertaining vignettes for his autobiography. But that was the difference between them: Niles sailed through life and past danger, but Paul wound up vomiting seawater, dragging broken mast and sodden sailcloth behind him.

Psilocybin for Niles had meant new colors and new insights. For Paul it had meant an entire day of panic, of sounds that hurt his ears and a visual world that had slipped beyond comfortable recognition. He had ended the experience curled in his dormitory bed with a blanket over his head, waiting for the drug to wear off, but at the peak of the experience he had been convinced that he had gone mad or even comatose, that his own body was out of his reach and he was doomed to spend decades prisoned in one tiny, walled-off section of his mind while his material form was wheeled around in a nursing home pushchair, dribbling helplessly down its chin.

In fact, he thought, *I should be terrified of that right now.* His body was no longer his to control, after all, his psilocybin nightmare made real—or virtual, anyway. But the world around him, false though it might be, seemed so genuine that he did not feel that same sense of claustrophobic terror.

He had been idly watching Calypso's urn bobbing on the waves, but it was only as he let the memories drift away that he realized something was wrong: it was a very strange shape for an urn, and in fact seemed to be draped across a collection of flotsam in a most un-ceramic way. He rose, wincing as he pushed himself upright, and squinted into the angled sun.

The urn was a body.

It was such a strange realization, the conceptual expansion of his current world from solitary to double-occupied, even if one occupant might be a corpse, that Paul needed long moments to grasp the situation and engage his sense of responsibility. It would have been different if there had been an obvious, easy way to reach the body, but the assaults of Scylla and Charybdis had not only destroyed the mast but also denuded his little craft of everything useful, including his long-handled oars. If he were going to perform a rescue, or more likely formalize the need for a burial at sea, he would have to swim.

It was a depressing, miserable thought. His arm was certainly sprained if not broken, the other castaway was almost certainly dead and probably hadn't been a real person to begin with, and God only knew what kind of Homeric monsters roamed these deeps. Not to mention that big fellow with the beard, Poseidon, programmed for some nasty dislike of the Odysseus sim Paul was currently inhabiting.

More importantly, he was feeling the need to go forward. Despite the setbacks, he had survived the journey to this point and was more than ever determined to get to Troy, whatever that might mean. He was struggling hard to take his fate back into his own hands—how much effort could he afford to waste on other things? How many wrong paths could he afford to take?

Paul sat and stared at the silent, motionless figure as the sun inched down the heavens toward evening.

In the end it was the paradox of need that decided him. If his own helplessness felt so great and so painful, how could he simply turn his back on another person? What would that make him? How could he even judge what was true self-interest in any case—what if the floating figure turned out to be another Nandi . . . or Gally?

Besides, he thought ruefully as he lowered himself over the side, *it's not like it's that easy to tell who the real persons are back in the real world either. You just have to do what's right and hope for the best.*

Despite the relatively short distance it was a hard, painful, and frightening swim; Paul had to keep lifting his head to make sure he was going in the right direction, resisting the small waves which wanted to tug him aside into green nothingness. When he finally reached the body and its floating bier, he grabbed the nearest timber—splintered scrap from someone else's wrecked boat—and hung on until he regained his breath. The victim was no one he recognized, which was not terribly surprising—a man dark as Nandi but much larger. The stranger wore nothing but a kind of skirt of rough cloth with a bronze knife shoved under the waistband; his exposed skin had the sun-reddened look of a plum. But most importantly, his chest rose and fell with shallow breath, which eliminated Paul's easy option of swimming back unencumbered to the raft, secure in the knowledge that he had done his best.

Clinging to the flotsam with his good hand, but still using his other arm far more extensively than was sensible, Paul first knotted together the ends of the feather-veil and looped it around the man's chest under his arms, then drew the stranger's knife and slipped it into his own belt. He pushed his own head through the loop, taking the veil in his teeth like a horse's bit, and gently slid the man off the wreckage and onto his back. It made an awkward configuration.

The trip back was even more harrowing than the trip out, but if sea monsters or angry gods lurked beneath the waves, they contented themselves with watching Paul's struggling, agonized, mostly one-armed progress. The veil dug painfully at the corners of his mouth, and the stranger seemed to come close to wakefulness several times, contorting himself and dragging at Paul's already less-than-Olympian crawl stroke. At last, after what seemed an hour fighting through the swells, each wave heavy as a sandbag, he reached the side of the raft. With a last heroic effort he dragged the stranger up onto the deck, then slumped beside him, gasping. Tiny prickles of light like infant stars swam before his eyes against the deepening blue of the sky.

She came to him in the dream, as she often did, but this time without the urgency of other visitations. Instead he saw her as a bird in a forest, flitting from tree to tree while he followed beneath her, imploring her to come down, afraid against all logic that she would fall.

Paul woke up to the gentle roll of the raft. The body that he had so laboriously brought back through the waters and wrestled onto the deck was gone. He sat up, sickly certain that the stranger had rolled off the raft and drowned, but the man was sitting on the other side of the deck, his muscled, darkly-tanned back to Paul. He had the broken top of the mast and a hank of sail on his lap.

"You're . . . you're alive," Paul said, aware that it was not the most perceptive opening he could have chosen.

The stranger turned, his handsome, mustached face almost a mask of indifference. He indicated the objects "If we make a small sail, we can reach one of the islands."

Paul was not quite ready to begin a conversation about boat repair. "You . . . when I saw you I thought you were dead. You must have been floating there for hours at least. What happened?"

The stranger shrugged. "Caught in that damned riptide outside the strait, smashed against the rocks."

Paul started to introduce himself, then hesitated. He was certainly not going to give his real name to this stranger, and even the name "Odysseus" could bring trouble with it. He struggled to remember what the ancient Greeks had made of words with "j" in them. "My name is . . . Ionas," he said at last.

The other nodded, but seemed in no hurry to reciprocate. "Hold this sail so I can cut it. What's left we can use to make a shelter. I do not want to spend another day in the sun."

Paul crawled forward across the deck and held the heavy cloth straight while the stranger sawed at it with his knife, which he had apparently reclaimed while Paul was sleeping. Nothing was said about the changes of possession, but the sharp and shiny fact of it was like a third person between them, a woman that they could not both have. Paul studied the man, trying to decide how he fit in. Although there had been much variation among Odysseus' subjects on Ithaca, the stranger still seemed too dark to be Greek, and he had the first mustache Paul had seen since entering this simulation. He decided from the man's careless skill with blade and sailcloth that the stranger must be a Phoenician or a Cretan, one of the seagoing peoples whose names still held a dusty place in Paul's memories from school.

They rigged the makeshift sail as the last light faded from the sky, using the broken piece of mast as an improvised yard, lashing it crossways to the rest of the mast with strips of cloth. As the cool breezes rose, the stranger made a crude tent with the rest of the sail, although there was no longer an immediate need.

"If we bear that way," the stranger said, frowning at the first stars of the evening, then pointing to the starboard side, "we'll hit land in a day or so. We just don't want to go anywhere near . . ." He stopped and looked at Paul, as though he had only just remembered the other man's existence. "Where are you bound?"

"Troy." Paul tried to look at the stars as though he could make sense of them, but had no more idea at that moment of where Troy was than he knew where his real, mundane and beloved England might be.

"Troy?" The stranger cocked a jet-black eyebrow, but said nothing more. Paul thought he might be considering taking the raft for himself—perhaps he was a deserter from the Trojan War, Paul suddenly thought, and had to struggle not to glance at the knife which rested back in the man's waistband. The stranger was at least three inches taller than Paul and a couple of stone heavier, and all of it looked like muscle. He suddenly felt apprehensive about going to sleep, despite the tug of fatigue, but reminded himself that the stranger had not harmed him after the rescue, when he had the chance.

"What is your name?" Paul asked suddenly.

The other looked at him for another long moment, as though the question were a strange one. "Azador," he said at last, with the air of settling someone else's argument. "I am Azador."

It was a good thing, Paul reflected, that he had grown used to his own company, because Azador was not exactly a fountain of conversation. The stranger sat in silence for nearly an hour as the stars wheeled through the immense blackness above and around them, responding to Paul's sleepy comments and questions with grunts or the occasional laconic non-answer, then at last he stretched out on the deck, pillowed his head on his arm, and closed his eyes.

Paul had also recently had the company of Calypso, and if most of the conversation had been sweet nothings or passionate exhortations, that was still much better than nothing, so he was more bemused than annoyed by the stranger's silence. Perhaps it was an accurate reflection of the ancient mind, he thought—the behavior of an era before social chatter.

It was not much longer before he fell asleep himself, needing neither blanket nor pillow in the balmy night. The slow, sky-wide pinwheel of stars was the last thing he saw.

He woke in the last dim hours of darkness, uncertain at first of what had brought him up from sleep. Gradually he became aware of a strange, soft melody as many-threaded as Penelope's tapestry, so faint at first that it seemed almost an exhalation of the sea and its luminous foam. He listened in sleepy absorption for a long while, following the rise and fall of the individual components, the strands of melody that emerged and then fell back into the greater chorus, until he suddenly realized that he was listening to the sound of voices singing—human voices, or something much like them. He sat up and discovered Azador was also awake, listening with head cocked to one side like a dog.

"What . . . ?" Paul asked, but the stranger raised his hand; Paul fell silent again and they both sat, letting the distant music wash over them. Because of the other man's obvious tension, what had seemed strangely beautiful at first seemed almost menacing now, although it had grown no louder: Paul found himself fighting an urge to put his hands over his ears. A weaker but more frightening inclination began to make itself felt as well, a whisper of suggestion that he might slip over the side into the comfortable waters and make his way toward the voices and thus discover their secret.

"It is the sirens," Azador said abruptly. In contrast with the distant melodies, his voice seemed harsh as a crow's. Paul found himself disliking the man just because he had spoken while the voices were singing. "If I had known we were even this close, I would not have slept."

Paul shook his head, befuddled. The distant music seemed to cling to his thoughts like spiderwebs. "The sirens . . ." He remembered now— Odysseus had sailed near them, making his men first stop their ears with wax while he himself stood tied to the mast so he could hear their fabled melodies without casting himself into the water.

The water ... the black water ... and ancient voices singing ... singing ...

Paul decided to focus on other distractions, anything to keep his thoughts away from the seductive, disturbing music floating across the black sea. "Have you been here before?"

Azador made another of his unhelpful sounds, then relented a little. "I have been many places."

"Where are you from originally?"

The stranger snorted. "Not here. Not this stupid ocean, these stupid islands. No, I am looking for someone."

"Who?"

Azador fixed Paul with a look, then turned back toward the singing darkness. "The wind is carrying us past them. We were lucky."

Paul reached down and slid his fingers between two of the planks, anchoring himself against the pull that, although weak, still troubled him. A part of him wanted to try to make sense of how this effect might work, to puzzle out the whys and wherefores of virtual sirens—he dimly felt there was something crucial to be discovered—but then, as the lure of the music grew a little less, a stronger, deeper emotion took a grip on him, an unexpected mixture of awe and delight.

Whatever this is, he thought, *this network, this ... whatever ... it is really quite a magical world.*

Somewhere in the failing darkness, perhaps with intent, perhaps as mindlessly as crickets scraping in the hedgerows, the sirens continued to create their terrible song. Safe now from its pull, Paul Jonas sailed slowly through a warm night in the ancient world, and for a little while gave himself over to wonder.

Azador was, if anything, even less forthcoming in the light of the following day: those of Paul's questions he did not deflect with a shrug or an uninformative grunt he simply ignored.

For all his recalcitrance, he was a useful companion. He knew far more than Paul did about the simple, important things that for the moment made up their world: wind and tides and knots and wood. He had managed to salvage enough torn ends of rope from the sail to splice together new braces, giving them far more control over the raft, and had also rigged a corner of unused sailcloth as a dew catcher, so when the sun rose they had water to drink. Later in the day the stranger even managed to catch a shining fish with a swift stab of his arm into the bottle-green waters off the raft's port side. They had no fire, and Paul as usual did not feel particularly hungry, but despite a certain queasiness there was still something marvelous about eating the raw flesh. Paul found that he was almost enjoying himself, an unusual sensation.

As he relished a cupped palm full of dew-water, taking a first tiny sip to sluice the fish taste from his mouth before letting the rest pour down, he had a sudden vision of himself doing the same thing, but somewhere else entirely. He closed his eyes and for a brief moment could see plants all around him, thick as a tropical jungle. He felt a trickle of sweet water going down his throat, then more water splashing against his face . . . a woman's voice, laughing . . .

Her voice, he suddenly knew. *The angel.* But it was nothing that had ever happened to him—not in the parts of his life he could remember.

The unlikeliest of things broke his concentration, and the memory blew away like smoke.

"Where are you from, Ionas?" Azador asked.

Dragged from what seemed an achingly significant memory, faced with an actual question from his taciturn companion, Paul goggled for a moment. "Ithaca," he managed to say at last.

Azador nodded. "Did you see a woman there, a dark-skinned woman? With a monkey for a pet?"

Nonplussed, Paul could only tell the man truthfully that he had not. "Is she a friend of yours?"

"Hah! She has something of mine and I want it back. No one takes what is Azador's."

Paul sensed an opening, but was unsure of how to keep the conversation going, and unsure also whether there was any point to it. Did he really want to know the precoded life story of some Phoenician sailor in a virtual *Odyssey?* The chances that a castaway would have anything useful to say to him were almost nil. In any case, there were more present and practical uses for Azador's sudden talkativeness.

"So do you know this part of the ocean?" Paul asked. "How long will it take us to get to Troy?"

Azador examined the fish skeleton eye to eye, like Hamlet considering the skull of Yorick, then flicked it high in the air over the side of the raft. A gull came down out of the sun, appearing as if from nowhere, and snatched it before it touched the water. "I don't know. The currents are bad, and there are many islands, many rocks." He squinted out across the water for a moment. "We must make a landing soon anyway. This broken mast will not last long before it splits, so we need more wood. Also, I must have meat."

Paul laughed at the serious way he said it. "We just had a fish—although it would have been nice to cook it."

"Not fish," Azador grunted in disgust, "*meat*. A man needs meat to eat or he will not remain a man."

Paul shrugged. It seemed like the least of their problems, but he was not going to argue with a fellow who knew how to splice rope and catch dew.

The beginnings of foul weather were blowing up in the late afternoon, a pall of clouds moving swiftly out of the west, when they caught sight of the island and its tall hills thick with vegetation. As the tiller and compromised mast creaked at the raft's crossways lurch into the wind, they could see no obvious signs of human habitation, no gleam of stone walls or whitewashed clay houses; if there were fires burning anywhere, they were lost in the deepening mist and clouds.

"I do not know this place," Azador said, breaking an hour's silence. "But see, there is grass high on the hills." He grinned tightly. "There will be goats, perhaps, or even sheep."

"There might be people living there, too," Paul pointed out. "We can't just take somebody's sheep, can we?"

"Every man is the hero of his own song," Azador replied—somewhat cryptically, Paul thought.

They beached the raft and made their way up through the rocky hills as the clouds drew closer. At first it was a pleasure simply to be off the ocean and onto dry land, but by the time that they could again see their craft on the rocky strand below, looking small as a playing card, thunder was murmuring overhead and a few fat raindrops had begun to fall. The stones grew slick beneath Paul's feet, but Azador's half-naked figure ranged up the hills ahead of him, agile as one of the goats he sought, and Paul could only curse quietly and struggle along after him.

After more than an hour had passed, with rain falling heavily now and lightning cracking across the sky, they reached the summit of the hill, climbing up out of a grove of beech trees that shivered in the rising wind to find themselves knee-deep in rough grass. The rocky spine of the hill thrust up before them in a last ridge, a massive outcropping several hundred meters across, fenced by wind-twisted pines. A huge hole, the entrance to a cave, opened into the stone ridge like the door of a misshapen house. It tugged at Paul's memory, and as the grass swished in the wind and sawed at his legs and the rain spattered down, he suddenly felt that they were terribly exposed.

Azador had already taken a step toward the opening when Paul reached out and grabbed his muscled arm. "Don't!"

"What are you talking about?" Azador glowered. "Do you want to stand here until the lightning comes down and cooks you? Who pissed in your head and told you it was brains?"

Before Paul could explain his premonition, something rustled in the grove of trees behind them, a faint but growing noise that was not the wind. Paul looked at Azador. Without a word, they both dropped onto their bellies in the grass.

The rustle became a rattle. Something big was moving through the grass stems only a stone's throw away. Lightning flashed, momentarily turning the twilight world white and black; when the crack of thunder followed a few seconds later, Paul flinched.

Azador lifted himself onto his elbows and pulled the stems wide so he could see. Thunder roared again; in the silence afterward, Paul heard a surprising sound. Azador was quietly laughing.

"Look," he said, and smacked Paul on the shoulder. "Look, you coward!"

Paul raised himself up a little way so he could peer through the space Azador had made. A flock of sheep was moving past them, a river of patiently suffering eyes and dripping, drooping wool. Azador had just clambered to his knees when they heard a new sound, a deep but distant thump. Azador froze, but the sheep seemed undisturbed and trotted on across the plateau toward the cave. The sound repeated, louder this time, then again, like the slow beating of a huge bass drum. Paul had time only to wonder why the ground was trembling when lightning painted the sky white again and their raft appeared, sailing toward them above the treetops.

Azador stared at the apparition, his jaw slack with shock. His hand crept up his chest as if it had a will of its own and made the sign of the cross. The thumping grew louder. The raft continued toward them, bobbing just above the top of the trees as though the swaying branches were ocean waves. Thunder followed the lightning, then lightning blazed afresh.

The man-shaped creature that crunched out of the trees, carrying their raft above his head, was the biggest living thing Paul had ever seen. Although the monster's legs were massively broad compared to human proportions, its knees were nevertheless as high above the ground as a tall man's head. The rest of the body, while of more ordinary dimensions, was still huge: the top of the creature's shaggy head loomed seven or eight meters in the air. Azador gasped something that was lost in the thunder, and Paul suddenly realized that his companion's head was visible above the grass. He shoved Azador to the ground even as the monstrous creature paused, still holding the raft high, and turned in their direction. The giant's mouth was full of broken teeth, its beard a wet tangle matted across its chest, but as it peered between the grass stems, it was the single eye big as a dinner plate that told Paul what they faced.

Again the lightning flared. The huge eye was staring right at the spot where they hid, and for a moment Paul was certain it had seen them, that any instant it would lumber toward them to twist their bones from their sockets. As they crouched in frozen terror the eye blinked, slow as a bullfrog blink, and then the Cyclops took a crunching step, then another, but away instead of toward them, trudging on toward its cave.

Paul was still holding his breath as the thing paused to prop the raft against the rock face, an ambulatory carpet of sheep crowding around its ankles. It bent and lifted away a stone that had bottle-stopped the shadowed mouth of the cave, then let the silent sheep file in. When they had cleared the doorway, the monster tossed the heavy, timbered craft in after them as though it were a tea tray, then followed.

When they heard the stone grind back into place, Paul and Azador leaped up and ran back into the trees as fast as their wobbly legs would carry them.

Paul lay huddled in the bottom of a culvert filling with rainwater. His heart was still racing but no longer felt like it might actually explode. His thoughts were a jumble.

"The bastard . . . has our . . . our boat!" Azador was so breathless he could hardly speak.

Paul lifted his chin out of the water and crawled a little way up the slope. Despite the terror, something else was tugging at him, something to do with Azador . . . and how he had crossed himself . . .

"Without it, we will die on this stupid island!" Azador hissed, but he had recovered himself and sounded more angry than frightened.

. . . But this wasn't even just ancient Greece, this was *Homer's* Greece, and therefore about a thousand years before . . . before . . .

"Jesus Christ!" Paul said. "You aren't from here at all! You—you're from outside!"

Azador turned to stare at him. With his curly black hair plastered to his head by the rain and his mustache draggled like otter whiskers, he looked a little less boldly handsome. "What?"

"You aren't from Greece—not this Greece, anyway. You're from outside the system. You're real!"

Azador regarded him defiantly. "And you?"

Paul realized he had given away whatever advantage the knowledge might have gained him. "Shit."

The other man shrugged. "We do not have time for such things. That big bastard will use our boat for his fire. Then we will never get away from here."

"So? What are we going to do, go knock on his cave door and ask for it back? That's a Cyclops. Didn't you read *The Odyssey?* Those things eat people the way you eat goats!"

Azador looked irritated, whether at the mention of reading

or the reminder of the goat meat he was not eating. "He will use it for his fire," he repeated stubbornly.

"Well, if he does, he does." Paul was struggling to think carefully, but the thunder was rattling his skull and he still had not recovered from the spectacle of a very ugly man as big as a two-story house. "Even if we could roll that stone out of the way, we couldn't get inside in time to stop him. But maybe he'll just add it to the woodpile. Or maybe he'll want to salvage some of the cloth and the ropes." He let out a shuddering breath and took another. "But we couldn't *do* anything about it anyway—Christ! You saw the size of that thing!"

"Nobody takes what is Azador's," the other man said harshly. This time Paul thought it sounded less like a code of honor than a symptom of insanity. "If you will not help me, I will wait until he comes out, then cut his hamstrings." He took his knife and waved it in the general direction of the top of the hill. "We will see how tall he is when he is lying on his belly."

Clearly Azador was going to get himself killed if Paul did not offer an alternative, but just as clearly there were not many alternatives to offer. If they remained on the island, it was only a matter of time until the thing came upon them in a place from which they couldn't escape. It might even have relatives—wasn't there something in *The Odyssey* about all the Cyclops living on the same island? They desperately needed an idea, but Paul doubted he was going to be able to come up with anything good. "We could build another raft," he offered.

Azador snorted. "We will cut down trees with my knife? And what will we use for a sail, this diaper I am wearing?" He pointed at himself, then at Paul's tattered chiton. "Or your little towel?"

"All right, all right!" Paul slumped back against the muddy side of the culvert. The rain was softening a little, but it was still like having someone drum their fingers against his head—not that he was brimming with brilliant plans anyway. An honors degree in Humanities might be a useful thing as far as recognizing various mythological monsters, but it was not all that helpful when facing them in the flesh. "Just let me think."

*   *   *

In the end, he could think of no better idea than to adapt Odysseus' original scheme to their own slightly different situation.

"You see, they were *inside* and needed to get *out*," he told Azador, who was not at all interested in the scheme's classical antecedents, and was busy lashing the hilt of the knife into the split end of a long deadfall branch. "We need to get *in*, but we also need him to be sleeping when we do it. It's a pity we don't have any wine."

"You are right there."

"I mean like Odysseus had—to give to the monster to make him sleepy." He clambered to his feet. His heart was hammering at the thought of what was to come, but he struggled to keep his voice casual. "Speaking of which, he must be sleeping by now—it's been dark for an hour."

Azador hefted the makeshift spear, satisfying himself with its balance, then stood. "Let's go and kill the big bastard."

"No, not like that!" Paul felt a sick panic sweep over him: it wasn't the greatest plan in the world to begin with. "Didn't you hear what I was saying? First we have to get the door open . . ."

His companion snorted. "I know—do you think Azador is stupid? Go now." He began to scramble up the side of the culvert.

They stopped on their way back to the hilltop to search for fallen logs of the appropriate width; eventually they found one that seemed acceptable, although it was narrower than Paul would have wished. It was just short enough for the muscular Azador to lift and carry, which he did after handing over his bladed spear. "If you lose my knife," he informed Paul with ceremonial dignity, "I will pull off your balls."

The rains had stopped, and although the long grasses outside the cave slapped wetly against their legs, the skies were clear and the moon gave them enough light to see the silhouetted bulk of the ridgetop before them. Azador moved to one side of the door, struggling to keep the log from dragging on the ground as Paul picked up rocks. When Azador was in position, Paul took another deep breath, then began to hurl the missiles against the stone that blocked the doorway.

"Ho! One-Eye!" he shouted as the rocks rattled against the door-stone. "Come out, you fat bastard! Give me back my boat!"

"Ow! Idiot!" Azador growled as one of the stones caromed from the door and bounced off his leg.

"Come out, One-Eye!" Paul bellowed. "Wake up! You're ugly and your mother dresses you funny!"

"I have never heard such stupid insults," Azador hissed, but then the great stone in the doorway creaked and grated as it slid to one side. The dying light of a fire inside made the opening glow like the mouth of hell. A vast shape moved in front of the embers.

"Who mocks Polyphemus?" The voice boomed across the hilltop. "Who is out there? Is that one of my shiftless cousins?"

"It is Nobody!" Paul's voice, already a songbird trill in comparison to the giant's rumbling bass, had suddenly become embarrassingly squeaky. As the Cyclops moved out onto his doorstep, the stench of wet fleece and rotting meat wafted out with him; Paul struggled against the powerful urge to scream and run. Remembering that Azador was within the giant's reach and that it was his job to distract the monster gave him back a little courage, but not much. "I am Nobody, and I am a ghost!" he screeched as impressively as he could, crouching low in the grass. "You have taken my ghost-ship, and I will haunt you until the end of your days unless you return it."

Polyphemus leaned forward and swept his head from side to side, his eye like a wide headlamp as it reflected the moonlight. "A ghost called Nobody?"

Paul had remembered something about Odysseus using that name, and although he couldn't quite remember why he had, it had seemed like a good touch. "That's right! And if you don't return my boat, I will haunt the hair off your head and the skin off your bones!"

The giant snuffled, great inhalations of air like a blacksmith's bellows. "For a ghost, you smell much like a man. I think I will find you tomorrow when it is less trouble, and eat you then. Perhaps with a little mint sauce." He turned back into the doorway.

In despair, Paul leaped up. "No!" He snatched up a stone as big as a grapefruit and ran toward the cave before flinging it as hard as he could. It struck the giant in its thatch of filthy hair

and must have bounced off its skull, but the giant only turned
slowly, a single shaggy brow lowering over the great eye. "Come
and catch me, if you think you're so clever!" Trembling with
terror, he stood in place, showing himself to the monster. "Maybe
I'll go visit your mother instead—I hear she *loves* to meet
strangers." He waved his arms in a manic semaphore. "Not just
meet them either, from what everyone tells me."

The Cyclops growled and took a couple of steps toward him,
looming like the prow of a battleship, stinking like a rendering
plant. It was all Paul could do to remain upright. "What kind of
little madman are you?" the monster thundered. "You can say
what you want about my mother—the old whore never gave me
a bone she hadn't sucked the meat and marrow from first—but
you have woken me up and wasted my sleeping time. When I
catch you, I will stretch you between trees like sheep's gut and
play a very unpleasant tune on you."

Almost hysterical with fear, Paul saw a movement in the shadows behind the Cyclops—Azador. Paul began to do a mad dance,
darting from side to side through the wet grass, leaping and waving his arms. The giant stepped nearer, the saucer eye now nar-
rowing in a squint. "Does it have the foaming-sickness?"
Polyphemus wondered aloud. "Perhaps instead of eating it, I
should grind it into paste and spread it on the rocks around the
meadow to keep wolves away from the sheep."

Although he wanted to keep the diversion going, the stink
and the horrible bulk of the thing coming toward him were too
much for his faltering courage. Paul snatched up the spear and
bolted back across the grass toward the forest, praying he had
given Azador time, that the man was not foolishly trying to drag
out the heavy raft himself.

The ground shook to a pair of heavy steps, and Paul felt his
heart climb up toward his throat.

*A dream . . . I've been in this dream before . . . and the giant's
going to reach down and grab me. . . .*

But the steps did not continue. When Paul reached the shelter of the trees a moment later, the huge shadowy shape was
still watching. Then it turned and trudged back to the cave. There
was a rumble and screech as it pushed the rock back in front of
the doorway—was there a hesitation, a moment's pause? Paul

held his breath. Only silence greeted him. Nerves like wires crisping in an electrical fire, he staggered back into the deeper shadows.

"I got the log into the doorway," Azador said when he had caught his breath. "It did not sound like the door closed all the way."

"Then all we can do is wait until he falls asleep." Paul actually wished that they could wait a great deal longer than that. The idea of creeping into the ogre's cave, with its escape-preventing walls and stench of putrid flesh, was paralyzing.

Why do I keep getting thrown into folktales? he wondered. *Awful ones at that—like the worst things the Brothers Grimm ever imagined.*

He eyed Azador, who was already settling himself against the sides of the depression, obviously planning to get some sleep. It was a good idea, but Paul's mind was full of flittering thoughts, and behind it all was the great fear of what they were about to do, too great to let him rest. He turned his attention to the mystery man beside him, who seemed to know much about the simulation but nothing about its source.

"Where are you from, anyway?" he asked quietly.

Azador opened one eye and frowned, but said nothing.

"Look, we're stuck here. We have to trust each other. Why are you in this network?" A sudden thought struck him. "Are you part of the Circle?"

His companion snorted his contempt. "A tribe of *gorgio* priests and fools." He spat.

"Then . . . then do you have something to do with the Grail people?" He only whispered the words, mindful of what Nandi had told him about the eavesdropping machineries of the network's masters. "Are you part of the Brotherhood?"

Azador's expression changed from scorn to something cold and reptilian. "If you ask me that again, then when the time comes that I have to save you from One-Eye, I will let him eat you." His tone had no hint of joking. "They are pigs."

"Then who *are* you? What are you doing here?"

The mustached man sighed, an exhalation of irritation. "I told you. I am looking for a woman who has something of mine. No one takes Azador's gold and walks away with it. I will find her, no matter in what world she hides."

"She took your gold?"

"She took something of mine."

The hair on Paul's neck lifted with a sudden memory. "A harp? Was it a golden harp?"

Azador stared at him as though he had begun to bark like a dog. "No. A cigarette lighter." He rolled over, deliberately turning his back to Paul.

A cigarette lighter . . . ? Paul kept thinking the universe around him could not become more strange, but he kept being wrong.

He woke from a shallow, unsatisfying sleep to find Azador kneeling over him, the blade-end of the makeshift spear near his throat. In the filtered moonlight the man's face looked hard as a mask, and for a moment Paul was quite convinced his companion intended to kill him.

"Come," Azador whispered. "It will be dawn in another hour."

Paul climbed to his feet, grogginess and disorientation a thin curtain in front of naked terror. For the first time in a while he thought longingly of coffee—If nothing else, the ritual of making some would postpone what was to come.

He followed Azador up the hill, sliding a step backward on the muddy ground for every few steps forward. The storm had passed, and when they reached the grassy hilltop, they stood beneath a sky dazzlingly full of stars. Azador held a finger to his lips—quite unnecessarily, thought Paul, who was already frightened almost into immobility by the idea that he might step on a twig and wake the monster.

They moved slower and slower as they approached the door of the cave, until it seemed that time itself had become something thick, weighty. Azador leaned into the shadows, then bobbed up, teeth bared in a mirthless grin, and beckoned Paul forward. The log had indeed kept the stone from sealing the doorway: a crescent of orange light revealed the gap.

The smell was even worse than Paul had remembered, meat and animal musk and sour sweat. His stomach had been squirming since he woke; as they stepped over the log and squeezed through the narrow space into the cave, it was all he could do not to vomit.

The monster's snores were deep and wet. Paul almost went limp with relief, and was equally heartened to see their raft leaning intact against a stone, but before he had time to savor the feelings Azador led him across the uneven floor. The cavern was high, and the dim glow of the embers did not penetrate every cranny, but he could see the great bulk of the Cyclops near the far wall, lying like a mountain range beside the fire. The sheep were crammed into a wooden pen that took up almost half of the large chamber. Stacked near it were the giant's implements, oddly domestic—buckets of pitch and a pair of shears that although bigger than normal must have been small and delicate as a surgical instrument in the Cyclop's oversized grasp.

Distracted by his observations, Paul kicked something which rolled across the stone with a heart-stopping clatter. Some of the sheep moved nervously, and for a moment the tone of the ogre's snores changed; Paul and Azador stood frozen until the rhythm stabilized again. The human skull, which had come to a halt upside down, teetering on its cranium, seemed to look back at them with grave if inverted amusement.

The job was Azador's now, and Paul would have liked nothing better than to stay near the door while his companion got on with it, but shame and something like loyalty forced him on. He groped his way forward a few inches at a time until he stood near the monster's feet, each one as long as he was tall and almost the same distance across, the skin more leathery and wrinkled than an elephant's hide. Azador inched around toward the creature's head, clearly torn as to which of his planned targets to strike, the lidded eye or unprotected throat. The Cyclops lay on his back with head tilted and a massive arm draped across his forehead: the angle was not good for reaching either spot. Azador climbed onto a rock shelf that brought him above the level of the giant's head, looked at Paul for a moment, then gripped the spear tightly and bent his knees before jumping down onto the Cyclops' chest.

As he sprang, one of the sheep bleated in alarm. The giant moved only a little, rolling in his heavy sleep, but it was enough for Azador's blade to miss the pit of the throat and tear down the side of the giant's neck instead.

Polyphemus woke, roaring like a jet engine, and slapped Azador off his chest. Paul's companion flew across the room, thudded into a corner, and did not rise.

Still roaring, his voice so loud in that closed place that it seemed he would shake the entire cavern into stone-dust, Polyphemus rolled onto his knees and then rose to his full height. His great, shaggy head swung around and his eye fixed on Paul, who took a stumbling step backward.

I was right, he thought as the giant's bloody hand reached out to close on him and crush him into paste, *it really wasn't a very good plan. . . .*

CHAPTER 13

Tending the Herd

NETFEED/NEWS: US, China to Cooperate on Antarctica Archaeology
(visual: Antarctic site seen from the air)
VO: The discovery of an archaelogical site on the Antarctic Peninsula, previously believed to have been uninhabited until recent history...
(visual: Chinese and American envoys shaking hands in Ellsworth)
... has brought the two most prominent feuding nations of the Zurich Accord together in a rare show of cooperation.
(visual: Chinese Cultural Minister Hua at press conference)
Hua: "This historic find must be protected. I know I speak for the entire Chinese people when I say that we will work happily and vigorously with the United States and other Zurich nations to keep this unique piece of human history safe so that it can be properly explored and documented..."

T was hard to watch the little kids running around on the playground with their nice Mamapapa-type clothes and their clean

faces and not wonder what that would feel like. But although he
could imagine a boy *like* him doing those kind of things, he could
never imagine *himself* doing it—not Carlos Andreas Chascarillo
Izabal. Not Cho-Cho.

He saw her come close to his hiding place, wandering by herself. He looked to make sure that the two teachers were still standing in the shade near the classroom, then he rattled the bushes.
She didn't hear him, so he rattled them louder, then whispered as
loud as he dared, "Hey, weenit! You deaf?"

She looked up, startled, and even when she recognized him
she still looked frightened. It made him angry, and for a moment
he thought of just leaving and telling *El Viejo* he hadn't found
her. "Come here," he said instead. "I gotta ask you something,
m'entiendes?"

The little girl turned and checked the teachers, just as he had
done. He found himself admiring her just a bit: for a little rich
white girl, she wasn't all stupid. She wandered closer to the fence,
but still kept a short distance away, as though he might reach out
and grab her.

"What?" she asked; then, "Is Mister Sellars sick?" She looked
really worried.

Cho-Cho made a face. "He ain't sick. He wants to know how
come you don't come see him or nothing?"

She looked like she wanted to cry. It made Cho-Cho want to
hit her, but he didn't know why. Probably just because the old
cripple liked her so much, had him running errands to see how
she was doing, like she was some kind of princess or something.

"My . . . my daddy took the Storybook Sunglasses. He says I
shouldn't have them." A nearby shriek made her jump. One of
her classmates had grabbed another kid's sweater, but was running off with it in the opposite direction, away from the fence, a
couple of kids chasing after him. "He's trying to find out why I
have . . . why I have them . . . and he won't let me go out and play
or anything until I tell him."

Cho-Cho frowned. "So you getting all punished? 'Cause you
won't tell them where the glasses from?"

The little girl—he could never remember her name right, even
when the old man said it all the time: Crystal Ball or something
stupid like that—nodded. Cho-Cho wasn't surprised she was keep-

ing her mouth shut, since where he grew up nobody told their parents anything about what *really* happened, if they even had parents, but he thought it was pretty interesting that she wasn't folding up right away. Rich little girl like that, he would have thought she'd give up as soon as they started the whippings, and they must have started those already.

"I'll tell *El Viejo*," he said.

"Does he want me to come see him?" she asked. "I can't— I'm grounded."

Cho-Cho shrugged. He was just doing his job. He wasn't going to waste time telling her all kinds of cheerful shit to make her feel better.

"La caridad es veneno," his father had always said, his poor, stupid, crazy father—*Charity is poison.* "It makes you weak, boy," was the explanation. "They give it to us like they give poison to rats. We're the rats in the walls, understand? And they want to make us weak so they can kill us."

Carlos Sr. could tell his family not to take handouts from the government or the church, but the problem was, he couldn't keep a job. He was a hard worker and a pretty smart one (one of the reasons it was still better to get fruit picked by hand), and if the man in the truck chose him to go to the citrus fields outside Tampa for the day, all morning that truck man would be thinking about what a good choice he'd made, because Carlos Sr. would be storming up and down the rows, filling twice as many orange or grapefruit bins as anyone else. But then someone would look at him funny, or one of the foremen would ask him a question that felt like an insult, and then someone would be lying on the ground with a bloody nose. Sometimes it was Carlos Sr., but usually it was the other person. And that would be that. Another job lost, another field where he couldn't work until they had a different man on the truck, a different foreman.

But he didn't take charity, as he was always pointing out. Carlos Jr.—never called Carlito, "little Carlos," because for some reason that, too, would have been an insult to his father—heard the speech so many times he could have recited it for him.

Carlos Sr.'s wife was not such a stickler for integrity, although she was never stupid enough to let her husband know that some of what she brought home to the honeycomb underneath High-

way 4 to help feed their five children was not merely earned from
her job at a grocery store, where she mopped the floors when
things spilled and carried boxes from one side of the warehouse
to the other, but in fact came from the very charity he hated, in
the form of state assistance to indigent families. Food vouchers.

It wasn't that Carlos Jr. particulary disagreed with any of his
father's philosophical positions. At a very basic level, he even understood and agreed with Carlos Sr.'s distrust of helping hands;
neither would he have liked to be known as "Carlito," so he felt
no loss there. His objection to his father was far more basic. He
hated him. Carlos Sr.'s bullying and bragging would have been
more tolerable if the Izabal family had lived a life of even middle-
of-the-road poverty, but they were poor as dirt. The father's comparison of their position to that of rats was horrifyingly true.

Carlos Jr. considered himself a man by the time he was eight.
Did he and his friends not bring in at least as much to their families as their benighted, hopeless fathers? What difference was
there between what others earned by sweat and what they earned
by thievery, except that the latter was less work and infinitely
more exciting? When he first met his friends Beto and Iskander
and they tried to call him Carlito, he hit Iskander in the eye and
kicked Beto so hard that the smaller boy had run home crying.
His reasons for not using that name were different than his father's,
but his determination was just as great. He had nothing against
nicknames, though. Later, when Iskander started to call him "Cho-
Cho" after a brand of rice candy that he particularly liked to
shoplift, he accepted the name graciously.

He and Beto and Iskander did a lot of things together, most
of which were meant to put money in their pockets, candy in their
sweaty fists, and dermal patches on whatever areas of their skin
could be spit-scrubbed clean enough for the chemical transfer.
They had a business, that was the truth of it, with diverse interests, some of which were as interesting and inventive as anything
conceived by people with college degrees. In fact, they were busy
with one of their projects—"tending the herd," as they called it—
on the night the terrible thing happened.

The International Vending Corporation had come up with a
new twist on the basic concept of food and drink delivery, something they rather preciously named "Walkabots"—vending ma-

chines on silent tank treads that covered entire neighborhoods, directed by simple codes to move from place to place. IVC did not expect to make even as much money from them as from simple stationary machines, but the big boxes were also mobile advertisements, playing up-tempo advertising jingles and greeting customers (once they came within range of the infrared eye) with cheerful canned chatter. It didn't take long for Cho-Cho and his friends (and hundreds like them in every major city) to realize that the machines could be physically removed to other neighborhoods, so that the IVC service people could not locate them (something a simple chip could have prevented if the vending machine executives had been a little less naive.) Once the machines were set roving on their new turf, the profits could then be safely harvested by Cho-Cho and his tiny business consortium until the box ran out of goodies. After they had jammed the credit slots which most people would have otherwise used, each machine still took in enough old-fashioned coin to deliver a tidy little profit at the end of each day.

Within a couple of months they had a free-range herd of Walkabot vending machines operating all over Tampa, so many that Cho-Cho and his friends had to surf the tramline for hours every night to collect all their takings. They were living so high that Cho-Cho even got himself an aspirational, Goggleboy-type neural access shunt installed in a dirty backroom surgery by a streetcorner can man, but they all knew that the time was short—the IVC people were busy snatching back every machine they could get their hands on—so they were pushing the enterprise as far and as fast as they could.

On the night the terrible thing happened, little Beto had located an unsheperded machine in Ybor City, an impressive new model with a holographic display of a fizzing drink being poured from a bottle hovering like a halo above a two-and-a-half-meter plasteel box. Beto was delirious with pleasure—he declared this would be the king of their herd—and despite Cho-Cho's reluctance to kidnap such an unusual-looking machine without investigating it first, he let Beto and Iskander have their way. In a matter of moments they had jacked it up onto the machine-rustling dolly which they had liberated from an auto garage and were heading across town.

The IVC Model 6302-B was meant to solve the problem that had plagued the last generation of mobile machines; many others beside Cho-Cho and his friends had discovered how to kidnap the mobile dispensers, and the company was sick of being a laughingstock. The worried executives at International Vending Company did not realize that they had made things dramatically worse.

As Cho-Cho and his partners took advantage of a late-night lull in traffic on the expressway to get their machine across—they were only boys, after all, and could not possibly have lifted such a large machine up the stairs to the pedestrian walkway—the Model 6302-B crossed the border of its designated vending area, which set off its defensive systems. An alarm as loud as an ambulance siren began to shriek, warning lights to strobe, and a theoretically harmless vegetable dye with ultraviolet trace elements sprayed from ports along the side of the drink machine to mark the machine rustlers.

Iskander was hit in the eyes by the dye. Terrified by the screaming alarm and his sudden blindness, he staggered away from the machine. Cho-Cho had also been sprayed in the face, and was rubbing his eyes frantically when Beto screeched in terror. Cho-Cho cleared the worst of the dye in time to see Iskander frozen in the headlights of an oncoming truck. They barely saw the impact, but the wet thump was so shocking that Cho-Cho let go of the heavy vending machine, still howling its warning cry as it teetered atop the dolly. A moment later it began to tip, the weight far too great for Cho-Cho to stop it even when he realized what was happening. Little Beto, wide-eyed as he stared at the spot where Iskander had been only a moment before, did not even see the huge box toppling on him. He disappeared beneath it without a sound.

Stunned, Cho-Cho had stood frozen for long moments. The car that had hit Iskander had stopped several hundred yards up the expressway, and other headlights were appearing now, slowing at the sight of the huge blinking machine lying on its side in the middle lane. Cho-Cho's muscles if not his wits returned to his control; he bolted into the darkness of the roadside, almost tripping on the dolly which was rolling slowly down the sloping expressway toward the shoulder.

The International Vending Company sustained such a blizzard

of negative publicity, the tabnets struggling to outdo each other with stories about how a "killer machine" had chased one child to its death on a freeway and killed another outright by crushing his skull, that within a month of the accident they declared Chapter 11 bankruptcy and sold their assets to another firm. Although Cho-Cho would experience other tragedies—his mother and younger sister were asphyxiated a year later when a trucker running his engine to stay warm during an evening's layover underneath the freeway accidentally filled their honeycomb with carbon monoxide—that night had already done much to form his expectations of life.

We are the rats in the walls, was the only thing of his father's that he kept when he ran away, making his way up the East Coast in search of cooler summers and less vigilant police. *They will trap us, poison us. They want us dead.*

Cho-Cho watched the little girl walk away with her head down, slow and sad like he had just told her he was going to burn up her house or something. Why had the old *vato* ever got involved with her in the first place? The old guy was weird, but he was pretty smart in his way—he knew lots of shit, that was for sure— so why did he get a little puppy dog like this to help him?

Because he hadn't had any other choice, the boy suddenly realized. He would have taken a street-smart animal like Cho-Cho if he could have, but they hadn't met in time. When they did, he had sent the little girl back to Mamapapa-land pretty quick.

This put a little spring in Cho-Cho's step as he made his way back through the walking park just beyond the school, but he still remembered to keep to the trees and stay out of sight of the paths. He was getting a little tired of eating the military rations the old cripple Sellars kept stacked in the tunnel, but he wasn't *that* tired of it—it was a lot better than not eating, and it also beat getting meals on trays in one of those kiddie jails, which was where he'd go if they caught him. If he was lucky, of course, and they didn't just take him out back of the base and shoot him instead—"snipe hunting," the *azules* called it. You couldn't trust the people who ran things. They talked all nice on the net, everyone said, but he knew they didn't like rats at all.

Sellars was different, but Cho-Cho still wasn't sure why. In fact, he wasn't sure about anything where the man in the wheel-chair was concerned. The old cripple was hiding from the army men, but doing it right underneath an army base. He was keyed into some kind of crazy part of the net that Cho-Cho had never seen—better than the best games or anything—but he wanted Cho-Cho to be the one to go, even though they could never quite make it work right, or at least not for very long. And he was always mumbling, like Cho-Cho's *abuela* in the mountains outside Guatemala City, who his dad had taken him to see once—a hor-rible sweaty boat ride that lasted days, just to meet an old lady living in some Indian village who didn't even have any teeth, and who kept a scrawny monkey on a leash right in her little house. She had seemed glad to meet her grandchild, but he couldn't un-derstand her language and his father couldn't be bothered to trans-late much of what she said. He knew he would never as long as he lived forget the smell of that place, boiled corn and monkey shit.

It wasn't much different living with Sellars, although *gracias á Dios* there was no monkey. But the things the old man mum-bled, even if they were in a language that Cho-Cho could actu-ally speak, still didn't make any sense—he talked to himself about his garden, like he still had a house of his own, and mumbled words like "platforms" and "Ay-eye structures" like even if he didn't have a house, he was going to build one. Which was pretty funny, because if ever there was an old *vato* who couldn't even lift a hammer, let alone use one, it was Sellars. He had arms like broomsticks and had to work so hard to breathe sometimes, even with that "oxygen nation" stuff he kept boiling all the time like some kind of ugly soup, that Cho-Cho sometimes couldn't even sleep for listening to him wheezing and coughing.

It was funny, though. He didn't want the guy to die, even if he was an old cripple. Not just because then he'd be on his own hiding from the army men, and the *mu'chita* probably wouldn't even bring food no more. There was also something strange about the way Sellars talked to him that he couldn't quite understand. It was almost like the old man liked him or something. Cho-Cho knew better, of course. People like Sellars, white people with houses of their own—or who had once *had* houses of their own, anyway—didn't like street rats. They said they did if someone was doing a net story on how sad it all was, or if the government or the church was opening some fancy *caridad* place, but people like that didn't really want to spend time with a dirty little kid with teeth knocked out and sores on his arms and legs that wouldn't stop oozing.

But Sellars was definitely strange. He talked softly and called Cho-Cho "Senor Izabal." The first time he did it, Cho-Cho almost kicked him right out of his chair, but it wasn't a joke, or at least not the kind Cho-Cho was used to. And Sellars thanked him for bringing him things. For a while Cho-Cho had been sure the guy was some kind of babybouncer—why else get friendly with a little *gatita* like that Christy Bell or whatever her name was?—and so he kept a sharp piece of metal he'd found in one of the base trash cans right in his hand when he went to sleep, his fingers curled around the sticky tape handle. But Sellars never did anything.

So was he just *un anciano loco*? But if he was, how did he get into that amazing place—a world better than the net, a world Cho-Cho had seen with his own eyes or he wouldn't have believed it? And why would Sellars only bring him online after he'd fallen asleep? He must have some lockoff big station he didn't want Cho-Cho to see, something worth monster *cambio*. The whole thing was so strange that it had to mean money somewhere, and Cho-Cho wasn't going to miss out. When you were a rat, you had to take what you could get, any time you could get it. Besides, he had to figure it out just so that if the burned-up old man died, *Cho-Cho El Raton* could still get back to that place on the net, to that utter tasty, wild place.

"SO her father has the sunglasses . . ." Sellars tried to keep his voice even, but it was shockingly bad news. It had been a dreadful gamble, but at the time he had done it, there had been no other choice—it was either give her the device or risk having her constantly coming to prearranged meetings at his hiding place, and how long could one hope to keep that up with a child before attracting notice?

Cho-Cho shrugged. "Is what she said." He was being unusually opaque today, even by his own standards. At the best of times the boy moved in a permanent dark cloud of suspicion and reflexive anger, but that meant he was fairly easy to read. Sellars had often brooded on the hopelessness of his own cause, but never more so than when he considered that his only real-world allies were the primary-school daughter of the man hunting for him and a boy only a few years older who hadn't slept in a house in years—a boy who at the moment was chewing the corner off a foil sack of RTE pudding so he could suck out the contents like a chimp with a marrowbone.

Sellars sighed. He was so tired, so very tired, but this latest crisis could not wait. It might even be too late already—the Storybook Sunglasses would hold up under a standard examination, but if someone researched the components, which Sellars had assembled over two years of stealthy mail fraud and fiddling with the base's records, they would realize that the receiving range for the device was very short indeed. Even if Christabel did not break under what must be terrible pressure, her father and his staff would know that whoever was narrowcasting to the sunglasses must be almost on top of them. Or beneath them.

If he had been the type to shudder he would have done so. Next up the line would be Yacoubian, and—although Christabel's father and his other subordinates might not know it—the entire weight of the Grail Brotherhood. The whole thing would be over in hours from the moment the deduction was made, so quickly that Sellars might not have a chance to do more than destroy himself and his records. In fact, the process might be in the chain at this very moment.

He steadied himself by thinking of his Garden, of the virtual plants twining and tangling. Nothing was ever simple, but that was true for his opponents as well as for himself. He would have to do something, that was all, and the obvious point of attack would be Christabel's father, Major Michael Sorensen. If Sellars had possessed the strange operating system the Brotherhood used, he could just reach out and hypnotize the man when he was next online, manipulate his mind. The sunglasses could be made to disappear, the entire subject to be forgotten. Of course, first he would have to be willing to interfere with the man's mind, to risk Christabel's father's sanity and perhaps even his life.

Sellars looked at Cho-Cho, whose grubby face was at the moment made grubbier still by the chocolate pudding smeared on his chin. Was there a difference between using innocents like Christabel—or even this child, who compared to Sellars himself was definitely an innocent—and mucking about in the mental plumbing of an adult?

"It comes down to choices, Señor Izabal," he said aloud. "Choices, as my friend Senor Yeats would have been the first to point out . . .

> ". . . *An aged man is but a paltry thing,*
> *A tattered coat upon a stick, unless*
> *Soul clap its hands and sing, and louder sing*
> *For every tatter in its mortal dress* . . .

". . . And coats don't get much more tattered than you and me, do they?"

Cho-Cho stared at him, rubbing his mouth and transferring pudding freely to wrist and forearm. "Huh?"

"A bit of poetry. I have a choice to make. If I make the wrong one, something very, very bad will happen. If I make the right one, something very bad might happen anyway. Have you ever had to make a choice like that?"

The boy regarded him from under long lashes, an animal quietly preparing for defense or flight. At last he said, "All the time I have to think, is like that—bad one way, bad the other. They always get you in the end. *Siempre.*"

Sellars nodded, but he felt something much like pain. "I suppose they do. Now listen carefully, my young friend, and I'll tell you what to go back and say to the little girl."

IT felt like four whole days had passed since she came home from school instead of only four hours, but all she could do was think about what the terrible boy had told her. She didn't even know for sure if Mister Sellars had really said that. What if the boy Cho-Cho was telling a lie? What if Mister Sellars was really sick, and the boy just wanted to do bad things? She saw someone on the net once saying that children like that boy didn't believe in the law, which she knew meant that they would steal and hurt people. He had pushed her down, hadn't he? Told her he was going to cut her?

She desperately wanted to go and ask Mister Sellars, really ask him his own self, but her mother was just a few steps away from the kitchen table, and even so she kept looking over her shoulder all the time, like she thought Christabel might try to sneak away.

She had been doing her homework, but all the thoughts had her so confused that she couldn't do her fractions right, couldn't remember which was the denumerator and which was the nominator or anything, and so she had just put in numbers and erased them, over and over.

"How are you doing, honey?" her mom asked, using her sweet voice, but she sounded worried, like she did all the time these days.

"Okay," Christabel told her. But she wasn't okay. She was afraid that her daddy wouldn't come home on time. She was even more afraid that if he did come home on time, something so bad might happen that nothing would ever be okay ever again.

It didn't help that her daddy was in a bad mood when he came in, swearing because he had kicked over a watering can on the porch that shouldn't have been there. Mommy apologized, then Daddy apologized, but he still wasn't in a good mood. He barely said hello to Christabel before he went into his study and closed the door.

Christabel looked at the clock on the wall above the sink and saw that there were only ten more minutes to go. She poured herself a glass of water but didn't drink any, and stared at the cartoons on the refrigerator, even though she'd seen them all before.

"I'm going to go talk to Daddy," she said at last.

Her mother looked at her carefully, like she did when Christabel said she didn't feel good. "He may just want some quiet time, sugar."

"I want to talk to him." She wanted to cry, but she couldn't let it show. "I just want to talk to him, Mommy."

So suddenly it almost startled Christabel into a squeak, her mother kneeled down and put her arms around her. "Okay, honey. Go knock on the door and ask him. You know how much we love you, don't you?"

"Sure." Christabel did not feel very good, and hearing about how her mommy and daddy loved her made it worse. She slipped out of her mother's arms and walked down the hall to the study.

It was only because she knew that just a few minutes were left that she managed to knock on the door, because it felt like she was standing outside a dragon's cave or a haunted house. "Daddy, can I come in?"

For a second he didn't say anything. When he did, he sounded tired. "Sure, baby."

He had poured himself a drink out of the are-you-going-to-have-one-this-early-Mike? bottle, and was sitting in his spinny chair with reports open all over the wallscreen. He looked up, and although he had started shaving again, something about his face seemed old and sad and made her heart hurt even more. "What is it? Dinner?"

Christabel took a deep breath. She tried to remember the words to a prayer, to pray that Mister Sellars had really sent her the message, that it wasn't just from the awful boy with the bad teeth, but all she could think of was *Now I lay me down to sleep,* which didn't seem right.

"Daddy, do . . . do you still have my Storybook Sunglasses?"

He turned slowly to face her. "Yes, I do, Christabel."

"Here?"

He nodded.

"Then . . . then . . ." It was hard to talk. "Then you have to put them on. Because the man who gave them to me wants to talk to you." She looked at the corner of the wallscreen, which said 18:29 in white numbers. "Right now."

Daddy's eyes went wide and he started to ask something, then he looked at the time and took his keys out of his coat pocket. He unlocked the bottom drawer of the desk and took out the black plastic Storybook Sunglasses. "I'm supposed to put them on . . . ?" he asked her. His voice was very quiet, but there was something in it that really scared her, something hard and cold, like a knife under a bedsheet.

It was even worse when they were on, because she couldn't see his eyes anymore. He looked like a blind man. He looked like a bug, even, or a space alien.

"I don't know what . . ." he started to say, then stopped. For a moment, there was silence. *"Who are you?"* he said at last, his voice angry and hissing like a snake, and because he was still facing her, for a moment Christabel had the terrible idea that he was asking *her*.

After a moment he said, in a different voice, "Christabel, you'd better leave the room."

"But, Daddy . . . !"

"You heard me. Tell your mother I'm going be a little late working on something."

Christabel got up and moved toward the doorway. Everything was quiet for few seconds, but as she closed the door she heard her father say, "All right, then. Show me."

He didn't come out.

An hour went by. Christabel's mother, who at first had been angry in a making-fun-of-it-way, began to get really angry. She went and knocked at the office door but Daddy didn't answer. "Mike?" she called, and rattled the door, but it was locked. "Christabel, what was he doing in there?"

She shook her head. She was afraid that if she said anything, she'd start crying so hard she'd never stop. She knew what had happened—the terrible boy had done something to the sunglasses. He'd killed Christabel's daddy. She lay facedown on the couch and buried her head in the pillow while her mother walked back and forth across the living room.

"This is ridiculous," Mommy was saying. She went back to the door. "Mike! Come on, you're scaring me!" There was a terrible sound in her voice, small but getting bigger, like a piece of paper tearing at the edge that would soon rip all the way through. "Mike!"

Now Christabel did begin to cry, soaking the pillow. She didn't want to look up. She wanted it all to go away. It was all her fault. All her fault . . .

"Mike! Open this door right now, or I'm calling the MPs out!" Mommy was kicking the door now, great thumps like a giant's footsteps which only made Christabel cry harder. "Please, Mike, please— Oh, God, Mike . . . !"

Something clicked. Her mother stopped shouting and kicking. Everything was quiet.

Christabel sat up, rubbing her eyes, feeling tears and snot running down her lip. Daddy was standing in the open doorway of the study, the sunglasses in his hand. He was as pale as an egg. He looked like he had just come back from outer space, or from monster land.

"I'm . . . I'm sorry," he said. "I've been . . ." He looked down at the sunglasses. "I've been . . . doing something."

"Mike, what's going on?" Christabel's mother said. She sounded only a little less scared.

"I'll tell you later." He looked at her, then at Christabel, but there was no anger or anything like it on his face. He rubbed his eyes.

"But what . . . what about dinner?" Mommy laughed, sharp and high. "The chicken is dry as a bone."

"You know," he said, "suddenly I'm not very hungry."

CHAPTER 14

Bandit Country

NETFEED/ENTERTAINMENT: Treeport Sues Wiggers
(visual: Treeport visiting children in hospital)
VO: Clementina Treeport, often called "The Saint of St.
Petersburg" for her work with Russian street children, is
suing the power wig group How Can I Mourn You If You
Won't Stay In Your Hole? over their use of her name and
image in their release "Meat Eats Money, Children Are
Cheap," which proposes that street children might be a
useful substitute for expensive vat-grown meats. The lyrics
to the release seem to suggest that Treeport and her Golden
Mercy hospice are trafficking in children for just this
purpose. Treeport has not made a public comment, but her
attorney states she is, "definitely very unhappy about this."
(visual: Cheevak, soundmaster for HCIMYIYWSIYH?, in
front of release promo)
CHEEVAK: "No, we're level with Clemmy. We think she's
ho dzang on this. It's, like, tribute, seen? She's a forward
thinker, we tell for true."

Renie was wrestling with an odd puzzle, one that frustrated her programmer's mind as much as it engaged it.

How do you engineer kindness?

They were taking their leave of the Library Brothers after a brief and restless night's sleep and an early breakfast in the Brothers' Refectory. Renie could not help wondering a little at the generosity the monks had shown them—something that went beyond mere reparation for their own accidental role in Martine's disappearance. It seemed unusual that coded creations should so thoroughly attempt to do good for strangers, and Renie was wondering how such a thing could come to be.

It's not like anger or something, where you could just program a hostile reaction to any deviation from normal routine, she thought as she clasped the abbot's hand in farewell. Brother Epistulus Tertius, standing beside him, actually looked a little teary, although Renie had no doubt he was just as happy to stay home. *I mean, it's hard enough simply to define kindness, let alone try to make it part of a response pattern on any level beyond stock phrases.*

The abbot leaned toward her and said quietly, "You will take good care of Brother Factum Quintus for us, won't you? He's quite brilliant, but a little . . . childlike in some ways. We would hate for anything to happen to him."

"We will treat him as one of us, Primoris."

The abbot nodded and let go of her hand. The others finished up their good-byes, all of Renie's party clearly a bit mournful except for !Xabbu, who was doing his best to appear nothing more than a monkey. The kindness of the Library Brothers was one of the few examples of genuine warmth they had encountered, and it was hard to leave it behind even though Martine's need took precedence over everything. Only gawky Factum Quintus seemed distracted, humming to himself as he paced back and forth, clearly anxious to be moving.

Genuine warmth—there I go again. How can it be genuine? These people aren't really people at all—they're code. She frowned. A neural net kept trying different strategies until it found successful ones, but how could you even make sure that kindness would *be* a successful strategy? Sometimes kindness was rewarded with treachery, just as the Quan Li thing had taken advantage of the Brothers' hospitality.

For the first time Renie had a genuine urge to get her hands on the inner workings of the Grail network, this so-called Otherland. She had presumed that what the Brotherhood had made with all its money and resources was simply a larger and more complex version of a normal simulation network—more details, more choices, more complicated "histories" for the created objects. But she was beginning to wonder if there wasn't something larger and stranger going on.

Wasn't there something in complexity theory about this kind of system? She watched golden dust drift through a shaft of light, struggling to remember her long-ago classes. *Not just that they can go bad, like Sick Building Syndrome, but that they can evolve, too—get more and more complex and turbulent, then take a sudden leap into a different state . . . ?*

"Renie?" Florimel could not entirely keep the sharpness of impatience out of her voice, but by her standards, it was a friendly inquiry. "Are you going to stand there staring at the bookshelves all morning?"

"Oh. Right. Let's get going."

She would put it away until later, but she promised herself she would not forget.

The Library Market, which seemed to be a permanent fixture, was in full swing; it took them the better part of an hour to get away from the worst of the crowds. Renie could not shake the feeling that they were being watched, although she found it hard to believe that the Quan Li thing, its disguise now revealed, would risk approaching them again so soon. Still, her flesh crawled as though they were being observed by some all-seeing eye. In Martine's absence, she would have liked to discuss it with !Xabbu, but her friend was still maintaining his pose as a simple animal and there was no chance for a quiet escape down a side passage for a conversation: Factum Quintus was setting a brisk pace, despite an almost nonstop monologue about the various architectural sights and the materials and methods used to create them.

The company returned to the line of the river and followed it for no little time, through settlements both poor and prosperous. As minutes became an hour, then more, Renie began to have doubts about their guide. It seemed unlikely that the person masquerading as Quan Li would have carried her so far from the scene of the kidnapping.

Factum Quintus stopped the procession. "This must seem a long journey," he told them, as if he had read her thoughts. "You see, it is simpler from our level to climb to the Campanile of the Six Pigs. Easier, but farther, yes. We can come back along the upper stories to the Spire Forest. So we are going to the farthest site first. The Campanile is not without interest in itself, though, so . . ."

"A friend of ours is in terrible danger." Renie could not bear another lecture on masonry at the moment. "We don't care about what's interesting. Every hour may be critical."

He raised a long, thin hand. "Of course. Critical. I am just apprising you of my method." He turned with bony dignity and set out along the riverwalk again.

Florimel dropped back from where she had been walking between T4b and Emily. "I am glad you said what you did, Renie. I am relieved to know we are not just accompanying this monk on a walking tour."

Renie shook her head. "We haven't even thought about what we'll do when we find her. *If* we find her."

"It is bad to worry too much without information. We should wait until we see the situation."

"You're right. It's just . . . I'm on edge. I keep thinking somebody's watching us."

"I have the same feeling." Florimel grinned sourly at Renie's expression. "It is not surprising, really. I think you and I are much alike—always we worry about everyone else. Always it is our responsibility to make sure others are safe." She reached out and gave Renie a tentative pat on the arm, a strangely awkward gesture. "Perhaps that's why we have had conflict. It is hard for two people both accustomed to the same position to sort things out."

Renie wasn't entirely sure if being told she was like Florimel was actually a compliment, but she decided to treat it as one. "You're probably right. But you've been feeling . . . that feeling, too? That we're being watched, even followed?"

"Yes. But I have seen nothing. I regret very much that Martine is not with us. I would say that I feel blind without her, but I fear it would sound like a bad joke."

Renie shook her head. "No, it's true."

"I will go back now, with the young ones. I feel more comfortable when I am close to them."

At first Renie thought the other woman meant she would be more comfortable because of T4b's size and impressive armored physique, but realized a moment later that she was talking about something quite different. "I feel the same way. Responsibility—it's tiring sometimes, isn't it?"

Again Florimel smiled, a little softer now. "We would not know what to do without it, I think."

A short time later Factum Quintus led them around a bend in the river and onto what seemed for a moment to be the opening of a sort of cave of polished marble, its huge, flat white floor cluttered with small buildings.

"The Grand River Stairs," the monk announced. "It is shocking how long it has been since I have visited this."

Renie saw that the broad landing did indeed mark the bottom of an immense staircase whose shadowed interior wound up and away from the river. The more recent structures on either side of it, slapdash constructions of wood and rough stone, almost swallowed the splendor of the stairs.

"But . . . but people have built all over it," said Renie, surprised. "Look, they've even built little huts on the stairway itself."

Brother Factum Quintus goggled at her shrewdly, and for a moment a look of amusement quirked his angular, ugly face. "And who is to prevent them?" he asked mildly. "The House is for those who live in it, surely. Surely. The Builders, if such exist, have never protested against later residents."

"But you love old things. Doesn't it make you sad to see them built over like this?" Renie was missing something, but she couldn't tell what. "Shouldn't it be . . . preserved or something?"

The monk nodded. "In an ideal House, we brethren would perhaps pick and choose where people could live. Yes, preserving the finest sites for study." He appeared to consider it for a moment. "But perhaps that in itself would lead to abuses—only the House itself is perfect, while men are fallible."

A little chastened, Renie could only lower her head and follow as Factum Quintus led them up the stairs, which were grossly narrowed by various flimsy constructions secured to the walls and the sweeping marble banisters. Only a few of these hovels were obviously occupied, but Renie could see lights and hear voices in the depths of the pile. It was something like a colony of coral, she thought. Or, to give it a more human shape, like one of the shantytowns or honeycombs of Durban.

People will find a place to live, she thought, *and that's all there is to it.*

The stairway dwellings became more infrequent as they climbed, and by the time they had mounted what Renie guessed to be three or four tall stories, the stairwell was pristine. The carvings now revealed were splendid, like something out of a Baroque church, although only a fraction were of things Renie could identify—human shapes, but other less familiar forms as well, and many objects whose models she could only guess.

"Who made this?" she asked.

Factum Quintus was clearly happy with the question. "Ah. Yes, well, I know there are many who believe this to be the actual work of the Builders themselves, but that is an old wives' tale. The House is full of such nonsense. The stairwell is ancient, of course—dating perhaps as far back as the First Crockery Wars or earlier—but certainly it was created within recorded history." He pointed at the balustrade. "See? There was gilt there once. Long gone, of course, long gone. Scavenged and melted down for coins or jewelry, no doubt. But the earliest building we know of happened long before such decoration. Ages ago. All stone it was, quarried blocks, joined without mortar—fascinating stuff . . ." And with that he was off again on another discursive ramble, rattling off facts about the House as Renie and the others trudged after him up the stairs.

The morning turned into afternoon. Although they eventually left the great staircase behind, it was not before they had climbed much farther than the few stories Factum Quintus had implied. Renie found both her spirits and her feet dragging. Only !Xabbu, with his quadrupedal advantage, seemed to find the climbing and walking easy.

Florimel still traveled with the air of one prepared to be sprung upon at any moment, although the feeling she and Renie shared had eased. T4b and Emily followed close behind her. The youthful pair had spent much of the day in quiet conversation. Emily's initial antipathy to the boy seemed to have eased considerably, and Renie wondered how long it would be until they were, in the old-fashioned phrase, "going steady," whatever that might mean in this bizarre universe, in this bizarre situation. She found herself missing Orlando and Fredericks, the other two teenagers, and wondered where they were, if they were even alive. It was a shame that Orlando, with the illness Fredericks had described, was missing out on this small chance for romance, since Emily certainly seemed ripe for some kind of relationship.

Her brother Stephen's small face and insolent grin suddenly came to her thoughts, bringing with it a pang of sorrow. Unless something changed dramatically, Stephen wouldn't even get the chance to be a teenager. He would never fall in love, never experience the joys and sorrows it brought, nor any of the other bittersweet pleasures of adulthood.

Renie could feel tears forming and overspilling. She reached up quickly to wipe them away before any of the others noticed.

"The Campanile of the Six Pigs is just a few stories above us now," Factum Quintus announced. He had halted the group in a great circular gallery whose wall was entirely covered by a single faded mural, figures being born out of clouds and flashing sun, striving and gesticulating in great muddled figure-groupings before being subsumed into the cloudstuff as the curving picture began again. "We should pause and rest, because there is one last climb. Very nice balusters coming, by the way." He looked around the group; his large eyes were wide, as though he still could not quite believe the company he was forced to keep. "And perhaps you would like to discuss strategy, hmmm? Something like that?" He spread his robe and sat, folding his long legs beneath him like a piece of campground furniture.

Not being able to talk to !Xabbu was beginning to chafe, and Renie particularly did not want to plan an assault on the Quan Li thing without his input. She looked at her friend helplessly. He stared back, his distress mutely obvious.

"One other matter," began Factum Quintus as the others slumped to the ancient carpet, which had been bleached to nearly nothing over the years by the sun that angled in through the gallery's high windows, so that its design was now little more than a pastel swirl. "Oh, mark that," he suddenly said, distracted by the base of the wall. "A figured plaster skirting. I have never seen that noted in any of the designs. And clearly added on later, too. I shall have quite a laugh at Factum Tertius . . ."

"You said 'one other thing'?" Renie tried to keep her voice pleasant, but her patience was rubbing thin. For one thing, she was worried about them chattering on like a picnic party when the Quan Li thing might be close by. "One other thing?" she prompted.

"Ah. Yes." The monk steepled his fingers on his knees. "I suspect that the ape can talk, and if it is staying silent for my benefit, there is no need."

Renie was stunned, but managed to say, "Baboon. He's a baboon. They're monkeys." What she really wanted to say was that !Xabbu was a man and a very fine one at that, but she had not lost all her caution. "Why do you think such a thing?"

"Monkey, ape . . ." Factum Quintus shrugged. "I have watched you passing significant glances all afternoon. It is like watching the two lovers whose tongues have been cut out in that play . . . what was it?" He frowned. "*Love's Larder Lessened,* something like that, an old Kitchen melodrama—very popular with the Market crowd . . ."

!Xabbu sat up on his haunches. "You are right, Brother," he announced. "What do you intend to do about it?"

"Do?" Factum Quintus seemed to think the question stranger than !Xabbu's human voice. "What should I do? Is it heretical for monkeys to speak where you come from? Is that why you have run away?" He smiled. There was more than a trace of self-satisfaction. "Because it is as clear as a glazier's dream that you are from some very distant part of the House. Hmmm. Perhaps even from one of the wild Preserves that legends tell of, the huge gardens wide as entire wings. Yes, indeed. Perhaps you have never even seen the interior of the House before, eh?"

Florimel stirred nervously. "What makes you say these things?"

"It is as clear as a . . . it is obvious. Things you say. Questions you ask. But it means nothing to me. Primoris has sent me to help you. There are many marvelous sights to see. If you were some demon creature from another House entirely, I would not care as long as you offered me no harm, and did not molest the wallpaper or chip the pilasters."

They had underestimated him, Renie realized. Although it made her nervous to see how easily they had been recognized as foreigners, it also gave her a little hope for their own quest as well. Brother Factum Quintus was not quite the idiot savant she had assumed; perhaps he would indeed help them find Martine, and even be some use getting her free again.

Silence fell in the wake of these revelations, but it did not last long. Factum Quintus stood, a process similar to a marionette being jerked upright. "I will explore the Campanile while you plan your strategies," he said.

"You?" Florimel asked suspiciously. "Why?"

"Because I am the only one your kidnapper does not know," he said. "Yes, that is right. I do not think I have ever met any of the dusting acolytes—we use more experienced hands in the crypts. Wouldn't trust the small ones among the parchments, do you see?" He shook his head; clearly it was a grim thought. "So if I happen to come across this . . . person you seek, I have a chance of being allowed to walk away. Everyone in the Library knows Brother Factum Quintus is mad for old structures. They're right, of course." His smile was crooked.

Renie found herself unexpectedly moved. "Be careful. He . . . he is small, but very, very dangerous—a killer. Several of us together could not hold him."

The monk drew himself up to his full gangly height. "I have no intention of scuffling with a bandit. I need these hands undamaged, to feel lacquer and test wood grain." He started toward the gallery's far doorway. "If I'm not back by the time the sun goes below the window . . . Well, trouble, I suppose."

"Just a moment," Florimel called after him, "you can't just . . ." But Factum Quintus was gone.

What must have been close to an hour spent imagining different scenarios and how they might respond to them did little to assuage the small company's mounting worry. The longer the monk was gone, the more it seemed certain they would have to go looking for him, and the more Renie felt they'd made a serious mistake not giving more consideration to the martial side of things.

They had no weapons and had not obtained any at the Library Market when they had the chance, although she had no idea what they would have used for money or barter. Still, just to throw themselves at Sweet William's murderer when he had nothing to lose except his place online, but they stood to lose everything, was too foolish for words.

They had just decided to break up some of the furniture they had seen back down one of the near corridors, so that they would at least have clubs, when they heard a sound at the door where Factum Quintus had vanished. A moment of heart-racing panic eased when the monk appeared in the doorway, but his expression was strange.

"The Campanile . . . it *is* occupied," he began.

"Is Martine there?" Renie demanded, clambering to her feet.

"Don't get up!" Factum Quintus lifted his hands. "Truly, it is better if you don't."

Florimel's voice held the same dull horror Renie was feeling. "What is it? What has happened to . . . ?"

The monk abruptly lunged forward, flinging himself to the ground in a ludicrous motion that Renie only realized had been involuntary when the other figures began crowding through the doorway after him. There were at least half a dozen, and Renie thought she could see more in the room just beyond. Their clothes were an assortment of coats and furs and scarves so filthy and ragged that they made the borrowed garments of Renie's troop look like dress uniforms. Most were men, but a few women stood with them, and every one of the strangers had at least one weapon and an unpleasantly gloating expression.

The tallest man, whose thick beard gave him even more of a piratical air than the others, stepped forward and leveled what looked like a flintlock pistol at Florimel, who was the closest person standing. He had a chest almost as wide as a door and not a single visible tooth. "Who are you?" she asked the bearded man coldly.

"Bandits," Factum Quintus groaned from his spot on the floor.

"And *you* are meat for Mother," the bearded man said, swiveling the pistol from Florimel to the other companions. His rasping laugh was echoed by his cohorts; many of them sounded even

less stable than he did. "It's festival night, y'see. The Mother of
Broken Glass needs blood and screams."

"*C*ODE Delphi. Start here.

"I cannot even whisper. These silent, subvocalized words will
only be retrievable by me, yet I think I will not live to collect
them. And if I do not, what will it matter? I will pass from the
world like a shadow. When this creature Dread kills me and my
heart stops, or however the virtual death will manifest itself in
reality, no one will find my body. Even should someone search
for me deep in the Black Mountains, they will never pass the security systems. My empty flesh will lie entombed forever. I thought
earlier that I had much in common with the person who had built
this vast house, but perhaps it is the Brotherhood's master, the
one my captor says appears only in the guise of a mummified
Egyptian god, who is my true soul mate. Lying for eternity in a
huge sepulchre of stone—that is what my unwillingness to enter
the world has gained me.

"These death thoughts will not leave me, and it is not only the
presence of my murderous captor sleeping in the chair only meters away, the stolen Quan Li sim even more deceptive in the false
innocence of slumber. No, death is even closer to me than that.

"What he brought back from his errand was a corpse. He trundled it through the door with all the casual good cheer of a sales-
man wrestling a heavy sample case into someone's living room.
Perhaps because that is what he has brought me—a sample.

"It is the body of a young woman which sits propped against
the wall beside me. I think it must be the girl of the Upper
Pantry Clerks who Sidri said had run away, but I cannot be
sure. The creature has . . . done things to the body, and for once
I am thankful that my senses are not visual. The outer silhouette alone, the altered shape of the thing as it sits with splayed
legs and sagging head, is enough to tell me I do not want to
know any more. The only saving grace is that it *does* sag—it
is apparently not the frozen sim of a murdered user, but the
corpse of a purely virtual person. Still, I have only to remember the sound of Zekiel and Sidri as they talked of their doomed,
overwhelming love for each other, or the pride in the voice of
Epistulus Tertius as he described his Library, to wonder what

would separate the horror and death-agony of one of these Puppets from that of an actual person. I am sure it would be just as terrible to witness, which is doubtless why my captor has turned a harmless Puppet with well-simulated fears and hopes into the mangled trophy he has dragged back, like a cat displaying its prey.

" 'Just cleaning up,' he told me as he set the thing in place and arranged the floppy limbs. He is a monster, truer to the black heart of evil than any invented ogre or dragon. The only thing that keeps hopelessness at bay is my desperation to see this creature punished. It is a slim hope, but what hope is not if the long run is taken into account? 'Happily ever after . . .' is only true if the story stops at that moment. But real stories never do—they end in sadness and infirmity and death, every one.

"Oh, God, I am so terrified. I cannot stop talking about what I feel coming. Without laying a finger on me since I have come here, he has tormented me until I feel like rats crawl beneath my clothes. I must . . . I must find the center again. All my life since I was plunged into darkness, I have sought the center—the place where a blind person knows what is what. It is the unknown and perhaps never-ending outskirts where fear takes hold.

"He wanted to know how we had followed him to the House simulation. I did not tell him our secret, of course—he can terrify me until I weep and beg, but I cannot let him turn me traitor. Instead I said that another gateway had opened in the same place as that through which he escaped and that we all went through. I could tell from body and voice that he did not entirely believe me, but the truth is so incredible—a baboon used a piece of string to show me how to summon the portal—that I have no fears he will guess it.

"With the mute example of his victim slumped against the wall, so close I could reach out and touch her with my foot if I wished, he produced the lighter from his pocket and reminded me that I was only useful if I could help him learn its secrets. I suspect he has examined the instrument in some detail already—perhaps even received advice of some kind, because for all his predator's intelligence he does not seem particularly schooled in technical matters—and much of what he asked at first seemed meant to test me, as though he would make sure I was giving him my honest best. Its shape and energy signature was so clear to my senses that I did not even need to face in its direction to know it was the same device on which I had spent so much time in the patchwork world—a thing of mostly locked potentialities, cryptic and powerful.

" 'One thing seems clear,' I told him. 'There are not many such objects on the network.'

"He leaned forward. 'Why do you say that?'

" 'Because there would not be a need for them. These Grail people have built the most phenomenal virtual network that can be conceived. Surely they have direct neural connections, and their interface with the network is such that they can make things happen simply with a thought or at most a word. The Brotherhood, at least here, must be gods of a sort.'

"The monster laughed at that, and told me something of his patron, the Lord of Life and Death also known as Felix Jongleur. Contempt fueled his description, and he spoke at surprising length. I sat silently so that I did not disrupt him—it is new information, and there is much in it to consider. At last he said, 'But you're right—I can't imagine someone like the Old Man needing something like this. So who would? Why?'

"I did my best to consider the problem—I might lie to him about how we arrived, but he had made it clear what would happen if I failed to give him answers to this question. 'It must be one of two things,' I said. 'It may be a guest key of some sort—an object given to a short-term visitor, if you see what I mean—or it may belong to someone who is more than a guest, but who spends little time in the network,' I explained. 'For most of the Grail Brotherhood, all the commands would surely be second nature, like whistling for a hovercab or tying one's shoes.' Despite my terror and disgust, I think I began to become a bit excited—I am someone who craves answers, and it is hard for me not to follow a trail once I have found it. For that brief moment, it was almost as though the monster and I were partners, researchers sharing a goal. 'This could well belong to someone who spends less time on the network than the others, but still has the right to access everything. Perhaps he or she also has many other codes and commands to remember in everyday life, and so it is simpler to keep the entire Otherland access system in one package, to be picked up online and then put away again.'

"The creature, who had told me that his master hated the name 'Dread'—and who in doing so had thus told me his name, which we had not known—nodded slowly. 'Either way,' he said, 'I'm betting that even if this device gets loaned to guests, the letter on it isn't just to make it look like an old-fashioned lighter—it's a monogram of the person who had it made.' His voice was still light, but I heard the hard, uncaring tone that was never far from the surface. 'Which should make it a lot easier to find out who it belongs to.'

" 'Why do you care about that?' I could not help asking. 'I thought you wanted to know how to use it.'

"He went still then. I cannot explain what my senses show me, but it was as though he turned cold all over—a change that may have been purely my own imagination as I realized I had gone too far. It was only the fact that I was still useful that saved me then, I know.

" 'Because I have plans,' he said at last. 'And they're none of your business, sweetness.' He stood up abruptly and walked to the corpse of the Upper Pantry Clerk, which had begun to slide down the wall. He put his fingers in her hair and jerked the body upright. 'You're not paying attention, *nuba*,' he said to the ca-daver—it might have been her name, or some word the system did not translate. 'Martine is working hard to prove how clever and useful she is—you should listen.' He turned, and I could feel the grin stretching his face, hear the way it changed his voice. 'Girls can be so foolish sometimes,' he said, and . . . and laughed.

"Horrified, my heart once more knocking at my ribs, I did my best to offer more observations about the lighter—wild specula-tion mostly, which in my panic I did my best to justify. At last he said, 'Well, I suppose you've earned a little rest, my sweet Martine. You've worked hard, and in fact you've earned more than that. You've earned another day!' He eased himself into the chair where he still remains. 'And Daddy needs some sleep, too. Don't get into any trouble.'

"Then he was gone, or at least the sim stopped moving. It is possible he has indeed gone offline to sleep or perform other tasks,

or else that he simply naps inside Quan Li's body like some ghastly
parasite.

"Can he have been the only one in the sim for all this time,
all these weeks? It is hard to imagine he would trust another, but
if not, how does he live? Where is his real, physical body?

"These questions have no answers now, and I doubt I will survive to discover the truth, but I have earned one more day—the
monster still needs me. I cannot help thinking of my own body,
tended by micromachines in my cavern home, separated from the
rest of the world by mountain stone as surely as I am separated
from it by the toils of the network. And what of the others, Renie,
!Xabbu and the rest—and what of their bodies? What of their
caretakers, Jeremiah and Renie's father, themselves imprisoned in
a mountain just as I am, but without even the solace of having
chosen it?

"It is odd to realize that I have friends. I have had coworkers
and lovers—sometimes one became the other—but just as the
mountain protects me, I have protected myself. Now that things
have changed, it no longer matters, because they are lost to me
and I to them.

"God, it seems, is fond of jokes. Or someone is, anyway.

"*Code Delphi*. End here."

IT didn't matter what he did, or where he went, or how thoroughly he pretended not to think about it. He was thinking about
it. He was waiting for it.

The netfeed news flickered on the tiny instrument console
screen, a ceaseless roll of disasters and near-disasters. Even isolated as he was, it was hard not to feel that things were getting
worse in the world outside: the news rumbled of mounting
Chinese-American tensions, and also of a feared mutation of the
Bukavu 4 virus, deadlier and faster-spreading. Smaller miseries
crowded in close behind, industrial disasters, terrorist attacks on
incomprehensible targets, the camera-drones transmitting pictures
of the latest carnage within seconds. The net throbbed with simple, everyday murders as well, with earthquakes and other natural
catastrophes, even a decommissioned satellite which had failed to
destruct, instead hitting a near-orbital passenger jet like a bomb
as it reentered the atmosphere, incinerating seven hundred eighty-

eight passengers and crew. All the commentators gravely commented how lucky it was that the plane was only half full.

Not all the netfeed was bad, of course. The media had the almost reflexive skill of self-perpetuation, knew as a bird knows it must migrate that they had to temper what would otherwise be an unremitting flow of bad news with pleasant stories—charity events, neighbors helping neighbors, criminals foiled by a quick-thinking bystander with a homemade stun-baton. The net also offered dramas, sports, education, and every kind of interactive environment imaginable. All in all, even with the primitive equipment which was all he had for access, it should have been enough to keep anyone occupied.

But all Jeremiah Dako was doing was waiting for the phone to ring.

He knew he should have found a sledgehammer and smashed the thing off its pillar days ago, but he had worried that somehow whoever or whatever was on the other end would know that something had changed, that the sudden alteration would signal life when Jeremiah and his charges needed secrecy. He had also had a less definable fear that even if he destroyed the ancient telephone, the ring would simply move to one of the base's other receivers. In a nightmare he had seen himself destroying all the equipment in the base, even shattering the controls to the V-tanks, only to find the chilling burr of the phone still coming out of empty air.

He woke sweating. And of course, the phone had been ringing again.

It was growing hard to concentrate on his work. Two helpless people were relying on him, but Jeremiah was consumed by a sound, a mere electronic signal. If it had only settled into a regular pattern he might have been able to cope, putting himself on the opposite side of the base, out of earshot, during the appointed times, but it was as randomly cruel as a snake crushed by a wheel but still alive. There might be nothing for hours, to the point where he thought he would be granted an entire day without hearing it, then it would start ringing again a few minutes later and continue on for hours, a dying creature emptying its venom into anything that ventured near.

It was making him quite mad. Jeremiah could feel it. It had been difficult enough to keep his spirits up after Joseph's defection, with only the V-tanked living dead for company, but with books and naps—something he had never had time for in the past—and a rationed dose of net, he had been getting by. But now this endlessly, crazily persistent device was all he thought about. Even when he was most occupied, caught up by something on the net to the point that he momentarily forgot where he was, a part of him was still tensely waiting, like a battered child who knows another assault will come. Then the shattering, clanging noise would return. His heart would beat and his head would pound, and he would all but hide beneath the desk until it stopped again.

But not today. Not ever again.

He was waiting for it, of course—he was always waiting for it these days—but this time he was going to do something. Perhaps it was dangerously foolish to answer it, but he could not take the miserable feeling of being probed at anymore, could not cope with the growing obsessive madness. And a thought had been gnawing at him until between that and the anticipatory fear of the sound, there was little room left for anything else.

What if he *had* to answer it to make it stop?

It had only been a casual idea at first. Perhaps it was some kind of automessager, programmed for random retries. Perhaps all that was needed—all that had been needed all along—was for someone to answer the call and either accept its message or demonstrate that the line was not equipped to carry information more complex than audible sound. Perhaps if he'd only picked it up the first time, that would also have been the last time.

He'd laughed when he'd thought that, a hollow wheeze of bitter amusement that felt like it might turn into something much uglier and more painful if he wasn't careful.

But maybe that's not all that will happen, another voice had whispered. *Perhaps it's some kind of hunter-killer gear, one of those things you see on the net, and it's just trying to get into the system here. Maybe one of those Grail people has sent it to kill the V-tanks.*

But if so, a more sensible inner voice suggested, *then why send it to an audio phone? And what harm can it do over audio lines, even if I pick it up?* Jeremiah didn't know much about technology, but he knew that someone couldn't send gear that would drip out of an old-fashioned phone and go crawling across the floor. He dimly remembered that Renie and the others had been talking about people like Renie's brother being struck down while using a low-cost station, but even so, that was a *station,* for God's sake, not an antique telephone!

The idea of answering, despite its attendant worries, had begun to grow over the last forty-eight hours. Every flinch-inducing ring of the phone bell had given the idea strength. He had actually meant to pick it up the last time it had rung, but the ring had sounded like the scream of a sick animal echoing in his ears, and his courage had failed. Now he was waiting again. He could do nothing else. He was waiting.

Jeremiah had dropped into a half-sleep, nodding over the V-tank console. When the phone rang, it was as though someone had poured a bucket of ice water on his head.

His heart was beating so swiftly he thought he might faint. *Idiot,* he told himself, trying to force his legs to lift him from the chair, *it's just a phone. You've been letting yourself be panicked by a twitch of electric current. No one knows anyone is here at all. Phones ring all the time. Just pick it up, damn you!*

He edged toward it as though afraid to startle the thing. The ring sounded for the third time.

Just pick it up. Reach out your hand. Pick it up.

His fingers closed on the rectangular handset just after the fourth ring. He knew if it rang again under his hand, it would feel like an electrical shock. He had to take it off the cradle.

It's just a phone, he told himself. *It's nothing to do with you.*

There's a spider on the other end, a voice whispered in his mind. *Forcing poison through the lines . . .*

Just a phone. A fluke. Pick it up . . .

He squeezed it and lifted it to his ear but said nothing. He felt himself swaying, and put out his free hand to the pillar. For a moment he heard only static, and relief began to climb through him. Then someone spoke.

It was a voice distorted, if not by mechanical means then by some incomprehensible malformation. It was the voice of a monster.

"*Who is this?*" it hissed. A second passed, then two. His mouth worked, but even if he had wanted to answer, he could not have. "*Is it Joseph Sulaweyo?*" Buzzing, crackling. It did not sound human at all. "*No, I know who you are. You are Jeremiah Dako.*"

The voice began to say something else, but Jeremiah could not hear it above the roaring in his ears. His fingers had turned lifeless as carved wood. The handset slipped from his grasp and clattered to the cement floor.

CHAPTER 15

Waiting For Exodus

NETFEED/ENTERTAINMENT: "Concrete" Revival
(visual: explosions)
*VO: The popular linear drama "Concrete Sun," which
finished its run only weeks ago, is already being turned into
a musical comedy. Writers Chaim Bendix and Jellifer
Spradlin are preparing a stage version for the opening of
the new theater at the Disney Gigaplex just being completed
in Monte Carlo.*
*(visual: Spradlin superimposed over footage of man
throwing a dog into a hovering helicopter)*
*SPRADLIN: "It's got everything—doctors in trouble, pets,
diseases—how could it not make a great musical?"*

FEELING more like a teenager than he had in some time, Orlando waited for the grown-ups to decide what they were all going to do. He was tired—exhausted—but too nervous to sleep and bored with sitting in one place. With Fredericks worriedly following, he set out on a slow journey around the Temple of Ra.

Unsurprisingly, the Wicked Tribe insisted on coming. After a negotiation punctured by many high-pitched shrieks of *"Not fair, not fair,"* Orlando wangled the concession that they remain perched on him or Fredericks at all times.

For any ordinary people, simply walking through the temple would have provoked continuous astonishment—even the architecture could only have been possible in a virtual world, the unsupported stone ceiling so high that it could have held Skywalker jets stacked like cordwood—but Orlando and Fredericks had been veterans of online fantasy worlds long before they had come to the Otherland network: they barely glanced at the magical carvings that flowed with life, the talking statues dispensing cryptic wisdom, or even the multiplicity of gods and goddesses, animal-headed and otherwise, who wandered the vast besieged temple, apparently as stifled and apprehensive as the two teenagers.

As the pair turned away from a fakir who had created twin serpents of red-and-blue fire, then set them to battling on the floor before a group of fascinated children, the monkeys began to complain loudly about not having any fun. The Wicked Tribe were still doing what they had been ordered to do, namely stay perched on Orlando and Fredericks and keep relatively quiet, but they were growing restless.

A large crowd had formed around Upaut's throne at the center of the room and Orlando found himself drawn toward it. A group of priests in white robes crouched before the wolf-god, already well into some ritual, chanting and knocking their heads against the stone flags; Upaut ignored them, gazing off into the air with the expression of a weary philosopher. Some of the siege victims crowded around the throne were calling out to him, demanding to know what was being done to protect them from the attack everyone seemed sure was coming, but the wolf had mastered the attitude of heavenly royalty if nothing else; their shouts went unanswered.

As Orlando led Fredericks to a spot between a bare-chested man with a child on his shoulders and a minor tutelary deity with the head of a goose, someone touched his arm. He turned to see Bonnie Mae Simpkins.

"Don't you say anything to that wolf," she quietly warned him. "He's got everyone in enough trouble. Goodness only knows what he'll do next."

"Who are those priests?" Orlando asked. "Are they his?"

"They belong to the temple, I suppose." She frowned at having to discuss heathen practices. "They're priests of Ra. You can tell by those gold disks. . . ."

"But if this is Ra's temple, where is Ra? Isn't he the . . . the big guy around here? Egypt, I mean?"

"Ra?" She shook her head. "He used to be, but he's pretty much retired now. Kind of like one of those Mafia things, I s'pose, where the old don isn't dead yet." She frowned. "Don't look at me funny, boy, I watch the net like anyone else. Osiris is the old fellow's grandson. He's the one who really runs things. They all give lip service to Ra, but all the old fellow does is sail through the sky in his boat, being the sun, or whatever the story is. But they still have to respect him, at least in public." Bonnie Mae's expression became something altogether grimmer. "That's why they'll wait until night before they do anything, when Ra is in the underworld. Why are you grinning? You think that what's going to happen here is funny?"

He didn't, not really, but the sudden notion of an Egyptian Mafia in linen skirts and heavy black wigs was hard to suppress. "Do you think they're going to attack tonight?"

"Nobody knows. But there are rumors that Osiris is coming back soon, and Tefy and Mewat sure won't want him to know about this—doesn't look good for them at all. So it seems likely. But we'll get you out of here before that, boy. Both of you."

"Yeah, but what about you and the others?" Fredericks asked.

Instead of answering, Bonnie Mae suddenly bent down and caught one of the Wicked Tribe, who had shinnied down Fredericks' robe to the floor. "I oughta find a tiny little stick to whup you with," she told the squirming primate before placing it gently back on Fredericks' shoulder.

"Didn't mean to!" it shrilled. "Fell!"

"Likely story." Bonnie Mae paused for a moment, then reached out and squeezed both boys' arms before heading back to the corner of the Temple where the Circle kept their camp.

"I don't like this waiting . . ." Fredericks began. A hoarse voice interrupted him.

"Ah! It is the gods from the river!" Upaut had spotted them, and was beckoning them toward his throne with long, hairy fingers. Orlando turned and caught Bonnie Mae's eye where she had stopped again; the look she sent back to him was full of helpless worry.

He and Fredericks stepped forward until they stood before the throne. Lifted by the high chair, Upaut's head towered almost three meters above them, but even at that distance Orlando could see that the wolf-god did not look good: his eyes were red-rimmed and his ceremonial wig sat slightly askew, partially covering one of his ears. He held a flail and a spear in his hands, and tapped the flail nervously against the side of the throne, a continuous and rather irritating beat. Fredericks stared at it as if hypnotized as the wolf leaned toward them, sharing a too-wide grin and carrion breath.

"Well, now!" His jollity sounded a bit hollow. "You have come to see me—and look! As I promised, I am leading heaven against those who have wronged me!"

Orlando nodded, trying to summon a smile.

"And you have come all the way here to join me—good, very good! It was the gift of your boat which brought me back from exile, after all. I shall be sure that your trust in me does not go unrewarded—your names will echo forever in the halls of heaven." He looked around the room. Perhaps reminded of his situation, he said in a slightly less emphatic voice, "You *have* come to join me, yes?"

Orlando and Fredericks exchanged a look, but there was little to be done. "We are here to defend the temple, yes," Orlando lied. "And help you in the fight against those two—against . . . against . . ."

"Taffy and Waymott," said Fredericks helpfully.

"Good, good," Upaut grinned, showing every tooth. He apparently cared little for the correct pronunciation of his enemies' names, or else had simply stopped listening to most of what was said to him. "Excellent. When the time is right, we shall burst from the temple like Grandfather Ra appearing on the eastern horizon and our enemies shall wail and throw themselves in the dust at our feet. Oh, they do not suspect our power! They do not know how mighty we are! They will weep and beg our forgiveness, but we are stern, and will punish dreadfully all who raised arms against us. We will reign a million years, and all the stars will chant our praises!

"Supreme one, beautiful in adornment,"

he abruptly sang, booming out the hymn to himself,

> *"Your armor bright as the barque of Ra*
> *Mighty in voice, Wepwawet! He Who Opens the Way,*
> *The master in the West,*
> *To whom all turn their faces—*
> *You are mighty in majesty . . . !"*

As the priests of Ra somewhat raggedly took up the tune—
most of them appearing a little less than wholehearted—Orlando
realized that the "we" Upaut claimed would do all those things
was Upaut himself, and that the wolf-god was as deranged as a
box of worms.

When the hymn had stuttered to a halt, and just before Upaut
could start the second verse he seemed eager to commence, Orlando hurriedly asked him, "Do you still have my sword?"

"Sword?" The huge yellow eyes squinted for a moment in
thought. "Sword. Hmmm. Yes, I think I may have put it somewhere—have a look behind the throne. Not really the weapon of
a king, you see. Oh, *armor bright as the barque of Ra*," he crooned
quietly to himself as his head nodded forward. His eyes closed
even farther, until they were only slits.

Orlando and Fredericks sidled around the throne until they
were out of his sight, then paused briefly to roll their own eyes
in a silently shared opinion of the wolf-god. They quickly discovered Orlando's sword, or more accurately Thargor's sword,
in an unpleasant pile of chicken bones and bits of hardened candle wax which had been swept behind the throne. Orlando lifted
it up and sighted along the blade. Except for a few notches and
dings that had not been there before, it was substantially unharmed, the same sword which Thargor had carried in his earliest adventures as a barbarian immigrant in the decadent south of
the Middle Country.

As they started back toward the Circle's encampment in a wide
swing meant to keep as much distance between themselves and
the throne as possible, the monkeys (who had been uncharacteristically silent during the audience with Upaut) began to dance on

Orlando's shoulders. Fredericks' own passengers immediately leaped across to join them.

> *"Mighty in smell, Wolfman!"*

they sang, growling an imitation of Upaut's voice between arpeggios of giggles,

> *"He Who Gets In the Way,*
> *To whom all turn their backs—*
> *You are mighty in stupidity . . . !"*

Orlando and Fredericks tried to shush them, but the monkeys had been forced to keep still too long. Orlando hurried his steps; as he glanced back, he was relieved to see that Upaut seemed completely sunk in his own thoughts, oblivious even to the priests at his feet. The wolf-god's long muzzle tilted slowly up and down as though he were just now scenting something that had already vanished.

An extremely large creature was stretched near the bronze front doors of the temple, the only thing in sight that seemed in scale with the massive portal. Even if the recumbent figure had not been so huge, Orlando could not have helped noticing it, since it occupied the middle of a large clear space—an oddity in itself with the temple so crowded. At first he thought it was Dua, the lavender giant who had met them on their way in, but this sphinx's skin was faintly orange, the color of sunset on stone. Saf, as his brother had named him, was no less impressive than his twin, the statuesque human head topping a leonine body the size of a small bus. The creature's eyes were closed, but as Orlando and Fredericks skirted the edge of the crowd, trying to work their way through the tangle of brown bodies, its nostrils flared; a moment later the dark eyes opened and fixed on them. Although the sphinx watched them without expression, and did not move even a paw in their direction, they still hurried to put several layers of the crowd between themselves and that serene but terrifying gaze.

Orlando had to stop for a moment and catch his breath. He

decided he would rather battle six red gryphons than either one of the Temple of Ra's guardians.

Fredericks might have been reading his thoughts. "Those things are a major shiver."

"Pah!" someone else said. "It's all shit—make-believe for idiots."

It took a moment before Orlando recognized the young man who had been introduced to them earlier as Vasily. Other than the slightly rakish way he had combed back his sim's dark hair and his cock-of-the-walk stance, his Egyptian sim looked like many others in the great room.

"What is?"

"This." Vasily made a broad gesture encompassing all of Egypt, or perhaps even the whole of the network. He fell in beside Orlando and Fredericks as they started to walk again. "This old rubbish. Pharaohs, temples, pyramids. Shit and Godlessness."

Looking around at the profusion of animal-headed deities, Orlando thought that godlessness was hardly the problem—if anything, the place had rather an excess of them—but he said nothing: there was something about the young man that made him nervous. Fredericks was looking at the newcomer with interest, though, and Orlando suddenly felt a pang of jealousy. "What would *you* do with a network like this?" he asked, in part to cover his own confusion.

Vasily scowled, then reached up to capture one of the Wicked Tribe, who had flown near his head on a reconnaissance mission. He examined the little monkey for a moment, then flicked it away in a dismissive manner that made Orlando angry. "Something better than this," the Russian youth said as the spurned monkey swooped back to Fredericks' shoulder, cursing shrilly and indignantly in a language Orlando did not recognize. "Something that would show the true glory of our Lord, not this shit. Egypt is dirt—it's a waste of space." His frown abruptly relaxed as a woman with the head of a bird walked past, talking anxiously to a group of white-robed priests. "Why does a stork stand on one leg?"

Orlando was caught by surprise. "Huh?"

"It's a joke, stupid. Why does a stork stand on one leg?" Vasily wiggled his fingers impatiently. "Give up? Because if he lifted it off the ground, he'd fall down!" He snorted with laughter.

Fredericks laughed, too, which set off another little depth charge of jealousy inside Orlando, but it was alleviated slightly when Fredericks leaned over and whispered in Orlando's ear, "He's so *scanny!*"

Vasily scooped up a small stone and began tossing it high in the air and catching it, first in one hand, then the other; after a while he began catching it behind his back, which required him to stop in the middle of the temple floor, forcing others to walk around him. Orlando did not stop to wait for him, and after a moment Fredericks followed, but it did not seem to matter much to Vasily, who was totally absorbed in his game. Orlando could not help wondering how old Vasily really was and what kind of crimes he'd been involved in: he'd heard that some of the Russian gangs used kids as young as ten or eleven.

Bonnie Mae Simpkins was waiting for them with the little-girl sim of the woman named Kimi. She asked if they'd seen Vasily.

"Over there." Orlando cocked a thumb. "He's playing with a rock."

Mrs. Simpkins knitted her formidable brow. "I suppose I'll have to get after him, then—the men wanted him to help. They want you boys, too, both of you."

"Help where?"

"At the gateway. Nandi's trying to find out if this idea of his works." She pointed down the wall to the far corner. "You go along there, where that door is. They're waiting for you. But not you, monkeys," she told the Wicked Tribe, who flapped and chattered their protests. "You can just come with me and stay out of the way." Her fierce look drew even the most reluctant monkeys toward her like a magnet. With the tiny yellow creatures settled on her shoulders, she started away toward Vasily, then paused. "You all be careful, now," she told Orlando seriously.

"I really don't have a good feeling about any of this, Gardiner," Fredericks whispered when the others had vanished into the crowd. "It's going to be dark soon. You *know* something bad's going to happen then, don't you?"

Orlando could only shrug.

Both the doorway in the corner of the great chamber and the small room behind it were deep in shadow as Orlando and Fredericks stepped through, but not for long. Something flickered and then began to glow beyond another door on the room's far side, drawing the pair on. In the farther room, Nandi Paradivash and the old man called Mr. Pingalap stood bathed in the golden light of a gateway. For a moment Orlando's heart rose, but as he and Fredericks hurried forward Nandi lifted a warning hand.

"Don't come too close! I hope you left the monkeys in some other place. We are waiting to see if anything is going to come through."

They stopped. All four stood silently until the gateway glimmered and then died, leaving only a small oil lamp to illuminate the windowless stone room.

"You let it close . . . !" Orlando protested.

"Quiet, please." Nandi raised his hand, then turned to Pingalap. "How long?"

The old man shook his head. "About thirty seconds, I would guess."

"We're trying to gauge the length of what we call the flare," Nandi explained, "—how long the gate will stay open without people passing through it—not unlike the sensor in an elevator, do you see?" He showed a little smile. "More importantly, though, we are also trying to determine how long before a randomized gateway shifts its connection to a new simulation—other people's experiences suggest it cycles almost directly after each use. We are nearing our answers, but there is still one important experiment left to perform. We can open a gateway here any time we want—the problem is, unless my guess about the larger cycle is correct, we can't know what simulation it's opening up *to*." He turned back to his companion. "Are you ready, sir?"

Mr. Pingalap nodded, then—to the surprise and embarrassment of both Fredericks and Orlando—stripped off his linen garment, which was as long as a bedsheet and only slightly narrower. He stood naked while Nandi tore the garment in half and knotted the two ends together, then the old man took the improvised rope and tied it around his waist.

Seeing the astonishment of the onlookers, Nandi smiled. "Mr. Pingalap is going to go through, but if he can't come back, what he discovers will do us little good."

"But there must be rope around here somewhere . . ." said Fredericks, who was trying hard not to stare at the old man's well-simulated and quite wrinkly nakedness.

"But do you see," Pingalap said a little crossly, "rope from this simulation will not exist in the next, whereas the clothes I wear will travel in some form." He smiled as if to make up for his bad temper. His few remaining teeth were an interesting variety of colors, none of which was white.

"I get it," Fredericks said.

"But I thought you said you knew which place the gateway was going to open to," Orlando protested. His dream of getting out and getting on with this exhausting adventure while he still had the strength suddenly seemed foolish.

"I think I do," said Nandi calmly. "But until we check, I won't know what part of the cycle we're in, so I won't know which of my guesses about what's coming next I am testing. Are you quite ready, Mr. Pingalap?"

The old man nodded and shuffled to the center of the room where the lamplight glinted on a solar disk carved across the floor. The trailing length of linen cloth looked bizarrely like a bride's veil. Nandi followed him to the edge of of the carving, then turned to the teenagers.

"Will you two take the end and hold it? I had planned that Vasily would help, but it seems he has wandered away."

"Wouldn't it be better if we tied it around us, too?" Orlando asked.

"Better in terms of security, but it would give him no room to move. He may have to take a few steps to be able to see anything useful. Just hold please, and pull him back when he gives two sharp tugs."

"Two sharp tugs!" echoed Mr. Pingalap cheerfully. He saw how Fredericks and Orlando averted their eyes; his breathy chortle as he gestured to his withered flesh was so high-pitched that it could have come from one of the Wicked Tribe. "The body itself is illusion—and this is not even a real body!"

Orlando did not explain that their reaction was as much aesthetic as modest. Nandi Paradivash made a few broad signals with his hand and a shimmering golden rectangle opened atop the solar disk. Mr. Pingalap stepped through, and Nandi quietly began to count.

"Hold tight," he cautioned between numbers. "We do not know what he will find."

Orlando adjusted his grip, but the length of cloth hung limp.

"Where is it you two wish to go, by the way?" Nandi asked. "If we are unlucky, Pingalap is at your destination right this moment and we will have to wait for the gateway to cycle through again. But out of all the possible simulations, it does not seem likely yours would be the first we try."

Orlando had a moment of sudden blankness. Fredericks nudged him and whispered, *"Walls."*

"Right. Priam's Walls—that's what the lady in the Freezer told us."

Nandi frowned, more in distraction than at Orlando's words, but a moment later he turned and said, "Priam's Walls? Troy?"

Orlando shrugged, uncertain.

"That is a strange coincidence," said Nandi. "No, I doubt it is coincidence . . ."

He was interrupted by Mr. Pingalap's sudden appearance in the gateway. Looking no worse for wear—but no better either, Orlando thought—the old man shuffled out of the rectangle of fiery light. As he began to speak, the gate flickered behind him, then vanished.

"It was like the Potala," he reported, "—a huge palace in the highest mountains. But it was not the Potala. It looked too . . . too . . ."

"Too Western?" Nandi asked. "That is likely Shangri-La, then." He looked down at the handful of tiles on which he had scribbled his notes. "Let us try again and see what we find."

Another gateway was summoned. As it smoldered into being, Orlando heard a loud wash of sound from the temple's great chamber, voices raised in alarm, people running. Mr. Pingalap vanished into the golden glow and the length of cloth abruptly snapped tight. Orlando was jerked forward; behind him, he could feel Fredericks stumble as he fought for balance.

"Hang on!" Orlando called as he was dragged nearer to the gateway. "Pull!"

"Don't pull him out," Nandi warned. "He will let us know— he is counting also, and he must have time to make observations."

"Observations?" Orlando shouted. "Something's trying to swallow him!"

Nandi reached out to help steady them. A moment later, Orlando was surrounded by a distracting cloud of yellow—the Wicked Tribe, swarming like bees. By the time Nandi had reached twenty in his slow count, Orlando felt what he thought was something jerking on the cloth rope through the steady pull. He threw all his Thargor-weight against it and yanked hard, half-expecting to drag some terrible monster through the gateway who had gulped the old man like a fishhook, but instead the venerable Pingalap popped out of the golden rectangle as suddenly as a cork from a bottle. The countervailing pressure gone, Orlando and Fredericks tumbled backward, Orlando landing on top of his friend.

The Wicked Tribe whirled delightedly above them like stars over a cartoon head injury. "Again!" they squealed. "Pull, pull, fall down! Again!"

"It was some sort of wind tunnel," Mr. Pingalap gasped. He was crouching as though he had just finished a marathon, his wispy hair sticking straight up and an expression of bliss on his face. "A canyon, in truth, but the wind caught me and dragged me right off the edge. I am glad you had me anchored!"

Nandi frowned at his calculations. "It should have been Prester John's African kingdom—could it have been that?"

The old man slapped his bony knees and straightened up. "I don't know. I saw nothing except rocks and trees.—I was busy flying like a kite at the end of a string."

"We'll have to do it again," Nandi said.

The Tribe had finally begun to settle. "What that shiny thing was?" Zunni asked, perching on Orlando's nose so that she was only a banana-colored blur. "Why door there, then no door?"

Orlando realized that the Tribe had never seen one of the gateways, and as he levered himself back upright, wondered again how the children had gone straight to this Egyptian simulation and been imprisoned, while he and Fredericks and everyone else connected through the Blue Dog Anchorite man had wound up in Bolivar Atasco's Temilun.

How . . . or why . . . ?

The thought was interrupted. Bonnie Mae Simpkins entered the chamber, Kimi and sullen Vasily in tow. "There's something happening at the front door," Bonnie Mae told Nandi worriedly. "The soldiers outside are all shifting around, and that big sphinx thing—what's his name, Saf?—is standing up now. He's not saying anything, but he's standing there like he's waiting. I don't like it." She saw the monkeys draped across Orlando and her eyes narrowed. "There you little monsters are. I'm going to put you rascals in a sack."

"Run away, run away!" the monkeys squealed, rising in a yellow cyclone and rushing past her, through the antechamber and back out into the temple's great hall.

"This is not *funny!*" Bonnie Mae shouted after them. "You all come back here!" For the first time since Orlando had met her she sounded genuinely frightened, but the monkeys had managed to get out of earshot quickly enough to escape the compelling force of her voice. "They're just kids—they don't understand this is dangerous," she said helplessly. "Vasily, Kimi, come help me catch them."

The two women hurried out, but Vasily stopped at the far door, gazing into the main chamber. "The fighting will start soon," he called back. The dreamy way he said it made it sound like he couldn't wait.

"All the more reason to help them find those children," Nandi shouted to him. "We have no time for distraction here." He turned and patted Mr. Pingalap on the shoulder. "Forward, please." As Orlando and Fredericks took up positions once more, wrapping the cloth around their fists for a better grip, the slender man summoned up another gateway. "Step through!"

As the naked old man disappeared into the light, Nandi told Orlando, "It is most strange you should be bound for Troy. I met a man who was also going there, or at least to another part of the same simulation. A very strange man indeed. Do you know someone named Paul . . . what was it?" He fingered his lip, trying to remember but clearly distracted by what was going on around him. "Brummond?"

Orlando shook his head. He looked to Fredericks, but his friend only shrugged: it was apparently not a name Orlando had missed during one of his illnesses.

A few seconds later Mr. Pingalap returned, bearing news of what Nandi seemed to think was the Prester John simulation he had mentioned earlier. He brightened a little. "I may have the pattern correctly now—it is a bit wider oscillation than I had guessed, that is all. The next one should be Kalevala, and then a place that I have never visited, but which my informants call the Shadow Country—apparently it is almost completely dark all the time." He frowned and shuffled his tiles full of calculations. "Even if we cycle through as fast as we can, and I am correct about everything else, it will take us almost an hour before we can open the gateway to Troy."

As the old man ran out his lifeline and stepped through the newest gateway like a very scrawny astronaut going for a space walk, Nandi suddenly said, "No, it was not Brummond—that was the first name he gave, but not his true name. I should have remembered, but my mind is very full just now. It was Jonas—Paul Jonas."

Orlando almost let go of Mr. Pingalap's rope. "Jonas! That's the one Sellars told us to look for!" He turned to Fredericks. "Wasn't that it? Jonas?"

Fredericks nodded. "Sellars said Jonas was a prisoner of the Brotherhood. That he helped him escape, I think."

Two jerks on the cloth rope reminded them of their duties; they reeled in Mr. Pingalap, who reported that he had seen acres of snowy forest and men in carts pulled by huge reindeer, which report pleased Nandi. "Kalevala, that's good." His expression darkened as he turned back to Orlando and Fredericks. "So the man I met was freed by your mysterious Sellars? Jonas told me he was being pursued by the Brotherhood, but he had no idea why. Did Sellars tell you why the Brotherhood imprisoned this man?"

"Sellars didn't tell us *fenfen*, really," Orlando said. "Didn't have time—somebody killed Atasco in the real world, and we all had to run."

Nandi's response was swallowed by a huge echoing *clang* that shook the floor and made them all jump. Outside the small chamber voices rose in screams and cries of fear.

"It begins." Nandi's face was grim. "That is bad. We have even less time than I had hoped."

Vasily bolted into the gateway room, feverish with panic and excitement. "They are breaking down the door! It is war! The Brotherhood is coming!"

"It is not the Brotherhood." There was an edge of quiet anger in Nandi's voice. "It is something happening just in this simulation and most of the participants are Puppets. Just help find those children. You will do the Circle no good if you get yourself killed."

Vasily did not seem to hear him. "They are coming! But the Lord has seen them, seen all the blasphemy, and there will be blood!" A series of ringing impacts filtered in from the great chamber, like someone striking a huge gong. Vasily darted back out into the main part of the temple.

Nandi shut his eyes for a moment; when he opened them, he wore a look of studied calm. "We work with the tools we have." He turned to Mr. Pingalap. "I think we must try one more time to confirm that I have not misunderstood some larger pattern, then we will start opening and closing gateways as fast as possible."

The old man sketched a little bow. He stepped into the newly opened gateway as a violent, grinding screech pierced the air, followed a moment later by a terrible crash that shook the very floorstones. After a moment's silence the screaming began again.

"It sounds like the temple doors have been thrown down," said Nandi. He saw Orlando's glance dart toward the door of the chamber. "Keep your grip," he cautioned. "We do not know for certain what is happening out there, but Mr. Pingalap needs you here."

"But why don't we just go through one of these things?" Fredericks pleaded. "We can do all this testing somewhere else, can't we?"

Nandi paused in his count. "It is not so simple. . . ."

"What do you mean?" Orlando was tired of being treated like a child. "Should we just wait here until they come and kill us? All these gateways open somewhere!"

"Yes," Nandi snapped, "and many of them to somewhere far worse than this." He stared hard at Orlando, and that momentary fierceness made him someone quite different—a warrior, a crusader. "You young people do not know what is in my heart—what I must consider. Many of the simulations are in deadly chaos and most of these gateways lead to worlds that now have only one working gate. If I take us to one of those worlds and that gateway shuts off also, then what? Even if we survive, we will have lost the fight!" He reached for some kind of equilibrium and found it. "This is what I was brought here to do," he said more softly. "I did not think I would have to solve such critical problems so fast, but it is my task and I will do it."

He was interrupted as Mr. Pingalap hurried back through the gateway. "I do not like that place," the old man announced, "but I think it is your Shadow Country—dark, it was very dark. Some faint lights, and things moving—large things, I think." He wrapped his bony arms across his thin chest.

"Then we must start cycling as fast as we can," Nandi declared. "You boys must go find Mrs. Simpkins and the others. Convince them to come back now. Be assured that if I can think of a place to take them all, I will. There is no point in unnecessary sacrifice—this is not our struggle anymore."

"Convince them?" Orlando was struggling to understand, but it was hard to be patient. "Can't you just order them or something?"

"If I could order them, our fellowship would not be a Circle." Nandi's face grew all too human for a moment, tired and frightened, but he managed a weak smile. "This is our great task, you see. Everyone has their own part to play. And this is my portion of that task." He turned and made the hand gestures to summon a new gateway.

The temple had gone strangely quiet.

Orlando and Fredericks moved cautiously out of Nandi's gateway chamber and across the darkened antechamber beside it until they stood in the doorway. They knew they had to find the other members of the Circle, but it was impossible to ignore what was going on at the far end of the enormous hall.

The patch of sky visible where the bronze doors had once loomed was night-dark, but the front of the chamber was now illuminated by hundreds of torches held by soldiers who filled the temple porch, rank upon rank. They were not the only ones who had come calling. A phalanx of weird, leathery men stood just inside the ruined doors, all of them shiny bald and covered in ill-fitting gray skin. Each wore a thick piece of plated armor around his torso from neck to groin that seemed somehow part of his body; each held a ponderous mallet, a thick handle of wood with a stone head. The temple's besieged inhabitants had retreated from the front of the temple until they were squeezed in a mass against the walls opposite the shattered doorway. Only the massive sphinx Saf stood before the invaders, but by himself he had created a standoff.

"So the fear of Osiris has proved greater than respect for Grandfather Ra," said a harsh voice near Orlando's knee. The ugly little domestic god Bes clambered up onto a ceremonial stand beside him, clearing away a lovely vase by toppling it to the floor before seating himself. In the nearly silent temple, even the sound of the clay shattering sent panic rippling through the crowd, but the besiegers and the sphinx remained as motionless as a wall painting. "See—they have brought the creatures of night into the temple of the sun." Bes pointed to the silent, leathery figures in the doorway. "Tortoise-men! I had thought them all slaughtered by Set in the red desert long ago. But now Tefy and Mewat have set them loose in the heart of Abydos—they have cast down the very doors of Ra's house." He shook his head, but the expression on his homely face seemed almost as intrigued as appalled. "What times these are!"

The tableau was so charged with potential violence that Orlando could not take his eyes off it. He reached for Fredericks' arm and found his friend almost vibrating with tension. "What . . . ?" Orlando began, but never finished the question.

The wall of soldiers parted, the torchbearers falling back into a line on either side until they had created a path of red-lit shadows leading up to the doorframe and its gigantic broken hinges. Two figures walked slowly up that path toward the temple. Something about them seized at Orlando's heart: as fearsome as were the soldiers and the stiffly silent tortoise-men, that dread was nothing compared to the sudden weight of illness and doom he felt at the sight of the two mismatched shapes. Many of the temple's defenders seemed to feel it, too, moaning and struggling to move even farther back, but they were pinned by the chamber's far wall and there was no room left for retreat. A woman lost her balance, screamed shrilly, and was sucked down into the close-packed crowd as though by quicksand. As she vanished beneath the crush of legs, the temple fell nearly silent once more.

"Orlando," said Fredericks in the breathy voice of someone

trying to wake up from a bad dream, "Orlando, we . . . we have
to . . ."

The two figures stepped through the doorway. One was so
grotesquely fat it seemed a miracle he could stand unaided, let
alone move so gracefully. A hood around his head at first seemed
to be a monk's cowl, but was actually part of his skin; the rest
of his massive body was clothed only in a loincloth, making it
easy to see the oily scales that covered him, black, blue, and gray,
patchy with disease. A long swollen tail dragged behind the cobra-
man like dead flesh.

The shape beside was only slightly less horrific, a tall but
stooped figure with the protruding chest of a bird, and with feet
that might have been human except that the toes stretched and
curled into long talons. But if the rest of the vulture-man was just
ugly, it was his face that was truly ghastly: his elaborate hooked
beak might have once been a human face before something had
melted flesh and bone and stretched the nose and jaw outward
like putty. But where either human or bird would have eyes, the
creature had only malformed flesh and empty sockets.

"Stop," the sphinx rumbled in a voice so deep that the soldiers all took a step back. Even the tortoise-men swayed a little,
like reeds in a stiff breeze.

The vulture-thing smiled slowly, showing teeth at the hinge of
his beak. "Ah, yes, the guardian known as Yesterday," he said in
a bizarrely sweet voice. "How appropriate, loyal Saf, since you
clearly fail to understand how things have changed."

"The Temple of Ra is the holy of holies, Tefy," the guardian
replied. To Orlando at that moment, watching from the doorway,
the sphinx's great bulk seemed the one thing holding the universe
in place. "That does not change. That will never change. You and
Mewat have overstepped your authority by assaulting the house
of the Highest. Turn and flee this moment, and perhaps your master Osiris will intercede for you with his grandfather. If you stay,
you will be destroyed."

Cobra-man Mewat laughed, a hoarse wheeze, and a glint appeared in the darkness of Tefy's empty sockets. "That might be,
Saf," said the vulture-man. "You and your brother are old and
powerful, and we are but young godlings, however high in our
Lord's favor—but we are not fools enough to pit ourselves against

you." He lifted his hands, the fingers long and thin as spider's legs, and clapped them together. The sound was picked up and echoed by the tortoise-men, who beat fists against bellies to make their shells echo to a slow drumbeat.

Saf crouched a little lower, as though preparing to spring. Muscles writhed like river current beneath his stony skin. The terrified crowd groaned and lurched backward yet again, surging against the chamber wall like a wave against a breakwater. People caught in the crush screamed for help, dull, muffled sounds that did not last long. "If you will not stand against me, carrion-eater, then who shall?" Saf growled. "I will crush your tortoise-men like Bast in a nest of rats."

"No doubt," said Tefy calmly. "No doubt." He began to back toward the doorway. Mewat, after showing his mouthful of crooked fangs in a sneer, followed him.

"They're going!" Fredericks exulted in a strangled half-whisper. Orlando, too, was feeling vastly relieved at the retreat of vulture and cobra until three tall figures stepped past the pair and through the temple doors.

"Oh, this impacts," Orlando murmured. "This impacts *plus*."

The three gods—and there was no doubt they were gods: larger than mere humans, they moved with the grace of dancers and the swagger of outlaw bikers—arrayed themselves before Saf, who rose to sit on his hindquarters, his head towering above everything except the temple roof. The drumming of the tortoise-men grew louder.

"Interesting," Bes said from his seat atop the dais, as calm as if he were watching an arm-wrestling match in a corner bar. "I wonder what Tefy and Mewat gave away to bring in the war gods."

"War gods?" But Orlando did not really need confirmation—one had only to look at the leader, a huge, bull-headed creature, to know it was true. Long and sharp as it was, the bull-man's curved sword was less frightening than were his naked arms, so thick with muscle he looked as though he could have twisted the temple doors off their hinges by himself. The other two attackers, a man and a woman, appeared no less formidable. The male god had gazelle horns jutting from his head; flickers of lightning played up and down his arms and crackled around the head of his war club. The goddess was the tallest of the three, dressed in a pantherskin and deftly balancing in one hand a spear that could skewer a dozen men at once. Orlando suddenly realized why Bes had treated their own claim of being gods of war with such droll contempt.

"Mont I can understand," the dwarf god went on. "He's the bull fellow, and he's got problems at home—wife running around with Amon like a bitch in heat, people talking behind his back. But Anth and Reshpu? Of course, she always likes a fight, and Reshpu's a new god—perhaps he's trying to make a name for himself. The harpers would sing forever of someone mighty enough to kill one of the great sphinxes."

"Can't anyone stop them?" Orlando demanded. The crowd was groaning like a wounded animal, trapped, terrified, mesmerized. The war gods feinted at the sphinx and the watchers exclaimed in terror. In a blinding instant, a bolt from Reshpu's hand crackled upward toward the ceiling, then dissipated with a snap of burning air. "Why don't you do something?"

"Me?" Bes shook his oversized head. "I was going to go home, but it's too late now. What I'm going to do instead is stay out from underfoot while the bigger children play." He slipped down from the stand, then hurried away along the wall, his bandy legs carrying him deceptively quickly.

"Where are you going?" Orlando screamed after the little god.

"One of the excellent things about my size," Bes called over his shoulder, "is that there are many fine hiding places available to me, O godlet from beyond the Great Green. Urns are my specialty." He vanished into the shadows at a trot.

A bellow of anger followed by another electrical flare dragged Orlando's attention back to the battle at the front door. Anth and Reshpu had attacked simultaneously; the goddess had sunk her spear into Saf's mountainous flank before dancing back, but the gazelle-horned god had not been so lucky and was caught squirming beneath the sphinx's paw. Lightning flared again; Saf pulled back his scorched claws, allowing Reshpu to crawl out of reach. Mont charged in, swinging his scimitar at the sphinx's face before dodging a swiping blow which would have hurled him against the wall. His sword bit at Saf's neck. No blood followed when Mont snatched the blade free, but the sphinx let out a rumbling cry of pain that made the air pulse. The tortoise-men beat their chests until it became a continuous thunder.

"They're going to kill him!" Fredericks shouted over the tumult. "We have to get out of here!"

"We have to find Bonnie Mae." Heart pounding, Orlando scanned for the others, but in the lamplight it was a nearly impossible task. The crowd at their end of the room was less tangled and compacted, but it was still a thicket of brown Egyptian faces and bodies and pale clothing, a chaotic mass of humans and petty gods struggling not to be crushed, trying to flee somewhere in a temple with few such places left.

Orlando grasped Fredericks by the arm and had just pulled his friend a few steps out onto the floor of the great chamber when a black cloud rushed through the demolished doorway. For a moment Orlando thought that Tefy and Mewat were pouring in poisoned smoke, and he felt his already racing heart falter.

I'm too tired for this . . . was all he could think.

"Bats!" someone shrieked, but they were only half right. The cloud was full of darting black shadows, but something else flew there, too—thousands of terrible pale serpents with translucent dragonfly wings, hissing like steam.

What had already been madness now became something else entirely. Ragged screams filled the air. The temple, already shadowy, became darker still as the cloud of flying things blocked the light from the wall torches. Shrieking people were running everywhere with no sanity or plan, as though trapped in a burning building; others had already been swarmed by bats and flying snakes and lay writhing on the floor covered with crawling, biting things.

A shape that might have been a woman barreled into Orlando from the side and knocked him sprawling before disappearing into the chaos. As he stood up, one of the besieging soldiers appeared before him, aiming at his stomach with a short stabbing-sword; Orlando had only a moment to react. Off-balance and unable to jump back, he fell forward instead, twisting so that the thrust only sliced the skin of his chest. He had almost forgotten his own sword, clutched in his hand so long the grip was sweaty, but his hard-won fighter's reflexes led him to an unthinking backhand blow into the soldier's unprotected legs behind the knee. The man screamed and fell forward. Orlando took the soldier's head off with a two-handed swipe, then batted away the sudden attack of a winged thing with the flat of his blade.

Before he could locate Fredericks, two other soldiers loomed out of the shadows. Loyalty tugged at them when they saw their comrade dead at Orlando's feet, but their faces were as disoriented as most of the others Orlando had seen, and after a moment they slipped back into the melee. Even Tefy and Mewat's troops seemed overwhelmed by the ghastly scene.

As Orlando waded into the crowd, he saw several people screaming on their backs with winged snakes wrapped around their heads, striking again and again at their faces. One bloodily wounded man crawled toward Orlando, his hand raised in a plea for help, but the two soldiers Orlando had seen earlier grabbed at the man's torn garment and pulled him back, stabbing his sides. Before Orlando could even react, another red-spattered body landed at his feet, nearly headless. The tortoise-man who had just killed the mother with its ugly stone-headed club now backed a screaming boy-child against the wall and raised the dripping cudgel once more. The leathery creature's face was expressionless, the eyes half-lidded, as though it could find scant interest in the nightmare scene.

Tired as he was, Orlando could not stand by while such a horror took place. He found his balance and took a loping stride toward the silent killer, bringing the broadsword around in a sweeping two-handed blow meant to separate bald head from lumpy body. At the last instant the creature saw him; as it straightened and turned his stroke caromed off the top of its shell, and although the tip of his blade struck the creature's face, smashing the eye socket and tearing away tissue and bone, the tortoise-man did not even stagger. Worse still, it made no sound despite the terrible wound, but turned slowly to face him.

Every muscle in the sagging Thargor-body ached; Orlando had to struggle to keep his trembling legs straight beneath him as he squared off against this newest adversary. Had he been in the Middle Country, the sagging-skinned monster would not have frightened him, but there was something in the thing's ruined face and remaining yellow eye that told him it had no sense of self-preservation—it would try to kill him even with all its limbs severed from its body—and he knew if he failed, he would not be bounced back to the real world. Also, every second that passed increased the chances that he would lose Fredericks and the others forever.

He gathered his strength then lunged forward. As he had feared, the point of his blade scraped then bounced off the shell covering the creature's midsection. Its return stroke was slow, but not as slow as he could have hoped: Orlando felt the wind of the great stone as it whipped past his face. He stumbled back and tried to catch his breath. The thing advanced.

He ducked beneath another swinging cudgel blow and grappled with the monster but its strength was frightening. He had time only to try one jab into the crevice in the thing's shell at the groin, but the space was too tight and the flesh at the leg joint was hard as an old boot. As he spun free, the tortoise-man switched hands with its cudgel—a dishearteningly clever move from a creature of such slow inhumanity—and caught Orlando a glancing blow on the shoulder with the stone head that almost knocked him to his knees. A flash of pain shot down his arm, and his fingers went numb. His sword clanged to the stone and he had to pick it up with his other hand. His wounded arm hung uselessly; he could not even make the fingers close.

As the tortoise-man turned and shuffled toward him again, the cracked face still with no expression except what might have been the ghost of a green-gray smile, Orlando backed away. He could turn and bolt for the back chamber—he could be there in seconds. Whatever gateway was open he could step through before anyone could stop him and be gone from all this. Wherever he landed, he would be alive. His last weeks or months of life would be his to spend, not wasted in this hopeless struggle.

But Fredericks would be lost. The monkeys—all the children—would be lost.

Something heaved in his chest and Orlando's eyes blurred. Even surrounded by what seemed like the end of the world, he was ashamed of his own tears. He lifted the heavy sword in his left hand, grateful that at least he could swing it—Thargor had labored through years of practice to be ready for just such a need—but knowing it would do him little good. The tortoise-man brought the club around in another rocketing sweep, so fast that Orlando had to jump back. He cut at the club handle but the wood was hard as iron. He crouched low to swing at a leg, but although the blade bit, only a gray trickle breached the wound and the creature almost caught him with a downstroke.

A cloud of bats so thick as to be almost a solid thing dropped down between them, hiding them both for a moment in chittering darkness. When they spiraled up again, Orlando realized that the tortoise-man was slowly driving him toward the melee, where his back would be completely unprotected and there would be bodies beneath his feet. He knew he would not last another minute in those circumstances. Gambling on a last attempt to reach the silent creature's neck, he feinted, the movement made soggy by weariness, and then rolled underneath the snapping backswing to climb the creature's plated belly. He could not bring the sword to bear at such close quarters so he dropped it, risking everything to wrap his hands around the tortoise-man's wattled neck before it could think to crush him between club and shell. The thing flailed as his thumbs found the place its windpipe should be, but its hide was too thick: he was hurting it, but he could not crush the leathery neck. It rammed one of its arms against Orlando's throat and began bending his upper body back, struggling for an angle to smash out his brains.

Again a cloud of shrieking darkness descended, wreathing the combatants in a chaos of velvet wings and claws, but Orlando, laboring for breath against the horny bar of the creature's arm, had already nearly lost the light. One of the winged serpents dropped out of the bat-swarm and coiled around his head, an almost certainly final indignity. Gasping, operating on pure vindictive reflex, he took a hand from the tortoise-man's neck, then snatched the serpent and shoved it into his enemy's shattered eye.

The tortoise-man abruptly loosed its grip, staggering back in slow, arm-waving distress as the serpent's tail whipped and lashed, the rest of its body already chewing halfway into the skull. As the tortoise-man dropped its club and tumbled to the floor, Orlando grabbed his sword in his good hand, steadying it with the hand now tingling with returning feeling, and put all his weight behind the blade to shove the point into the creature's throat.

The tortoise-man did not die quickly, but it died.

Orlando was on his knees sucking for air, feeling certain he would never, ever get enough of it into his burning lungs, when he heard Fredericks screaming his name from the front of the temple. He dragged himself to his feet and waded toward the shattered door. Bloody madness and dying innocents were all around him, but he was in a desperate hurry and lifted his sword only to slap away winged serpents or knock grasping hands and claws from his ankles. Still it took him long minutes to drag his exhausted body across the temple, a journey through the worst corner of hell.

The terrible dance of combat at the front door had slowed but not ended. The goddess in the pantherskin lay in a crumpled heap against one of the walls, an arm and both legs twisted at hideous angles, her spear broken across her, but the sphinx was dragging one foreleg and was covered with cuts and gouges that leaked sand instead of blood. The god Reshpu had his antlers dug into one of Saf's sides; small lightnings crackled there, blackening the tawny skin. Bull-headed Mont, ribboned with bloody wounds and with both eyes swollen shut, clung with his great arms to the sphinx's throat.

As Orlando cleared the worst of the slaughter, stepping out into the clear space where the besieged sphinx had crushed anything that had come too close, he saw something that made him forget the temple guardian's heroic struggle in an instant.

Framed between the twisted bronze hinges which were all that remained of the great doors stood Tefy and Mewat. The bloated cobra-man held a small, struggling figure; his vulture-headed companion was examining it as though for purchase.

"Orlando!" Fredericks' shriek was cut off by a flick from Mewat's blunt, scaly finger. Orlando's friend sagged in the cobra man's grip, knocked senseless. Fear washed out over Orlando like winter wind.

Tefy looked up, beak curling in a dreadful smile.

"Citizens," he purred. The word might have described some particularly tasty treat. "Look at this, my beautiful brother—not just one Citizen, but two! Just when all nice little visitors should have gone home, we find them still roaming in our network, up far past their bedtimes. We wonder why, don't we?" Tefy reached out a long finger to stroke Fredericks' slack face; the claw scratched the skin, drawing blood. "Oh, yes," Tefy said happily as he licked the talon with his purple-black tongue, "we have so many questions!"

Third:

BROKEN GLASS

Two Gates the silent House of Sleep adorn;
Of polish'd Iv'ry this, that of transparent Horn:
True Visions thro' transparent Horn arise;
Thro' polish'd Iv'ry pass deluding Lies.

—Virgil's *Aeneid*, translated by John Dryden

CHAPTER 16

Friday Night at the End of the World

NETFEED/NEWS: Anford to Undergo More Tests
(visual: Anford at campaign rally, waving and smiling)
VO: President Rex Anford is slated to undergo more tests,
although the White House staff still declines to explain the
exact nature of his illness, or even to confirm that the chief
executive is ill. Rumors have dogged the course of the
Anford presidency, his infrequent appearances and moments
of public confusion leading to rumors that he is suffering
from a brain tumor or degenerative muscular disorder. The
White House claims this latest round of tests is merely part
of a routine medical checkup, and doctors at Bethesda
Naval Hospital are, as usual, silent on the state of the
president's health. . . .

HER wallscreen held a six-meter-square collage of files. Her living room was littered with an afternoon's and evening's worth of snacks and empties and notes. In a tiny apartment the clutter piled up quickly. Calliope surveyed the mess and made a logical Friday night decision.

I should get out of here for a while.

It wasn't like she was getting anything useful done—that hey-it's-the-weekend feeling had settled into the back of her mind over an hour earlier like a bored, lazy relative who tired everyone out just by being there. And it wasn't as though she'd been devoting a lot of attention to her private life lately either.

A memory of the sullen waitress at Bondi Baby suddenly woke a desire in her for pie and coffee. Or just coffee. Or perhaps just a seat at the edge of the holographic ocean and a chance to flirt with Little Miss Tattoo. She looked at the wallscreen whose printed words suddenly seemed as impenetrable as top-secret military code and flicked her fingers to shut it off. Calliope stared out the window at the stately curve of the Sydney Harbor Bridge, an arc of lights like a pictorial representation of a Bach fugue. Sometimes she found the view itself to be enough to ease her craving for contact with the real world, but not tonight. She was definitely going out. No one could work all the time.

The apartment elevator was incredibly slow. The trip down from the 41st floor to the parking garage seemed to take months. When she reached the bottom and stepped out, a whoop of laughter and a murmur of other voices came echoing to her. A troop of homeless people had paused in their migrations to have what sounded like a party outside the garage gates. Calliope was not looking forward to trying to get the car out without letting any of them in. This was a depressingly common experience, since the neighborhood itself was fairly poor. In fact, as Calliope's friends had pointed out to her several times, other than the view, there weren't a lot of nice things to say about her apartment. A police detective did not earn a huge salary, and if said detective was determined to look out at the bridge and the harbor, she either had to accept an apartment in a pretty seedy part of town, or an apartment so small you couldn't swing a cat in it (Calliope fortunately had no urge to own a cat for any purpose at all), or—if she was sending part of her paycheck every month to her widowed mother in Wollongong—both.

After much sawing back and forth, she had just backed the car out of the incredibly narrow parking space when she realized she had left her wallet and pad upstairs. There wasn't enough room in the garage to leave the car out without blocking anyone else who might want to pass, and she certainly wasn't going to leave it on the street while those people were having their Homeless Festival or whatever it was. Swearing in a way that would have left her old-fashioned father pale and shaking had he heard it, she laboriously injected the car back into the original parking slot and trudged across the garage to the elevator, her brief, winged moment already a bit bedraggled.

Both wallet and pad were sitting on the small *tansu* stack near the door. As she leaned in to snatch them up, she saw the "urgent message" light blinking on the wallscreen. She was tempted just to leave it and go, but her mother had been ill and one of the neighbors had been going over to check on her in the afternoon. Surely she would have called hours ago if there had been anything wrong . . . ?

Calliope cursed and stepped back in, cueing the message. It was only her semi-friend Fenella inviting her to a drinks party next week. Calliope stopped the message halfway through—she knew how it would go—and cursed herself for giving the woman her priority code in a moment of weakness the year before, when Fenella had been trying to set her up on a date with an out-of-town friend. Fenella was a politician's daughter and liked to be at the hub of power, even if it was just running a dyke arts salon: every invitation was to an "event," although Calliope had discovered that "event" just meant a party with photographers where the guests didn't know each other. She headed back down.

Somewhere around the twentieth floor she realized she had left her car keys on the table where the wallet and pad had been.

By the time she made it back up the elevator, any last bit of interest in going out had been crushed, a casualty of the invisible (but clearly omnipresent and all-powerful) God of Work. After a brief period of glowering at the apartment, since it had been a major player in the conspiracy against her Friday night, she waved a bowl of pseudoberry crumble, spooned the last of the ice cream on top of it, and—with extremely bad grace—brought the Merapanui files back up on the wallscreen.

*   *   *

If the final compilation of files on John Wulgaru had been printed out on paper, they would barely have filled fifty pages— a pathetically and even suspiciously small amount of information considering the boy had spent most of his life in one institution or another. Over half that material had come from Doctor Danney's fragmented case notes, and a good proportion of those notes were useless for Calliope's purposes, little more than scores and dry observations of various behavioral tests.

A search of various record banks had turned up a few other pages here and there, including a solitary death notice found in one of the backwaters of the police system, now appended to his few remaining sheets from the criminal justice files (John Wulgaru, aka etc., had been hit by a car while crossing a street in the Redfern district, and thus his case was to be marked closed.) But all in all there was very little, as though someone with a crude but fairly thorough grasp of government information systems had done their best to remove any record of his existence and had mostly succeeded.

The death notice caught her attention, and although the date given for the fatal accident was depressing—if it were true, John Wulgaru had died more than half a year before the Merapanui murder, which would certainly qualify as an alibi—there was something else about the notice that nagged at her like a loose tooth, but although she shuffled back and forth through the various documents until the flasher for the evening news appeared on the wallscreen, she could not put a finger on it. She clicked off the flasher, deciding she would download the news later. As she had surveyed the death notice, which mentioned that Wulgaru had no surviving relatives, a new thought had suddenly arisen and she was afraid she might lose it.

Calliope had a hearty dislike of the term "intuition," which she thought was usually what people called good detective work if it was done by someone the rest of the department didn't like much, especially female cops. What the hell *was* intuition anyway? Guesswork, really, and a surprising amount of police work had always been just that. You had to get the facts first, but often what put them together was that eye for subtle yet familiar patterns that all good law enforcement people developed after a while.

But Calliope had to admit at least to herself that she sometimes went a step farther, getting hunches on things based on perceptions so ephemeral that she couldn't even explain them to Stan. That was one of the reasons she was so much more hands-on about detective work than he was: she needed to touch things, smell things if she could. And she was having such a moment just now.

She brought up the pictures of the suspect again—three of them, each in its own way quite useless. The juvenile authority processing picture was of a young boy, his Aboriginal heritage obvious in his dark skin and close-curled hair, but with unexpectedly high cheekbones and a pronounced Asian shape to the watchful eyes. Beyond that the likeness revealed little. She had seen abused children enough to know the look—closed, as impenetrable as a wall. A child full of secrets.

The only remaining booking photo from his reentry into the system as a young adult was even less useful. Due to some equipment malfunction, missed at the time, the camera's focal length had gone off slightly and the face was blurry—it looked like one of the flawed experiments from the early days of photography. Only a certain faith would connect the shadowy presence (booking number superimposed at the bottom of the frame) with the stone-faced little boy of the earlier picture, and not a witness in the world could identify the person in the photo beyond color of skin and rough shape of head and ears.

The last picture was from Dr. Jupiter Danney's own files, but here as well fate had conspired to keep John Wulgaru's true likeness a secret. The picture had been shot over the shoulder of a dark-haired girl—Calliope could not help wondering if it might be Polly Merapanui, but Danney had not remembered and the notes held no clue—but the young man seemed to have moved just as the picture had been taken. Instead of a face, there was only a blur of motion, a glint of feral eye and smear of dark hair, with all else as liquid as dream, as though some demonic presence had been caught just as it dematerialized.

Devil-devil, the minister's wife had said. *Devil-devil man.*

The absurdly melodramatic thought nevertheless sent a chill through her, and for a moment she could almost believe she was not the only person in the tiny apartment. She barked an order at the system to close the blinds, cross with herself for doing so but suddenly wanting to be a little more private.

Calliope went back to the juvenile picture again, to the boy with a face like a shuttered house. Little Johnny. Jonny Dark.

It was obvious once you saw it, but she would have trouble explaining where the idea came from, or—more importantly— what she thought this intuition proved even if it were true. John Wulgaru's mother claimed he had been fathered by what the juvenile justice report called "a Filipino boatworker with a criminal history"—which meant a pirate, Calliope knew damn well, one of those human predators who waylaid boats and small ships on the Coral Sea, pilfered the cargo, even took the hijacked craft itself if it was worth the risk of a black market sale in Cairns, then machine-gunned the sailors and passengers to make sure there were no witnesses. Calliope had been a police officer in this part of the world long enough to know what a "boatworker with a criminal history" was, and she had also seen eyes shaped like little Johnny's many times: it wasn't just a rumor that the boy had an Asian father.

So little Johnny's Aboriginal last name didn't come from Daddy's side. His mother Emmy's real last name, the few remaining social worker reports agreed, was Minyiburu, although she was better known by various Anglo-sounding aliases, the most frequent being "Emmy Wordsworth." So where did "Wulgaru" come from? It might have been from one of the men who serially shared her life, an attempt to legitimize her boy through a stepfather's name, but from what the report had to say about her short-lived, violent liaisons—none mentioned as being with Aboriginal men of any sort, anyway—Calliope had a strong hunch that the name had come from somewhere else.

So where would that be? Why would his Aboriginal mother give her boy the name of a monster from her people's folklore?

Calliope was considering this, and feeling a vague certainty beginning to form that even the most scornful could have labeled intuition and she would not have been able to argue, when the other nagging concern, the one about the death notice, suddenly came clear to her and blew the question of Johnny's name out of her mind like a strong, cold wind.

*   *   *

She was so full of what she had just discovered that when the call was picked up on the other end she was only mildly bemused by the fact that her partner appeared to have been processed through some kind of reverse-time machine that had taken twenty years off his age. It wasn't until she noticed the acne that her scattered thoughts rearranged themselves into some kind of sense. She struggled to remember Stan's older nephew's name, but it came at last.

"Hi, Kendrick. Is your uncle there?"

"Oh, yeah, Ms. Skouros." He seemed to be watching something above her, and did not look away even when he shouted, "Uncle Stan!" It took Calliope a moment to realize she must be in a window at a corner of the wallscreen.

"So how are things with you?" she asked the boy. "School going well?"

He made a face and shrugged, not willing to take his eyes completely off whatever was banging and screaming on the other part of the screen. That was pretty much it for conversation, but he was a polite young man and did not simply ignore her: they both sat waiting patiently until Stan Chan arrived, at which point Kendrick evaporated from her view, moving to get a better angle on the wallscreen.

"What's up, Skouros?" Stan was wearing one of his horrible weekend shirts, but Calliope bravely resisted the urge to comment.

"Working. And you're babysitting. For a Friday night, this pretty much locks, Stan. At least one of us should definitely be having a date."

"I *did* have a date."

She raised an eyebrow. "You're home early, then." Stan refused to be drawn into further discussion on the subject, so she said, "It doesn't matter anyway. I found something. I was ready to give up and go out, go drinking or something, but I made myself work a little longer—you might try that sometime, Stan—and I think I hit paydirt."

Now it was Stan's eyebrow that tilted up. "Paydirt? Is that from a flick or something?"

"Shut up. I think I've had a big breakthrough. Shit—now I *am* talking like a flick. Here, I want to show you something. I'm putting it on your screen."

His eyes flicked up as his nephew's had done, examining the document; he had his little I'm-not-impressed quirk to his mouth, but he was reading carefully. "So?" he said when he had finished. "It's a report by some guy named Buncie to his parole officer that he met our Johnny on the streets of Kogarah. It's years old, Skouros—what's the point?"

"*Damn,* Stan, I wish you would read the files. Didn't you check out the notice of death?"

For a moment she saw a flash of defensiveness. "We only got them this afternoon, Skouros, after I was officially clocked out. Do I have to apologize for not being on the job twenty-four hours of every day?"

"I'm sorry." Behind him on the couch, she could see his younger nephew wrestling with Kendrick over something or other, could hear their breathy laughter. There were better things than work to do on a Friday night. "You're right, Stan. Sorry. Do you want me to save this until Monday?"

He laughed. "After calling me up in the middle of '*Romeo Blood: DEATH PACT SEVEN—The Return of Scourge*' and making me miss the arch-villain's careful explanation of all the things he's going to do to destroy the world, so now I'm going to have to have it repeated to me by these two couch monkeys? Chance not, Skouros. You better have come up with something worthwhile, that's all I got to say."

"Okay. Right. Well, this guy Buncie told his parole officer . . ."

"Why do we have that anyway?"

"Turned up in the cross-check. If someone was editing out Johnny Wulgaru stuff, they missed it. Anyway, Buncie claims he had a conversation with Johnny on September 26th, about nothing much—Buncie said our boy 'much sliced him,' didn't give him a lot of respect. The kind of thing that sticks in a street beast's mind."

"So? Or have I said that before?"

"You have, Stan. Come on, take your eyes off Romeo Blood for a second. That's *two whole weeks* after the date of death on the death notice!"

Stan shrugged. "I saw that. But Buncie-boy has probably got charge damage like crazy, and the statement was made a year after the fact. I think it's more likely he got his dates wrong."

"I thought so, too, Stanley." She couldn't resist a small note of triumph. "But I checked, just to make sure . . . and you know what? Buncie might have a skull so pounded by bad gear he wouldn't know when he last saw his own mother, but he was in prison until three days after the date when Johnny Wulgaru is supposed to have died. So either he made the whole thing up for no conceivable reason, he was talking to a ghost, or somebody falsified a death notice. Me, I don't think little Johnny Dread died before Polly Merapanui. I think he killed her, and you know what else I think? I think the bastard's still alive."

Stan was silent for a long moment. His younger nephew asked him something Calliope couldn't quite hear, but Stan ignored him.

"Know something?" he said at last. "You should swear off going out for good, Skouros. You do your best work when you're home feeling sorry for yourself and spilling ice cream on your sweater." As she looked down to see the glob of white she had completely missed slowly oozing its way into the fibers, Stan continued. "You are one smart person, partner, and that is the truth. Now I'm going to watch the end of the Romeo Blood program, 'cause I think any moment now they're going to start blowing up all kinds of stuff."

"Is that all?"

"Well, even though I love you, I'm still not going to work through another weekend. But on Monday I think we start to hunt Jonny Dark for real. Okay?"

She smiled. It felt good. "Okay."

It was only after she broke the connection that she remembered she had forgotten to tell Stan her idea about the name.

ON a sunny day like today, with the shop banners moving in the breeze along Spring Street, the windows full of artsy animated displays and the sidewalks a continual parade of interesting-looking people, Dulcie Anwin remembered again what it had felt like when she first moved to New York.

Her mother, who had no idea that her daughter had already lost her criminal virginity while still a student hacker at Stevens Institute (a swift slide from stealing tests to a credit card scam that kept her in the kind of clothes her roommates couldn't afford), could never understand why her daughter would leave the relative safety of Edison, New Jersey, for a dangerous, dirty place like Manhattan. Ruby Anwin had carefully constructed what she thought of as an exciting life for herself in the suburbs—friends who were musicians and artists and philosophy professors, lovers who became husbands, or some who simply stayed lovers, including one or two women just *pour épater le bourgeois*—and couldn't understand why her only child would want something more. The idea that a permissive upbringing could lead to rebellion had occurred to Ruby, of course, and she had feared raising a daughter who might become a religious zealot or a slot-eyed Republican, concerned only with material goods. In fact, since all she knew of her daughter's current profession was that she worked with information technology and traveled a lot, she was quietly convinced that Dulcie had veered toward the latter. What had never occurred to her was that a child raised in a household in which her own high school teachers were doing drugs in the downstairs bathroom during her mom's parties might need to go even farther afield to find her individuation.

Born into an earlier generation, Dulcie might have become a political extremist, a bomb builder, someone willing to sacrifice her own life—and those of occasional bystanders—in an assault against the System. But when Dulcie had begun to discover who the secret masters of the world truly were, instead of rebelling against them, she had gone to work for them.

So when her mother said with the aggressive cheerfulness that was her hallmark, "Dulcie, honey, I know you're busy, but why don't you come visit for a week anyway? You can do your work here. I have a system, you know—I don't live in the Stone Age," Dulcie couldn't tell her the truth. She tried instead to explain it away in terms of bandwidth, and business calls coming in at weird hours from other parts of the world, and all her reference material being at home, and even in terms of needing proper security: her own system was almost alive, teeming with evolving antivirals, tiny A-Life gear that adapted and learned and changed. But the truth was that if she wanted to, she could get a fast enough link from her mother's house to work off her own system from there. The reason she didn't go home for more than a few hours at a stretch, even after eight years of living only a short drive away, was that she didn't want to. Her mother made her feel like a little girl, and Dulcie had spent far too much time building credibility with international criminals to like that feeling very much.

The piece in the gallery window had caught her eye, and she was standing in a ray of sunshine, squinting against the glare and wondering whether she shouldn't be wearing sunblock, when her pad beeped.

The artist had taken a group of little builder toys—the kind you could buy in any souvenir store or on most street corners— and put them into an intricate grid made of glass pipes. But what gave the piece its jolt was that he had supplied them with building materials too large to be manipulated within the narrow confines, thus frustrating the monomaniacal automata completely.

Is that supposed to be some comment on modern life? she wondered. The pad beeped again, this time with a second tone—a priority signal. She felt her heart speed a little. She felt pretty certain she knew who it was.

He was not transmitting visuals, but his voice, even with slight distortion, was unmistakable. "I have to talk to you."

She stilled the hammer of pulse as best she could. Why did he have this effect on her? It was like something at the pheromone level, if pheromones could travel over satlinks from Colombia to New York, something subliminal that made her feel she was being stalked by an interested male despite the lack of any outward signs. Whatever the cause, it was something she could not understand and did not entirely like.

"I'm outside at the moment." She couldn't assume he was getting visuals on his end. "I've got you on my pad."

"I know. Go home. I need to talk to you now."

The voice was flat, and Dulcie bristled at the tone of command—one of her early stepfathers had tried the Dad Voice on her, as she thought of it, and had received permanent contempt as his reward. But she had another response as well, a more placatory urge. He was her employer, after all. He was a man used to dealing with men—stupid men, or at least men who needed to be ordered around, from what she'd seen. And was that an undertone of real need in his words, something he did not want to let her see? Was that why he had blanked the picture?

"Well, you've probably saved me spending a lot of money,"

she said, keeping her tone light. The little builders in the gallery window were trying to get a stainless steel pin around an S-bend in their pipette, something that wasn't physically possible for them, but they weren't giving up; she had a feeling if she came back the next day they'd still be shoving the same pin at the same bend, still without result. "I was about to indulge in some serious shopping . . ."

"I'll call you in thirty minutes," he said, and was gone.

The palm-reader at the main street entrance was even slower than the one on her own door. The thing was ridiculously old, and miserable in chilly weather when you had to take off your glove to operate it.

As she wrestled her bags through the door, someone called a greeting to her. She looked up to see the guy with the artistic haircut who lived a few doors down from Charlie, waving as the elevator door hissed closed.

The bastard. Did he ever think I might want to use it, too?

Every time she wondered about the life she had chosen for herself—hurrying home on a Friday evening, not to get dressed to go out somewhere, but to take a call from an international terrorist—she thought of how pleased her mother would have been to see her hooked up instead with somebody like Mister Elevator Wave, and it all fell back into perspective. She knew that type only too well. He would be big on personal freedom when it came to things like getting his own way—oh, the Bohemian clichés that would be flung around then!—but it would be quite a different story if someone was having a loud party upstairs when he wanted to work, or if she wanted to go somewhere he didn't.

Dulcie waited for the elevator, hating a man with whom she had never spoken.

But the thing was, she thought as she got out on her own floor, what other kind of man was she going to meet? She worked too hard, even when she was on the road, and when she came back to New York she barely ever had the energy to go out. Was that her range of options—criminals and neighbors?

Even someone like Dread, someone who was at least *interesting*—how could you have a relationship with someone like that? It was stupid. Even if there had been a spark of some kind, even if her own strange feelings were in any way reciprocated, what future could there be?

Still, even a fling had its attractions.

She stood waiting for her own door to recognize her, wondering if she'd gone too far now ever to turn back, to be a normal person. Was it just the adrenaline? Surely she could get that somewhere else—skydiving, jaywalking on freeways, something. The whole thing had seemed so exciting when she had first started, but that's what people always thought before everything went bad. Dulcie wasn't stupid: she knew that. Was it all worth it?

It was the dreams that were unsettling her, she told herself as the door grudgingly decided to let her in. The bad dreams. There was nothing very mysterious about them. Her little cocker spaniel, Nijinsky—her mother's choice of name; Dulcie had called him "Jinkie"—the one who had been hit by a car when she was ten, was suffering. She didn't know how or why exactly (in the dream there was no car, no blood on the little dog's muzzle as there had been in real life) but she knew she had to put Jinkie out of his misery. "End his suffering," as her mother had said. But in the dreams there was no veterinarian's office either, no smell of alcohol and pet hair. In her dreams she had a gun, and as she touched the barrel to the little dog's head, he rolled his eyes toward her without seeing, responding only to the feeling of the metal bumping against his skull.

It didn't take a Park Avenue specialist to tell Dulcie what the dream was about, that it was not Jinkie she was dreaming about, but a Colombian gear monkey named Celestino. She had been pleased with herself for how easily she had done the deed—a neat, quick performance, like swatting a spider with a rolled-up newspaper—and she had been proud of how little it had affected her. But night after night she saw Jinkie's small body trembling with fear as she approached. Night after night she woke up sweating, calling for the lights in a shaky voice.

It happens, Anwin, she told herself. *So you thought you'd get off lightly—you didn't. But the world is full of innocent little children getting killed every day, starved, raped, beaten to death, and you're not losing sleep over them. Why worry about a lowlife like Celestino? He was putting every other person in that operation at risk. You were a soldier, and he was a risk to everyone. You did your job.*

Which might be true—she wasn't quite sure anymore—but there were moments, especially at two in the morning, when the idea of working for a normal company and being married to a man whose idea of wild behavior was making love on the living room couch instead of in the bedroom seemed to have its charms.

Packages shed, Jones purring in and out around her ankles, Dulcie made herself a drink. She was irritated with herself, both for her self-indulgent mood and for hurrying home just because Dread had ordered her to. She had just finished adding soda to the scotch when the calm voice of the wallscreen announced a phone call.

"I'll be brief," he said when she opened the connection. Whatever he had been doing lately, whether online or in Cartagena, must be agreeing with him: he looked sleek and happy, like a well-fed panther. "First, expand for me a bit on your report."

"The virtual object—the lighter?" She took a sip of her drink, trying to summon her thoughts. She should have gotten her notes up directly on coming through the door, but a schoolgirl rebelliousness had sent her to the scotch first. "Well, as I said, it's hard to tell without having the object in its matrix to experiment with. It's a very nice simulation of an old-fashioned lighter . . ."

He waved his hand dismissively, but did not lose his grin. She wondered why he seemed so speedy—from what she knew of the shared account, an account she had not used recently because he was so busy with it himself, he was in the network about sixteen hours a day or more, which must be exhausting. "I know I didn't make it easy for you," he said. "Don't waste my time with the obvious—I've got your report. Just explain what you mean by 'can't reverse without breaking the hard security.' "

"It means I can't reverse-engineer the thing just from the copy I made."

"You made a copy?" The snap of sudden chill was familiar now, but it didn't get any more pleasant.

"Look, this thing of yours is hot, in more ways than one. It's a live object. I can't just bang on the buttons until something happens, especially if you don't want anyone to know you've got it."

"Go on."

"So I had to copy it off to my system, where I've got the tools. Not that it was easy—I had to crack about five levels of encryption just to get the low-level functions to replicate. But there are levels beyond that I couldn't copy—couldn't even access. I'm going to have to do some major work just to get to them."

"Explain to me."

His tone was more agreeable now. She liked that. He *did* need her. There was a reason her price was high, and she didn't want him to forget that reason. "This thing is at root an effector—it sends positional information out, and interprets what comes back from the matrix. That's just for the low-level functions, like moving the user through the network. Basic stuff. Actually, strictly speaking, I guess you should call it a 'v-fector,' since all the information it deals with is about a virtual space. It's not describing the user's real position, just their position within the network. Right?" She hurried on as he nodded. "But with this system, nothing is simple, and certainly not access to even the most basic kinds of information. See, we found out a long time ago that most of the network is security-banded, to keep users who aren't owners from doing anything they shouldn't. So even the positional information coming to this device from the matrix is shielded—it's like with those areas around top-secret military test grounds in the real world, where you can't buy a map anywhere for miles because they don't want people trying to figure things out from what's shown and what's not shown. To be able to get that information, I'll have to pretend I'm one of the people who's supposed to receive it—and I'm guessing that's only these Grail people. They all have passwords or some other kind of access, and I have to learn how to mimic that, especially if you want me to mess with the protocols enough to show it inactive while still keeping it active."

"So what you're saying is that it needs more work." His expression was distracted, as though he was adding this information to a much larger whole. "You need more time."

"Yeah." She hoped he didn't think she was just stalling. "I did manage to find a way to corrupt the telemetry, which means that even if someone tries to turn it off before then, the system won't be able to find it. I've sent you the instructions on how to do it. But after you do it, you won't be able to use the thing until we switch it back. If the telemetry is wrong, none of the other functions will work right either. For all intents and purposes, once you change those settings, you have a dud effector."

Dread nodded. "I see."

"Whoever this belonged to must be an idiot," Dulcie said, pleased to have reestablished her credentials. "Either that, or it's taking them a hell of a long time to realize it's missing. They could have found the device any time if they'd tried. I mean, it's a hot v-fector, for God's sake—it's just been sitting there waiting for the network to ask where it is."

"Then maybe I should do what you said—change the telemetry. I'll think about that." He cocked his head as though listening to faint music. The smile came back, but it was a bit more natural this time, less stretched and gleeful. "I've got some other important things to discuss with you, Dulcie. I'm closing down the Cartagena office. 'Sky God' is now officially boxed, and the Old Man's got some other jobs he wants me to do."

She was still nodding, but caught by surprise. Both relief and loss were pulling hard on her at the thought that this man would be leaving her life. She opened her mouth but for a moment could think of nothing to say. "That's . . . well, congratulations, I guess. It's been a pretty wild ride. I'll finish up my work on the v-fector and send it along. . . ."

One of his eyebrows crept up. "I didn't say *my* project was finished, did I? Just that I'm closing down the Cartagena office. Oh, no, there are a lot of loose ends I still have to deal with." The grin, flashbulb-white this time. "I want you to come to Sydney."

"Sydney? Australia?" She could have kicked herself for saying something so stupid, but he did not waste energy with the obvious put-down, waiting instead for an answer to his request—a request that suddenly seemed to her far more complicated than she could easily understand. "I mean . . . what do you want me to do? You . . . I haven't used the sim for a week or so."

"I need your help," he said, "and not just with this device. This is a very complicated project I've begun. I want you to . . . help keep an eye on things." He laughed. "And then I can keep an eye on you, too."

She flinched, just perceptibly, but there was none of the menace in his voice he had used when warning her to keep her mouth shut. A thought came to her, a surprising, frightening, altogether overwhelming thought.

Maybe . . . maybe he wants to spend time with me. Personal time.

She covered her confusion with another long, slow sip of her scotch and soda. Could that even be true? And if it was, would she be a fool to go? He fascinated her in a way no one else had—would she be a fool *not* to go?

"I'll have to think about it."

"Don't think too long," he said. "Train's pulling out." She thought she detected a slackening in his good cheer, weariness perhaps. "You'll be paid your regular contractor's rates."

"Oh! Oh, no, that's not what I . . . I just meant it's not easy to . . . to pick up and . . ." She bit her lip. Babbling. Chizz, Anwin, just chizz. "I just have to think about arrangements."

"Call me tomorrow." He paused. "I've been working with another contact of mine, doing research on this lighter, but all the time I've been working with her I kept wishing it was you instead." His smile this time was odd, almost shy. "Enjoy your Friday night." His image winked off the wallscreen.

Dulcie downed the rest of her drink in one long swallow. When Jones jumped into her lap, she scratched the cat behind the ears by reflex, but if it had been another cat entirely she would not have noticed. Outside the windows the sun vanished, the stone and cast-iron canyons of Soho darkened, and lights began to come on all over the city.

THROUGH the whole strange progress of the last few days, Olga Pirofsky had been almost numb. If a part of her was positive that she had found her purpose, something that would finally give the rote repetitions of work and home-life meaning, another part of her was still capable of seeing that from the outside this would all look like madness. But no one outside could feel what she had felt, experience what she had experienced. Even if this wasn't madness, even if it was, as it seemed to be, the most important thing she could ever do, she understood now the allure of lunacy in a way she hadn't even in the sanitarium in France.

The voices arguing inside of her scarcely touched the outside.

She had gone on making arrangements, sending mail, informing the necessary functionaries, moving through her life with the slow caution of someone who has been badly bruised. The only time Olga had cried again was when the people came to take Misha away.

They were a childless couple, both in management of some kind, fairly young in years by Olga's standards, but already a near-complete sketch of their own middle age. She had picked them from the three or four inquiries because the man had a kind sound to his voice, something that had reminded her inexplicably of her lost Aleksandr.

After she had told them she was moving, they had showed the good taste not to ask too many more questions, and although Misha had been his usual suspicious self, they had seemed to like the little dog very much.

"He's just zoony," the woman said, using an expression Olga didn't recognize, but which seemed to mean cute. "Look at those ears! We'll give him such a good home."

As they loaded him into the dog carrier, Misha's eyes had bulged at the horror of Olga's treachery and he had leaped against the barred door until she was terrified he would hurt himself. His new owners assured her that he would soon be happy again, eating out of his very own bowl in his new house. Misha's sharp bark was only cut off by the closing of the air seal on the car door. When the shiny machine had disappeared around the corner, Olga finally realized that tears were streaming down her face.

She was thumbing down the pressure strip on the last of the boxes when a squeal outside brought her to the attic window. A little way down the street a compact hover-runner packed with teenagers was making dizzyingly small circles under one of the bright white streetlamps, the girls in the back seat screaming and laughing. A boy loped out of a nearby house and climbed in among them, provoking more laughter. The car straightened out, but not before an overcompensated turn took the the hover-runner over a flower bed. As the car picked up speed and skimmed away, a brief but colorful display of decapitated blossoms sprayed from under the skirts into the gutter.

Just another Friday night at the end of the world, Olga thought, but she did not know exactly what she meant, where the words had come from. It had been weeks since she had paid much attention to the news, but she didn't think things were much worse than usual—wars and murders, famine and pestilence, but nothing extraordinary or apocalyptic. Her own life might be changing, might even be winding down into some inexplicable darkness, but surely everything else would go on? Children would grow up, teenagers would misbehave, and generation after generation would march on—wasn't that the point of everything she had done with her life? Wasn't it the point of what she was doing now, the only point? The children were what mattered. Without them, mortality was a bleak pratfall with nobody laughing.

She pushed the thought away, just as she had pushed away the desperation in little Misha's bark. It was better to be numb. If a great task had been set before her, she could not afford to feel pain. There would be much more to come, but she would square her shoulders and bear up. That was one thing Olga had learned to do, one thing she did well.

She slid the last of the boxes into place, almost all her worldly goods stored like the effects of a dead pharaoh put aside for the afterlife—and, she thought, with about as much chance of getting used by their owner again—then closed and locked the attic.

For a while the voices had been curiously silent.

In the first days after she had left her job, Olga had spent most of every day in the station-chair, link in place, waiting for guidance. But whether she hovered in the lowest level of her own system, bathing in gray light like a frog half-submerged in a lily pond, or roamed through the active strata of the net, the voices still did not speak to her again. No matter what she did, the children remained absent, as though they had moved on to some other and more interesting playmate. The desertion left Olga frightened and heartsore. She even began to monitor the Uncle Jingle show again—fearful that she might somehow incur another one of the murderous headaches, but even more terrified that she had thrown away what life she had over some kind of hallucination. It was strange to see Uncle's clownish tricks and songs from her new distance, to see him as something almost sinister, a white-faced Pied Piper, but although watching the show only made clear to her how unlikely it was that she could ever go back, nothing else happened. No pain in her skull like a jagged blade, but no children either—at least none who were not part of Uncle Jingle's shrieking Krew.

Every evening she had connected to the system and stayed there, Misha curled in her lap, until fatigue drove her to her bed. Every morning she woke up in the wake of turbulent but unremembered dreams and returned to the chair. It was only at the end of the first week of her new life that something changed.

That night, Olga fell asleep with her fiberlink in place.

Slipping out of the gray nothingness of the first-level system into slumber was as gentle and unnoticed as the turn to twilight, but instead of entering the blurry carnival of the freed subconscious, she found herself floating through silent, empty space, adrift in a chill, featureless void like a dark little moon. She could not help noticing that her thoughts were far too clear and complete for a dream. Then the visions began.

At first she saw little—only a shadow within the greater shadow—but gradually it became a mountain, impossibly tall, black as the night that surrounded it, thrusting high against the stars. It frightened her, but she was drawn to it through the frozen dark, pulled toward its negative brilliance as helplessly as a moth to a tongue of flame. But as the mountain loomed ever higher, she suddenly felt the children gathering around her in an invisible flock. The deep, killing cold eased, although she knew somehow that the zero chill was only held at bay.

Suddenly, with the fluidity of more ordinary dreaming, the mountain was no longer a mountain but something more slender—a tower of slick black glass. Dawn or some other cool light touched the sky and edged back the night, and she could see that the tower rose from water, like a castle surrounded by a moat, like something in the stories her mother had told her long ago.

The children did not speak, but she could feel them drawing close around her, frightened but also hopeful. They wanted her to understand.

The last thing she saw before waking up was a spark from the rising sun, a line of fire along the tower's smooth obsidian skin. But in the final moments she had also heard the children's voices again, which had eased her heart like wind in tree branches after a sweltering afternoon.

South, they whispered to her. *Go south.*

Olga surveyed her packing. Her shoulders hurt and her back throbbed from the bending, but the dampness of her blouse and the hairs sticking to the back of her neck were a pleasant indicator of things accomplished; even the aches proved that she was finally doing something.

It was strange to see how little she needed after so many years of living with *things.* It was like traveling with her family again, and with Aleksandr, only the important things carried along because the road was not kind to clutter. Now she was leaving decades of her life behind, taking only two suitcases. Well, three.

The chair had of course gone back to Obolos, but Olga had saved more than a little money over the years: beside the big bag with her clothes and the smaller one with her toiletries stood a slim little case about the size of an old-fashioned children's picture book. Inside was a top of the line Dao-Ming travel station, something the young man at the store had assured her in a faintly condescending way would allow her to do anything she could possibly want. It had taken a while to get him to produce the machine—he clearly thought she might be planning no more than a few phone calls to relatives while she vacationed, or perhaps writing an old woman's travel memoirs—but eventually money stimulated his attention. She had been firm but reticent, though she had allowed herself a polite smile when he told her that Dao-Ming meant "Shining Path," as though that might be a factor in whether she bought it. There wasn't really any way to make sense of the voices, and she herself did not know why she thought she needed such a powerful station, but she had reached a place where a certain kind of faith seemed more important than any other considerations.

With the button of the telematic jack she had also bought now in place on her neck, she could finally feel content: the children could speak to her when they wished. A channel was always available now, and every night she laid her dreams open to them. They had told her many things, some she remembered on waking, some that faded, but always they whispered for her to go south, to find the tower.

She would trust them to help her on the way.

A horn blared outside. Olga looked up in surprise, wondering how long she had been lost in thought. That would be the cab to take her to the Juniper Bay train station for the first part of a journey whose ultimate length and destination she could not guess.

The driver did not get out to help her until she had dragged the luggage down to the sidewalk. While he flopped the two suitcases into the trunk, she went back to check that the door was locked, although she strongly doubted she would ever be coming back. When she got into the back seat and reminded the man of her destination, he grunted and pulled away from the curb. Olga turned and watched her house dwindling until it was obscured by a tree.

A car was coming slowly down the road toward them. As it passed, Olga's attention was caught by its driver. A glint of streetlight through the windshield lit his somehow familiar face for just a moment. He was staring straight ahead, and it took her a moment to summon up the profile from her memory.

Catur Ramsey. At least it had looked like him. But surely after she had told him she didn't want to talk, surely after he had left all those messages and she had not replied, he wouldn't come all the way up here?

For a moment she hesitated, thinking perhaps she should go back and at least speak to the man. He had been kind, and if it was truly him, it seemed terribly cruel to drive away and leave him to knock on the door of an empty house. But what could she say? How could she explain? She couldn't. And she might have mistaken the face anyway.

Olga said nothing. The cab reached the end of the street and turned, leaving both her house and the man who might or might not be Catur Ramsey behind. Olga Pirofsky, despite being wrapped in the strange, invisible security of the voices and their plan for her, could not help feeling that something grave had just happened, some slippage of universal forces that meant far more than she could understand.

She shook off the disturbing idea and settled back in the seat, wrapping herself in her coat. All done now. Choices made, no turning back. Without even quite realizing it, she began to sing quietly as the streetlights gleamed past the windows.

"... *An angel touched me ... an angel touched me ...*"

She had never sung it before. If asked, she could not have said where she had learned it.

CHAPTER 17

Our Lady and Friends

O'MEARA: "Are you kidding? It's going to cost them major, baby. Wild credits."

THE forced march up the stairs to the Campanile of Six Pigs was not a pleasant one. Their bandit captors were armed not just with swords and knives, although there were plenty of those on display, but also with antique guns. The blunderbusses, as Renie supposed they were, had huge bell-shaped mouths and convoluted shapes that made them look more like musical instruments than anything else, but she did not doubt they would do terrible damage when fired. The man behind her, who seemed to do nothing but giggle and hiccup, kept bumping his against her back every few steps, so that she felt sure any moment a jiggle of contact would set it off and that would be the last thing she ever felt.

Worse, in a way, was the stink of liquor that hung over the bandit party like a fog. They seemed giddy with dark amusement, heedless, a volatility that suggested that no compromise or bargain, no matter how much they might benefit, would interest them.

This did not stop Florimel from trying. "Why are you doing this?" she demanded of the huge, bearded leader. "We have done you no harm. Just take what you want from us, although we have nothing worth stealing."

The toothless giant laughed. "We are the Attic Spiders. We decide what is worth taking. And we have a use for you, missy. Yes we do."

The man guarding Renie giggled even more shrilly. "The Mother," he said, almost to himself. "It's her day. Be her birthing-day gift, you will."

Renie suppressed a shudder. The gun barrel bumped against her back again and she almost leaped up onto the next step.

Even before they climbed the final flight, they could hear what sounded like a riotous party above them—tuneless singing, the scraping of a fiddle, many boisterous voices. The Campanile was a vast open space, hexagonal, with arched windows opening to the late afternoon sky in all six walls. In the angle of each wall was a statue of a standing pig wearing human clothes; one was dressed as a greedy priest, another as an overly fashionable lady, each of the six apparently a satire on some different human folly. A cluster of giant bells so covered with verdigris that it seemed doubtful they'd been rung in years hung from the center of the roof. Two or three dozen more bandits were cavorting beneath the bells, swigging from jugs or metal goblets, bellowing boasts and imprecations. Two men with faces covered in blood were wrestling on the stone tiles, and a few of the others had paused to watch them. At least a dozen of the party-goers were women, dressed in the bosomy style of a Restoration comedy, as cacklingly drunk and foulmouthed as the men. When the revelers noticed Renie's captors they let out drunken cries of pleasure and welcome, staggering forward to surround the returning bandits and their prey.

"Eee, they look fat and healthy," one slattern said as she leaned forward and poked terrified Emily with a crooked finger. "Let's roast 'em and eat 'em!"

As others cheered her suggestion—a rough joke, Renie prayed—T4b puffed up like a blowfish and put himself between Emily and the crowd. Renie leaned forward and grabbed his robed elbow, clutching his hidden spikes by accident. "Don't do anything stupid," she whispered, wincing as she massaged her injured palm. "We don't know what's going on here yet."

"Know these dirt-hoppers better not go touching," the youth growled. "Take some heads off, me."

"You're not in a gameworld now," Renie began, but was interrupted by a high, lazy voice from the back of the crowd.

"My lads and lassies, you simply must move. I can see nothing of these newcomers. Clear away, there. Grip, let me see what you and your wastrels have fetched home."

The ragged, reeking crowd parted, so that Renie and her friends had a direct view to the far side of the Campanile and the two people sitting there.

At first she thought the long, slender figure slumped in the high-backed chair was Zekiel, the runaway cutlerer's apprentice, but this one's pallor came from powder, largely sweated away at forehead and neck, and the white hair was an ancient periwig, slightly askew.

"Mother preserve me, but they are an odd-looking lot." The pale man's finery seemed no newer or cleaner than that of any of the other bandits, but the fabrics were brocades and satins; his languid movements caught gleams of the afternoon light. He had a narrow face, handsome as far as Renie could tell, but with cheeks heavily caked in rouge and a sleepy, careless expression. A smaller man in a harlequin's costume slumped on a cushion at his feet, apparently sleeping with his head against one of the pale man's legs. The harlequin's colorful mask had been pushed down until only his cheeks showed in the eyeholes. "Still," the tattered dandy said, "odd or not, none of them seems capable of flight, so they will serve our purpose. Grip, you and your cutthroats have done well. I have saved four barrels of the best, just for you."

Renie's captors let out a howl of joy. Several of them bolted to the far side of the Campanile to open the casks, but enough remained, weapons raised, to remove any thought of trying to escape just yet.

The masked harlequin stirred and swiveled his head from side to side, then seemed to realize after a moment the reason he could see nothing. He raised his finger with the controlled concentration of a brain surgeon and pushed the mask up his nose until his eyes appeared in the slots. The eyes narrowed, and the man in the patchwork clown costume sat up.

"Well, well," he said to Renie. "So you are still on your grand tour, are you?"

The pale man on the chair looked down at him. "Do you know the sacrifices, Koony?"

"I do. At least we've met." He lifted the mask away, revealing black hair and Asian features. Renie's first dreadful thought, that they had been delivered straight to the Quan Li creature, slowed her realization of where she had seen the face before.

"Kunohara," she said at last. "The bug man."

He laughed, sounding almost as drunk as the bandits. "The bug man! Very good! Yes, that is me."

The pale man sat a little straighter in the chair. His voice, when he spoke, had a dangerous edge. "This is rather tedious, Koony. Who are these people?"

Kunohara patted the other man on his silk-sheathed knee. "Travelers I have met before, Viticus. Do not worry yourself."

"But why do they call you by another name? I do not like

that." Viticus now sounded petulant as a child. "I want them killed now. Then they will not be so tiresome."

"Yes! Kill them now!" Those of the Attic Spiders whose mouths were not full of drink took up the chant. Renie jumped in startlement as something grasped her leg, but it was only !Xabbu climbing from the floor into her arms.

"My thought is that we should try to stay alive until they fall asleep from their liquor," he whispered in Renie's ear. "Perhaps they will chase me if I flee, giving the rest of you some time . . . ?"

The thought of !Xabbu, even in his swift baboon body, being chased through an unfamiliar place by gun-wielding thugs made Renie's throat clench with fear, but before she could say anything a deep, vibrating hum filled the room. The bandits fell silent as the sound reached a loud ringing tone and then dropped away once more.

"There is our sign," said the pale leader. "The bells have rung. The Mother is waiting." He began to say something else, but was taken by a fit of coughing. It went on far longer than seemed normal, ending in a tubercular hack that bent him double in his chair. When it had finished and he was regaining his breath, Renie saw a spot of blood flecking his chin. Viticus pulled a dirty handkerchief from his sleeve and wiped it away. "Bring them," he wheezed, flipping a limp hand toward Renie and her companions. Immediately the Attic Spiders surrounded them again.

As they were herded from the Campanile, past a marble pig wearing the mortarboard of a scholar and an expression of swollen self-esteem, Kunohara sidled up to Renie.

"He is consumptive, of course, the White Prince," he said, as though continuing some casual conversation. "Quite impressive that he should have made himself a ruler over this crude lot." He had dropped the harlequin mask somewhere, and now made a goggling face at !Xabbu, who was still crouched in Renie's arms, exactly as if !Xabbu had been a real monkey in a zoo. If Kunohara was not drunk he was doing a very good imitation.

"What are you talking about?" Renie asked. She heard a sharp voice and turned to watch T4b; the youth was not handling the jostling contact well, but Florimel had moved close to him and was speaking softly. The bandits led them down a flight of stairs, then through an arched doorway into a long, dark corridor. Some of the Attic Spiders carried lanterns, which threw shadows up the walls and onto the carved ceiling.

"Viticus, the chieftain," Kunohara continued. "He is a scion of one of the richest families, those who have their great houses along the Painted Lagoon, but even among those old and strange dynasties his habits were too controversial, and he was forced into exile. Now he is the White Prince of the Attics, a byword for terror." He belched, but did not apologize. "A fascinating story, but the House is full of such things."

"Is this your world, then?" !Xabbu asked.

"Mine?" Kunohara shook his head. "No, no. The people who made it are dead, although I knew them. A writer and an artist, husband and wife. The man became very rich because of a net entertainment he devised—something called 'Johnny Icepick'?" Kunohara swayed a little as he walked and bumped against the gun of Renie's escort, the same man who had prodded her up the staircase to the Campanile. "You will move a little farther back, Bibber," Kunohara directed.

For once the bandit did not giggle—Renie thought she even heard a quiet grunt of resentment—but he obeyed.

"In any case, the man and his wife took their money and made the House. A labor of love, I suppose. It is one of the few places in the network I will truly miss—a quite original creation."

"You'll miss it?" Renie said, wondering. "Why?"

Kunohara did not answer. The troop of bandits and prisoners now turned down another corridor, just as empty as the first, but dimly lit from above. Skylights in the roof, constructed of something bluer and more opaque than ordinary glass, turned the dying afternoon light into something like the bottom of the sea.

"Are they going to kill us?" Renie asked Kunohara. He did not reply. "Are you going to let them?"

He looked at her for a moment. Something of the sharpness she had sensed in him at their first meeting was gone, dulled by something more than just alcohol. "If you are still here, then you are part of the story, somehow," he said at last. "Even though I am not, I confess to being interested to see what will happen."

"What are you talking about?" Renie demanded.

Kunohara only smiled and slowed, so that Renie's part of the procession passed him by.

"What did that mean?" Renie whispered to !Xabbu. "Story? Whose story?"

Her friend, too, had taken on a distracted look. "I must think, Renie," he said. "It is strange. This is a man who could tell us much, if only he would."

"Good luck." Renie scowled. "He's a game-player. I know the type. He loves all this, being the only one who knows."

The thought was interrupted by Brother Factum Quintus, who had angled his way between the other prisoners until he reached Renie and !Xabbu. "I have never been here before," he said, almost in wonderment. "This corridor is on no map I have seen."

"Map!" Behind them, Bibber allowed himself a full chortle. "Hark at that! Map! As if the Spiders need a map. All the Attics are ours." He began to sing in an off-key warble.

> *"Who's that lurking on the stair,*
> *Weaving webs as fine as air,*
> *To catch the foolish unaware?*
> *Bow down to the Spiders!"*

Other drunken voices chimed in. As they turned again into yet another dark hall, half the company was singing, banging their weapons together, making a din like a circus parade.

> *"Here and there on silent feet,*
> *Leave the bitter, steal the sweet,*
> *Death to every foe we meet,*
> *Bow down to the Spiders . . . !"*

The blue-lit hallway was lined with massive mirrors in heavy frames, each one taller than a man, each draped with a dusty, sagging piece of cloth that did not entirely hide the reflection of the bandits' lanterns. Factum Quintus leaned out, craning his gawky neck to look at these objects more closely. "It is the Hall of Shrouded Mirrors," he said at last, breathlessly. "A myth, many thought. Wonderful! I never thought I would live to see it!"

Renie, with some difficulty, restrained herself from pointing out that he might not outlive the experience by much.

A weary voice called from somewhere back in the line, "Do

not go rushing in, my bravos. There are observances to be made, you know." The company slowed as they reached the end of the corridor and its draped mirrors; as Viticus walked forward his out-law tribe parted to let him pass. "Where is Koony?" he asked when he reached the front.

"Here, Viticus." The man in the harlequin suit stepped out of the crowd. He seemed tired and distracted now. Renie wondered what that might mean.

"Come along, then, old fellow. You wanted to see how we honor the Mother, didn't you?" The pale chieftain strode through the door at the end of the hall with Kunohara beside him.

Renie and the others now found themselves hemmed in the midst of the unwashed bandits, who gleefully poked and prodded them. "Do you think Kunohara will protect us?" Florimel asked softly. Renie could only shrug.

"I don't know what he'll do. He's strange. Maybe we should . . ."

Her sentence was never finished. As if at some signal, the en-tire crowd of bandits surged forward through the door at the end of the corridor, carrying Renie and the others with them. After jostling their way with much show of evil temper through the bot-tleneck of a small but high-ceilinged anteroom, the bandits spread out into the wide space on the far side, a rectangular chamber even larger than the Campanile, full of chill air. Windows lined the two long sides, although the glass had been smashed from every one on the left and several on the right as well, starting at the far end of the room. Through these gaping apertures the rooftops, turrets, and spires of the House could be seen stretch-ing endlessly into the distance, tinged a dull red by the last of the setting sun. Cold wind blew in across the few remaining spikes of glass that clung to the frames. Those windows still unbroken were of stained glass, huge multicolored squares, their subjects hard to discern by the dying light, although Renie thought she saw faces.

Their captors marched them forward until they had almost reached the far end of the room, where Viticus kneeled before an oil fire smoking in a wide bronze bowl while Hideki Kunohara stood a short distance away, watching. On the far side of the fire a shadowy shape loomed higher than a man, lit in a weirdly glint-

ing manner by the flames, its silhouette somehow rough and unstable. The tall, seated figure, robed and hooded, had hands clasped
on knees and a face shrouded by the sagging hood. Renie had a
terrified moment before she realized that the thing was a statue;
a fear almost as deep returned when she realized it was composed
entirely of shards of broken glass.

Most of the bandits had held back, unwilling to approach the
idol too closely, but the bearded giant Grip and a dozen more
pushed Renie and her companions down onto their knees.

Pale Viticus turned from the thing of glass. His eyes were
hooded as though he could barely keep himself awake, but there
was still somehow a bright watchfulness to him. "It is the Mother's
day," he said, examining Renie and the others. "All praise her.
Now, which of these shall be her gift?" He turned to Kunohara.
"It is sad, but we can only give her one in the proper way." He
gestured to the nearest unbroken window, whose picture was entirely unrecognizable now that the sun had vanished behind the
far rooftops. "Even so, in a few more years we will have no more
windows, and we will have to find another spot . . ." He paused
as a cough shook him, then dabbed at his lips with his soiled
sleeve. "We will have to find another place to bring the Mother
of Broken Glass her gifts." He squinted, extending a languid finger toward T4b. "We have not given her a man the last two years—
she will thank us for this strapping fellow, I think."

Grip and one of the other bandits seized T4b by his arms and
dragged him toward the first intact window. The teenager fought
uselessly: when his sleeve fell back and exposed his glowing hand,
Grip started and leaned his head away, but still maintained his
hold.

"No!" Florimel struggled with her own captors. Beside her,
Emily let out a cry of true terror, ragged as a death rattle.

"It is only a little time to fall," Viticus assured T4b. "Only a
moment of cold wind, and then you will have nothing to fear ever
again."

"Kunohara!" Renie shouted. "Are you going to let this happen?"

The harlequin crossed his arms on his chest. "I suppose not."
He turned to the bandit chieftain. "I cannot let you have these
people, Viticus."

The powdered man regarded the prisoners, then Kunohara. He seemed more amused than anything else. "You are being dreadfully boring, Koony. Are you certain?"

Before Kunohara could reply, the bandit named Bibber stepped forward, face contorted in fury. "Who's this little dung-monkey to say no to the White Prince?" He leveled his blunderbuss at Kunohara, trembling with outraged traditionalism. "Who is he to tell the Spiders how to honor the Mother?"

"I don't think you should do that, Bibber," said Viticus mildly, but the bandit was so outraged he paid no attention to the chieftain whose honor he was defending. His finger curled on the trigger. "I'll blow this little crease-wipe clean out of the House . . . !"

Kunohara made a small gesture and both Bibber's arms suddenly burst into flame. He immediately dropped to the floor, shrieking and thrashing, surrounded by an ever-widening circle of nothing as his comrades hurried to get away from him. Kunohara waved his finger and the flames were gone. The bandit lay curled beside his forgotten gun, stroking his forearms and weeping.

Kunohara laughed quietly. "It is good, sometimes, to be one of the gods of Otherland." He still sounded a bit drunk.

"Can we use none of them?" Viticus asked.

Kunohara eyed Renie's companions. Emily was crying. T4b, reprieved, had sunk to his knees again in front of the window. "The monk?" the harlequin said, half to himself. "He is not one of you, after all," he pointed out to Renie. "He is . . . well, you know what I mean."

Renie was outraged, although what he said was technically true. "Brother Factum Quintus has just as much right to live as we do, whether . . ." She paused—she had been about to say *whether he's a real person or not,* but realized that might not be the kindest or the smartest thing to bring up. "It doesn't matter," she said instead. "He *is* one of us."

Kunohara turned to Viticus and shrugged.

"So, then," said the White Prince. "Grip?"

The giant bent and scooped whimpering Bibber up from the floor. He took a step to one side to get around T4b, then—with Bibber already squealing in unbelieving horror as he realized what was happening—got a good hold on his captive and heaved him through the stained glass window, which exploded outward around him.

The scream went on for long seconds, growing fainter all the way down. In the silence that followed, a few remaining pieces of glass slid from the frame and chinked to the floor.

"Thank you, Mother, for all you have given me," Viticus said, bowing toward the statue of glass shards. He bent and with his long fingers tweezed up the pieces that had sprayed from the shattered window, then tossed them onto the statue's lap. For a moment it seemed to swell a little, a trick of the guttering firelight.

Renie, frozen in shock at the callous murder, suddenly felt the cold room grow colder still, although the wind had not risen. Something was changing, everything somehow shifting sideways. For a moment she was certain it was another of the bizarre hitches in reality, like the one they had experienced when they had lost Azador on the river, but instead of the entire world shuddering to a halt the air only became thicker and colder, clingy as fog. The light changed, too, stretching until everything seemed farther away from everything else than it had been only instants before. Some of the bandits cried out in fear, but their voices were distant; for a moment Renie felt certain the statue of the Mother was coming to life, that it was about to step down from its plinth, claws creaking open. . . .

"The window!" gasped Florimel. "Look!"

Something was forming in the very place where only seconds before Bibber had plunged to his death, as though the stained glass were growing back to cover the gaping hole. A pale blur in the middle became a rough sketch of a face. A moment later it grew clearer, a faint, smeary image of a young woman, dark eyes staring blindly.

"The Lady . . ." someone cried out from the crowd behind Renie. All sound was distorted—it was impossible to tell whether the words were spoken in joy or horror.

The face moved in the cloudy plane that filled the frame, sliding from corner to corner like something trapped. *"No!"* it said, *"you send me nightmares!"*

Renie felt !Xabbu clinging, his head only inches from her own, but she could not speak; nor could she take her gaze from the suggestion of a face surrounded now by a halo of dark hair.

"I do not belong here!" Her indistinct gaze seemed to take in Renie and her companions. *"It hurts me to come here this time! But you summon me—you send me my own nightmares!"*

"Who . . . who are you?" Florimel's voice was barely audible, as though someone had gripped her throat in strong fingers.

"He is sleeping now—the One who is Other—yet he dreams of you. But the darkness is blowing through him. The shadow is growing." For a moment the face grew even dimmer; when it reappeared, it was so faint that her eyes were little more than charcoal smudges on the pale oval of her face. *"You must come to find the others. You must come to Priam's Walls!"*

"What do you mean?" Renie asked, finding her voice at last. "What others?"

"Lost! The tower! Lost!" The face dwindled like a cloud torn by high winds. After a moment there was only the square hole where the window had been, a gaping wound opening into night's deeps.

It was long moments before Renie could feel anything again. The deep cold had gone, replaced by the lesser chill of the wind skirling in the turrets outside. Outside, evening had turned into night; the only light remaining in the high chamber was the inconstant flicker of the oil fire.

The bandit chieftain Viticus was sitting flat on the floor as if blown there by a great gale, his rouged face slack with surprise. "That . . . that is not what usually happens," he said softly. Most of the rest of the bandits had fled; those who remained were facedown on the floor in positions of supplication. Viticus hoisted himself onto his trembling legs and purposefully dusted his breeches. "I think it likely we will not come here again," he said, and walked to the doorway with careful dignity, although his shoulders were tensed as though he expected a blow. He did not look back. As he passed through, the remainder of his Attic Spiders clambered to their feet and hurried after him.

!Xabbu was tugging at Renie's arm. "Are you well?"

"Enough, I guess." She turned to look for the others. Florimel and T4b were both sitting on the floor, and Factum Quintus lay on his back talking to himself, but Emily was in a limp tangle near the far wall, just beneath one of the broken windows. Renie hurried to her side and reassured herself that the girl was still breathing.

"She's just fainted, I think," Renie called over her shoulder to the others. "Poor child!"

"Priam's Walls, is it?" Hideki Kunohara was sitting cross-legged beneath the jagged likeness of the Mother, his expression distant. "You are indeed in the center of the story, it seems."

"What are you talking about?" Florimel snapped, regaining a little of her composure. She came to join Renie at Emily's side, and together they turned the girl until she was resting in what seemed a more comfortable position. "That means Troy, does it not? The fortress of King Priam, the Trojan War—no doubt another one of these damned simulations. What does it mean to you, Kunohara, and what do you mean, 'center of the story'?"

"The story that is taking place all around you," he said. "The Lady has appeared and given you a summons. Quite impressive, even I have to admit it. You are wanted in the maze, I suppose."

"Maze?" Renie looked up from Emily, who was beginning to show signs of waking. "Like with the Minotaur?"

"That was in the palace of Minos, in Crete," Florimel said. "There was no maze in Troy."

Kunohara chuckled, but it was not a particularly pleasant sound. Again Renie felt something wrong about him, a certain febrile wildness. She had thought it was liquor, but perhaps it was something else—perhaps the man was simply mad. "If you know so much," he said, "perhaps you can answer all your own questions, then."

"No," Renie said. "We're sorry. But we are confused and frightened. Who was that . . . that . . . ?" She gestured at the window where the face had appeared.

"It was the Lady of the Windows," Brother Factum Quintus said behind her, his voice full of awe. "And I thought I had experienced the full run of marvels, today. But there she was! Not just an old tale!" He shook his head as he sat up, as oddly articulated as a stick insect. "They shall be talking of this at the Library for generations."

He seemed to have missed entirely the fact that they had almost been hurled to their deaths, Renie thought sourly. "But what did she want, this . . . Lady? I couldn't make any sense of it at all." She turned to Kunohara. "What in hell is going on around here?"

He lifted his hands and spread them, palms up. "You have been summoned to Troy. It is a simulation, as your comrade said, but it was also the first simulation the Grail Brotherhood constructed. Near the heart of things."

"What do you mean, 'the heart of things'? And how do you know so much—you said you weren't part of the Grail."

"I am not part of the sun either, but I know when the afternoon turns hot, or when night is coming." Pleased with this epigram, he nodded.

Florimel growled, "We are tired of riddles, Kunohara."

"Then Troy will hold many disappointments for you." He slapped his thighs and stood, then sketched a mocking bow to the statue of the Mother before turning to face them once more. "In truth, you cannot afford bad temper—you curse riddles, but where does wisdom come from? Have you solved those I posed for you earlier? Dollo's Law and *Kishimo-jin*? Understanding may well be important to your own part of the story."

"Story! You keep saying that!" Renie wanted to hit him, but could not rid herself of the memory of Bibber's horrified face, of the flames Kunohara had summoned which had momentarily engulfed him. In an unreal world, who could say what was real? Kunohara had called himself one of the gods of Otherland, and in that he was correct.

"Please, Mr. Kunohara, what does this mean?" said !Xabbu, reaching for Renie's hand to calm her. "You speak of a story, and the woman—the Lady of the Windows—spoke of someone who dreamed of us. Dream is *my* name, in the language of my people. I thought we were in a world purely of mechanical things, but now I am not sure it is true. Perhaps there is a greater reason I am here, I wonder—a greater purpose. If so, I would like to know it."

To Renie's surprise, Kunohara looked at !Xabbu with something like respect. "You sound a bit like the Circle people, but more sensible," the bug man said. "As far as dreams, I do not know—there is much in a network this complicated that cannot be known by anyone, even the creators, and there were also many details that the Brotherhood kept hidden from the rest of us. But

as to what I said about story, surely you have seen something of
that. The entire network has lost its randomness, somehow," he
paused, musing, ". . . or perhaps randomness itself is only a name
for stories we have not recognized yet."

"You are saying that something is guiding the network?"
Florimel asked. "But we knew that already. Surely that is the Grail
Brotherhood's purpose—it is their invention, after all."

"Or perhaps the operating system itself . . ." Renie suggested.
"It must be very complicated, very sophisticated."

"No, I mean something even more subtle is at work." Kunohara shook his head impatiently. "My idea is not something I can
explain, perhaps. It does not matter." He hung his head in mock-
sorrow. "The fancies of a solitary man."

"Please tell us!" Renie was frightened he might disappear again,
as he had done to them twice before. Despite his sarcasm, his discomfort at the situation was palpable—this was not a man who
felt comfortable with others.

Kunohara closed his eyes; for a moment, he seemed to be talking to himself. "It is no good. A story-meme? Who would do such
a thing. Who *could* do such a thing? You cannot infect a mechanism with words."

"What are you talking about?" Renie reached to touch his arm,
but !Xabbu's warning squeeze stayed her. "What's a . . . a story-
mean?"

"Meme. M-E-M-E." He opened his eyes. His expression had
grown tight and angrily mirthful. "Do you wish to go to Troy?"

"What?" Renie looked around the little company. T4b was
cradling Emily, who was still only half-conscious. Factum Quintus was across the chilly room, apparently oblivious to their conversation as he inspected the frame of one of the broken windows.
Only Florimel and !Xabbu were paying close attention.

"You heard me—or you heard the Lady of the Windows. You
have been invited, or commanded, or implored. Are you going?
I can open a gateway for you."

Renie slowly shook her head. "We can't—not yet. Our friend
has been kidnapped. Will you help us get her back?"

"No." Kunohara now seemed distant, glacial, but the half-smile
remained. "I have spent too much time here as it is—intervened,

broken my own rules. You have your part in this story, but I do not. None of it concerns me."

"But why won't you just *help* us?" Renie said. "All you give us are these irritating riddles, like something out of a . . . a story."

"Look," said Kunohara, ignoring her troubled expression. "I have done more than I should. Do you want honesty from me? Very well—I will be honest. You have set yourself up against the most powerful people in the world. Worse than that, you have invaded their own network, where they are more than people—they are gods!"

"But you're a god, too. You said so."

Kunohara made a scornful noise. "A very small god, and with very little power outside my own fiefdom. Now be quiet and I will tell you the honest truth. You have set yourself an impossible task. That is your business. Somehow you have stayed alive so far, and that is interesting, but it is nothing to do me with me. Now you ask me to intervene—to join you, as though I were some friendly spirit standing by the path in a children's tale. But you are not going to succeed. The Brotherhood may destroy themselves someday with their own cleverness, but that will have nothing to do with you. Instead they are going to capture you, either here or in the real world, and when they do, they are going to torture you before they kill you."

He swiveled from one member of the company to another, swaying a little, but making eye contact with each of them, some for the first time. "When it happens, you will tell them anything they want to know. Should I give you information from the privacy of my own mind so that you can give it to them? Should I provide you a tale of how I helped you work against their interests, so that you may tell it to them between screams?" He shook his head, staring down at his own hands; it was hard to tell who was the target of his disgust, Renie and her companions or himself. "I told you—I am a small man. I want nothing to do with your imaginary heroism. The Brotherhood are far, far too strong for me, and I exist here and enjoy my freedom of the network only because I am not an impediment. You think I speak in riddles just to torment you? In my way, I have tried to help. But should I lay down everything I have for you, including my own small life? I think not."

"But we don't even understand those things you told us . . ." Renie began. An instant later she was talking to nothing but cold air. Kunohara had vanished.

"You're safe," Renie told Emily. She felt the girl's forehead and checked her pulse, knowing as she did so that it was a pointless exercise with what was at best a virtual body, and which might not even belong to an actual human being. How could you tell if code was seriously ill, anyway? And what if the code claimed to be pregnant? The whole thing was crazy. "You're safe," she said again. "Those people are gone."

With Florimel's help she got Emily into a sitting position. T4b hovered nearby making attempts at assistance that wound up interfering more than helping.

"Say my name," the girl requested. Her eyes were still almost shut; she sounded like someone half-dreaming. "Did you say it? I can't remember."

"You are . . ." Florimel began, but Renie, remembering what the girl had said before, grabbed Florimel's arm and squeezed, shaking her head.

"What do you think your name is?" Renie asked instead. "Quick, tell me your name."

"It is . . . I think it is . . ." Emily fell silent for a moment. "Why are the children gone?"

"Children?" T4b sounded frightened. "Those raggedy ma'lockers, they hit her? She funny?"

"What children?" Renie asked.

Emily's eyes flicked open, scanning the room. "There aren't any here, are there? For a moment I thought there were. I thought the room was full of them, and they were making lots of noise . . . and then they just . . . stopped."

"What's your name?" Renie asked again.

The girl's eyes narrowed as though she feared a trick. "Emily, isn't it? Why are you asking me that?"

Renie sighed. "Never mind." She sat back, letting Florimel finish checking the girl for any sign of damage. "So here we are."

Florimel looked up from her ministrations. "We have much to talk about. Many questions to try to answer."

"But finding Martine still comes first." Renie turned to the monk, who was inspecting the statue of the Mother with rapt fascination. "Factum Quintus, do you know how to get to that other place from here? The one you said we'd check second?"

"The Spire Forest?" He was bending at the waist, a gaunt shape like a drinking-bird toy, his nose only inches from the glass-shard face of the Mother. "I suppose so, if I can find the main Attic throughway. Yes, that would be best. We can't be more than a few hundred paces away in a straight line, but we will have to find a route, and the Attic is a bit of a maze." He turned to face her, his expression suddenly intent. "Hmmm, yes. Speaking of mazes . . ."

"I'm sure you want to know what that was all about," Renie said wearily. "And as you can tell, we need to talk about it ourselves." She wondered how much it would be permissible to tell Factum Quintus without threatening the monk's sanity. "But our friend comes first, and it feels like we've wasted hours."

"There are unfamiliar stars in the sky," !Xabbu said from his perch on the windowsill. "I cannot recognize any of them. But it is true the sun has been down for some time now."

"So let's move." Renie stood, realizing for the first time since they had been captured how sore and exhausted she was. "Martine needs us. I just hope we find her in time."

As T4b helped Emily to her feet, Florimel turned to Renie, speaking softly. "One thing we have learned—no approach without a plan next time. And we *must* succeed. Even if we rescue Martine, we will be helpless if we do not recover the lighter as well."

"Amen." Renie nervously watched !Xabbu teetering on the windowsill, trying to remind herself that in this world he wore the body of a monkey, and clearly had a monkey's balance and climbing skills. But it was still hard to watch him leaning out into the cold night air through which a man had just fallen to his death a few minutes earlier. "!Xabbu—we're going."

As he hopped down, Florimel said, "But I have to admit Kunohara's words haunt me. If he had not been here, we would have been helpless in the hands of those quite ordinary bandits. How are we going to strike at the masters of this network? What chance do we have?"

"It's not what chance do we have," Renie replied, "it's what *choice* do we have."

Silent then, they turned and followed the others out the door, leaving the room of broken windows to the night and the wind.

CHAPTER 18

Dreams in a Dead Land

PAUL felt small as a mouse, a cornered thing squeaking out its last moments of life. As the Cyclops' massive hand stretched wide he stumbled backward, terror draining the strength from his legs.

Nothing around you is true, the golden harp had told him, *and yet the things you see can hurt you or kill you . . .*

Kill me, he thought dazedly, groping on the cavern floor for something to use as a weapon. The giant's roar was so throbbingly loud his own thoughts seemed about to blow away. *Going to kill me—but I don't want to die . . . !*

He found the monster's shears, far too short and heavy to be a useful weapon. He heaved them up and flung them as hard as he could, but Polyphemus only swatted them away. Somewhere behind the Cyclops lay Azador, knocked aside by a blow, his skull probably crushed. The great stone that sealed the cavern had not been pushed all the way closed, but Paul knew he could not wriggle through the narrow space before the monster caught him.

He snatched at something that felt like a rock, but it was too light; only after he had bounced it uselessly off the Cyclops' broad chest did he see it was a human skull.

Mine . . . ! The thought swirled past like a spark. *The next fool who tries that—he'll use mine . . .*

The vast hand slammed down, narrowly missing him. Paul tripped and staggered back. The Cyclops leaned closer, blood from Azador's failed attack on the monster's neck and hand, his growling, gap-toothed mouth stinking of rotten flesh, and the difference between real and virtual shrank to absolutely nothing.

Paul heaved up a pitch bucket and threw it at the Cyclop's face, hoping to blind him. The bucket fell short and broke on the creature's breastbone instead, covering his mighty chest in black ooze, but the giant was not even slowed. Paul sprang to the side and dodged behind their raft, which was leaning against a cavern wall near the fire. Polyphemus flung it aside as though it were paper; it crashed down on the far side of the room, timbers cracking. The monstrosity's lips curled in pleasant anticipation as Paul fled again, backing into a corner, his only weapon a deadfall branch from the pile of firewood. Both of the giant's enormous hands came up, hemming him in, and Paul smacked uselessly at the dirty, squat fingers.

Suddenly, the Cyclops lurched upright, bellowing out a scream which threatened to burst Paul's eardrums as he swatted at something behind him. Azador stumbled back from the Cyclops' leg, the shears which Paul had flung earlier now quivering in the monster's thick calf muscle. The giant made a move toward this new attacker, then turned to peer with his vast, bloodshot eye at Paul, who still cowered in the corner. Polyphemus shambled to the wall of the cavern and snatched up his shepherd's staff, a slender tree trunk half-a-dozen meters tall, shod in bronze, then whirled with surprising speed and swung it at Azador, who had only an instant to fall to his belly as the log hissed toward his head. Polyphemus lifted the staff high, intending to spear him like a fish.

Desperate, Paul threw the piece of wood he had been holding, but it bounced harmlessly off the Cyclops' back. He sprang forward and heaved up the giant's wooden dinner bowl, but realized it would be no more of a distraction than the firewood. The Cyclops jabbed at Azador, forcing him to roll out of the way again and again, but he was running out of room to maneuver. Paul's helpless terror was so great that it took a moment for him to realize that he was standing on something that was burning his foot.

The Cyclops had raised the staff to pin Azador against the cavern wall when Paul put his foot against the shears wagging in the monster's calf and shoved them farther into his leg. The giant roared and turned, swatting at Paul with the back of his hand, but Paul had expected the blow and was able to duck beneath it before flinging the bowl full of burning coals into the monster's face.

He had hoped only for a moment's distraction, to blind the creature long enough for them to make a try for the cavern entrance. He had not expected the pitch splashed on the creature's face and body to ignite, crackling up the creature's beard and setting it ablaze.

Flames enveloped the Cyclops' head. The creature's shriek of pain was so loud that Paul sank to the earth and clutched his head. Polyphemus turned and shoved his way through the front doorway, sending the great stone spinning; Azador pulled Paul out of its path just before it wobbled to a halt and crashed to the cavern floor.

For long moments Paul could only lie curled on his side. His skull felt like it had been smashed to pieces inside his head, and he could hear nothing but a single insistent tone. When he looked up, Azador stood before him, bloody but alive. He was speaking, but Paul could not make out a word.

"I think I'm deaf," Paul said. His own voice seemed to come from the other side of a vast space, faint as a whisper, all but subsumed by the painful ringing.

Azador helped him up. They looked at the open doorway, both wondering how long until the giant would return with flames extinguished, burned and vengeful. Azador gestured to the raft, clearly wanting to seize it, but Paul only shook his head as he staggered toward the cavern entrance. There was no knowing how long the giant would be gone: to remain a moment longer would be suicidal folly. He could not hear the other man, but he knew Azador was cursing his cowardice.

The first light of dawn was in the sky outside, revealing the giant's track where it had smashed its way through the trees, perhaps stumbling in search of water. They followed along the line of destruction, but stayed hidden in the trees on either side. The path zigzagged down the hill toward the ocean far below.

They found the Cyclops facedown on a shelf of stone, wreathed in smoke like a defeated Titan flung blazing to Earth from Mount Olympus. Flames burned fitfully in the sheepskin garment, fanned by the wind. The creature's head still smoldered, a lump of black ruin atop the shoulders. It was quite dead.

Paul slumped down on the stone beside it, so happy to be alive and underneath the sky once more that he burst into tears. He could not make out Azador's scornful words, but it was easy to read the other man's expression.

Even with the monster destroyed they could not get off its island, nor were they in much of a hurry to do so.

They spent the first day simply recovering from the struggle, sleeping and nursing their aching bodies. Most of their wounds were little worse than cuts and bruises, but Azador's ribs had taken a hard blow and although his hearing had returned, Paul was burned on his feet and in several places on his hands and chest where the coals had touched him. As the sun fell down the sky toward evening, Azador suggested they sleep in the giant's shelter, but Paul did not want to spend any more time in that reeking den than necessary. To Azador's disgust he insisted that they make their campsite in front of the cave instead, exposed to the elements but breathing clean air.

Azador caught and killed one of the Cyclops' sheep, which had strayed all across the hilltop after their master's death. For

Paul the smell of roasting meat was a little too reminiscent of what they had just survived, but Azador ate with gusto. By the time he had finished his meal he seemed quite recovered, and even grudgingly congratulated Paul for his quick thinking.

"That was good, the fire," he said. "Bastard went up like a torch—*foof*!" Azador wiggled his fingers to mime flames. "And now we eat his meat."

"Please, no," said Paul, nauseated by the choice of words.

The raft was too large to carry down to the water so they reluctantly dismantled it into a half-dozen smaller pieces, carefully saving all the rope for later use, and dragged them out of the cave and down to the beach for repair.

"He was a big strong bastard, I give him that," grunted Azador as they trudged along the hillside with a length of bound logs. "The way he carried it up over his head like that—when I saw it coming over the trees, I thought it was Saint Kali the Black."

Paul stumbled on a root and almost let go of his end. "Saint who?"

"Saint Kali. She is special to my people. We carry her in her boat down to the ocean every year." He saw that Paul was staring at him. "A statue. On the saint's day she is carried to the water. She is called Black Sarah, too."

Paul had been astonished not by the outlandishness of the ritual, but because Azador was sharing something of himself. "She's . . ." He paused. "Who *are* your people, anyway?"

Azador lifted an eyebrow. "I am Romany."

"Gypsies?"

"If you like." Azador himself did not seem to like, because he was silent for the rest of the trip to the beach.

They were able to use the giant's own tools, although they found them heavy and clumsy. Of particular use was a bronze knife with a scalloped edge, long as a sword but twice as wide, handy for sawing at tree branches. Over the course of two days, slowed by an occasional rain shower or their own aching muscles, the two men managed to reassemble the raft and fashion a new mast from the pliant trunk of a young tree, but it was much harder work than Paul's first round of boatbuilding. More than once he found himself wishing that Calypso's magical ax had survived the attack of the monster Scylla.

On the evening of the second night, with plans to cast off again at dawn and leave the island of Polyphemus behind, they held a celebratory feast.

Besides the luckless animal whose leg was crackling on a spit above the flames, Azador selected several more of the giant's fattest sheep to take with them on the raft. The thought of a fresh stock of meat put him in a good mood. As their fire leaped high into the air, sparks whirling above the trees, he did a dance and sang a song whose words the machineries of the network could not or did not translate. As the gypsy grimaced through some of the more difficult steps, his face locked in a scowling concentration that was nevertheless oddly joyful, Paul found himself warming to the man.

The mutton and the Cyclops' last jug of sour but potent wine might have put Azador in a buoyant mood, but his tongue was no looser than usual. When he had finished dancing and eating, he rolled himself onto his side without further conversation and went to sleep.

The winds were up and the sea was restive all the next day after they cast off, and their rebuilt raft responded to it as to a new and ardent lover. Disturbed by the constant pitching, Paul spent most of the day crouched on the deck with his arms around the mast, wondering how a virtual experience could cause such profound discomfort to his inner ear. The winds calmed a little at sundown, and as a balmy evening settled on them Paul found himself feeling much better about everything. Azador steered by the stars, using a dead reckoning method that Paul had read about in books, but which had never seemed of any more practical use than mummification or alchemy. Now he was extremely grateful to have a companion who knew such antiquated things.

"Will we reach Troy soon?" he asked as the moon ran behind the clouds and the ocean and sky darkened. The rush and murmur of the sea and the great starless emptiness around him was like being inside a vast seashell.

"Don't know." Azador sat at the back of the raft, one hand

lightly on the tiller, perched above the waves as calmly as if he sat on a mat in his own home. "Depends on many things."

Paul nodded as though he understood, but it was only to save the now familiar—and generally unrewarded—effort of getting Azador to explain. Weather, he guessed, and navigational uncertainty.

Sometime after midnight Azador lashed the rudder into position and took his turn sleeping. The moon had gone for good now and the black sky was afire with stars. Paul watched them pass through their slow dance above his head, so close it seemed he could reach up to them and freeze his fingers against their cold light, and vowed that if he ever found his way home he would never take the heavens for granted again.

In the late morning of their third day since leaving Polyphemus' island they saw land again. Another squall had passed over them just after sunrise, forcing them to furl the sail, and the sea had been unruly ever since. Azador was struggling with the ropes, trying to find a healthy tautness of sail. Paul was kneeling at the front of the raft, holding one of the lines but mainly feeling queasy, when he saw something dark on the horizon.

"Look!" he said. "I think it's another island!"

Azador squinted. A column of sunlight sharp as a knife blade suddenly sliced down through the toil of clouds, making the distant green hills glint across the dark water.

"Island, yes," Azador agreed. "Look at her, winking at us like a beautiful whore."

Paul thought that seemed a little harsh, but he was too happy to have sighted it to care. He was much less sad and fearful now that the raft was rebuilt and he had a strong, skilled companion, but he was still growing a little tired of the monotony of the Homeric seas—a bit of dry land would be a good thing. He thought of berries, and even bread and cheese if there was a town or city below the distant green slopes, and his mouth watered. It was odd that he seldom felt hungry, but could still feel the *desire* for food very strongly, could think of tastes and textures with great pleasure and longing. Undoubtedly a by-product of his body being kept alive on machines—drips and tubes providing his nutrients, most likely. But it would be good

on that day when he was not only back in his own England,
but back in his real body once more as well. Like the star-
sprayed skies, it was something he would never again take for
granted.

As the day wore on past noon and they drew nearer to the island, the clouds drifted away; although a mild breeze remained,
the sun soon warmed the skies and sea, and Paul felt his mood
becoming even more optimistic. Azador, too, seemed to catch a
little of the feeling. Once, turning quickly, Paul almost caught
him smiling.

The island growing before them rose at its center to a collection of steep grassy hills which took the sun like green velvet. A mile or more of white sand lay before them along the
water's edge, curiously mimicked in the blankets of white flowers that covered many of the hillsides, thick as snow. Streams
and rivulets glittered in the meadows, or splashed down from the
rocks of the highest hills, the cataracts making more spots of
white. Paul saw no human inhabitants, but thought he saw regular shapes that might be low buildings atop some of the lesser
hills. In truth, it would have been astonishing if there had not
been some sign of the works of men, for the island was the
loveliest he had seen in this whole imaginary Mediterranean
world. Even the scents that the wind had brought them for some
time now, blossoming trees and wet grass and something less definable, something pungent as perfume but somehow also as subtle as the spray from a waterfall, made Paul feel that for this
moment anyway, life was good.

As they dragged their raft through the gentle surf and onto
sand fine as bone ash, Paul realized that he was laughing with
pleasure.

He and Azador raced up the slope to the first meadow, bumping and shoving like schoolboys let out early. Soon they found
themselves hip-deep in soft bushes covered with thick white flowers, the petals as translucent as smoked glass. The flower field
stretched away for almost a mile, and they waded into it with
their hands above their heads so as not to damage the beautiful
blossoms more than they needed to. The scent was even stronger
here but harder to define, as heady as an ancient brandy. Paul

thought he could happily stay in this place, experiencing only this one glorious scent, for the rest of his life.

Halfway across the field their raft seemed not just a long distance away but a long time away as well, something from another life. People appeared in the doorways of the long white houses on the hills before them and began to walk slowly down the path to meet them. By the time the islanders had reached the edge of the flowering meadow, where they waited for Paul and Azador, they were laughing, too, with the sheer joy of the meeting.

They were handsome folk, men, women, and children, all tall, all shapely. Their eyes were bright. Some were singing. Little boys and girls took Paul and his companion by the hand and led them back up the winding road to their village, its broad roofs and white walls shining in the sun.

"What is this place?" Paul asked sleepily.

The smiling, dignified old headman of the village nodded slowly, as though Paul's question contained the very essence of wisdom. "The Island of Lotos," he said at last. "Treasured of the gods. Jewel of the seas. Welcomer of travelers."

"Ah." Paul nodded, too. It was a lovely place. All those names were understatement, if anything. He and Azador had been fed a meal more sumptuous and delectable than even the nymph Calypso's ambrosia. "*Lotos.* Lovely name." And familiar, too, an exotic word that tickled his mind pleasantly but did not compel further consideration.

Beside him, Azador nodded even more slowly. "Good food. Everything is very, very nice."

Paul laughed. It was funny that Azador should say that, since there hadn't been amy meat to eat at all, only bread and cheese and honey and berries and—oddly but somehow appropriately—the white flowers that shrouded the hillsides. But it was good to see the gypsy man enjoying himself, his usual dour expression gone, as though carried away by the warm breeze. Several of the local girls had already noticed Azador's dark good looks and now sat around him like the acolytes of a great teacher. Paul might have been jealous, but he had a fan club of his own only slightly smaller than the gypsy's, all watching his every move and hanging on his words as though they had never seen his like before, nor had even imagined such a paragon could exist.

It was good, Paul decided. Yes, things were good.

He was having trouble keeping track of time. He dimly remembered that the sun had vanished more than once, perhaps slipping behind clouds, but darkness had been as pleasurable as daylight and he had not minded. Now it was dark again. Somehow, when Paul had not noticed it, the sun had set. A fire had been lit in a ring of stones on the bare ground, even though the beautiful city was all around them, but that just made things feel more homely. Many of the Lotos people were still entertaining the newcomers, although others had finally wandered off, doubtless to their lovely, comfortable houses.

Azador disentangled himself from the long limbs of a dark-haired, comely young woman and sat up. The woman protested sleepily and tried to pull him back down again, but Azador wore an intent expression.

"Ionas," he said. "My friend, Ionas."

Paul stared for a moment before he remembered it was the name he had given himself. He laughed—it was funny that Azador should call him that.

Azador waved his hand, trying to concentrate despite the caressing hands of the woman. "Listen," he said. "You do not know it, but I am a very clever man."

Paul had no idea what he meant, but it was pleasantly amusing to listen his friend's voice. The slightly halting English was exactly how an Azador should talk.

"No, stop laughing," Azador said. "The Brotherhood, those bastards—I am the only person ever to escape from them."

Puzzled, Paul tried to remember exactly who the Brotherhood was, but he felt so good that it seemed like a waste of time to think too hard. "You got away from someone . . . escaped . . . ?" he said at last. "Is that the woman? The one with the cigarette monkey and the lighter?" Something was wrong about that sentence, but he couldn't figure out what.

"No, not the woman, she is nothing. Never fear, I will find her soon and take back what is mine." Azador waved his hand.

"I am talking about the Brotherhood—the men who own this place, and all the others."

"The Brotherhood." Paul nodded his head gravely. He remembered now, or thought he did. A person called Nandi had told him about them. Nandi . . . the Brotherhood . . . something about the subject nagged at him, but he gently pushed it away. The wide ivory moon sliding along the sky behind a thin net of clouds was so beautiful that for a moment Paul forgot to listen to what Azador was saying.

". . . They do not simply use the few children they have stolen," Azador was saying when the moon disappeared behind a thicker cloud bank and Paul's attention returned.

"What are you talking about?"

"The Grail people. The Brotherhood. It is strange to think about now. It seemed so important." Azador laid his hand on the dark-haired woman's brow. She pulled it to her mouth, kissed it, then gave up on persuasion and slid back down to sleep curled beside him. "They took the Romany first, of course."

"The Romany . . ."

"Gypsies. My people."

"Took them first for what?" It was nice to talk to Azador, Paul reflected, but it would be good to sleep, too.

"For their machines—their live-forever machines." Azador smiled, but it was a little sad. "It is always the Romany, of course. No one likes us. I do not mean here. Here on this island, everyone is kind, but outside . . ." He drifted for a moment, then made an effort to recover himself. Paul too tried to concentrate, although he was not sure why Azador's words were any more important than the night birds and the distant sound of the ocean. "In any case, they took our young ones. Some disappeared, some were taken, some . . . some the parents turned a blind eye, telling themselves that although they never heard from them anymore, the money from the companies meant that the children were alive and well and giving satisfaction with their work."

"I don't understand."

"They use the children, Ionas. This network, it is made with the brains of children. Thousands they have stolen, like my people, and thousands more they have crippled, who they control with their machines. And then there are the million never-born."

"I still don't understand." He was almost angry with Azador for making him think. "What are you talking about?"

"But they could not hold me—Azador escaped." The gypsy seemed almost not to remember Paul was there. "Two years I have been free in their system. At least I think it is that long— it was only when I had the lighter that I knew what time it was in the real world."

"You escaped from . . . from the Brotherhood?" He was trying as hard as he could, but the scent of the night pressed down on his eyelids like a cool, gentle hand, urging him to sleep.

"You would not understand." Azador's smile was kindly, forgiving. "You are a nice man, Ionas, but this is too deep for you. You cannot understand what it is to be sought by the Grail Brotherhood. You are trapped here, I know. It has happened to many others besides you. But you cannot imagine what it is like for Azador, who must travel without being discovered, always one step ahead of the bastards who own all this." He shook his head, moved by his own bravery. "But now I have found this place, where I am safe. Where I am . . . happy . . ."

Azador lapsed into silence. Paul, quite satisfied not to have to think anymore, let himself drift down into comfortable darkness.

At some later point the sun was up, and Paul again took a meal with the island's handsome, friendly inhabitants, savoring the sweet blossoms and other wonderful dishes. The light on the island was oddly inconstant, sliding almost unnoticeably from bright day to darkness and back, but it was a small enough irritation when weighed against the deep satisfactions of the place.

During one of the intervals of bright sunshine he found himself staring down at something that seemed inexplicably familiar, a piece of shimmering cloth bearing the emblem of a feather, a pretty thing that had fallen to the ground. Having admired it for a moment, he was about to walk away, following a group of singing voices—the islanders loved to sing, another of their many charming habits—but he could not quite bring himself to leave the cloth behind. He stared at it for what seemed a long time, although it became harder to see as the sun dipped behind a cloud again. A cool breeze sprang up and ruffled it. Paul leaned down and picked it up, then stumbled off again in pursuit of the singers, who were now far out of sight but not yet inaudible. Even the feeling of the soft, slippery weave was somehow familiar, but although it was clutched in his hand, he had already nearly forgotten it.

He did not remember lying down to sleep, but he knew somehow that he was dreaming. He was back in the giant's sky-castle, in the high room full of dusty plants. Somewhere far above him he could hear the sound of birds murmuring in the treetops. The winged woman stood close, her hand on his arm. Leaves and branches surrounded them, a bower of green, intimate as a confessional.

The dark-eyed woman was not sad now, but joyful, full of a bright and almost feverish happiness.

"Now you can't leave me," she said. "You can't ever leave me now."

Paul did not know what she meant, but was afraid to say so. Before he could think of anything to say at all, a chill wind slid through the indoor forest. Paul knew without understanding how he knew it that someone else had entered the room. No, not just one. Two.

"They're here!" she gasped, breathless with sudden alarm. "Butterball and Nickelplate. They're looking for you!"

Paul could only remember that he feared them, but not who they were or why. He looked around, trying to decide which way to run, but the bird-woman clutched him harder. She seemed younger now, little more than a girl. "Don't move! They'll hear you!"

They both stood frozen like mice in the shadow of an owl. The noises—leaves rustling, stems snapping—came from either side. Paul was filled with a deep, heart-thudding horror at the idea that the two searchers were closing on them like pinching fingers, that if they stayed a moment longer they would be trapped. He grabbed the woman by her arm, conscious despite his terror of the avian frailty of her bones, and pulled her deeper into the thick greenery, searching for another way out.

For a moment he could hear nothing but the crunch of fallen branches and the whip and smack of leaves, but then a wordless cry was raised somewhere behind him and echoed by another, equally cold voice. An instant later he crashed through the last of the vegetation and against the hopeless obstacle of a blank white wall.

Before he could turn back to the sheltering jungle a vast eye appeared in the wall, blinking slowly, red-rimmed and implacably cruel.

"The Old Man!" the woman beside him howled, but her cry was swallowed by the deep rumble of a voice more inhuman than the roar of a jet engine.

"BEHIND MY BACK!" It was so loud that Paul's eyes filled with helpless tears. Birds sprang into the air, squawking in terror, loose feathers sifting down like multicolored snow. The winged woman fell to the ground as though she had been shot. "BUT I SEE YOU!" the voice bellowed, and the eye widened until it seemed bigger than the room. "I SEE EVERYTHING . . . !"

The floor shook with the voice's power. Staggering to stay upright, Paul leaned down to pull the woman to her feet, but when she turned, her look of panic was gone, replaced by one of stern intensity.

"Paul," she said. *"You must listen to me."*

"Run! We have to run!"

"I do not think I can come to you again in this world." Even as she spoke, the huge, dusty garden grew faint. The roar of the Old Man's voice faded to a wordless rush of sound. *"It pains me to be in a place where I have a reflection. It pains me terribly and makes me weak. You must listen."*

"What are you talking about . . . ?" He remembered now that he was dreaming, but he still could not understand what was happening. Where was the horrible Eye? Was this another dream?

"You are trapped, Paul. The place you now are—it will kill you, as surely as would any of your enemies. You are surrounded by . . . by distortion. I can hold it back, but only for a little while, and it will take most of my strength. Take the other one with you—the other orphan. I may not be able to come to you again, with or without the feather."

"I don't understand . . ."

"I can only hold it back for a little while. Go!"

Paul grabbed at her, but now she was fading, too, not into

darkness but into a dull half-light. Paul blinked, but the ugly gray light did not disappear, was not replaced by anything better.

He pushed himself up onto his elbows. All around him lay the dreariest view imaginable, nothing but mud and stunted leafless trees, made even more depressing by the pale dawn light. Things that at first he took to be more excrescenses of the muddy earth slowly revealed themselves to be pathetic shelters made of sticks and stones and lopsided bricks. More disturbing still were the scrawny human figures, tangle-haired and toothless, seated like nodding beggars or lying in the mud, limbs slowly moving as though they swam through the deepest and thickest of dreams. Everything was muck and misery—even the clouds smearing the gray sky were thick and damp as mucus.

Paul clambered to his feet, knees trembling. It was hard to hold up his own weight—how long since he had stood? Where was he?

Distortion, the bird-woman had said. The meaning came slowly, horribly.

I've been . . . here all along? Sleeping here? Eating here?

For a moment he thought he would be sick. He choked back the burning liquid that had risen in his throat and began to stagger blindly downhill, searching for the sea. She had told him to take the other with him—what had she said? The other orphan? She must mean Azador, but where was he? Paul could hardly stand to look at the mewling, whispering human shapes that lolled among the crude shelters. And he had thought them beautiful. How could such a madness happen?

Lotus-Eaters. It floated to the surface of his memory and popped, like a bubble. *The flowers. I should have realized . . . !*

But even as he slid through the muddy wreck of a village the wind changed direction and the scent of the white blossoms came down the hillside. The breeze that carried their sweet, pungent odor was warm—everything was growing warmer. The sun appeared, and the clouds instantly evaporated above him, revealing the great seamless blue sky beyond.

Paul stopped, arrested by the bright, whitewashed stone of the village, the orderly paths and walled gardens, the bright-eyed people gathered in the shadows of the olive grove, sharing talk and song. Had it simply been a nightmare, then—the decay, the mud?

There was no other answer, surely. The heady, perfumed air from
the meadows had simply woken him to the truth again. It was
impossible to see such beauty surrounding him again and regret
the loss of such a dreadful vision, even as its last cold strands
still troubled his thoughts.

Azador, he thought. *I was looking for Azador. But surely I can
find him later at the evening meal, or even tomorrow. . . .*

Paul realized he was clutching something in his hand. He
stared at the veil, once pristine, now so spattered and smeared
with gray mud that the embroidered feather was almost hidden.
He suddenly heard the woman's voice again as clearly as if she
stood at his shoulder.

*"I can hold it back, but only for a little while, and it will take
most of my strength . . ."*

He did not want to lose the safety of the stately village and
the warm sun, but he could not forget her voice—how appre-
hension had made her words harsh and jagged. She had been
pleading . . . begging him to think, to *see.* The muddied feather
was in the palm of his hand, the fabric creased where he had
clutched it.

The sky began to darken, the village to dissolve back into ru-
ination, as though some evolutionary wheel had been sped forward to the end of time or back to the pathetic precursors of
civilization. Paul pulled the veil tight against his chest, terrified
that the magic of false beauty would overcome him again, leaving him trapped and blind forever, a prisoner of the mire.

"Azador!" he screamed, struggling to keep his footing on the
foul, muddy hillside. "Azador!"

He found his companion in a tangle of bodies, the wet, naked
forms intertwined like mating snails. He leaned down and grabbed
the gypsy by a slippery arm and dragged him loose from the pile.
As thin, bruised arms reached up to pull them both back down,
Paul gave a shout of disgust and kicked at the nearest muddy
figure. The arms all jerked in unison, like the polyps of a startled anemone.

At first Azador hardly seemed to understand, and allowed himself to be propelled down the hill toward the beach and their raft,
but as Paul coaxed the raft out past the first set of breakers and
the scent of the lotos-flowers grew less, the other man tried to

fling himself into the surf and swim back to shore. Paul grabbed him and held on. Only the fact that Azador was still in the grip of the flower-spell, frail and trembling, allowed Paul to withstand the man's increasingly manic struggles.

At last, as the island dropped out of sight below the horizon and the winds washed the air clean of anything but sea tang, Azador stopped fighting. He dragged himself away from Paul and lay sprawled on the deck of the raft, dry-eyed but sobbing, as though his heart had been yanked from his body.

CHAPTER 19

A Life Between
Heartbeats

---

*NETFEED/ART: Thank God She's Not Pregnant Again
(Review for Entre News of staging by Djanga Djanes
Dance Creation)*
VO: "... *Those who suffered as I did through the entirety
of the occasionally fascinating but generally excruciating
spectacle of Djanes' pregnancy and delivery, including the
unintentionally hilarious final moments, with choreographed
doctors and technicians slipping in blood and fecal matter,
will be pleased to know that although her subject matter is
still unabashedly self-absorbed, Djanes will be giving us a
little more of the terpsichorean and a little less of the
cloacal in her new piece titled, 'So I waited in front of the
restaurant for about three hours, Carlo Gunzwasser, you
pathetic little man'* ..."

ORLANDO was so tired he could barely stand. One arm dangled at his side, almost broken by a blow from a tortoise-
man's club. Except for the rumbling, growling breath of the sphinx

fighting for its life, the shadowy temple was almost silent: the few survivors of the siege were whimpering in dark corners or hiding behind statues, but to little avail. The air was nearly empty of flying creatures now, but only because most of them had settled down to feed—the temple floor was dotted with writhing piles of bats and serpents clumped in the rough shapes of human beings.

But dying sphinxes and winged serpents were the least of Orlando's problems.

The larger of the two grotesqueries before him was dangling his unconscious friend Fredericks like a gutted fish. Mewat's snaggletoothed smile showed how much the bloated cobra-man was enjoying himself, reveling in the power he and eyeless Tefy wielded. Despite all the fearful things Orlando had seen and survived, these two filled him with a terror he could barely resist, a chest-squeezing panic that made his heart stumble. He dredged up what felt like his final reserves of strength and lifted his sword, hoping that in the guttering torchlight his enemies could not see how it trembled. "Let her go," he said. "Just let me take her away. We don't have any argument with you."

Tefy's vulture-beaked grin pulled wider still. "Her?" He peered at Fredericks' male Pithlit-the-Thief sim. "So it is masks and costumes, is it? But—let her go? I think not. No, it is you who will come with us, or we will peel her apart in front of you. Do you want that? You and the rest of your people must have noticed by now that there is no escape from the network—that what happens to you here will be all too real."

Orlando took a step closer. "I don't care. If you hurt her I'll take at least one of you with me. I've already sixed one of your turtle-boys." He felt no need to add it had almost drained his last strength to do so.

Fat Mewat goggled his eyes in enjoyment and let out a loud, rolling belch. "Ooh, aren't you a wicked lad?" he hissed at Orlando. "Aren't you, now?"

A loud impact from just behind him made Orlando jump. He whirled to see the door sphinx Saf being dragged to the ground by the bull-headed war god Mont, who clung to the sphinx's neck like a terrier. Antlered Reshpu drove his prongs into Saf's side again and the great sphinx let out a long, low moan like wind rushing down a deserted street. The massive guardian struggled back onto his lion's legs once more, but he was clearly losing strength.

"It is nearly finished here." Tefy stilted a step closer to Orlando. "You and your people have lost. If you come along without struggling, we will release your friend—we will need only one of you, after all. You see, when we take you to our hidden place you will tell us all that you know and wish you had more to tell."

My people? Do they know about Renie and the others? Orlando could make no other sense of Tefy's words. The vulture-man knew Orlando was a Citizen, a real person—he couldn't think he was anything to do with this local insurrection in the Egyptian simworld.

No, he realized suddenly, *they think we're part of the Circle.* A group that actually *was* a threat to the Grail people, or meant to be. Was there some way he could use this to his advantage? The fear made it almost impossible to think, and he was so tired.

"Right," he said out loud. It was easiest this way—if they took him, they would be trading Fredericks for damaged goods. There was little chance he would live through an interrogation, and he had nothing much to give them in any case: he knew little of the Circle, and could not even be sure Renie and the others were still alive. "All right. Let her go. Take me."

Mewat extended a scaly hand. "Come here, then, my lad. Don't be afraid . . . you may even enjoy parts of it. . . ."

Allowed to sag until her feet touched the floor, Fredericks' eyes flickered open and surveyed Orlando blearily for a moment, then caught sight of Tefy's angular form.

"Run, Orlando!" Fredericks struggled uselessly, then was heaved up into the air again, hanging from Mewat's meat hook paw. "Just run!"

"They're going to let you go," said Orlando, trying to keep his friend calm. If there was any hope of getting out of this, they could make no mistakes. "Just don't do anything sudden, Frederico."

Fredericks thrashed helplessly. "They won't let me go! You're scanning major if you think they will!"

Orlando edged closer. "They said they would." He eyed Tefy,

who was rubbing his impossibly long and bony fingers together, cheerful as a child at a birthday party. "Right?"

"Goodness, yes." The distorted beak pulled down in a look of wounded solemnity. "In our way, we are . . . men of honor."

Orlando took another step forward. The aura of terror around the pair beat at him like a stiff cold wind; it took all his courage not to turn and run. How could Fredericks stand it without shrieking?

"Now," he said as he came within just a few meters of Mewat, "let her go." He lowered the sword until it pointed at the thing's immense, pale, oily stomach.

"When I can touch you," the cobra-man said.

Fighting his terror, Orlando gave Fredericks the most significant glance he could muster. This would be delicate—how much pain could he cause this monster if he struck at that flabby hand?

A sudden impact made the floor vibrate and drew the cobra-man's gaze to the side. The great sphinx had tumbled again, and this time was writhing on the floor with the two war gods atop its chest.

"Dua!" The sphinx's bellow threatened to crumble the temple's walls. *"Dua, my brother, I have fallen! Come to my aid!"*

Orlando seized the moment, lashing at the hand that held Fredericks suspended. "Run!" he shouted. As Mewat jerked in startlement, Fredericks managed to twist free. Orlando leaped in with his blade to cover her escape, slapping at the snarling, jagged-toothed face, but Mewat deflected the blow with his wounded hand, then struck with terrible, unlikely speed, dashing the hilt from Orlando's grip. His partner Tefy stilted after Fredericks and snagged her in his long fingers before she had taken two steps.

A huge arm coiled around Orlando and pulled him suffocatingly close. He struggled, but there was no breaking that grip. Mewat's mouth brushed his ear.

"After you talk, and talk, and talk about what we want to know . . . I think I will eat you up." The thing belched again, engulfing Orlando in a fog of decay. Bright spots shimmered before his eyes, but they were only sparks against the rapidly encroaching blackness.

A booming voice echoed from the temple's stone walls. *"I come, my brother!"*

Orlando's captor paused. Out of the shadows at the back of the temple another huge shape was pulling itself across the floor. The second sphinx's back legs dragged uselessly, and a gush of desert sand leaked from its wounds in a dully sparkling trail.

"I have deserted my post, O my brother," it moaned, *"for the first time since Time itself was born."* The skin that had been a faint sunrise lavender was now pale gray. *"But I come to you."*

Orlando's captor looked to Tefy, who held Fredericks entangled in his long pinions. They appeared to be communicating soundlessly, perhaps considering how safe this spot might be with two massive sphinxes about to join forces in a death struggle. Dua crawled through a phalanx of attacking tortoise-men toward his brother, almost oblivious to their blows. Several vanished beneath Dua's bulk with their mouths stretched wide, still voiceless in their death agonies. Screams and even stranger noises began to fill the shadowed temple again as the bats and serpents, disturbed at their feeding, whirled up like a storm of black snow.

"Now to our hidden place . . ." Tefy declared when a shrieking gust of air from the temple's front doorway knocked him sideways and sprawling. Fredericks almost broke free, but Tefy quickly secured her and staggered to his splay-toed feet. The much chunkier Mewat had wobbled but held his balance. They could all hear a rising howl outside the temple, as if a tornado hovered overhead.

A soldier crawled in through the doorway, battered and bleeding.

"He is coming!" the man screeched. "The Lord Osiris is coming! He rides the bird Bennu, whose wings are the storm and the dark flame, and in his fury he strikes down even his own worshipers!" He fell face-down on the floor, sobbing.

The look of pure fear that flashed between Tefy and Mewat this time was much easier to interpret, but Orlando took little satisfaction from it. Even if the two servants were terrified of their master, the arrival of Osiris would surely only make things worse for Orlando and Fredericks. Hadn't Bonnie Mae Simpkins said that he was one of the highest Grail masters?

The skirling, shrieking winds rose to such a pitch that the humans still alive in the temple began dropping to their knees, bleeding from ears and nostrils. Suddenly a great stone large as a house fell from high in the ceiling near the front doorway and crushed a group of tortoise-men, then split into several huge chunks that tottered and fell, smashing others who had survived the first impact. Those who could still move tried to drag themselves away from the doorway. More massive stones vibrated out of the walls, tumbling to the floor like bombs. The war gods and a few tortoise-men fought on against the failing sphinxes, oblivious, but the world seemed to be ending around them.

As Orlando struggled uselessly against his captor's clammy grip, the howl of wind outside the temple increased to an even more frightening pitch. Orlando's ears popped, the pain sharp and hot. The entire front of the temple heaved, as though the stones were the belly of a single, gigantic living thing, then the wall collapsed inward.

He had time only to see an impossibly large shape in the night sky just outside, a black something big as a passenger jet with flapping wings outlined in flame, filling the ragged hole in the temple facade, then one of the huge door-stones cartwheeled past them, striking the cobra-man Mewat a glancing blow which threw him sprawling on top of Orlando.

For a brief instant, smothering beneath the monstrous weight, Orlando could feel the final darkness as close as a whisper in his ear. The roar of wind was stilled, replaced by a great pulsing silence. Something urged him to let go, to step away, that freedom and rest awaited him.

But I can't ... was his only thought. There was something he still had to do, although in the throbbing stillness he could not imagine what that thing could be.

A little air rushed back into his lungs, burning down his throat. The great mass of the cobra-man had pinned his head and shoulders against the stone floor; he was drowning in a foul-smelling, scaly blackness. He heaved, but there was no dislodging Mewat's limp bulk. He shoved with his arms, trying to push himself backward, but could find no room to get his elbows bent for leverage. The exertion brought up his own personal blackness again. The first saving breath had not been replaced, and now he could almost feel his rib cage collapsing.

I can't do it anymore ... Simply staying alive seemed a heavier weight than anything—a Titan's burden he had shouldered too long. *I give up* ...

It was only when he abruptly slid a few inches backward, just enough that he could finally suck in that second breath, that he realized something was pulling hard on his leg. The shift was enough to allow him finally to draw in his elbows so his rib cage could expand. Even with oxygen in his lungs it was a miserably hard, noxious job to worm his way backward from under Mewat's belly, but the search for light and air had his adrenaline pumping, and whoever had a grip on his ankle was still pulling. After a horrible, inching time he finally squirted out from beneath the blubberous stomach.

When he was out into the windy chaos of the shattered temple once more, wheezing and choking, he was startled to find it was not Fredericks holding his leg but the little domestic god Bes.

"The view isn't much better out here," the god informed him, grinning.

Orlando struggled onto his knees. The temple's front wall was gone. The giant bird shape had landed, though the fire-tipped wings were still spread and beating, driving fierce winds through the ruined hole where the temple facade had been. A pale figure was seated on its neck, mummy wrappings smoldering as they streamed and snapped, golden-masked face the embodiment of angry power. Orlando wanted nothing to do with it. He scrabbled on his hands and knees through the rubble until he found his sword, then suddenly remembered.

"Fredericks! Fredericks, where are you?"

"Over there," said Bes, looking up from his inspection of Mewat's huge, silent form. "You can probably help him if you hurry."

Orlando cursed the little god's blitheness and dragged himself to his feet, close to tears. This wasn't fair, any of it. He wanted only to be left alone. He wanted sleep. Didn't anyone care that he was a sick kid?

It was hard to see in the darkened temple, and hard to make sense of what he was seeing anyway, but after a moment he spotted Fredericks and Tefy rolling on the floor beyond one of the fallen door-stones. Whatever advantage the surprise of the great god's entrance might have given Fredericks was now gone: eyeless Tefy had wrapped his long fingers around Fredericks' neck and was forcing her head backward until it seemed certain her spine would break.

Every step Orlando took toward them increased his terror, as though the vulture-man were surrounded by some kind of poisonous fog, but Fredericks was helpless and needed him. He heaved his sword up in both hands and forced himself into a stumbling sprint, then spun into a flat, swinging attack that Thargor used for disemboweling dangerous beasts. But he was not looking for a body blow, not with Fredericks struggling clamped between the creatures's bony legs.

"You!" Orlando screamed as he bore down on them. "You scanning, ugly . . . bird-faced mamalocker!"

Tefy looked up, blind gaze inscrutable, as the sword hissed inches above Fredericks' flailing hands. With all Orlando's momentum behind the blow Tefy's scrawny neck offered little resistance: the beaked head snapped free and flew end over end through the air like a misshapen football. As the bony body collapsed, Fredericks fought her way free, sucking air.

"You're alive!" she said when she could breathe again. "I thought that big slug sixed you!"

Orlando was so exhausted he could not speak. He put one hand on Fredericks' arm for support, then bent double until the black spots began to go away.

"You really don't have time for that," Bes called from nearby. As if in answer, Fredericks let out a sudden screech of disgust and terror.

Orlando laboriously straightened to look around. Tefy's body was scuttling away across the floor, fingers clawing at the tiles as it searched for its head. A few yards away, Mewat was beginning to drag himself upright despite a massive dent in his skull that had popped one of his reptilian eyes out onto his cheek.

"The gateway," Orlando gasped, pulling hard on Fredericks' arm. "We have to get to the . . . we have to . . . the gateway."

"What happened to the Circle people?" Fredericks asked as they staggered away from the temple's ruined doorway. "And the monkeys?"

Orlando could only shake his head.

"WHERE ARE MY SERVANTS?" a voice thundered from the doorway. Osiris seemed as large as either of the sphinxes, but unstable, as though not entirely made of matter. A sickly light oozed from between his bandages. "TEFY? MEWAT?"

Just keep going, Orlando told himself. Others were running too, shrieking and stumbling, besiegers and besieged both driven mad by the appearance of Osiris. *Step, another step, another step . . .*

An angular shape loomed before them—it seemed to stretch to the distant ceiling. "You have done me wrong!" it screeched. Orlando, convinced Osiris had caught them, stumbled and nearly collapsed. Wolf-headed Upaut, abandoned by the few of his followers who still lived, stood atop his throne as though surrounded by floodwaters, his eyes glowing a baleful yellow.

It took Orlando a confused moment to realize that the wolf-god was not shouting at them, but at the billowing form across the temple's acres-wide floor. "Injustice! You took what was mine, Osiris! You mocked me!"

Orlando could not imagine anything more foolish than lingering near this idiot god. He tugged at Fredericks' arm and they lurched past the foot of Upaut's throne. The would-be usurper was almost dancing with indignation and rage, pointing at distant Osiris.

"But see! I have turned your land against you!" Upaut screamed, then a vast cloud of pulsing white light rolled toward him across the temple. Fredericks snatched Orlando by his long barbarian hair and jerked him away. As the glaring wave flowed across Upaut, the wolf-god's bellow became a brief, whistling shriek of agony. The throbbing glow gave off no heat; as it slowed and stopped just a half-meter away from them, Orlando was so bemused that he almost reached out to touch it, but Fredericks dragged him on until the light began to recede again, revealing the throne. Upaut still stood atop it, arms thrown out in righteous fury, but after a moment Orlando realized that the god was not moving. Scorched to carbon in moments, he was now a perfect wolf-headed statue of fine ash. A moment later the replica collapsed in a silent gray implosion, leaving only a tiny pyramid of powder on the seat.

Lit now only by the inconstant glare of Osiris' own person and the thin, distant radiance of stars, the ruined temple was full of crazy shadows. Figures appeared in front of them and disappeared; the floor was covered with dark obstacles. Orlando barely noticed. He clung to Fredericks' arm, conscious only of the need to put distance between himself and the terrible figure of the Lord of Life and Death.

Why did we ever think we could fight them? Orlando wondered. *They are gods. They really are. We never had a chance.*

A heart-stopping groan reverberated across the vast room, a sound like the timbers of a wooden ship being torn asunder—the death cry of one of the great sphinxes. More stones were toppling from the ceiling. The entire temple seemed ready to collapse.

Orlando and Fredericks reached the temple's far wall, their progress fearfully slow. Here, on the edge of things, bodies still moved, a living tableau of Hell's torments. Shadowy figures rolled on the floor, tearing at each other—temple dwellers, soldiers, tortoise-men, all tangled in a horizontal tapestry of destruction. Some of the shell-bodied creatures even seemed to be fighting among themselves, biting at each other's faces in ghastly silent combat.

As the two friends struggled to force their way through the door at the back of the temple, which was half-blocked by a dam of contorted bodies, the god's powerful voice again blasted through the temple, so loud he might have been standing right behind them.

"OF COURSE I'M BLOODY WELL ANGRY, YOU USELESS IDIOTS! AND PUT YOUR DAMNED HEAD ON WHEN I'M TALKING TO YOU!"

In another universe Orlando might have laughed, but nothing here was even remotely funny.

Something struck him, rattling his skull, and the floor abruptly rushed up to meet him. He felt Fredericks pulling at him, but he could not immediately remember how to make his limbs work. Only a meter away something that might once have been young Vasily from the Circle had been twisted into a terrible, almost shapeless knot. Fredericks got an arm around Orlando's chest and somehow he managed to find his feet, but he felt strangely disconnected, as though his head were floating free of his body . . . spinning in air like Tefy's vulture head . . .

"Bonnie . . . Nandi . . ." he murmured. They couldn't just leave them behind. And the Wicked Tribe . . .

"Stand up, Gardiner!" his friend shouted. Fredericks dragged him forward, deeper into the room. "Somebody help us!" On the far side of the chamber a flicker of light suddenly became a wall of golden flame.

That means something, Orlando realized, but it was too hard to think. A whirlwind of black shapes came spinning toward him— bats or monkeys, monkeys or bats. He couldn't remember which was which, or why he should care.

"Help us!" Fredericks shouted again, but it was faint now, as though his friend had fallen down a deep tunnel.

The golden light was the last thing Orlando saw, a wavering gleam that held out against the dark for a long second after everything else was gone, but at last even that spot of brightness shrank and was extinguished.

THERE was no protocol for something like this, Catur Ramsey knew. It was like being the first delegation to an alien planet. When you were in the presence of parents whose child was dying, there were no words, no gestures, that could ever bridge such an incomprehensible gap.

He shifted, uncomfortably aware of the scratchy rattle of his disposable hospital sanitaries. It made no difference, though; he suspected he could have fired a gun in the air and the parents would still not have taken their eyes off their child's pale, wizened face.

Sunk deep in the slow machineries of the coma bed, with cheeks sunken and skull almost visible beneath the translucent skin, Orlando Gardiner resembled nothing so much as the corpse of some superannuated ruler put on display for public viewing. And yet he was still alive: some tiny flickering thing in the depths of his brain kept his heart beating. A tiny thing, yet when it ceased, so much would change. Ramsey felt guilty looking at the dying child, as though he were trespassing on something private—which in a way he was, perhaps the most private thing of all, the final and most solitary of journeys. Only the shiny button of the neurocannula, still planted in the boy's neck like a plug that might keep the last of his life from draining away, seemed out of place. It troubled Ramsey, reminding him of things he should say— things he did not want to say.

Orlando's mother reached out and touched the boy's slack face.

Her expression was so terrible that Ramsey could not watch any longer. He sidled to the door and stepped out into the hallway, full of guilt at his immediate sense of relief.

The hospital's Family Center did not make Ramsey a great deal more comfortable than the wards. It had been decorated in an aggressively cheerful style, which, although he understood the reasoning behind it, depressed him. The toys and holographic displays and bright, overstuffed furniture did not disguise the pain and fear that hung over a place like this, whatever the decor—you had only to look at the families huddling together waiting for visits, or pulling themselves together after such a visit, to see the truth. Instead the toytown furnishings merely made it seem that expressing that pain or fear would somehow be an expression of ingratitude. *Be a team player,* the teddy bear lamps and the cartoons flickering on the wallscreen seemed to urge. *Smile. Watch what you say.*

If that was the message, Vivien Fennis and Conrad Gardiner were not getting with the program.

"It's so . . . it's so hard." Vivien brushed a strand of hair from her eyes, heedless as a famine victim shooing a fly. "We knew it would happen. We knew it would only be a matter of time—progeria kids just don't last very long. But you can't live your life that way, waiting." She stared at her hands, fighting anger. "You have to go ahead as though . . . as though . . ." Tears formed, and her anger seemed aimed at herself as she wiped them away. Her husband only stared, as though he were surrounded by a glass box and knew reaching out was useless.

"I'm so sorry." Ramsey did not reach out either, did not even offer her one of the tissues that sat in the middle of the table. It felt like it would be an insult.

"It's kind of you to come," Vivien said at last. "I'm sorry—it just doesn't seem important at the moment. Please don't give up on us. I'm sure it will mean something later, when . . . when we're a little less crazy."

"Did you find someone for us to sue?" Conrad Gardiner's joke was so dreadfully hollow, so hopeless, that Ramsey flinched.

"No, not really. But . . . but I have run across some strange things." It was time to tell them about Beezle, he knew. It might be too late to save their son—it was hard to look at the child and imagine otherwise—but how could he deny them the chance at communication? "I noticed that Orlando's neurocannula is still in place . . ." he said, trying to find a way to raise the subject.

"Yeah, it drives the doctors crazy." Vivien laughed, a short dry rasp. "They're eager to take it out again. But we saw what happened the last time they tried. It was horrible. And even if that wouldn't happen now, why take the chance? Anyway, there's still brain activity." She shook her head at the strangeness of the idea. "Still . . . And if it's a comfort to him somehow . . ."

Conrad stood up so suddenly his chair caught on the carpet and toppled backward. Vivien started to rise, too, but her husband waved her off and staggered away from the table. He wandered seemingly at random for long seconds until he stopped in front of a tropical fish tank. He leaned against the glass, keeping his back to the room.

"Our own fish are all sick," Vivien said quietly. "We've hardly cleaned their tank in weeks. We've hardly done anything. We're living at this damned hospital, pretty much. But it's better than being somewhere else when . . . when . . ." She swallowed hard, then smiled a smile that was as hard for Ramsey to look at as Orlando himself had been. "But you do what you need to, don't you? So what do you have to tell us, Mr. Ramsey? Don't wait for Conrad—I'll pass along anything important."

And now here it was, the moment in all its inevitability when the secret should be shared, but Catur Ramsey suddenly realized that he did not want to tell this brave sad woman anything about it. What could he offer them? A story that would be hard for anyone to understand or believe, let alone the parents of a boy who was clearly on the very edge of death? And even if he could convince them that Beezle's unlikely-sounding tale was true—that the software agent could talk to Orlando even in the depths of his coma, and that the boy himself was somehow trapped like a lost spirit in some kind of alternate universe—what if Beezle could not make contact with Orlando again, could not find the proper dream-window to reach him? How cruel would that be, to raise their hopes, confound all the thankless, miserable work they had done to come to terms with what was happening, and then not be able to deliver? It wasn't as though Ramsey himself had actually spoken with Orlando. It was all secondhand, all hearsay from a piece of gear that considered itself a talking bug.

Suddenly he felt paralyzed. It was too great a risk. He had thought that he had no other honorable choice, but now, seeing Vivien with grief heavy on her, as though Orlando's coma had lasted years instead of days, seeing her husband weeping quietly against the fish tank, he did not trust his earlier conclusion. One of the headiest things about his career, back in the early days, had been the godlike feeling of holding people's lives in his hands—confessor, interlocutor, sometimes even savior. Now he would have given anything to let the cup pass.

But can I really take away their only chance to say good-bye? Because I'm afraid it might be a mistake?

A small, cowardly part of him whispered, *If you don't tell them today, you can always change your mind tomorrow. But once you speak, it's too late—you can't unsay it.*

To his shame, he listened to that whispering part and found himself agreeing.

Vivien was trying to pay attention, but she was clearly having trouble concentrating. "So you're saying it was some kind of thing in this gameworld of his? Someone . . . lured him?"

Conrad had returned, but seemed willing to let Vivien ask the questions. He was making a pile on the table before him of tiny little pieces of tissue, tearing each one from the now-ragged larger sheet and then setting it down on top of the others.

"I suppose, although it's not really clear yet why someone would want to lure him or any of the other kids that might have run across this thing."

"This . . . picture of a city."

"Yes. But from what I can tell, someone went to a lot of trouble, and must have spent a lot of money, too—everything I can discover about this makes it seem like a lot of work went into it. But why? I still have no real idea."

"So someone *did* do this to Orlando." For the first time Vivien's voice had something like a normal tone—the tone of an outraged parent.

"Perhaps. It would be a strange coincidence otherwise, especially considering that Salome Fredericks is also in a coma, and she was helping Orlando look into it."

"That damned Middle Country—I hate that place! He practically lived there the last few years." Vivien suddenly began to laugh. "Monsters! My poor son wanted monsters he could kill. No surprise there, I guess, considering the real stuff he couldn't do anything about. He was very good at it, too."

"That's what everyone there tells me."

"So let's sue the bastards." She looked to her husband, who offered a ghost of a smile, acknowledging her return of his earlier serve. "Those Middle Country bastards. Let's make them pay. It won't bring Orlando back, but it may help some other kids."

"I don't really think they're the problem, Ms. Fennis." Ramsey had decided to avoid the painful subject of communication with Orlando, but here was yet another place where he did not feel comfortable. Everything he had discovered about Orlando's case so far screamed out like a tabnet shoutline—Worldwide Conspiracy! Science Fiction Plot to Steal Children! He couldn't really start talking about stuff like this to grieving parents until he had more proof. "Let me look into it a little more, then maybe next time we get together I can make some positive recommendations. Don't worry about the hours, please. The Fredericks are still paying me, and I'm doing some of it on my own time, too."

"That's very kind of you," Vivien said.

He shook his head, embarrassed. "No, I didn't mean it that way. It's just . . . it's caught me, that's all. I need to get to the bottom of it now. I hope if I solve it, it will . . . I don't know, bring you and your husband a little peace. But I couldn't stop caring about this if I wanted to."

He realized he'd said all he could say. He rose and stuck out his hand. Conrad Gardiner took it carefully, squeezed it for a moment, then let it go. Vivien's handshake was only a little more robust. Her eyes were shiny again, but her mouth was set in a firm line.

"I don't really care about suing anyone," she said. "Not unless they've done something wrong, not unless they hurt my boy somehow. But it's all just so strange. It would be nice to have some answers."

"I'll try to get you some. I truly will."

As he turned and headed across the colorful puppies-and-kitties carpet toward the exit, she left her husband at the table and walked with him. "You know the worst thing?" she asked. "We were ready for this—we really were, as ready as any parents could ever be for something so terrible and unfair. We had been getting ready for this for years. But we always thought we'd at least have a chance to say good-bye." She stopped somehow, as though she had struck some kind of invisible wall. When Ramsey hesitated she waved for him to go on, then turned to walk back to the husband who was waiting for her, waiting to return with her to the alien world of grief that normal people could not enter.

Ramsey took his own far different pain with him out through the lobby and into the parking lot.

IT was hard to make his way back out of the darkness—harder than it had ever been. Something held him, not in a cruel way, but with a grip as elastic yet implacable as a spiderweb strung wide between the stars. He fought it, but it merely gave, and all the energy of his being burned uselessly; he fought on anyway, for a span that might have been centuries. After a while, it seemed pointless to continue struggling. How long could anyone fight the inevitable? Forever? Maybe someone else could, but he couldn't.

When he relaxed the darkness did not become deeper, as he had expected. Rather, the darkness itself began to glow, warming almost imperceptibly from ultimate black into some deep, polar range of violet, a light he could only feel, not see. Then something spoke to him—not a voice, and not in words, but he understood it, and understood that it was somehow separate from himself, or at least separate from the part of him that thought.

You have a choice, it said.

I don't understand.

There are always choices. That is the pattern beneath all things. Universes appear and disappear with each choice—and worlds are destroyed with every breath.

Tell me. I don't understand.

A place in the soft violet darkness began to glow a little brighter, as though the fabric of negation grew thinner there. He could see shapes for the first time, oblongs and angles that made no sense, but simply seeing them made him hungry for life again.

That is your choice, his voiceless, wordless adviser told him.

And as the imprecise vista became clearer, he realized that he was looking down on something from above. At first, the lines and odd shapes made him wonder if he hovered over some alien landscape, but then the shadows and brightnesses resolved themselves into a face, a sleeping face . . . his face.

Hospital, he thought, and the word seemed something icy and hard—a knife, a bone. *That's me. Dying.* His features, so strangely shriveled by his disease and yet so cruelly familiar, hung just on the other side of an imperfect barrier like a fogged window. *Why are you showing me this?*

It is part of your choice, it said. *Look closer.*

And now he could see the huddled, dark forms beside the bed, one of them extending a shadowy hand to touch the insensible mask of his face—his own face!—and he knew who they were.

Vivien and Conrad. Mom and Dad.

The presence, the companion that was not a companion—was in fact nothing but a certain illogical knowledge—said nothing, but suddenly he saw the choice before him.

I can go back and say good-bye . . . he said slowly, or would have if there had been any words to speak, sounds to hear. *I can go back and see them before I die—but I'll leave my friends behind, won't I? I'll lose Fredericks, and Renie, and Bonnie Mae, and the others . . .*

He could feel the presence beside him, silently assenting. It was true.

And I have to choose now?

No reply, but none was needed.

As he stared at the shadowy forms, a terrible loneliness swept over him. How could he not return to them, even if only for a last touch, a last sight of his mother's face before the final, dark door opened? But Fredericks and all the children, all those poor lost children . . .

The time he had spent resisting the initial darkness was nothing to that which seemed to pass now as he hung between worlds, between something more subtle and complicated than simply life and death. It was an impossible decision, but it could not be avoided. It was the single most terrible thing imaginable.

But in the end he chose. . . .

*   *   *

It took a while before Orlando realized he was dreaming now, just dreaming. At first the strange filtered light and the half-glimpsed shapes seemed almost a continuation of what had gone before, but then the blurriness lifted and he found himself staring at . . . a bear. The animal was sitting on its rump on wet gray concrete with its leather footpads extended. A collar of nearly white fur around its neck made a startling contrast to the rest of its black pelt.

Something bounced off the bear's chest. It snapped downward with its jaws, but the peanut had fallen away, skittering into the cement moat and out of reach. The bear's eyes were so piercingly sad that even though it was a dream of the remote past, Orlando found himself weeping all over again. Conrad's head appeared at the edge of his vision, poking in past the netting his parents used to keep Orlando safe from both bright sunshine and prying eyes.

"What's wrong, honey? Does the bear scare you? It's called a sun bear—see, it's friendly."

Something moved on his other side. Vivien's hand came through the netting and took his fingers, squeezed them. "It's okay, Orlando. We can go somewhere else. We can go look at some other animals. Or are you tired? Do you want to go home?"

He tried to find the words, but the six-year-old Orlando—far too old for a stroller if he had been a normal child, but condemned to one by his frail bones and easily overtaxed muscles—had not been able to explain the deep sadness of the bear. Even in this dream-version he still could not make his parents understand.

Someone tossed another peanut. The bear waved at it with its paws, and for a moment almost had it, but the peanut slithered down its belly and into the pit. The bear looked mournfully after it, then looked up again, bobbing its head, waiting for another throw.

"Boss?" someone said. Orlando looked down. He was holding a shelled peanut in his own bony, knob-knuckled little hand, a peanut he was afraid to throw for fear he would not even be able to make it across the moat, but the peanut was moving. Tiny legs had sprouted from its side and waved helplessly in the air. *"Boss, can you hear me?"*

He stared at it. Vivien and Conrad were still talking to him, asking if he wanted to see the elephants, or maybe something smaller and less frightening like the birds. Orlando did not want to lose them, did not want to miss what they were saying, but the squirming of the peanut was distracting him.

"Boss? Can you hear me? Talk to me!"

"Beezle?"

"I'm losing you, Boss! Say something!"

The peanut, the peanut's voice, his parents, the white-collared sun bear, all began to fade.

"Beezle? My parents, tell them . . . tell them . . ."

But the dream had evaporated, and Beezle and his parents were gone—so completely vanished that he felt certain he had left them all behind forever.

The diffuse light made everything almost gray. This time there was no mechanized womb of an expensive hospital bed, no angel's-eye-view of a dying boy, only the inconstant light of burning embers gleaming through translucent fabric.

The wind mounted outside, fretful and searching. Something was beneath him—a bed, but rough and unfamiliar. It felt like nothing so much as a pile of coats, as though someone had put him down in the spare room during one of his parents' parties and then forgotten to come back for him.

Orlando tried to sit up, but even the effort of trying almost pulled him back into oblivion once more. Dizziness so great he would have thrown up if it had not been too much trouble, if he had anything in him to throw up, swept over him.

Weak, he thought. *So weak. I can't do this again—can I? Start over?*

But he had to. He had made his choice. If he had lost his last moments with Vivien and Conrad, it had to be for something. He closed his eyes and tried to take inventory.

We were in the temple, he remembered. *And what's his name, Osiris, came and broke down the walls. Then we were running for the back room and something hit me on the head. Did I make it through the gateway?* All he could remember was light, flickering like the light on the fabric around this bed.

He slowly turned his head to one side. He could see dark walls beyond the thin cloth of the bed hanging: he seemed to be in a sort of cabin made of rough boards. The bit of the roof he could see was dry thatch. A brazier full of coals smoldered near the farthest wall. The energy it took to move his head exhausted him, and for a while he only lay, staring at the play of fire across the embers.

When he felt a little more strength returning, he shoved himself back until he found something soft and yielding behind his head. He steeled himself for the effort and pushed with legs that did not feel quite like his own until his head slid up onto whatever lay rolled behind him and tipped upward, so that he could see what was in front of him.

The cabin or hut was large, several meters wide, and almost entirely empty. The floor was pounded earth; light leaked in at the bottom edges. A graceful handled jug stood on the ground near him, and beside it lay a rolled cloth bundle. The only other objects in the room stood opposite the brazier—one very long spear and a few slightly smaller versions, a short stabbing-sword he had never seen but which seemed inexplicably familiar, and a huge round shield leaning against a weird figure like a truncated scarecrow.

The manlike shape was armor on a crude stand, the bronze polished until it glinted—a breastplate, some other pieces, and a helmet with a horsetail crest perched on top.

Orlando sighed. Fighting, then. Of course.

They don't need me for my smile or my sense of humor, he thought. *Not much left of either of those, anyway.*

So where was he? It looked old-fashioned, but he was too tired to think about it much. Troy? Had they been lucky with the gateway?

A shadow skimmed across the bottom of the wall as something moved outside the hut. A moment later a man pushed open the door and stepped inside. He wore simpler armor than that which hung on the stand, boiled leather held together with rope and straps and buckles, and a kind of skirt made of leather strips. He dropped to one knee inside the doorway, his dark, bearded face turned down to the ground.

"Forgive me, Lord," the soldier said. "There are many who wish to speak with you."

Orlando could not believe it was all starting again so soon.

Where was Fredericks? Bonnie Mae and the others? "I don't want to see anyone."

"But it is the Great King, Lord." The soldier spoke nervously, startled by Orlando's refusal but determined to deliver his message. "He sends a messenger to say that the hope of the Achaians rests on you. And Patroclus also asks to see you."

"Tell them all to go away." Orlando managed to raise a trembling hand. "I'm sick. I can't talk to anyone. Maybe later."

The soldier seemed about to say something else, but instead nodded and rose to slip quietly back out of the cabin.

Orlando let his hand drop. Could he make himself do it all again? How? It was one thing to make a choice, another to have the strength to see it through. What if he couldn't? What if he didn't get any stronger?

Something scratched on the cabin wall, a quiet but insistent noise. Orlando felt a surge of indignation—hadn't he just told them all to leave him alone? He gathered his energy to shout, but found himself staring openmouthed instead as a small shape crawled in through the gap where wall and floor did not quite meet.

"You are confused?" the turtle asked, turning its head to fix him with an eye like a drop of tar. "Do not worry—I will tell you what you need to know. The Great King is Agamemnon, and he fears you are upset with him over the matter of a slave girl."

Orlando groaned. It was like another stupid Thargor adventure, but one he did not even have the energy to participate in. "I just want them to leave me alone."

"Without you, the Achaians cannot win."

"Achaians?" He closed his eyes and let his head sag back, but the voice of the turtle was not so easily silenced.

"The Greeks, we will call them. The federation that have come to conquer Troy."

So he had reached Troy after all. But he could not find any pleasure in the knowledge. "I need to sleep. Why do they want me? Who the hell am I supposed to be?"

There was a pause as the creature made its way to the section of dirt floor just beside his trailing hand. "You are Achilles, the greatest of heroes," it said, nudging his fingers with its cool, rough little head. "Aren't you pleased?" Orlando tried to sweep the turtle away, but with surprising nimbleness it moved just beyond his reach. "Great Achilles, whose deeds are legend. Your mother is a goddess! The bards sing of you! Even the heroes of Troy tremble at your name, and you have left the burned wrack of many cities behind you . . ."

Orlando tried to shut out the lecturing voice, but even fingers in his ears would not silence it. He missed Beezle more than ever.

"Please leave me alone," he murmured, but apparently not loud enough for the turtle to hear. It continued on, reciting his fabulous history with the hideous cheer of a tour guide, even after Orlando had rolled over and pulled the bedding close around his head.

CHAPTER 20

Elephant's House

NETFEED/NEWS: It's Silly Season Again, Says Investigator
(visual: Warringer investigating at Sand Creek)
VO: The destruction caused by a satellite falling from orbit
and the discovery of ancient habitations in the Antarctic
have started a new round of what writer and investigator
Aloysius Warringer calls "silly season journalism," bringing
the UFO debate back into the public eye.
(visual: Warringer at home in front of wallscreen)
WARRINGER: "It happens every few years. We've been
searching for intelligent life beyond our planet for decades
and haven't found it, but any time something having to do
with space comes up, the conspiracy theories come out of
the woodwork. 'There are aliens and the government's
hiding them!' Roswell, Sand Creek in South Dakota, all the
perennials get trotted out. Meanwhile, what about the real
questions? What about Anford's conspiracy with
international anti-monetarists to return the country to the
gold standard? What about the Atasco assassination? The
continuing fluoridation of our water?"

"I CAN'T believe you." Del Ray Chiume rolled his eyes in a theatrical way that made Long Joseph want to kick him. "How could you not know how to get back? What would you have done if you hadn't met me?"

"Met you?" Joseph pushed off from the wall, away from Renie's irritating ex-boyfriend, but two steps took him out into the drizzling rain and he quickly moved back beneath the cement overhang. They were drinking their coffee on the street. Even in this backwater sector of Durban, the restaurant proprietor had taken one look at Del Ray's stained, rumpled suit and Joseph's slightly lurching gait and asked them to take their coffee in travel cups and their business outside. If the man hadn't been black, Joseph would have called it racism. "Met you? You crazy? Seems to me you came at me with a gun, boy."

"Probably saved your life, too, although you've done your damnedest to make up for it." Del Ray cursed as hot coffee squirted out of the foam container and down his chin. "Why I let you talk me into going back to that hospital . . ."

"I had to see my boy." Despite the misery of the experience, Joseph felt no qualms. That was why he had left that mountain place, after all. Why was it so surprising he didn't know how to find his way back—was he supposed to have made a map or something?

"Well, we're going to have to figure it out. It's up in the Drakensberg—you don't just walk around up there hoping to stumble onto some government base." He frowned. "I wish my brother would hurry up."

Joseph was looking at a black van parked at the far end of the street, the silver antenna strip above its windshield pounded underneath a torrent of water draining off one of the roofs. It was one of the fat ones people in Pinetown called a "pig," and it seemed a little rich for the neighborhood. He thought about pointing it out, but didn't want to send Del Ray off on another long speech about how foolish they'd been to go to the hospital, and how they were probably being followed by Boer hitmen . . .

His thoughts were scattered as an old car pulled up beside them. Joseph felt a moment of alarm when he recognized it as the one into which he had been thrown before, then realized that of course it was the same car, and the same brother who had driven it. As Del Ray climbed into the front, Long Joseph opened the other door to find three small children playing a noisy game of I-smack-you, you-smack-me on the back seat. "What the hell is this?" he growled.

"You brought your kids?" Del Ray's voice soared high with irritation. "Gilbert, what are you doing?"

"Look, man, their mama's gone out." The brother, who Joseph was seeing properly for the first time, had the worn look of a man who had been babysitting all morning. "I don't have a choice."

"I'm not getting back there with no children," Joseph declared. Grumbling, Del Ray got out and slid in with his niece and nephews. By the time Joseph got his long legs properly folded under the dash—Del Ray's brother was short, and had the seat close to the wheel—they had driven past the spot where the black van had been parked, so Joseph didn't get a closer look at it.

"Look, I can't drive you and this old man around all day," Gilbert said. "I already spent enough time sitting around outside that hospital. Where are you going?"

"Yes, and nice to meet you, too," Joseph snarled. "Last time we spending any time together, you were perpetrating a crime on me. You lucky I don't call the police on you. Old man, is it?"

"Oh, please shut up," groaned Del Ray.

"Wasn't my idea," his brother said quietly. "I have a *job*."

"Don't start with me, Gilbert," Del Ray snapped. "Who got you that job, anyway? We're going to see Elephant. He lives over in Mayville." He gave directions, then slumped back, pausing to pull the two boys apart, but not before they had inflicted scream-provoking injuries on each other.

"Elephant!" Joseph shook his head. "What kind of name is that? I'm not going to no game park."

Del Ray sighed. "Very humorous."

"I did an elephant in school, Uncle Del," the girl beside him announced. "I colored him all green and my teacher said that wasn't right."

"Your teacher is foolish, girl," Long Joseph called over his shoulder. "Schools are full of people who can't get no regular job, think they know everything. You can have any color elephant you want. You tell your teacher that."

"Look," snarled Gilbert, the car rocking on its aged springs as he negotiated a narrow turn, "don't start in telling my child to disrespect her teacher. You and my brother want to run around playing Johnny Icepick, that's your affair, but don't start with my children."

"I'm just telling her to stand up for herself." Joseph was deeply wounded. "Don't blame me 'cause you not doing your duty."

"Oh, for God's sake," said Del Ray. "Everyone please just *shut up*."

Gilbert dropped them in front of Elephant's building, a warehouse tower built in the early part of the century, a right-angled pile of alternating brown-and-gray concrete slabs. Under the dark skies and cold rain, Joseph thought it was almost as depressing as the hospital. Del Ray thumbed the intercom and the downstairs door unlocked with a loud click.

There was no elevator, and Joseph was complaining vigorously by the time they reached the third floor. Some of the widely-separated doors had little nameplates next to them, but many more were blank. Every door, though, had some kind of additional security locks, and some were so festooned with chains and pressure bolts that it looked like terrible monsters must be imprisoned behind them.

"What good that going to do you when you inside?" Joseph asked. "How you going to lock all that nonsense?"

"This isn't a flatblock, it's storage." Del Ray was breathing only a little less heavily after the climb than Joseph. "People don't live in these, they just want to keep other people out." He corrected himself as they stopped in front of one of the featureless, nameless doors. "People don't live in *most* of these."

The door popped open almost immediately at his knock. It was nearly dark inside, so Joseph hung back to let Del Ray step through first while his own eyes adjusted.

"What is this?" he asked. "Looks all old-fashioned."

Del Ray shot him an irritated glance. "He likes it this way. Just don't start in with your usual charm, will you? He's doing us a favor—I hope."

The huge, windowless room was indeed like something out of one of the net dramas of Joseph's youth, one of those science-

fiction things that had always filled him with scorn. It looked like
an aging space station or a mad scientist's laboratory. Machinery
covered every surface, and had colonized the room's other spaces
as well, hanging in nets from the ceiling or piled on the floor in
haphazard stacks. Everything seemed to be connected, thousands
of individual conduits flowing together to share one electrical circuit; huge bundles of cables ran almost everywhere so that it was
hard to find somewhere to put your foot down. There were so
many little scarlet readout lights blinking and so many palely
glowing dials and meters that even though only one ordinary
source of illumination burned at the center of the room, a tall
floor lamp with a crooked shade, the cavernous space was as full
of twinkling light as a Christmas display in some Golden Mile
shop window.

An ancient, peeling recliner stood in the middle of the lamp's
glow. Its occupant, a large black man in a striped wirewool jumper,
whose head was shaved except for a topknot like a bird's crest,
sat hunched over a low table. He turned to peer at them for a moment before returning to whatever was in front of him. "Del Ray,
utterly weird that you called," he said in a childish, high-pitched
voice. "I was just thinking about you."

"You were?" Del Ray picked his way through the seemingly
random piles of equipment; Joseph, following close behind,
couldn't figure out what any of the machines were supposed to
be or do. "Why?"

"Cleaning out some memory and found this thing I put together for a presentation a while back—remember that thing I did
for your Rural Communications Project, the bit with the little
dancing bullyboxes?"

"Oh, yes. That was a while ago." Del Ray pulled up beside
the recliner. "This is Joseph Sulaweyo. I used to go out with his
daughter Renie, remember?"

"Doubt not. She was fine." The chunky young black man nodded in appreciation. He glanced at Joseph but did not get up or
offer his hand.

"How come you got a name like Elephant?" Joseph asked.

Elephant turned to Del Ray. "Why'd you tell him that? I don't
like that name."

"You don't? But it's a term of respect," Del Ray said quickly.

"You know, because an elephant doesn't forget anything. Because they're wise, and they get their noses into everything."

"Yeah?" Elephant wrinkled his forehead like a little boy who still wants to believe in Father Christmas.

Long Joseph thought he knew where the name came from, and it wasn't anything to do with respect. Not only was the young man's belly wider than his shoulders, he had the sagging skin and gray pallor of someone who didn't get outside in the sun very much. A mulch of food wrappers, squeeze bottles, and wave boxes surrounding the table testified to the truth of it.

"And I need a favor," Del Ray hurried on, "like I told you. And you're the only one I can trust to do it right."

Elephant nodded sagely. "Couldn't talk over the phone, you said. I hear that—man, your old bosses at UNComm, they're all over everything now. Can't fart without someone showing up at your door, talking about EBE."

"Electronic Breaking and Entering," Del Ray explained to Joseph, who could not have cared less. "Hacking, in an old-fashioned word. My man here is one of the world's true experts on data acquisition—legitimate, very legitimate, that's why he did so much work for us at UNComm!—but there's so much red tape, tollgates, you name it. . . ." He turned back to the large young man. "And now I need you to find something for me."

The respect due to his eminence now duly rendered, Elephant inclined his head. "Tell me."

As Del Ray passed along Long Joseph's fragmented recollections of the military base in the mountains, Joseph wondered idly if this fat young man might have any beer. He considered asking, but after weighing it against another annoying lecture from Del Ray, figured he would do better looking around on his own. The cavernous warehouse space seemed big enough to hide anything, including a refrigerator full of something pleasant, and anyway it was something to do. As he wandered off, Elephant was already making pictures appear in midair above the desk, a succession of bright shapes that threw long shadows from the equipment towers.

"Op that, man," Elephant said proudly. "Hologram display like this, you won't find another one in private hands south of Nairobi."

*   *   *

The huge horizontal refrigerator, which at first had filled Long Joseph with such glee, seemed to contain only soft drinks—row after row of squeeze bottles like Chinese soldiers awaiting inspection. Joseph finally found a single bottle of something called "Janajan" behind the plastic bags of components inexplicably stored alongside Elephant's cola reserves and pop-up wave packs. It had an irritatingly fruity taste, but it was still beer—it even had a tiny bit of a kick to it. Joseph nursed it slowly as he strolled through the artificial fairyland, not sure when he might get his next one.

He had no urge to hurry back to where Del Ray and his large friend sat huddled before the shining, cartoonish display. All this blinking-lights nonsense was what had taken his son from him. What use was it? Didn't even kill someone, like fire had killed his wife, so you could bury the dead and get on. Instead, it just turned them into a machine—a machine that didn't work, but you couldn't unplug it. The fat man was excited about his toys, but the whole thing left a sour taste in Joseph's mouth that no fruity beer could take away. Renie had tried to explain this kind of foolishness to him when she was studying, had dragged him to the school lab, full of excitement, to show him how people made the things he watched on the net, but even then he had found the whole thing strange and confusing, and he hadn't liked his young daughter showing him so many things he was ignorant about. Now that it had taken Stephen—and Renie, too, for that matter— he had even less interest. It all just made him thirsty.

"Joseph!" Del Ray's voice pulled him out of his thoughts. "Can you come over here?"

Long Joseph realized he had been standing in the middle of the room for long minutes, looking at nothing, slack as a rag doll. *What's becoming of me?* he thought suddenly. *Might as well be dead. Just thinking about the next drink.*

Even that realization just made him want the drink more.

"Hey," Del Ray said as he approached, lean face carnival-painted by the lights from Elephant's display, "I thought you said this place was a big secret, this military base."

Joseph shrugged. "That's what Renie told me."

Elephant looked up from a luminous snake's-nest of data. "It's called 'Wasp's Nest,' not 'Beehive.' "

"Yeah, that is right." Joseph nodded. "I remember now."

"Well, it *is* a secret, but someone's been checking into it." With a gesture of Elephant's meaty hand, another squirming tangle of shapes, numbers, and words appeared in the air before him. "See? Careful, very quiet, but they've been nibbling at the edges, looking it over."

Joseph squinted at the display, as meaningless to him as the most aggressive sorts of modern art. "That must have been that French woman, what her name, Mar-teen. She was all around, helping get it ready for Renie. And some other old man they were talking to, him, too."

"Within the last couple of days?"

"Don't know." He shrugged again, but he had an uncomfortable feeling in his stomach, as though the fruit-flavored beer had been a little off. "But it seem like they were all done with that a while ago. That Mar-teen, she was with Renie and the little Bushman fellow, whatever they were doing, wherever they went."

"Well, someone has been sniffing around." Elephant sat back and folded his arms across his breasts. "Checking the communication lines, testing the links." He frowned. "Does that place have phones?"

"I think so. Yeah, that old kind you hold up to your mouth."

"I think someone's been trying to call." Elephant smirked as he turned to Del Ray. "I've got your maps for you, man, but I am utterly glad *I'm* not going anywhere near the place." He waved his arm and the bright visuals vanished so swiftly that it left a dark hole in the air where they had been. "Take it from me, there's nothing worse than pranking around with secrets that aren't quite secrets anymore."

HE felt weak and ashamed, but that had not prevented him from coming. Even he sometimes needed relief.

He closed his eyes and felt the air wash over him, relaxing already under the ministrations of the silent slaves and their palm-frond fans. The bower of Isis was always cool, a refuge from the desert, from the noise of the palace, from the stresses of mastery. He felt a part of himself, a steely, cold part, resisting the urge to let go. It was hard to turn that part off—the habit of self-reliant command, of sharing his thoughts with nobody, was very strong, and more important than ever now in these last days—but even he could not go without forever. Still, he had waited long before returning this time.

Even with his eyes closed he knew she had appeared, her presence like a cool hand on his brow. Her scent, already strong simply because it was her room, became even more potent, cedar and desert honey and other things more subtle.

"My great lord." Her voice was the sounding of delicate silver bells. "You honor me." She stood in the doorway, slim as a reed in a gown of pale, moon-colored cotton, her feet bare. Her half-smile affected him as powerfully as a once-favorite song heard after years had passed. "Will you stay with me a while?"

He nodded. "I will."

"Then this is a happy day." She clapped her hands. A pair of slaves filtered in, quiet and swift as shadows, one bearing cups and a pitcher, the other a tray of sweetmeats. "Let me feed you, my husband," said Isis. "We will forget the world and its cares for a little while."

"For a little while, yes." Osiris leaned back on the couch, bidding his sentry-self to be silent, and watched the goddess pour him a cupful of foaming, golden beer, her every movement an unspoken poem.

". . . And so I returned to find that those two imbeciles had allowed a full-scale rebellion to flower in my absence—then, in an effort to cover up their own incompetence, they had even violated the temple of Ra and slain its guardians, Dua and Saf."

"Your anger must have been great, my husband." Her look of sympathy was perfect, containing nothing but intelligent regret for his discomfort.

"They are spending some time in the punishment circuits," he said. She frowned the tiniest frown at the unfamiliar word, but did not allow herself to be distracted from stroking his knee. "I will have to release them soon, though. Sadly, I still need them to find the man Jonas."

Isis shook her head, her shining pale hair swinging like a curtain. "I am sorry you must have servants who displease you, my lord. But I am even more sorrowful at the idea that others would rebel against your gracious rule."

Osiris waved the thought away. Here in this safe place he had allowed his wife to unwrap the mummy bandages from his hands, exposing the wan, deathly fingers with their gilt nails. "None of this is what truly upsets me. There are always those who resent the powerful—those who cannot build for themselves, who are not strong enough to take what they desire but still think that they should be given a share by those who can and are. Real peasants or automata—coded simulations—they are always the same."

A slight blankness passed over her face, but despite terms and concepts foreign to her, the warm sympathy of Isis did not flag. Her wide green eyes remained fixed on him as a flower follows the sun. She was the perfect listener, and no surprise: she had been designed that way. In her porcelain beauty he had resurrected something of his first wife Jeannette, dead for more than a century, and in her selfless solicitousness he had memorialized something of his mother as well, but those traits had only been imposed on Isis out of his own memory. She was entirely unreal, a singular piece of code, his only trustworthy confidante. She might not understand him, but she would never betray him.

"No," he said, "I am at a crossroads and I have a terrible decision to make. The clumsiness of my servants is only an irritation, one that I have dealt with already." He allowed himself to dwell for a moment, not without pleasure, on how he had swept down upon Ra's temple on the back of the immortal bird Bennu and ended the rebellion in a single instant. Servants and rebels alike had thrown themselves on their faces, weeping at the terror of his majesty. He had felt his own power as a real and tangible thing, seen it ripple out from him like the blast pattern of an explosion. And that was what Wells and the others—even canny Jiun Bhao—did not understand. They thought his involvement with his simulations an old man's hobby, a sign of weakness, but how could you prepare to live forever in a virtual universe if you did not become part of it? And how could you rule such a universe without caring about it?

The rest of the Grail Brotherhood, he suspected, would find eternity hanging upon them very, very heavily. . . .

Thought of the project returned him to his worries. Isis was waiting, as still as a pool in the high mountains.

"No," he said, "the problem is that I do not trust my own operating system—the Other, that thing you know as Set."

Her face clouded. "Dark he is. Lost and troubled."

He could not help a tiny smile of satisfaction. Even though she was nothing but code, she spoke sometimes in a way that transcended her own narrow universe. She was a well-made machine. "Yes. Dark and troubled. But I have come to rely on it . . . on him. His power is great. But now that the time of the Ceremony is almost upon us, he is more restless than he has ever been."

"You spoke of the Ceremony before. That is when you will come to live with me all the time?" Her face was shining, eager, and for a moment he saw something in her he had not seen before, a girlishness that came neither from Maman nor Jeannette.

"Yes, I will come to live here for all time."

"Then nothing must go wrong with the Ceremony," she said, shaking her head gravely.

"But that is where the problem lies. There may be no second chance. If something does go amiss . . ." He frowned. "And as I said, Set has been restless."

"Is there no other magic you can use to perform the Ceremony? Must you rely on the Coffined One?"

Osiris sighed and leaned back. The cool stone room was a place of refuge, but his problems could not be avoided forever. "One other might be able to provide the magics I need—but he is my enemy, Ptah." Ptah was known to the rest of the world as Robert Wells, but Jongleur had slipped into the soothing rhythms of Osiris now and was reluctant to break the spell.

"That yellow-faced schemer!"

"Yes, my dear. But he is the only one who might be able to provide an alternative system . . ." He checked himself. "He is the only one who might have a magic powerful enough that I can do without Set."

She slid from the couch to kneel by his feet. She took his hand in her own, her pretty face earnest. "You control dark Set, my husband, but you do not control Ptah. If you give him such power, will he not use it against you?"

"Perhaps, but neither of us, Ptah nor myself, wishes the Ceremony to fail. It *must* work, for all of us—we have waited too long, worked too hard, sacrificed too much . . . and too many." He laughed sourly. "But you are right. Afterward, if I made Ptah my confidant, if I used his power to insure the Ceremony and the continued functioning of the Grail Project—what certainty would I have that he would not turn it against me?" Speaking these worries out loud was both painful and glorious—the freedom, the relief, of letting his fears be witnessed, even by a creature constructed only of code, was almost overwhelming. "Ptah hates me, but he fears me, too, not least because of the things I have kept secret. What would happen if that balance changes?"

"You control Set, but you do not control Ptah," Isis repeated stubbornly. "Your enemy is like an asp, my lord. His yellow face hides a heart that is black and faithless."

"It is always good to speak with you," he said. "It is far too much of a gamble to hand this weapon to Wells . . . to Ptah. He will certainly use it against me—the only question is when. If you give a man eternity, then he has much time to scheme."

"I am glad that I have pleased you, my lord." She rested her head on his thigh.

He stroked her hair idly, thinking of things he might do to improve his position. "Jiun Bhao will not be the only one to hang back," he said, but almost silently, forgetting for a moment that his companion could not read his mind any more than a true person could have. He turned and spoke to her directly. "I myself will wait with Jiun . . . I mean with wise Thoth . . . and I will see. If the Other proves untrustworthy—well, I will have some temporary solution in place, and Thoth and I will solve the problem together. If the others suffer because of this, or even do not survive the Ceremony . . ." He allowed himself a wintry smile. "Then Thoth and I will salute their sacrifice."

"You are most wise, my husband." Isis rubbed her cheek against his leg like a cat.

With the return of confidence, Osiris felt something stirring inside him, something that he had not experienced in many long years. He let his finger follow the curve of Isis' neck and trail down to the rough softness of her dress. He had not performed the physical act for almost a century, and even with the false vigor of virtuality the urge had not survived his loss of ordinary physical capability by more than a few decades. It was odd to feel it again.

And I'm such an old man, he thought. *It scarcely seems worth it—all that sweat, all that bother, and for what?*

But although nothing in his real physical form responded but a faint electrochemical glimmer from brain to ganglia and back, he still felt that almost forgotten pressure at the back of his mind, and found himself bending to kiss heavenly Isis on the nape of her neck. She lifted shining eyes to him. "You are strong, my lord, and beautiful in your glory."

He said nothing, but allowed her to climb back onto the couch and curl against him, her breasts pushing gently against his bandaged ribs, her perfumes a sweet cloud around him. She had her mouth against his ear, breathing, murmuring, almost silently singing. He began to forget himself in the seashell whisper of her endearments until her voice, her soft, unintelligible words, and everything else began to be subsumed by the rushing of his blood. All but the melody . . .

His hand, gently pinioning her wrist, suddenly tightened. She cried out, more in surprise at first than in pain. "My lord, you are hurting me!"

"What is that song?"

"Song?"

"You were singing. What is it? Sing it to me so I can hear."

Eyes wide at the raggedness of his voice, she swallowed. "I did not . . ."

He slapped her, rocking her head backward. *"Sing!"*

She began, falteringly, tears sparkling on her cheeks.

> ". . . *An angel touched me, an angel touched me,*
> *The river washed me, and now I am clean . . .*"

She paused. "That is all I know, my lord. Why are you so angry with me?"

"Where did you hear that?"

Isis shook her head. "I . . . I do not know. It is only a song such as my handmaidens sing, a pretty little song. The words came into my head . . ."

In fury and terror he struck her again, toppling her from the couch onto the floor, but the silent slaves did not change their rhythms; the palm fronds continued to beat slowly up and down. Isis looked up at him, full of terror. He had never seen the expression on her, and it upset him almost as much as the song.

"How could you know that?" he raged. "How could you know it? You are not even part of the Grail system—you are separated, sealed off, a dedicated environment that no one else can access. It cannot be!" He stood, towering high above her. "Who has touched you? Have you betrayed me, too? Told them all my secrets?"

"I do not understand your words," she cried helplessly. "I am yours, my husband, only yours!"

He fell upon her and beat her until she could not speak, but even then her silence only goaded him on. A black terror was swirling inside him, as if a door into nothingness had swung open and he was being forced through it. His childhood nemesis stood waiting for him on the other side—the inescapable Mr. Jingo, full of mocking laughter. Lost in a dreadful darkness, Jongleur thrashed her until she was a thing of rags and sagging limbs, then fled her bower for the other worlds of his manufactured universe, all of them suddenly suspect, all of them without solace.

Silence fell in the cool stone room. The stolid slaves continued to wave their fans up and down, up and down, over the unmoving shape sprawled on the floor.

"**I** DIDN'T think your brother give you this car in a million years," Joseph said after they had dropped Gilbert off. The entire ride back from Elephant's place had been spent in argument between the two brothers. Joseph had enjoyed that so much he had not even bothered to offer his own opinion, which was that the car was an ugly old thing anyway and should be replaced by something a bit more luxurious. It was amazing that something so large and clumsy should have so little room for Joseph's long legs.

"I gave him the down payment," Del Ray said grimly. "He owes me. And it's not like we can take a train to the Drakensberg—not that part of the mountains, anyway."

"Could have rented something nice. You got cards, don't you?" Renie had taken Joseph's away from him, something which still galled, but she had given him an ultimatum—if she had to earn the money and balance the books, she wasn't going to have him buying rounds for what she called his "lazy, drunken friends."

"No, I couldn't have rented one," Del Ray snapped. "All of my cards have been cut off. I don't know whether Dolly did it or . . . or those men who were after me. I don't have anything, damn it! Lost my job, my house . . ." He fell silent, face set in a scowl that made him look years older. Joseph felt obscurely pleased.

They swung out onto the N3, entering the stream of traffic without trouble. The rain clouds had rolled through and the skies were clear. Joseph saw no sign of a black van, or of any van at all: the cars in their immediate vicinity were small commuter runabouts and a few long-haul trucks. He relaxed a little, enough to feel the urge for a drink come drifting up. He fiddled with the car's music system and found a dance hall station. After reaching a tense compromise with Del Ray about volume, he settled back.

"So why you break up with my Renie?" he asked.

Del Ray glanced at him but said nothing.

"Or did she break up with you?" Joseph smirked. "You didn't have all them nice suits and such in those days."

"And I don't have them anymore." Del Ray looked down at his wrinkled trousers, dark at the knees with dust and smeared mud. He drove in silence for a few moments more. "I broke up with her. I left her." He gave Joseph a brief look of irritation. "What do you care? You never liked me."

Joseph nodded, still in a good mood. "No, you are right."

Del Ray seemed about to say something unpleasant, but paused. When he spoke, it was as if he were talking to someone else, a third passenger who might actually be sympathetic. "I don't really know why we broke up. I mean, it seemed like the right thing to do. I think . . . I just . . . I was too young to have a family, get into all that."

"What are you talking about?" Joseph squinted at him. "She didn't want no family. She wanted to study all that university foolishness."

"She had a child, or just as good as. I didn't want to be a father."

"Child?" Joseph rose higher in his seat. "What are you talking about? My Renie didn't have no child!" But a panicky voice inside him asked, *Did you miss that, too? How much went past after her mama died, while you were trying to drink yourself to sleep every day?*

"You ought to know," Del Ray said. "I'm talking about your son, Stephen. Renie's brother."

"What foolishness is this?"

"Renie might as well be his mother is what I'm saying. You weren't there most of the time. She raised him just like he was her own child. That's what I wasn't ready for, I suppose—having a little boy of my own while I was still just a boy myself. It scared me."

Joseph let himself relax. "Oh, Stephen. You just talking about Stephen."

"Yes." Del Ray's voice was full of sarcasm. "Just Stephen."

Joseph watched the hills slide past, the suburbs of Durban as strange to him as another continent, full of lives he could only imagine. It was true, Renie had tried to step in when Stephen's mother had died. Well, that was a woman's nature, wasn't it? It wasn't Joseph's fault. He had to earn a living, make sure they both had food to eat. And when he couldn't work anymore—well, that wasn't his fault either, was it?

A vision of Stephen in his hospital bed, the blurred shape beneath the plastic tent, made Joseph flinch. He leaned forward to fiddle meaninglessly with the music controls. He did not want to believe it was the same Stephen as the little boy who had climbed up the tree in Port Elizabeth that one time and then refused to come down until he found a monkey nest. It was easier to think of them as two separate people—the real Stephen and the terrible fraud in the bed, curled up like a dead insect.

When his wife Miriam had been lying in the burn ward, the light slowly fading from her eyes, he had wished that there were some way he could go down after her, follow her into death and then carry her back out to the world again. He had thought he would do anything, risk anything, suffer any pain to find her and bring her back. But there was nothing he could do, and that had been a far worse pain than anything he could have imagined. Drink? If the ocean had been wine, he would have drunk it down from shore to shore to make the hurting stop.

But wasn't that what Renie was doing? Going after Stephen, no matter how little hope there was, trying to find him and bring him back from death?

For a moment, as they moved out from behind a truck to change lanes, the afternoon sun stabbed through the windshield into Joseph's eyes, dazzling him. To think that there was so much love in her, growing on sorrow like a green vine curling up out of the ruin of a dead tree. It was as though the terrible secret of how Joseph had felt while Renie's mother lay dying had jumped from him to his daughter without words. It was a mystery, a great and terrible mystery.

He was silent for a long time, and Del Ray seemed to like it that way. The music played on, lively, bouncing rhythms, something to chase away care. Durban vanished into the late-afternoon gloom behind them.

THEY waited only two minutes after Gilbert's ancient sedan had pulled away from the warehouse building before spilling out of the black van. The three men, two black, one white, moved quickly. One pushed a card into the front door slot, overriding the palmreader. They filed silently up the stairs. It took them only a few moments to find the door of Elephant's rented space.

One of the black men slapped an adhesion-cup of shaped hammer gel onto the door just above the handle, then all three stepped back. The contained explosion shattered the bolt and fried the door's internal electronics, but they still had to slam against it two times before it popped open.

Elephant had a spike into the warehouse's security cameradrones, which had given him almost a minute's headstart, plenty of time to dump his system memory (the resident memory only, since he had backups scattered on various nodes under various coded designations) and replace it with a carefully-constructed and legally irreproachable subsitute. When the three men smashed through the door he was sitting with his hands held up in plain sight, a look of injured innocence on his round face.

All of which would have been fine if the trio had been a UN-Comm flying squad, as Elephant had expected. But Klekker and Associates had a much different agenda than UNComm, and—

unfortunately for Elephant—a very different *modus operandi* as well.

They had already crushed two of his fingers before he even had a chance to tell them how willing he was to share whatever information they wanted about his earlier guests. He could tell these men were not the types to bargain, so he did not try to make a deal, but admitted that the information Del Ray Chiume and his friend had wanted was available to anyone with the skills to find it. Maps of the Drakensberg and information about an abandoned military base called "Wasp's Nest" was all he had given Chiume and the old man. It had been dumped out with the system memory, but Elephant hurried to assure the new arrivals he would be happy to find it again.

Klekker and Associates had made one mistake already, assuming that an old woman named Susan Van Bleeck was not going to survive the attack on her house. She had, at least temporarily, and that was an error they would not make twice.

Two small-caliber bullet wounds in the back of the skull did not make for much bleeding, but the red puddle was still slowly growing on the desktop beneath Elephant's head when the three men had gathered up the last of the things they wanted. One of them paused at the doorway to toss a small dispersive incendiary back into the cluttered room, then they went down the stairs, moving swiftly but without obvious haste.

The van was half a kilometer away before the building's fire alarms went off.

CHAPTER 21

The Spire Forest

NETFEED/ART: Artistic Suicide Challenge
(visual: Bigger X at Toronto arraignment)
VO: A guerrilla artist known only as No-1 has challenged
the better-known forced involvement artist Bigger X to a
suicide competition. No-1's broadside against Bigger X,
which calls him a "poseur" because "he only works with
other people's deaths," suggests a suicide competition
between the two artists, to be broadcast live by
"artOWNartWONartNOW." The one with the most
artistically interesting suicide would be judged the winner,
even though he or she would not be around to collect the
prize. Bigger X, who is wanted by the police for
questioning in a Philadelphia bombing, has not been
available for comment, but ZZZCrax of
"artOWNartWONartNOW" called it "an intriguing story."

"WE have a short time left before the sun rises," said Brother Factum Quintus. "Renie, Florimel—perhaps you would accompany me?" He gestured to the stairs.

Renie looked at T4b, busy comforting Emily, who had been

stumbling like a sleepwalker since their encounter with the Lady of the Windows hours ago. The pair were seated on a dusty, threadbare couch which looked like it might collapse under the weight of T4b's armored form at any moment, but otherwise the small tower room seemed safe enough. "You two stay here, will you?"

"We will not go far from them," the monk reassured her. "It is only a small distance. But if we do not want ourselves revealed to watching eyes, we should go before the sun rises."

!Xabbu hesitated only a moment, then joined the small procession as they mounted the stairs; Renie knew he was restraining himself, since in his baboon form he could have climbed much faster.

"This tower is on the edge of what is called the Spire Forest," Factum Quintus said. "A very fascinating part of the House." He was breathing a little heavily, but otherwise had weathered being kidnapped by bandits and the unexpected appearance of a religious revelation far better than Renie and her supposedly more hardened comrades. The monk had an almost childlike quality of being interested in everything, even the dreadful and the dangerous—a good trait in many ways, but Renie could not help worrying about his safety.

Oh, Jesus Mercy, she reminded herself, *he's a bloody Puppet. Might as well start fretting about the characters in netflicks, too.*

But the idea of Factum Quintus as an artificial being—not even a living creature, but an amalgam of coded behaviors—was hard to hold on to when those coded behaviors were walking beside her, slightly flushed, murmuring to themselves in pleasure over a newel-post.

"Why does it matter whether it is sunrise or not?" Florimel asked.

"Because the place we are going has many windows—and so do the other places. You will see." The monk paused on the landing, about to say something more, when suddenly the entire universe shrugged as though trying to dislodge something crawling on its back.

Renie had time only to think, *Oh, not again . . . !* before everything went sideways.

In an instant her surroundings blurred, retreating in all directions as though she were being shrunk to the size of an atom, but at the same time they seemed to topple in on her, as though reality itself were enfolding and crushing her. For half an instant, a terrible, jagged bolt of pain passed through her, as though her nerves were the teeth of a comb being dragged along a rough brick wall. Then the pain vanished, and so did everything else.

She had experienced these reality-quakes before, but never one that had gone on so long. She had been floating in darkness for a long time—she knew her time-sense must be distorted, but she had been able to think about many things while the darkness persisted.

I feel . . . different. Than the other times. Like I'm actually somewhere. But where?

She could feel her body, too, which was unusual. As far as she could remember, in the earlier episodes she had always been bodiless—a floating mind, a witness to a dream. But now she had the sense of her self, a knowledge that extended all the way to her fingers and toes.

What is that called, that sense-of-the-body? Had the word gone, like so much of her university vocabulary and other minutiae, swallowed up afterward in the day-to-day of grading exams and trying to stretch limited resources into legitimate lessons? *No, it's . . . it's proprioception. That's the word.*

A small warm glow suffused her, satisfaction at having remembered. But with it came an increasing sense of something wrong, something different. Proprioception was indeed the word, and her proprioceptive senses were sending her strange messages. She had been in the network so long that it took a while before she finally understood.

I feel like I have a body again. A real body. My body!

She moved her hands. They moved. Strange currents beat at them, strange pushes and pulls buffeted her, but she was feeling her own hands. She touched herself, running her hands over her arm, her breasts, her belly, and was startled by how dazzlingly ordinary her body felt. Her fingers slid up to her face and encountered tubes . . . and a mask.

It's me! The thought was so bizarre she could not quite grasp it for a moment. The confusion of real and unreal had become a normal way of thinking, hard to put aside on such short notice, but the facts seemed indisputable: she was touching her own naked body. The bubble-mask with its dependent tubes and wires was again clamped to her face. The thought of what it all meant was slower, but when it finally arrived, it had the force of epiphany.

I'm . . . I'm back!

The strange flow of forces across her skin must be the gel in the V-tank, temporarily offline from the reality-mimicking circuits of the Otherland network and generating random patterns. That meant . . . that meant she could simply pull the inside release handle on the tank and step out! After all these weeks, the real world was only inches away.

But what if it was temporary? Or what if the same thing was not happening to !Xabbu, and he would be left behind in the network? It was hard to think—the excitement of the world that had seemed so far away now being so near was making her claustrophobic. How could she float here, deep in the unlit depths of the tank, while real air and real light were only a few movements away? Even seeing her father, the miserable old bastard, would be such a joy . . . !

The thought of Long Joseph brought with it the memory of Stephen and her excitement suddenly turned cold and heavy. How could she leave when she had done nothing for him? She would be free, yes, but he would still be stretched like a corpse in that horrible tent, wasting away.

Adrenaline sped through her like a brushfire. Whatever she was going to do, she might have only minutes or even seconds before this ended. She pushed at the inconstant gel, forcing herself toward one of the sides of the tank. Her hands encountered something hard and unevenly smooth—the tank's interior wall and its millions of pressure-jets. She curled her fingers into a fist and tried to find an area where the counterpressure was weaker, then rapped at the wall. A dull sound like a gong wrapped in a blanket came back to her, so quiet that she despaired anyone would ever hear it until she remembered that she was wearing not just a mask but hearplugs. She knocked again, over and over, and the more she did so without result, the stronger grew the urge to throw aside all responsibilities and simply open the tank. Escape. Escape would be so wonderful. . . .

"H-hello?" It was very hesitant but very close.

"Jeremiah? Is that you?" His voice in her ear brought his face with it, a pure spark of memory, as though he had suddenly appeared in the darkness beside her. "Oh, God, Jeremiah?"

"Renie?" He sounded even more surprised than she was, his voice shaking. *"I'll . . . I'll let you out . . ."*

"Don't open the tank! I can't explain, but I don't want the tank opened. I don't know how much time I have."

"What's . . ." He stopped, clearly overwhelmed. *"What's happening with you, Renie? We weren't able to talk to you after the first few minutes you went in. It's been weeks! We had no idea what . . ."*

"I know, I know. Just listen. I don't know if this will do you any good, but we're still in the network. It's huge, Jeremiah. It's . . . I can't even explain. But it's strange, too. We're still trying to understand everything." And yet they understood almost nothing— how could she possibly relate what they had experienced? And how would any of it be of any use? "I don't know what I can say. There's something keeping us online—this is the first time I've been off the network or whatever it is since we first hacked our way in. There are other people involved, too. Damn, how can I explain? Somebody just told us we're supposed to go to Priam's Walls, which I think is some kind of simulation of the Trojan War, but we don't know why, or who wants us to go, or . . . or anything . . ." She took a breath, floating in darkness, separated from life by a thin wall of fibramic crammed with micromachinery. "Jesus Mercy, I haven't even asked about you, about my father! How are you? Is everything okay?"

Jeremiah hesitated. *"Your father . . . your father is fine."* There was a pause. Despite her racing heart, Renie almost smiled. Clearly, he was driving Jeremiah crazy. *"But . . . but . . ."*

She felt a sour tug of fear. "But what?"

"The phone." He seemed to be struggling for words. *"The phone here has been ringing."*

Renie could make no sense of this. "So? It's old technology— that's what phones used to do."

"No, it's been ringing, and ringing, and ringing." A burst of static swept through her hearplugs, almost obliterating the last repetition. His words jumped back, very clear. *"So I answered it."*

"You did what? Why in the name of God did you do that?"

"Renie, don't yell at..." Another blizzard of noise swept through. *"... Until I was going crazy. I mean, after your..."* Jeremiah's pause was his own this time, although more distortion soon followed. *"Anyway, I ... up ... other end ... said ..."*

"I can't hear you! Say that again."

"... it was ... me ... frightened ..."

"Jeremiah!"

But his voice had grown distant, like a bee buzzing in a paper cup several meters away. Renie shouted to him again, but it was too late: the connection was gone. Within moments she felt her sense of her surroundings diminishing as well, as though something had reached down and grasped her mind in powerful yet velvet-soft fingers and was drawing it right out of her body. She had time only to wonder what would have happened if she had actually left the tank, then she was sucked back into the void again. Darkness lasted only another instant, then the world—the virtual world—reassembled itself around her in a fluttering explosion of particulate color, like a tumbled card-tower flocking back together, until the stairs were beneath her feet once more and Brother Factum Quintus' face was before her, lips still parted in preparation for speech.

"In fact..." was all he had time to say before Renie astonished him by sagging and then collapsing onto the stairs.

"So Factum Quintus didn't feel anything," Renie said quietly. She had passed off her collapse as a dizzy spell, and the monk had already begun to mount the stairs again. "For him, it was like it didn't happen. He just turned off and then turned on again."

"That is no doubt because he is a Puppet," Florimel whispered—caught up as Renie was in the strange courtesy of not letting Factum Quintus suspect he might be artificial. "My experience was more like yours. Of all these ... spasmic occurrences I have been through in this network, this was the strangest. I felt myself back in my own body. I ... I felt my daughter beside me." She hesitated, then abruptly turned to follow the monk.

"What happened to me was different," !Xabbu said, padding along at Renie's side. "But I would like to think about it for a little while before I tell you."

Renie nodded. She was still too shaken by the brief moment

of return to want to talk much at all. "I don't know that we can make any sense of it anyway. *Something's* happening—I can't believe it's normal when everything goes crazy like that. But what it all means . . ."

Renie fell silent as they stepped up onto the landing, which turned out to be the entrance to the top of the tower. The room was only a few meters wide, an octagon with a window of thick, old-fashioned leaded panes in each wall. The sky outside was cobalt blue, but already at the edges night was beginning to burn away; a faint glow of dawn outlined the strange horizon.

But horizon, Renie decided, could not really be the right word. What horizon they could see was only the most distant parts of the House still visible—she could not help wondering for a moment whether the House-world curved like the natural globe, or was as flat as it was apparently infinite—but all around them stood the much more absorbing vista of the Spire Forest.

It was obvious what had occasioned the name. Unlike Renie's other view of the House, which had been mostly flat rooftops, cupolas, and domes, what surrounded their tower windows was a profusion of vertical shapes in astounding variety—windowed obelisks, clock towers, attenuated pyramids and needle-thin spikes, Gothic protrusions clotted with dark carvings, even vast crenellated belvederes so ornate they looked like entire castles perched in the sky. Even in the dim light, Renie could count hundreds of the spires looming far above the House's sea of roofs.

"I know the names of some, but not all," Factum Quintus said. "Many of the older names are lost forever, unless we find them perhaps in the translation of old books. That tall thin one is Cupboard's Dagger. Nearer is Weeping Baron's Tower, and closer still is one called Jelliver's Heart, for reasons no one knows. I think that more elaborate shape in the distance might be the Pinnacle of the Garden Kings—yes, it seems to have the famous carbuncles, much argued about in their day—although it is too dark to be sure."

"And . . . and our friend is in one of these?" she said at last.

"It seems likely. And her abductor as well, which is why we want to see rather than be seen, and thus needed to arrive here while darkness remained. But there is another serious problem, I'm afraid." Brother Factum Quintus' worried look, though sincere, did not entirely overshadow the fascinated gleam in his eyes as he surveyed the garden of spikes just warming into three-dimensionality with the sun's first rays. "The piece of figured plaster that began this search tells me your friend's captor has likely passed through the long corridors built during the Alliance of Chambers era, which link most of these towers. It stands to reason that a criminal would pick one of these high spots as a lair—an 'eyrie' would be a better term, perhaps—since they are remote and yet still close to the Library. But as to *which* of all these actually contains your friend . . . I'm afraid I have no idea at all."

"That's ridiculous," Renie told them flatly. "It's too risky." She was exhausted, desperate for sleep, but this had to be dealt with now. "We can't afford to search with anything less than our full numbers. That's how that monster got Martine in the first place, when she fell behind us—culled her from the herd like a lion taking an antelope."

"But what he says makes sense, Renie . . . " Florimel began.

"No! I can't accept it."

!Xabbu sidled across the floor of the dusty chamber, not quite upright, but not on all fours, blurring the difference between his real inner self and his sim body in a way that always made her nervous. "I appreciate that you are concerned for me, my friend, but I believe it is the best way."

Her fatigue was making her stupidly stubborn—it was hard to argue with !Xabbu's logic—but Renie would not let go easily. "So we're supposed to just let you go off by yourself? Not just after a murderer, but climbing around hundreds of feet above the ground?"

"Can we six this so I can get some 'zontal?" T4b snarled. "He's a monkey, seen? Monkeys climb."

Helplessly looking for allies, Renie turned to Factum Quintus, who shrugged. "It is not my argument," he said. "But as I told you, it will take us days to walk up and down corridors and stairs, searching all these towers on foot, and in very few of them would we be able to reach the upper rooms without warning any occupants."

Renie clenched her teeth, biting back an angry reply that would convince no one. It was useless to antagonize her friends. The most pressing argument of all was one she could not make, not without announcing her own selfishness: she was terrified she might lose !Xabbu. After all they had experienced together, she could not imagine where she might find the strength to go on without him. With Stephen as good as dead, the small man was the closest thing she had to loving family.

"We are tired, Renie." Florimel was clearly finding it difficult to keep resentment out of her voice. "We must sleep."

"But . . ."

"She is right," !Xabbu said. "I will not change my mind, but it may look different to you after you have rested. I will take first watch—I shall not go anywhere until it is dark, in any case, so we can sleep through as much of the day as we need."

"I don't want to sleep." It was Emily, her voice tremulous. "I want to go home. I . . . I *hate* this place."

Renie fought for patience. "You've been in worse."

"No." The girl sounded quite certain. "It makes me feel sick to be here. It's bad for my baby, too."

Renie wondered if there was something going on that they did not understand, but had no strength to pursue it. "I'm sorry, Emily. We'll leave as soon as we can get our friend Martine back."

"Don't want to stay here at *all*," Emily grumbled, but quietly, like a child back-talking a parent who had already left the room.

"Sleep," Florimel grunted. "Sleep while you can."

The minutes of silence that followed were not restful ones, and the sleep Florimel recommended seemed impossibly distant. Renie realized she was clenching and unclenching her fists. She could sense !Xabbu looking at her, but she did not want to meet his eyes, even when he sidled closer.

"There is a story my people tell," he said to her quietly. "Perhaps you would like to hear it?"

"I would enjoy hearing it, too," announced Brother Factum Quintus, "—oh, that is if I am not being rude!" he added hurriedly, but he was clearly abrim with anthropological interest. Renie could not help wondering in what sort of scholarly archive !Xabbu's tale might end up, another thread in the strange tapestry that was the House. "And if the others don't mind, of course."

T4b groaned in a way that confirmed for Renie once and for

all that he truly was a teenager, but despite the noise of protest, did not actually object.

"Does what we others think matter at this point?" Florimel grumbled.

"It is a good story," !Xabbu assured them. "One of my people's favorites. It is about Beetle and Striped Mouse." He paused and settled himself in a comfortable position, sitting on his haunches. They had drawn the chamber's heavy curtains—unlike the tower room above, it had only one window—but a thin spear of morning light had found its way through a gap in the fabric. Floating dust shimmered in the beam like silver.

"Beetle was a very beautiful young woman," he began. "All the young men would have tried to make her their own, but her father Lizard was a sour old man and did not want his daughter to leave him. He put her in his house, a hole deep under the earth, and would not let her out into the sunlight. He would let no man court her.

"All of the First People went to Grandfather Mantis to complain, saying that it was unfair for old Lizard to keep a lovely young woman like Beetle hidden away so that none of their sons could marry her and her beauty was not shared. Grandfather Mantis sent them away, saying he must consider what they said.

"That night, Mantis had a dream. He dreamed that Lizard had taken the moon down into his hole in the earth as well, and that without it in the night sky, the First People were lost and terrified. When he awakened, he decided that he could not allow Lizard to hide his daughter away.

"Mantis sent for Long-Nosed Mouse, who was a beautiful fellow, and told him what had happened. 'It is for you to find the place she is hidden,' Grandfather Mantis said. Long-Nosed Mouse was one of the best of all the First People at finding things, so he agreed, and went in search of Lizard's daughter.

"When at last Long-Nosed Mouse came near the hole in the earth, Beetle saw him. In her excitement, she could not help herself. She called out, 'Look, look, a man is coming!' Her father heard this cry, and when Long-Nosed Mouse entered into the earth, Lizard fell upon him in the dark and killed him.

"'Who shall tell a father what he may and may not do?' said Lizard. He was so proud and happy he did a dance. Beetle wept.

"When Mantis heard what had happened he was sad and afraid. The kinsmen of Long-Nose Mouse heard also, and one by one they went down into Lizard's hole to avenge their brother, but Lizard lay hidden until each one was lost in the dark tunnels, then fell upon him and killed him. Soon all of the men of the long-nosed mice had been slain. Their wives and children set up a great cry of mourning so loud that it pained Grandfather Mantis, so loud that he could not sleep for three days.

"When at last he fell asleep, he had another dream, and when he awakened from it he called all his people together. 'In my dream I have seen Lizard killing the long-nosed mice, and that is something that cannot be. In my dream I have spoken to myself, and I have thought much, and I find that it is the Striped Mouse who must now go and save the young woman, Beetle.'

"Striped Mouse was young, quiet, and clever, and he knew that the dreams of Mantis could not be ignored. 'I will go,' he said and set out. But when he came to the place where Lizard lived, and where so many had fallen before him, Striped Mouse thought, 'Why should I go down that hole into the dark, when I know Lizard is waiting? I will dig a hole of my own.' And so he did, scratching his way into the earth, for the Striped Mouse is a good digger, until he came at last into the tunnel where Lizard lay in wait. But because he had been quiet and clever, Striped Mouse had dug his own hole in behind the place where Lizard was, and so he was able to fall upon Lizard from behind. Long they fought, until Striped Mouse at last began to win out.

"Lizard shouted in fear and unhappiness, 'Why do you kill me? Why do you raise your hand against me?'

"'I am, by myself, killing to save friends,' cried Striped Mouse, and with that Lizard fell dead before him. Striped Mouse found Beetle, and although she was frightened he led her forth out of the hole and into the light. As he did that, a wonderful thing happened, for all the long-nosed mice who had fallen came back to life, crying 'I am here!' Each stepped out into the sunlight behind Striped Mouse and Beetle, each one carrying a fly-whisk, which he lifted over his head like a flag. Striped Mouse was very proud as he walked beside Beetle, and happiness was great inside both of them, because he already felt himself to be the husband of the young woman, and she felt herself to be his utterly.

"When they reached Mantis, he got up and followed them. As they came to the village where the long-nosed mice had lived, waving their fly-whisks, the grass of the plain began to wave, too. All the wives and children of the long-nosed mice came rushing out, making glad cries to see that their men were alive again, and Grandfather Mantis watched with amazement and joy, not a little surprised by how well he had dreamed."

Oddly enough, Renie did feel more relaxed as !Xabbu finished his story, but she could not entirely free herself of nagging worries. "It was a lovely story," she told him, "but I'd still like to try to think of some other way to search for Martine."

Even after all this time, it was still a little hard to read the baboon expressions, but he seemed to be smiling. "But that is what my story is about, Renie. Some tasks can only be done by one person—by the right person. I feel that I am that person. And sometimes, as the story also tells, we must all trust in the dream that is dreaming us."

There was nothing to argue with—no crevice into which she could get the fingernails of logic—and exhaustion was weighing heavily on her. Renie yawned, tried to speak, but yawned again. "We'll talk about it when you wake up . . . when you wake *me* up for my turn at sentry," she said, starting to stumble over her words.

"You sleep now," he said. "Look—the others are sleeping already."

She did not bother to look. She could hear the steady rasp of Florimel's breath a meter away, and the longer she listened, the more it seemed to pull her down, down, down.

"He's *what*?" She shook off the lethargy of waking, her heart suddenly tight as knotted wire in her chest. "The bastard! He told me we would talk about it some more!"

"He waited until dark, but he was determined, Renie." Florimel had been the final sentry, and thus the only one to see !Xabbu leave. He had never wakened Renie. "You could not have stopped him—you could only have made it more difficult."

Renie was furious, but she knew that Florimel was right. "I'm just . . . what if we lose him, too? We're falling apart, fragmenting . . ."

Florimel took her arm in a tight grip. Afternoon light was leaking in through the drapes: it was easy to see the other woman's face, hard to ignore her anger. "The others are waking up. They do not need to hear such things from you of all people."

"But you know I'm right." Renie shook her head. This was the problem with holding so tightly onto control as everything pulled harder and harder against it—when things began to slip, the temptation simply to give up was very strong. "Quan Li and William and Martine already gone, not to mention Orlando and Fredericks—and now !Xabbu. What's the point? Is it going to come down to you and me arguing about which cliff we should jump off?"

Florimel's laugh was sudden and unexpected. "It would probably be a long argument, Renie. I'm sure I would be a much better judge of cliffs."

It took a moment for Renie to realize Florimel had made a joke—the German woman was turning into a regular comedienne. Renie felt a bleak amusement of her own. Perhaps as the group shrank, everyone would begin to take on new roles. What would be next, T4b as the group's diplomat? Emily as the sergeant-at-arms? "I don't think I'll have the energy to argue, Florimel," Renie said at last, and did her best to smile. "Tell you what—I promise I'll let you pick the cliff."

"Bravely spoken, soldier." Florimel smiled back and patted her on the shoulder. Her clumsiness with the friendly gesture made Renie suddenly like her more than she ever had before.

"Right," she said. "So we wait. Jesus Mercy, I hate waiting! But if we can't do anything about !Xabbu, we can at least plan what we want to do when we hear from him, I suppose."

"Why are we here?" Emily said groggily from the bench, where she had pillowed herself in what seemed a fairly uncomfortable way on T4b. "I don't want to be here anymore."

"Of course you don't." Renie sighed. "But the rest of us are having such a lovely time, we thought we'd stay."

Renie's improved spirits did not last long. Although they used the time waiting for !Xabbu's return to scavenge a few weapons— splintered table legs and heavy curtain rods for clubs and spears, even a ceremonial sword found hanging neglected in an alcove in one of the lower halls—there was only so much planning and preparation they could do. As evening passed into night, and night itself stretched on and on with no sign of the man in the baboon sim, the tightness in Renie's chest became overwhelming.

"I told you we shouldn't have let him go by himself!"

Florimel shook her head. "He has many towers to investigate. And even if something happens to him—and of course we all pray it does not—that would not make his plan wrong. The rest of us cannot go where he can go, wearing that body."

Renie knew it was true, but that did nothing to alleviate the helplessness, the terrible, despairing pressure building inside her. "So what do we do? Just sit here until doomsday, knowing that monster probably has both of them now?"

Factum Quintus looked up. "Unlike your monkey friend, we do not need darkness to search," he said. "In fact, we will do better in daytime, since we will be able to see which hallways are full of undisturbed dust—I have noticed a few such in our exploration this evening."

"So if !Xabbu isn't back by dawn," Renie said, "we can start looking." It was amazing how much relief came from the simple notion of *doing something*.

"Then let us all try to get some more sleep now," Florimel said. "We have been working hard since your friend left us and we are still tired. We do not know what a search will lead us to."

"Talkin' smart," T4b agreed. "Like wearing a car, this armor."

"So take it off," Renie growled.

"You crash for total?" T4b said, shocked. "Like, fly around dangling my *churro*?"

Emily giggled. Renie waved her hand in disgust and went back to sharpening the end of her curtain rod on the exposed stone wall.

Night crept on, but no one could sleep. !Xabbu did not return. At last, everyone had run out of things to do, and sat, wrapped in silent thoughts and worries. Outside, the moon passed slowly over the Spire Forest, as though trying not to prick itself on the thorny towers.

"CODE *Delphi.* Start here.

"Something strange and frightening has happened. Even now

I find it difficult to speak, but I doubt I have much time so I must use this chance.

"The monster who had impersonated Quan Li, the thing that calls itself 'Dread,' has been working me hard, exploring the nature of the access device. Some of his questions are so strange and unexpected that I am certain now he is consulting outside sources as well—not surprising since, unlike us, he can leave the network and then return to his stolen sim whenever he pleases. But there has been an edge to his explorations as well. I think it likely that he is using the outside knowledge in large part to test *me*—to make sure I am giving him legitimate data. Fortunately, although I lied about how we came to the House, I have been honest in all my other discussions of the access device. He is too frighteningly clever for me to risk trying to trick him, and I do not fool myself he will keep me alive an instant longer than suits him.

"But no, this is not what I wished to record. In my upset state, I have gone about these thoughts wrong-way 'round, since Dread is not the subject. When I awakened a little while ago from a short, exhausted sleep, he had disappeared again, perhaps to confer with his other sources, and I was alone. Or so I thought.

"As I went through my groggy ritual, checking more in reflex than in hope to see if I was still securely tied to the fixture above my head and that the thing itself was still firmly attached to the wall, I only slowly became aware that something in my prison room was different. It did not remain a mystery for long, though. There were now two corpses leaning against the wall, sharing my captivity.

"My heart sank, and I found myself praying that the new body was only another sim, and not one of my own companions who had been captured or even killed trying to find me. But as I concentrated, I discovered something very, very strange. The first corpse was still the familiar virtual cadaver of the young woman Dread had killed. The second body, though, seemed to be her twin. Everything about this second unmoving form mirrored the first— shape, dimension, position. Somehow, Dread had murdered a victim just like the other, then propped her up in identical pose while I was sleeping. But how? And why?

"Then the second corpse began to speak.

"I screamed. I should be used to the madness of this network by now, but even though I knew the first body was virtual, it was still a corpse to me, and the second was just as cold, just as still. Until it began to talk. And the voice—it might once have belonged to the original Puppet, the sad, dead young woman of the Upper Pantry Clerks, but it was being used now by someone unused to speech, a sound midway between an automated reader and a stroke victim. I cannot reproduce it. I will not try, for even to think about it makes me queasy.

" '*Help . . . is . . . needed,*' the corpse said. '*Flowpatch. Reroute. Help.*'

"If I made a sound in response, it must have been a moan. I was shocked, caught completely by surprise.

"It said again, '*Help is needed,*' with exactly the same intonation. '*Unexpected feedback. Danger of subroutine overwhelming central directive.*' It paused as a shiver or something similar passed through it. The plump arms moved in random ways, and one of the hands thumped against the twin corpse beside it. '*Help is needed.*'

" '*Who . . . who are you?*' I managed to ask. 'What kind of help do you need?'

"The head rotated toward me, as though it had not known where I was until I spoke. '*Speech is secondary functionality. Subroutines are confused. Nemesis Two needs clarification, or reroute of . . .*' It then spewed out a string of numbers and designations that must have been programming code, but they were mixed up with other lumps of barely comprehensible noise that didn't sound like any gear-scripts I have ever encountered. '*Nemesis One has been made nonfunctional by operating system problem,*' it said slowly. '*No contact, X abort threshold X cycles. Nemesis Three still operant, but has closed on the greater anomaly, no contact, X abort threshold X cycles. For White Ocean read Sea of Silver Light. Strong pull. Nemesis Three operant, but must be considered nonfunctional.*' Despite the strange, mechanical voice, there was something in its words that suggested a kind of devastation, like the deceptively ordinary speech of someone who has survived a terrible disaster. '*Nemesis Two caught in expanding subroutine loop. Cannot prosecute X Paul Jonas X search. Help is needed.*'

"I took a breath. Whatever it was, it did not seem like it meant to harm me, and the name 'Paul Jonas' had set me tingling. Sellars had spoken of a man named Jonas—was this something Sellars had created to find him? Or something of the Grail's? Whatever it was, it was clearly having problems. 'Is . . . is Nemesis Two—is that you?' I asked.

"It tried to stand, or at least that's what I think it did, but the attempt did not work. The copied corpse flopped onto the floor of the small room, face-first. One of the jerking hands touched me and I quickly pulled my legs away from it. I could not help it.

"*'Cannot detach,'* it said. *'Nemesis Two cannot detach from observation. Anomaly is folded here. Not X Paul Jonas X . . . but not NOT X Paul Jonas X. Nemesis Two cannot detach.'* It lay, hapless as a beached whale. I swear that its inhuman voice was plaintive. *'Help is needed.'*

"Before I could say anything else, it vanished. One moment it was there, thrashing slowly, then the next it simply was not, and I was alone with the original corpse sim once more.

"Whatever it may be, I feel as though I have been visited by a restless spirit. If it is some program meant to find the man Jonas, then Otherland itself has been too much for it, as I am beginning to feel it is for all of us. Like a trained laboratory rat whose pleasure button suddenly begins to dole out electrical shocks, the thing seems to be throwing itself at something it cannot understand and is helpless to avoid.

"I hear noises—Dread is returning. Perhaps this will be the time I can no longer keep him interested. I am not sure I care. I am so tired of being frightened . . .

"*Code Delphi*. End here."

"**C**OULD you be wrong?" Florimel asked Brother Factum Quintus. The group was sitting in a dispirited huddle on the stair landing. "Could the monster be keeping our friend somewhere other than the Spire Forest? Perhaps the piece of plaster was a false clue?"

Renie spoke up before the monk could answer. "Why would there be such a thing? The murderer didn't know we were coming, and he couldn't have known we would be able to find someone like Factum Quintus to tell us so much from that one little piece."

After eliminating all the hallways whose undisturbed dust suggested that they had not been traversed by anyone for a long time, the company had begun to force one tower door after another, eliminating every possible hiding place before moving to the next structure. The remoteness of the Spire Forest, which according to Factum Quintus had been deserted for decades except for bandits and a few runaways and eccentrics, had left them with a less daunting task than it had seemed at first, but although they had mustered up their courage to force open door after door, each time with weapons ready and hearts thumping, through the whole of the morning and afternoon they had found nothing but empty rooms. The one or two which had shown any hint of recent occupation had still clearly been deserted for years.

"I am sorry we have not found your friend." Factum Quintus spoke a little stiffly; the long day's work had clearly worn him out. "But that does not change what the ballflower fragment tells me. They were not in the Campanile of Six Pigs, so they must be somewhere here. Or at least the hiding place must be here—whether this person you seek is still using it, who can say?"

That was too depressing a thought for Renie to entertain. The only hope they had was that the Quan Li thing had not bothered to move its lair since taking Martine. "They HAVE to be here. They have to be. Besides, if they're not, then where in hell is !Xabbu?"

"Maybe he had an accident," Emily said. "Fell or something."

"Shut up, Emily," Florimel said. "We don't need suggestions like that."

"Just trying to help, her," muttered T4b.

Renie resisted an impulse to put her hands over her ears. There must be something they were missing, something obvious . . ."Wait!" she said suddenly. "How do we know he hasn't found some way to move ABOVE the floor—on ropes or something?"

The others looked interested, but Factum Quintus frowned. "Hmmm. It is an ingenious idea, but think back on those halls we eliminated from our search—there were no ropes remaining behind, and the walls themselves were dusty, too. Surely it would be hard for someone to swing or climb above the ground, carrying your friend's . . . carrying your friend, then remove these ropes after himself without leaving a trace. Besides, as you said, would this person really anticipate determined pursuit? More likely he would simply have hidden himself close to the hallways that *are* traveled, so as not to be tracked by bandits or other predatory searchers."

Renie thought back on the ancient hallways, thick with the silt of ages, silent and ghostly, and of the dozens of empty, uninhabited towers they had so fearfully explored. Another idea suddenly seized her. "Hang on," she said, "maybe we're the ones who are going over the top."

"What does that mean?" Florimel could not muster the energy to sound very interested.

"Because he has plaster from a tower window ornament in his cuff, we've been assuming that our man is living in one of the tower rooms. But maybe he just uses one for, what do you call it, surveillance? Maybe he's actually tucked in somewhere a couple of floors lower, where there are more exits." As soon as she said it, she felt certain she was right.

"So . . . so we have to look through all the buildings again?" Florimel scowled, but she was thinking. "All the floors we didn't bother to check?"

"No." Brother Factum Quintus stood up, the light of engagement bright in his fishy eyes. "No, if you are right, he would be using one of the towers with a good view all around for his observation post—perhaps to watch out for bandits, or for searchers from the House below. I would guess Weeping Baron's Tower."

"Which one is that?" Renie was gathering up her weapons, her table-leg club and curtain-rod spear.

"Do you remember the round tower? We saw that someone had been in the topmost chamber, I thought perhaps even recently, but since there was no sign of anyone actually staying there, we went back down again."

"I remember it, yes."

"A few floors down there was a landing—we climbed right past it, following the tracks on the stairs. The windows were broken out, and it was covered with leaves."

Renie could not forget. Factum Quintus' expression of sorrow and disgust at the state of the building had been almost comical. "But there weren't any doors off that landing, were there?"

"No," said Florimel, who had risen to her feet as well, "but there were tapestries—I remember, because they were discolored by the water that came in through the windows."

"Right. We're going. God, I hope we're not too late."

As T4b helped her to her feet, Emily 22813 wailed, "But I thought we were resting!"

Renie stopped them on the floor before the landing. "Emily," she whispered, "you and Factum Quintus at the back, because you're not carrying any weapons. Just try to stay out of harm's way."

"Quietly now," Florimel added. "He may have both !Xabbu and Martine. We don't want to frighten him into harming them."

Weeping Baron's Tower—in an uncharacteristically discreet mood, the monk had refused to explain its name, saying that it was too unpleasant a story for just now—was clearly one of the later additions to the House, its much-repaired stone facade only a skin over a skeleton of heavy timbers. The wood of the stairs and the landing was even less impressive, and years of weather through the shattered windows had also taken their toll. Some of the steps gave alarmingly; before they had climbed even a dozen, one of them let out a squeak that although barely audible, grated on Renie's nerves like a sudden scream.

Worried that the boards of the landing might be similarly noisy, Renie waved the others to stay behind at the top of the stairs, then continued with as much stealth as she could muster, gently lifting the sodden tapestries one by one. She found nothing but mossy wooden walls beneath any of them until she reached the last tapestry by the window. As she twitched up the corner, the light of the setting sun revealed a door sunk into a recess in the wall.

Heart pounding, Renie motioned for T4b and Florimel, lifting the tapestry a little farther so they could see what she had found. When her two companions were standing beside her, Florimel round-eyed with nerves, the teenager inscrutable behind his helmet, Renie tapped T4b on the arm. She and Florimel grabbed the edges of the tapestry and tore it away from the wall. It dropped like a wet corpse into Renie's arms. T4b hiked his robe up above his gleaming silver-blue armored legs with the delicacy of a dowa-

ger going wading, then kicked the door off its hinges and stepped
inside.

The clatter dropped into silence. Everything beyond was
shadow.

"I think it's . . ." T4b began, then a gout of flame and noise
erupted from the darkness.

Knocked to her knees, half-smothered in the heavy tapestry,
Renie thought a bomb had gone off until she saw T4b stagger
away from the door with his chest on fire, his robe and armor
melted into a smoking hole in his midsection. The teenager jit-
tered backward, flailing at himself with his hands, then slipped
and tumbled down the stairs, missing Emily, but carrying Factum
Quintus down with him in a flailing black snowball.

Before Renie could even struggle to her feet another explosion
knocked Florimel backward into the landing rail. She dropped
limply and did not move, a doll with its stuffing gone.

Ears ringing, her head as cloudy as if she had sunk into deep
water, Renie at last kicked free from the tapestry, but she had only
crawled a few meters back toward the stairs when she felt something step on her leg. She rolled over to see the Quan Li thing
standing above her, the familiar face contorted as though by demonic possession, stretched in a gleeful smile. It held a flintlock
pistol in each hand, one of them still dribbling smoke.

"I wish I'd been able to find more than one of those old blunderbusses," it said. "Good choice for Bang-Bang the Metal Boy,
though, wasn't it? As good as a shotgun. But these little black
powder guns aren't bad either." It glanced at the smoking pistol,
then smirked and tossed it over the landing. Renie heard it clatter downward, tumbling, falling. "One shot apiece. A bit Stone
Age . . . but then, if I'm going to treat myself to some extended
play with one of you, I only need one more shot anyway." It
glanced at Emily, cowering in shock at the top of the stairs, then
turned the familiar, terrifying grin back onto Renie.

"Yeah, I think I'll keep the little one," it said, and lowered the
pistol toward Renie's face.

CHAPTER 22

An Unexpected Bath

NETFEED/INTERACTIVES: GCN, Hr. 7.0 (Eu, NAm)—
"Spasm!"
(visual: Pelly being airlifted from building roof)
VO: Pelly (Beltie Donovan) and Fooba (Fuschia Chang)
think they have found the missing children, but the sinister
Mr. B (Herschel Reiner) has a surprise waiting for them—a
heart-attack ray! 2 supporting, 63 background open,
previous medical interactive pref'd for hospital strand. Flak
to: GCN.SPSM.CAST

IT was windy, and the Lollipop Family kept blowing over in the middle of their tea party. Christabel didn't feel very much like playing, but her mommy had told her to go out and play, so she was sitting on the ground next to the fence in the front yard, under the big tree. She had put a rock on top of the table so it wouldn't tip, but she couldn't do anything about how every time Mother Lollipop reached for the tea she lost her balance.

They were really indoor toys. It was stupid to play with them out in the yard.

Everything was all wrong, that was the problem. Christabel

had been so happy that the Storybook Sunglasses hadn't killed her daddy when he put them on, and even happier that after that he hadn't yelled at her anymore about the secret with Mister Sellars. She had been certain that now everything would be all right. Things would go back to the way they were before—Mister Sellars would come up out of his hiding place in the ground and go back to his house, and Christabel would visit him, and the terrible Cho-Cho boy would go away, and everything would be good again. She had been certain.

But instead, things had just got more wrong. At first, Daddy hardly came out of the study at all, coming home straight from work every evening and locking himself in. Sometimes she even heard him talking to someone, and she wondered if it was Mister Sellars, but her daddy wouldn't say what he was doing and her mommy just seemed scared and unhappy all the time and told her to go play.

The worst thing was the fights that her mommy and daddy had. Every night they had an argument, but it wasn't even like other arguments. They did everything really *quiet*. When Christabel stood beside the door of the study or her parents' room when they thought she was asleep, she could hardly hear a word they were saying. At first she thought they were trying to hide the fighting from her, which was scary. That was what Antonina Jakes' parents had done, then one day her mother had just left the base and taken Antonina away with her. Even on the day her mother came and took her out of school, Antonina had said, "My parents don't never fight," because someone had teased her about Divorce.

So at first, that was what had scared Christabel. *Divorce.* That word that sounded like someone slamming a door. When your mommy and daddy didn't live together, and you had to go away with one of them.

But when she had finally made herself brave enough to ask, her mother had been very surprised and said, "No, no, Christabel! No! We're not fighting! Your daddy's worried, that's all. I'm worried, too." But she wouldn't tell Christabel what she was worried about, except that Christabel knew it had something to do with the Storybook Sunglasses and Mister Sellars' secret, so whatever it was, it was Christabel's fault.

When her parents went on with their whispering-but-scared arguments, Christabel had another idea. Her parents were afraid someone would hear them, but maybe it wasn't Christabel they were hiding from. The arguments were a secret, but who were they trying to keep the secret from?

In her mind Christabel saw something from a kid's show on the net, a story about the North Wind, a frightening, angry face that appeared in the sky. Something like that was all around, maybe, listening, trying to catch her parents talking out loud. Something as thin and slippery as the air, as dark as a rain cloud. Something that could listen at every window.

Whatever the problem was, nothing was right any more. Christabel wished she'd never met stupid old crippled Mister Sellars.

Last night had been the worst. For the first time in days the arguing had gotten loud. Her mom had been crying, her dad shouting in a kind of scratchy way. They were both so unhappy that she wanted to run in from the hall and beg them to stop, but she knew they would just be angry at her for listening. This morning, when Christabel had come down for breakfast, her daddy had been out in the garage and her mommy had looked very sad, her eyes red and puffy-outy and her voice very quiet. Christabel had hardly been able to eat her cereal.

Something was wrong, more wrong than ever, and she didn't know what to do.

Christabel had finally switched off Mother Lollipop, because if she didn't keep trying to pick up the teapot at least she wouldn't fall over, when she heard a noise behind her. She turned around, expecting to see the dirty-faced boy with the broken tooth, but it was only her father's friend Captain Ron looking different than usual. He was wearing his uniform, but she was used to that— she hardly ever saw him in anything else. It took a moment before she could figure out that what was different was the look on his face. He seemed very serious, scowly and cold.

"Hello there, Chrissy," he said. She hated the name, but she didn't make the face she usually did. She felt like running but that was silly. "Is your daddy home?"

She nodded. "He's in the garage."

He nodded, too. "Right you are. I'll just pop in and talk to him for a minute."

Christabel jumped up. She wasn't sure why, but she felt like she wanted to run ahead and warn her daddy that Ron was coming. Instead she walked a little way ahead of him all the way across the lawn, then only ran the last couple of steps.

"Daddy! It's Captain Ron!"

Her father looked startled, and for a moment it was like the time when she pushed open the bathroom door and went in by accident when he was naked out of the shower, but he was only taking the seats out of the big van—when he was in a good mood he called it "the Vee-Hickle"—and setting them on the garage floor. He was dressed in shorts and a T-shirt, and there were black smears on his hands and arms.

"That's fine, honey," he said. He didn't smile.

"Sorry to interrupt your Saturday, Mike," said Captain Ron, stepping into the garage.

"No problem. You want a beer?"

Ron shook his head. "I've got Duncan working with me today and you just know he'd be mentioning it in some report somewhere. 'I noted an apparent smell of alcohol when Captain Parkins returned.'" He frowned. "Little prick." He suddenly noticed Christabel standing near the door. "Oops. Pardon my French."

"Why don't you run along and play, honey," her father told her.

Christabel went back onto the lawn, but she found herself slowing down when she was out of sight of the open garage door. Something was different than usual between her father and Captain Ron. She wanted to find out. Maybe it had something to do with why her mother was crying, why they were arguing every night.

Feeling very, very naughty, she quietly walked back and sat down on the path near the garage door where the men couldn't see her. She was still holding Baby Lollipop in her hands, so she made a little pile of dirt and sat him on top of it. He moved his fat little arms slowly back and forth, like he was losing his balance and about to fall.

". . . Tell you these things pop in and pop out," her daddy was saying, "but I'm telling you the sonsabitches are lying. I've already scraped all the skin off my knuckles on the damn bolts." It sounded almost like his normal cheerful weekend voice, but something was not quite right. It made Christabel squirm like she needed to go to the bathroom.

"Look, Mike," Captain Ron said, "I'll make this quick. I just found out about this little vacation you're taking . . ."

"Just a few days," her father said quickly.

". . . And I have to say I'm not real pleased about it. In fact, I'll be honest with you, I'm pretty goddamned pissed off about it." For a moment as his voice got louder, Christabel got ready to run away, but then she realized he was only walking back and forth between the door end of the garage and where her daddy was. "I mean, now of all times? When we've got the Yak breathing fire about that damned old man? You're just going to cut out for a few days for a little family trip and dump it all on me? That suctions, Mike, and you know it."

Her father was quiet for a while. "I don't blame you for being upset," he said at last.

"Don't blame me? *That's* a lot of help! Man, I never thought you'd do something like this to me. And not even talk to me about it first! Shit." There was a clumpy, clanky sound as Captain Ron sat down on one of the trash cans.

Christabel was excited and scared and confused by the bad language and Ron's angriness, but most of all by this talk of a vacation. What vacation? Why hadn't her mommy or daddy said anything? She suddenly felt very frightened. Maybe her daddy was going to take her away somewhere. Maybe he and Mommy were going to do a Divorce after all.

"Look, Ron," her daddy said. "I'll tell you the truth." He waited for a moment. Christabel slid a little nearer to the garage door, quiet as she could be. "We've—we've had some bad news. A . . . a health problem."

"Huh? Health problem? You?"

"No, it's . . . it's Kaylene. We just found out." He sounded so strange as he talked that for a moment Christabel couldn't really understand what he was saying. "It's cancer."

"Oh, my God, Mike. Oh, Jesus, I'm so sorry! Is it bad?"

"It's one of the bad ones, yeah. Even with those whatchamacal-lits, the carcinophages, it's still not very good odds. But there's hope. There's always hope. Thing is, we just found out and she has to start treatment right away. I . . . we wanted to spend a little time away, with . . . with Christabel. Before everything started."

Captain Ron just kept saying he was sorry, but Christabel couldn't even listen any more. She was cold all over, as though she had just fallen off a bridge into the darkest, deepest, most freezing water she could imagine. Mommy was sick. Mommy had *cancer,* that terrible pinchy black word. That was why she was crying!

Christabel started crying, too. It was so much worse than she had even imagined. She got up and stared at the ground, her eyes so full of tears that little Baby Lollipop was just bubbles of color. She stamped him into the dirt, then ran into the house.

She had her face pushed into her mother's lap, crying so hard she couldn't answer any of Mommy's questions, when she heard Daddy stomp in from the garage and say, "Jesus, that was horrible. I just had to tell Ron the most awful, awful . . ." He stopped. "Christabel, what's going on? I thought you were outside playing."

"She just came in here sobbing," Mommy said. "I can't get any sense out of her at all."

"I don't want you to die!" Christabel shrieked. She pushed her face into her mother's stomach and wrapped her arms around her mother's thin waist.

"Christabel, sweetie, you're mashing me," her mother said. "What are you talking about?

"Oh, God," said Daddy. "Did you . . . Christabel, were you listening to that? Oh, honey, were you listening to Daddy and Uncle Ron?"

Christabel was hiccuping now and it was hard to talk. "Don't d-die, Mo-Mommy!"

"What's going on here?"

She suddenly felt her daddy's strong hands curl under her arms. He pulled her away from her mother, although it was not easy, and lifted her up in the air. She didn't want to look at him, but he pulled her close with one arm, holding her against his chest, then took her chin with the other and lifted her face toward his.

"Christabel," he said. "Look at me. Your mommy's not sick. I made that up."

"She . . . she's not?"

"No." He shook his head. "It's not true. She's fine. I'm fine, you're fine. Nobody has cancer."

"Cancer!" Her mommy sounded really frightened. "For the love of . . . what's going on, Mike?"

"Oh, God, I had to tell a lie to Ron. It was bad enough, doing that to him . . ." He put his other arm around Christabel and pulled her close to his chest. She was still crying. Everything was wrong, it was wrong, everything was crazy and wrong. "Christabel, stop crying. Your mommy's not sick, but there are some important things we have to talk about." He patted her on the back. He still sounded funny, like something was squeezing him around the neck. "Looks like we need to have a little family meeting," he said.

IN Cho-Cho's dream he was back on the beautiful island in the secret part of the net, the place with the sand and palm trees, but he was there with his father, who was telling him not to believe any of it—that the blue ocean and white sands were just a trick, that the rich gringo bastards just wanted to trap them like *bichos* and kill them.

Even as he said it, Cho-Cho's father was stuck to the sandy beach like flypaper. It was pulling him farther down, but all the time he kept yanking on Cho-Cho's arm, saying "Don't believe them, don't believe them," even though he was going to pull Cho-Cho down into the sticky sand with him.

Struggling, trying to scream with a throat that didn't work, Cho-Cho realized that the old man, Sellars, was the one who was pulling on his arm. He wasn't on the beach, he was back in that tunnel, and *El Viejo* was trying to wake him up.

"Cho-Cho, it's all right. Wake up, please."

Cho-Cho pulled away, wanting only to go back to sleep, but the funny-looking old man kept tugging at him.

"What the hell is this?" said a new voice.

Without thinking, Cho-Cho snatched his homemade knife from the rolled coat he used as a pillow. He scrabbled to the far side of the tunnel and put the wall at his back, then raised the shank of sharpened metal scrap before him, pointing it at the stranger.

"Come near me, I cut you!"

The man was wearing normal clothes, not a uniform, but Cho-

Cho knew a cop when he saw one and this was definitely a cop—
but there was something else familiar about him, too.

"You didn't say anything about there being anyone else, Sellars," the man said, staring at Cho-Cho with hard eyes. "What's
going on?"

"I admit that I forgot to mention my friend here, Major
Sorensen," Sellars said, "but I assure you he is involved. He must
be a part of any plan."

The man glared at Cho-Cho. "But there isn't room in there! I
didn't plan on another person, even a child." He shrugged and
turned his back on Cho-Cho, who was astonished. Was it a trick?
Cho-Cho looked at Sellars, trying to figure out why the old man
had sold him out.

"I'll tell him everything," Cho-Cho said out loud to the old
man. "Everything about you and that little *much'ita* stealin' food
for you, and all that. Little Christy whassername, Bell."

The big police man turned back around. "Christabel? What
about Christabel?"

Cho-Cho suddenly realized why the man was familiar. "*Claro
que sí,* you her papa, huh? You in on this?" Maybe this explained
some of the weirdness—maybe the little girl's daddy was playing some money game on his bosses, and Sellars was helping him.
There had to be some explanation for all this. People like Sorensen
didn't just come down into stinking places like this for no reason—you could see it on his face how much he hated the smell,
the damp walls.

"Except for Cho-Cho here," Sellars said calmly, "I have explained everything to you truthfully, Major Sorensen. The boy is
here because he sneaked onto the base, and because if I had turned
him out, he would have been sure to mention it to you and your
associates when he was finally caught."

"Jesus," said the man sourly. "Jee-zus. Okay. I'll think of something. For now, we better get moving. I'll just put him in the front
seat with me until we get to our place."

"I ain't going nowhere." Cho-Cho was beginning to think this
was just an excuse to take him quietly. Men like this Sorensen
guy were the kind who vacuumed up street kids and disappeared
them. Cho-Cho'd seen guys like this before, white and clean-
looking, but hard and nasty, too, when no one was watching.

"My dear Señor Izabal, we have no choice," Sellars told him. "This place is not safe for us any longer. Do not fear—I am going, too. Major Sorensen is going to protect us."

"Major Sorensen," the white guy cop said, scowling, "is beginning to think that a court-martial and firing squad might be a less painful alternative."

It took them a couple of hours to clean everything up. The little girl's father didn't want them to leave anything behind.

"But surely we are only slowing ourselves down," *El Viejo* said, but mildly, the same way he talked to Cho-Cho.

"Look, if someone finds this place and sees someone has been living here, they'll go over every square inch with a particulator. They'll find stuff from you, but they'll find stuff from my daughter and now me, too. Forget what I said before—I may be committing career suicide, but I'd prefer it wasn't the other kind as well." The man named Sorensen took apart the old man's wheelchair and put the pieces into bags, which he hauled up out of the tunnel two at a time. Next he took a folding shovel and went off to dig a hole in the grass a long way from the concrete building that hid the tunnel entrance. When it was done, he came back and took away the chemical toilet to empty it into the hole.

When the toilet and the little stove and the old man's other stuff were all loaded into the van outside, he made Cho-Cho and Sellars lie down between the back seats so they would be hidden. At first the man tried to get Cho-Cho to give up the homemade knife, but Cho-Cho wasn't taking *that* credit, and at last he gave up and let him keep it.

"If we stop, don't make a noise," Sorensen said as he pulled a blanket over them. "I don't care what happens, don't you even breathe."

Cho-Cho was still not sure he trusted any of this, but the old man wasn't kicking about it, so he decided to go along. The van only drove for a little while. When it stopped and the blanket was pulled away, they were in somebody's garage.

"Mike?" A woman was standing in the doorway, wearing one of those night-time robes like the ladies on the netshows. "You were gone so long—I was worried." She sounded more like she was about to scream, but she was trying hard. "Is everything all right?"

"It took a while to get the place cleaned up," he grunted. "Oh, and we have an additional guest." He took Cho-Cho by the arm, a strong grip but not too rough, and hoisted him out of the van. Cho-Cho shook him off. "Sellars here forgot to mention that he had company."

"Oh, dear." The woman stared at Cho-Cho. "What are we going to do with him?"

"Mess with me, I'll six you, *ma'cita.*" Cho-Cho gave her his best cold stare.

"There isn't room for him in the compartment, so he'll have to ride with us." The man shook his head. "I guess if anyone asks, we'll have to say he's Christabel's cousin or something."

"Not looking like that, he wouldn't be." She frowned, but it wasn't the angry kind. Cho-Cho couldn't figure out what any of this was about. "You'd better come with me, young man."

He brandished the knife. Her eyes widened. "Ain't going nowhere, seen?"

She put her hand out, but slowly, like she was letting a mean dog sniff it. Somehow that made him feel much worse than the way she'd frowned at him. "Give that to me right now, please. You're not bringing that into our house."

"Please cooperate, Senor Izabal." Sellars had just lifted himself out onto the van's steps and he was breathing hard.

Cho-Cho stared at the woman. She didn't look like a real person to him at all—she was pretty and clean like someone on a commercial. What did these people want with him? He gripped the knife tighter, but her hand stayed out.

"Please give that to me," she said. "No one's going to hurt you here."

He looked from her to her big policeman-type husband, who wasn't saying anything, to Mister Sellars, who nodded, his strange yellow eyes very calm and peaceful. At last Cho-Cho reached out and set the knife down on a little bench near the door, next to a plastic box of nails and screws. He was putting it down because *he* wanted to—no one was going to take it from him.

"Good," said the woman. "Now follow me."

*   *   *

When the water had been turned off, the woman stood up. Cho-Cho had been too busy looking at all the strange things in the room—little kid toys and dried flowers and about nine hundred kinds of soap, most of which looked more like candy than anything else—to pay much attention, so when she said, "In you go," it took him a moment to figure out what she was talking about.

"In . . . in there?"

"Yes. You're certainly not going anywhere the way you are right now. You . . ." She almost shuddered. "You are absolutely filthy. I'll deal with those clothes."

He stared at the warm water, the white towels hanging on the racks. "You want me to get in there."

She rolled her eyes. "Yes. Go on, hurry up—we don't have much time."

Cho-Cho reached up for the tab on his jacket, then paused. She was still standing there, her arms crossed on her chest. "What you doing?" he asked her. "You funny or something?"

"What are you talking about?"

"I ain't taking no clothes off with you in here!" he said angrily.

The little girl's mother sighed. "How old are you?"

He thought about it for a moment, wondering if there were some trick hidden in the question. "Ten," he said at last.

"And what's your name?"

"Cho-Cho." He said it so quietly she asked him again.

"All right," she said when he had repeated it. "I'll be outside, Cho-Cho. Don't drown. But throw those clothes outside as soon as you take them off. I promise I won't look." Just when the door was almost shut, she opened it again, just wide enough to say, "And use soap! I mean it!"

When the little girl's father came in about half an hour later, Cho-Cho was still angry about his clothes.

"You robbin' me," he said, close to tears. "I'm gonna get my knife back, then you sorry!"

The big man looked at him, then at the woman. "What's this about?"

"I threw those horrible clothes away, Mike. Honestly, they

smelled like . . . I don't even want to talk about it. I let him keep his shoes."

Cho-Cho's choice had been either to go naked or to put on the clothes she gave him, so he was wearing a pair of the man's pants, rolled several times at the cuff, and held up with a belt. That wasn't so bad—with such baggy legs, he looked a little like a Goggleboy wearing 'chutes—but the shirt he was now clutching to his naked, damp chest was another story.

"I ain't wearing it."

"Look, son." The man kneeled down beside him. "Nobody's really happy about all this, but if you make a fuss and we get caught, we're *all* in trouble. Trouble as big as it gets. Do you understand? They'll put me in the brig and you in one of those children's institutions—and not the nice kind either. I bet you know what I'm talking about. So please just give us a break, will you?"

Cho-Cho held out the shirt, trembling. "This? 'Speck me to wear this *mierda*?"

The man looked at the picture of Princess Poonoonka, the pink fairy-otter, then turned to the woman. "Maybe you could find him something a little less . . . girly?"

"Oh, for goodness sake," said the woman, but went to go look.

The man astonished Cho-Cho then by smiling. "Don't you dare tell her," he said quietly, "but I have to agree with you, kid." He patted Cho-Cho on the shoulder and walked back down the hall to the garage, leaving the boy even more confused than he had been this whole, crazy night.

When her mother woke her up, it was still dark outside, although the sky was turning purple. "We're leaving on our trip, Christabel," she said. "You don't have to get dressed—you can sleep in the car."

But when she had put on her warm slippers and pulled her big coat on right over her pajamas, Mommy said something so strange that for a moment Christabel almost thought she was still asleep and having a dream.

"Mister Sellars wants to talk to you before we go."

Daddy was in the kitchen, drinking coffee and looking at maps. He smiled at her as her mommy led her by, but it was a small, tired smile. Out in the garage all the van's doors were open, but Christabel didn't see Mister Sellars anywhere.

"He's in the back," her mother said.

Christabel walked around to the far end of the van. Her daddy had taken out the tire and the other things that were usually under the floor in the van's back part. Mister Sellars was lying in the empty space, curled up on an unrolled sleeping bag like a squirrel in its nest.

He looked up and smiled. "Hello, little Christabel. I just wanted you to see that I was all right before your father put the top back on. See, I have water—" he pointed to a couple of squeeze bottles lying beside him, "—and a nice soft place."

She didn't know what to say. Everything was so strange. "Is he going to put the top back?" she asked.

"Yes, but I'll be fine." He smiled again. He looked tired, too. "I'm used to confined places, and besides, there are things I can do while I'm in here and things I need to think about. I'll be fine. Besides, it's only for a little while. You just do what your mommy and daddy tell you to do. They're being very brave, and I hope you'll be brave also. Remember how I told you about Jack when he was climbing up to the giant's castle? He was scared, but he did it anyway, and everything turned out for the best."

Her mother, standing a little way behind her, made a funny noise, kind of a snort. Christabel turned to look at her but her mommy just shook her head and said, "Okay, sweetie, come on now. We have to get going."

"I'll see you real soon," Mister Sellars said. "This is still a secret, but not from your mommy and daddy anymore, and that's very good for everyone."

Her daddy came out of the kitchen wiping his hands. As he started to put the floor of the van over Mister Sellars, talking to the old man in a quiet voice, Christabel's mother helped her up into the middle part where the seats were.

"Now if anyone asks," her mommy said, "you tell them Cho-Cho's your cousin. If they ask you any other questions, just say you don't know."

Christabel was trying to figure out why her mommy would say something like that when she saw the terrible boy on the back seat, wearing one of her daddy's jackets. Christabel stopped,

scared, but her mother took her arm and helped her sit down. The
boy only looked back at her. It was funny, but he suddenly looked
much smaller. His hair was wet and close to his head, and the
jacket and pants were so big that he seemed like a really little kid
dressed up.

She still didn't like him, though. "Is he going with us?"

"Yes, sweetie." Her mommy helped her fasten her seat belt.
Christabel squeezed over to one side, so there would be lots of
space between her and the terrible boy, but he wasn't even looking at her anymore. "Everything is a little . . . unusual today," her
mother said. "That's all. You sleep if you can."

She couldn't sleep, and she couldn't stop thinking about the
boy Cho-Cho, who was just a few inches away, staring out the
window. She also couldn't stop thinking about Mister Sellars lying
under the carpet in the back. Were they going to take the boy
back to his home outside the Base? Why did Mister Sellars want
to bring him along? And why was Mister Sellars hiding if Daddy
and Mommy knew about him and knew that he wasn't bad? She
hoped it wouldn't hurt his legs to be curled up like that. She hoped
he wouldn't be scared. He had said he had work to do, but what
could he do in the dark, in a little small place like that?

There was just a hint of light in the sky as they drove toward
the front gate of the Base, enough to make the trees look like
black cutouts. Most of the houses had a light on in front or inside, but the ones that didn't looked dark and sad.

Her daddy talked to the soldier at the first guardhouse for a
few minutes. She thought another soldier looked through the window at her and Cho-Cho, but she wasn't sure because she was
pretending to be asleep.

They stopped for less time at the second guardhouse, then they
were out beyond the fences and driving. She could see the sky
now, all gray but with light behind it. Her mother and father were
talking quietly, but they weren't arguing. The terrible boy had his
eyes closed.

Christabel couldn't think about anything any more. The gentle bump, bump, bump of the car and the noise of the engine
made her want to go to sleep for real, so she did.

*   *   *

"I *REALLY* thought we were done here," Ramsey said.

"Don't blame me," Beezle replied. *"I didn't pass you that note."*

Catur Ramsey sighed. The streets and alleys of Madrikhor were becoming depressingly familiar. "Which way did you say it was?"

"Street of Silver Coins," the disembodied voice told him. *"Take a right when you get to the Ogre Fountain. It's not too long a walk."*

"Easy for you to say," Ramsey grumbled.

He had been following up the last of several leads developed from the files he had received from the Polito kid—better known here in the Middle Country as the wizard Dreyra Jarh—and like all the rest it had come to nothing. Like the others, it had also come to nothing in a particularly Middle-Countryish way, requiring a long walk to somewhere. The contact—another pretend wizard—turned out to have vacated his enchanter's cottage in the Darksome Wood, but as Ramsey had stood on the picturesquely shabby front porch, cursing the fruitless visit, he had discovered a cryptic note in his own pocket, a folded square of parchment reading "Blue Book of Saltpetrius" that he knew damn well hadn't been there at the beginning of the expedition.

"How did it get there?" he had demanded of Beezle.

"Search me," the agent had said, his gear sufficient to convey a verbal shrug. *"One of those black squirrels maybe. There were a lot of 'em out today."*

Ramsey had only been able to shake his head. How could you properly pursue a case of life-or-death importance where you had to track down teenage sorcerers and information was dropped into your pocket by hired squirrels?

"Hey, Beezle, isn't that the Scriptorium over there?" Ramsey pointed to a large impressive tower looming several blocks away above the local skyline, basalt walls smoldering in the torchlight of midnight Madrikhor, roof covered with gargoyles like nuts on an ice-cream sundae. "We're going the wrong direction."

"Nah," his invisible companion said. *"That's the Scriptorium Arcanum—where they keep the books of magic spells and like*

that. Real high-volume operation, lotsa visitors. The Saltpetrius thing is some kinda local government document, so we're going to the Scriptorium Civilis. See, that's it right there."

Ramsey at first had no idea what Beezle was referring to, since the building in front of them was tiny and rundown even for this part of Madrikhor. He took a few steps forward, squinting, and saw the plaque above the front gate—*"Scrip or um."* Apparently they had a bit of a woodworm problem.

Like most of the places in Madrikhor, especially near the center of town, the Scriptorium was bigger than it looked on the outside, but since it had looked pretty damn small from the outside that wasn't a very impressive trick. What lay beyond the front door was a dark room lit by a few meager lamps, its floor-to-ceiling bookshelves stuffed with scrolls and bound volumes in many varieties of neglect and decay.

The ancient creature behind the front desk took so long to respond to his question that at first Ramsey thought it was an uninhabited sim. When the gaunt, bearded thing finally moved, stretched, yawned, scratched itself in several spots, then gestured to a small stairwell near the back of the room, it was like watching a mechanical toy ratcheting through the last spasm of a winding.

"You take me to the nicest places, Beezle," he subvocalized.

"Huh. You like this joint?" Apparently the agent was not geared for sarcasm.

The clerk on duty downstairs at first seemed to provide a marked contrast to the upstairs employee. The young elf prince was the complete package—tall, slender, golden-haired, with pointed ears and an angular catlike face—but as he listened to Ramsey's query with a look of dull disinterest, the lawyer noticed that the elfin sim's face was no more detailed or individual than that of a mannequin, as though the clerk had been forced to settle for some kind of unmodified starter set.

"Saltpetrius?" The elf prince frowned like counter help in a fast-food depot asked to detail the heritage of the vat-beef. "Dunno. Back there, somewhere." He hooked a pale thumb in the direction of a narrow corridor between two leaning shelves. "Under 'S,' prob'ly. Unless it's under 'B' for 'Blue Book' . . ."

Working his way back to Adventurer Class on minimum wage, Ramsey guessed.

This downstairs room was if anything darker and more cramped than the prisonlike conditions of the ground floor. It took Ramsey long minutes of squinting and fumbling in the shadowy "S" aisle, not to mention a few near misses with death-by-book-avalanche, before he found the volume in question, a small tome with a greasy leather cover. It was fortunate that the name "Saltpetrius" was printed prominently on the spine, because he would have needed to build a bonfire with several dozen of the other volumes to be able to make out the color.

Ramsey carried it out into the closest thing to useful lighting the room provided. The clerk was slumped behind the counter, his bland face looking at nothing as he tapped his pointy-booted foot aimlessly to some stirring adventurer's anthem he alone could hear.

The book itself was an impenetrable tangle of densely packed, illegible handwritten characters. Ramsey was feeling his bemusement curdle into disgust when a square of parchment dropped out of the pages and drifted to the floor. He picked it up quickly, sneaking a look at the clerk, but His Elfin Majesty didn't seem as though he would have noticed if Ramsey had turned into a crocodile and begun singing "Streets of Laredo."

Step through the back door, the note read. Ramsey compared it with the note he had found in his pocket. It looked like it had come from the same source.

"*They want me to go out the back door,*" he subvocalized to Beezle. "*Do you think it's an ambush or something like that?*"

"*Seems like a lot o' trouble just to knock your head in,*" the agent pointed out. "*You can hire a couple of guys in any tavern around here who'd beat you to tapioca in broad daylight for half a tankard of beer each.*"

God, listen to me, Ramsey thought in disgust. *Ambush. Like I was somewhere it mattered, instead of in a role-playing game.*

"*Right,*" he told Beezle, and stuffed the second note into the pocket of his cloak. "*Then I think I'll go find the back door.*"

It wasn't hard to locate, although getting to it meant stepping over piles of unfiled scrolls against the back door. Ramsey guessed they probably didn't have fire marshals in the Middle Country.

The alley was suitably damp and dark. After Ramsey took a look around and saw no one waiting, or any object big enough to hide someone, he let the door fall shut behind him.

"I feel like the new kid at summer camp," he told Beezle. *"The one who keeps getting sent out to find left-handed smoke-shifters . . ."*

Something flared in front of him so abruptly that he staggered back, instinctively raising his hands before his face to keep from being burned. But not only did the pulsing white thing give off no heat, despite its bright glare the alley around it also remained sunken in shadow.

"What the hell . . . ?" Ramsey said. He grabbed at his sword, struggling to wrestle it out of the sheath even as the white shape coalesced into something vaguely human in outline. It raised the raw shapes that were its arms, but did not step toward him.

"Good evening, Mister Ramsey," it said, just quietly enough to suggest discretion. The voice was obviously filtered; it sounded like nothing human. "I apologize for all the mystery, but it really is necessary, whatever you may think. My name is Sellars . . . and I think it's time the two of us had a conversation."

CHAPTER 23

Buried in the Sky

NETFEED/MUSIC: Horrible Animals to Split Even Farther (visual: Benchlows at home in pool)
VO: Twins Saskia and Martinus Benchlow, founding members of My Family And Other Horrible Horrible Animals, broke up their band this year, but now they have decided to split in the old-fashioned way, too.
(visual: close-up on connective tissue)
VO: The Benchlows, who are conjoined twins, have decided that they can best lead their individual artistic lives if they surgically separate themselves.
S. BENCHLOW: "It's a big step, but we both need to spread our wings and hit the ground running. It's hard to say good-bye, but we can always keep in touch the way other twins do . . ."
M. BENCHLOW: "That's so true, you know, because we both have jets, but we've never used more than one of them at a time."

IN the instant before the Quan Li thing killed her, Renie felt a surprising stab of regret that she would never see her father again.

I can't even tell him he was right—I was a fool to come here. . . .

Before the hammer of the flintlock drew back, something with clawing hands and feet flew into the murderer's face. It wrapped around his eyes in an instant and wrenched his arm upward so that he lost his balance and staggered backward, bellowing in rage. The murderer and the clinging, tawny attacker whirled across the landing like a single mad creature trying to bite its own tail. The Quan Li thing's shout of surprise had electrified Renie. She clambered onto her feet, then ducked as gun and arm whirled past at head level.

"!Xabbu!" She was full of wonder and terror. The man in the baboon sim was all over the Quan Li thing, but the gun had not yet been fired, and if their enemy could get his arm up for one clear shot . . .

She took one step toward them and tripped over something. It was only when she fell onto her hands and knees, skidding in blood, that she realized it was Florimel's limp body. She staggered up, fighting to get footing, then flung herself forward. She tackled the spinning thing and threw the Quan Li creature back against the wall near the broken windows. Their enemy sagged but did not fall. He was struggling to tear clinging !Xabbu away from his face, but had managed to twist the gun free of the baboon's grip; before he could point it at either one of his attackers Renie grabbed the slender wrist in both hands and smashed it back against the wall. The gun clattered free and bounced across the floor and off the landing, down into shadow.

Renie turned back in time to see the complicated shape made by !Xabbu and the Quan Li thing reel a few steps back toward the window. The sill hit the dark-haired woman's form in the back of the legs; the Quan Li creature threw out his arms for balance, but he was confused and blinded by the clawing monkey. He tipped, grabbed at nothing, then fell backward into the evening sky with !Xabbu still clinging to its head.

Renie screamed, but the window now framed only emptiness. A noise from outside sent her hurrying to the sill to look down.

To her amazement, !Xabbu and the Quan Li thing had not plummeted to their deaths, but had dropped onto a pitched roof half a dozen meters below that extended from the side of the tower like an awning and ended in a narrow parapet. Beyond that parapet was only air, a final fall down to the roofs of the House far below. !Xabbu had slid halfway down the roof. The Quan Li thing had the high ground.

The murderer had found a long rod with a metal hook on one end, a tool left behind by some long-dead workman, and was swinging it like a scythe, forcing !Xabbu farther down the slope and onto the parapet. As Renie watched fearfully, the thing in Quan Li's body snapped the rod out again and again, slashing at !Xabbu as he danced back along the plastered rail. Only his small size and quick reflexes saved him, but he had to drop over the parapet to avoid the last blow. He swung by his hands for a heart-stopping moment before pulling himself back up again, but the Quan Li thing was still swinging the rod in swift, wicked arcs, intent on driving him to the corner of the parapet. Renie desperately wanted to help !Xabbu, but she knew she could not drop such a distance and keep her balance on that steep slope.

The gun! she thought, then remembered that it had fallen off the landing. Even if it hadn't already shattered into several antique pieces, by the time she found it !Xabbu would surely have been killed.

Something scraped behind her. She whirled away from the windowsill to find T4b staggering up the stairs toward the landing.

"He shot you," Renie said, conscious of how stupid that sounded even as the words escaped her.

"Seen." He hesitated for a moment at the top step, where Emily crouched weeping with her face in her hands, then stepped over Florimel without looking down, but with a certain care nevertheless. T4b's armored chest was a puckered, blackened mess of what looked like melted plastic. All that remained of his voluminous robe was tatters. "That's why I got a Manstroid D-9 Screamer. Sixin' gear."

"Help me get down there—he's got !Xabbu trapped on the roof."

T4b peered at the window, then back at Renie. "You sure?"

"Jesus Mercy, of course I'm sure! He'll kill him!" She scrabbled on the ground for the the sharpened curtain rod she had lost in the shock of the first gunshot, then set it by the window and climbed up onto the sill, grateful at least that the broken glass had fallen out long ago. "Just take my hand, then brace yourself and let me down as carefully as you can. I'll try to find some handholds or footholds."

T4b made a doubtful noise but did as she had told him, grabbing her wrist with his gauntleted hands. She could feel a tingling from the hand that had been seemingly vaporized in the patchwork simworld, but it seemed otherwise as strong and sturdy as the other. As she let go of the windowsill and felt herself swing out into space, she looked down. The Quan Li thing still had !Xabbu pinned at the edge of the roof, forcing him to use his simian skills to the utmost just to stay alive. The enemy turned and gave Renie a swift, seemingly casual glance, but took a moment to pull a long, ugly knife from his belt before turning back with disheartening swiftness to lash at the baboon again. !Xabbu had tried to take advantage of the distraction to scramble down from the parapet, and now had to swing back up once more. The rod hissed so close to his retreating form Renie thought it must have touched his fur.

She swayed above the pitched roof and forced herself to concentrate on finding a grip. T4b had only the low windowsill to lean against so she could not expect him to lean very far.

"I'm . . . I'm . . ." T4b sounded like he might be sick.

"Just hold on." Even now the Quan Li thing might have knocked !Xabbu off the parapet and moved beneath her with that sharp knife, waiting, grinning . . .

Don't think about it!

There were cracks in the plastered facade of Weeping Baron's Tower but nothing that would support her weight. She stared between her dangling feet at the steeply sloping roof, careful to look no farther than just beneath her. It wasn't that far down, really, and the spot where the tower joined the roof was covered with ornamental moldings. If she dropped carefully and caught at those moldings, she should be all right. If there hadn't been a fatal drop just a few meters downslope, she knew she wouldn't even be hesitating.

"I'm going to grab your wrist and then let myself fall," she

said breathlessly to T4b. "It's not so far. Just let me do it myself."

"This . . . this is bad, Renie."

"I *know*." She fought panicky anger—she had no time to reassure the young man, fear of heights or no fear of heights, and
in any case, who was the one jumping? She held tight to T4b's
gauntleted wrist and spread her feet wide for better balance, then
let go. The tower wall had a slight outward slope of its own which
could have spun her away down the pitched roof, but she was
able to get one foot behind her; when she thumped down onto
the tiles she snatched at the moldings. To her incalculable relief,
they held.

She looked over her shoulder. The murderer was watching her
even as he lazily swung at !Xabbu, but he made no move to stop
her. His casualness was baffling, but Renie was not going to waste
time wondering about it. "Throw me down that spear," she shouted
at T4b. She caught the curtain rod and then turned to move carefully down the steep slope, mindful of every step. Two chimney
pots stood in the center of the slanting roof like lonely trees on
a mountainside, but other than that nothing but the half-meter
parapet would keep her from falling to her death should she slip.

She tried to angle her move toward the Quan Li thing to force
him away from !Xabbu, but the enemy kept moving, stopping occasionally to lunge at !Xabbu with the pole, forcing the man in
the baboon sim into another heart-clenching drop over the edge.
The Quan Li thing was calmly playing a game, keeping himself
between Renie and her friend. The monster began to laugh.

He's enjoying this! she realized. *But even if he falls, he won't
die—he'll just drop offline. We won't be so lucky.*

She risked a cautious attack, plunging the sharpened curtain
rod toward the Quan Li face, but the monster was terribly quick;
he twisted away and snatched at the makeshift spear, almost pulling
it from Renie's grasp. Even though she managed to yank it away
again, she slipped to her knees and had to clutch at the tiles to
keep her balance. She scrabbled back just in time to avoid a swinging return blow from the hooked staff.

T4b shouted down to her, "I'm . . . I'm coming, Renie!" His
voice was an adolescent honk, squeaky with panic.

"No!" she shouted. "Don't!" She could think of nothing more

disastrous than having a blundering, terrified T4b on the roof with her. "Don't do it, Javier! Go back and help Emily and the others!"

T4b was not listening. He had already draped his armored form over the windowsill, and was trying to get both his legs beneath him while hanging on.

The murderer was distracted for a moment by the spectacle. !Xabbu leaped down from the parapet and bounded up the roof toward Renie. He was bleeding on his hands and legs, but his only concern was for her. "You cannot fight him," he gasped. "He is very fast, very strong."

"We'll never get off this roof if he's alive," said Renie, then disaster struck.

T4b had swung down from the window and was dangling, kicking his legs as though that might somehow bring the roof closer to him, but the ancient wooden sill had taken all it was going to take and now tore loose in a shower of plaster, dropping T4b to the sloping roof.

For a moment, as the youth windmilled his arms, she thought he might catch his balance; but as his pale face swung up and he saw the forest of towers around him and the yawning spaces between them he panicked and threw his hands out, yearning toward the window far out of his reach. His legs went out from under him. An instant later he was rolling down the pitched roof like a cannonball.

Before Renie could even take in breath to scream, T4b hit the parapet. It was no more strongly made than the rest of the tower, only plaster and timber in the semblance of stone. As it snapped and splintered outward, T4b snatched at it desperately and managed to stop himself before he rolled out, but only his belly and upper body were still on the roof. As he clung to the sagging timbers, he began to shriek, his legs dangling in emptiness.

!Xabbu was already hurrying down the roof toward him, a golden streak on all fours. Renie wanted to shout at her friend to stay away, that there was nothing he could do but be pulled down himself in T4b's wild terror, but she knew the little man wouldn't listen to her.

!Xabbu threw himself onto the parapet and wrapped an arm around T4b's head like a lifeguard with a drowning swimmer. He grabbed at the shattered parapet with his other long arm even as the wreckage shifted and T4b slid a little farther over the edge. !Xabbu was now stretched as though on a medieval torture device between T4b and the remains of the parapet. There was another squeal as the timbers moved again; ancient nails popped and plaster dust rose like smoke. Renie opened her mouth to call a warning.

She saw the shadow in the corner of her eye too late to duck. She managed to get her hand up and deflect the worst of the blow, but the rod still knocked her reeling sideways. She scrabbled blindly up the slope, away from her attacker, but an even harder blow caught her low in the back, an explosion of pain as though she had fallen on a hand grenade. She screeched and collapsed.

Something grabbed her and roughly turned her over; a weight immediately dropped onto her chest. The leer was gone from the Quan Li thing's face, replaced by a curious masklike slackness, but the eyes seemed alive in a completely inhuman way—the burning, dilated stare of some transcendent biological urge. Fingers as remorseless as surgical restraints clamped Renie's hair and twisted her head back, baring her neck. She heard !Xabbu calling her name, but he was hopelessly far away. The knife curved above her, the blade as dimly gray as the lead roof, as gray as the sky.

There was a crack like a dropped plate and a simultaneous smack of movement—surprisingly light, like a slap on her belly. Renie felt herself showered with sticky fluid.

My throat is slit . . . she thought in bleak wonderment, then the Quan Li thing dropped heavily onto her face. Renie struggled in reflexive panic, expecting to feel her own failing strength leak away, but instead she was able to shove back the clinging weight and crawl out from under, dizzy and nauseated.

The Quan Li thing had already stiffened like hot wax poured into water. The eyes were open, but the look of animal exultation was gone. The neck and throat were a ribboned mess of blood and tissue.

Renie could barely understand what had happened, let alone why. She turned her head and was lashed by dizziness and nausea. !Xabbu and T4b were still clinging to the parapet a few meters down the roof. She crawled toward them, then stopped, afraid that even at a distance her added weight might hasten the parapet's collapse. She caught at one of the chimney pots, wrapped both her arms around it in an embrace that shoved her cheek against the cold brick, and then inched the lower half of her body down the roof until she was stretched full length. She was so battered and exhausted it was difficult to speak; the words came in panting increments.

"Grab . . . my legs . . . if you can."

She could not look back, and in fact would not have watched if it were possible. She stared back up the roof slope instead, waiting to feel a grip on her ankle and praying to hear no more cracking of timbers. A shape was draped across the windowsill up above, like a handpuppet discarded on its stage. Blood drooled down the wall beneath it, slow drips that had become long red lines. Renie could not see who it was, and at the moment did not care.

A small hand grabbed her foot.

She grunted in pain as !Xabbu first got a solid grip, then gradually let her help him take T4b's weight. It took only a minute, but it felt like days. Renie's joints burned. Her head felt like something had reached into her skull and harshly stirred her brains with a spoon.

At last she felt the burden lessen as T4b, with !Xabbu's help, was able to pull his body up onto the roof. She heard the youth collapse onto the tiles, gulping in air and letting it out again in a sobbing wheeze. !Xabbu did not rush up the roof to her side immediately; she could hear him talking quietly to T4b. Renie could only guess at how much pain her friend must be suffering himself after having held the battle-suited T4b's weight for all that time.

At last they all summoned enough strength to crawl up the slope toward the wall below the window. As they reached the base of the wall, the huddled shape on the sill above them lifted a bloodied face. Florimel looked down at them for a long moment in which there seemed to be no recognition, then nodded in dull satisfaction. The left side of her face was almost completely obscured by blood, and her hair on that side jutted stiff and black, scorched like grass in a prairie fire. She raised the flintlock pistol in a trembling, red-slicked hand.

"Got that bastard," she grunted. "Got him."

*   *   *

Although she took charge immediately, shouting for Emily to come help Florimel while she herself checked !Xabbu and T4b for serious injuries, it was a while before the numbness lifted and Renie could begin to think properly again. Twice in a few minutes she had been so close to death that she had given herself up to it. Being alive felt almost like a burden.

She left her two companions squatting below the window and made her way carefully back down the roof to the spot where the Quan Li thing lay sprawled in an odd pose, a three-dimensional photograph of its dying moment. The sim had stiffened in a sort of arch, as though Renie's own form still lay beneath it.

But he's not dead. He's just been pushed offline. The thoughts bobbed through her mind like untethered balloons. *He almost killed me. He was going to do it. It was like sex for him. But I'm the one who's still here.*

She shook herself, trying in vain to dislodge the coldness that seemed to have soaked into her spirit, then bent and began searching.

Although the body was as rigid as something cast in bronze, Renie's earlier presence beneath the dying sim proved a stroke of luck. The peasant tunic had bunched up when the monster fell forward, leaving the inside pocket open even after the sim and its clothing had turned solid. She flattened her hand and reached in, wondering a little at how disturbing it was to touch even a simulated dead thing. Her fingers closed around a heavy, smooth shape.

"Thank God." She lifted the lighter. The bulky little metal shape was almost invisible against the gray sky: the daylight was vanishing quickly. "Thank God."

What if the pocket hadn't been open? she wondered. *Can you cut through the virtual cloth on a sim after it's gone terminal like this? Is it just impossible, or could you do it with a blowtorch or whatever those things are, a filament saw? Not that we'd have found either of those things in this world.*

She stood and crawled back up the roof, grateful at least for this one stroke of luck. The idea of dragging the Quan Li corpse all over the House in search of something capable of cutting into the clothing was a very unpleasant one.

Emily's mostly ineffectual attempts to lend first aid were being further undercut by her desire to gaze down from the splintered window like some crop-haired Juliet at her hero T4b, so !Xabbu climbed up to help tend Florimel. Watching him make his way nimbly up the wall, Renie paused.

"How do we get the rest of us back inside?" she wondered aloud.

!Xabbu looked over his shoulder. "Brother Factum Quintus is coming up the stairs," he said. "He can help us. We can use one of these cloth hangings to pull you up."

The monk appeared at the windowsill, squinting and holding his hands to his head.

"I am sorry I was no help," he said, "but I am glad to see you are alive. Was that your enemy? He was a rare and dangerous creature. He looks amazingly like a woman, though." He leaned on the sill and groaned. "I believe I have struck my head on every stair on the staircase."

"Florimel needs more help, Renie," !Xabbu announced. "She is very cut and bloody, and one of her ears is gone. We need to find a place that is warm and protected."

"I . . . never liked the ears . . . on this sim . . . anyway," Florimel said wanly.

"Somebody has to shoot you before you make a joke?" Renie asked. She tried to keep her voice light, but it felt as much of an effort as dragging !Xabbu and T4b back off the parapet. "Okay, let's go. But before you start pulling us up, can you throw down one of those tapestries?"

!Xabbu dropped to the floor inside. A moment later he returned, dragging the heavy piece of fabric. "It is a little torn where I pulled it from the wall," he explained as he slid it over the sill to Renie.

"Doesn't matter," Renie said. "I just . . . I just want to cover Quan Li."

"That was not Quan Li, that was a monster," snarled Florimel, grimacing with pain as !Xabbu returned to examining her lacerated face. "The one who killed William, and maybe Martine."

"Jesus Mercy," Renie said. "Martine—has anyone looked for her? !Xabbu?"

But the little man was already gone, scampering toward the room from which the monster's ambush had begun.

"She is here!" he shouted. "She is . . . I think she is all right, but she is . . . not awake." A moment later he remembered the word. "Unconscious! She is unconscious."

"Thank God." Renie swayed a little. "Just . . . just give me a moment to do this," she said. "There may have been a monster wearing this sim, but it was Quan Li's once—the real Quan Li—and she was one of our companions, if only for the first hours." She moved back down the roof and carefully draped the fabric over the hardened form. "I think that . . . monster told the truth about one thing anyway," she said, looking back to the others. "I think the real Quan Li must be dead. I wish we could bury her properly. It feels so terrible, leaving her here." She dipped her head.

"The people," T4b said suddenly, "the Indian people . . . some of them do this."

Renie and the others turned to look at him. The young man fell silent, suddenly shy. His pale face plastered with lank black hair looked even more vulnerable protruding from the outsized, cracked shell of his armor.

"Go on, T4b," Renie said gently. "Javier. What do you mean?"

"Some of the Indian tribes, they put the dead ones on platforms up in the tree branches. Sky burial, they call it. Leave 'em for, like, the birds and the wind." He was serious and solemn; much of his street persona seemed to have dropped away. "This is kind of like that, seen? 'Cause we couldn't carry her all the way to some ground or nothing anyway, could we?"

"No, you're right." Renie nodded. "I like that. We'll just leave her here . . . buried in the sky." Renie pulled back the top of the tapestry until Quan Li's head was exposed, then left the empty sim and climbed back toward her companions. Behind her, the small dark shape lay on its side facing the edge of the roof, like a child who had fallen asleep watching the first stars begin to gleam above the needle-shadows of the Spire Forest.

As !Xabbu had reported, Martine was alive. Except for a knot on the back of her head behind her ear, she also seemed to be unharmed, although she was still unconscious: she scarcely stirred as they cut her loose from the pipe to which she had been bound.

Florimel had not been so lucky. When the group finally made their way down Weeping Baron's Tower to a carpeted, window-less room on the lower floor—T4b had insisted there be no view of the Spire Forest and its precipitous angles—Renie continued their companion's medical care while !Xabbu stacked broken fur-niture in a fireplace that looked to have been unused for decades, if not longer.

"Your ear is gone," she told Florimel, who seemed as stunned and disassociated by her experiences as Renie was by her own brushes with death. "And I can't tell for certain until I get the blood cleared away, but your left eye doesn't look very good ei-ther. It's swollen closed right now." Renie winced as strips of fa-cial tissue shifted like sea kelp under her careful cleaning. Knowing that the body, and hence the damage, was purely virtual did not make the task less disturbing. "It looks like the bullet missed you, though—except for maybe the ear, I think the damage is all from the gunpowder. I guess we got lucky."

"Just clean it and bind it," Florimel said faintly. "And find something else to wrap around me—I am cold. I am afraid of shock."

They draped a velvet wall hanging around her shoulders, but Florimel continued to shiver. When !Xabbu got the fire lit, she moved closer to it. Brother Factum Quintus found some ancient linen napkins packed in an old chest in one of the other rooms; torn into strips and tied together, they made decent bandages. When Renie had finished Florimel looked like something out of a horror movie, her head bumpy and misshapen with knotted ban-dages, but the worst of the bleeding had finally been staunched.

Florimel's one good eye peered fiercely out from the strips of linen. "That is enough," she told Renie. "Rest and warmth are what will help me most now. See to the others."

The rest of the damage was surprisingly light. T4b's armor had protected him from almost everything except cuts and scrapes on his face and his natural hand—the other still glowed faintly, and showed no change—but Renie felt sure that underneath his rup-tured chestplate his torso must be a bloody, bruised mess.

He waved her away. "Don't want to take it off, do I? Probably holding me together, like."

Renie doubted that, but she couldn't help wishing he would let her clean out any scraps of the shattered armor that had worked their way into his virtual skin—who knew what kind of opportunistic infections might be coded into this quasi-medieval House world? But T4b seemed to prefer wincing stoically at every movement, which brought tears of sympathy to Emily's huge eyes as she sat holding his hand.

"What happened to you?" Renie asked !Xabbu as she cleaned the cuts on his creased monkey hands. The repressed emotion made her voice quiver; she hoped she didn't sound like she was angry with him. "You were gone so long—where did you go? I was so worried. I mean, we all were."

Before he could reply, Martine abruptly groaned and tried to sit up. The effort failed; the blind woman rolled onto her side and made dry retching noises.

Renie crawled to her side. "Martine, it's okay. You're safe. That thing, that monster—he's dead."

Martine's eyes rolled, unfocused. "Renie?" Tears formed. "I did not think to hear your voice again. He is dead? Truly dead, or just pushed offline?"

"Well, he's out of the network." She stroked Martine's hair. "Don't try to talk—you've been hit on the head. We're all here."

"He didn't want me making noise," Martine said, "didn't want you to know he was waiting." One quivering hand stole up to touch the bump behind her ear. "Even though he was behind me, I sensed the blow coming. I leaned forward, so he did not hit me directly. I think he meant to kill me." She covered her eyes with her fingers, a curious and pathetic gesture. "I wish he were truly dead. God, how I wish it!"

Renie touched Martine's arm. Martine snatched at her hand with a surprisingly desperate grip and held it.

"We cannot go anywhere until we are healed, at least a little," said Florimel slowly. "We can stay here while we plan what we will do next. Unless there are other dangers we do not know about . . . ?"

Brother Factum Quintus, who had been quietly making bandages, looked up. "Other than bandits, some of whom you met the other day . . ." He frowned, considering. "Hmmm. Perhaps you should gather up your enemy's guns. Yes, yes. Even if we cannot find powder or shot, they might convince a potential foe to leave you alone."

Renie nodded. "Good idea. But you have already more than done your duty to us, and we're sorry it's brought you into so much danger. If you want to get back to the Library now . . ."

"Oh, I will, when I have helped as much as I can here. And my own small suffering has been more than worthwhile—I have seen enough new things to keep me writing and studying for years." His look turned shrewd. "But I think I see disappointment in your face. Could it be I have offended you in some way, that you are tired of my company?"

"Oh, no! Of course not . . . !" Renie stammered.

"Then I suspect it is because you have things to discuss you do not feel comfortable speaking about in front of me." The monk folded his hands in his lap. "I know that your group is unusual, and I could not help but notice that you spoke of your enemy as being other than 'truly dead,' but instead as being 'off the network.'" Factum Quintus wrinkled his brow. "What sort of net might that be? I rather doubt you are talking about the cords we use to protect the books in the Library. What do the ancients say of the word?" He paused for a moment to recall. "Yes, I believe the citation is, 'anything reticulated or decussated, at equal distances, with interstices between the intersections . . .' Hmmm. Unhelpful." His homely face brightened. "A metaphorical meaning, perhaps? A network can mean a political faction, or even a sort of maze. Whatever the answer, clearly there are things here I do not understand . . . and perhaps cannot understand. But even if you wish to send me away, I would ask first to hear your ape companion's tale, as the Spire Forest is largely unexplored in our day, and I cannot help wondering if he has made any interesting discoveries."

A strangely bitter smile curled along !Xabbu's baboon muzzle. "I have no objection to telling my story, although it brings me no happiness."

"Go on," Renie told her friend. Something about the monk's words or the way he said them had left her oddly troubled, and she wanted time to understand why.

"During the first hours, little happened," !Xabbu began. "I climbed many of the towers, peered in at windows, but found nothing. It was not fast work—almost every time I had to climb back down to the level of the roofs after I had finished my search, so I could be sure I was not missing any of the towers in the dark. There are many! Perhaps a hundred, and each a different kind of challenge.

"Late in the evening, as I was resting on a stone rainspout, partway up one of the larger towers, I heard voices. At first I thought they came from inside the tower. I listened carefully, thinking it might be the bandits we had already met or others like them, but I realized after a moment that the people speaking were above my head on the tower roof!

"I climbed cautiously until I found a place where I could hide behind an ornament on the roof corner and watch them. There were perhaps a dozen all together, mostly men, but I heard at least one woman's voice, and a few of the shapes were small enough to be children. They had built a fire right on the roof tiles, up against one of the chimneys, and seemed to be cooking dinner. They were even more shabby than the bandits we had met, their clothes and faces so dirty that the people themselves were hard to see even from a short distance away. Their speech, too, was unusual—I could understand much of it, but only by listening carefully. The words had strange shapes, and they pushed them together in strange ways."

"Steeplejacks!" declared Factum Quintus with deep pleasure. "They are few—in fact, some believe that there are none left. They have lived atop the House so long that they are supposed to have become part bird. Did they have wings or beaks?"

"No, they are just people," !Xabbu said. "And there are more than a few left, if I understood them correctly, since they seemed to speak of other families. But there are fewer of them now than when I found them," he added sadly.

When he had been silent a few moments, Renie asked him, "What do you mean?"

"I will come to it. Anyway, I watched them from my hiding place. They had long thin spears and nets and ropes with hooks, and I saw that they were roasting small birds over the fire. I should have left, but I stayed, hoping that they would say something that might prove useful, and they did, although it was not for a long while.

"When the birds were ready, and they had divided up the small amount of meat between themselves, two of them began a friendly argument about a shadow one of them had seen more than once in an empty place they called ... Whipping Burn Tor—the one who had seen it swore it was a person. The other said that no lights and no fires burned there after dark, and that no one from the House—he said 'bellaroofers', which I think meant 'below-roofers'—would live without candles or oil light, which he called 'Houselights'.

"When another arrived late to the gathering, climbing up onto the roof from the far side, and asked them what they talked about, they pointed away toward where Whipping Burn was—I could see the tower I thought they meant, a faint dark shadow against the sky.

"Whipping Burn Tor," said Factum Quintus, nodding his head. "Weeping Baron's Tower."

"Yes, although I did not remember hearing the name," !Xabbu said. "I should have been thinking more clearly about many things, but I was fascinated by their talk, and by the idea that the unusual shadow the man had seen might be our enemy. I did not stop to think that there might be other late arrivals to the gathering, and that they might climb up from other directions.

"I heard them just before they stumbled on me, but too late to find a better hiding place. They climb quickly and silently, these Steeplejacks of yours. We surprised each other very badly. I was so startled that I actually jumped in the direction of the people gathered around the fire, almost into their arms. In a different place it might not have made any difference, because most people would stop and stare, which might have given me a chance to swing down off the roof and make my escape. But these people were hunters, and I think they seldom see much meat at a time. Climbing roofs is hard work, and the birds they catch are mostly small, I guess. In any case, only a moment went by before someone cried out and flung a net over me."

"They do not entirely live off birds, if the old stories are true," Factum Quintus said. "They poach from the rooftop gardens and grazing places. Some even say that they will come through windows in the higher parts of the house and make away with things, shiny things to wear sometimes, but mostly food."

"I can believe anything of them," !Xabbu said. "They are quick and clever. In a way, they remind me of my own people, squeezing out a living in a hard, hard place." He shook his head. "But I had no time for sympathy. I barely escaped from under the net before they could draw it tight—if I had been a true beast, I would be roasting on a spit by now, or I would already be gnawed bones. I went over the side, scrambling down the tower walls as quickly as I could in the dark, but I had lost the advantage of surprise. Several of them came after me, hunting like a pack, whistling to each other as they spotted me moving in the darkness. Everywhere I turned it seemed another was in front of me, calling to his companions."

"!Xabbu!" Renie said. "How horrible!"

He shrugged. "Hunters and hunted. We are almost always one or the other. Perhaps it is a good thing to experience both. I have certainly been hunted more than once since we came to this network.

"I could not let them catch me, but neither could I lose them. They knew the rooftops much better than I did, and when I was down off the tower and onto the rooftops where the danger of falling was less, they could spread out and try to surround me.

"The chase went on for hours, from roof to roof. Sometimes I would find a place to hide and catch my breath, but always I would hear them coming closer, surrounding me, until I would have to run again. Again, a real animal would have had no chance, for several times they threw their spears at me, which had long cords to keep them attached to their owners. Because I was a human—because I have hunted with a spear myself—I knew that I could not let them get a good throw at me, and I always managed to dodge just as the spear flew. They must have thought me one of the cleverest or luckiest animals they had ever hunted. But even luck cannot hold out forever, and I was growing very tired.

"I made my last attempt at escape by climbing a very high, very thin tower, up to a place where I thought they could not reach me, so far up the tower spire that I did not believe they could even get close enough to throw a spear. I huddled there, clinging to an iron needle far, far above the rooftops. The sun was rising. I had no idea where above the House I was, but I thought at least I was safe.

"But the Steeplejacks are not just grown men and women. They sent a boy up after me. He was perhaps eleven or twelve years old, but he climbed as well as I do, even without the advantage of this baboon body. He drew himself up hand over hand until he found a solid foothold only a few meters beneath me, easy range for a spear throw. With the cord attached to his weapon he could simply keep trying until he hit me. Small as he was, he was still much larger than I am, so I could not even hope to catch the spear without him simply pulling me off.

"His eyes were wide, although his face was so dirty that even with the dawn sunlight I could not make out much more than that. He was clearly excited to be able to go where none of the older men could reach, joyful to be the one who would bring this prize back to his people. Perhaps this was his first hunt with the grown men. He was singing to himself or praying as he drew back his arm.

"I shouted, 'Please, do not kill me!'

"His eyes grew even wider, and he screamed 'Dimmon!'—it may have been someone's name, or just the way he said 'demon.' He tried to slide farther down, but instead he lost his balance. For a moment, as his feet went out from under him and he clung by one hand only, he stared as though despite his terror of me I might somehow save him . . . but I could do nothing. He fell. The men climbed quickly to where he had landed. One picked him up and clutched him to his chest, but the boy was clearly dead. They turned their backs on me then, as though I no longer meant anything, and took the boy and headed back toward the rest of their tribe." !Xabbu's eyes were unusually hard, as though he had decided not to speak about something that had made him very angry. "I did not dare come down for some time, and they disappeared quickly. I could only follow in the general direction they had gone. It took me much of the day to find my way back to the Spire Forest—the roofs of this House are truly endless—and another painful hour to find the place they had called 'Whipping Burn.'"

"But you did find it, !Xabbu," Renie said gently. "And you saved my life. Again."

!Xabbu shook his head. "He was only a child."

"A child who was trying to kill you," she pointed out.

"So his family could eat. I have done the same thing many times."

"It is sad, yes," said Brother Factum Quintus suddenly. "Perhaps some of us who share this House owe a little more to our less fortunate brethren than we have given. There is something in that to think on, indeed. But I am amazed to find that there are Steeplejacks on the very roofs above the Library. Amazed. What a great deal I have learned!"

"I think I am tired of being an animal," !Xabbu said quietly.

"CODE *Delphi*. Start here.

"I will try to compose my thoughts, but it is not easy. Ever since Renie and the others took me from that small room, I have felt as though my skin has been stripped from my body. I am cold, raw. I weep easily. Something has changed me, and it does not feel as though it is for the better.

"We have come through again—passed through another portal, entered another world. I can smell the ocean and can perceive the points of demarcation that must be stars in a broad, broad sky. But no, it is too soon to tell this. Order. I must find some order. If the universe has none, or at least none we can discern, well, then it is our job to give it some. I have always believed that.

"I think I still do."

"I will start again.

"We could not leave the House immediately, even if we had all been healthy—but of course we were not. Florimel in particular was badly injured. It is a fluke that she was not killed. I think she was saved only by the unreliability of such ancient weapons, because Dread shot at her point-blank. As it is, she is still very ill from her wounds and loss of blood, and has only one eye, as we feared. Renie once said she had trouble telling the three sims apart—Quan Li's, mine, and Florimel's. That is no longer the case.

"But even had Florimel been well enough to move the first day, we would not have been able to leave the House simulation. We had recovered the lighter from the corpse Dread left behind, but it was all !Xabbu and I could do with it last time to open up a gateway we already knew was there. We had no idea if there was a gate anywhere near Weeping Baron's Tower, and it was too long a march for Florimel back to the place we had first entered the House. We used the opportunity to examine the lighter.

"I had learned more things from Dread than he supposed, which was some assistance. I was surprised the device was even functioning, since he had asked me pointedly about how easy it might be to trace, and I had told him that it seemed likely a working model could be located by its owner. For some reason, though, Dread had chosen not to turn it off.

"The abstract shorthand that !Xabbu and I had developed before was not . . . robust, I suppose would be the word . . . was not robust enough to let us use the device the way we needed to. Renie had explained to me about their strange encounter with what the monk called the Lady of the Windows, and although I had no better idea than Renie about *why* it had happened, it seemed foolish to ignore her summons, since it might have been Sellars forced into one of his indirections, trying to give us information. But even though we had the device, simply wanting to move to a Troy simulation world was not enough, any more than having a car and a map would help someone who had never learned to drive.

"It is hard to explain what passes between !Xabbu and me when we collaborate on these problems. His understanding is almost purely impressionistic—augmented, I believe, by the fact that he is now perceiving network information in the same direct way as he once learned to read signs in wind and scent and drifting sand. Although we have found a sort of language where we can meet to share information, I only grasp what he has learned or sensed, not how he has learned it. The information I share with him is equally personal, equally subjective, so our progress is slow at best. Fortunately, I have enough new and practical information gleaned from Dread that Renie has been able to lend her own virtual engineering expertise to our experiments, suggesting why certain things might cause certain others, and what sorts of basic functions are likely to be performed by the device.

"I am glad we had this work to do. T4b and the child Emily are always content to live in the moment, and the monk kept himself busy making lists and drawings of the furnishings and architecture. Florimel has been too debilitated to do much except rest. But Renie chafes without things to keep her busy.

"Nevertheless, even with the huge challenge of the access device to occupy her mind, she has still been distant and distracted. I could not understand it at first, so oppressed have I been by my own feelings of vulnerability, but on the second night after my rescue, she confessed to me that Brother Factum Quintus' words had troubled her.

"She said, 'What are we trying to do? When all is said and done?'

"I told her we were trying to solve a mystery, and most importantly save the children like her brother who had been harmed by the Grail.

"'But what if we have to destroy the network to save them—to free them?' The unhappiness in her voice was impossible to ignore. 'Not that we have a chance in hell of doing it. But what if we do, somehow? What happens to Factum Quintus? Look at him! He's planning to spend the next few years writing about all this. He's as happy as a pig in muck. He's alive! If he isn't, who is? But what happens to him and all the others if we destroy the network? The Library Brothers, those young lovers we met, your flying people in that other simworld—what happens to them all? It will be like condemning a whole galaxy to destruction!'

"I tried to tell her these were problems we couldn't afford to consider at this point, that they were so far away from being real that we had to put our energy into other things, but she remained troubled. And so do I. I cannot help remembering the kindness of the flying people in Aerodromia before Dread murdered one of their tribe. There was an entire intricate world in that valley, and there are uncounted other worlds within this network.

"In any case, with much work !Xabbu, Renie, and I managed to solve some of the problems of using the access device, but were still unable to summon a gateway where no mechanism already existed, so on the third day we set out for the place we had first entered the House—the Festival Halls, as Factum Quintus called them. Even with Florimel much improved, it was more than a day's march, so we slept that night still in the upper stories, then continued down until we reached the level of the Festival Halls. Factum Quintus still had to descend several more floors to return home, so after drawing us a map that Renie said was so detailed it looked like an engraving, he left us. It was a strange, sad parting. I knew the monk only a little, and my feelings about this world will always be steeped in the horror of that tiny room, but he had clearly become a genuine friend to the others. They were all very, very sorry to see him go.

" 'I do not know what I have been involved in,' he said as we parted, 'but I know you are good people, and I am glad if I've helped. Yes, glad. I hope when your task is finished, you will return to us at the Library and tell us what you have seen and found. I shall save a chapter in my book just for your new discoveries!'

"Renie promised that we would return when we could, but it felt like a terrible lie told to spare a child's feelings. As we watched his tall, angular shape vanish down the corridor, I could sense she was crying. It is almost impossible not to agree with her—if Brother Factum Quintus was not a living being, then I must admit that I do not understand the meaning of the words. And the great House itself, though forever tainted for me, has a peculiar beauty. For its people, it is the world, and it is a world like no other.

"What have these Grail monsters created? Do they understand? Do they even care, or like the slave masters of old, are the lives of others so unimportant to them that they cannot conceive of anyone but themselves having dreams and desires?

"The departure of Factum Quintus brought up another and more surprising realization for me. The pain I felt as we watched him go was part of a larger and more confusing feeling. Far more frightening, in a way, than anything Dread made me feel about my own imminent death, as shattering as that experience was.

"I have friends now. And I am terrified of losing them.

"For so long, I have isolated myself—always keeping something back, even from my occasional lovers. Now I am connected. It is a painful, frightening feeling. A couple I once knew from my university days told me, when they had their first child, that they had given a hostage to Fate and would never be comfortable again. I understand now. It hurts to love. It hurts to care.

"There. Now I have made it hard to talk again. It is ridiculous. I am glad the others are asleep, and cannot see me.

"We reached the Festival Halls and the room where the gate was. The remnants of our first fire were still there, a circular scorch mark and a pile of ashes. It was strange to realize we had

been there only days before, no more than a week. It felt like a
year had passed.

"!Xabbu and Renie and I continued to work hard in the hours
after returning to our entrance point, until we felt sure we had
solved all the most crucial problems. We would not be able to
manipulate the environment in the way one of the Grail Brotherhood might, but we could open up some of the access channels.
It was not easy—we struggled, and we worked. . . .

"My God, I am tired, so tired. I cannot tell it all now. So much
has happened, and all I want to do is sleep. We made the lighter
work. We stepped into our newly-summoned gateway, leaving the
gloomy magnificence of the House behind as we walked into the
golden light and passed on to another place, just as we had hoped.

"But for the first time since we entered the network, we have . . .
changed.

"No. This must wait. If I were writing this as the ancients did,
with paper and ink, the pen would long since have dropped from
my hand. We have changed. We are in a new land, the ceilings
and dim lanterns of the House exchanged for endless night skies
and stars that blaze, not twinkle.

"I do not fear for myself, not anymore, but I am more frightened than I can say for these dear, brave people who are my
friends. We are few, and every day it seems we are fewer.

"I am so tired . . . and the others are calling me.

"*Code Delphi*. End here."

THEY were all around him in the darkness, although they were
scarcely more solid than darkness themselves—the shadow-faces,
the animal men, the hungry things, all the Dreamtime monstrosi-
ties, all shifting and changing as they moved closer.

But closest of all was her face, *her* face, grinning, cold, enjoying his misery. He was trapped in darkness with all the terrors
that ever were, and she had put him there.

Death could not claim her. He could kill her a million times
and she would still be there, still trying to fill him up with shadows, still trying to crush his heart.

The face shifted, but it remained the same. He struggled to put
a name to it as the shadows drifted away, but names were meaningless. It was her. *She* had done this to him.

His whore mother.

That little Polly—another dream-raddled slut.

The faces rippled past, thousands of them, screaming, begging, but still beneath it all they were triumphant. They were all one. They could not die—*she* could not die.

As he swam up from the nightmare, the last face hovered before him, bloody and smirking.

Renie Sulaweyo. The bitch who killed me.

Dread sat up. The dream, if that was what it had been, still clung. He shuddered, rolled out of the chair and onto his knees, then was violently sick.

So that's what it feels like to die, he thought, resting his head against the cement. *That's as bad as anything the Old Man's ever done to me.*

After he had wiped the floor, then stumbled to the bathroom to wash out his mouth, he settled himself on the edge of the chair and stared at the white walls. The room, his new Sydney base of operations, was all but bare. The carpet was being installed later in the day. The coma couch was at the warehouse, waiting to be delivered. Dulcie Anwin would be arriving in a little over twenty-four hours. There were things to do.

He could not make himself move. Something was blinking at the edge of his vision, indicating a waiting message, but for the moment all he wanted to do was sit and let the rest of the dream fall away.

God damn the bitch. How had it happened? Had she stabbed him, or had she been hiding a gun all along? He shook his head and brought up a little music, a quiet course of Schubert lieder designed to soothe his aching head and singed nerves. He had forgotten the Old Man's mantra, *that* was what had happened—*Confident, cocky, lazy, dead.* A virtual death, but still quite a useful lesson. A stupid death. He had played with them the way he would have played with a single victim, the quarry for one of his hunts. He had underestimated them. He would not do so again.

The singer's silvery tones washed over him, relaxing him a little. This was a setback, but only a temporary one. He still had Dulcie's copy of the lighter, and a lot more information about everything than the Sulaweyo bitch and her friends. He would find them. He would cut them away from each other one by one and destroy them. He would save the African whore for last.

Yeah, it's a flick, he thought. He changed the Schubert to something more brutish and stirring, strings wallowing and drums rattling, the sound of something with a very small brain being killed by something faster and meaner. *But they don't know that I'm writing the script. They don't know this is only the middle. And they're going to hate the ending.*

It was time to get ready for Dulcie's arrival, time to start the most important phase of his plan. Dealing with that gang of losers was only a sideshow, after all. He needed to remember that.

He brought up the message, extinguishing the annoying glimmer at the corner of his eyesight. Klekker appeared, huge and startlingly ugly. The South African operative had reputedly been rebuilt after surviving a near-fatal bombing—cellular restoration and almost complete skeletal replacement with fibramics, especially around the face and hands. Without having seen his original face, it was hard to tell whether the surgeons were geniuses or monstrous failures.

"The Sulaweyo woman and her companions are in an abandoned Air Force base up in the mountains outside Durban," Klekker's recorded image rasped. "We should be able to secure them in a matter of seventy-two hours or so, depending on the security they've got in place. I'll take four men and some specialty equipment, if you authorize."

Dread frowned. He didn't just want Renie Sulaweyo's meat, he wanted her soul. He wanted to hold her naked terror in his hands. On the other hand, having her body made for a potentially useful bargaining chip, and he was fairly sure that the little Bushman was with her, too, which might be an even greater pull on her loyalties than her own physical safety. Even Martine, sweet, terrified, blind Martine might be slumbering away beside them, if she had somehow survived his little parting gift.

He keyed Klekker's number in. When the man answered, his face swollen and emotionless as a thunderhead, Dread said, "You're authorized. But I want them alive, and I want the woman's body and the Bushman's body untouched. In fact, anyone who appears to be online, I want them left that way. Don't unplug them unless I tell you to."

Dread brought his internal music up louder as he clicked off. His good cheer was returning, the Dreamtime ghosts banished by daylight and activity. The hero had experienced a setback, but that's the way these stories always ran. Big things were going to start happening very soon now, and lot of people were going to be surprised.

Very, *very* surprised.

CHAPTER 24
Serious Games

*T*HE wine-dark seas.

That was what Homer liked to call them, Paul remembered—one of the phrases, like "rosy-fingered Dawn," that came up again and again, to the delight of Classics instructors and the dread of bored schoolboys. It was a way to give form and shape to things, a way to help the bards remember as they passed along the old, strong words, generation after generation, before alphabets and books.

But they weren't just dark like wine, of course, these Homeric seas. As Paul sat on the raft through days of storm and sun, the sea proved itself even more changeable than the sky. There were moments it turned a blue so light and transparent it seemed to go ice-white at the edges; other times it grew as coldly opaque as stone. When the sun was low in the morning, it would sometimes bring the entire surface to dazzling fire, but then as it climbed overhead the sea might become a field of strangely mobile jade. When the great disk went down in the evening, burying itself in the tangerine clouds on the horizon, there would be a moment, an instant's flash, when the sea went black and the sky itself turned an unearthly green—the precursor to the appearance of the most splendid stars Paul had ever witnessed.

Despite his impatient longing for home and peace, there were moments as Paul watched heaven and its oceanic mirror reflecting and distorting each other that he felt something that could only be called joy—although it was a joy he kept to himself. Since their escape from Lotos, Azador had regained all his earlier reticence and more, retreating into an even more sullen silence, all spines, like a hedgehog curled into a ball. It was as much as Paul could do simply to get the man to confirm that they were indeed sailing slowly toward Troy.

There were worse places to be functionally alone; Paul found he did not mind the silence as much as he once had. Since the winged woman's last visitation, he found himself full of elusive thoughts and speculations. If his own memory still contained locked doors, there was no reason he could not try to guess what might lie behind those barriers, especially now that he finally had a few clues.

The first and greatest puzzle was of course the woman herself. Her brief appearance when he was clutching the spar of his broken boat, near drowning, had been different from her other visitations: all the other times she had come to him, in dreams or in the simulations themselves, she had been dressed in something appropriate to the setting. The early twentieth-century clothes she had worn for that one appearance, although antique, had not been particularly strange in themselves—he had seen her in many exotic guises—but they had had nothing at all to do with ancient Greece or the giant's castle of his dreams. The vision had sparked something in him. He wondered now whether he had seen something closer to her true self, or at least closer to his buried memories of her.

So who was she? Someone who knew him, obviously, unless she was simply part of the network and coded to behave as she did. But that did not explain why he felt so sure that he knew her, too. If he put aside the frankly chilling possibility that *both* of them had somehow been manipulated to remember a purely imaginary relationship—a consideration which opened speculations about his own reality Paul did not even want to touch—then it left one likely possibility: they did know each other, but it had been obliterated from his memory, and from hers as well. The obvious candidates for such tampering had to be the Grail Brotherhood. Nandi's explanations of their nature and plans had been confirmed by Azador in his lotos-trance, even if he was now resolutely refusing to discuss it further.

But that led Paul to an entirely different and unanswerable question. Why? Why would such powerful people care a jot about Robert Paul Jonas? Why, even if they did, would they keep him alive on their expensive system instead of simply pulling his plug? Did that mean that somehow his body was not in their possession? But why then on the occasions they had almost captured him hadn't they simply destroyed him? Surely in this virtual universe, where he had been warned that the dangers to him were real, the horrible Twins could simply have arranged to have a bomb dropped on him once they found him.

Clearly, there were no obvious answers.

Paul tried to summon up his last useful recollection, hoping that discovering where the obliteration of his memory began might give him some hint at what came after. Before his flight through the worlds of the network—before what he thought of as his starting place, the now-dim horrors of the First World War simulation—came . . . what? The memories before that point were from the routine of his daily life, the boring story he had lived for so long—walking out to Upper Street in the mornings, the quiet click of the electrical bus filled with English commuters busily ignoring each other, then the descent into gloriously-named Angel Station (which didn't quite live up to that, but what could?) and the morning tube ride down the wheezy Northern Line to Bankside. How many days had he started off in just that way? Thousands, probably. But how could he guess which had been the last one, the last clear stretch before the fields of recollection disappeared in silvery fog? His days had been so mundane, so similar that his friend Niles had used to tell him that he was hurrying toward middle age the way other people hurried to meet a lover or a long-lost friend.

Thinking of Niles brought with it a flash of something else, something vague as a distant night sound. Niles' teasing had finally begun to sting. Shamed by his more cosmopolitan friend, Paul had begun to mourn his own not-so-distant past, the years of his youth when there had been more to look forward to than the yearly winter holiday in Greece or Italy. In his normal, ineffectual, well-that's-Paul-isn't-it style he even had begun to brood about it, secretly knowing that nothing more exciting would come of this urge to break out than a short, disastrous love affair or maybe a holiday to somewhere a little more exotic—Eastern Europe, or Borneo.

And then one day, Niles had said . . . had said . . .

Nothing. He could not remember—it was hidden beneath the silvery cloud. Whatever wisdom had issued from his friend's mouth was lost, and no matter how he tried, he could not summon it back.

Unable to penetrate the mists in his own head, Paul found himself returning to the mechanism of the false universe around him. If the woman, Vaala or whatever her name was—he was beginning to feel like an idiot, thinking of her always as "the bird-woman" or "the angel"—was also resident in the network, why did she appear in so many ways and so many guises, while he himself stolidly remained Paul Jonas, despite the occasional change of clothing? How could there be more than one version of her, as when Penelope and the winged incarnation had faced each other across the fire on that windswept beach in Ithaca?

Perhaps she's not a real woman at all. The thought filled him with sudden dread. *Perhaps she really is just code, like the other people in this bloody place—a slightly more complicated sort, but basically no more human than an electric pencil sharpener.* But that would mean that other than a few travelers—"orphans," had that been her word?—like Azador and the woman Eleanora, he was alone in this tent-show universe.

I can't believe that, he thought. The majesty of the robin's-egg skies momentarily lost their ability to charm. *I can't afford to believe it. She knows me, and I know her. They've just taken those memories away from me, that's all.*

Did her multiplicity of guises have something in common with the Pankies, the bizarre couple who looked so much like the Twins, but were not? There was something to ponder there, but he did not have enough information.

Whatever the truth, there was no questioning the sheer technical marvel created by the evil plutocrats that Nandi had described—just this spectacular journey across the ocean, more real than real, would have been top-of-the-queue news on all the tabnets. Was Azador right—was it somehow a system built on the minds of stolen children? But even if it was, how did it work? And what was going to happen when they reached Troy?

That last thought had been irritating him for days. He was in a simulation of *The Odyssey*—he was himself Odysseus!—but he had started at the end and was going backward to what should have been the beginning of his character's story, the Trojan War. Did that mean that he would reach the place and find the war had ended as it had in the epic tradition, which was what had allowed Odysseus to begin his doomed journey home? But what if someone else wanted to use the Trojan War simulation right now, one of the rich buggers who had paid for it? It seemed bizarre to think that just because Paul himself was wandering around hundreds of kilometers away pretending to be Odysseus, even the people who built the network would only be able to experience a burned and blackened wreck where the walls of Troy had once stood.

The boy Gally had told him that in the Eight Squared, the Alice-through-the-Looking-Glass simulation, all the chesspiece people strove against each other until the game ended, then everything went back to the beginning and they started again—liter-

ally, at square one. Did that mean the simulations were cyclical?
Again, it raised the question of how its owners might feel if they
wanted to bring a party to Pompeii to watch the eruption, for instance, only to find the ash had just fallen and it would be days
or weeks until the spectacle would happen again.

Paul could not wrap his head around the logic. There might
be simple rules behind the whole process that made it little more
than a board game for the people who had built it, but he was
not one of those people; he had none of their information and
none of their power. And if he started to think about it as a game
and forgot to take this world seriously, it would probably kill him.

As dawn broke on the morning of the third day and the sea
mists began to clear, they saw the coastline.

Paul at first thought the line of gray on the horizon was simply more mist, then the overcast cleared, the sun broke free, and
the rest of the sea warmed to turquoise-blue. As the raft drew
closer and the sun mounted higher, gray became the pale gold of
hills that edged the plain like sleeping lions. Although he knew
it was only make-believe, Paul could not hold back an apprecia-
tive sigh. Even Azador grunted and stirred, sitting up straighter
from his crouch beside the tiller.

As the waves rolled them toward the wide, flat beach which
ran for kilometers in either direction, Paul moved to the front of
the raft and knelt there, watching one of the most storied places
in all the world appear before him.

Ilium, he recalled, schoolboy swot-work suddenly come to life
and shimmering in the distance. A fake, yes, but a magnificent
falsehood for all that. *Helen, whose face launched a thousand
ships. Achilles and Hector and the wooden horse. Troy.*

The city itself stood on a promontory just before the hills, with
wide, strong walls that seemed chiseled out of the naked rock,
flat as the facets of huge gems. The palace loomed above all at
the city's center, its columns painted red and blue, its roofs adorned
with gold, but there were many other impressive buildings as well.
Troy was alive; the citadel was still unbreached. Even from this
distance, Paul could see sentries moving on the walls and the thin
smoke trails of domestic fires.

There were fires on the beach as well, where a river curled its way down from the plain to the all-embracing sea, where the thousand black ships of song were drawn up onto the sand, row upon row. The Greeks had surrounded their landing place with a huge enclosure built of stone and timbers, filled with countless tents and numberless inhabitants. The Greek encampment was just as much a city as ·was Troy, and if it had no painted columns, no glittering golden roofs, that only made its purpose more grimly clear. It was a city that existed only to bring death to the fortress on the hill.

"Why are you here?" Azador asked suddenly.

It took Paul a moment to draw his attention away from the scurrying, tiny shapes in the Greek camp, the distant twinkle of armor. "What?"

"Why are you here? You said you must come to Troy. We are here." Azador scowled and gestured to the lacquered ships and the walls glaring white as teeth in the bright sun. "This is a war, here. What are you going to do?"

Paul could not immediately think of a reply. How could he explain, especially to this brusque gypsy, about the dream-angel and the black mountain—things that made no sense even to him?

"I'm going to have some questions answered," he said at last, and found himself hoping painfully that it was true.

Azador shook his head in disgust. "I want nothing to do with this. These Greeks and Trojans, they are mad. All they want to do is stick a spear into you, then sing a song about it."

"You can leave me here, then. I certainly don't expect you to endanger yourself."

Azador frowned but did not say anything more. He might not be a representative of an ancient type, as Paul had first thought, but he was clearly of almost a different species than the chattering classes among whom Paul had spent most of his life: the man used words the way a traveler in the desert rationed his last canteen of water.

Poling hard, they managed to turn the raft aside from the beach to the mouth of the river. When they had made their way far enough against its flow that the raft would be safe from the changeable ocean, they waded to shore and drew the salt-crusted collection of logs and rope up onto the bank. The Greek encampment was still half a kilometer away. Paul untied the feather-scarf from his wrist and knotted it around his waist, then began to walk toward the forest of leaning masts.

Azador fell in beside him. "For a little while, only," he said gruffly, not meeting Paul's eyes. "I need food and drink before I leave again."

A moment of wondering whether Azador truly did need food, or whether it was only a habit he had carried over into the network and was reluctant to shed, was ended by the sight of two figures coming toward them from the Greek encampment. One was slender and appeared frail, the other bulked as large as a professional strongman, and for a moment Paul felt a feverish rush of terror at the idea that the Twins might already have found him again. He hesitated, but the figures trudging toward him along the sandy ground did not give him the sense of panic he had come to expect. Reluctantly, ignoring Azador's look of irritation at this stopping and starting, he moved toward them. The smaller figure raised its hand in a kind of salute.

If I really am Odysseus in this simulation, he thought, *then the system has to fit me in somehow. I have no idea what I'm supposed to do here, but Odysseus was one of the important lads at Troy, I remember that much. I need to watch, and listen, and try not to make things awkward.*

The wind changed, bringing the scents of the Greek camp down on him, the smell of animals and men at close quarters, the raw smoke of many fires.

But if these two were not the monsters who had been pursuing him, he suddenly thought, perhaps they *were* the reason that Penelope and her other incarnations had sent him here. Perhaps someone was looking for him—someone real. Perhaps someone actually wanted to help set him free from this apparently endless nightmare.

The knee-weakening thought of rescue was almost as debilitating as the thought of the Twins; Paul pushed it away and tried to concentrate. The approaching pair were easier to see now. One was a tiny old man, his beard whitely vigorous, his thin arms nutbrown where they were exposed by his flowing garment. The large man was dressed for battle, wearing a chestplate that looked like boiled leather trimmed with metal and a kind of metal skirt. He held a bronze helmet under his arm and carried a terrifyingly long spear.

You could stab something with that thing without being in the same county, Paul thought uncomfortably. Azador's reluctance to get involved with these people's war suddenly seemed very sensible.

As the strangers drew near, Paul realized that the old man wasn't little at all: it was the warrior who was huge, well over two meters tall, with a bristling beard and a brow like a rock overhang. Paul took one look at the big man's stern face and massive neck and decided he would go a long way to avoid offending him.

"May the gods be good to you, Odysseus!" the old man called. "And may they turn their smiles on the Greeks and our venture. We have been looking for you."

When Azador realized it was Paul being addressed, he shot him a look half of amusement, half of contempt. Paul wanted to tell him that it hadn't been *his* choice to be Odysseus, but the old man and the giant were already upon them.

"And stalwart Eurylochus, too, if I remember correctly," the old man said to Azador, giving him a nod that seemed little more than perfunctory. "You will pardon an old man if I have your name wrong—it has been many years since Phoinix was in his full bloom, like you two, and my mind sometimes forgets. Now, I must speak to your liege lord." He turned to Paul as though Azador had disappeared. "We beg you to accompany us, resourceful Odysseus. Bold Ajax and I have been sent to plead with Achilles that he join us in battle, but he is prideful as always and will not come out. He feels that our leader King Agamemnon has done him a terrible wrong. We need your wits and your clever tongue."

Well, there's a neat little summing-up, Paul thought. *The system handing me what I need to go forward? I still wish I remembered all this better, though,* he thought sourly. *This would be bliss for a real Classics major—all except the maybe-getting-killed part.*

"Of course," he said to old Phoinix. "I'll go with you."

Azador fell in behind them, but neither of the other two seemed to notice.

The gate of the Greek camp was made of timber bound with

heavy bronze, guarded by several armored men. The camp itself looked like something that had started out as a temporary bivouac, perhaps in the springtime of the invaders' hopes, but a decade on the Trojan plain had turned it into something far more involved, although still without any real homelike feeling. A deep ditch formed the outermost ring, with palisades of sharpened logs on either side. Inside the ditch rose a wall of piled stones twice as high as a man, reinforced by giant timbers. An ominously huge mound of dirt and sand had been raised a short distance inside the wall, as if in imitation of the distant hills. Smoke leaked from it in several places: there had been a great burning, and the remains were still smoldering. With a little thump of dismay that even the knowledge of virtuality could not entirely cushion, Paul realized what had been burned and entombed there. The slaughter must have been dreadful.

Ajax received a great deal of attention as they made their way across the Greek settlement, respectful nods and the occasional shouted greeting, but Paul himself, as Odysseus, received no less. It was incredibly strange to walk into this archaic fortress and be greeted with cheers by ancient Greek soldiers, a returning hero who in actuality had never been here before. He supposed it was the kind of thing that the Grail Brotherhood loved, but it made him feel like an impersonator.

Which, he supposed, was exactly what he was.

It really was a city, Paul realized. For every single Greek warrior, and there seemed to be thousands, there were two or three others, both military and civilian, working in support. Drovers with supply sledges, grooms for the chariot horses, water-bearers, carpenters and masons working on the fortifications, even women and children—the camp bustled with activity. Paul looked up to the shining walls of Troy and wondered what it felt like to be trapped inside for years, to look down each day and see this incredible human machine working tirelessly toward your destruction. The plain had probably once been the home of livestock and herdsmen, but now all the animals were penned inside the two cities, the great and the temporary, and the people also had drained away, making their choice between besiegers and besieged. Except for carrion birds, flocks of crows like earth-hugging storm clouds, the plain was as empty as if some great broom had swept away everything that did not have deep roots.

As they made their way through the camp, Phoinix and the massive Ajax continued to behave as though Azador were not present, but the gypsy had fallen into one of his watchful silences and seemed not to care. They walked to the water's edge, where the ships pulled onto the sand lay in a long row, hull by tilted hull, huge craft with twinned banks of oars on each side as well as a number of smaller, faster vessels. All were stained a shiny black, and many had sterns that curled high above their decks like the poised tails of scorpions.

The foursome headed through a field of rippling tents toward a large wooden hut, which even if it had been of the same material would have stood out from the others by its ornamentation, the painted doorposts and the beaten gold on the lintel. Paul at first thought it must belong to Achilles, but Phoinix stopped before the guardian spearmen on either side of the doorway and said to Paul, "He is angry at Achilles, but he knows it was his own foolishness that began this. Still, he is highest among us and Zeus has given him the scepter. Let him say his piece and then we will hurry to the son of Peleus and see if we can calm him."

Ajax grunted, a deep, angry, rumbling sound like a bull who had backed into a nettle. As they stepped into the building, Paul wondered which of the disputants the giant was unhappy with, and could only be glad it was not him.

Paul had difficulty seeing at first. The smoke of a large fire clouded the air inside the cabin, despite the hole in the ceiling. There were many shapes, mostly armored men, but a few women as well. The old man made straight for a gathering at the cabin's far side.

"Great Agamemnon, High King," Phoinix said loudly, "I have found clever Odysseus, wise and well-spoken. He will go with us to Achilles, to see if we can unknit the anger that is in that great warrior's heart."

The bearded man who looked up at them from the bench was smaller than Ajax, but still large. His ringleted head sat low on his wide shoulders, a circlet of gold on his forehead the only mark of kingship; if he had the belly of a man who ate well, he was still muscular and imposing. His small eyes were set deep beneath his brows, but they glinted with prideful intelligence. Paul could not imagine liking such a man, but he could easily imagine being afraid of him.

"Godlike Odysseus." The high king withdrew a broad hand from beneath his thick purple cloak and waved for Paul to sit. "Now is your wisdom needed more than ever."

Paul took one of the rug-covered benches. Azador squatted beside him, still darkly silent, still seemingly of no more interest to the others than a housefly. Paul wondered what would happen if Azador spoke—would they continue to ignore him? It did not seem likely he would find out, since the gypsy had not uttered a word since the beach.

There was some talk back and forth about the fortunes of the siege, to which Paul listened carefully, nodding in agreement when it seemed appropriate. Some of the details seemed different than what he remembered of *The Iliad,* but that wasn't suprising: he felt sure a system this complex, with characters so sophisticated as to be indistinguishable from real people, would come up with countless different variations of the original story.

The siege was going badly, there was no question about that. The city had held strong against attack for almost ten long years, and the Trojans, especially King Priam's son Hector, had proved to be fierce fighters; at the moment they were also taking heart from the absence of the Greeks' greatest warrior, Achilles. Several times in past days they had not only pushed the Greeks away from the walls but had almost reached the Greek fortifications, with the ultimate aim of setting fire to the Greek ships and stranding Agamemnon's assembled army in a hostile country. The list of the fallen on both sides was heartbreakingly long, but the Trojan warriors—led by Sarpedon and Hector's brother Paris (who had stolen the beautiful Helen in the first place, starting the war), but most especially by the powerful, seemingly unstoppable Hector—had been doing tremendous damage to the Greeks, who were beginning to lose heart.

Paul could not help smiling inwardly as great Agamemnon and the others talked, laying out all the important points. Whoever had programmed this had taken into account that even the few folk who had actually read Homer, like Paul himself, would have done so a long time before, and perhaps without the most careful attention.

"... But as you know," Agamemnon said heavily, tugging his beard in unhappiness, "in my greed I offended Achilles, taking from him a slave girl who had been given him as a prize to make up for the loss of my own prize. Whether Zeus the king of gods has turned his heart against me—everyone knows that the Thunderer watches over Achilles' destiny—I cannot say, but I do know that I feel a great doom hanging over the Greeks and their well-benched ships. If lordly Zeus has turned against us, I fear we will all leave our bones here on a strange shore, for no man can overcome the desires of the immortal Son of Time."

Agamemnon quickly listed all the glittering, generous gifts he would give to Achilles as recompense for the stolen prize, if only the great warrior would forgive him—the girl herself returned, augmented by objects of precious metal and swift horses, and the pick of the spoils if Troy should finally be overthrown, not to mention lands and a royal daughter in Agamemnon's own Argos—then urged Paul to go with Phoinix and Ajax and win Achilles back. After they had drunk wine with him from heavy metal cups, and also spilled some as offerings to the gods, Paul and the others stepped back out onto the sand. The sun had gone behind the clouds and the plain of Troy suddenly looked dead and dreary, a gray, brown, and black marsh that had already swallowed whole armies of heroes.

Ajax was shaking his huge head. "It is Agamemnon's own stiff neck that has brought this on us," he growled.

"It is the stiff necks of both of them," aged Phoinix replied. "Why are the greatest always so quick to fury, so swollen with pride?"

Paul felt that he was expected to say something, perhaps offer some wise Odyssean aphorism on the foibles of the mighty, but he was not quite ready to attempt improvised rhetoric of the kind that all this Classical conversation seemed to require. He tried to compensate by looking properly concerned.

Hang on a bit, he suddenly thought. *I damn well should be concerned. If the Trojans come down on us and drive us into this ocean—and there's no reason that might not be in the cards on this go-round of the simulation—then it's not just a bunch of Pup pets that get killed, spouting poetry. It'll be me and Azador, too*

Lulled by the familiarity of names, almost charmed by seeing such a famous place brought to life, he had lost track of just what he had sworn he would never forget.

If I don't take it seriously, he reminded himself, *it will kill me*

The camp of Achilles and his Myrmidons was at the far end of the Greek flotilla, almost on the beach; Paul and his escorts walked a long way in the gray shadows of the boats. The Myrmidon soldiers sat or stood around their tents, dicing, arguing, full of what seemed to Paul like raw nervous energy. As he and the others approached, the men watched with faces either angry or sullen with shame; none greeted them as others had so cheerfully elsewhere in the camp. The split between Agamemnon and Achilles was clearly doing nothing good for morale.

Achilles' hut was only a little smaller than Agamemnon's, but workmanlike and undecorated—a place for a famous warrior to sleep and nothing more. A slender, handsome young man sat on a stool before the door, his chin propped on his hands, looking as though he had lost his best friend. His armor did not seem to fit him correctly, as though the pieces had been improperly tied. When he heard the footsteps he lifted his head and looked at Paul and the others nervously, but with what seemed no recognition.

Old Phoinix clearly recognized him, though, and greeted him "Please, faithful Patroclus, tell the noble Achilles that Phoinix with bold Ajax and famed Odysseus, would speak with him."

"He's sleeping," the young man said. "He's not well."

"Come—surely he will not turn away his old friends." Phoinix could not entirely disguise his irritation. Patroclus looked at him, then at Paul and massive Ajax, as though trying to decide what to do.

Something in the young man's hesitancy set Paul's revived sense of danger on edge. It was natural that in such a delicate situation, caught between the wishes of honored comrades-in-arms and the pride of his lord, Achilles, that this Patroclus should find himself uncertain of how to proceed, but something about the youth seemed subtly out of place.

"I'll tell him," Patroclus said at last, then disappeared inside the hut. He emerged a few moments later with his face set in an expression of disapproval and nodded them inside.

Someone had put in an effort to make the dwelling clean; the sandy floor had been swept with a branch, and the armor and few other possessions were all neatly placed along one wall. At the center of the room, stretched on a bed of boughs that had been covered with a wool rug, lay the focus of everyone's worries, Trojans and Greeks alike. He, too, was smaller than Ajax, who seemed to be the largest man in the whole countryside, but he was tall by any other standard and built like a marble statue, every muscle beneath his sun-browned skin sharply defined. Half-naked, with a cloak drawn over him like a sheet, he looked like a romantic painting come to life.

Achilles lifted his handsome head of dark golden curls and stared at them. He tilted his head to one side for a moment, as though listening to a voice no one else could hear, then turned back to face his guests. He did not look ill—his color, as far as Paul could tell inside the dark hut, seemed to be good—but there was a great lassitude to his movements.

"Tell Agamemnon I . . . I am sick," he said. "I cannot fight. There is no use sending people to ask me, even . . ." again he paused, his eyes focusing distantly, ". . . even you, Phoinix, my old tutor."

The aged man looked to Paul, as though expecting him to offer the first arguments, but Paul did not want to dive in quite so quickly. Instead, as Phoinix took up the slack by describing Agamemnon's generous offer of reparations in intricate detail, Paul watched Achilles' reactions. The famous anger was absent, or at least suppressed. Although he was clearly annoyed, it seemed the petty frustration of a man awakened from a nap to no useful purpose, which suggested that Patroclus had told the truth. But Paul could not remember anything about Achilles being sick in *The Iliad*. Perhaps this was one of the variations, sprung from the complexity of an endlessly reiterating environment.

Phoinix's blandishments did nothing to change Achilles' mind. Ajax spoke brusquely about the duty that Achilles owed to the other Greeks, but that did not seem to impress the golden warrior either.

"You don't understand," he said, his voice rising a little. "I cannot fight—not now. Not yet. I am weak and sickly. I don't care about all your gifts." He hesitated again as if trying to remember something, or as if a small voice spoke in his ear. "A man can win prizes," he continued at last with slow deliberation, as though quoting a famous saying, "but there is no winning a man's life back again when it has passed the guard of his teeth."

He would say no more, and even Phoinix was at last forced to turn away in frustration and lead Paul, Ajax, and silent Azador out again.

"Will you come with us to give Agamemnon this sorrowful news?" the old man asked as they paced back along the row of beached ships. He looked ten years older, and Paul was again struck by how deadly serious these matters were to all those here.

"No, I wish to be alone and think," Paul said. "There is nothing I can say to make it better, but there may be some . . . device that I can come up with. That my mind can conceive." He didn't know why he was bothering to try to talk like them, really. The system would adapt to whatever form of speech he chose.

As Phoinix walked off to finish his sad mission, accompanied by hulking Ajax, Paul suddenly realized what was troubling him. He almost said it out loud to Azador, then decided he would be better off keeping his own counsel.

They didn't quite talk like everyone else, or act like everyone else, he thought. Achilles did a little better than his friend Patroclus, but even he sounded like he was getting some prompting. Could they be outsiders—visitors on the network? Of course, that was no guarantee that they wouldn't be enemies. They might even be members of the Grail Brotherhood having a pleasant holiday in one of their billion-credit playgrounds. He would have to keep an eye on them, think carefully. He was here for a reason, he had to believe that—Penelope, Vaala, whatever her name was, must intend something to happen for him at Troy.

The black mountain. She said I had to find it . . . but there aren't any mountains at all around here.

"I am going back to the raft," Azador said suddenly. "You see these people—they will all kill each other soon. I have no reason to let them kill me, too."

"Where will you go?"

The gypsy's shrug was eloquent. "It does not matter. Azador, he can take care of himself, whatever may happen. But you, Ionas . . ." He smirked, suddenly. "*Odysseus.* You are going to wish you had gone with me. This sort of thing is too dangerous for you."

Paul was a little stung, but tried to sound matter-of-fact. "Could be. But I have to stay here. I'll wish you good luck, though—I won't forget you. Thank you for your help and your companionship."

Azador barked a laugh. "You must be an Englishman, with those manners—they smell of some English fancy-school. Are you an Englishman?" Paul's irritated silence made him laugh again. "I knew it! You, my friend, you will need more than good luck." He turned and walked up the beach.

What the hell am I doing? Paul thought. *He's right—I should get bloody well out of here. This place is going to turn into a killing field—it's going to be as bad as anything in the First World War. But here I'll be, playing guessing games and trotting around trying to figure out why some angel sent me here while a bunch of overmuscled madmen with spears try to kill me. An idiot, that's what I am, and I'm tired of it.*

But what else can I do?

Somewhere on the far side of the wall a flock of crows rose from the field and spun upward like a lazy black cyclone before breaking apart and scattering across the sky. Paul watched them go, wondering how anyone could possibly conceive of that as anything other than a bad omen. He kicked the sand, considering what to do next.

I suppose it wouldn't hurt to explore a bit—look around the camp, talk to a few people. Then maybe later I'll drop back in on Achilles, greatest of warriors. . . .

CHAPTER 25

A Job with Unusual Benefits

NETFEED/NEWS: Silence from Mars Base
(visual: MBC project footage—construction of base)
VO: The largest construction project on Mars has gone
silent and work has stopped. Space agency officials say they
suspect a reproduction error may have infected the buglike
builder robots.
(visual: General Equipment VPPR Corwin Ames at press
conference)
AMES: "The problem is, we don't control these things. We
just built the originals and sent them out. These are highly
complex systems that reproduce themselves mechanically. If
something in the blueprint mutates—changes for some
reason, like a scratch on one of the templates—nothing
except natural selection is going to stop it. We just have to
hope that the bad changes have a high enough mortality
rate that the breeder-builders weed them out in the next
generation. . . ."

BRIGADIER General Daniel Yacoubian simply appeared in the imaginary dining hall; if his entrance had been accompanied by a puff of smoke, it would have made a very fine conjuring trick. "I got your message," he growled. "It better be important—I'm on the road and I'm in the middle of about a thousand things."

Robert Wells seemed to take an almost perverse pleasure in presenting himself honestly, even in VR. On close inspection, his sim showed every day of his one hundred and eleven years—the skin dull in some places, shiny in others, the movements slow and brittle. The anti-aging treatments were keeping him alive and even active, but they could not make him young, and he allowed his virtual presentation to reflect this important truth. Yacoubian found it perversely irritating.

"You are on a secure line, Daniel, aren't you?" Wells asked.

"Of course I am. I'm not an idiot. Your message said it was a priority matter."

"Ah. Good. Thank you for responding so quickly." Wells seated himself and waited for Yacoubian to do the same. Just beyond the open wall the Pacific Ocean seethed in the rocky coastal channels, tossing up confetti handfuls of spray. The general wondered idly if it were purely code, or whether Wells' engineers had done the easy thing and used actual images of the real-life ocean. He had a feeling that Wells would not do it the easy way, even for an environment that so few other people would ever see.

"So what's up? I don't think we've either of us got much time to waste, with countdown at T minus seventy-two hours or whatever it is."

"You sound a little nervous, Daniel." Wells had the unnerving habit of sitting very, very still, whether in RL or VR. It made Yacoubian positively itchy. The general drew a cigar from his breast pocket but did not light it.

"Jesus, is that what you got me on the line to talk about? Whether I'm nervous or not?"

Wells lifted his hand. The bones showed beneath the nearly translucent skin as he waved it. "No, of course not. We're all a bit . . . concerned, of course. Even after all these years of planning, of anticipation, it's hard to face the moment without feeling a little uncertainty. But it *is* the Ceremony I wanted to talk about."

Yacoubian put the cigar in his mouth, then took it out again. "Yeah?"

"I've just had the strangest call from Jongleur. I don't quite know what to make of it. For one thing, it was the first time I've ever talked to the Old Man when he wasn't wearing his Curse-of-the-Pharaohs sim. He called me up and left it on voice-only—blank screen. The whole experience was quite . . . old-fashioned."

Yacoubian scowled. "Are you sure it was him?"

"Please, Daniel. Do I ask you whether you're certain you're bombing the right country or defoliating the right jungles? It was the Old Man, all right."

"So what did he want? Jesus, Bob, you take your sweet time getting to the point."

"What are you, Daniel—seventy or so? It's charming that you're still young enough to be impatient. We're going to have a long time, a very long time, to think about these things after the fact if we do them right, but no time at all if we do them wrong."

"What are you talking about? Now you've got me worried." Yacoubian stood up and walked to the edge of the room. Outside, the Pacific stretched away on either hand as far as he could see, hugging the intricate coastline like an unimaginably large two-piece jigsaw puzzle.

"I just mean we shouldn't hurry things, Daniel. That's how mistakes get made." Wells pushed his chair back a little bit and rested his hands on the edge of the table. "Jongleur doesn't want me to go through the Ceremony when everyone else does. He wants me to sit it out with him and Jiun Bhao—fake it, I guess you would say."

"Jesus Christ!" Yacoubian whirled, his face contorted with anger. "What the hell is *that* about? Is he going to bump the rest of us off or something?"

Wells shrugged minutely. "I don't know. It wouldn't make much sense—we all need each other to make this work. I asked him why, of course. He said that Jiun Bhao wants to wait and go through the Ceremony last and Jongleur didn't feel he could refuse. The Old Man said it didn't seem fair to me, as one of the three project managers, if I didn't get to do the same."

"That's horseshit and you know it."

"Mostly, yes, I'm sure it is. But there's something going on that I can't grasp. It wouldn't do any good to talk to Jiun about it—you'd have better luck getting a rock to tap dance. I figure that they're nervous. They want to hold back because they're not sure it will work properly, and they want me because I'm the only one who can get the technical problems solved if something goes wrong."

Yacoubian's hands were balled into fists. "So . . . so the rest of us are just some kind of . . . guinea pigs? Canaries in a goddamn mine shaft?"

"Not you, Daniel." Wells smiled gently. "I told him that he had to include you in anything I was doing."

"You . . . oh." The general seemed uncertain of what to do next. "I . . . that's . . . thank you, Bob. But I still don't get it."

"I don't either, and all of this happening at the last minute leaves me a little uneasy. Let's make a few calls, shall we? Just listen, if you don't mind—I won't put you on view to any of them."

In marked contrast to Wells, Ymona Dedoblanco, the owner of forty-five percent of the stock of Krittapong Enterprises and thus one of the globe's wealthiest people, maintained a public sim that was aggressively misleading. Its physical appearance was pegged to her time as a Miss World contestant—a moment of ancient history that was of little import to anyone except Dedoblanco herself.

The former Miss Philippines pushed her shiny black hair away from her face. "What do you want? I am terribly, terribly busy. There are so many legal things to settle . . ." She glared. "Well?"

"And it's a pleasure to see you, too," Wells said, smiling. "I just wanted to see if you had any last-minute questions."

"Questions?" It was hard not to see the lion-goddess face Jongleur had created for her as she shook her head in annoyance. "I have been waiting for this for twenty years. I have asked all my questions. My lawyers and . . . science people, whatever they are called, they have looked at everything."

"Are you worried at all? It's a big step for all of us."

"Worried? Such things are for little people, timid people. Is that all you wanted to know?"

"I guess so. I'll see you at the Ceremony, then."

She did not waste time with a long farewell, breaking the connection so quickly that Yacoubian could almost hear the transoceanic silence before Wells selected another number.

Edouard Ambodulu, although obviously pleased to be the subject of Wells' concern, had nothing to add. The African president-for-life was busy with his own arrangements, many of which had resulted in various human rights groups making special pleas to the United Nations, all of which had been dutifully moved to the most distant part of the calendar by UNCov bureaucrats who knew hopeless causes when they saw them. Neither did Fereszny nor Nabilsi nor any of the other Grail Brotherhood inner circle seem to have any new concerns, at least none that Wells could turn up with his delicate probing. Of all the busy autocrats, only Ricardo Klement did not seem to resent the interruption.

The Latin American businessman—a euphemism which would have made even the most grasping, hardened graduate of Harvard's MBA program quiver with indignation—was a little reticent at first, perhaps because of Robert Wells' known enmity to Jongleur. Klement had hitched his wagon to the Old Man's star early, and had kept that wagon hitched by an ever more embarrassing descent into flattery and abject approval of anything Jongleur proposed. Yacoubian, watching invisibly, could not help but be impressed by how Wells dealt with him, relaxing the other man with small talk, making it clear that this was not some last-minute attempt at a political maneuver against Klement's beloved master.

"No, I'm just checking to see if anyone has any questions," Wells said. "We've had our differences, you and I, I'm not pretending we haven't, but we're all in this together, after all. We succeed or fail together."

"We will succeed," Klement said fervently. Oddly, of all the Brotherhood Wells had contacted, the Argentinean was the only one who shared Robert Wells' own brutal self-honesty. His sim showed him just as he was, festooned with tubes and half-obscured by dermal patches—a man struggling to hold off death in a private Buenos Aires hospital. "We have worked too hard not to succeed. Señor Jongleur has created a miracle. With your help, too, of course, Señor Wells."

"Thank you, Ricardo. That's kind. So . . . everything is ready?" Unspoken was the knowledge that Klement more than anyone else was waiting desperately for this long-delayed moment. The black marketeer had bargained everything on a number of aggressive therapies, sacrificing any chance of long-term physical salvation, even of the macabre type that sustained Jongleur, to keep his multifold cancers out of his brain stem until he could undergo the Grail process.

"Oh, yes. With Señor Jongleur's permission, I have created a beautiful setting—you will remember I discussed it at our meeting? It will be a tribute to this great day. We will have the proper surroundings to become gods!"

"Ah, yes." Wells had clearly not been paying much attention at the meeting, and neither did he want to spend too much time talking about what were for all intents and purposes party decorations. "I'm sure it will be splendid, Ricardo. So, any word from the Old . . . from Jongleur?" Wells kept his voice light. "I have not had a chance to speak to him lately, with all the last-minute details to oversee."

Klement shook his head. If he was hiding anything, he was doing a good job. "Only the invitation. I am certain he has many things on his mind, too. Señor Jongleur is a man with many, many responsibilities, many subtle thoughts."

"He certainly is. Well, I will see you at the Ceremony, Ricardo. *Vaya con Dios.*"

"Thank you . . . Robert. It was kind of you to call." Nodding happily, Klement clicked off.

Wells laughed. "Did you hear that, Daniel? 'It was kind of you to call.' From a jumped-up grave robber, yet. Oh, we are a genteel and respectable bunch, aren't we?"

"If any of them knew anything, I sure didn't see it."

"I didn't either." Wells frowned slightly. "Which doesn't really prove anything. I don't suppose we have much choice, though— I think we have to say yes to the Old Man's offer, even if we don't know exactly what it means."

"Damn it, Bob, is this thing going to work?" Yacoubian's sim retained its customary tanned appearance, but his voice suggested a man going a little pale around the edges.

"Relax, Daniel. We've done every test you can imagine—not to mention the Old Man's prisoner, the one who flew the coop on us. *He* went through the process, and he's doing fine as far as we can tell. A little too well, actually."

"Speaking of 'X,' or whatever you call him, what happened to that agent of yours that was tracking him down? You said you were having problems with it."

Wells shook his head. "I won't lie to you, Daniel. The whole thing has me puzzled. We're not receiving anything useful back from Nemesis at all. My boys and girls on the J-Team say the gear has 'gone native.' We're looking into it, but it really doesn't have anything to do with the Ceremony. Unlike the Grail Project, I'm afraid we rushed the Nemesis code a little bit, and now we're paying for it."

"Unlike the Grail Project."

"Don't say it like that. It's going to work. The Grail is something we've been working with a long time, and as I said, it's already tested solidly through thousands of trials. These are machines, Daniel—complicated, but still machines. We haven't added any new functionality to the system since Mr. X got processed and escaped. It works. It'll work for us."

"But now we've got the Old Man playing some kind of game. God, I *hate* that old bastard. I can't believe we let him keep control of so much of this process."

"It was his ball, Daniel," Wells said mildly. "We had to let him make the rules for the game, at least some of them."

"All the same, I'd happily kill him. What is it the kids say? I'd six him for shorts."

"I think it's 'chorts,' actually. As in 'chortles.'" Wells smiled, a stretching of lips that did not change the expression in his quiet, yellowed eyes. "You *are* bloodthirsty, Daniel. You didn't wind up in the military by accident, did you?"

"What's that supposed to mean?" Yacoubian sat down and smacked irritably at his pocket, then realized he still had an unlit cigar in his hand. He ignored the matches that Wells flicked into existence on the tabletop.

"Nothing, really, Daniel. Let's not fight—we still have a great deal of discussion ahead of us if we're going to take Jongleur up on his suggestion."

"What are we going to do?"

Wells nodded. "What else is it the young people say? 'Smile sweet, pack heat?' We'll say 'Yes, thank you,' to the Old Man, but I think we'll have a few surprises of our own prepared, just in case."

"Good." Yacoubian withdrew a large gold lighter from his pocket, sparked the minisolar flame, and lit his cigar. Outside the imaginary room, the sound of the hungry ocean rose.

THEY were stacked up over the new airport for an hour and a half, turning in a broad, four-sided pattern that took them out across the Tasmanian Sea, then back over the heart of the metropolis. Except for the overabundance of planes waiting for landing strips, the skies were clear. Dulcie Anwin, too tense to read, watched the city as it rotated past every fifteen minutes like a miniature display in a shop window.

She thought Sydney's famous opera house, subject of millions of postcards and calendars, looked less like the billowing sails of ships everyone always cited than it did a pile of quartered hard-boiled eggs. The little Tupperware boxes her mother had sent with her to school, filled with celery sticks or eggs—or even, when her mother was feeling exotically lazy, with leftover *dim sum*—were one of the few homely memories she still retained from her childhood.

As the harbor fell away behind the wing of the plane each time, and the angle changed, the opera house for a moment took on other, less nostalgic shapes—curls of melon rind, or even the chitinous, articulated length of a crustacean.

Like a shrimp, she thought. *A prawn. Wonder if all these food thoughts are a metaphor for sex or something.*

The harbor, the bridges, she had been living with all of them for months as the view from Dread's virtual office. It was strange to realize that she was actually now seeing something so familiar for the very first time.

That's modern life, though, isn't it? she told herself as the pilot announced that they were finally ready to land. *Our lives aren't even about doing real things, most of the time. We think and talk*

*about people we've never met, pretend to visit places we've never
actually been to, discuss things that are just names as though they
were as real as rocks or animals or something. Information Age?
Hell, it's the Imagination Age. We're living in our own minds.*

No, she decided as the plane began its steep descent, *really
we're living in other people's minds.*

Dread wasn't there to meet her, but she hadn't expected him
to be. She was a grown woman, after all. He was a boss, not a
boyfriend, and whatever suspicions she might harbor about his request for her presence—suspicions rooted in feelings too am-
bivalent to be called either hopes or fears—she was not going to
put herself in an awkward position by presuming anything other
than Business As Usual.

Besides, she had the feeling that her decidedly unnerving employer wasn't the type who picked *anyone* up at the airport.

The new Sydney Airport, opened only a few years earlier, squatted twenty-five kilometers offshore on its own artificial atoll, linked
to the mainland by a long, straight causeway standing on hundred-
meter-wide fibramic pillars sunk deep in the ocean floor, their
great lengths layered with pressure distributors to minimize damage from seismic instability. The causeway itself, lined with ho-
tels, shops, restaurants, and even a few apartment buildings, had
become an adjunct neighborhood of the city. As Dulcie sat on the
high speed tram, watching the doors puff open at each stop—
Whitlam Estates, ANZAC Plaza, Pacific Leisure Square—she wondered if with so many businesses happy to invest in these clean
new causeway developments, the next city that built an offshore
airport might not go twice as far off the coastline and double the
commercial buy-in. Eventually, as all the Pacific Rim cities thrust
farther and farther out into the ocean, the day might come when
they would all meet in the middle, and someone with enough time
on her hands and a high threshold of mall-boredom would be able
to walk from commercial atoll to commercial atoll and cross the
Pacific on foot.

What should have been an amusing notion, strolling from shop
to shop and lobby to lobby while sharks and other deep-ocean
creatures swam invisibly beneath, instead felt strange and unset-

tling. *So this is what happens when you actually go places,* she thought. *Maybe there's something to be said for VR after all. . . .*

The tram reached dry land but sped onward, continuing to the old airport complex on Botany Bay, which served as the new airport's transportation hub. Dulcie spent an additional quarter hour in the taxi line, but eventually found herself in the back seat of an old-style wheeled cab heading north. The driver, a garrulous young Solomon Islander, almost immediately asked her if she would have dinner with him.

"I need to learn more about America," he explained. "I could be your special friend in Sydney. You need something, need to go somewhere? I will drive you."

"You *are* driving me," she pointed out. "And I need to go to Redfern, like I said. But that's all I need, thank you."

He did not seem unduly disappointed, and even offered to stop and buy her an ice cream in Centennial Park. "I am happy to get it for you, and I will pay," he said. "I am not expecting sex in return."

Amused despite herself by this completely mad young man, she nevertheless refused this offer, too.

Her research on various travel nodes had portrayed Redfern as a district on the rise, so Dulcie was surprised and a little depressed by her first view of it; if this was rising, the low must have been very low indeed. There were a lot of Aboriginal people on the streets, but few of them had the cheerful look of the dancers and actors and small business owners in the nodes' wraparound advertising. The district had its share of restaurants and bars, but at this time of day they were mostly closed. Dulcie told herself that things might be very different after dark, with lights and music all around.

"Oh, it's better now," the driver told her. "This used to be very bad. My cousin, he lived here, he was robbed three times. And he had nothing worth stealing!"

The address proved to be a featureless walk-up in a largely shuttered commercial street that was less run-down than some of the others, but completely empty of pedestrians. She was not thrilled with the idea of being left by herself on the sidewalk, but Dread did not answer when she called his number from her pad, and after checking again to make sure she had the street address right, she paid the driver and asked him to wait a few minutes, willing for safety's sake to risk a misunderstanding that might lead to more social overtures.

Dread's voice from the speaker by the gate was startlingly clear, as though he were standing right beside her. *"Dulcie? Come on in."* The gate tumblers shot back. She waved good-bye to the taxi driver, who smiled and blew her a kiss as she turned to walk up the damp cement stairs. The door at the top swung open through no visible agency, ominous as the beginning of a horror flick.

She paused on the doorstep. *Maybe I should have just stuck with the taxi guy . . .*

The main room was startlingly large, an area that once might have held several tiny apartments or a small factory, and was almost completely empty. It had been painted entirely white, and a new white carpet covered the floor. The tall windows had been covered with blackout curtains, which themselves were shrouded in white bedsheets.

Dread stood by the far wall, inspecting something that looked like a mobile execution device. As with the famous opera house, but in a far more unsettling way, Dulcie was conscious of the oddity of seeing such a familiar face for the first time. He had not misrepresented himself. He was no taller than she was, and dressed all in black.

Dread walked toward her and to her surprise and confusion stuck out his hand. After a moment she took it. He squeezed once, firmly, then released her. "It's good to see you. Hope your flight was all right. Was that you who called a few minutes ago?"

"Y-yes, I guess so. I wanted to make sure you were here before . . ."

"Sorry I didn't pick up. I've been trying to figure out this bloody bed."

"Bed?"

"Yeah. Coma bed. So I can stay online for long stretches without bedsores and cramping and whatnot. All these little microfiber loops, lots of oxygen and skin massage." He smiled, a brief but dazzling display of wide white teeth. "Come give me a hand with it, then we'll get something to eat."

He turned and strode back across the naked room. Dulcie was left trying to sort out her thoughts. *He's lit up like a Christmas*

*tree. Is he on something? But he seems to be in a good mood—
that's something, I guess.* She stood, hesitating. It was hard to get
moving. A part of her, she realized, was hurt by the perfunctory
greeting. *Business As Usual,* she reminded herself. *Business.*

"It's a nice piece of work, that bed," he said. "Top of the line,
right? Like a Rolls-Royce Silver Shadow or a Trohner machine
pistol."

"So I take it you're planning to spend a lot of time online? In
the Otherland network?" She smiled reflexively at the hovering
waiter, but what she was really feeling was nervousness and irritation.

"We're not done yet," Dread told the young man in a flat voice.
"Piss off for a while. No, get us some coffee." He turned back
to Dulcie and his lazy smile returned, but his dark eyes were
frighteningly intense. "Oh, yes, I've got plans. I've just found out
some very interesting things—very, *very* interesting. I got knocked
offline, see. That was yesterday. And I used your copy of the
thing," he lowered his voice a little, "the *device,* trying to get back
on. But I ran into something. Did you know this system is run
by some kind of AI? That thing they were all complaining about
when they were first in Atasco's simworld?"

"Slow down. I'm having trouble following you." Dulcie was
beginning to feel the jet lag. He had done nothing but talk a blue
streak since she had arrived, but his openness was the opposite
of flattering—she felt sure he would have done the same with
anyone halfway qualified, halfway interested, halfway trustworthy. "I don't think the system is run by an artificial intelligence,"
she said, "—not in the conventional sense. It's a weird neural net
of some kind—or a bunch of them, distributed. I haven't been
able to break into the architecture at all. But nobody does AIs
anymore, they're clunky and unreliable. They certainly wouldn't
be using one to run something this complex."

He shook his head in annoyance. "Whatever. Not an AI, then,
but one of those other things—an ALife system. But I'm telling
you, there's something alive on the other end of that wire. Something that *thinks.*"

She started to argue, then stopped. "How did you get knocked
offline?"

"I got killed." He stopped, staring at the waiter, who had arrived with the coffee. The young man clinked a cup hard as he set it down, perhaps from nerves, then hurried away. Dread shrugged. "Stupid thing—an accident. I wasn't paying attention."

"And the rest of those people?" It was odd—she missed them, missed their personalities and their odd courage, even missed the adventure of the whole thing. It had been difficult sometimes as she had inhabited the Quan Li body to remember that *she* was not trapped online as they were, that she could go offline at the end of the day and sleep in her own bed with no fear that a mistake in the virtual universe, a moment of bad luck or carelessness, might kill her.

He curled his lip; his stare was feral. "I don't give a shit about them. Are you going to listen? Who's paying you anyway?" For a moment he seemed about to reach across the table and grab her throat.

"Sorry. I'm tired."

"There's something on the other end, that's what I'm telling you. If it's not an AI, then you pick the name—that's your job, not mine. But I know it's alive, and I know it wants to keep me out. We lost the Quan Li sim and so we've lost that access to the network."

"Could you find out something through . . . through your employer? I mean, this is his system, after all."

"Christ!" It was a hiss. If it had been a shout it would only have startled her, but instead it froze her into complete immobility. For a moment, her concern that he might grab her seemed laughably mild. "Have you forgotten *everything?* If the Old Man even guessed I might be messing around with his network, he would . . ." He sat back, his face suddenly blank, distant. "I'm beginning to wonder if I made a mistake, bringing you here."

A part of her knew she was supposed to beg forgiveness. Another, perhaps healthier part wanted him to order her onto a plane back to New York. But something had settled into her spine, a cold inertia. "I told you," she said, speaking almost as flatly as Dread himself. "I'm tired."

The mask softened in an instant. The teeth reappeared. "Right. I'm being pushy—I'm just excited about this. We can talk more tonight, or even tomorrow. Let's get you back so you can get a nap." He snatched the check from the table so suddenly she leaned away from the force of his movement. Within seconds he had flashed a card over the reader and was heading for the door. It took some moments before she could assemble her thoughts to get up and follow him.

"The room's fine," she said slowly. "I just thought . . . I'd be staying in a hotel. Or something."

He was bouncing with energy again. "No, no. Wouldn't work. I'm going to need you here all kinds of hours. Sometimes you're going to have to sleep with the monitors on. You're going to earn that high consultant's rate of yours, sweetness."

She surveyed the room, made up in a spartan simplicity that matched the larger studio space down the hall. In a strange, almost touching gesture, he had already turned back the comforter and the top sheet. "Okay. You're the boss."

"Oh, don't worry," he said, grinning. "You play your cards right, you're going to come out of this better than rich."

"Great." She slumped onto the bed, unable to keep up with him anymore. Her head felt like it was stuffed full of wet laundry. Any concerns—or hopes, for that matter—that he might make a pass at her had subsided into the numbness of her jet lag. "That's great."

"I'm not joking, Dulcie." He paused in the doorway and looked at her carefully, measuring something she could not even guess. "How would you like to live forever?" he asked her. "Seriously, I want you to think about it. How would you like to be . . . a god?"

CHAPTER 26

Dawn at the Gates

NETFEED/NEWS: Concerns of Cosmetic Ethicists
(visual: young man with twelve fingers)
*VO: The World Association of Cosmetic Surgeons, meeting
for their annual conference in Monte Carlo, find themselves
with a bit more on their hands than usual. Cosmetic
generation, an offshoot of stem-cell technology
advancements, has been a fad among the rebellious young
for several years, but recent advances now permit not just
the generation of extra digits, but the actual addition of
limbs and even nonhumanoid features such as tails.*
*(visual: artist's rendition of Goggleboy with dorsal fin and
horns)*
*VO: Some surgeons and bioethicists worry that teenage fads
are not the real problem.*
(visual: Doctor Lorelei Schneider speaking at conference)
*SCHNEIDER: ". . . We are already receiving troubling
reports from some of the poorer parts of the world that
manual laborers are being pressured to undergo limb-
augmentation—to have not just extra digits generated, but
extra hands and even arms. Those who refuse are less able
to compete in a very, very tight market. . . ."*

THEY had come through, but things had changed. Many things had changed.

Renie reached out to put her hand on the stone wall, as much to keep herself upright as to feel its reassuring solidity. Above the deserted garden, above the tiled paths and the empty pond, above Renie and her disoriented companions, the stars burned ferociously, as different from the dim sparks in the sky above the House as a wolf was from a lapdog. But the new stars were the least of anyone's worries.

"I'm . . . I'm a man," Renie said. "Jesus Mercy, Martine, what happened?" She ran her hands down her body, feeling the hard muscles of the chest through her wool garment, her solid thighs, the alien *something* between her legs. Her hands pulled back as though they had a volition of their own, as though they did not want to reconnoiter this suddenly foreign territory. "Did you do this?"

"Did everyone come through?" Florimel asked. She at least looked much as she had before, bandaged and bloodied, clothed in rags, although what Renie could see of her face was different. "Are we all here?"

"God, of course. I'm sorry." Renie began counting heads, but it was hard to believe the strangers around her were truly her companions. "!Xabbu? Is . . . is that *you*?"

The slender young Greek man laughed. "Somebody heard my request, it seems. It is . . . odd to stand with my back straight."

"How did . . ." Renie forced herself to swallow her questions. "No, let me do this first. T4b, that's you, right?" she asked a tall youth dressed in the kind of armor usually seen in museums or portrayed on ancient pottery, the only one of them who looked ready to fight in the Trojan War. When he confirmed his identity, she looked to the small shape on the ground by his feet. Emily had kept her own face, but her hair was longer and had gained a distinct curl. Her crude smock dress had been replaced by a long white gown, but although her costume had changed, the girl herself had not, if her weeping was any indication. "What's wrong?" Renie asked.

"She's been doing this since we came here," T4b said helplessly. "Worse than ever—just, like, crying."

"It hurts!" Emily yelped.

"Not so loud, please." Renie kneeled and put her face close to Emily's, trying to calm her. They seemed to have the darkened garden all to themselves, but if they were really in besieged Troy, someone shouting in one of the courtyards would not go unremarked for long.

"But it does hurt!" the girl sobbed. "Everywhere you take me, it hurts."

"What does?"

"I don't want to be here. I don't belong here!"

Renie shrugged and stood up, leaving T4b to offer comfort. The last figure, sitting on the edge of the dry pond, also wore a pale dress. "Martine?"

She took a moment to respond, as though she had been lost in her own thoughts. "Yes, it is me, Renie."

"What's going on? Why am I a man?"

The blind woman gave a tiny shrug. It was hard to see her face by starlight, but she seemed exhausted. "I had to make choices," was all she said.

"Is this really Troy?"

"As far as I can tell. You can see what people are wearing, which I cannot. Do the clothes seem correct?"

Renie shot a sidelong glance at T4b's crested helmet. "I suppose so, yes."

"It was not like the other time, going through," Martine said slowly. "We had to find a particular simworld this time, not just open a gateway—you remember that we were trying to find a way to access the central index for the network. We had to find the actual listings for the . . . the . . ."

"Nodes?" Renie prompted.

"The individual world-nodes, yes. And when I found it at last and the gate was opening, I was suddenly given an array of choices. I suppose the Grail Brotherhood or their guests receive such a prompting each time they change simworlds, but this is the first time we have entered one through the front door, I suppose you would say. Anyway, I had to choose quickly, so I did. I was afraid to stay connected to the central system any longer than I had to— after all, our device, the lighter, was stolen from one of the Brotherhood. They may even be looking for it—I'm not sure it's safe for us to keep it near us."

"We do not dare separate ourselves from it either," said Florimel wearily. "It is the only victory we have won so far. Should we just bury it in a hole and trust we can get back to it again?"

"We can talk about all that later," Renie said. "You had to make choices, you said. Are we inside Troy? Inside the city itself?"

Martine nodded. "The apparition you saw, the Lady of the Windows, said *'You must come to find the others. You must come to Priam's Walls.'* Until we know otherwise, we must take it literally. Unless we are inside Troy, there is no guarantee we could ever reach the walls."

Renie grimaced in frustration. "Look, Martine, I don't claim to know the Trojan War stuff very well, but I do remember one thing, which is a big damned wooden horse and a bunch of Greeks setting the whole city on fire. We're going to be slaughtered if we stay here!"

"It was a ten year war, Renie," Martine replied. "We have no idea at what point we've arrived—or if it's even following the same pattern."

"Martine had to make decisions very quickly," Florimel said, chiding her, Renie knew. And Florimel was right.

"Look, I'm sorry. It's just all been kind of a shock. I mean, suddenly becoming a man—it's so strange. I have . . . a . . . a penis!"

"Many people have managed to overcome that and still lead useful lives," Florimel pointed out.

Renie laughed despite herself. "Did you have a choice about that, too, Martine?"

"Yes, but not for very long." The blind woman sounded as though she were about to fall asleep sitting up. "I tried to make the best decisions I could, but who knows? I will tell you my thoughts. We do not know what we are doing here, or who wants us here. Perhaps if we are lucky, it is Sellars, who has found a way to enter the system and meet us. But even if so, there is no guarantee that the walls are what he actually meant as a meeting place—it could be anywhere in this Trojan simworld, including out there on the plain or in the Greek camp."

"I'm with you so far," Renie said.

"This is a city at war. No one is going to be allowed out of the gates except men, fighting men. I thought you might prefer to be able to accompany !Xabbu and T4b if they had to go out."

Renie wasn't sure whether Martine meant that she knew Renie wouldn't trust anyone but herself to lead such an important expedition, or whether she meant Renie would not want to be separated from !Xabbu, although she was probably right about both things. Renie's irritation melted into shame. Martine had thought very quickly and carefully under the circumstances. "Go on."

"Florimel is badly hurt, and I am going to be more use at finding things out in here, I think, than out in the chaos of battle. Emily is a child, or acts like one, and seems to be pregnant. She certainly should be kept inside, where she will be safe as long as possible. So for that reason I made the three of us women."

"Are we supposed to be anyone in particular?" Renie asked. "Achilles or . . . Paris, or any of those folk?"

"You and !Xabbu and T4b are not any of the truly famous heroes," Martine said. "I did not want to put you at the center of things. My memory of the Trojan War, at least from *The Iliad,* was of heroes fighting against each other with spears, with one of them dying almost every time. If this simulation follows Homer's poem, that is too great a risk. As ordinary fighting men, you can stay out of the melee as much as possible."

"You have thought wisely, Martine," !Xabbu said. "We are lucky to have you with us."

She waved her hand, too weary to bear the weight of a compliment. "The rest of us are women of the royal family. That will keep us as informed as it is possible to be, and extend our freedom a little—women were not allowed much independence in the Greek world."

"Don't get it, me," T4b said suddenly. "We in some kind of swords and sandals army? Like one of those Hercules flicks? Who we fighting?"

"You're a Trojan," Florimel told him. "This is your city, Troy. The Greeks are outside, trying to conquer it."

"Crash," said T4b, nodding. "Gonna six me some Greeks, then."

"Jesus Mercy," said Renie. "There have to be easier ways than this to save the world."

* * *

Despite their fatigue, Renie and her companions had much to discuss; an hour passed quickly.

"We still don't know why we are here," Florimel pointed out. Of all of them, she was most in need of rest—her wounds were obviously still hurting her—but she had insisted on participating anyway, a form of self-denial Renie recognized. "What if it is not Sellars trying to reach us? What if it is some fluke of the system, or even somehow a device of our enemies? Remember that Nemesis thing Martine told us about? We just have no idea who's out there looking for us and what they might want."

"I do not think we are enough of a threat to our enemies for anyone to go to such trouble," !Xabbu pointed out. "So far, we have been like flies on an elephant—worth a flick to dislodge us, but nothing more."

"We haven't even met our real enemies yet," said Martine. "We have met their minions, the Twins—if your Tinman and Lion were indeed them, as this Azador man claimed. And Dread we have had far too much of, God help us. But Dread's master and the others, they are still above us, beyond our reach. As Kunohara said, they are like gods."

"So we should simply wait and hope?" demanded Florimel. "I think that is an invitation to destruction."

"Do you have a better plan?" Renie asked. "I'm not being sarcastic. What other choice do we have? We're still trying to make sense of all this. We have the lighter, so we have a little more control than we did, but we can't use it to bring down the whole system any more than . . . than we could use a key to tear down a house."

"I think there is more going on," !Xabbu said suddenly. "The man Kunohara said we were in a story. I do not understand his meaning, but I feel truth in what he said. Perhaps the word I am looking for is 'faith'—we need to have faith that things will become clear to us."

Renie shook her head. "I don't see any difference between that and what Florimel is complaining about, waiting and hoping. You know I respect how you see things, !Xabbu, but I'm not you—I don't believe that the universe is going to save me, or that it even makes sense."

He smiled sadly. "The universe has certainly never gone out

of its way to save my people, Renie, whatever they may have believed." He brightened, and Renie realized she hadn't seen his human smile for quite some time; it was good to see it now. "But you yourself may have given a clue, Renie. That is why you are like the beloved Porcupine."

T4b, largely uninvolved in the discussion, nevertheless snorted at this. Florimel, too, was puzzled. "Porcupine?"

"Grandfather Mantis' best-loved," !Xabbu said. "The one who sees the ways forward when others do not. Renie sometimes does not even know it herself, how truly she sees."

"Enough." Renie was embarrassed. "What are you talking about, a clue?"

"You said we could not use the device to destroy the system any more than a key could bring down a house. But a *key* can bring down a house. It unlocks the door, and then others can come in, either those who will rob and ruin the house or those who will see what has been hidden there and can overcome it."

"You mean, like the police?" She wasn't at all sure. "I suppose if we ever get out of here alive, and if we hold on to the lighter, we might be able to turn it over to someone at the UN or something . . ." But it was hard to remember Del Ray's treachery and remain confident.

"It is an idea only," he said. "But I wanted to point out that there might be hope after all. Whether our story has an end that is already written or not, we can only trust to our luck and do what is before us. But hope is never an unwelcome companion."

She nodded. For the first time since they had left the House, the new sim really seemed to be the !Xabbu she knew and loved. *What if we had to live like this all the time?* she wondered, *moving from body to body? Would it make love easier, or more complicated?* Just now she felt herself physically attracted to !Xabbu in a way that had been inhibited by his baboon form—his new sim was young and reasonably attractive, and the !Xabbu-ness still showed through—but that desire was making itself felt while she was wearing a male body herself, a situation which was almost as off-putting, in a strange way, as when !Xabbu had worn the monkey sim.

I suppose there are worse spots for one man to be in love with another man than in the Greek army, she consoled herself.

"Who are you?" a voice called suddenly from the darkness.

Renie jumped, startled, and clambered to her feet, cursing their complacency—she and the others had almost forgotten they were in a strange place, a city at war. But the man walking toward them from the shadows at the edge of the garden was so tall and broad-shouldered that for a moment she was positive she was seeing a familiar barbarian sim.

"Orlando? Is that you?"

The man stopped, just visible in the starlight. "I do not know that name, but since I see noble Glaucus there among you, as well as my sister, you must know mine. Cassandra, what are you doing away from the women's chambers? Our mother Hecuba is full of worry."

To Renie's surprise, Martine stood up. "This . . . this girl was frightened by a nightmare, brother," she said, then pointed to Emily, who sat huddled on the tile path. "She ran away and we went in search of her. These soldiers helped us find her."

The newcomer swiveled his glance across Renie and her companions. He did not seem entirely to believe the story. "My family owes you thanks, Glaucus," he said at last to T4b, who stayed nervously silent. "You Lycians are the noblest of men, it is true, and the most redoubtable of allies. But now I can take these women back, soothing their fears, and you can return to the rest of your company by the Skaian Gate." He looked sternly at Renie and !Xabbu. "Do not dally, you men. Soon it will be time to put your armor on—bloody deeds will be done when the sun rises, and great honor won."

Renie felt her heart sinking. Battle! And they had barely been an hour inside Troy.

"Great . . . Hector," said Martine, hesitating as though she were not sure she had guessed the right name, "are the Greeks so close to the walls, then? Is there no chance for even a few days' peace?"

She had evidently guessed his identity correctly. "The Greeks still sleep by their well-benched ships," he said, "but the gods have spoken and told us that godlike Achilles has fallen out with Agamemnon and will not fight. Now is the time for us to bring great force against them and drive them back into the sea, while their greatest warrior is sulking beside his black ships. But I have said enough. It is not right that I should speak too much of war to you women, which will only deepen your worry."

Martine and Florimel helped Emily onto her feet. "I don't belong here!" the girl said, but she seemed so feeble and disconnected she might have been talking to herself.

"We are none of us protected against the will of the changeable gods," Hector told her, his commanding tone softened. "Come, girl. I will at least see you safely back to the women's quarters." As he stepped forward, the starlight picked out his features in greater detail, his pale brow and long straight nose beneath jet black hair.

One of the male leads, Renie could not help thinking. *Handsome bastard, at least in this version. But I think he gets killed in the end, so what good is it to him?*

As he led the women across the garden toward the arched door that led back into the palace, Hector turned and called to T4b, "Glaucus, tell noble Sarpedon I will be at the gates an hour before the sun rises. If your men are lacking anything of weapons or armor, take them to the armory near the Skaian Gate and tell the men there I said to give them what is needed. Every man now within Troy's walls must be ready when we face the Greeks and their bold spears."

Renie was still watching long moments after they had disappeared.

"What are you thinking?" !Xabbu asked her.

"I'm just wondering about this system again—it's so astonishing!" She sighed. "I could spend years studying this network. But we'd better get moving if we're going to find some armor. If the Greeks are anything like Hector, I want to be well-protected even if we're going to spend most of our time running away and hiding."

Renie had been worried about finding their way through the Trojan citadel in the dark, but other armed men were moving down to the gates as well, and Renie, !Xabbu, and T4b fell into the flow.

"See, what I'm trying to figure out is how much hard-coding there is in this thing." She spoke quietly even though the small group of levied soldiers just ahead of them were singing, with the aggressive tone of those who want to prove they are not frightened, a drunken song about the slopes of Mount Ida. "You saw Hector—he had doubts about Martine's story, even though he had no doubts that she was his sister. So these Puppets have to be very flexible, have to incorporate changes. I suppose what I'm wondering is how quantum-mechanical this whole thing is. That is, if there were no outsiders, like us or the Grail Brotherhood, would the same story just play out over and over again like clockwork? Is it only having real people in the mix that alters things? Or is it a turbulent system—so complicated that it can never do the same thing twice, even if there aren't any real people involved?"

"Difference not," T4b grumbled. "Puppets trying to six us, seen? 'Less we six them first, seen? All there is to know."

"Are you saying we shouldn't try to figure out the system?" Renie was stung, although she knew she shouldn't be. "Understanding how this thing works may be our only hope to get out of here."

T4b shrugged, at the limit of his interest in conversation. *Oh, my God,* Renie thought, *he's such a teenager.*

"I think I understand you, Renie," !Xabbu said. "But I wonder if there is even such a thing as . . . what would be the word? As . . . an uncorrupted environment anymore. If, as Azador said, there are things like the Twins moving from simulation to simulation, and the Grail Brotherhood and people like Kunohara entering wherever they want, the entire system is no longer what it first was."

Renie nodded. "True. I wonder if that's part of what's going on—those breakdowns, where the whole system freezes. Maybe the system is just getting too complicated and unpredictable things are starting to happen, major collapses, all kinds of stuff."

"Then the Otherland network would be very much like the real world," !Xabbu said. He was not smiling.

The armory was a vast storeroom connected to an equally large smithy across the courtyard from the massive, shadowy Skaian Gate. At this late hour it was the only well-lit building in the area, its forges brighter by far than the fires of the soldiers camped in the open area behind the gates. As they entered, they were enfolded by steam and the scents of sweat and molten metal. The gymnasium-sized room was a magnificent clutter, an archaeologist's dream, full of the acoutrements of war—dismantled chariots, stacks of spears with splintered shafts, helmets damaged in ways that suggested their previous owners were probably not coming back to claim them—but Renie had little time to take it all in. The forge workers, almost uniformly old or crippled and thus exempted from serving as soldiers, came crowding forward to look at the newcomers, eyes wide. The torchlight revealed the reason.

"As it is sung," one of the oldest armorers said, looking reverently at T4b, "noble Glaucus wears armor without peer."

T4b stared down, astonished. His fitted chestplate, arm guards, and the greaves which stretched from his knees to his ankles were all made of bright-gleaming gold. Apparently the machineries of the network had improvised on the armor his sim had already been wearing when he crossed into the Troy simworld. The armorers crowded around the young man like autograph seekers around a professional athlete.

"Is it true your grandfather Bellerophon wore it when he slew monsters?" asked a man with one arm.

"Glaucus has been struck in the throat," Renie improvised. "While . . . while wrestling. His voice is weak."

T4b shot her a grateful glance.

"As long as his arm is still strong," the man who had spoken first said. "There will be much blood and weeping when the sun rises. Let Father Zeus grant a prayer that most of it will belong to the Greeks."

The armorers, honored to serve the companions of the (apparently) famous Glaucus of Lycia, hurried to outfit Renie and !Xabbu. As the workers handled her with casual familiarity, Renie tried hard not to flinch, reminding herself that she was a man now. They tied a sort of padded linen mat around her chest, then draped a two-piece bronze cuirass over her torso and knotted it at the sides. As she experimentally lifted her arms, wondering how someone could run away in such a heavy thing, let alone fight, they added a dangling plate to protect her abdomen and groin, then fitted linen-padded bronze greaves on her lower legs. !Xabbu was patiently undergoing similar treatment, and Renie could not help admiring his trim, slender figure. It was so nice to see him as something other than a baboon! He saw her watching, and smiled in amusement.

Damn it, woman, this is for real, she chided herself. *It doesn't matter how good he looks, or how you look either, or even if you're a damned man now. There are people outside those gates who want to shoot you full of arrows and whack your head off with an ax.*

Suitably self-chastened, she allowed herself to be led to a pile of discarded helmets and was given something not at all like T4b's huge gold helm. It was instead a sort of cap of stiff leather with flaps that hung down over the ears, covered all over in rows of split animal tusks which had been drilled at either end and stitched onto the leather. She hoped the tusks were more use than simple ornamentation.

"You're lucky," the one-armed man told her. "That's a fine piece of work."

When !Xabbu had received a leather helmet of his own, they were allowed to choose from a waiting stack of wooden shields shaped like circles and figure eights, covered in stretched oxhide and banded with bronze. Renie picked a round one, hoping that the smaller size would allow more mobility, and !Xabbu followed her example. After being given a short stabbing-sword each, they stepped up to choose from the small forest of spears leaning against the wall, all more than twice their own height. Renie's new armor, instead of making her feel more secure, left her feeling heavy and confined. Already the cuirass chafed her unfamiliarly flat chest. As she examined the bronze-tipped spears, she could not help thinking of all the Greeks outside the gates who would be trying to skewer her with similar instruments, and she felt a moment of stomach-dropping dread.

We don't belong here. We are in over our heads again.

"If I may ask, noble Glaucus," an old man said to T4b as he knotted Renie's scabbard onto her belt, "why do your friends have no armor of their own? Is there some tale to tell? The Greeks often take armor as tribute, but not without killing its owner."

T4b, who had been daydreaming while Renie and !Xabbu were fitted, looked up in surprise.

Is he calling us cowards? Renie wondered. *You could spend a year here trying to figure this out, but we have to fall into the middle of everything.* She tried to think of something plausible. "Our . . . our horses ran away with our belongings." So far, every Puppet she had met except Brother Factum Quintus had taken what she said at face value; she hoped these Greek slaves and freedmen would be the same.

The old man proved her right. "Ah, it must have been a difficult journey for you from Lycia, then, if your horses were lost." He nodded, his expression serious. "But we are grateful you are here. Without you Lycians and Dardanians and others, Troy would have fallen years ago."

"Always happy to help." Renie cocked her head toward T4b. He took a moment to catch on, then waved his arm, beckoning them to leave with him. The armorers came to the doorway again to send their good wishes and to have one last look at his golden armor.

The encampment beside the Skaian Gate was huge. For a moment, Renie felt a return of confidence. Even if the Greeks could mount a force of equal size, surely there were enough men here for her and her friends to lose themselves somewhere away from the front lines.

One of the sentries recognized T4b and led them to Sarpedon, who seemed to be some kind of relation to Glaucus. The chief of the Lycian allies was another movie-star type, not quite as imposing as Hector, but still tall and built like an Olympic gymnast. He accepted Renie's hurried explanation for T4b's silence without question.

"As long as your arm is still strong, noble Glaucus," he told T4b, giving him a brisk slap on the shoulder that made the young man stagger. "There will be bloody deeds to do when the sun comes up, and the Greeks will not wait to hear you speak before trying your strength with their sturdy spears."

T4b's smile was sickly, but Sarpedon was already off again, striding manfully from campfire to campfire, pep-talking the Lycian troops. Renie was beginning to feel heartily sick of the Trojans and their muscular nobility. If she heard one more person talk about the bloody deeds that would come with the morning, she thought she might scream.

They found a place beside one of the fires. After an exchange of nods with the dozen or so men huddled there, T4b wrapped his cloak around his gleaming armor and sat quietly. !Xabbu crouched beside Renie and watched the wavering flames, perhaps thinking of other fires in more familiar places. For the first time Renie could observe the other soldiers, the levied troops who had come to the aid of Troy. As the men sat staring at the fire or whispered quietly among themselves, Renie saw something she had missed before, but which was now all too apparent in their hooded eyes and hunched postures. For all the brave talk of the leaders like Hector and Sarpedon, these soldiers, these average men, were terrified of what the morning would bring.

"CODE *Delphi.* Start here.

"Except for Emily, who has been softly, helplessly crying since we arrived, it is quiet now in the women's quarters. I am feeling the strong pull of sleep myself, although a part of me screams that every minute not spent trying to solve this or that puzzle is a minute wasted. I will take time to record these thoughts, since there is no effort in a soundless whisper, but I have no further strength.

"We are in Troy. Again, our group has been split apart, but this time it is by my choosing. I made the choices as carefully as I could, but any decisions with so many ramifications, taken in such haste, will inevitably seem dubious. As Emily, Florimel, and I were led away by great Hector, the lion of Troy, I already feared I had made a terrible mistake. I have left Renie and the others to bear the heaviest burden of my decision—within hours they will be part of an attack on the besieging Greeks. I feel like a very small, very petty god, one who has been given the power of life and death without any of the usual certainties of divinity.

"Even so, for all my guilty fears, I cannot help being drawn into the wonder and complexity of this simulation, cannot see Hector or his wife or parents without thinking of their well-known dreadful fates, and of the thousands of years they have been part of human thought. In a way, I know too much. Perhaps T4b, in his seemingly total ignorance of anything that happened before his own birth—and of much that has happened since—is in the best position of any of us. He will simply see and react to what is before him. But I cannot help what I know. I cannot shut off the life I have lived before coming to this strange, strange place.

"Hector led us through the palace to this suite where the women were sequestered. Except for a few torches the hallways were dark, and empty but for a token force of guards. For the first time in a while I resented my blindness. The other senses have been invaluable to us in this network, but I would have liked to see the frescoes. Based on the details I *have* been able to discern here, I am certain the Grail Brotherhood made sure the wall paintings were as accurate as possible. When I was a child, I fell in love with the frescoes of Knossos in Crete, which were reproduced in gorgeous color in one of my parents' books: leaping dolphins and birds and bulls. I would have liked to see how the walls of Priam's palace were decorated.

"Hector's wife Andromache and his mother Hecuba were up and waiting for us, worried about me—or rather worried about Cassandra, whose persona I have assumed. If I remember correctly, Cassandra was the king's daughter given the gift of prophecy by the god Apollo, who later poisoned the gift by decreeing that none of her predictions would be believed. Perhaps I chose poorly—perhaps I will even come to regret it later on—but to the best of my recollection, Cassandra figures little in most of the Trojan War.

"Andromache was even more pleased to see her husband Hector than she was to see me, and obviously hoped that he would stay, but he is a brusque and businesslike man for all his romantic silhouette, and he made it clear that now the three of us were safely delivered he was heading back to the Trojan army camped inside the gates. Trying to hide the depth of her unhappiness, his wife lifted their little son Astyanax for a farewell kiss, but Hector had already donned his bronze helmet with its huge horsehair crest, and the sight of his father turned into such an alien creature frightened the child.

"Watching, I was quietly stunned, for this is one of the most terrible moments of *The Iliad,* although acted out in a slightly different setting in the poem. Knowing what no one else in the room knew, with the possible exception of Florimel—that tall, brave Hector would never return alive, and that even his body would be dishonored before his family's helpless eyes—completely overwhelmed my certainty that these were Puppets, mere coded actors. In fact, as Hector kneeled and removed his helmet to stop his son's tears, it was almost impossible to believe that such a human gesture, no matter how famous or how often discussed, could be purely the product of an engineer's algorithm.

"I am tired, so tired, but the memory will not leave my head. What could be worse—for Hector and his family to live this sad moment once, as real people, or to be condemned like Dante's sinners to repeat the tragic event over and over and over, with no hope of salvation?

"It is foolish to think so much on these ghosts, for in a way that is what they are, when there are so many tasks to be undertaken to serve my real, living friends. It is exhaustion that keeps me cycling back through that instant again and again—Hector kneeling and taking off his helmet with its nodding plume, reaching out his arms to the crying boy, who is not yet sure it is really his father. Andromache and aged Hecuba watch with grim smiles, guessing even if they cannot admit it that although it seems the child is being needlessly fearful, what he has truly seen is the presence of Death in their house.

"It has been a long day—it started in another world, after all. I am running out of words. The women have all taken to their beds. Florimel is snoring heavily beside me. Emily has at last dropped into shallow sleep, mumbling and tossing, but no longer crying. I am positive there is something wrong with her that goes beyond her youth and callowness—she has not been right since Renie and the others rescued me—but I have no strength to think anymore. Like the tragedy of this city, foreordained to destruction by the capricious gods, my thoughts loop over and over. . . .

"Sleep. Tomorrow, we can try to make better sense of things. Sleep . . .

"*Code Delphi.* End here."

IT had been a strange dream, the kind that went with shallow, disturbed sleep. Stephen had been tied to the front of a huge wooden horse, calling to her that he could see everything, that he could see their flat in Pinetown and his school, while Renie had leaped and leaped without success, trying to reach him to pull him back down to the ground and safety.

They're going to use that horse, she thought. *They're going to use it to break down the gates and Stephen will be crushed. . . .*

As she surfaced from sleep, a contradictory thought flitted across her dreaming mind: *No, wait, the horse is going to save us, because only we know about it. We're going to get into it and escape.*

But they couldn't get into it—the horse was on the outside of the walls, full of angry children with claws and shadowed faces, and she and the others were on the inside, helpless, waiting. . . .

She gasped and opened her eyes. !Xabbu was leaning close, the still-unfamiliar face full of concern. "You were making bad noises," he said. "As you dreamed, I mean. It did not sound happy."

She looked around, reorienting herself. The ground was dew-moist. The sky overhead was still dark, but most of the camp-fires had burned down to coals. Above them loomed Troy's famous gate, only faintly touched by ember-light, the watchtowers on either side jutting like great square tombstones.

"It was just . . . I was dreaming about Stephen." She shook herself. Several others at the campfire were also sleeping uneasily; T4b was one of them. "Just another dream."

They talked quietly about nothing important for a few moments, sharing impressions of their new bodies, trying to find a tone of normality although both of them knew there was nothing normal about their situation. Runners were going from campfire to campfire, quietly alerting the soldiers. The eastern sky was beginning ever so slightly to lighten.

T4b woke up withdrawn and grim, his earlier bravado gone. Renie felt better—he would be less likely to do something youthfully stupid.

"We gonna have to, like, fight up on the walls?" he asked, surveying the high ramparts. His eyes were wide, the whites plainly visible.

"I don't think so—I think we're going out to attack the Greeks on the plain." She frowned. "But I don't want you to fight *anybody* if you can help it. Do you hear me, Javier? Don't make that face—we've been through enough for me to call you by your real name."

He shrugged.

She turned to include !Xabbu. "We can be killed out there. We're not code, like these men. Our job is to stay alive. Don't get caught up in all this glory-and-honor foolishness—it's like a netflick. It's not real. Do you understand me?"

!Xabbu smiled at her, but it was a small one. T4b hesitated a moment, then nodded. "Are you . . . clenched?" he asked quietly. "Like, scared?"

"Damn right." Renie could hear the runner exhorting the men at the next campfire, hear the soldiers clambering to their feet, slapping the dew from their armor and weapons. The rattle of movement and talk was growing louder. "I'm scared to *death*. Those spears and arrows are just as dangerous to us as they would be in RL. Keep behind your shields. We'll all stick together and protect each other. *Don't get separated!*"

As the messengers reached their group and summoned them to join the rest, Renie stood and put on her helmet, then picked up her heavy spear and shield.

It would have been nice to have some martial-arts training or something, she thought sadly as they jostled with the other men toward the standing mass just inside the gates. *Instead of learning on the job.*

!Xabbu reached out and squeezed her arm below the bronze shoulder guard. On her other side, his golden armor still hidden beneath his cloak, T4b's lips were moving as though he prayed.

Hector stood tall on a stone beside the gate, a living monument. His spear was three times his own height, but he waved it as easily as if it were a bamboo fishing pole.

"Trojans, Dardanians, all our allies, now is the time!" he shouted. "Let us sweep down on the Greeks. Let us take fire to their black ships. Let us avenge every one of our cities sacked, every one of our wives and daughters taken to bed in slavery. Let every man face death with courage, so that the gods themselves weep at the bravery of Troy!"

As the quiet noises of the massed soldiers rose to an animal roar, the rising edge of the sun notched the eastern hills and within an instant became a burning, spreading gash of fierce light.

The Skaian Gate heaved open, its mighty hinges shrieking like birds of prey, and the army of Troy surged out onto the plain.

Fourth:

SUNSET ON THE WALLS

"You have taken the east from me, you have taken the west from me, you have taken what is before me and what is behind me; you have taken the moon, you have taken the sun from me, and my fear is great you have taken God from me."

—*The Irish Girl's Lament,* collected by W. B. Yeats

CHAPTER 27

On the Road Home

NETFEED/NEWS: Arizona Denounced for "Slave Labor"
Camps
(visual: Youths marching to work at Truth And Honor Rancho)
VO: Civil rights groups denounced a bill passed by the
Arizona state legislature that would channel most of the
state's juvenile offenders through "youth service facilities"
which the civil rights community says are nothing more than
slave labor camps.
(visual: Anastasia Pelham, Rightswatch, in front of
Legislature Mall)
PELHAM: "We've already seen this in Texas, and it's
horrible—twenty children died in the Texas system in one
year from heat exhaustion and exposure. It's institutionalized
murder."
(visual: State Senator Eldridge Baskette)
BASKETTE: "Yes, I've heard all that nonsense—Auschwitz,
that kind of crap. The fact is, we've got huge facilities
jammed with youthful offenders, many of them rotten, violent
kids, and we're spending millions to support them. So all
we're saying is, 'You want a holiday at state expense? Well,
you're going to work for it.' Pretty fair, if you ask me."

WHEN Fredericks came back, Orlando was struggling to sit upright on his bed of branches. The sun had vanished, and the light from the brazier of coals was the only thing that illuminated the hut, forcing Orlando to bend close to the object of his scrutiny.

"What are you doing?"

"Just . . . just trying . . ." The effort had worn him out already, but he was determined. Orlando managed to secure his balance, then began the difficult process of folding his leg so he could look at his foot. "Just trying to look at my heels."

"You mean like your *feet?* Scanning is what you do best, Gardiner, that's for true."

"If I'm Achilles, there's supposed to be something wrong with my heel. Haven't you ever heard that expression? Don't you ever do anything when you're out of school besides hang around hoping to get invited to Palace of Shadow parties?"

"Get locked." Fredericks was not so certain as she sounded. "What do you mean, wrong with your heel?"

"That's how Achilles got killed—it's in all the old stories. I don't know how, I just know that's what happened."

"Then put some shoes on. Quit that." Fredericks did not want to talk about Orlando getting killed, that was clear. "We have to do something, Orlando. All these people keep coming over begging you to fight the Trojans."

"I'm not going to, so they can beg all they want." The effort to examine the backs of his feet had tired him without revealing any telltale weakness. He groaned and let himself slump back into a horizontal position, head pounding. "I can't do it. I just can't. I don't have the energy. That stupid Egyptian temple almost finished me off."

"We'll get out of here," Fredericks said a little desperately. "Then you'll be okay."

Orlando did not bother to point out what they both knew. "No, we have to stay, at least until we see if Renie and the others are coming here."

"They must be. That woman in the Freezer said so."

"No, she said we'd find what we were seeking here, or something like that—she never promised our friends would show up. You've done enough of these prophecy things in the Middle Country, Frederico—they sound like they mean one thing, but then turn out to be something else. They're tricky."

"I just want to get going. I want to find a way out of here." Fredericks lowered her head, the new, handsome Patroclus body contrasting oddly with the slumped, sullen posture. "I want to see my mom and dad again."

"I know." Orlando could not let the silence go on too long—there were a few things he didn't want to think about either. "Did you find anything while you were out? Any sign of Bonnie Mae or the kids?"

Fredericks sighed. "No. At least, nobody was talking about them. Seems like if a bunch of yellow monkeys were flying around, someone would notice."

"Unless they changed, too. Like we did."

"Yeah." Fredericks made a face. "So what are we supposed to do, ask everyone we meet, 'By the way, did you used to be a monkey?' We have to do everything here the hard way! It's worse than being back in the real world."

"You didn't see if they followed you when we came through from the temple?"

"I didn't see anything, Gardiner! There were bats, and . . . and monsters, and that guy Mandy just said, 'Into the gateway!' So I pushed you in and went with you."

"Nandi. His name was Nandi."

"Whatever it was, I didn't get a chance to see what they were doing."

Orlando could not help worrying about the Wicked Tribe, left in the crumbling Egyptian simworld to face a raging Osiris. They were just kids, after all, just micros. "We should never have let them out of that pot," he said gloomily.

"That was too far scanny." Fredericks frowned. "Were they just waiting there the whole time? While we were in that cartoon place, and the bug place, and everything? Just sitting in a jar like they were peanut butter?"

"I don't know." Orlando yawned despite himself. Napping all day had not made him any less tired. It was one thing to decide he was saving his energy for some coming crisis, but where would that energy come from? He didn't feel strong enough at the moment to carry a kitten across the room. "Somebody's messing around with this network. Everybody has adventures in a sim-world—that's what *happens* in simworlds. But to have somebody show up in the Freezer, then *bang,* she's an Egyptian goddess in a whole different simulation? And she's telling us where to go, helping us? I can't figure it out." He shook his head wearily. "Any of it. Is someone really trying to communicate . . . ?"

He was distracted by a noise from outside, the sound of voices raised in protest or argument. It did not sound too serious—most likely one of the frequent arguments that broke out over dice games among Achilles' bored, nervous troops—but Orlando's Thargor reflexes sent his hand searching weakly for his sword, which was still leaning against the armor-stand on the other side of the hut.

"The soldiers, whatever they're called, the Mermadoos or whatever . . ."

"Myrmidons," Orlando said. Getting up for the sword was too much effort; he let his hand drop. "Don't you ever listen to the turtle?"

"Too many names. I can't keep track. Every time that thing opens its mouth, it's 'And that is Bonkulus, son of Gronkulus, hero of the Kissmybuttians' . . ."

Orlando smiled. "Myrmidons. They're our soldiers, Frederico. You better remember their name—you might need them to save your life someday soon."

"They want to fight the Trojans. Every time I go out there, they ask me if you're going to put on your mighty armor and lead us against the Trojans. It's not just King Agawhozit—*everybody* around here utterly wants you to fight."

Orlando shrugged and nestled deeper in the bed. "I can barely sit up yet. I'm not going to get us both killed just to impress a bunch of virtual spear-jockeys."

The voices outside were still raised, but the anger had turned into some kind of loud discussion. Fredericks listened for a moment, then turned back to Orlando. "But I think they wonder how come we're in here all the time, the two of us. They probably think we're soft boys or something."

Catching him by surprise, it took a moment for the laugh to work its way up from Orlando's belly to his mouth, but when it finally exploded out of him, it was so loud that Fredericks jumped up from her seat on the floor, startled. "What? What's so funny?"

Orlando waved at him weakly, tears forming at the corner of his eyes. If Fredericks could not see the humor of a girl in a man's body worrying about whether a bunch of imaginary people thought they were queer . . .

Someone knocked at the door. Fredericks turned to look at it helplessly, uncertain whether or not Orlando's attack, which had now weakened to a hiccuping froth of giggles, was evidence of some graver problem.

Orlando caught his breath. "Come . . . come in."

The door swung open to reveal one of the bearded Myrmidons scowling with embarrassment. "It is the King of Ithaca, Lord," he said to Orlando. "We told him to go away, but he demands to speak with you."

"Who?" asked Fredericks.

"It's Odysseus," a voice said from behind the soldier. "I am sorry to disturb you, but I think it's important we speak again."

Orlando groaned quietly, but said, "Let him come in."

Odysseus bobbed his head in greeting to Fredericks, then to Orlando, then found himself a stool and sat. Exhausted and depressed, Orlando had not paid much attention to the man on his first visit earlier in the day. Now he looked him over closely. There was a watchfulness to the newcomer's manner, a sly reserve that suggested he was not quite as likely as the other Greeks Orlando had met to start spouting poetry about the nobility of hand-to-hand combat.

"What is it?" Orlando asked.

"I felt there were things that were not talked about when I was here with Ajax and Phoinix," the King of Ithaca said. "I thought perhaps we could have a conversation without those two and see if it goes more easily."

"Turtle," Orlando subvocalized, calling for the agent. In just a day, he had already begun to rely on it, although its limitations made him miss Beezle all the more.

"Tortoise," it said in his ear. *"I have told you, I am a tortoise."* It did not need to be visible to make its annoyance clear.

"Just tell me what I need to know about this Odysseus guy."
Aloud, he said, "I don't think there's really much to talk about.

I cannot fight. I am sick. I am not well." He tried to think of something pertinent to say about the gods, but couldn't muster the strength to improvise.

"Odysseus, son of Laertes, King of Ithaca," whispered the tortoise. *"He is the cleverest of the Greeks, renowned for his stratagems. But although he is a mighty warrior, perhaps the best archer among the invaders, he did not wish to come to Troy and pretended to be mad . . ."*

The man whose biography was being recited in Orlando's ear was speaking again, and Orlando had missed the first few words. ". . . find an understanding between us."

"We don't know what you're talking about." Fredericks sounded alarmed. Orlando hurriedly gestured for his friend to be silent.

"I did not hear what you said—my illness makes it hard to think clearly, sometimes. Please say that again."

"An illness?" asked Odysseus. His smile did not soften the harshness of his tone. "Or a voice in your ear? Is yours a bird, or something else? A bee? A fly? A goddess, maybe?"

Orlando felt his heart turning cold as wet clay. "I . . . I don't understand you."

"Come now—I'm taking a risk, too." Odysseus leaned forward, his expression again shrewd and careful. "You are not from here, are you? You are not really part of this whole thing, this . . . simulation."

Fredericks short sword hissed as she drew it from her scabbard. Odysseus did not move, even when Orlando's friend had touched the sword to the side of the stranger's neck. "Should I . . . should I kill him?" Fredericks asked.

You could at least try to sound a little more convincing, Frederico. Orlando felt weak and short of breath, as helpless as in a bad dream. Again he mourned his former vitality. As Thargor in his prime he could have tied even this rugged warrior into a knot if need be, but he had no such confidence about Fredericks, whatever sim his friend might be wearing. "Let him talk," he said hopelessly. If the Brotherhood had really found them, killing the messenger was not going to do much good, even if they could manage it.

"Good." Odysseus stood up, then spread his arms wide and showed his empty hands to make clear the movement was peaceful. "I said I was taking a risk—I'll go farther out on a limb, just to show you I mean well." He looked from Fredericks to Orlando, then briefly over his shoulder, as though to make sure no one was lurking in the shadows. When he spoke, it was with the solemn formality of one ambassador greeting another. "The golden harp has spoken to me."

Orlando waited for more. Apparently, none was forthcoming. "What are you talking about?"

"The golden harp." Odysseus narrowed his eyes, clearly expecting the words to have some profound effect. "The *golden harp*."

Orlando looked to Fredericks, wondering if he had missed something along the way, but his friend only looked back at him, a matching bookend of blankness.

"We don't know what you're talking about." Orlando had a sudden thought that raised the hairs on the back of his neck— was this some kind of Brotherhood code word? Had they gone too far in admitting that they were not of the simulation, then by not recognizing the code confirmed they had no right to be there? The only solace was that Odysseus, too, seemed completely taken aback by the failure of his overture, far more baffled than suspicious. He peered at Orlando, clearly uncertain what to do next.

"Perhaps . . . perhaps I've made a mistake." The stranger sat down again. "I suppose it's too late to pretend that I've come to try to convince you to fight the Trojans?"

Orlando almost smiled, but the fear was too close, too deep. "Just tell us who you really are, then maybe we'll have something to talk about."

The King of Ithaca spread his hands. "Are you going to tell me who you are, without any kind of certainty who you're talking to? I didn't think so. Well, you can understand my position, then."

Fredericks was still standing, sword in hand. Orlando examined the stranger and considered. Whatever else might be true, their physical safety did not seem immediately threatened. One shout would bring Achilles' warriors through the door, and he had little doubt the Myrmidons would be of the stab-first, ask-questions-later school. "Okay, we'll talk. Why don't you move your stool back a little, so that none of us is too close to each other."

The stranger nodded slowly, then did as Orlando had suggested. When he was seated again, midway between the bed and the door, he showed a crooked smile. "This is a bit of a logic problem, isn't it? We all know things that we can't say, because we don't know exactly to whom we're speaking." He bit his lip, considering. "Let's talk generalities, shall we? We can discuss what we *do* know, but stick to things that won't put anyone on one side or another."

Fredericks looked worried, but Orlando could see nothing wrong with the suggestion. "Okay."

"I don't mean to be critical," Odysseus said, "but it wasn't that hard to guess you weren't part of the simulation. You just don't talk like these other people. You use too many contractions, for one thing—whoever programmed this went for the old-fashioned, operatic effect."

"I'm better when I'm not so tired," Orlando said, a little embarrassed. "It's . . ." he caught himself just short of using Fredericks' name—had the stranger tried to lure him into doing just that? "It's Patroclus here who gets bored of talking that way and starts saying . . . things. Things the way he normally would."

"Thanks a lot." Fredericks glowered.

"We all know it's a simulation," said Odysseus. "We know it's part of a big simulation network, right?"

Orlando nodded. "Of course. Anyone would know that."

The stranger started to say something, but checked himself. "Good, so we agree on that," he continued a moment later. "Most of the people here are Puppets, but some are from outside. From the real world. Like the three of us."

"With you so far."

"And if I mentioned a certain . . . brotherhood?" Odysseus continued.

Fredericks gave him a worried look, but Orlando knew it was an obvious direction—one that could not in fact be avoided. "The Grail Brotherhood, right?"

"Right."

But neither side wanted to talk too much about the Brotherhood: to betray support or revulsion might immediately topple the careful structure of trust they were building.

It was maddeningly slow work—they went on minute after

careful minute, for the better part of an hour, advancing careful observations about the nature of the network, hampered at all times by the need to keep things vague and general. The coals burned down until the room was mostly shadows. Outside, somebody called the midnight hour as the sentries changed.

At last Orlando felt he could wait no longer—if nothing changed, this kind of fencing match might go on for days, and he had long since decided that time was not his friend. "So tell us about this golden harp," he said. "You came in here saying that it had spoken to you. What is it? How much can you tell us?"

Odysseus ran his fingers through his beard. "Well, without giving away too much . . . it was a message someone left for me. It told me . . ." He stopped to consider. "It told me that there were people looking for me. And that they would know me if I told them I had spoken to the golden harp." He cocked an eyebrow. "But you said that you've never heard of it."

"No," Orlando said. "But I'm beginning to have an idea." He hesitated—it was like reaching into a dark hole in the ground, a pit that might contain treasure or some terrible, venomous guardian. "Did this harp . . . did it start out as something else?"

"Something else?" Odysseus had suddenly gone very still. "What do you mean?"

"You heard me." The tension was beginning to make Orlando giddy; he felt he might suddenly laugh or scream. "It was your stupid harp—you tell me."

The stranger seemed to have turned to stone. "No," he said at last. "But . . . after it was a harp, it turned into something else."

"*After?*" This threw Orlando off-balance—he had been thinking about the vision of the golden city, which for Renie and the others had appeared first as a small golden gem. Still, he had committed himself and he was running out of energy; even with the possible fate of his friends hanging in the balance, he could not play these spy games forever. In the grip of a sort of downhill fatalism, he said, "Okay, yes, *after* it was a harp, was it . . . was it still golden?"

"Yes." It was like watching someone turn over a card in a high-stakes game. "Yes. It was a . . . small, golden thing."

"*Dzang!* That's just like what Sellars sent out!" said Fredericks excitedly.

"Fredericks!" Orlando's skin went cold. He turned back, but the stranger was not leering at him, not rising in theatrical menace. Instead, he seemed even more puzzled than he had been.

"Sellars?" His confusion was plain. "Who's Sellars?"

Orlando stared at him, trying to be certain this was not a ploy. "Let's make sure we're talking about the same thing. Someone gave you a harp, or showed you a harp, and after it gave you a message, it turned into a little golden . . . what?"

The stranger showed no emotion, but he took a long moment before he answered. "A gem. Like a diamond, but made of gold, and with a kind of light inside it."

Orlando felt a wave of relief. Either the Brotherhood was going a very long way around trying to chase down Sellars' people, or the stranger himself was one, too. "A gem. That's what we found, too."

"I'm confused," Odysseus said. "Did you—how did you get one? I thought I was the only . . . I thought there was no one else like me."

"No, there are quite a few of us." A sudden, sad thought flickered. "At least there were. But for some reason you didn't make it to the golden city, so you didn't meet them, didn't meet Sellars."

"Golden city?" He shook his head in confusion. "You've mentioned the name 'Sellars' twice. Can you tell me who that is?"

Orlando considered for a moment. "Did your . . . message say anything else?"

The man they knew as Odysseus paused, then recited, "'*If you have found this, you have escaped. You were a prisoner, and you are not in the world in which you were born.*'" He frowned, struggling. "That's pretty much it. I should have memorized it word for word," he apologized, "but . . . well, things have been a bit hectic."

"Was that all?"

"No. '*Nothing around you is true, but the things you see can hurt you or kill you. You will be pursued, and I can help you only in your dreams . . .*'"

"Dreams . . ." said Orlando. The hairs on the back of his neck lifted again, this time in a kind of fearful wonderment. "In dreams . . . ?"

"*'The others I am sending will look for you on the river. They will know you if you tell them the golden harp has spoken to you.'*" The stranger paused. "Does any of this tell you anything?"

"Is your name Jonas?" Orlando asked suddenly.

For a moment he thought the bearded King of Ithaca would leap through the door and disappear into the night. The stranger's eyes grew wide and bright, a deer stepping out of the brush into a hunter's flashlight beam. Then Orlando saw that they were glossy because they were filling with tears.

"My God," he said quietly. "Yes, I'm Paul Jonas. Oh my God. Have you come to get me out of here?"

"It's Jonas!" Fredericks said excitedly. "*Dzang,* Gardiner, we did it! This is so utterly, utterly chizz!"

But Orlando saw the hope shining in the bearded man's face, and knew that when the stranger discovered who it was who had found him, and how helpless they were themselves, he would regret this cruel moment of belief.

When the conversation slowed at last, Paul Jonas sat back on his stool. "You look tired," Jonas told him. "We've been up all night already, and we could go hours more, but we should all get some sleep."

"I am tired," Orlando said. "I'm not . . . I'm pretty sick. In real life."

Fredericks looked at him worriedly. Orlando tried to smile.

"I just can't get over this," Jonas said. "After all this time. It's all so strange, the things that have happened to you—the bugs, the cartoons." He laughed self-consciously. "I suppose some pretty odd things have happened to me, too, for that matter."

Even in the depths of his own misery, Orlando could not help feeling sorry for the man. "I couldn't do what you did," he said. "Going on like that without knowing why."

"You could and you would," Jonas replied. "Because what else does one do? But we still don't really know why, do we? About any of this. I can't get over the fact that you've met the bird-woman, too."

Orlando thought he almost sounded a little disappointed. "But we don't *know* her—not like you do. She just . . . I don't know, took an interest in us."

Jonas tugged at his beard, thinking. "There's so much still to try to figure out. Who is she, and why is she moving from simulation to simulation, like . . . like an angel? And the Twins . . ."

"I think that's the scanniest part," Fredericks offered. "They're so horrible, just from the one time we met them. I utterly can't imagine what it must be like to have them always hunting for you."

"As bad as you might guess," said Jonas darkly.

"Sellars told us that the Brotherhood were holding you prisoner." Orlando was having trouble keeping his eyes open, but there were so many things to consider he didn't want to sleep, no matter how sick he was. "That you must be a threat to them somehow. That's why we were supposed to look for you."

"Well, I wish your mysterious Mr. Sellars had told you *why* I was supposed to be a threat. Not only don't I feel very threatening, it would make me feel a little better about the huge hole in my memory. God, when you said my name, I . . . I thought you were going to give it all back to me. Tell me why this was happening." His face cleared. "But enough—a moment ago I called the mystery woman an angel. I was thinking about all that when I first came to this world, when I found that there could be more than one version of her in the same place—just like those people the Pankies I told you about were like the Twins, but they *weren't* the Twins."

"Man, those Pankies sound like my aunt and uncle from Minnesota," Fredericks said. "They were still giving me dolls when I turned fourteen. Yick."

"I've been thinking there might be as many as four different categories of people here in this network," Paul continued, ignoring Fredericks' unsolicited bit of family history. "Puppets, of course—the ones that are pure code, part of the simulations—and people like us. Or like the Grail Brotherhood, for that matter. Real people—Citizens, I think is the term." He stopped at a noise outside, clatter and conversation as new-wakened soldiers in the Myrmidon camp began to stack wood for a morning fire. "Good God," said Jonas, "it's almost dawn. But let me finish this thought. Other than Puppets and Citizens, I think there are two other types in this Otherland network, which I'm calling Angels and Orphans. The Angels are like the version of the bird-woman that came to me in dreams and here in the Odyssey world, and who was a goddess for you in Egypt—they can go from simulation to simulation, always retaining something of themselves. I guess the Twins might be that, too, unless they're really just some mad sadistic bastards working for the Brotherhood. Don't know which would be worse." He offered a grin without much humor in it. "But as for Orphans . . . I think they're like the boy I met, Gally, and like the versions of the bird-woman that I met in the Mars world, and as my character's wife here in ancient Greece. They kind of . . . take root in the simulation, somehow. Fill a space in it, perhaps in the same way that real people take on character roles, as you've done with Achilles and Patroclus, and I've done with Odysseus."

"Yeah, and who the hell is Patroclus, anyway?" Fredericks asked. "We know Achilles is the guy with the bad heel, but we've never heard of this Patroclus guy."

Orlando thought Jonas looked a little worried by the question, but was trying to hide it. "I'll tell you about that later. Let me get through this—it's slippery."

Fredericks nodded, abashed. "Chizz."

"So who would these personalities be," Jonas asked, "these Orphans, just floating around until they find a character to fill?"

Despite exhaustion, Orlando felt his interest quicken again. "The children, the ones like Renie's brother?"

"It seems possible."

"Whoo." Orlando shook his head, wonderingly. "And like those children in the Freezer, too. That would be so scantagiously weird." He considered. "But wouldn't that make your bird-lady one of them, too?"

"I suppose it's possible." Jonas seemed a little unsettled by the idea. "It doesn't quite feel true—but how can you judge anything around here?"

"Do you remember who she could be from your life? I mean, from your life before all this. . . ?"

"A little sister? A teenage girlfriend?" Paul shrugged. "No. But anything's possible."

"Jeez, there's just so much!" Orlando complained. "This whole thing—it gets weirder and weirder and weirder."

The reply from Jonas was interrupted by a rap at the door of the hut. Fredericks got up and opened it, revealing aged Phoinix, barely visible in the predawn light. The old man did not wait for formal greetings.

"Lords, I come to tell you that the Trojans are spilling out through the great Skaian Gate, a vast army of them. Already they are rushing across the plain, the wheels of their chariots roaring. Odysseus, your men of Ithaca are in confusion, not knowing where you are."

"Oh, my God," Paul said softly. His eyes darted, as though he were looking for somewhere to hide, or a convenient back door that would allow him to walk out of the simulation.

"I'm not fighting," Orlando said. "I can barely keep my eyes open—I can't even stand up yet!"

"Please, noble Achilles," Phoinix begged, "forget your quarrel with Agamemnon. The Trojans are coming down upon us, intent on putting fire to our well-benched ships so that we cannot return to our lands and our families."

"If he says he can't fight, he can't fight," Jonas told the old man brusquely. He turned to Orlando and Fredericks. "I can't just walk away from this," he said quietly. "Not without a risk of throwing the whole thing into chaos."

"You're not going to fight, are you?" Orlando was horrified by the idea they might lose Jonas so soon after having found him.

The man the Greeks called Odysseus turned to Phoinix, who was fidgeting in the doorway, torn between fear and excitement. "Go back and tell the Ithacans I'm coming. Achilles is still not well enough to fight. Hurry—there must be others who need your help. I will be right behind you."

Phoinix hesitated, then bobbed his head and hurried away.

"I'll do my damnedest not to get killed," Jonas said when the old man was gone. "Believe me, I'm not interested in having any songs made about me. But if the Trojans crush the Greeks, we'll never get into the city, if that's really where we're supposed to go, except as prisoners. If I remember the damn poem, everything was very evenly balanced, especially with Achilles not fighting. If all the troops who came with Odysseus bolt and run because I'm not there, that may skew the whole thing—the Trojans might be setting your ships on fire in a couple of hours."

Orlando watched him walk toward the door. Paul Jonas had described himself as a nobody—a museum curator, the kind of person who spent his weekends putting up shelves and reading the newspapers. But he was walking into a full-scale battle, risking his life in the hope of holding things together long enough for his questions to be answered.

Orlando could only hope he wasn't watching a very brave man going out to die.

Even though she had been in the States for more than a week, and had traversed the old Mason-Dixon line days earlier, it was only when she crossed into Georgia that Olga Pirofsky finally began to feel that she was truly in another country.

There was no obvious reason why that should be so. It was true that the eastern seaboard of the U.S. had been mostly indistinguishable from Canada—the polite fiction of North American solidarity held up far down the coast—but there was not a great deal of difference between Atlanta and any of the larger northern cities she knew, like Toronto or New York. Only the famous red clay, the odd, salmon-colored mud that showed through the greenery like slow-healing wounds, told her that the faceless, dignified suburbs were not her own, or that the cluttered squatter camps hidden off the main roads were full of Georgians rather than Pennsylvanians or even Canadians.

If there was anything that marked a real change, it was in the undertones—in the unspoken assumptions of the local broadcasters, in the slightly sullen tenor of the religious advertisements on walls and billboards and even in the bright holographic marquees, scintillatingly colorful images of Jesus, as well as more secular but equally magical figures—smiling Chicken Boy, Hungry Hillcat, The Price-Killer—that appeared like apparitions beside the freeways at night, flashing for a few heartbeats against the dark mass of buildings before vanishing in the rearview mirror.

Have You Thanked God Today? inquired neon-red letters along the side of a barnlike structure that Olga assumed was a church. *It's Time To Seek Truth* read another, marching slowly around the circumference of a floating kiosk two hundred feet off the ground, like the first proclamation from an alien spacecraft.

Not all these urgent communications could be read in the dark.

In true democratic fashion, some who could afford no more than a can of spray paint posted their own messages. *The Lord came Back,* read one scrawling graffiti on a freeway overpass, *and the Jews Killed Him again.* She supposed that referred to the Keever Cult, whose leader had been shot down in Jerusalem a decade earlier in an attempt to take over the Dome of the Rock.

Olga had grown sensitive to voices, and thought she heard something in these signs and wonders that might almost be the voice of dreams. Dark dreams. Worried dreams.

It's always those who have lost, and lost something important and painful, who cling to secrets, she decided. *Who believe in signs.* She thought back on her own youth among the gypsies and other circus folk, their strange certainties, their constant struggle with a universe that held tight to its mystery. *But these people lost their war two hundred years ago. They're rich and powerful, modern. What are they still looking for?*

It seemed mourning was not always easy to put aside.

She had abandoned the train in Washington, D.C., because her own voices seemed to be growing faint. She knew that she was going in the right direction—knew it the way a sunburned woman would know the direction of the sun—but the voices had become irregular and indistinct, as though something was frightening or distracting them. The vision of the great black spike still came to her as she slept, but now it often seemed only a memory of the earlier dreams. Olga could feel the radar in her head, which at first had led her so inexorably, beginning to become confused. She needed to get out of the fast-moving metal bullet that had rushed her down from Toronto. She wanted to smell unrecycled air, to feel wind against her face. The black mountain was out there—farther south somewhere—but she needed to feel the world properly to know where exactly in the world it was.

From time to time, while driving her rented car through the thick dark greenery of upper Georgia, or while unobtrusively taking up a seat in a roadside restaurant, she could look at herself as an outsider might—a fifty-six-year-old woman who had quit her excellent job and left her home and even her country behind, rushing toward something she did not understand because voices in her head made her feel she must—and knew that if she were that outsider, she could only judge herself insane. Who else had voices in their heads, after all? Who else would be positive that the children of the world were speaking to them in dreams? Crazy people, mad people. Oddly, though, the idea did not bother her.

I'm not worried about being mad, she realized one evening, waiting for a tired waitress to remember that she hadn't taken her order yet. *Not as long as I can understand that's how it is. There's still a lot of me that's Olga—still a lot of the same me.*

It was strange, to live both inside herself and outside, but it was also oddly calming. Despite her intellectual understanding that what she was doing made no sense, that it was in fact a textbook demonstration of some kind of schizophrenia, it was too powerful to resist. The voices might be imagination, corruption of the brain, but they were a part of her too, just as the more measured part was, and they were the deepest and most true thing she had felt for a long time. She had to treat them with respect— to do anything else would be a form of self-obliteration, and Olga was not the suicidal type. If she had been, she would never have found herself here, sitting in a poorly-lit restaurant waiting for a cheese sandwich, still alive decades after her beloved Aleksandr and their baby had died.

She drove out of Atlanta and through southern Georgia into Alabama, following the freeways past woods and scrubland crammed with trailers and even less permanent dwellings, or through soaring midtown metroplexes where the mirrored towers of the telemorphic barons filled the skyline, each shining structure proclaiming that even in a world where information ruled, information came from somewhere, was itself ruled from somewhere. *This is that somewhere,* the buildings announced on behalf of their owners. *Here, among the office castles, here and in thousands more across the globe. We control the gateways. We own the very electrons. The timid and downtrodden among you can wait for Jesus if you want to, but in the meantime, we are the Earth's rulers, the masters of the invisible spaces. We shine.*

Each night, Olga found herself lying in bed in one of an interchangeable array of roadside motels, the roar of trucks muted almost to silence by the override of her telematic shunt, her head full of pictures and soft voices. The children surrounded her like shy ghosts, each whispering sadly of a personal past that seemed lost, each seemingly content to recite that story over and over as part of a fragmented chorus. Like doves, they closed on her, nudging and murmuring, and each night they led her to a place where she could see the great thrusting shard of black standing against the sky.

Closer now, the murmuring throng told her. *Closer.*

She awoke each morning tired but peculiarly exalted. Even the occasional flaring pains in her skull, which only weeks before had filled her with constant dread, seemed almost worthwhile, just more proof she was connected to something important. For the first time in years something was happening to her, something that *meant* something. If the headaches had led to this, then despite the terrible pain they had not been a curse but a blessing.

The holy martyrs in the old days must have felt this way, she realized one morning as she pulled out onto Interstate 10 with an insulated coffee-pack in her hand, the cushioned mylar warming against her palm like some small creature stirring into life. *Every wound a gift from God. Each blow of the whip a divine kiss.*

But the martyrs died, she reminded herself. *That's what made them martyrs.*

Even this thought could not perturb her. The sky was gray and cold, the huddled birds unmoving knots along the road signs, but something inside her was so alive that she almost could not believe in death.

In some inexplicable way, a thousand miles from everything that was familiar, and thousands more from the place she had been born, Olga Pirofsky knew she was finally coming home.

CHAPTER 28

A Coin for Persephone

NETFEED/SITCOM-LIVE: "Sprootie" for Better Sexual Life!
(visual: Wengweng Cho's living room)
CHO: Chen Shuo, help me! I cannot find my Sprootie implant, and Widow Mai will be here for our date any minute. With no implant, she will mock my impotence!
SHUO: (whispers to Zia) Your father has too much faith in that Sprootie philosophical implant. (Out loud) Here, Mayor Cho. I have found it.
CHO: Thank Heavens! (rushes off)
ZIA: You are a wicked man, Chen Shuo. That was my panda implant for biology class.
SHUO: Make sure there are enough bamboo shoots in the refrigerator!
(audio over: laughter)
CHO: (offstage) I am glad I can now give proud, bumptious sex to the Widow Mai—she is so attractive! Her eyes, her wet nose, her beautiful fur . . . !
(audio over: rising laughter)
SHUO: That is what happens when a foolish man thinks Sprootie will solve all his sexual problems.
(audio over: laughter and applause)

THE Trojan attack seemed more a force of raw nature than an assembly of humankind—an armored mass flashing with bronze and silver that came howling out of the Skaian Gate and onto the plain like a terrible storm. The Greeks were still struggling into their own armor as the first of the Trojan chariots reached the wall around the Greek encampment. Arrows flew over the barricade and hissed down in a fatal rain. Soldiers stumbled and fell on their faces in the sandy earth, bristling with feathered shafts. Their companions could not even pull the bodies to safety or separate the wounded from the dead—corpses and living men alike were trampled as the Greeks rushed to find shelter from the Trojan archers.

The sun had barely appeared above the hills and the gate of the Greek encampment was already the site of a fierce struggle. Huge Ajax, so large in his armor that he seemed to be a god who had taken sides in the battle, had been caught outside when the gate was hurriedly closed and bolted; he was holding strong against the first Trojan assault, but he had only a few men beside him, and already several had dropped, skewered with arrows.

Paul had never seen anything so impersonally terrifying in all his life. As the first wave of Trojan charioteers and archers pulled their horses back from the wall and sped away along the edge of the great defensive ditch, the second wave wheeled in with hooves thundering like muffled kettledrums. One of Paul's Ithacans went down with a black-feathered arrow in his gut, coughing and spewing blood, calling to the gods to save him.

How can I avoid a battle that's right on top of me? Paul wondered desperately as the wounded man clutched at his legs. He crouched lower, doing his best to ignore the dying, bubbling thing beside him. Two arrows thumped into the shield, jolting his arm. *What am I supposed to do?* The spear clutched in his hand already felt as heavy as a lamppost. *I can't fight with one of these bloody things—nobody taught me how to do this!*

The Greek archers began scrambling up onto the embankment behind the wall, some with only half their armor. Many died before they could even get their bows strung, but others were able to begin returning fire. The Trojan archers and their charioteers could not use their shields while they were shooting, so when arrows began coming back from the Greek wall, the chariots pulled back to a safer range.

A ragged cheer went up from Paul's Ithacans as the hail of arrows slowed, but if any of them were foolish enough to think they had repelled the Trojan attack, that misunderstanding did not last long. The last wave of Trojan chariots was nearing the ditch, but this time they were not wheeling in to shoot and then gallop away. As the Trojan foot soldiers came roaring across the plain in a vast wave, the chariots' passengers dismounted and strode forward, hidden behind tall shields except for their expressionless, insectile helmets and their long spears.

But one moved faster than any of the others, rushing toward the Greek wall as though he meant to throw it down by himself.

"Hector!" shouted one of the Greeks. "It is great Hector!" Paul could feel dread ripple through the men around him. Elsewhere along the wall a few shouted insults down at Priam's son, but even those had a nervous sound.

"We cannot face him without Achilles," muttered one of the Ithacans. "Where is he? Is he going to fight?"

The Trojan leader did not respond to any of the insults, but hurried forward as though afraid that one of his own comrades might reach the wall first. By the time he had gone down into the ditch and begun clambering up the other side his shield was pincushioned with Greek arrows, but he carried it as lightly as if it were made of paper. He vaulted up to the base of the wall and brushed aside a thrown spear with his shield so that it caromed away and stuck quivering in the ground; a moment later his own long spear flicked out, swift and deadly as a bolt of lightning. The archer impaled on the spearpoint had only a moment to shriek before Hector jerked him off the wall like a harpooned fish and finished him with a brutal thrust and twist of his short sword.

The other Trojans leaped out of their chariots. Some were already scrambling up out of the ditch behind Hector, carrying not just spears and swords, but also long boards like ship's timbers. As their comrades in front and the archers on the far side of the ditch kept the Greeks busy, these men began digging beneath the edge of the wall, trying to find leverage to unseat some of the stones. Some were pierced by arrows and fell, but others continued the grim work. Paul knew that if they were given enough

time, they would succeed—the defenses of the Greek camp, unlike the ramparts of Troy, were not meant to withstand a determined siege.

Chaos swarmed around him as the morning sun rose higher,
with Greek defenders hurrying to this or that part of the makeshift
wall, wherever it seemed the Trojans were about to gain a foothold
and scramble over, always just managing to repel the assault. King
Agamemnon himself, accompanied by the hero Diomedes—Paul
had heard several people call him the best Greek fighter after
Achilles, and he had only to watch the man to know that he was
a star and not a bit player—made a sortie over the walls to save
Ajax, who had lost almost all his men, and had been reduced to
clubbing Trojans into bloody ruin with one of their own wall-
toppling timbers. Hector spotted Agamemnon from a hundred meters away down the wall, but by the time he could make his way
through the crush of his own men, fighting for their lives along
the Greek defenses, the high king and Diomedes had rescued the
giant. A fiercely-defended ladder allowed them all back over the
wall and left Hector raging in futility along the base of the ramparts, pounding his spear against his great shield so that it could
be heard even above the clamor of battle, demanding that they
return and measure themselves against him.

A Greek soldier found Paul and summoned him to Agamemnon, who stood spread-legged and trembling a short distance behind the walls, covered in bleeding scratches.

"Even now, noble Odysseus," the high king panted, "I can feel
the scales of Father Zeus tipping. Our side is plunging down,
down toward Hades, while Priam's cursed Trojans are lifted up
toward Heaven. Ajax and Diomedes have hurried back to the fighting, but I think neither of them can stop Hector, who clearly has
the hand of a god upon him. What will we do?" He wiped sweat
from his face. "Only Achilles can stand against him. Where is he?
Will you go to him, beg him to stand with us in this our dark
time?"

It was hard to look at this powerful man gone gray and quivering with strain and not feel at least a little pity. "He's ill. He
can barely stand—I've seen it with my own eyes."

Agamemnon shook his head and sweat flew from his ringleted
beard. Only a short distance away, one of the Greek defenders

fell back from the wall shrieking, a spear all the way through him, the bloody point standing out from his back. "Then some god has put this upon him, as Apollo earlier brought us plague for dishonoring a priest. Olympus must wish our destruction." The high king crouched, still panting. "It is hard. Have we not given them all the sacrifices they were due?"

"It's Hector, isn't it?" Paul said. "If we could stop him, that would take some wind out of the Trojan sails, wouldn't it?"

Agamemnon shrugged heavily. "I do not think even godlike Diomedes can stop him—have you not seen Hector as he slaughters Greeks and calls for more? Priam's son is like a lion, roaring in the middle of a village, while all the dogs hide beneath the houses."

"Then we shouldn't fight him one to one," Paul said. Something had to be done now or whatever purpose had brought him here, had led him to the boys Orlando and Fredericks, would disappear in a sea of blood. "We should drop a rock on him or something."

Agamemnon looked at him oddly, and at first Paul thought he was going to be denounced for insufficient nobility. Instead, the high king said, "You are indeed the cleverest of the Greeks, resourceful Odysseus. Go and find Ajax and tell him to come to me."

Paul hurried across the encampment. Already the ground was strewn with bodies that had been hastily dragged back from the walls so as not to impede the other defenders, and in many places so much blood had drained out that the mud was stained a sickening red.

How can they do it? was his helpless thought as he drew closer to the knots of combat rippling along the top of the Greek wall, each one a pair or more of men struggling to kill before they were themselves killed. *This . . . organized murder? Even in the real world, how could anyone rush into something like this, knowing that thousands of people are waiting to drive a spear into your guts or put an arrow in your eye?* He could hear Ajax's bellowing war cry now, loud as an angry bull. *But why am I here, for that matter? Why don't I just hide until this is over? To protect those two kids so they can help me find out why all this has happened to me?*

Whether you call it rotten luck or you blame it on the will of the gods, he decided as the screams of the wounded rose to the skies, disturbing the calm circling of the ravens, *I suppose it's what you do when all the choices left are bad ones.*

Paul was forced to take Ajax's place on the wall, and his more philosophical considerations were pushed aside by the necessity of not being killed.

The Trojans came on and on like an ocean beating against the rocks. For all the hundreds of them swarming along the walls of the Greek camp, there seemed to be thousands more just behind, pushing to take their places beside their comrades. At times it seemed as though the gods had indeed fired the Trojans with some kind of madness; no matter how many were killed, there were always others willing to drag the bodies aside and step into their places.

Several Trojan heroes fought in the assault—Paul heard their names shouted by both their companions and foes, as though the war were some kind of wild, dangerous sporting event, the foot soldiers on either side as thrilled as they were terrified to be sharing the field with legends like Sarpedon, Aeneas, and Deiphobus. But grandest and most terrifying of all was Hector, King Priam's son, who seemed to be everywhere at the same time—threatening to break open the camp gate by sheer strength here, then moments later leading an assault on a weak part of the Greek defenses. The Greeks offered champions of their own, Diomedes and aged Nestor, and Helen's spurned husband, Menelaus, but at this moment none of them could stand against Hector, who even managed to impale two Greek soldiers with one thrust of his spear so that they were pressed together like spoons in a drawer as they coughed out their lives. Hector did not stop to marvel at his own might, but put his foot against the nearest and pushed the bodies down the length of the shaft; they fell in a heap together on the ground as Hector turned his attention elsewhere. He seemed truly, as Agamemnon had called him, a lion among hounds.

Paul's existence had devolved into a constant rhythm of stabbing and retreating, taking lives to preserve his own. This ancient warfare was not like anything he had seen, no measured attack and counterattack of trained swordsmen. When the arrows and the long spears had hissed out and fallen, the survivors charged forward, shouting. Shields were locked so the combatants could stab at each other with their short blades. It was maddening, everyone so close in the thickest clinches that Paul could feel other men leaning on him as they fought, and there was little way to distinguish friend from enemy. He was himself injured several times, the worst a long bleeding runnel on his arm, an aching but fairly shallow wound from a spear that had partially pierced his shield. He wanted nothing more than to be off the wall and out of harm's way, but as the sun rose blood-red over the plain, it was clear that the Trojans smelled victory, and with Hector in his glinting armor savaging hapless Greeks like a jungle beast turned loose at a children's party, Paul began to feel his own weakness and weariness mirrored in the other defenders. It would all be over soon. He would finally get the black peace he had often wished for, now when he least desired it.

Trojans were massing again at the gate for another push. Paul stood, gasping for air, and watched them jostling up the gulley toward him and the other exhausted Greeks. With their shields above their heads, the invaders looked more like insects than men—Paul almost seemed to be looking down on a horde of cockroaches. Only one face could be seen: black-haired Hector stood in their midst like a warrior god, unafraid of Greek arrows, his blood-slicked spear held high in one hand as he used the other to shove his countrymen toward the vulnerable gate. Diomedes had dropped down from the wall in an effort to engage Hector, but the Greek hero had instead been hemmed in by other Trojan fighters; although he had killed several of them, he was still beset, several dozen meters away.

Just as Paul felt himself slipping into a sort of doomed fever-dream, hypnotized by the wave of shields slowly rising toward him, there was a heavy thump near his feet, then a hand like an industrial vise tightened on his ankle. He raised his stabbing-sword with exhausted languor, realizing only after a long instant that he had been grabbed from behind—from the Greek side of the wall.

The giant Ajax stood on the ground below him. He lifted the hand that had clutched Paul's leg.

"Help me up, Odysseus."

Paul braced himself, then reached down so Ajax could grip his

wrist and found that it was all he could do even to bear a por
tion of the massive hero's weight. Ajax pulled himself up onto
the wall, then took a moment to catch his breath, looking down
with distant malice on the swarming Trojans.

"I would have returned sooner," he rumbled, "but that pretty
boy Paris got over the wall with some of his men. We chased
him back out quick enough." Ajax was red-faced and sweating,
clearly exhausted, but his presence was still startling. If Hector
was a warrior god, this was some older, less subtle deity, a god
of mountains, of earth, of . . . stone.

Paul stared in amazement as Ajax bent and lifted the boulder
he had set down on the wall by Paul's feet, then gulped air and
straightened. "I wouldn't have wanted to carry this much farther,"
he rasped, the tendons on his neck swelling and stretching tight.
The stone looked like it weighed as much as a small car.

Heroes, Paul thought. *They're bloody heroes, and meant to be
so. That's what it said all through* The Iliad—*"a stone that ten
men of our day could not lift."*

"Now, where is that bastard Hector?" rasped Ajax. It took him
only a moment to find Priam's mighty son, who was shoving his
way to the front of the assault. "Ah," the giant grunted, then with
a creaking of muscles so loud Paul winced and shied away, he
heaved the boulder up above his head and held it there, tree-trunk
arms trembling. "Hector!" he shouted. "I bring you a gift from
the Greeks!"

Hector's handsome face turned upward just as Ajax hurled the
great stone down at him. The hero of Troy had time only to jerk
his shield up above his head and brace himself before the stone
smashed him to the ground. Rolling away, it killed three men, and
the Trojan line fell apart, bellowing in surprise and fear. A few
of them had the presence of mind to pull Hector's limp body
back with them as they retreated into the mass of the Trojan forces.

"You killed him!" Paul said, stunned.

Ajax was slumped, bent almost double with his forearms on
his thighs, trembling all over. He shook his head. "Great Hector
still moves—that I saw as they dragged him away. He is too strong
for one rock to kill him. But he will not fight again beneath today's
sun, I think."

Paul watched, amazed, as defeat eddied out through the Tro

jan ranks like the smell of a brushfire through a herd of deer. The soldiers assaulting the walls pulled back, and although arrows continued to fly, the great number of Trojans retreated with Hector's senseless body to the far side of the ditch. The gods, it seemed, had withdrawn their favor from Priam's forces . . . at least for a while.

"CODE Delphi. Start here.

"The sun is up, and all the royal household are atop the watchtower trying to make sense of what is happening in the battle by the Greek camp, which to those on the wall, at such a distance, can be little more than a scurrying of ants. The fighting has been going on for hours. Everyone knows that there must already be many dead on both sides. What a dreadful thing, to wait helplessly to find out who has survived, who has not! And I understand Priam and Hecuba and all the others only too well, for my own friends are somewhere on that field of slaughter. Even in this imaginary world humankind seems to be a machine built solely to damage itself. If the hand of evolution is at work, if somehow violent death serves some greater purpose, I cannot see it.

"Of course, I cannot see anything. What a fool I was, to think that these new senses, my new adaptation, made me any less blind. I am lost in the dark.

"No. Order, I must have some order. I do not know how long before something momentous happens—the Trojans parading back in victory or hurrying toward the gates in defeat. My own friends may need help when they return. If they return. No. I will make some order.

"I could sleep only a little after I last made a journal entry. As dawn approached, I woke from an unsettling dream where I was again lost in the blackness of the Pestalozzi Institute with the voices of lost children moaning down the hallways. I could not get back to sleep, nor did I try to for long. There is little enough I can do now, since I have cast the dice and sent my friends off to war, but there are things I can accomplish that are certainly better than lying on my back in the last hours of night, sleepless and brooding.

"Emily awoke when I got up. She was fractious, like a very young child, but perhaps some of the dream was still with me, because for the first time my heart truly went out to her. Whatever she is, she clearly did not ask to be drawn into our troubles and she is suffering because of it. In fact, she is suffering in ways that perhaps mean something important . . . but I am ahead of myself again. Order, Martine.

"Florimel was still sleeping, thank God—she needs rest badly—and the girl was afraid to stay by herself in the women's quarters, so I took her with me. I had no idea where I was going, but was determined to learn something of this famous city. We are here for a reason, I must believe that. The manifestation—the Lady of the Windows, as the monk named her—could not have been just a part of the House world, since she spoke of this simulation. Someone communicated with us, or tried to. Someone wanted us here. But who . . . and why? And where in this vast place, exactly, are we meant to go?

"As we went out from the women's quarters and through the palace, I heard voices in many of the rooms—prayers, quiet arguments, even weeping. Emily and I were not the only ones waiting uncomfortably for the dawn. Several times we were stopped by men of the palace, some armed, some apparently hurrying to King Priam's chambers with messages, but they were all distracted and seemed to want little more than to make certain we knew to stay away from the gates where the men were mustering. I had wondered if Priam himself might somehow be the focal point of our assignation from the Lady of the Windows, but could not see why. In any case, I had decided to wait to explore the king's quarters until daylight, when he and his advisers would be distracted by the battle on the plain, since this night it would be full of Troy's male leadership.

"Outside, all of the fabled city seemed to lie still but rigid with tension, like someone feigning sleep. As we went out across the great square, with even my expanded senses blurred by the mists that would disappear with dawn, the palace behind us seemed a dream-object, something that would not be as easy to return to as it had been to leave.

"Emily was quiet but watchful beside me, anxious as a cat stepping into an unfamiliar room. 'Do you feel something?' I asked her.

"She nodded, but almost reluctantly. 'I could . . . there is no word—smell, hear, see, all are misleading . . . I could *sense* a certain contraction of her attention, as though circumstance forced her to retreat into herself. 'Something . . . I feel . . . something.'

"Leading her like a horse that might bolt at any moment, I tried to distract her with small talk and little touches while slowly heading in the very direction which seemed to trouble her most. I have an idea, one that I cannot explain any more than I can name the senses that have been given to me in place of my sight, that Emily might somehow be sensitive to anomalies in the system, or at least to the particular anomaly which led us here. Renie has told me that the appearance of the Lady of the Windows struck Emily almost like a physical shock. I hoped that her discomfort was more than general, that perhaps now it meant we were near some similar locus.

"It was cruel. I do not like what I have had to do, and I fear that I will have worse things on my conscience before the end of all this, but I also know that we are desperate—that our ignorance has wasted time and lives.

"Long before we left the center of Troy, Emily's discomfort was so strong that I felt certain we were near something significant. We crossed through the market, the empty stalls like eye sockets, a few cloth banners still flapping, forgotten in the confusion of war. At one point, when she was shaking like a palsy victim and crying to go back to the palace, I perceived that a large building of some sort lay at the end of the street where we had stopped. I urged her forward, promising that soon we would turn back, and although her fear had almost overwhelmed her, managed to lead her to the steps of the huge, columned box. I had an idea what it was, but I wanted to be certain.

"'I know you're afraid, Emily,' I said. 'Let me go and see what this is, then I'll come back to you.' But to my astonishment, she insisted on going with me, more afraid of being alone than of her own internal agonies.

"Robed men stepped up to meet me as I entered through the great bronze doors. They were priests, and as I had suspected, this was the famous Temple of Athena. When they recognized me— I have not chosen to be Priam's daughter Cassandra out of pride or a desire for luxury, but for relative freedom—they stepped aside and let me enter.

"Despite the curtains that hid it, my senses told me that the shape at the back of the tall-roofed chamber was the huge wooden statue of Athena known as the Palladium. Recollections of the role of Athena in *The Iliad,* coupled with my guess at Emily's sensitivities, suggested that this might be the place for a nexus, or at least where a presence like the Lady of the Windows might make an appearance—there is a strong sense of the metaphorical in this Otherland network, perhaps part of the original design, perhaps what Kunohara referred to as our 'story.' But to my surprise, even when we neared the shrouded altar, Emily did not experience any greater degree of unease—if anything, the solid stone walls of the temple seemed to reassure her. She stood and waited almost patiently as I surveyed the room, trying to detect any sign of a hidden entrance that might lead to the maze Kunohara had mentioned, but without success.

"I led her out again, deciding that I must come back again in the daytime, when I could explore at leisure without inflicting pain on Emily and thus distracting myself. But to my further astonishment, her discomfort appeared again after we left the Temple of Athena, until by the time our circuitous route had almost brought us back to the palace she was not only shaking again, but weeping quietly. At last it got so bad that I had to let her sit on a low stone wall to try to compose herself. We were in what must have been, in Trojan terms, a relatively old and undesirable part of the acropolis. The temples and other buildings were small and, as best I could tell, in poor repair. The trees that lined the little street had grown until they almost completely blocked the sky. Water dripped somewhere onto stone, making a solemn, lonely sound.

" 'Is she ill?' someone asked me—a sound so unexpected in the last hour before dawn that I jumped. 'I can offer you shelter. Or did you wish to make an offering?'

"The stranger seemed to be a man bent with age, leaning on a staff, wrapped in a heavy if threadbare wool cloak. I could not see his face, of course, not as a sighted person would, but the information it gave me suggested he was not just old but very old, with no hair but a wisp of beard on his chin, and the way he held his head suggested he might be blind. The irony was not lost on me as I thanked him and told him we were almost home.

"He nodded. 'You will be from the palace, then,' he said. 'I can hear it in your voice. A few others have wandered down from there in the last weeks, seeking otherwise forgotten gods and goddesses.'

" 'Are you a priest?' I asked.

" 'Yes. And my patroness, Demeter, puts a special burden on her priests for the care of women and their misfortunes. Still, considering the terrible flowering of widowhood, you would think my lady's temple would not be so deserted, the altars empty of offerings. But since her daughter Persephone is the unwilling wife of Death himself, perhaps it is not so surprising after all.'

"Something in his words set me tingling. 'May I see Demeter's temple?'

"He pointed to a place away from the road, even deeper in the trees, where a small and unprepossessing facade was backed against a hilly prominence. 'Come with me. I fear that with my eyes useless, it is not so clean as it used to be. I will have help when it is time for the Mysteries, but the rest of the year . . .'

"Emily suddenly leaped up. 'No!' she cried, "no, don't go, don't go in there!' She seemed hysterical, but would not take a step closer to the tiny temple, even to drag me away. 'Don't— oh, take me back! I want to go away!'

"My heart was beating fast as I made my apologies to the priest and pressed an *obolos*—a small coin—into his hand. Emily was so relieved that she almost ran the rest of the way back to the palace, every step increasing her happiness. As for me, I was— and still am—full of thoughts, full of frustration at my dim memories of Classical mythology, but also full of hope.

"Demeter, the goddess to whom that neglected temple on that lonely road is dedicated, was the Earth Mother, but she was also the mother of Persephone, a girl kidnapped by Hades, Lord of the Dead, and Demeter herself went down into Hades' kingdom to bring her daughter back. There is much I do not recall—I seem to remember that Persephone ate pomegranate seeds while a prisoner underground—and thus her mother could not bring her back to the sunlight again—but I believe I can remember one important thing. The Elysian Mysteries—the Mysteries to which I am sure the ancient priest referred—were a ritual journey through death and into life, a religious ceremony of the highest order. And, if I remember correctly, the participants are led through a maze. Yes, I am certain . . . a maze.

"There is much to consider, but perhaps we have at last received a piece of luck in our favor. If so, then we also owe something to Emily—perhaps our lives. Already I feel sorry for the times I have been able to feel only annoyance toward her.

"Much to consider. Order is still out of reach, but I think I perceive the first suggestions of something like it taking shape. My God, but I hope that is true.

"*Code Delphi.* Hmmm. My choice of a code phrase to mark out these entries begins to seem . . . rather Delphic. In any case . . .

"*Code Delphi.* End here."

EVEN in the depths of one of the weariest, most bone-sick slumbers of his life, Paul could not escape his dreams.

The vision coalesced out of darker and more indeterminate dream stuff like bright coral growing on the blackened, decaying timbers of a mud-bound shipwreck. The shadows in his mind began to glimmer with red light, which quickly became vertical streaks stretching up, up, up, until they described a vertex lost from sight, the outline of a great scarlet-splashed, black arrow pointing upward and away into infinity—a mountain, unimaginably large, incomprehensibly high. The uppermost part of the cone that he could see bulked cold and dark—lifted out from the blackness of vacuum space into visibility only by those few blood-colored reflections skittering along its convoluted surface—but the base of the impossible mountain, set continent-wide on the endless plain where Paul stood, was awash in fire.

He watched the flames licking along the base of that great black mass and knew that he had seen it before in another dream. It was no real surprise when he heard her voice.

"Paul, the time is growing ever shorter. You must come to us."

He could not see her, could not see anything but the tall endlessness of the mountain sitting in its nest of flames. His eyes were drawn back to the place where the black of the mountain became inseparable from the black of space. A point of light hovered there, where before there had been nothing, as if the mountain's uttermost peak had scraped a star loose from the firmament.

Slowly, as gradually as a feather falling off the wind on a mild spring day, it was drifting down toward him.

"How do you come to me like this—in dreams?" he asked. "How is it that I can talk to you, but I know I'm dreaming?"

The voice grew closer and more intimate, even as the sparkle of light spun slowly down toward him. *"Dreaming—that is a word that means little,"* she said in his ear. *"You are not a thing, separate from everything else. Not here. You are like a shoal of fish in the ocean—you are a concentration, a congregation, but still the sea flows through you, around you, over you. There are times when you are at rest, and the current of the ocean in which we all swim flows well from me to you."* The gleaming point seemed larger and more diffuse now, a shining, diaphanous shape, an "x" made of watery light, as though she did indeed come to him through the pressures and refractions of some liquid medium.

At last he could see her face. Despite all the confusion and misery, the familiar features warmed him. "Whatever you call it, a dream, not a dream, I'm glad you've come to me again."

Her expression was more troubled than tender. *"I am strained to the utmost, Paul. I do not think that I can force myself across this distance again, even through what you call dream. You must understand that time is short now."*

"What can I do? I can't come to you if I don't know where you are." He laughed, an angry, sad sound that he had never heard in a dream before. "I don't even know what you are."

"What I am is not important now, because if you do not come to us, I think that soon I will be nothing."

"But what can I do?" he demanded.

"The others you seek—they are close to you. You must find them."

"That boy Orlando and his friend? I found them already . . . ?"

"No." He could hear her frustration, although her face was still little more than a tissue of light, a will-o'-the-wisp faint against the silhouette of the black mountain. *"No, there are others, and they are waiting between the old wall and the new. All are needed. I will try to lead you to them, but you must search carefully—my strength is limited. I have forced the mirror too many times."*

"Forced . . . What does that mean? And even if I find them, where are you? Where can I find you?"

She waved a hand, her light beginning to fade. At first he thought it was a gesture of farewell, and he shouted in frustration—he could dimly feel his body, a distant thing, twitch in weak response—but then he realized she was pointing, even as she flickered and vanished.

"*The . . . mountain . . .*" Her voice came to him from far away, then followed her shining form into oblivion.

The black mountain had changed. The endless, razor blade vertices had twisted and wrinkled, the shape transformed as though some galaxy-wide hand had twisted its proud rigidity like paper. It still loomed, still stretched to the sky, but it was crooked along its length now, the flame-lights painting texture up its broad reach, to the place where it spread wide across the sky like a black mushroom cloud, like . . . like a tree.

Paul yearned toward it, desperate to make sense of what he was seeing, intent on memorizing everything, but already the fires were beginning to burn low and the black tree to disappear into the background of night. As it finally merged with the blackness, his perspective changed, as though he grew or the god-tree shrank. Something that had not been there before gleamed in the uppermost branches.

He squinted. It seemed shiny, curiously cylindrical, a silvery shape perched in the boughs. It was only in the last moments before it disappeared entirely that he recognized it for what it was.

A cradle.

Paul dragged himself to his feet, groaning. All around him, the Ithacans who had survived the day slept where they had sat down at battle's end, lying at odd angles with slack mouths or contorted brows, as though mimicking the unhappy dead.

The Trojans had only retreated a short way back from the Greek settlement, and although the setting of the sun had brought the battle to an end, for the first time in a long time the Trojans were camped on the plain instead of hidden behind the walls of their great city. There was no doubt they would press hard when dawn came, trying to recapture the momentum from the day before and push the Greeks into the sea.

How can a virtual body hurt this much? Paul wondered. *Or if it's my real body hurting, why did these bastards code the thing so I could absorb so much punishment through the system? Was it really that important for a battle to feel realistic?*

He shuffled toward the wall and climbed to where he could see the lights of the Trojan fires, and beyond them the slumbering bulk of the distant city. The dream was still so much with him that he half-expected to see a vast black peak blocking the stars, but nothing disturbed the line of low hills behind Troy.

What did it mean? A cradle? In the treetop, like "Rock-a-bye Baby"? He massaged his throbbing arm and looked out across the Trojan encampment, a thousand fires gleaming like cracks in a cooling lava flow. *And who is out there?* He had to assume that "between an old wall and a new" meant on the plain. Why did the woman, whoever she was, have to speak so cryptically? It was like being dragged through one of the Greek myths, all prophecies and tragedy.

There's a reason, he told himself. *There must be. I just haven't figured it out yet. Something about the system, maybe—or about her.*

Paul wrapped his cloak more tightly, then made his way down from the wall and headed across the sleeping camp toward the gate, amazed to find so much stillness in a world that only hours earlier had been as mad as a Bosch painting. He would tell the guards that he was going out to spy on the Trojans—hadn't Odysseus done something like that? He would much rather have slept and nursed his wounds, but he knew this might be his last chance to find those unspecified others waiting between the walls. After all, if things went the same way tomorrow, there might no longer be a new wall, and he himself might not be around to care.

SALOME Melissa Fredericks was not an average girl.

Her mother had found that out early, when her daughter had rejected not only her given name, but "Sally," "Sal," "Melissa"— a failed flanking exercise—and even (and perhaps least surprisingly) "Lomey," her mother's last desperate attempt to avoid "Sam." But Sam she was, from the time she was first old enough to make it stick, which she achieved by the civilly disobedient means of refusing to answer to anything else.

Her father, who had never liked the name Salome, had acted as a fifth column, constantly "forgetting" his promise to his wife not to call Salome by that terrible, masculine name, and so Enrica Fredericks had finally given in.

This early experience had confirmed Sam in the value of quiet noncompliance. She was known to her teachers as a good, if not deeply motivated, student, and to her friends as a quiet but surprisingly self-confident companion. Many of her schoolmates had been experimenting with sex since before the official dawn of their teenagerhood. Sam Fredericks did not know exactly what she *did* want in the way of romance—she had a lot of thoughts and imaginings, none of them quite clear—but she knew much better what she *didn't* want, and that definitely included being groped by any of the boys with whom she went to school. Drugs hadn't made much of a blip on her radar either. What Sam really wanted more than anything else, more than good grades, acceptance by her peer group, or the startling array of sensations, real and virtual, that were available to a young person of her age, was to be more or less free from the pressures of her parents and her classmates until she was grown up and could make up her mind about what she wanted out of life. She saw this watershed as coming in the distant but not impossible future, perhaps by the time she was sixteen or so.

Meeting Orlando Gardiner had confused her in a number of ways, none of them immediately obvious to a girl as self-assured as Sam, who made friends easily even if she didn't connect deeply, who played soccer so well she had been elected team captain twice (and refused the honor both times), and who convinced teachers by the serenity of her countenance that she probably knew answers that she in fact didn't, causing them to turn and expend their vital teacher-charisma on some more needy student. Even in the world of role-playing Sam had always been a good-natured individualist, never a leader, never a follower, until Pithlit the Thief had encountered a young barbarian named Thargor in The Quirt, a seedy little tavern which was one of the nicer spots in Madrikhor's Thieves' Quarter. Thargor, already a semilegendary figure in the Middle Country, knew Pithlit by reputation as well, having heard that the slender man was unusually trustworthy for a thief, and since Thargor was in need of a lock-picking specialist on his quest to liberate some objects from a rich warrior baron, he had offered Sam's alter ego a reasonable percentage.

The theft had gone well, once the barbarian had dealt with an unexpected trio of mastiff-headed, human-bodied sentries, and the casual partnership had rolled over into other ventures.

A year later, Sam Fredericks had been astonished to realize that Orlando Gardiner, a boy she had never seen, had somehow become her best friend in the world, and the only person besides her parents (not counting a previous obsession with Pain Sister, one of the musician/heroines from the *PsychiActress* show, which despite all the allowance money she had spent on posters, holographs, and interactives, was now relegated in Sam's mind to the status of stupid kid stuff) that Sam could honestly say she loved.

It wasn't the kind of love you saw on all the teenage shows on the net—it didn't seem to have anything to do with sex, for one thing. Even Pain Sister, for all the cartoonish nature of her presentation, had inspired a bit of a warm itch, but what Sam felt for Orlando was something much less obvious. She had wondered once or twice if it might be that kind of love, of course—the kind that led people like her parents to get married, and led people on netshows to blow up banks or drive off cliffs or shoot themselves—but it seemed like something far different. Before she had known about Orlando's condition, she had often wondered what he looked like, and had even constructed a sort of imaginary version of him in her mind—skinny, with floppy hair, old-fashioned eyeglasses, and an endearingly crooked smile—but the idea of meeting him in person had never been anything other than odd and, increasingly as time went by, uncomfortable.

Uncomfortable, of course, because Orlando Gardiner thought Sam Fredericks was another boy.

So as the months slipped past, and as one year of friendship became two and more, she had grown increasingly conflicted in her feelings toward him. Their rapport was deep. Their ability to joke and even insult each other without ever wondering if the other person would be offended was one of the greatest freedoms she had ever known. His sharply mocking sense of humor was an idealized version of her own, and Sam was just selfless enough not to resent that, just quick enough to appreciate it properly. She thought that, in his own way, Orlando was as sharp as the peo-

ple who got paid millions of credits on the net to be clever for a
living. And she was his best friend, too, the one person he all but
admitted he could not do without. How could she not love him?

At the same time, although she had not realized it, she had become increasingly committed to a friendship that would never
leave the net, because to meet face-to-face was to reveal how,
without intending to, she had let their relationship deepen under
false pretenses. What had felt comfortable to her, being treated
like another boy, being allowed that freedom to be tasteless and
crude and pushy without her parents or other friends judging her,
had become increasingly precious.

She hadn't realized until the horrible moment of discovery, and
the aftermath in which Orlando revealed his own secret, that the
knife could cut both ways. The idea that when she had thought
Orlando was opening his soul to her, so much so that she had felt
stabbed with guilt at her own duplicity, he had been hiding a secret even more important than hers, was surprisingly painful.

But the horrible wonders of the Otherland network had distracted them both, and in recent days Orlando had been even more
obsessed by his own condition, that dreadful downhill slide that
he clearly wanted to discuss, but which Sam could not bear to
talk about. She was too smart to think reality could be changed
just because she did not like it, but she was also superstitious
enough to believe in some deep part of herself that she might be
able to make something stay away longer by ignoring it. Despite
her occasional troubles and confusions, Sam Fredericks had led a
happy life in the suburbs of Charleston, West Virginia, and she
was smart enough to know she was not equipped to handle something like this.

Orlando was sleeping, his golden, muscular Achilles body
stomach-down and his thin garment disarranged. He looked, she
thought, like some kind of ad for men's cologne. If she was ever
going to find herself excited by sharing a room with a boy, this
should be the time, but all she could think about was how sick
he was, how brave he was being.

The battle had come so close during the afternoon that she
could hear Trojan voices screaming insults at the Greek defenders. Achilles' Myrmidon soldiers, so desperate to fight that they

trembled like leashed dogs, had given her regular reports of the progress of the attack, and although the Trojans had been pushed back at the last, no one seemed to doubt that some kind of heavenly balance remained in their favor. Several of the Myrmidons had even risked being labeled cowards—apparently a fate worse than death in this place and time—to suggest to Orlando that they should take to their boats. After all, if they weren't going to be allowed to fight, the soldiers had pointed out, why should they sit still and be slaughtered when the Trojans came over the wall tomorrow?

Orlando, who had been fighting waves of weakness since they came to Troy, had at this point been able to do little except listen, eyes bleary and head barely upright. Much as it pained Sam to see him that way, she was even more frightened of what might happen if the soldiers were right. Even in her current sim she could not carry his Achilles body more than a few hundred meters—if the Greeks broke through, she would either have to desert Orlando or they would die together. The man Jonas had confirmed what she and Orlando had already felt in their bones: getting killed here would be the real thing.

Paul Jonas himself had not returned to them after the day's fighting, which might mean nothing, but might just as easily mean he was one of the corpses lying in a mass grave beside the camp wall, or even one of the unlucky bodies stiffening out on the plain. Had she dared to leave Orlando, she would have been looking for Jonas even now. She was desperate for advice.

Sam Fredericks was not a reader, as Orlando never tired of pointing out to her, but she was not in the least bit stupid either. She could read perfectly well, but life just seemed too short to spend much time squinting at text when you could find all the stories you wanted on the net, or make your own. But Orlando's gibes had not gone entirely unfelt, and his constant harping on *The Lord of the Rings* had made her feel she was missing something—if nothing else, a key part of her best friend's identity. So without telling him, she had downloaded a text copy and read it. It had not been easy, and had taken her the best part of a year as she picked it up and read a little, then got bored and gave it up again for easier pursuits. Even when she had finished the monumental task—who could even *dream* of writing so many words about something?—she had not mentioned it to Orlando, in part because she really hadn't liked it very much, and had been mostly unmoved by the long, flowery descriptions of trees and hiking and meals. But she had believed she understood a little better what it meant to Orlando—so much of it was about losing things you loved. In fact, as she thought about it now, watching the sleeping Achilles who was also her best friend, it made even more sense.

But one thing in particular that had stuck with her, and which she knew was as important to Orlando as anything else in the book, was what it meant to be a hero. He always talked about how the real heroes weren't like Bulk U Six in *Boyz Go 2 Hell* or one of those kind of things—not just people who could slaughter everyone else and make clever comments while they were doing it. Real heroes were like the characters in that man Tolkien's story, who did what they had to even if they hated it, even if it took their own lives away from them.

Sam was frightened. She didn't know what was going to happen next, but she had little doubt that the next morning would see the Trojans coming over the wall, because the Greeks' greatest warrior, Achilles, was currently the sim of a dying teenager. All day long the messengers had come from Agamemnon, promising the Earth if only Achilles would come out and fight, reminding him how just the sight of him in his armor would fill the hearts of the Greeks with joy and those of the Trojans with terror.

She stared now at the polished armor on its stand. In the red light of the coals, it seemed made of rubies, or lacquered in blood.

There was a character in *Lord of the Rings* with her name. He had been the companion of the main hero, and when the hero had been sick, almost dying, it had been that Sam who took up the burden and went forward. It had been Sam's time, Orlando never tired of saying. Time be a hero. *When it comes,* he had often said, *you know it. You may not want to know it, but you know it.*

She had thought he meant make-believe heroes, like his own Thargor, Scourge of the Middle Country, but she believed now he had really been talking about himself, about just getting out of bed to make it through each day. She was also beginning to suspect that way back then he had been speaking to a version of herself that hadn't arrived yet—talking to the Sam Fredericks who was sitting here tonight, huddled on a cold dirt floor in a camp on the Trojan plain, while Orlando tossed in shallow, unsatisfying sleep. And now she finally understood.

It was Sam's time to be a hero.

CHAPTER 29

Some Roadside Attractions

NETFEED/NEWS: "Coralsnake" Creator Claims Free Speech Rights
(visual: Möven under arrest outside Stockholm house)
VO: Freelance gear writer Diksy Möven, creator of the "Coralsnake" virus which destroyed nodes and disrupted service all over the net last year, says he is going to argue at his trial that his arrest represents an illegal suppression of free speech.
(visual: Attorney Olaf Rosenwald)
ROSENWALD: "My client's position is that the net belongs to everybody—it's a free medium, like the air we breathe. UN guidelines make it clear that all citizens of the world have the right to free expression—what difference, then, between words and lines of code? My client is no more to blame for people accepting his code and then having it damage their equipment than a journalist who writes about crime is to blame for people reading that book and then committing a crime. My client happens to like expressing himself by writing complicated strings of symbols—symbols that, if improperly used, might happen to destroy some property..."

CALLIOPE Skouros had already been in the Yirbana Gallery for half an hour when Stan arrived, grumpy and out of sorts. "You couldn't think of a better place to meet for lunch?" He was trying to work his glasses back into place by nose-wrinkling, since his hands were shoved deep in his coat pockets. "Do you know what it's like trying to park here?"

"You should have taken public transport," she said. "We won't need the car this afternoon."

"We didn't need to leave the office, for that matter," he said. "We could have called out for *yum cha.*"

"If I eat another dumpling this week, I'll die. Besides, I had a reason for wanting to come here." She pointed to the exhibit, an array of lovingly carved wooden posts that might have been an Expressionist sculpture of a city skyline. "Know what those are?"

"Betting you'll tell me." Stan slumped onto the bench. For a man who spent a lot of time in the gym, he hated to run anywhere.

"Tiwi grave posts. Funeral markers."

He squinted at the collection of unique wooden shapes. "Yeah? You looking for some kind of ritual angle? Seems to me that it was your victim Polly Merapanui who was Tiwi, not the suspected murderer."

"But as far as we can tell, he didn't really have an Aboriginal identity of his own. Dr. Danney said he hated that stuff. His grandmother had a strong tribal heritage, but Dread himself never had a chance to connect with it directly, since his mother apparently ran away when she was quite young, and by the time our boy came along, Mom was way too busy working the corner and putting black ice in her veins to be joining any Aboriginal Cultural Revival groups."

"Well, our late friend Polly doesn't seem like the ACR type either."

"I know, but . . . but there might be something there. I have some ideas, I just can't make them gel." She leaned forward to read the display screen, which seemed to float a ghostly inch in front of the wall. "It says, 'Tiwi grave markers were known as *pukumani,* a general term which could mean sacred or taboo. They were erected above the grave, sometimes months after the actual burial, and became the centerpiece for complicated mourning ceremonies which might include several days of singing and dancing.' "

"Sorry I missed that—things seem pretty quiet now."

Calliope scowled. "Look, there's something going on, I'm just trying to figure it out. There has to be a reason for the woolagaroo number—the stones in the eyes. There also has to be a reason why he picked Polly Merapanui to murder. He knew her from Feverbrook Hospital. How did they wind up together in Sydney? What did she do to make him so angry?"

"All good questions," Stan said evenly. "So what do they have to do with wooden grave posts?"

"Probably nothing," she sighed. "I'm reaching. But it's one of the most famous Tiwi exhibits in the city—I just thought I'd have a look."

His smile was surprisingly kind. "Maybe we should go grab some lunch—this is our break, after all. Isn't there a coffee bar or something in here?"

Calliope was having a salad week, and even bravely avoided the feta cheese she could, with fairly clean conscience, have crumbled on top. She was determined to knock off a little weight. She still hadn't gone back to see the waitress at Bondi Baby, and was using the prospect as a dangling carrot: lose five kilos, get a new outfit, go see if the girl with the tattoo had really been giving her meaningful glances or had just forgot to put in her contact lenses.

Stan, who was one of those nauseating people who could eat like a pig and still remain thin, had loaded his tray with not just sandwich and crisps, but two desserts.

"I have a theory," said Calliope, mournfully prodding a section of tomato. "Just listen to it and don't tell me I'm full of shit until I finish, okay?"

Stan Chan grinned around an excessive mouthful of sandwich. "O aheah—ire aray."

"Ever since I realized this, it's been bothering me. Our boy Johnny's real name, or at least the name on the birth records, is John Wulgaru. But his father was almost certainly this Filipino guy . . ."

"Uh irate."

"The pirate, yeah. And none of his mother's long-term

boyfriends were Aboriginal. And Wulgaru wasn't a last name she used, nor did it turn up anywhere in the three generations of her background I tracked down." Calliope gave up trying to spear the tomato and picked it up with her fingers. "So what does it mean? Why would she give him that name? If it was just a name that didn't mean anything, I'd say forget about it, but it's the name of a particularly creepy Aboriginal monster, a wooden doll that comes to life, and it's also the MO for how he killed Polly Merapanui, so it has to mean *something*."

Stan had finally swallowed. "I'm with you so far, but everything up to 'what does it mean' is the easy part."

"I know." She frowned. "Now we get to my theory. The woolagaroo was—what did Professor Jigalong say? 'A metaphor for how the white man's attempts to control the native people may eventually backfire on him,' something like that. Maybe that's what his mother meant him to be from the very first. Maybe she meant him to be a monster—or at least an instrument of revenge."

"Slow down, Skouros. You already said his mother was too busy hooking and hyping to join any political groups."

"I'm not necessarily talking about something *political*." She realized that her voice was getting loud; several tourists at other tables had turned to see what the argument was about. "I'm just talking about . . . I don't know, hatred. If you were an Aboriginal woman in the Cairns ghetto, maybe beaten and raped by your own father—there's suggestions of it in the social services files— and certainly beaten and raped by customers, isn't it possible you might want to strike back at the world somehow? Not everybody poor can be noble about it." She leaned closer. "The few juvenile records we've got from Jonny Dark's childhood are horrible— you've seen them. Whipped and burned, locked in closets for days, thrown out to live in the streets once when he was three years old just because he pissed off one of his mother's so-called boyfriends. Who's to say some of it wasn't intentional? That she wasn't . . . molding him. Turning him into a weapon against the world that had hurt her."

Stan was already on his first dessert, and for a moment, as he speared and chewed, she thought he had not been listening. "It's interesting, Skouros," he said at last. "And there may be some truth to it, but I've got a couple of problems right up front. First, he *hated* his mother—you heard that Doctor Danney guy. If she'd lived, he would have killed her himself. Why should he take up some crusade on her part?"

"But that's what I think happened! I think his mother raised him to be this . . . woolagaroo, this killing monster, but what she mostly made him do was hate *her.*"

"So where does our victim come into this?"

"Maybe she tried to be his friend, and was just too close to something dangerously damaged. Worse, maybe in the way girls do sometimes, she tried to take care of him. Maybe . . . maybe she tried to be his mother."

Stan slowed down as he started on his second dessert, as though taking the word "ruminate" literally, and did not speak for almost a minute. "Yeah, I see what you're saying," he finally said. "I'm not sure about it, but it's interesting. I'm not certain it helps us forward any, though, and I sure as hell don't see what it has to do with grave posts."

Calliope shrugged, then reached out her fork and pilfered a corner off Stan's piece of pie. He raised his eyebrows but said nothing—it was an old dance of theirs. "I can't tell you. I just have a feeling that this Aboriginal myth stuff isn't simply window-dressing. He didn't mutilate that girl just to make some mocking point about his cultural heritage. No, it's more like . . . like he was trying to liberate himself from it, somehow. Turn it back on his mother, tell her, 'This is what I think of your plans.' But she was gone, already dead. He had to find someone else to act all that anger out on."

Stan pushed back a little way from the table so he could cross his legs. The slanting sunlight through the high windows, the green of the trees in the Botanical Garden, the shrill voices of children as they skidded along the food-service aisle, all made Polly Merapanui's death seem almost fantastically remote. *But that's the point, isn't it?* Calliope thought. *We do what we do so that people can feel that the bad stuff is in boxes, kept separate—that when someone does something horrible, people like us are right behind them, ready to take them off the streets.*

"I've been doing some thinking of my own," Stan announced suddenly. "But first, I have a question. Tell me again why exactly they threw this case out of the "Sang" killer investigation—or the

"Real" killer, or whatever the hell they're calling it this week . . . the "Sang-Real-Good" killer, maybe—why did they throw Merapanui back out again?"

"The only reason the task force picked it up in the first place was because the weapon was the same—their killer uses one of those big Zeissing meat-choppers too. Oh, and some of the wound-pattern stuff was slightly similar, mostly because of the size and shape of the knife, probably. That and lack of forensic data. But everything else is different. The Real Killer—they only called him that because his first victim's name was Real, and because he never shows up on surveillance footage—goes after well-to-do white women, usually youngish, but certainly not girls like Polly. The mutilations on his victims are a lot less bizarre than with Merapanui, too. Why?"

"Because something's been bothering me about the information in this case, and . . . well, it's just strange the way the records have been erased."

"People hack into systems all the time, Stan, even our system. Don't you remember that multiple-murder on Bronte Beach, where the guy's girlfriend . . ."

"That's not what I'm talking about," her partner said impatiently. "I'm not surprised someone hacked into the system and jiggered this guy's records, what's suprising is the way they did it. I know about this stuff, Skouros—I did an academy refresher in it just a couple of years ago. It usually goes two ways. Either they work and work at it until they manage to get into one system, but don't realize how many parallel systems there are, and leave all the cross-referencing, or they do a sensible, professional job once they're in and drop a dataphage."

"Some of that data-eating gear."

"Yeah. Which will systematically follow the name or whatever from system to system until everything's gone—everything, including stuff about people with the same name! You can buy the service from any black market hackshop. But what our boy's done—if it was him—is somewhere in between. He's left little bits of information lying around all over the place. Kind of sloppy, in fact. It's like he managed to do stuff no normal gear-jockey can do, in terms of getting into lots of different systems without being detected, but didn't know enough basic stuff to get a data-eater and do the job right."

Calliope wasn't sure where this was going. "So?"

"So it just made me wonder about the Real Killer and his weird luck at staying off surveillance systems, camera drones, you name it. I don't know. I'm still thinking about it."

"That seems like a real stretch, Stan. Besides, if the task force didn't find any hard connection between our murder and all of theirs, we'd probably be spinning our wheels worrying about it. Let's face it—we've got a small-time case and we should just get used to it."

Stan nodded. "Maybe, but you haven't heard the rest of what I'm thinking about, and some of what you've said today, your theory, just makes me wonder about it more. Let's assume that what you've said is true, right? This kid was raised in a brutal environment, with a mother and a succession of boyfriends we *know* abused him—that much isn't speculation. But let's go with your idea, that his mother systematically tortured him, trying to turn him into some kind of human terrorist weapon. Filled him full of monster stories, religious mania, all but put the knife into his hands and told him 'kill, kill, kill!' Okay. The profile fits—he's been in trouble since he was little, there are suspicious deaths all through the record, as well as what we know are a few actual murders, whether or not you buy into the polite fiction of temporary insanity. Then he goes into Feverbrook Hospital and scares the bejesus out of everyone with how smart and quick and evil he is—old Doctor Danney comes up about a fingernail short of calling him the Antichrist—where he meets Polly Merapanui. Then, a short time later, our Jonny Dark aka John Dread, he suddenly dies. But we don't believe that now, do we? In any case, all his records are buggered, so it's hard to know what's really going on. A few months after our boy's so-called death, Polly Merapanui dies, brutally mutilated, a real psycho number. All this sound more or less right?"

Calliope had been hungry, but she did not feel like finishing her salad now. "Yes. More or less right."

"You see where this is going, don't you?" Stan put his feet on the floor and leaned in, his eyes intent. "Little Johnny Dread has been shaped from birth to inflict pain and suffering. He's gotten away with everything so far. He's an intelligent, cruel, sociopathic bastard—maybe he is the Antichrist, for all we know." His grin was without humor. "So . . . why would he stop killing? He's like an adult in a world of children, as far as he's concerned. He can get away with anything. *Why would he stop killing?*"

Calliope sat back and closed her eyes for a moment. "He wouldn't, of course."

Stan nodded. "That's what I think. So he's either gone—way gone, America, maybe Europe—or he's here. Could even still be in Sydney. Right under our noses. And he's still murdering people."

As the sun went behind a cloud, a shadow passed across the tall windows of the museum restaurant. It might have been Calliope's imagination, but for that single moment everyone in the wide, echoing room seemed to fall silent.

THEY stopped to get out and stretch their legs along the motorway. The Drakensberg stretched above them, sharp and forbidding. The dim late afternoon sun had already begun to drop behind the peaks; shadows blanketed the mountainside and the patches of high snow seemed weirdly luminous.

"This . . . I haven't been here before." A puff of Del Ray's vaporous breath swirled in the crisp, cold air as he squinted up at the line of jagged peaks. "It's impressive, I guess. I can't say it looks like a very nice place to spend a lot of time."

"You are just ignorant, man," Long Joseph said cheerfully. He had been here before, only a few weeks earlier, and felt a certain expansive possessiveness about the place. Besides, it was always good to one-up a young know-all like Renie's ex-boyfriend. "This is your heritage. It is . . . it is part of history, you see? Those little people, those Bushmen, they used to live all up around here. Before the white man came and shot them all."

"Some heritage." Del Ray clapped his hands together. "Come on. I don't want to be looking for this base in the dark, and God knows how far we'd have to go to find a place to stay for the night."

"No, you don't want to be running 'round here in the dark," Long Joseph said. "Very tricky."

*   *   *

The ride up had been long and tedious, but once Joseph had established his right to play the radio and occasionally sing along— a right granted in return for a promise that he would keep his feet off the dashboard, whether he thought the leg space was too cramped or not—he and Del Ray had worked out a reasonably practical arrangement. The tenor of the day had further improved when Joseph found a handful of coins wedged in the crack of the seat, and made Del Ray pull over at a combination store-and-she-been along the motorway, a place too small to have a hologram, or even a neon sign, but whose painted advertising carried the only words that mattered—"COLD DRINKS." Despite a few desultory protests from Del Ray that the money by rights belonged to his brother Gilbert, since it was his car, Joseph spent his wind-fall on four bottles of Mountain Rose. He drank half of one be-fore they were out of the muddy parking lot, but then, remembering that there would be no alcohol at the Wasp's Nest base, put the cap back on, and congratulated himself on his restraint.

While Del Ray drove, Joseph gifted him with some of his philosophies and thoughts, and handled the map when the situation called for it, since the trip-reader in the old car had long since given up the ghost. To Del Ray's astonishment, Joseph proved useful with Elephant's map, and he even congratulated the older man once when he guided them through a particularly tricky set of back roads successfully.

Joseph, in his turn, would not have gone so far as to say he *liked* the young man, but he had managed to get past some of his prejudices, both acknowledged and unacknowledged—the former being his distrust of anyone who wore suits and spoke netcaster-style English, the latter being Joseph's dislike of anyone who would break off with his daughter. Long Joseph might think Renie was a bit of a nag and a know-all, but that was *his* privilege. For anyone else to disapprove of her—well, that seemed little different than disapproving of Joseph himself. She was his daughter, wasn't she? Everything she was, she owed to his hard work and thoughtful care.

So the thaw had been slow, but it had been a thaw nevertheless, and as they wound their way up the mountain roads, the car rocking on inadequate springs, Joseph found himself thinking that perhaps there was hope for this young man after all. Poke a hole in some of his college-boy ideas, rub a little dirt on him—although that part seemed to have happened already—and maybe he and Renie would make a match after all. This fellow was broken up with his wife, and when all this virtual, military-base nonsense was done with, he would be able to get a new suit and a nice new job, wouldn't he? That university degree had to be good for something besides making a man talk funny.

Joseph could not help thinking that it would be nice to see Renie settled. After all, a woman without a man—she couldn't really be happy, could she? She was certainly going to find it hard to give her father proper attention in his declining years if she had to be working all the hours of the day.

"Is this the road?" Del Ray asked, breaking into a sunny reverie in which Joseph was enthroned on the couch of his expensive new flat, with a big Krittapong wallscreen always on, entertaining his grandchildren with stories of how contrary and difficult their mother had been. "It's hardly a road at all."

Joseph peered out the dusty window. When he saw the brush-choked cut in the road, he didn't need to look at the map. "That is it," he said. "Looks like we clear it out a bit when we brought that car of Jeremiah's through—it was more tangled up before. But that is the road."

Del Ray swung onto the narrow track; within moments it widened into a well-maintained road which angled up the mountain in a series of steep switchbacks, hidden from below by the tall brush and trees. The sun was gone now, although the sky was still a thin, pale blue; the mountain's flank was mostly shades of purple and gray, the vegetation more shadow than anything else.

"One thing or two I have to tell you about this place," Joseph said. "It is very big. And it is a military place, so you don't go touching anything I don't tell you to touch. Whatever your Elephant friend say, it is a secret, and we are going to keep it that way."

Del Ray made a noise that almost sounded impatient. "Right."

"The other thing I have to let you know, this man Jeremiah Dako?" Joseph pointed up the mountain in the general direction of the base. "The man who is staying there, helping me with things? Well, he is a homosexual man." He nodded. He had done his duty.

"And?" said Del Ray after a moment.

"And what?" Joseph raised his hands. "There is no 'and,' man. I am just telling you, so you don't do something foolish. You have no cause to insult him—he has never done anything to you."

"Why on Earth would I want to insult him—I haven't even met him!"

"That's fine, then. He and I, we had to work things out. I mean, I had to make him understand how things were. But he is a human being, you see. He has feelings. So I don't want you to say anything foolish—besides, I don't think you his type. He likes mature men. That is why we had to have some conversation, he and I, so I could let him know for certain that I am not that way."

Del Ray began to laugh.

"What?" Joseph scowled. "You think it is a joke, what I'm telling you?"

"No, no." Del Ray shook his head, dabbing at the corner of his eye like it itched. "No, I was just thinking that you are a piece of work, Long Joseph Sulaweyo. You should be on the net. You should have your own show."

"I don't think you mean that for real." Joseph was displeased. "Think it's supposed to be a joke on me. I'm going to have to stop paying attention to you, you act like that. Leave you on your own, make all the mistakes you want."

"I'll try to muddle through," Del Ray said, then: "Jesus!" He stomped on the brake and the car skidded a bit on the gravel. Del Ray flicked up the high beams. "I almost didn't see it."

"That is the gate," Joseph pointed out, willing to bend his new rule of silence at this crucial juncture.

Del Ray pushed open his door, then leaned back in and set the parking brake. Joseph got out and walked with him to the chain-link fence. "It's locked. I thought you said you had to break it open before."

"We did. I made Jeremiah step on the gas even though he was frightened, we went through just like that fellow in *Zulu 942*, where they have the armored car. Boom!" He clapped his hands together. The sound died quickly in the thick, damp brush that hemmed the road. "We just knocked it open."

"Well, it's locked now." Del Ray shot him an irritated sideways glance. "We're going to have to climb over the top. Let me go turn off the engine, and you go find me a stick to push up the razor wire so we can squeeze underneath without getting our skin peeled off."

Joseph, although annoyed to be given the go-fetch part of the job, found a piece of broken branch that seemed adequate, then remembered the precious cargo he had left in the car. He put a bottle of Mountain Rose in each of his pants pockets, then the two remaining containers in his shirt.

Del Ray had just slid the toe of his scuffed, once-stylish boot into the wire of the gate, preparing to climb, when Joseph suddenly put a hand on his shoulder.

"What?"

"Just . . . I am just thinking." He stared at the shiny chain that joined the two halves of the gate, the very formidable-looking lock. "Who put this chain here?"

Del Ray put his foot back on the ground. "I assumed it was your friend Jeremiah."

"I told you, he isn't my friend, he's just a man who is in the mountain, and I was in the mountain, too." Joseph shook his head. "But Jeremiah didn't put no lock here, I don't think. Isn't no easy way to get out of that base—it took us most of a day to get in, and we had help from that old man and that French woman." He rubbed at his beard stubble. "I don't know. Maybe I am thinking too much, but I don't make sense of there being a chain on this gate—it being all locked up tight like this."

Del Ray looked around. "Maybe there are . . . I don't know, park rangers or something. Isn't this part of one of the nature preserves?"

"Maybe." Joseph could not help seeing in his mind's eye that shiny black van and its dark windows. He felt a glimmer of regret he had not mentioned it to Del Ray before. "Maybe, but I don't like to see it."

"Well, if you didn't come out this way, how did you get out?" Del Ray took the stick from Long Joseph and poked at the chain. It made a very solid *clink*.

"One of those, what do you call them, air shafts." He pointed. "It come out on the far side of the hill, round over there."

Del Ray sighed, but he looked troubled. "So you think—what?

That there could be someone who came in after you and Renie did? Who could that be?"

Long Joseph Sulaweyo knew that this was the time to mention the van, but couldn't think of any way to do it that wouldn't give Del Ray the right to yammer at him about what an old fool he was. "I don't know," he said finally. "But I don't like to see it."

They turned Gilbert's old car around in the open space in front of the gate and drove it a few hundred meters back down the road. Del Ray found a spot where the brush was high along the side, and although the increasingly slippery, bumpy ride and the ugly scraping sounds from the undercarriage suggested that getting it back on the road might be more difficult than getting it off had been, they hid it there before heading back uphill. As the twilight failed the mountain air rapidly became colder, and Joseph shivered as they made their way back across the uneven terrain, wishing he had brought warmer clothes with him. At first, with the squeeze bottles bumping in his shirt, he had felt like a guerrilla fighter with a bandolier of grenades. Now the bottles just felt heavy.

Even though it was getting dark quickly, they picked a spot well away from the road and gate for climbing the fence. Del Ray managed to prop the razor wire well enough that he got over with only a few rips in his already tattered clothes, but the stick popped out just as Joseph was pulling his leg through and he tumbled down the fence to the ground, cursing Del Ray's incompetence. The wounds were painful but not deep, and the polymer bottles had survived the impact handily, so Joseph at last decided it was worth continuing. He put on an expression of not-so-cheerful martyrdom and limped up the hill after Del Ray, heading for the base's huge front door.

The scrub was low, so Del Ray said they should get down and crawl. Joseph thought this was the kind of foolishness that came from too much time watching netflicks, but the younger man insisted. It was cold, uncomfortable work, and since Del Ray refused to turn on the flashlight he had brought with him, they spent almost as much time climbing out of thorny ditches or struggling back around unclimbable rocks as they did moving forward. When they finally reached a spot where they could see the entrance, they were both scratched and breathing hard. Joseph's urge to knuckle the back of Del Ray's stubborn head was cooled by the broad smear of light along the mountain stone and the sound of voices.

His first feeling when he saw the vehicle parked in front of the massive door was actually relief that it wasn't a black van. The truck standing with its back gate down was something larger and more primitive-looking, almost like a safari wagon, covered with thick gray plating. A spotlight on top of the cab illuminated the concrete slab that barred entrance to the mountain retreat. Three men, their shadows thrown in stretching black along the stone, were huddled in front of the code-box. Another pair sat on the gate of the truck, smoking. The faces of these two were hard to see, but one of them had a large, ugly-looking automatic rifle across his lap.

Joseph looked to Del Ray, hoping in a strangely dreamlike way that the other man would say something to make everything normal and acceptable, but Del Ray's eyes were wide with fear. He reached out and grabbed at Joseph's arm so hard it hurt, then pulled him back and away from the immediate vicinity of the squat, gray truck.

They stopped fifty yards down the hillside, now panting even harder.

"It's them!" Del Ray whispered when he had caught his breath. "Oh, Christ! It's that Boer bastard, the one that burned my house down!"

Joseph sat on the ground, filling his lungs. He couldn't think of anything to say, so he didn't bother. He pulled the open bottle of wine out of his shirt and had a long drink. Strangely, it didn't make him feel any better.

"We have to get out of here! They're murderers. They'll rip our heads off just for fun."

"Can't do it," Joseph said. It didn't even sound like his own voice.

"What are you talking about?"

"They trying to get in the mountain. You said these people, they are angry at Renie. You think I can just go off and leave my daughter in there? You don't understand what I said before, do you? She in a big old machine. She . . . she is helpless."

"So what are we going to do? Walk up to them and say, 'Excuse us, we just want to go inside, but we hope you don't mind waiting out here?' Is that what we're going to do?" Sarcasm and terror made an unpleasant combination. "I've dealt with these people, old man. These are not some local bad men—these are killers. Professionals."

Joseph could hardly make sense out of anything, but he had a picture in his brain of Stephen lying in that terrible hospital bed, covered in plastic like some piece of meat in a store, and it filled him with shame. Everything else in his head was in shadow except that picture. Stephen and now Renie, too, both caught like animals in traps. His own children. How could he walk away again?

"Why don't we go in the way I come out?" Joseph said suddenly.

Del Ray stared at him as though he had lost his mind. "Then what? Hide in the mountain and wait for them to break in?"

Joseph shrugged. He had another drink of wine, then put the cap back on and slid the bottle into his shirt. "It is a military place. Maybe there are some guns in there, we can shoot the bastards. But you don't have to go—I suppose it is not a place for a fellow like you." He stood up. "Me, I'm going."

Del Ray was staring at him as though faced with an entirely new kind of animal species. "You're crazy. How much of that wine have you drunk?"

Joseph knew that the other man was right about how foolish this was, but no matter how he tried, he could not lose the picture of Stephen in the bed. He tried to make another picture, a sensible one of himself getting in the car with Del Ray and driving away down the mountain, but he just could not imagine it. Sometimes there were things you had to do. Wife died, leaving you alone with two children? What could you do? You went on, even if you had to stay drunk most of the time to manage it.

Joseph began clumsily to make his way back up the moonlit mountainside, this time angling away from the entrance, circling toward the spot on the far side where he remembered coming out. A rustle in the brush startled him so that he almost wet himself. Del Ray had caught up to him, eyes still wide, breath steaming. "You are crazy," he whispered. "We're going to get killed, you know that?"

Joseph was already out of breath, but he doggedly continued to clamber up through the jagged outcrops. "Probably."

For some reason, it was far more difficult getting back in through the air shaft than it had been getting out. Four bottles of Mountain Rose clicking and sloshing in his clothing might have had something to do with it, not to mention a continuous mumbling litany of complaint and disbelief from Del Ray, who was crammed into the shaft behind him.

"Why don't you drive away, then?" Joseph said finally, wedged into an angle of the shaft and taking a breather. "Just go."

"Because even if they kill you and your entire damned family, that doesn't mean they won't come back and get me, too, just to leave things neat." Del Ray bared his teeth. "I don't even know what this is *about*—not really. Maybe we can find out what they want to know from Renie. Cut a deal, something."

The cramped, unpleasant journey came to an end when they reached the far end of the air duct and discovered that the screen Joseph had originally removed had been replaced, neatly screwed back into its socket.

"For Christ's sake, man," Del Ray fumed. "Just kick the bloody thing out."

Joseph gave it a good sharp crack with the heel of his shoe, enough to strip one of the bolts and shove a corner free. After a few more kicks the screen clattered down to the cement floor.

They hurried through the wide, cavernous garage and into the base, Del Ray staring all around. At a different time, Joseph would have been happy to give him a proprietorial tour, explaining what all the things were—as far as he had been able to discover during his wandering explorations—but for now all he wanted to do was find the deepest, most secure part of the underground fortress and pull everything in on top of himself. He was already regretting the foolishness of his heart that had forced him to climb the air shaft. The empty base was full of echoes and shadow. The thought of being chased through it by men with guns made him want to throw up.

It took a little while to find the elevator. When it dropped them down into the hidden basement lab and the door hissed open, something anticipatory about the darkness outside the car made Joseph pause, his heart beating hard.

"Jeremiah . . . ?"

"Step out," a voice said, squeezed and tight and not immediately recognizable. Joseph stepped out. A sudden light in his face dazzled him.

"Oh my Lord, it is you. Sulaweyo, you fool, what have you been doing?" Something clicked and the overhead fluorescents warmed halfway, filling the tomblike lab with yellow light. Jeremiah Dako stood before them with a flashlight in his hand, wearing a dressing gown and unlaced boots. "And who is this . . . ?" he asked, staring at Del Ray.

"No time to talk," Del Ray said. "I'm a friend. There are men outside, bad men, trying to get in . . ."

Jeremiah spoke briskly and evenly, but he was clearly frightened. "I know. I thought you were them. I was going to hide and try to hit someone with this, then go hide again." He lifted the metal table leg he had been holding in his other hand. "If I had time, I would have jammed the elevator. I suppose we'd better do it now—let's push that table into it."

"How did you know?" Joseph demanded. "How did you know about those men? And how is my Renie?"

"Your Renie's fine, more or less," Jeremiah said, then scowled. "If you're so worried about her, why the hell did you take off?"

"Good God, man, you are not my wife!" Joseph stamped his foot on the floor. "How did you know about those men outside?"

"Because I've been talking to someone, and he told me about them. He's a friend, or at least he claims he is." For the first time, the strain Jeremiah was under truly began to show. When he spoke again, it was with the exhausted resignation of a man who had just sighted a flock of winged pigs, or received incontrovertible proof of snow flurries across Hell. "In fact, he's on the phone right now. He says his name is Sellars. Do you want to talk to him?"

CHRISTABEL was tired, even though she had slept in the back seat for a lot of the trip. She didn't know where they were, but she had a feeling her daddy had been driving in some kind of big circle. They had stopped several times, always in campsites or turnouts that were out of sight from the main roads, and every time her daddy had gone back to take off the wheel-compartment cover and talk to Mister Sellars. The terrible boy was still being quiet, but he had eaten a whole candy bar Christabel's mommy had given them to share, and even had licked the chocolate off his fingers, like he never got to eat candy or something.

They were driving slowly through a city. Christabel had never seen it before, but the name "Courtland" was on lots of the stores, so she thought that might be its name.

"We need to stop for a few minutes," her father said. "I have to do something. I want the rest of you to stay in the car. I shouldn't be too long."

"Is that the reason we came all the way up into Virginia, Mike?" her mother asked.

"More or less, but I thought it wouldn't hurt to take a bit of a roundabout route." He looked out the window for a while and didn't say anything, then steered the van into a service station. "Fill it up, honey, will you?" he asked Mommy. "And use cash. I'll be back in twenty minutes. But if I don't check back in with you by half an hour, just go on along this street until you get to the Traveler's Inn. Cash there, too. I'll catch up to you." He suddenly smiled, which was good, because Christabel had not liked how serious his face had been. "And don't eat all the pillow-mints before I get there."

"You're scaring me, Mike," said her mommy, almost too quietly for Christabel to hear.

"Don't worry. I just . . . I don't want us to do anything stupid. I'm still trying to figure all this out." He turned around in his seat so he could look at Christabel. "You do what your mother says, okay? I know things are a little strange at the moment, but it's all going to be all right." He looked at the boy, who looked back at him. "That goes for you, too. Just listen to what the senora has to say and do it, and we'll all be fine." He tossed the keys to Mommy and got out of the car.

While her mother went to give money to the man in the glass box, Christabel watched her father walk around to the back of the station, where he disappeared. She was just about to turn away when she saw him come out the other side and walk across the parking lot toward a building which had a big sign over the front door that said *Jenrette's*. It looked like the kind of place they stopped to have lunch when they were on other car trips, restaurants where they had pies under little glass bowls on the front counter, and it made Christabel think about food. Her father walked in through the front door. She couldn't help being sad when it swung closed behind him.

It was all very upsetting and confusing. She was glad her mommy and daddy had met Mister Sellars and they wanted to be his friends—that terrible big secret had begun to feel like something alive in her stomach that would never lie still. But ever since it had happened, everything was different. They were going somewhere, but no one would tell her where, and Mommy and Daddy still had lots of whispering arguments. Also, there was the strange thing of leaving Mister Sellars curled up in the back of the truck, hidden in that small place like one of those Egypt mummies Christabel had seen on a really interesting and creepy program on the net, until her mother had noticed she was watching something about dead people and made her switch to another node so she wouldn't have bad dreams. But that was just what it was like, except he wasn't dead, and she didn't know what to feel about that, exactly.

Her mother was having a long conversation with the man in the glass box. Maybe trying to use paper money was confusing to them—Christabel had almost never seen her mother do it before, but Daddy had got a whole lot of it out of the bank before they left, a big pile of paper with pictures on it, just like in old cartoons.

"Afraid your mama gonna take off and leave you with me?" the terrible boy Cho-Cho said behind her. "You ain't taked your nose off that glass since she left, *mu'chita*. What, think I'm gonna eat you, something?"

She looked at him with her best You-Go-Away look, but he just grinned. He did look smaller and less scary now that he was clean and wearing other clothes, but the broken-out tooth made her nervous. He always looked like he might get close enough, then bite.

She wasn't sure why, but she suddenly got up and pulled open the van door. "You're just stupid," she told the boy, then slammed the door and ran to her mother.

"What do you want, sweetie?"

She couldn't quite explain why she had gotten out, so she said, "I need to use the bathroom."

Her mother asked the man in the glass box something, and he pointed to the side of the building. Her mother frowned. "I don't want you in there by yourself," she said. "And I've got my hands full. You see that restaurant there? The one that says 'Jenrette's'? You just go over there and ask to use their bathroom. Don't talk to any strangers except the ladies behind the counter. Understand?"

Christabel nodded.

"And come right back. I'll watch you till you're in the door."

Christabel skipped across the parking lot, turning back once to wave to her mother. The van looked faraway and strange, a familiar thing in an unfamiliar place, and she couldn't help thinking about Mister Sellars, lying there curled up in the dark.

The restaurant was busy, with lots of women and men in brown clothes going from table to table, taking food to people and pouring water. The seats were the kind she liked, squishy booths where you could slide from one end to another, something that always drove her father crazy. 'Christabel,' he would say, 'you are a child, not a ball bearing. Just stay in front of your plate, will you?'

Her daddy was in here, she remembered. Doing something, maybe making a call. She didn't really need to use the bathroom, not much, so she stood on tiptoes near the front counter, looking around the big room trying to find him.

He wasn't in the back, by the comm box. To her surprise, he was sitting in one of the booths, only a short way away, with his back to her. It was him—she knew the back of his head almost as well as the front—but there was someone else sitting in the booth with him.

For a moment it felt like another big, bad secret, and she wanted to turn around and walk back across the parking lot and get into the van, even if the boy was going to smile at her and say things that made her squirm. But the man her daddy was talking to didn't look scary, and also she wanted to see her daddy's face, see if he was smiling or serious or what, because she needed something like that to make the confusing parts less confusing.

She walked toward the booth so slowly that two different women in brown almost ran into her. "Mind where you're going, muffin," one of them said, and by the time Christabel had finished apologizing to the woman's back as she hurried on, her daddy was staring at her.

"Christabel! What the . . . what are you doing here, baby?" He looked as though another thought had just come to him. "Is everything okay?"

"I just came in to use the bathroom." She looked shyly at the man sitting with her father. He was wearing a brown-gray suit, and had very dark skin and black curly hair cut close to his head. When he saw her looking, he smiled. It was a nice smile, but she didn't think she was supposed to smile back, even if her daddy was right there.

"Well . . . well, damn," her father said. "I'm kind of in the middle of something, honey."

The man sitting across from him said, "That's okay, Major Sorensen. Maybe your little girl would like to sit down for a moment."

Daddy had a funny look, but shrugged. "I can't stay much longer anyway—my wife's just filling up the van."

"What's your name?" the man asked her. When she told him, he stuck out his hand to shake. His palms seemed very pink because the rest of the skin was so dark, almost like they had been scrubbed clean, but they were dry. He didn't squeeze too hard, which she liked. "Nice to meet you, Christabel. My name is Decatur, but my friends just call me Catur."

"Say hello to Mr. Ramsey," her daddy said.

"Oh, please, not Mr. Ramsey. Like that old joke, Mr. Ramsey's my father. Or, I suppose it would be more accurate to say *Captain* Ramsey is my father. You see, I've had a bit of experience with the military myself. Lived on more than a few bases, growing up." He turned to smile at Christabel again. "Do you like the base where you live, pumpkin?"

She nodded, but she could tell from her daddy's face that he didn't really want her here, so she didn't say anything as she climbed up onto the seat next to him.

"Look, Major," the other man said, "we've had a chance to look each other over, and I hope I've passed the test. I can understand you wanting to get settled in, especially with this young one here—she must be tired after a day on the road. But how about I come by your motel tonight? I need to meet this Sellars face-to-face even more than you needed to see me. There's . . . there's just so much to talk about."

"I'm with you there, Ramsey." Her father rubbed at the side of his head for a moment. "I don't mean to seem . . . suspicious, or difficult, but you can understand that things have been happening very fast the last few days."

"For me, too," Ramsey said, and laughed. "Oh, have they ever." He reached for the check. "So if you need an evening to yourself, I'll understand. Heaven knows, I've got a lot of casework backed up. I can spend my evening in gainful employment with just my pad and a motel desk. But I can't hang around in town forever, and I really need to have a proper conversation with Sellars, face-to-face."

"It . . . well, as far as that goes, you should brace yourself. He's a little startling to look at."

Ramsey shrugged. "I'm not surprised. I got the feeling from the few conversations we've had that he spends a lot of time indoors."

"About the last thirty years, yeah." Her father's short laugh had an edge to it that Christabel didn't understand.

"Well, in any case, this whole thing scares me to death, but I'm looking forward to meeting him in the flesh, too—whatever he looks like. He must be a pretty amazing human being."

Her father laughed again, but this time it definitely sounded unhappy. "Well, that's the really interesting part. See, he's not really a human being in any normal sense of the word . . ." He stopped suddenly and for the first time in a couple of minutes, looked at Christabel, as if he had just remembered she was there, gently kicking her heels against the bottom of the booth. His face was just the same as the time he had complained to her mommy that it was "pretending-to-be-Santa-time again," without realizing she was sitting on the kitchen floor where he couldn't see her.

Christabel didn't understand what he meant, and was just about to ask him when she realized that someone else was standing right behind her father. The man named Catur Ramsey was looking up at this person with his eyes narrowed. Christabel turned at the same time her father did. For a moment, it was confusing, because it was a face she knew so well that she couldn't figure out why it seemed so wrong.

"Well, here you are," said Captain Ron. "Jesus, Mike, when you get lost, you really get lost. I've been looking all over North Carolina for you, and here you've slipped off to another state on me."

Christabel's daddy was very pale. For a moment she thought he was going to be sick, the way her mother was that time when they had started to talk about making a brother or sister for Christabel, and then stopped talking about it. For days her face had been the gray color Christabel's father's was now.

"Ron. What the hell are you doing here? How did you find me?"

Captain Ron waved his hand. A few people across the aisle turned to look at the man in uniform, but then turned away again. "We've got an APB out on you, asking for help. Some of the local smokeys picked you out and passed it on."

"What's this about?" Her daddy tried to smile. Across from him, Mr. Ramsey had gotten very quiet, but his eyes were bright. "Can't a man get away for a few days, Ron? You . . . you know we need some time off. Some kind of disaster at the base? I can't imagine why else you'd be . . ."

"Yeah, disaster, you could call it that," said Ron, cutting him off. Now that she looked at him, she could see that something was wrong with him, too—he had the same tight look on his face he'd had the last time he came to the house. "Seems like our old buddy General Yak is on the warpath. Seems like he wants to talk to you personally—personally, got it?—and that means all leaves are canceled and all bets are off." For a moment his face changed again, as though something was shifting behind a mask. "I'm sorry, buddy, but this is a direct order from the top of the food chain, and there ain't a thing I can do about it. I don't know what's going on, and I hope I'm still your friend, but you're going to have to come with me." He paused and fingered his mustache for a moment. "We're not going far—Yacoubian's set up a command post right in town here. Don't know if that's anything to do with you. I hope not." For the first time he seemed to see Christabel. "Hello, Chrissy. How are you, sweetie?"

She didn't say anything. She wanted to run away, but she knew that would be the worst thing. She could almost hear Mister Sellars' voice in her ear saying, "Secrets are scary, Christabel, but if there's a good enough reason for them, then they might be the most important thing in the world. Be careful."

Ron turned back to her daddy. He had looked at Mr. Ramsey a few times, but it was almost like he had decided the other man wasn't there. "Let's leave your little girl with her mother and then we can get going."

Her father shook his head. "Kaylene . . . she's off running errands. We're just waiting for her. Won't be back for an hour or so—we were going to get a little lunch."

Ron frowned. "Well, then I guess we'll have to bring her along with us. I'll leave a number here at the restaurant for her to call, find out where to pick up your daughter."

Even Christabel noticed that he said "pick up your daughter," not "pick up you and your daughter." She was really, really scared.

Her father didn't move or say anything. Captain Ron nodded his head toward the front of the restaurant, and for the first time Christabel noticed that a couple of soldiers in MP helmets were standing outside the glass by the front door. "Let's just make it quick and painless, shall we, Mike?"

"I should introduce myself," Mr. Ramsey said suddenly. "My name is Decatur Ramsey, and I'm Major Sorensen's attorney." He turned those bright eyes on Christabel's daddy, as if warning him not to say anything different. "Is this an arrest?"

"This is military business, sir," Captain Ron said. His voice was polite, but he looked angry. "I don't think it's any of your affair . . ."

"Let's decide that when we have a better idea of what's going on, shall we?" said Mr. Ramsey. "If this is just a routine matter, I'm sure there won't be any problem with me coming along to wait for . . . for Mike. I can even stay with Christabel until her mother comes. But if this highly unusual procedure *is* of a legal nature, then I think it will be to everyone's advantage to have me along." He sat up a bit straighter. His voice had turned very hard. "Let me make it a bit clearer, Captain. You have MPs, and you are directing Major Sorensen to accompany you, even though he's on a granted leave. If this is a formal arrest, then your jurisdiction is clear, and I'll work with the system as appropriate. If this *isn't* a formal arrest, and you insist on taking my friend out of here against his will without letting me accompany him . . . well, I know a surprising amount of people in local law enforcement here in Virginia, and I know for a fact there's a couple of State Troopers having some coffee and pie over in the corner of the room. I'd be happy to bring them in to help discuss the legality of dragging a man out of a public restaurant without proper authorization."

Christabel did not understand what was happening, but she knew that she wanted more than anything in the world for it to stop happening. Nothing went away, though. Her daddy and Captain Ron and Mr. Ramsey all just sat or stood where they were without saying anything for what seemed like a long time.

When Captain Ron spoke he sounded more unhappy than mad, although there was still plenty of angry in his voice. "All righty, Mr.—what did you say your name was? Ramsey? You come on along. We'll bring the little girl, too, make it a family outing. As I said, all I know is that a very high-ranking officer wants an immediate conversation with this man on a matter of military security. So we'll all play nice. Do you want my serial number?"

Mr. Ramsey's smile was very cold. "Oh, I don't think that's necessary, Captain. I'm sure we'll have plenty of chance to get to know each other."

As they stood up, the two MPs came in through the door and stood, waiting. Christabel held her daddy's hand while Captain Ron went to the front counter and left a message for Mommy, then they all walked together out through the doors of Jenrette's restaurant. All the people at the tables and booths were staring now.

Outside, a dark military van was waiting. Christabel could not help looking across the parking lot toward the service station, wondering if her mommy was watching and might come over to help, but the family van wasn't there anymore.

Her father squeezed her hand, then helped her up into the military van. The two MPs got in with them. They were young men, the kind who waved to her when they drove past at the base, but these young men had faces like statues and did not smile or say a word. There was wire in the glass between where they sat and where Captain Ron sat in the front of the van next to the driver—like Daddy and her and Mr. Ramsey had all been loaded into some kind of nasty animal cage.

And her mommy and Mister Sellars had gone away somewhere.

Christabel decided she was probably too brave to cry, but she wasn't completely sure.

CHAPTER 30

Heaven's Plaything

NETFEED/FINANCE: Discreet Sell-Off of Krittapong Shares
VO: Traders are taking note of what one veteran of the international markets called "a very careful sell-off" of Krittapong shares. Sources in the electronics industry suggest that Ymona Dedoblanco Krittapong, the globe-trotting widow of company founder Rama Krittapong, has been quietly reducing her own large percentage of the Thailand-based consumer electronics giant, perhaps in anticipation of rumored product liability lawsuits. . . .

It had been the most terrifying day of her life.

Renie was exhausted, so tired that her bones felt heavy, but she could not sleep. The night was almost silent, but the clatter of weapons and the shrieks of wounded men still seemed to surround her. She lay with her head on !Xabbu's chest, a cloak drawn over their bare legs, and knew that she could not survive another such day of bloody madness.

Renie also knew that when the sun came up, it would all start again.

*   *   *

There had come a point in the middle of the hideous afternoon, the sun so far away in the sky that the battle seemed to be taking place on some desolate planet at the rim of the solar system, every second crawling past as though time itself had grown weary, that Renie had thought she finally understood warfare.

It came as a single flash of insight as the battle raged around her, a sea of chaos in which spears and muscle-knotted arms and shouting faces appeared and disappeared so quickly that they might have been the temporary creations of turbulent raw matter.

Patriotism, loyalty, duty—different words that served the same purpose. Most people would fight for friends and family, but why would a normal person consent to murder strangers on behalf of other strangers? Humans needed order; killing each other for no reason—*risking* being killed for no reason—was meaningless, poisonous. When chaos swept you up, you had to believe in something, however vague. Renie had suddenly realized that you had to sprinkle the fairy dust of *love of country* or *duty* over the nearer group of strangers—convince yourself that somehow they were bound to you and you to them—or else you would go mad.

As bizarre as it was to kill or die for strangers, her own worst problem during the battle had turned out to be the exact opposite—watching her virtual Trojan comrades fall at her side and forcing herself to ignore their agonized calls for assistance. *These are not real people,* she told herself time after time, although every bit of sensory information screamed otherwise. *If I try to help one of them, I'm risking my own life*—and thus the life of her real companions, and even of her brother and the other lost children. Still, it seemed a hollow distinction.

One such terrible moment had come as a dying Lycian soldier, speared in the back, had come staggering toward her. The young soldier, who only minutes earlier had offered Renie a drink from his water skin, had headed straight for her through the madness of battle as though he could see no one else, the spear that had murdered him protruding through his ribs, its long shaft dragging behind him like a stiffened tail. As his strength ended, he had reached out his hands, the clutch of a drowning swimmer, a man sinking in his own blood. Renie had stepped away, afraid he would clutch at her and leave her defenseless. The look in his fast-glazing eyes had burned her so badly she thought she would never forget it.

Is this what's coming? she had wondered in helpless horror. *Is this what the future will be like? We'll make worlds where anything is possible, see real, breathing, sweating people killed before our eyes every day—even murder them ourselves—and then sit down to dinner afterward as though nothing has happened?*

What kind of future were human beings creating? How could the human mind, an organ millions of years old, sort through such mad, science-fictional riddles?

The day had crawled on.

Charge to the attack, hemmed and pushed by those behind. Dodge and duck, work back to the rear, keep the shield up at all times against the rain of biting arrows. Keep an eye open for !Xabbu and T4b, remember that they are the only real things in this wasteland of shouting ghosts. Duck, dodge.

Spears had jabbed out at her from behind shields like vipers hiding among rocks. Without warning, entire sections of the battlefront had gone shoving past, so that the worst fighting was suddenly behind her instead of in front, and for all her caution she and her companions found themselves in the middle of the conflict again.

Start over. Dodge and duck. Work back to the rear again . . .

And all around, death. It was not a quiet presence during the long day—not a pale-faced maiden bringing surcease from pain, not a skillful reaper with a scalpel-sharp blade. Death on the Trojan plain was a crazed beast that roared and clawed and smashed, which was everywhere at once, and which in its unending fury showed that even armored men were terribly frail things; in a moment, all that solidity could be turned into bloodmist and bubbling cries and soft, tattered flesh. . . .

Renie sat up, trembling.

"!Xabbu?" She could barely find her voice. "Are . . . are you awake?"

She felt him move beside her. "I am. I cannot sleep."

"It was so horrible . . . !" She covered her face with her hands, wishing like a small child that when she took them away everything strange around her would be gone, the too-bright stars and their dim reflections, the thousand campfires. "Jesus Mercy, I thought this post-trauma stuff wasn't supposed to hit for a few years." Her desperate laugh almost began a fit of weeping. "I keep telling myself it's not real . . . but it might as well be. People really did that to each other. People really *do* that to each other . . ."

He reached out and took her hand. "I wish that I could find something to say. It was indeed horrible."

She shook her head. "I just don't know how I can go through that again. Oh, God, it will be light again in a few hours." She had a sudden thought. "Where is T4b?"

"He is sleeping." !Xabbu pointed to a shadowy shape curled a couple of meters away from the fire. Relieved, Renie turned back to her friend and marveled for a moment at how quickly she had grown used to !Xabbu's new human body, a vessel which had quickly filled with !Xabbu-ness. The slender, youthful face, that of a stranger a day earlier, already helped soothe her simply by being in her line of sight.

"Sleeping. He's got the right idea. God, maybe all those battle-games are good for something. Maybe they harden you."

"He was frightened and upset, just as we were." !Xabbu squeezed her hand. "If he is sleeping, then perhaps he will be more alert tomorrow. We must all protect each other, as we did today."

"We were lucky. We were damned lucky." Renie did not want to think of the chariot wheel that had almost ground !Xabbu into the dirt or the spear that had hissed over her own shoulder, a hand's span from her face. It was terrifying to remember how close she had come to losing him. She ached to take him in her arms, to build something together that would shield them even for just a little while against what had been and what was to come.

"What . . . what's flying?" T4b sat up, a dim shape made even stranger by the black hair straggling across his face like a mourning veil. "Is it starting again?"

"No." Renie tried to smile, but gave up. "Not yet. We've got a few hours."

T4b brushed his hair aside. There was a gaunt intensity to his face that had appeared with the struggle atop Weeping Baron's Tower and which had not left since. "Look, why don't we just lock off and fly. Just . . . get out." He produced the smile that Renie had not been able to summon; seeing the effect, she was glad she had failed. "Yeah, yeah," he said, "it's wild funny—the guy in the Manstroid suit wants to run away. But I . . . I don't care, seen? Never thought it would be like this, me. Never would have . . ."

Renie wanted to offer him some comfort—fear and unhappiness almost throbbed off him—but as she leaned over to touch his arm, he shrank away. "We're all terrified, and we're doing our best not to get killed," she said. "I won't stop you from doing anything you want, Javier—this isn't the military. You didn't enlist. But I believe we're here for a purpose, and I can't run away if there's a chance to fulfill that purpose."

Jesus Mercy, she thought. *I sound like some kind of army chaplain.*

T4b was silent for a moment. Somewhere, an owl hooted, a sound so nature-documentary normal that it was only as T4b began to speak again that Renie realized it was the first noise they had heard other than their own in hours. They were on the far rim of the Trojan bivouac, and although she felt sure the feelings of dread and misery were similar all through the army of Troy, not to mention among their Greek enemies, the nearest Trojan campfire was a long stone's throw away, too far for normal conversation to drift to Renie's ears. They might almost have been alone beneath the blazing stars.

"They're not going to turn back tomorrow, are they?" T4b said slowly. "That guy Hector, he's screamin' for it, seen? He's one of those *tchi seen* six-knockers—you have to kill him to stop him. And he's bulk scorching now, 'cuz he got hit with that rock and they had to carry him off in front of everybody." He seemed to be thinking deeply, working something out in his mind. "So there's like possibility major we're all going to get sixed, huh?"

Renie could think of nothing to say—she knew that in the same situation she would not want to hear anything but the truth. "It will be at least as bad as today. And we were lucky."

"Then I want to tell you something. Tell both of you." He paused again. "It's been bothering me, seen?—but if I'm gonna get boxed . . ."

"Renie." It was !Xabbu, an odd, quiet urgency in his voice, but Renie could feel T4b working up to something.

"Wait."

"Renie," he said again, "there is someone in our fire."

It took a moment for what he said to sink in. She turned abruptly to stare at !Xabbu, then followed his gaze to the low flames. She could not see anything like a person, or any shape at all, but the fire did seem to have some new quality—or rather it had lost some quality that had been present before, as though it had been simplified somehow, its flames made less chaotic or its colors reduced.

"I don't see anything." She glanced at T4b, who was staring intently at the fire, too, arrested on the verge of some painful admission.

"It is . . . I think it is . . ." !Xabbu squinted, leaning closer, so that his cheeks and forehead were brushed with motile golden light. "A face."

Before Renie could ask the obvious question, a female voice spoke in her ear, almost inside her head—distant but crisp, like a bell made to ring with the sound of a human throat.

"Someone is coming to you. Do not be afraid."

The others heard it too—T4b grabbed his spear and struggled to his feet, looking around wildly. The fire was once more only a fire, but something was moving now at the edge of the circle of firelight. As if summoned by the mysterious voice, a figure walked toward them out of the darkness. For a moment the robe and hooded face made Renie wonder whether in this created world, Death had been given a traditional form after all.

"Stop," she hissed, some instinct keeping her voice low. The shape did as she commanded, then slowly lifted and spread its hands, showing that it bore no weapons. The hood was nothing more than a fold in a thick wool cloak, which had been wrapped across the stranger's shoulders and pinned across the chest. Bright eyes looked at her out of the shadowy depths. "Who are you?" she hissed.

T4b took an aggressive step forward, spear thrusting toward the hidden face.

"Don't!" said Renie sharply. The stranger had taken a step away. Now, as T4b halted, the stranger threw back the hood to reveal an unfamiliar bearded face. "I asked you before," Renie said. "You are running out of chances. Who are you?"

The stranger looked slowly from Renie to her two companions, then back. There was something strange in his hesitation—Renie felt sure that anyone caught and challenged while wandering around a military encampment at night would claim to belong there, truthfully or not.

"I . . . I was led here," the stranger said at last. "By a floating thing. A shape, a light. I . . . I thought I recognized it." He peered at them. "Did you see it?"

Renie thought of the fire, but kept her mouth shut. "Who are you?"

The stranger put his hands down at his side. "What's more important is who I'm looking for." He seemed to be taking a step he feared he could not retrace. "This may seem a strange question. Do . . . do you by any chance know someone named Renie?"

T4b drew in his breath sharply and began to say something, but Renie waved a hand at him. Her own heart was hammering, but she kept her voice as calm as she could. "We might. Why do you . . ."

She was interrupted by T4b, whose excitement had overcome him. "Is that you, Orlando?"

The stranger looked at him sharply, then smiled a weary, relieved smile. "No. But I know him—I have talked to him only a few hours ago. My name is Paul Jonas."

"Jesus Mercy! Jonas!" Renie reached out almost unconsciously for !Xabbu's hand and squeezed it, then pointed a trembling finger at a space beside the fire. "You'd better sit down. Somehow . . . somehow I thought you'd be taller."

Renie found herself watching the newcomer closely, not so much out of suspicion—although her time in the network did not encourage her to trust anything or anyone—but more in curiosity at a man who had survived so much. The strangest thing was that Jonas' description of himself seemed exactly true: he was nobody special, an average and unremarkable man caught up in things he did not understand. Still, he was clearly not a fool. He asked intelligent questions, and thought carefully before replying to those Renie and the others asked him in turn. He had also paid attention to the things he had encountered along the way, and had struggled to understand the nature of the experience. Most unusual of all, in the midst of his terrible trials he had retained a dry, self-mocking sense of humor.

"You really are Odysseus," she said aloud at one point.

He looked up, startled. "What do you mean?"

"Just . . ." She was embarrassed she had spoken the thought aloud. "Just what you've been through. Lost and trying to find your way home through strange lands, persecuted by the powers-that-be . . ." She waved her hand, encompassing not just the battlefield but the whole of the network. "It's like you've become the character who's the most like you."

His smile was a weary one. "I suppose so. I've become a survivor, is what's happened. Wouldn't read too well on a CV, but it speaks volumes in these parts."

"I wonder, though . . ." Renie looked to !Xabbu. "Things like that, it's like what Kunohara said—as if we were in a story. But what does that mean? That we don't have free will or something?"

!Xabbu shrugged. "There are other possible meanings. We could be participants, but someone else could be trying to give things a certain shape. There are many ways to understand the workings of the world—any world." He gave Renie a shrewd glance. "Did we not have this discussion before, you and I? About the differences, if any, between science and religion?"

"But it doesn't make sense—who would be shaping a story, and how?" Renie did not want to rise to !Xabbu's bait: for all her happiness at learning that Orlando and Fredericks still lived, the larger truth was that Jonas did not bring any obviously useful answers. Before this moment, she had thought that if they ever found Sellars' escaped prisoner, he would be like a spy in some old-fashioned drama, full of hard-earned secrets. The information Jonas possessed was indeed hard-earned, but none of it shed any light on the most crucial questions. "The only candidates to be messing around with our lives that way are the Grail people themselves. Or perhaps this mystery woman." She turned back to Jonas. "I heard her voice, just before you arrived, telling us not to be afraid. It was the same woman who appeared to us as the Lady of the Windows, I swear it was."

Jonas nodded. "Yes, she led me to you. Orlando and his friend have seen her, too—Orlando seems to have had almost as much contact with her as I have, in fact. I'm certain that she's important—that she's more than just one of the fairground attractions, if you see my meaning. I've felt since the first that she means something to me, but what that might be, I still can't get to."

"Means something? You mean, like you knew her before?" Renie thought back, but the apparition they had seen in the House had been as tenuous as the end of a dream. "Can't you think of anywhere you might have known her in your life? Lover, friend . . . sister, daughter . . . ?"

Jonas hesitated. "Something was there for a moment, when you said that, but it's gone now." He sighed. "We need to talk all together, perhaps. Is this all that remains of your group? Orlando seemed to suggest there were many more than this."

"No, we've left three people inside Troy." Renie shook her head in frustration. "We were told 'Priam's Walls,' but we had no idea where or why, so we split up."

"Got no clock for this," T4b said suddenly. He had been listening with surprising attention, but now it seemed his youthful patience was growing thin. "Let's just get on and bust Fredericks and Orlando out of that camp and fly back to Troy Town."

!Xabbu nodded. "T4b is right. The clash will begin again at dawn, and look . . ." —he pointed to the eastern sky— "the Morning Star is on his way back from his hunt across the night. At any moment now, he will be kicking up red dust along the horizon."

"True—we can't just be sitting here when the hostilities start." Renie turned to Jonas, but the newcomer was looking at !Xabbu.

"You have a poetic way with words, friend," he said. "Are you sure you're a real person? You'd fit in well with the Greeks."

!Xabbu smiled. "Renie taught me it is impolite to question whether someone is real, but I am fairly certain I am not just code."

"He's a Bushman," Renie said. "Originally from the Okavango Delta. Did I say that right, !Xabbu?"

Jonas raised his eyebrows. "You're a fascinating group, there's no question. I can see we could spend days telling stories, but we'd better get into the Greek camp before dawn." He frowned, thinking. "I don't think they'd take too kindly to me bringing home some Trojan friends for breakfast, so perhaps you'd better be my prisoners." He stood up. "Let's bundle up your weapons so that I can carry them, then I can walk behind you with a spear and make it look good." He saw the glowering expression on the youngest of their company and smiled sourly. "You're going to have to trust me . . . what was your name again, sorry? T2v? There's just no other way."

"T4b, but you can call him Javier," said Renie, giving the teenager a stern look. "It's easier to remember."

T4b glared back at her, but having his true name revealed had taken some of his starch out, and he meekly handed his spear over to Jonas.

They had only gone a hundred paces before T4b stopped in midstep and jumped back, swearing. "Shit!" he said. "Give me that sticker back!"

"What are you talking about?" Renie snapped. "We explained . . ."

"It's a locking big snake!" T4b said, pointing. "Right there!"

Renie and !Xabbu could see nothing.

"I ain't dupping!"

Paul Jonas stepped up beside the quivering teenager. "Ask it what it wants."

"Can *you* see it?" Renie asked.

"No, but I think I know what it is," Jonas replied. "I had one earlier—it was a quail."

T4b turned back to them, more shaken than before. "Did you hear that? It talked to me!"

"It's part of the system," Paul said. "I think everyone gets one—certainly all the important characters do, I suppose so they can get the details right. Orlando had one, too." He turned to T4b. "What did it say?"

"Told me I was heading for the Greek camp, seen? Which was, like, a bad idea—but that if they captured me, I should ask for some Greek guy named Die-Tommy-Tees or something, because he knows my family."

"Diomedes—he's one of the likely lads on the Greek side." Paul inclined his head. "Well, your snake could have been more useful, but at least it sounds like you're important enough that I might be able to get some ransom for you."

It took T4b a long, distrustful moment before he realized the man was joking. "Oh, chizz, man," he growled. "Wild funny, you."

*   *   *

The eastern sky had lost a few layers of black when they reached the gate. The soldiers standing watch there recognized Odysseus and were excited to see he had brought back Trojan prisoners. The high flames of the watch fire also revealed something that Renie and her companions had completely forgotten.

"By the Thunderer!" One of the soldiers gaped at T4b. "Look at his armor—all of gold!"

"Odysseus has captured a hero!" one of the others said, then turned and shouted to a nearby group of soldiers, just stirring awake, "Crafty Odysseus has captured Glaucus of Lycia! The man with the golden armor!"

Much to Renie's distress, they were quickly surrounded by a cheering throng of soldiers and camp followers. The mob shoved them toward Agamemnon's headquarters, intent on sharing the good news.

Paul Jonas leaned close to her as people clapped him on the back and congratulated his daring. "We can't afford this. The bird-woman, the angel . . . she said time was running out."

"Don't look at me!" Renie hissed in frustration. "You're supposed to be the smartest man in Greece—think of something!"

Roused by the noise, Agamemnon came out of his cabin. Half-buckled into his armor and with his plaited hair disarranged, the big man looked like a bear jostled from hibernation. "Ah, god-like Odysseus, you have indeed performed a feat for the ages," the high king said with a hard grin. "Sarpedon's heart will be heavy in his breast when he discovers we have his kinsman alive. Even courageous Hector will wonder if the gods still favor his cause."

"We haven't much time," Jonas said. "I have questioned these Trojans, and they say the attack will come with dawn." He looked to Renie and !Xabbu, who nodded—even their few sparse exchanges with other Trojans after the battle had made that clear. "This time Hector and the others intend to drive us all the way into the sea."

Agamemnon held out an arm so one of his men could tie an ornate bronze guard onto his forearm. "I guessed as much. We will all be ready, though—you, noble Odysseus, and my brother Menelaus, and mighty Ajax, and Diomedes, master of the war cry. The Trojans will find out what kind of men are born in the Greek isles, and much Trojan blood will stain their own earth."

Renie was almost ready to scream with impatience as Agamemnon summoned them all back into his cabin so he could finish dressing. Despite Jonas' assurances that the prisoners had surrendered and no such precautions were necessary, she and her two companions found themselves surrounded by helmeted spearmen, all of whom wore expressions of frightened anger that made her even more nervous than Agamemnon's pragmatic nastiness.

"There might be more these enemies have held back," said the high king. "We will prick them a bit and let out some blood, and thus discover whether they have told all they know."

"Please," Jonas said, fighting to keep desperation from his voice. "I will work on them with more . . . subtle means. Leave them with me."

Agamemnon had finished pouring ritual libations on the fire and was hesitating, clearly relishing the prospect of torturing a few Trojans, when there was a commotion outside and an old man came through the door, flapping his hands in the air.

"The Trojans are at the walls!" he wailed. "Apollo's golden chariot has not risen above the hills, yet they are already slavering at our gate like wild dogs!"

Agamemnon clapped his meaty hands together, calling for his high, plumed helmet. "We will go, then. Leave the prisoners to these guards, noble Odysseus—your Ithacans await you, and the fighting will be fierce."

"Give me just a few moments more," Jonas begged him. "I suspect there is something these Trojans can tell me that might bring great Achilles out to fight—surely that's worth the time?"

The high king cocked his head. His plumes waggled like a peacock's tail. "Certainly, although I doubt anything you can do now will sway that stiff-necked man." He marched to the door, his retinue falling in behind him. Just as Renie was breathing a sigh of relief, he stopped and turned, a look of mistrust twisting his face. "Did you not swear to me, clever Odysseus, that Achilles could not fight because he was ill?"

"I did," Jonas said, caught off guard. "Yes, I did. But . . . but

perhaps it is a plague brought by the gods, and if they have turned
in our favor, perhaps they have made him well again."

Agamemnon stared at him for a moment, then nodded heavily. "Very well. But I cannot help remembering that you also were
reluctant to join us, Odysseus. I hope that you have not become
changeable again on this day of our great need."

The door creaked closed behind him, but half-a-dozen armed
soldiers still remained in the cabin, along with the rest of Agamemnon's household, several women and old men. The din of conflict was already loud outside, and Renie could almost feel the
advantage of having found Paul Jonas sliding away from them
like water down a drain.

"Let's do something!" she whispered to him. He started, as
though he had been daydreaming.

"I just . . . something was on the tip of my tongue," he told
her quietly. "From something you said earlier, about the woman.
You said 'sister, daughter . . .' and I almost heard a name." His
eyes again became distant. "Avis? Could that be it?"

"We know it is important, Mr. Jonas," !Xabbu said quietly,
"but perhaps we could talk about it at some later time . . . ?"

"Good God, of course." He turned to face the guards, who had
been suspiciously watching their quiet conversation. "We must
take these people to Achilles," he announced to them.

One of the soldiers, a clean-shaven man with a scar across his
broken nose, elected himself spokesman for the others. "The high
king said you were to question them . . ."

"Yes, but he didn't say I had to do it here," Jonas declared.
"Come with us if you like, but we must take them to Achilles.
What they have to say could mean the difference in this war."
His face hardened. "Where are you from?"

The soldier looked startled, as though he expected Jonas to
know. "Argos, noble Odysseus. But . . ."

"Do you want a chance to see it again? You saw what happened yesterday, didn't you? Without Achilles to help us, who
will stop the Trojans?" The soldiers still hesitated; Renie saw Jonas
make a decision. "The gods decree it! Are you calling me a liar?
How do you think I captured mighty Glaucus and these others in
the first place? The gods sent me a dream!"

This clearly shook the guards, and Jonas was not going to give them time for any lengthy theological pondering. He picked up the bundled weapons and prodded Renie, !Xabbu, and T4b toward the door. After an exchange of troubled glances, the soldiers fell in behind them and followed them out into the shouting and confusion of the Greek defense.

They were scarcely a dozen paces away from Agamemnon's cabin when the huge gate of the encampment burst inward, swinging so wildly on its hinges that two men were killed just by the force of its collapse. Great Hector loomed in the opening, still holding the massive log with which he had smashed the bolt, and the Greeks stumbled back from him in superstitious terror. Just hours before Priam's son had been carried from the field; now he stood glowering before them, recovered from injuries that would have killed any normal man. A moment later his Trojans came pouring through the shattered gate like floodwater over a crumbling dam, slaughtering all before them. Desperate Greek defenders leaped down from the walls to try to halt their advance, and any semblance of order vanished. The fire of battle now raged in the center of the Greek camp.

The guards who had followed Renie and the others from the high king's hearth rushed forward to join their comrades, leaving the prisoners alone. "Hell!" Jonas fumed. "The Trojans are between us and Orlando! We'll never sneak past without someone seeing us."

Already a group of warring soldiers had spun out of the battle toward them, locked breast to breast and oblivious, as though the conflict itself were throwing out a tentacle toward Renie and her companions in an attempt to draw them in. Jonas threw down their bundled weapons and slashed the cord with his short sword, but it was almost too late: a Greek soldier rushing to aid his comrades saw T4b and abruptly changed direction to try to put a spear through him. The intended victim snatched one of the newly untied spears from the ground just in time to knock away the first lunge, but the other man had a shield and he did not. Even as Renie scrambled for a spear of her own, a Trojan arrow struck the Greek in his unprotected back and flung him onto the ground. He crawled away, leaving a red trail on the sandy soil.

"Take off that damned armor!" Renie snarled at T4b.

"You crash?" he screamed back at her. "Take it off . . . ?"

"We're not going to have a chance if everyone keeps recognizing you." They were all backing toward the slight shelter of Agamemnon's striped cabin, but she had no illusions it would help for more than a few moments. "Take it off!"

"If you're lucky, they'll think you're a slave," Jonas said. "I'm serious—these maniacs are too busy killing each other to attack slaves—it's not approved behavior."

So furiously unhappy that it seemed he might burst into tears, T4b shucked his golden armor until he stood in only a simple, wrinkled chiton. Renie heaved the pieces of armor past the wall of Agamemnon's hut, hoping no one would notice them until she and the others were long gone.

"We have to get to Orlando and Fredericks," she said. "If he's still sick, they're helpless." She looked up to see Hector and some of the other leading Trojans surging toward the nearest of the Greek ships, torches blazing in their hands. Even now, the sun had barely topped the distant hills.

"We'll never make our way through that," Jonas said miserably. The Trojans were consolidating their position in the middle of the open area behind the gate, but the Greeks were flinging themselves at the invaders from all angles, throwing lives away in an effort to keep them from advancing farther, like antibodies trying to destroy a cluster of germs. "We have to go down to the ocean, see if we can make our way up the beach. Damn!" He pointed. "Orlando and Fredericks are all the way over there, at the opposite end of the camp."

"Follow me," said !Xabbu, then turned and trotted away between the tents.

The others scrambled after him. Although several Greeks rushing toward the battle at the gate shouted in anger at Odysseus, and an occasional arrow dropped out of the sky without warning, they managed to avoid serious harm all the way down to the beach, where they discovered that groups of Trojans had already reached the water's edge while their comrades kept the Greek defenders occupied in the center of camp. A dozen or so exultant attackers had already clambered into the rigging of one of the long black ships and were busily setting it on fire. Flames ran up the mast, lifting tendrils of tar-black smoke into the morning sky.

A contingent of Greeks had seen them and were climbing onto

the ship's deck to stop the assault even as Renie and the others reached the spot. Individual battles broke out among the fires. Renie saw one Trojan's head almost hewn from his neck by the blow of a sword, but the victor staggered away a moment later with a spear in his chest and fell shrieking into the flames.

Hell, she thought. *War really is hell.* The ancient cliche would not leave her brain; it repeated itself over and over as she sprinted along the beach, like some idiot nursery rhyme.

Ahead of them, several more of the Greek ships were already running with flames, little waves of fire that swept through rigging and up pitch-smeared masts to explode in the bundled sails. A hundred meters away Hector had burst through the defenders, armor gleaming in the slanted morning light as he led a group of shouting men down on one of the other ships. The Greeks at the back of the larger melee were peeling away in a frantic attempt to get between their chief enemy and the precious vessels, but Priam's son seemed an unstoppable force. In the few short moments Renie was watching, Hector smashed his flaming brand into one man's face and gutted another with his spear, then kicked both bodies aside as though they were no heavier than footstools. His line of assault moved unstoppably forward toward the ocean, a wall of screaming, battle-maddened Trojans that now separated Renie's company from their goal.

!Xabbu stopped a few paces ahead of the others, hesitating.

"We're never going to make it," Renie gasped.

Jonas was pale. "A trick, maybe? Something? We can't just let them . . ."

"They think T4b's a Trojan—except for you, they think we're all Trojans. Maybe that will help." She couldn't believe they were going to have to stand and watch as Orlando was captured or slaughtered.

"Like that's going to make em say, 'Go ahead, problem not!' or something?" T4b said, stopping to suck in air. "This a lockin' gang war! You don't run into the middle, saying 'Scuse me!' "

He was right, of course. Full of helpless dread, Renie sank to one knee as Hector in his bright armor reached the ships, completing the barricade of armed men across their path. The Trojan hero threw his torch high into the air; for a brief moment all the battlefield seemed to grow still as faces tilted up to watch it. It

spun end over end, trailing flame like a comet, and stuck in the
rigging of the nearest beached ship. Within moments the ropes
were ablaze.

"Now Zeus has given us a day that pays all back!" Hector bellowed. The approving din of the Trojans swelled around him.

Renie was trying so hard to think of a way to overcome the
apparently hopeless situation that at first, even as the clamor increased, she did not understand that something had changed. Men
were shouting excitedly, and where the fighting was less intense,
they waved their spears in the air in salute. But for the first time
that morning, it was the Greeks who were cheering.

"The Myrmidons have come out!" someone shrieked. "See—
they fall upon the Trojans from the side!"

"Myrmidons?" Renie squinted. There was indeed a commotion
on the far side of Hector's assaulting force; she could see what
looked like horses and chariots rushing toward the thickest part
of the struggle, dirt flying from beneath the horses' hooves.

Jonas looked stunned. "The Myrmidons . . . those are Achilles'
men."

"You mean . . . ?" Even as she tried to make sense of it, some
soldier closer to the struggle began to shout in excitement that
might have been joy or terror.

"Achilles! Achilles! The son of Peleus has entered the battle!"

A figure in bright armor stood in the lead chariot, holding himself upright with rather less grace than would be expected of a
hero, but holding a spear high over his head. Just the force of his
presence had already sent some of the nearest Trojans scattering;
several of them could not escape fast enough, and were run down
by the foaming horses. As his charioteer steered around a larger
group, the shining figure leaned out and jabbed with the spear.
More chariots and a surging mass of armored men came rushing
up behind him, and together they plunged into the battle like the
thrust of a knife.

"Jesus Mercy, what is he *doing?*" Renie shouted. *"Orlando!
Don't be a fool!"* But it was hopeless—if he had been standing
ten meters away he would have had trouble hearing her above
the screams of men and terrified shrilling of wounded horses,
but he was a dozen times that or more, leading his Myrmidons
into the thickest part of the Trojan force.

The return of Achilles sent a flash of confidence through the Greeks, as suddenly as if the gods themselves had poured courage back into their hearts.

"He's too sick for this," Renie said worriedly. "Where is Fredericks? Why would he let his friend do something like this? Over an imaginary battle!"

"It would not have been imaginary if the Trojans burned the ships and overran the camp," !Xabbu pointed out.

The Trojans, who had been scenting victory only moments before, now fell back toward the gates in a disorganized muddle. Hector and his men had been cut off from the rest of the attacking force; surrounded and in danger of being taken, Priam's great son began a dogged, bloody march away from the ships and back to the mass of his comrades.

"And see—they are falling back," !Xabbu said. "Orlando has done what was needed."

"Op that," said T4b, impressed.

"More than what was needed." Jonas stood on tiptoe, trying to make sense out of the swirl of bodies in the middle of the camp. "The young idiot has got the Trojans on the run, but now he and his men are chasing them back out through the gate. God, if only he could hear us!"

!Xabbu clambered up onto the nearest of the beached ships, all but abandoned now as the fighting had shifted all the way back to the settlement walls, where the Trojans were trying to keep some order in their retreat. Renie and the others followed him, scrabbling along the ship's slanting deck until they reached the prow. "What's happening?" Renie asked. "Where is he?" Part of the battle had already spilled back out through the gate and onto the plain, the Greeks now actively in pursuit as the Trojans fought a desperate rearguard action.

"Orlando in his wagon is chasing some of the Trojan wagons. No, chariots—isn't that the word?" !Xabbu shook his head. "It is hard to see, but I think that is Hector, who has fought his way back out again, and now is getting into his own chariot."

As Renie watched, the rest of the combatants rushed out the gate and onto the plain like sand pouring through the neck of an hourglass. "We have to go after him," she declared. "Orlando, I

mean. We can't leave him out there—Hector will cut him to bits
if he catches him."

"Go out there?" T4b demanded. "Without armor?"

"We'll find you some on our way," Jonas said. "There's plenty
of men who won't need theirs anymore."

"We have to go," Renie repeated. "Now we've all found each
other, we have to stay together." She began to work her way back
along the deck. "If we're lucky, we can catch up to him—pull
him away from the fight and then just keep going."

"Keep going where?" Jonas said, jumping down onto the sand
beside her.

"Troy?" Renie shrugged. "If we can avoid getting killed until
we reach Orlando, we'll worry about it then." She gave him a
sour grin. "Welcome to how things work around here."

!Xabbu swung down from the prow and led them back through
the camp. The sun was only a short way into the sky, but had almost vanished behind the pall of the burning ships, bringing a
premature twilight to the battlefield. As they stepped over the
sprawled corpses that littered the camp and bloodied their hands
searching among them for new armor for T4b, the little voice
began to sing in the back of Renie's head again, reminding her
over and over again just exactly what war was.

ORLANDO awoke from a rare dreamless sleep to a world that
seemed subtly different.

He could feel the rough blanket under his back, the leaves and
boughs beneath it prodding at him like small, gentle fingers. He
could smell smoke from a fire, sharp and crisp, although the fire
in the brazier in the corner held only dark ashes. He could hear
men's voices, but the noise was far away, murmurous as the ocean.
None of those things were new.

No, I feel . . . stronger. He sat up, and although it made him a
little dizzy, the sensation passed quickly. *In fact, I feel pretty good.*

The last wave of illness, which had almost drowned him after
the escape from the temple of Ra, seemed to have receded. He
was nowhere near completely healthy—the world around him
seemed less than totally real, and he felt fragile, as though his
body were made of flexible glass—but he still felt better than he
had in days.

The shadowed cabin was empty. He shouted, "Fredericks!" but no one came. He was not hungry, yet he had a tremendous urge to eat something anyway, to drink, to feed the furnace of his system with something more substantial than whatever dripped nutrients were keeping his real body alive.

But anything you eat here wouldn't really be too substantial, now would it, Gardiner?

He didn't care. He was alive again, more or less. He wanted to celebrate.

He swung his legs to the floor and felt dirt beneath his toes. That was pleasure enough; he spent a moment enjoying it. When he did stand, his legs wobbled a bit before his knees finally locked, but the terrible vertigo that had kept him in his bed most of the time since he had arrived was gone. He took a few steps. It worked.

I'm alive! For a while, anyway.

After a few more careful steps he leaned against the doorpost to check the state of Orlando again and found it fairly good. He pushed the door open and stepped out into the morning sunlight, blinking. The sky was blue, scribed with odd streaks of black cloud. The smell of burning wood was very strong.

Where is everyone?

He shouted for Fredericks again, without response. The camp seemed to be deserted. A few fires still smoldered, but they did not seem enough to account for the strong smell of burning in the air. He stepped out farther and looked around, but there was no sign of any of the Myrmidon soldiers.

As he walked through the eerily empty camp his view of much of the Greek siege-city was blocked by the prows of the large black ships, but he could see a few human forms in the distance and could hear faint voices. Startled by a shadow moving across the sun, he looked up and saw that the trailing clouds were not natural, but were the wind-tattered outer edges of a vast funnel of black smoke—smoke that was rising from only a short distance away, back along the row of ships.

"Scanny!" Eyes fixed on the smoke, he stepped on a sharp stone; he cursed and hopped for a moment, then turned back to the cabin to get his sandals.

As he stooped to pick them up from the floor, he noticed that something else had changed since he went to sleep. The armor and weapons that had stood in one corner of his cabin were gone, nothing left behind but the empty armor-stand, sad as a roadside grave marker, and a single long spear lying on the earthen floor.

Sandaled now, but fighting another slight wave of dizziness, he banged back out the door of the cabin again and almost collided with a bent old man who was carrying an armful of firewood. The man took a staggering step back, goggled at Orlando for a moment, then shrieked and dropped the logs.

"Where is everybody?" Orlando demanded.

The old man scuttled sideways like an arthritic crab, but could not seem to look away, as though Orlando were something monstrously strange. He opened his mouth as if to answer, but only moaned.

"Oh, chizz—what, are you brain-damaged?" Orlando looked around, but there was no one else in sight. "Can't you tell me where everyone's gone?"

"Mighty Achilles, is it you?" The old man's toothless jaw worked.

"Yes, it's me." Orlando gestured at the cabin. "I live here, don't I?"

The crouching man almost whimpered. "Then who was it who led the brave Myrmidons into battle?" He shook his head. "Have the gods led us astray with some terrible trick? Cursed be the day we ever came to this place!"

"Led the Myrmidons . . ." Orlando felt a chill. Suddenly, the odd translucency of his vision seemed nightmarish, as though he himself were fading away while all else remained solid. "Me? You saw *me?*"

"It must have been you, my king. All know your shining bronze armor, your famous shield, your sword with its silver-studded hilt. Surely you remember! The Trojans were pressing hard through the Greek camp—some of the ships had already been set aflame, and Hector was raging among our soldiers like a wounded boar. All was nearly lost, then you came out girded for war and leaped into your chariot. The Myrmidons let out a great cry of gladness! How my own heart swelled at that moment!" His look of remembered pleasure suddenly disappeared and his face crumpled like a paper bag. "But you are here, when I myself saw you chase the fleeing Trojans out onto the plain not an hour ago."

"Oh, my God," Orlando said slowly. "Fredericks. Oh, Fredericks, you scanmaster!"

The old man cringed. "I do not understand your words, my king. Have you been killed on the field, brought down by the Trojans like a bear beset by hounds? Is this your ghost which pauses here before going down the dusty road to Hades?"

"Just shut up, will you?" Orlando stood beneath the reemerging sun, smelling smoke. The world had just turned inside out. Fredericks, who even avoided tavern brawls in the Middle Country, had put on the armor of Achilles and led the Myrmidons against the Trojan army. The idiot! Didn't she know she could be killed here? "What's your name?" Orlando demanded of the old man.

"Thestor, my king. Not Thestor the father of Calchas, or that other who fathered Alcmaeon, or even that other Thestor, son of Enops, who met his death on the battlefield at the hands of your friend Patroclus . . ."

"Enough." The sun was now out from behind the trailing smoke, and Orlando could see faint signs of movement on the plain, but they were far away, almost in the shadow of Troy's great wall. What could he do? Go charging into the middle of a battle unprotected, without weapons?

"You see, there are many Thestors," the old man went on, "and I am but one of the humblest . . ."

"Enough, okay? I need armor. Where can I find some?"

"But I saw your famous bronze armor when you rode out—like a god, you looked . . ."

Orlando turned away. The old man was worse than useless. He had a sudden thought. *"Turtle!"* he called. "Turtle, come here!"

"But my name is Thestor, great Achilles . . ."

Orlando ignored him. A moment later a small round shape emerged from beneath the cabin, blinking its eyes. "As I have pointed out several times, I am actually a tortoise."

"I need armor. I need weapons. Where can I find some?"

"If you could wait a night, your immortal mother might apply to Hephaestus, god of the forge, to create some for you. He does very nice work, you know."

"No time. I need some armor right now."

The tortoise closed its eyes as it consulted the current state of the simworld. The old man Thestor, whether because the system itself had removed him from the loop, or because divine madness was an unremarkable thing in heroes, seemed content to wait while his master Achilles talked animatedly to nothing.

"For some reason, the armor of Glaucus of Lycia has been discarded," the tortoise announced, "and even now lies behind Agamemnon's cabin. It should fit you, and it has a long and heroic lineage . . ."

"I don't care. It'll do." He turned to Thestor. "Do you know where Agamemnon's cabin is?"

The old man nodded, trembling. "Of course . . ."

"There's some armor behind it. Go find it and bring it back. All of it. Run!"

"My legs are frail, great king . . ."

"Then jog. But get going!"

Thestor obediently creaked off. Orlando went back into the cabin and picked up the single spear left behind. It was hugely heavy, and so long that it was not easy to steer it back out the door, but it fit his hand with a familiarity that was strangely satisfying.

The tortoise eyed it complacently. "Your great spear—it was too much weapon for brave Patroclus, although he took everything else."

"Is he—Patroclus—is he alive?"

"Only the gods know what men cannot see," the tortoise said. "He rode out onto the plain, driving the Trojans before him like sheep. Great was their terror when they saw the armor of Achilles."

"Oh, jeez, Fredericks, why didn't you stop once you turned away the attack?" Orlando groaned. "You utter scanbox!"

With the help of the tortoise, Orlando had discovered a replacement sword and shield by the time Thestor returned, panting beneath the burden of Glaucus' armor. The chestplate gleamed like a gaudy punchbowl.

"It's gold!" Orlando said, impressed

"From carrying it, I would have guessed lead," wheezed the old man. "But heroes are stronger than ordinary men—doubtless you shall scarce notice the crushing weight, my king, the weight which has nearly killed an old freedman."

"Help me put it on."

As Orlando first tried to wait, then in impatience tried to speed up the process by tying on those pieces he could manage himself, he finally began to consider the old man fumbling at the greave-ties as something other than a bit of the background. Whatever else was going on, whatever code determined his behaviors, ancient Thestor truly seemed to be what he was meant to appear—a frightened, weary old man with shaking hands. Orlando began to regret his short temper.

"That's all right." He gently but firmly tugged the groin-piece from the man's grip. "I can do that myself." The man's white-stubbled jaw suddenly reminded him of his own father, unshaven on a Sunday morning, trying to pretend that it was another normal weekend day like everyone else's, despite the fact that he and his son were not going to be going out to any baseball games or museums, or strolling in the park. Despite the slightness of the memory, it hit him like a fist in the stomach: for a moment Orlando was afraid he might burst into tears.

"Do you . . . do you have any kids?" he asked Thestor.

The old man eyed him warily. "Goats? No, my king. I have never owned anything except a white pullet, and once a pair of dogs, but I could not afford to keep them fed."

Orlando cursed his own stupidity. "No, I mean children. Do you have any children?"

Thestor shook his head. "I had a wife, but she died. I have traveled with your household now for many years, Lord, in many lands, but I have not found another who pleased me as she did." He straightened. "There. You are girded for war, my king. You look like Phoebus Apollo himself, if I may say so without incurring the god's wrath." He lowered his voice. "They are a touchy lot, Lord, if you did not know it."

"Oh, I know it, all right." Orlando sighed. "Believe me."

The horse was picking up speed, jouncing him almost off its bare back as they hurried across the battlefield. All around him the bodies of Greek and Trojan soldiers lay in frozen stillness, as though some wall sculpture from a museum had crumbled and fallen to the floor. The slaves who had remained behind as the battle surged back across the plain, capably plundering the Trojan corpses on behalf of their masters or perhaps themselves, stood up and pointed as he passed, astonished both by his bright golden armor and the sight of a warrior riding on a horse's back.

Here it comes, Orlando thought grimly as he kicked his heels into the horse's ribs, urging it forward. *The world's first and smallest cavalry.*

Ahead, and growing closer every moment, lay the glinting, seething ruck of battle. He could hear men's voices, tiny, thread-like screams of fury and agony rising to the skies. Carrion birds circled above, following the movable feast with patience bred through thousands of generations.

Here I come, Fredericks. Please don't be dead. Just hang on until I get there.

The horse pounded on across the smoky plain.

CHAPTER 31

The Hall Wherein
They Rest

NETFEED/NEWS: Node for Homeless Draws Criticism
(visual: portal to Streethouse)
VO: Streethouse, a nonprofit node established for the
homeless has drawn fire from retail nodes with similar
names, like StreetSmart Apparel.
(visual: StreetSmart spokesperson Vy Lewin)
LEWIN: "... No, look, we're totally supportive of the
homeless—we give lots of money to charities every year—
but this directly interferes with our business. People looking
for that Streethouse node just come wandering into our
showrooms and annoy our customers. We had a group of
gypsies, or whatever you call them these days, who moved
into the big and tall showroom of our main retail node and
wouldn't leave. Once they find a node like ours with lots of
entertainments and private dressing rooms, they keep
coming back with different aliases. It's a real problem."
(visual: Condé Del Fuego, spokesperson for Streethouse)
DEL FUEGO: "Basically, the retailers just want poor
people to go away, even online. It's the same old story—
'Yes, it's too bad, but go suffer somewhere else....'"

IN the flick that was always running in the background of his thoughts, Dread was now a knight in shining armor, a lone hero girding himself for battle. His castle was a converted warehouse in the Redfern district, his squire a young woman named Dulcinea Anwin whose mind he was slowly, carefully destroying. In place of breastplate and buckler, he had strapped himself into a Clinsor LR-5300 Patient Care Station (known more prosaically as a coma bed) and, with connections less physical but no less real, into the matrix of his own heavily-modified system. Instead of a gleaming sword, the man who had once called himself Jonny Dark bore the only weapon he truly trusted, the white-hot fire of his own mind—his *twist*.

"How are the meters?" he asked, taking care of a few remaining details. He did not flinch as he inserted the catheter.

Dulcie looked up at him, bedraggled, eyes hollow from jet lag. "Good. Everything's working."

Burning with impatience and three tabs of Adrenex, he had pushed open her door in the middle of the night. She had struggled up from sleep, eyes wide, fearful—a look that Dread was usually pleased to evoke from his female acquaintances—but he had a more important use for this particular woman, at least for the time being.

He had let the adrenaline flow through him like hot gold, carefully channeling his exultation into charm. He sat on the edge of her bed, amused by a seeming intimacy that only he fully understood, and apologized for how distant and abrupt he had been since her arrival. He told her how important she was to him, how much he needed her help. He even pretended to be a bit embarrassed as he hinted that his feelings for her might be more than mere collegiality and professional respect. A momentary dislocation of her attention, a flash of confusion that turned into a blush, had confirmed his guess.

Just before leaving her room, he had leaned across and cradled the back of her head in one gentle, firm hand as he pinioned her wrists with the other, then kissed her softly on the mouth. Pretending that he had surprised even himself by the moment of passionate indulgence, he had said an awkward good-bye and then slipped back out the door.

He was fairly sure she hadn't gotten much sleep after that.

Dread smiled now, watching her move among the display screens like a sleepwalker, fatigued and confused. He was well on the way now, whipsawing her back and forth between fear and desire. If he played his cards correctly, there would come a point when she would throw herself from a high window or walk in front of a speeding car if he asked her to—not that he would leave her inevitable death to something so impersonal, so unsatisfying. But that ultimate pleasure would have to wait: for now, she was far more useful to him alive. He was going into the unknown, to fight a monster. He needed someone loyal to watch his back.

"I'm going to leave a channel open," he said. "I don't know if it will still work after I penetrate the network, but I'll be able to talk to you at least until then."

She nodded. Her hair hung down, curtaining her face.

"Right. Wish me luck, sweetness."

"Of course. Good luck."

Dread subvocalized a command and dropped into the empty surface level of his own system. He closed his eyes, centering himself, reaching out along the ganglia of the system matrix which he knew as well or better than he did his own body. He tested the new capacities, the greater speed and vastly increased memory, and found it all good. He had only a vague idea of what he might find, and what might happen when he found it; he wanted to be prepared for all contingencies.

But something was missing, he realized. The hero was going into battle with no music. Dread considered for a moment. It was dangerous to squander even a tiny amount of his resources, surely—but what about style? Wasn't it part of being a hero to waste a little energy on swagger? He summoned up his catalog—he was not going to be so foolish as to try to manipulate an invented score during an assault like this—and settled at last on an old, old friend, Beethoven's *Ninth.* Some might consider it a cliche. Fine. Let the snotty bastards step in with him and face the dragon, or if not, shut up. Better, let them step in and face Dread himself. A little music might actually help focus his resolve, and if it became a drain on either his resources or his attention, he would shut it off.

As the first portentous string figures drifted up, he called up the entry sequence on Dulcie's copy of the stolen access device. When he had first tried to reenter after being knocked out of the system, the response had been swift and savage—a bolt of hideous input like bad charge, worse than anything the Old Man had ever done to him. This time he was prepared. He had found a way to hide his point of connection while the Otherland system considered the request. Any attack would be pointless, and would pinpoint the source of resistance.

But to Dread's surprise, instead of another retaliatory stroke, the sequence keyed through and the system opened, presenting him with an initial choice of parameters—a kind of visitor's lobby for the exclusive environs of the Otherland system. Elated that Dulcie's tinkering had solved the access failure from last time, he was about to make his first set of choices when he became aware of an unusual sensation.

Something was waiting for him.

It was bizarre—it made no sense at all—but Dread's instincts were very sharp, and like the predator he was, he always trusted them. He paused to think about what he was feeling. He was in one of the preliminary levels of the Otherland system, far too distant from the VR environments to be receiving information in anything other than straightforward ways, sound and vision. Any normally sensible person would discount the sensation as an effect of his own nervousness and get on with making selections, but Dread had never been a normal person.

He hesitated, then initiated the first of the subroutines he and Dulcie had created for this incursion, this one a secondary call-up, a falsified but very realistic request from an access line other than his own. When it had connected with the preliminary level, it randomly made a selection from the presented choices. A second later it had been rubbed out of existence.

Dulcie's voice purred in his jawbone, a little interest adding color to her dulled tones. *"The secondary call-up just got sixed. Not just ended, but something blew it up completely—the line is out of service now, too."*

A security system that could set traps and then brutally dispatch what it captured. Dread smiled. *You are a clever bastard, aren't you?* It was impossible to feel that vast patient malice just behind the facade of the system and not think of it as a person—

and judging by its swift, skillful viciousness, a person not that different from himself. *Neural net, ALife—whatever you are . . . I'm going to enjoy taking you down.*

In her examination of the access device, Dulcie had found what she thought was an override—a priority access, just the sort of thing that members of the Grail Brotherhood would demand, especially in those days when they'd been forced to share the system with others not of their cabal. Dread brought in the tertiary call-up and gave it that priority, which seemed to work—this probe was not attacked, and within moments had opened up the outer level. The system threw up auxiliary defenses, some of which Dread and Dulcie had only been able to anticipate in the most general of ways: since their access device was a copy, it had not been regularly updated. Dread saw the probe halted by a light-swift array of queries for which it had no immediate answers. He decided it was time to get aggressive.

He routed his original call through what was now the active line, inhabiting that probe into the secondary level of the Otherland system as though it were a suit of clothing, while his peculiar ability—his *twist*—began slowly to work. The levels of complexity, the layer on layer of subroutines, were so much more Byzantine than even the Atascos' top-flight security system that for a moment he despaired, but he clung to the crack he had opened in the system and began to look around.

Dulcie was boosting him with every tool they had prepared— she even improvised a few—but although his probe was not being attacked as the first one had been, neither was it able to penetrate the next level of security. If it had been a simpler system, this might have been the point at which failure of their assault became automatic, but the Otherland system seemed able to live with the paradox of a priority code that was nevertheless incomplete. They held their beachhead, but could not move farther.

The *Ninth Symphony* had finished and begun again, a low, muscular pulse of strings just at the edge of Dread's hearing, when he finally found a weak point. He had been using his twist sparingly, conscious that unlike the rest of the arsenal he and Dulcie had assembled, it was organic and prone to fatigue; now, as he assayed another test of the Otherland system's responses, he discovered something he could only think of as a hesitancy, a space where the system which was resisting him so assiduously showed an almost imperceptible lag.

An ordinary intruder, reliant on numbers and experience, might have missed it, but Dread's odd gift was only coincidentally something that could be used against information systems: whatever genetic mystery had caused it, it was a part of him. Dread was a hunter, his talent a hunter's talent. When the system hesitated on each cycle, the split instant of delayed reaction was still far too swift to be noted by any normal animal senses—but through the twist he felt it, as a shark might smell a spoonful of blood in the water a mile distant.

He let everything slide away—Dulcie, the subroutines, his own meat body—until only the twist mattered, a pulse of energy at the farthest extension of his mind. He ignored the now constant migrainous pain, slowed his breathing, then extended his understanding out along the tendrils of his consciousness and beyond, until he himself became that point in conceptual space—until he was the twist. And he waited.

The Otherland system might seem to have put an impenetrable wall between his probe and what he sought, but it was only a wall in the same way matter appeared to be solid—a false seeming, a concession to the limits of perception. Just as solidity itself was an illusion of whirling, bonded energy, the fire wall with which the system held him at bay was an illusion of unbreachable speed. Deep within the nearly continuous flash of information, there was an all but imperceptible hitch.

Dread waited, his consciousness extended like an antenna, the potentiality of his probe waiting like a synapse poised to fire. The cycles of the resisting system sped past. Dread waited. Then, trusting an impulse too inexplicable even to be called instinct, he *twisted* hard.

It was an impossible feat, like throwing a broomstraw unscathed through the whirling blades of a propellor. He succeeded.

The system fell open before him, an astonishing array of conduits connecting an almost equally vast collection of information nodes, all open, all as accessible as if he had built them himself. The system, or at least its security apparatus, lay behind him now, evaded and neutralized. He could go anywhere, assume any form, with the same godlike ease as the Brotherhood wielded. He had as much power within the network as the Old Man himself.

He felt like a huge gray wolf who had found a valley full of fat, unshepherded sheep.

Dread paused to rest and nurse the dull red ache behind his eyes. Once again the twist had served him well. He brought the volume back up on the Beethoven, just in time for the tenderly melodic opening of the third movement.

"It worked," he told Dulcie. *"Can you hear me? Is the spike carrying this back out?"*

She did not hear him, or did not reply, but he was not bothered. His joys had always been solitary.

Should he move immediately to find and destroy that Sulaweyo bitch and her friends, which would now be as easy as swatting flies, or should he play closer to the vest so as not to risk his long-term goal—the destruction of the Old Man and the usurpation of his power? Dread was considering all the exciting possibilities when something else, something unexpected, tugged at his imagination.

What *was* the Otherland system? Was it an ALife, or some even stranger and more revolutionary form of flexible operating system, the product of some accidental discovery in the code-mines of Telemorphix? Dread knew this was one way in which he was still not the Old Man's equal—he had power, but he lacked knowledge. Perhaps there was a way to hack the operating system itself, cause trouble for the Old Man there? If true, he might be able to remove the protections of the Old Man and his Grail Brotherhood cronies—make them just as vulnerable to real harm inside the system as Sellars' recruits were. If so, he might accomplish his goal much more quickly, not to mention save himself a great deal of risk later on.

Yeah, but—confident, cocky, lazy, dead, he warned himself. *It's a crazy system. You don't want to let one victory go to your head, mate.*

Still, if he was careful, it couldn't hurt to have a bit of a look.

He opened himself to the machineries of Otherland and began to explore. Primed by Dulcie's explanation of the likely architecture, and with her prepared reports instantly available, he pushed at this interesting structure and pulled at that one, probing deeper wherever he found resistance, brandishing his stolen access permission like the badge of a Papal Inquisitor to penetrate level after level of security. He had gained the inner circle, therefore all that had happened before was meaningless: if the security system had considered him a possible intruder earlier, that was negated now by the simple fact of his penetration—he was in, therefore he deserved to be in. Machines did not hold grudges. From his privileged position, he began to unravel the complexities of the platform, looking for the central place from which the orders were issued.

He found it at last, an unimaginably complex core that had no obvious source within the system—the nerve stem, as he guessed, by which the operating system controlled the entire network and its miraculous machinery. He had one instant in which to gloat, and then something—*something*—came down on him like an arctic wind.

Visual input, auditory input, sight and sound, both abruptly disappeared. Even his own volition seemed smothered in all-enveloping, frigid blackness. Dread flailed without connection or purchase. In a far distant place a body that had once been his, its physical responses suppressed by the telematic jack connection, struggled to scream but could not.

Something blasted into his brain, changing the blackness in a microsecond to flaring white, all-devouring light. He felt his true self slipping away, his thoughts burning, shriveling like ants in a blue-white gas flame.

It was not hiding any longer, he dimly realized, this something at the heart of the network. He had stuck his fingers into it, bruised it, mocked it, and now it had him.

And it *hated* him.

THE bandaged hand extended, indicating the long, low hallway and the black walls incised with carvings that glittered in the light of the dying sun. "And this is the Passage of the Way of Shu, open to the air. The procession will begin here." The mummified figure turned, deathmask face wooden but the voice tinctured with irritation. "I am taking the time to give you a private tour, Wells," complained Osiris, known elsewhere as Felix Jongleur. "Now, of all days, my time is very valuable. I'm sure yours is as well. You could at least pretend to be interested."

The second mummified figure turned from the wall carvings. The yellow face of the god Ptah showed a very tiny smile. "I am sorry, Jongleur. I was just . . . thinking. But this is all very impressive—a suitable location for the Ceremony."

Felix Jongleur made a noise of disgust. "You haven't even seen a fraction of it. This is a favor, you know. I thought you might like to walk through the Ceremony with me, to prevent surprises later on. Let me be frank. We are unlikely allies, and I want you to understand everything that will happen—we don't want to confuse things by suppositions of treachery." He allowed himself a hard little smile of his own. "Well, except for the properly prudent amount, of course."

"Of course."

Jongleur floated on, his feet a hand's span above the polished silver of the floor. Wells chose to walk on the ground, a bit of homespun stubbornness that amused Jongleur mightily. "This is the Passage of Ra," he said as they moved through the second hall, wider than the first and pillared in shining electrum. "The farthest place the sun's light will reach. And this corridor, where the images of the gods stand in shrines along the walls, is named The Hall Wherein They Rest. You will notice that your own likeness is no less flattering than any of the others, Wells. I have never been a petty man."

"Of course not."

Jongleur led him across the great vertical shaft known as the Hall of Hindering—Wells was forced to levitate himself briefly until he reached the far side—and up the vast ceremonial corridor simply called The Ramp, whose wall paintings glowed not just with life but with music and subtle movement, the one offense Jongleur had allowed against perfect classicism, since Ricardo Klement had begged to be allowed to make the last stage of the procession "more dramatic." Even the Lord of Life and Death had to admit the results were surprisingly subtle and tasteful—the upward-slanting corridor seemed open on both sides to a beautiful, stylized Garden of the Afterlife, where the gods disported gracefully in the shade of sycamore trees, singing and eating dates and other fruit brought to them by nubile servants.

"You really like this stuff, don't you?" Wells said suddenly.

Jongleur, who had forgotten where he was, lost in the dream of his own imminent conquest of the enemy he had fought so long—an enemy far older and more formidable than Robert Wells—paused for a moment, wishing to regain the measured tone with which he had begun the tour. "Yes. I do like 'this stuff,' Wells. More than that, it is as necessary to me as the blood—or what passes for blood, these days, chemicals whose names I no longer remember—which keeps my physical body alive."

As Jongleur slid above the ramp, smooth as a maglev train, Wells found himself beginning to hurry to keep up. Faced with a choice of indignities, he chose the lesser of the two; within moments he had floated abreast of the older man. "Necessary, you said?"

"Yes. Because the world is too small."

A long moment's silence passed. The painted tomb scenes slid past on either side and light rippled across the two gods' faces, the butterskin yellow and the pale green that was midway between putrescence and vegetative rebirth.

"Explain, please."

"The world is too small for belief, Wells. You and I, we have taken the raw stuff of chaos and out of it we have built empires. Either of us wields more power than any pharaoh ever did, more than any satrap of Babylon or emperor of Rome. We have all the powers they had. We lift a finger or blink an eye and men die. At our word, navies sail, armies march, countries are conquered, even if sometimes those countries do not realize it. But we have powers the ancients did not. We drain oceans. We raise mountains where no mountain stood. We populate the sky with our own constructed stars." He paused for a moment, as though his attention had been caught by some detail in the passing display. "Soon we will do what even the greatest monarch of Egypt only hoped might happen, but did not truly believe—for if he believed, why did the great king spend so much money and time building monuments to his own immortality and badgering the gods to protect his soul? The pharaoh, methinks, doth protest too much." A bleak, wintry grin. "In a matter of hours, we will in truth become gods. Measurably, reliably, scientifically. We will live forever. Our power will never die." He nodded slowly, but did not continue.

"Forgive me, Jongleur, but I don't quite understand . . ." said Wells at last.

"What? Ah. I am saying that if you do not *live* like a god, you will never be able truly to *be* a god. It requires bravery and intellect and immense resources to spit in the face of Mister . . . of Death. But I think it also requires something more. *Panache,* perhaps is the word. Style. To put oneself on an equal footing with the universe, and say 'I am the measure. There is no other.' Do you understand?"

For a passage of some little time, Wells said nothing. The Ramp flowed away beneath them, having at some point imperceptibly transmuted into faceted diamond, so that their own shapes were multiplied beneath them a millionfold.

"You . . . you are very eloquent," Wells said at last. "You give me much to think about."

Jongleur inclined his massive head and crossed his arms on his chest as they rose from the end of the ramp and into the final chamber. They hovered before an immense gilded expanse, walls and floor and ceiling all polished and gleaming like the sun, although only one of Ra's vertical rays spiked down through a hole in the roof hundreds of meters above them. A wide circle of green marble chairs so magnificent that even the word "thrones" seemed insufficient stood around the pool of light at the room's center, glittering like some jeweled desk set replica of Stonehenge. On a raised platform beside each seat lay a huge and ornately decorated sarcophagus of shining, blood-colored stone.

"This is where the Ceremony will take place," Jongleur said solemnly. "It is called the House of Gold. In the tomb of a mere pharaoh, in this spot where he at last became one with the gods, it would be a place little larger than a parlor room. I thought this more in keeping with the number and nature of our own ritual."

The pair stood for a long time in silence, watching as the single ray of sunlight, veiled and unveiled by the passing of unseen clouds, brought as much change to the vast golden room as a stone dropped into a still pond.

"It is . . . astonishing," Wells said at last.

"It is meant to be so." Jongleur nodded, satisfied. "I am pleased to say that Jiun Bhao had the same reaction." He rubbed his hands together, fraying the ancient bandages between the fingers. "When the time comes, we will all raise our cups in a toast. Yours and mine—and those of the two others, of course—will not, metaphorically speaking, contain that which is given to the rest of our Brotherhood. You may drink it or not—I am sure you can prove to your own satisfaction that I have no trick up my sleeve—but if you and Yacoubian and Jiun and I are not seen doing what all the rest are doing, questions will be asked. I will make sure that in all other ways we appear to go through the same experience." He turned to the other bandaged god. "Speaking of your colleague Yacoubian, where is he? I would have thought with his suspicious nature he would have been first in line to see what I've shown you today."

Wells did not seem bothered by the question. "Since the four of us will be completing the Ceremony later, Daniel felt that he could put some time into a pressing matter having to do with his own work—something that he wants to have wrapped up before taking the Grail. He told me this morning that he has it in hand now, and is certain that all will be resolved shortly after the Ceremony, and he will then be completely free."

"Good." Jongleur could not say it with much conviction. "In any case, if you will excuse me now, I have some matters of my own that need tying up."

"One last question. The rest of the Brotherhood are not trusting types, as you know. Surely some of them must have worried that you or I might do something just like this . . . ?"

Jongleur shook his head. "There is no benefit to treachery, not really—you and I are simply waiting out the first version of the Ceremony. We could even make the case that we *should* do this for their own good, so that those who know the system can solve any problems that might crop up."

"Sounds good, but I can't see someone like Ymona Dedoblanco being convinced."

Jongleur chuckled sourly. "No, nor can I. But even the most suspicious of the Brotherhood should know they have nothing to fear. With all of us diverting huge percentages of our assets into this system, we have just managed to keep it going, and even when we become immortal ourselves, there will be much more expensive work to be done before we can truly make the system permanent and indestructible. We need the whole Brotherhood alive within the network but still in control of their resources in the outside world. Unless they are idiots, they must realize that."

"Wealth and power don't prevent someone from being an idiot—present company excepted, of course." Wells showed a yellow smile. "I'll let you get back to your other business. You've been very generous." He made a tiny bow, only his head moving; it was not, as far as Jongleur could tell, part of the etiquette circuitry of Abydos-That-Was. "Perhaps you and I will find in the future that working together is of more benefit than working . . . at occasional cross-purposes."

Jongleur's gesture was magisterial. "We will have plenty of time to examine all possibilities. Farewell."

In the next moment, Ptah's sly smile and quietly penetrating eyes were gone.

Jongleur bathed in the white nothingness of his most neutral environment, trying to regain his equilibrium. It had been terribly hard, after the horror that had been visited on him in the boudoir of Isis, to re-enter his once beloved Egyptian realm, but he could not let squeamishness stand between him and the Grail.

He had wondered several times whether Wells had known of the treachery, might even have instituted it, and had found himself chewing over the man's words for hidden meaning the way a Taoist monk studied the ineffability of the Way, but with no success. If Wells *had* penetrated Jongleur's own private realms so thoroughly, all the more reason to keep him neutralized, wondering what Jongleur might intend—it was always easier to watch over an ally than an enemy. And right until the moment that he himself had tasted the Grail, Jongleur needed the American's insurance against the vagaries of the Other.

Now it was all coming to a climax. Decades of waiting, far more than a century's worth of fear, to be faced and slain in a single night. Events could yet conspire to thwart him, but it would not be for lack of years of obsessively careful planning, not to mention a gambler's instinct that had dropped entire nations into his grasp, and which had left him the single oldest human being on Planet Earth.

He let his thoughts cool, instructed the expensive medical plumbing that had long ago replaced his heart to slow its minute pulsations. All was in place. Now he need only wait for the Ceremony. He might even sleep a little.

One more time the sun would rise outside his huge glass tower on Lake Borgne, and one more time Felix Jongleur would wake into the burden of his ancient, ancient flesh. Then the next dawn to which he would open his eyes would be the measureless light of Eternity.

THERE was nothing left in the entire deserted universe but Dread and the thing.

Through emptiness that was all light and no light, it closed on him. Numbed, helpless, he felt it reach into him and pull him open, so that everything that made him an entity seemed to fall away before the assault. As though flicking switches, it neutralized the governors for his autonomic nervous system, and the vague notion that was his distant body began to break down: his heart started to race, his breathing to grow shallow, and the spasms of seizure took hold of him. Numbness gave way to pain as his body began to tear itself to bits—a searing agony so great that it overwhelmed the telematic buffers, as though every single nerve he had was being pulled writhing from its sheath.

But it was the pain that saved him. Of all human creatures, few knew it better than the man who had been Johnny Wulgaru. It had been his true mother, his first teacher, at times his one constant, and thus his only real friend. From his infancy pain had shaped him, made him sharp and remorseless, kept him as quiveringly alert as a lidless eye. Pain defined him.

And now, in the nothingness that had engulfed him, it was something familiar he could grab—a lifeline. He seized the pain even as it savaged him. As he had done through countless childhood beatings, through the pack-cruelties of bigger children in the institutions, he curled up behind pain as though it were a shield, hiding his sense of self from destruction, riding out the assault. But it would not be a long respite.

Reduced to a tiny point of fraying consciousness, he tried desperately to understand.

Whatever the attacking thing was, it was part of the Otherland system. The Grail Brotherhood would not build anything so important without being able to control it, so that meant somewhere there must exist the means of control.

Hero, he thought, rallying himself, and the image brought an eruption of fury from the center of his being. *Can't do this to me.* The thing battered him, ripping at the core that was his consciousness, using his treacherous meat body against him, but Dread fed on his own rage. He knew how to take a beating, knew how to protect that which was himself, the single greedy point that could never be cowed, which sustained itself against all damage by waiting to leap free and devour everything. He made himself small and hard as a collapsing star, condensed his *twist* to an almost infinitely narrow spike of will, and let his consciousness slide out along its length.

The thing was all around him, but he suddenly realized the thing itself was somehow bound. He knew these must be the Brotherhood's controls, the mechanical safeguards that could keep such a complicated and responsive intelligence behind walls; if he could find them, he could use them. He reached out, his special gift piggybacked on the investigative algorithms he had triggered in his assault on the system, and let the billions of node-points that made up the system matrix flash past, knowing he had no time for conscious examination.

The twist was all he had left. He let the complexity of the network's inner workings flash past him as he groped for the one thing he needed.

It was no use. Somewhere his body was in full clonic contraction, his lungs frozen, his heart beating so desperately that it had lurched into stumbling arrythmia. His brain was all but out of oxygen. The blazing, murderous point that was Dread, a single dwarf star in a vast empty universe, was about to collapse entirely.

Then he found it. He was far gone, and his understanding of these systems was limited by his own disinterest even at the best of times—did a dancer need a degree in gravitational science?—but as he stopped the scan and probed deep into the matrix, he knew that he had located the structures which bounded and restrained the Otherland operating system. Randomly, desperately, he reached out and seized the first one he could distinguish, then twisted it.

The monstrous thing that enveloped him flinched back—there was no other word to describe the suddenness and violence of the reaction. The effect was so dramatic that it almost broke the frail membrane that still held Dread in the world of the living. Somewhere, his body arched and sucked in air—he could almost see it, see Dulcie Anwin standing over the bed and its shrieking alarms, her face contorted with fear and hope—and he expanded his strangled consciousness to fill the space that had been given back to it. He twisted again, and again the thing that had attacked him heaved away, retreating in all directions, dispersing itself through the system like a cloud evaporating in bright sunlight. As it retreated, Dread finally let go, closer to death than he had ever been in a life full of mortality.

For a long time after that, Dread simply *was*—a leaf drifting on a puddle, a drop of dew poised and fat on the end of a grass blade. The seamless gray of the system platform had returned; he floated in it, and it waited for his commands. He slowly gathered back his strength and his will, putting them on as though redonning the armor of a questing knight, fitting each piece over limbs which had been scorched almost to cinders by the dragon's breath.

But I won, he thought. *I did it—me. The hero. The solitary pure one. The one who sees through lies. The one who can't be broken.*

He allowed the Beethoven to climb back up again, the fourth movement beginning its stirring quick-march tempo in his skull. *Hero.*

He reached out and found the controls of the Otherland system once more. There was much that was odd about them, even to his keen but unsophisticated perceptions. He experimented, and found that the safeguards were a strangely imprecise tool. Even a system this complicated was at base a machine, and thus susceptible to simple commands—stop, go; on, off. But as he triggered one of them, and felt the thing which had almost killed him—felt it even though it had made itself remote from the intruder and his fiery, painful sting—he thought he could feel something like a shudder pass through the system.

The more he considered, the more it seemed to Dread that the

Brotherhood controlled their unusual operating system by pain, of a sort. And if there was anything that Dread knew about, if there was any language of which Dread was a living master . . .

The last movement of the Ninth was swelling in his head now, the chorus shouting like warrior angels flying to the attack, buzzing his bones with the mighty "Ode to Joy."

> *Freude, Schoner Götterfunken,*
> *Tochter aus Elysium,*
> *Wir betreten feuer-trunken,*
> *Himmlische, dein Heiligtum!*

The thing which had tried to kill him, the security system, had broken and fled, and was now hiding in the most shadowy reaches of its impossibly vast matrix. But Dread had learned how to inflict pain on it. It feared him. Whatever it truly was, artificial being or fantastically complicated neural net . . . it had run from him.

Everything else could wait. The Old Man, the Sulaweyo bitch, everything.

"Feuer-trunken." That means "Fire-drunken." Drunk with fire. Like a god . . . Dread laughed, echoing the music, almost shouting with the pleasure of his victory and his returning strength.

It was time to hunt.

CHAPTER 32

Trojan Horse

NETFEED/NEWS: Can Chemistry Make Good Citizens?
(visual: virtual test subject)
VO: Despite complaints from numerous human rights
groups, the US Senate has passed a bill to fund
investigation into the feasibility of mandatory chemical
rebalancing of individuals with what some lawmakers called
"an organic propensity toward bad behavior." Complaints
from Rightswatch, the UNCLU, and various other groups
could not prevent the Margulies-Wethy Bill passing by a
wide majority.
(visual: Gojiro Simons of Rightswatch, press conference)
SIMONS: "It's a bad, illegal, unconstitutional combination
of prior restraint and Doctor Frankenstein. It's just an
unutterably dreadful idea. What's next? Thought control?
Behavioral implants like they're using in Russia, but put
into law-abiding citizens just to make sure they don't do
anything wrong . . . ?"

F OR a single shimmering moment, everything was right.

* * *

Sam Fredericks had spent a largely sleepless night wrestling with ideas that seemed far too slippery to be described by words like *duty* and *loyalty,* and when she slept briefly in the last hours before dawn, her mind was still not completely made up. When she woke to the sounds of battle, screams and curses and the dull smack of blade on armor, so close it might have been happening in the next room, she was terrified—not just by what she heard, but by what she now knew she must do.

Orlando was still sleeping, deeper and more peacefully than he had in weeks. Even the Myrmidons rapping on the cabin door, begging their king to come out and lead them before the Trojans destroyed the camp, did not stir him.

Sam crouched for a moment beside the bed. Orlando's face, or at least the face of Achilles that he wore, was as beautifully composed as something in a museum. She felt a clutch of helpless misery as she realized that the statues in museums were of people long dead. She reached out and touched him, sliding her fingers down his temple and into his tousled, golden hair.

Would I be in love with him if he looked like this? she wondered. *Big and strong and beautiful?*

It was hard to look at him. There was too much wrapped up in it, too many feelings that had no names. Sam stood up.

It was not easy to put on the armor, but she had been helped with her own by slaves, and she had tried to pay attention. She knew she really should call someone—that it was vitally important everything fit properly—but she did not want to give away the secret, and was even more reluctant to have someone intrude on the silent connection between herself and her sleeping friend.

Achilles' armor was heavier than her own, which had been heavy enough; she was grateful the system had given her a heroic male form and the muscles that went with it. When she had finished fitting the heavy bronze to her body, she returned to Orlando's side. She hesitated, then bent and kissed him on the cheek.

Outside, the soldiers were dashing back and forth, armored for combat but unable to do anything because their king had forbidden it. Fredericks stood in the doorway of the cabin as she cinched the leather strap of the borrowed helmet under her chin. One of the men noticed her and almost staggered with surprise. He dropped to one knee in a spontaneous gesture of fealty that made

Fredericks blush hotly with shame and even a kind of secret pleasure.

Others saw her and a shout arose. Some hurried to surround
her, full of questions which she did not answer; others hurried to
tell the rest of the Myrmidons that their king was going to war.
Sam gestured to the nearest charioteer, who sprang to life as though
electrified and bellowed for his comrades. Within moments drivers
had begun harnessing the horses, both men and animals almost
trembling with excitement.

Achilles' own chariot appeared, the yoked horses snorting and
stamping, the driver fighting hard just to keep them from bolting
across camp toward the curling black smoke and the clamor of
battle. Doing her best to imitate the nonchalance of a hero, Fredericks handed him her borrowed spears, then vaulted up behind
him. The Myrmidons, both the chariot riders and the foot soldiers,
formed up loose ranks around her; she scarcely had time to find
and get a good grip on the leather strap attached to the chariot's
rim before her own horses began to rear, almost jerking the car
out from under her. The driver used the whip to settle them, but
they seemed wild as demons.

Someone pointed down the beach. Fredericks turned in time
to see a mass of men surge out from behind one of the ships,
locked in a vicious dance of spear and shield. The Trojans were
so close! She thought she should shout something inspiring, but
could think of nothing that wouldn't sound like bad high school
drama; more importantly, she didn't want to risk giving away her
secret. Instead, she raised her spear and jabbed it toward where
the Greeks were desperately fighting to keep the torch-bearing
Trojans away from the line of ships, then shouted "Go!" in her
charioteer's ear, trying to pierce the din of the excited Myrmidon
soldiers.

The chariot shot forward so quickly that only the strap kept
her from tumbling out the back. With a rising, animal howl, her
troops surged out behind her.

The Trojans who had reached the ships, where they had a slight
numerical advantage over the straggle of defenders, looked up in
shock at the sound of the Myrmidons bearing down on them.
When they saw Sam waving a spear, doing her best to stand erect
in the bouncing chariot, their expressions of surprise turned quickly

to terror. Within moments they had disengaged from the Greeks and were stumbling in a disorganized rout back across the camp. Several went down, arrow-pierced, as Sam's charioteer pulled hard on the reins and turned the horses in pursuit.

All across the Greek settlement knots of battling men frayed and collapsed within moments of sighting Sam and the Myrmidon soldiers, a wave of astonishment that spread outward faster than men could run. By the time she and her chariots had reached the middle of the camp, the Trojans were fighting to get back out the gate. The Myrmidon assault smashed into the bottleneck of fleeing soldiers. Sam clung to the chariot rim as shouting men heaved around her. She had not yet struck a blow, but men were dying beneath the chariot wheels, and the survivors were being speared by her infantry like fish caught in a draining pond. The Myrmidons chanted the name of Achilles as though it were a magical spell, hacking and stabbing at everything in their path.

The clog at the gate abruptly loosened as the men who only a quarter hour before had all but overwhelmed the Greek defenses now spilled out onto the plain in panicky flight. A terrible joy rose through Sam, up from her groin and along her spine, unfolding in her head like a hot bloodflower. How mighty she felt! It was like being a god—wave your spear and whimpering men threw themselves into the mud.

As her charioteer steered the horses through the crush at the gate, a Trojan warrior who had fallen twenty meters ahead clambered to his feet without his weapons or shield and ran away across the uneven ground, so terror-struck he did not turn away to one side or the other, but only went tripping and stumbling on before the chariot. Sam lifted the long, heavy spear and balanced it. She might not be Achilles, might not even be Orlando, with his long experience as Thargor in half the wars of the Middle Country, but this simulation had given her a hero's muscles, a hero's arm, a hero's aim. She drew the spear back and flung it.

For a single shimmering moment, everything was right.

In Sam's favorite sports, soccer and baseball, there were instants of pure clarity when it was only you and the ball, when the world went silent and the second stretched. With a runner sprinting down the base path, you cocked, strode, and threw, and even if you weren't the strongest arm in the world, there were times, golden times, when the throw was perfect—when even if the ball was going to bounce once or twice, you knew as you released it that it would nestle into the fielder's glove at just the right height, and everything would come together, runner, base, ball . . . but you would already be strolling off the field, because you knew what was going to happen.

The spear flew from Sam's hand as though it were on a rail, flexing slightly as it hissed through the air, but even though the man was stumbling over the uneven ground, Sam knew as it left her that the line of flight and the line of the target would intersect as neatly as if they had been drawn with a ruler.

The spear struck the fleeing Trojan like a thunderbolt, the impact so great that he was flung forward off his feet. He crashed on his face and skidded; the spearhead that had shoved through his chest gouged the muddy earth like the blade of a plow, making the long shaft waggle. A scream of hungry approval went up from the Myrmidons as they saw what their leader had done, as though deeds of blood had finally sealed the truth of the miracle.

Sam's chariot reached the body so fast that the charioteer made no attempt to swerve. The heavy wheels rolled across the dead man's arm and head with a quick, sickening crunch.

And suddenly Sam Fredericks remembered where she was.

Oh, my God. In the midst of the triumphant Myrmidon chariots surging across the plain like a riptide, the riders hacking the legs out from under fleeing Trojans and leaving them to the merciless spears of the foot soldiers, Sam felt like she was going to throw up. *Oh, my God, these people are killing each other. What am I doing here?*

But it was too late. Even if she screamed to the charioteer to turn back, he would not hear her, and the other chariots were pressed in too close to allow it. Nothing would stop the Myrmidons' thundering, headlong assault until they reached the thickening mass of armored men in the middle of the plain, where the Trojans had finally stopped to face their pursuers, turning murderous spears outward like the defensive spines of some massive creature.

It's too late. She clung to the chariot as it jounced wildly over the torn ground. Around her, the war cries of Achilles' soldiers rose like the belling of a hunting pack. *Oh, Gardiner, what have I done?*

"**I**T'S hopeless," Renie gasped. "There must be five thousand men between Orlando and us—I can't even see him anymore."

The four of them were struggling to catch their breath on the outskirts of the battle. They had traveled far up the beach beneath the slipping afternoon sun, but as the Greeks and Trojans continued to hack away at each other like overwound clockwork toys, Renie and her companions had stopped to rest in this comparatively peaceful spot where there were far more slaves than warriors and more wounded men than healthy ones. If their long-lost friend had not been battling for his life in the middle of the plain, it would have been a good place to be.

!Xabbu had scaled an outcropping of rock. "I think I see Orlando," he called down. "He is still in his chariot, but he is in a great crowd of soldiers. The chariot is stopped."

"Jesus Mercy, this is making me crazy!" Renie threw down her spear. "It would be a suicide mission to try to get close to him."

"Be worse for me," T4b pointed out. "Least you got your own mamalockin' armor." He was not happy with the trade of his golden armor for the bits and pieces they had scavenged from the battlefield.

Paul Jonas leaned heavily on his spear, his Odysseus beard dripping with sweat. "So what do we do?"

Renie shook her head, exhausted. Beside enduring several skirmishes in which they had fought off roving bands along the fringe of battle, she and the others also had run the better part of two kilometers in heavy bronze plate, carrying shields and weapons. "Just let me think." She peeled off her helmet and dropped it, then stooped and put her hands on her knees, waiting until the blood circulating in her head felt like something other than molten metal. She straightened. "One thing we have to do is get word to Martine and the others. We have to do that right now—tell her Orlando and Fredericks are alive, and that we've found you."

"What good will that do?" Jonas asked. "You said they're being kept in the women's quarters. It's not like they're going to come riding out and save us."

"No, but what if the battle just goes on? What if Orlando survives and we have to spend another night out here trying to get to him? Martine doesn't even know that !Xabbu and T4b and I are still alive!"

The Bushman had scrambled down from the rock and was catching his breath. He was clearly less weary than his companions, but even he was starting to flag. "Shall I go, then?" he asked. "I can run a long time in a day, Renie, and then run more if I have to—that is one thing my childhood has given me. We are closer to Troy now than we are to the Greek camp. I can reach it in an hour, perhaps less."

She shook her head. "It's not just getting there, it's getting in as well." She turned to T4b. "You should be the one, Javier," she said.

"Quit calling me that!"

"Listen to me. You're the one that everybody recognizes. I don't know who this Glaucus was, but he must have been Troy's version of Miss Congeniality. The best chance of getting in without trouble will be to claim you've got a message for the king or something like that, and you're probably the most likely of us to get a break."

T4b was sullenly considering it as !Xabbu touched her arm. "But I should go with him, Renie. If they won't open the gate, he may need to climb the wall to get into the city. That may take two people working together." Especially, he did not need to say, if one of them was T4b.

"Climb? Like, up *that*?" T4b gestured at the distant white stone of Troy's outer wall. He did not look happy.

"But . . ." She realized !Xabbu was right. "Of course. It's safer for two than for one, anyway. It is a battlefield, after all." She grabbed at her friend's hand, then dragged him to her and hugged him. "God, please just be careful. Both of you. If you can find Martine, tell her what's happened. Her Trojan name is Cassandra, and she's the king's daughter, so you shouldn't have much trouble locating her. Tell her Orlando's in the middle of the battle and we're trying to think of a way to get him out."

"I just remembered something from the poem, in case you need it," Paul Jonas said. "There's a place on one of the walls that's easier to climb—I think it's the west wall, beside a fig tree. I remember some teacher of mine making a bit of a fuss about it."

!Xabbu nodded. "That is good to know."

"So . . . over the wall?" T4b asked, hesitating.

"If he doesn't want to go, I could do it," said Jonas.

"No, you wouldn't recognize any of them, and there's not enough time to risk a mistake. Javier and !Xabbu can do it." Renie reached out and took T4b's shoulders. "You probably won't have to climb anything. Just act important, and if they ask you too many questions at the gate, get scorchy on them. Now take care of yourself."

He allowed a brief hug before pulling away. "Might as well get going," he said gruffly, then turned to !Xabbu. "You flyin', too?"

!Xabbu nodded and gave Renie a last smile, then the pair jogged away toward distant Troy, the city's congregated towers pale and perfect as an ivory chess set.

"The Bushman—he's important to you, isn't he?" said Paul Jonas as they watched the two figures obscured by swirling dust.

"Yes. Yes, he is."

"Oh, God, I've just thought of something else," Jonas said unhappily. "Where do you think Orlando's friend is? We didn't stop to see if he might still be at the camp."

Renie shook her head. "I don't believe it. Those two are like Siamese twins—if one of them's out there, the other is bound to be right next to him or right behind." She squinted, then swore. The windblown dust was spouting from beneath chariot wheels. A ragged arm of Trojan cavalry had swung wide in an attempt to encircle the Greek flank, and Renie and Paul Jonas were uncomfortably close to the line of attack. Already other stragglers from the battle's edge were hurrying toward them, fleeing for their lives. Renie snatched at Jonas' arm and yanked him back toward the sloping beach and its only relative safety.

"Jesus Mercy, I'm an idiot!" she groaned as they stumbled down a slope. "!Xabbu and T4b—we forgot to agree on a place to meet up." Arrows, fewer now than earlier in the day, but still just as deadly, flew over their heads and dug into the sandy soil.

Jonas was trying to run while keeping his shield over his head,

and not doing a very good job of it. "We can worry about it whe
we get there," he panted. "If we live that long."

To Sam Fredericks, caught in a crush of men and chariots i
the middle of the field, the walls of Troy still seemed remote,
dream-castle from a fairy tale standing pale and untouched abov
the muck. Around her men screamed and died. Most of the Myr
midon heroes and their resurgent allies had climbed down from
their chariots to engage the Trojans hand to hand.

"Now is the time, O King," her driver called above the dir
"Now you can break this last stand of Priam's folk and send ther
fleeing back to the walls, where we will slaughter them."

Sam felt paralyzed. When she had decided to put on the armo
she had been able to think only as far as keeping the Trojans awa
from Orlando. She had seen herself making a brave show, per
haps even giving the rest of the Greeks a moment to recover thei
courage and throw the Trojans back, but she had imagined noth
ing like this—almost under the walls of Troy, with death all aroun
her and the battle perhaps resting on what she did next. . . .

The charioteer swore an oath as a badly-thrown spear rattle
off the body of the chariot and for a moment became tangled i
the horses' harnesses. One of the proud beasts stumbled for a mo
ment, and Sam was again almost pitched out, but sheer terror ha
quickly made her an expert at holding on.

"There," she shouted, pointing to an open space beyond th
stew of men and spears. She had to get out this scanhouse be
fore her nerves failed entirely. "Go there!"

The charioteer gave her a strange look, but lifted the reins an
whipped the horses through a gap in the swirl of battle. Even a
they burst out to relative safety, the battle behind them broke apar
again with the Greeks pressing forward. Dozens of Trojans drev
their chariots away and hastened back toward the walls of thei
home. Seeing the retreat, others broke from the struggle and joine
them, and for a moment Sam felt like she was the leader in som
strange race, her chariot in front, the fleeing Trojans right behind
with her own allies sweeping along after them, shouting loudl
as they sensed victory within reach.

For long seconds she could only cling as they hurtled alon
over the uneven ground, the chariot bouncing and creaking lik

he world's most poorly maintained carnival ride, until the huge
white walls were only a long stone's throw away. Abruptly, the
charioteer yanked hard on the reins and the horses veered sharply
to the side, coming around in a broad circle to face the Trojan
horde stampeding back toward the shelter of Troy.

"Now they will see you and know fear, my lord!" the charioteer shouted.

"What? Are you scanning *utterly*?"

Sam had put down her spear so she could cling with both hands
to the side of the chariot, which was up on one wheel and seemed
about to tip over at any moment. The idiot charioteer was about
to turn her simple attempt to get out of the fighting into some
kind of heroic death-stand against a hundred terrified Trojans. She
slipped down until centrifugal force pressed her against the inside
of the chariot, then reached out and snatched at his greaved leg,
trying to get his attention. They completed their turn, the walls
directly behind her now. She thought she could even see tiny figures on the battlements.

"Stop!" she shouted, pulling on the driver's leg. "What's wrong
with you? Stop!"

He looked down, clearly astonished to find great Achilles kneeling on the floor of the chariot. An instant later something snapped
into his chest. He let go of the reins to grab at the black shaft
quivering there, but the chariot bounced and he was gone, hurled
away like unneeded ballast.

The one mercy was that Sam had only a moment to think about
it. The careening chariot began to wobble, then the wheels struck
something solid, which almost knocked the entire car sideways.
It bounced, rose, then struck again even harder as something splintered with a terrible, final sound. Another impact sent Sam flying
through air.

She struck the ground hard, rolling so fast that her thoughts
were like rapidly beating black wings—around and around and
around and then she hurtled into nothingness.

At first Sam thought she had gone blind. Her eyes stung, and
she could see nothing. Her swollen, aching head seemed about to
burst like a water balloon.

You're an idiot. You're the uttermost idiot in the world. . . . she told herself as she struggled up onto her hands and knees. When she wiped at her face, her hand came away slick and wet. Terror made her whimper as she rubbed her eyes.

Light.

For a moment she could see only a little shimmer, a smear of gray and brown, but after the momentary blindness it seemed as sumptuous as full-color stereoptic wraparound. She wiped again and now could see her own hands through eyes made cloudy by the same blood that was dribbling from her fingers.

I've ripped my face off. Oh, God, I'm probably all torn up, all ugly. A thought whisked past—she could die in this network, but what about getting a disfiguring injury?—leaving her with another even more terrible idea. *How do I know I'm not dying anyway?*

A bad head injury. Even the words had the stomach-clenching sound of the End of the Road.

She had rubbed away enough blood that she could see around her, although her eyes still smarted. The chariot lay a dozen meters away, or at least the largest piece of it did. One of the horses was clearly dead, the other still kicking fitfully. Men in other chariots were wheeling toward her over the rough ground, but she had no idea which side they were on.

Sam found one of the spears and used it as a prop as she struggled to her feet. A fiercely burning ache ran all the way down her side—only the cracked-eggshell feeling in her head had prevented her from noticing it before now—but as far as she could tell, none of her limbs were broken.

She watched the distant chariots speeding toward her and wondered what to do next. She did not realize that others had been closer until the voice spoke from behind her.

"So we will test our arms after all, son of Peleus. I see you have lost your chariot. What else will you lose this day, I wonder?"

Sam Fredericks turned so fast a jolt of dizziness nearly knocked her down. The man standing before her seemed impossibly large despite his perfect proportions. His eyes glared from the slot of his helmet. "Who . . . ?" she croaked.

The man banged his long spear against his shield; the noise made Sam's head feel like it was collapsing in on itself. "Who?" he roared. "You have slaughtered my kinsmen, sacked my father's cities, and yet you do not know Hector, son of Priam, when you meet him face-to-face?" The man pulled off his helmet, setting free his thick knot of black hair, but even as he did a peculiar look came over his handsome, scowling features. "You look strange to me, Achilles. Has falling to the ground changed you so much?"

Sam tried to back up and found herself teetering on the edge of a shallow ditch. "I'm . . . I'm not . . ."

"By Olympian Zeus, you are not Achilles at all, but Patroclus in his armor! Has all this rout then been in fear of something that was not so?" He snorted like an angry horse. "Have you put Troy's power to flight with naught but the effigy of Achilles?" His expression hardened as though a cold wind had blasted it to freezing. He raised his massive spear. Sam stared at its huge bronze point with horrified absorption. "Well, you will not live to enjoy your joke . . ."

Her shield was out of reach. She almost thought she heard someone call her name—a distant voice, like the last words of a dream heard while waking up—but it was meaningless now. Sam could only cringe back, raising her hands to her face as Hector took a few running steps and sent the black spear whistling toward her.

THERE were moments, as he urged his horse across the plain, that he seemed to be riding through some ancient tapestry from a museum, past frozen vignettes of men struck down while fleeing and of fallen warriors locked with enemy soldiers in mutually fatal embraces—dozens of small but varied illustrations of the Folly of Mankind. He skimmed above it all, still seeing with some of the strange, high clarity with which he had awakened, but intent on hurrying forward.

Even in the spots the active battle had left behind, it was hard to make really good time through the corpses of men and horses and the clouds of crows and other scavengers. Although Thargor was one of the finest bareback riders in all the Middle Country—and Orlando, to his gratitude, had apparently retained some virtual command of those skills—he still found himself wishing desperately for a saddle.

Beggars can't be choosers, he reminded himself. It was not a very inspiring war cry.

*   *   *

Orlando thought he could see Fredericks in the distance now, the polished bronze armor—Orlando's own armor—glinting in the occasional spray of sunlight. The wind was growing stronger. Whirling horizontal dust clouds sprang up and rushed past him as he dug in his heels and leaned forward over his straining horse's neck. The morning's clarity was beginning to fade, leaving him with only a dogged sense of the task in front of him. At times it seemed like the fever had returned and he thought he could hear whispering voices all around him.

Although there were more men here on the fringes of combat than he had encountered on his ride across the plain, few raised a hand against him. Some clearly mistook him for the man whose armor he wore; he ignored their cries of recognition as he galloped past. Here and there others who wished to challenge him rose up in his path, both Greeks and Trojans, but Orlando did his best to ride around them, not wanting to waste time on meaningless combat. When forced, he used the momentum of his horse and his long spear to shove them away; if he killed one or two, it was more by accident than design. But for the most part the survivors who had made their way to the battle's edge, or had been left there when its strongest tide swept past, seemed to have little wish to oppose the lone rider in golden armor. Most hurried to get out of his way.

This much was familiar to Orlando. By the time Thargor had fought in his last great battles, at Godsor Rim and in the Pentalian Swamps, his reputation was such that only the most famous heroes or a few suicidal overachievers hoping to make a reputation of their own would fight him on open ground, one-to-one. It was strange, as he floated along almost separate from his own body, to remember those make-believe wars. In the Middle Country he had been full of adrenaline and roaring good humor, the barbarian lord of the battlefield, cutting down men by the dozens and leaving a wake of mangled bodies all across the field—fighting two, three, even four men at once just for the glory of the challenge. Now he wanted only to survive long enough to accomplish a single small task.

He was closing on the thickest part of the battle, which had crawled across the plain like a living organism until it was almost within bowshot of Troy's mighty walls. As he jerked the horse's harness to avoid a wounded man crawling on the ground, he caught a glimpse of something shiny bursting free from the middle of the conflict, heading for the walls as though bearing some crucial strategic message for Troy's defenders. It was Fredericks, he felt sure—the gleam was his friend's figure crouched low behind the charioteer—but Orlando could make no sense of what was happening. A few of the nearer Trojan chariots sped in pursuit, and two or three more curled out from another part of the chaos as though to catch Fredericks in a pincer, but they were all too far behind to catch up.

But what was Fredericks doing?

Ever more desperate now to reach his friend, Orlando saw open ground before him and dug his heels into his horse's sides. Fredericks' distant chariot suddenly veered away from the walls in a wide circle, curling back on its own path.

Doesn't she see those men are after her? Orlando reached back and spanked his horse's flank hard with the butt of his spear, then let the reins go slack as he leaned in and grabbed a fistful of braided mane, clinging as the animal belted toward a gap in the fighting.

Something had happened to Fredericks' chariot. It rose for a moment, cresting a bump, then smashed down and rose again, but this time only one on side. For almost three full seconds it careened on one wheel, then suddenly chariot and horses were down in a single confused mass, tumbling over and over. A wheel flew up into the air and spun several times like a flipped coin before falling away to one side. Orlando's view was blocked by the chariots now wheeling toward the wreckage.

He screamed his friend's name, but only a few heads even turned—the battle around him had become a grim, final struggle, and no man's life was safe. A helmeted man stumbled out of a clump of soldiers right into his path. He did not even see Orlando before the horse ran him down.

Within moments the dense mass of the battle's center was falling away behind him and he was again speeding across open plain. As he passed the first of the chariots that had been pursuing Fredericks, Orlando raised his spear to skewer either the crouching driver or his armored passenger.

No, they're just Puppets, he told himself and veered away. *Like windup toys. Don't waste energy getting angry.* But he was angry. Instead of the laughing excitement of Thargor's Middle Country battles, he was full of cold, detached fury.

He could see the wreckage of the chariot clearly now, only a few hundred meters away; his heart stuttered as he saw a body crumpled grotesquely beside it, but a moment later another figure crawled out of the high grass and lurched up onto its feet. The armor it wore was his own. Before he could even feel relief, a huge bronze chariot wheeled to a skidding stop and a tall man jumped out of the cart and jogged toward Fredericks.

"Stop!" Orlando shouted, but the wind snatched his words away. "It's me you want!"

Fredericks was hobbling badly, and made no attempt to flee the armored man. Orlando kicked at the horse's ribs, reaching toward the two small figures as though a few more inches could allow him to stop what was about to happen. The larger man raised a spear, then skipped forward and heaved it at Fredericks.

Orlando's friend took a helpless backward step and tumbled into a ditch. The spear sliced through the spot where she had stood and flew another twenty meters before it hit the ground and dug deep into the earth.

Other chariots were pulling up as Fredericks struggled up onto the edge of the ditch and crouched there on hands and knees. Orlando kept his head against the horse's neck, closing the distance, but slowly, so slowly . . . ! The man who had missed his throw returned to his chariot where he snatched another spear from his driver.

Orlando could faintly hear the man's voice now. "The gods have saved you, Patroclus. You have your own spear—try your arm, and see if it is strong enough to dent my shield."

Fredericks wavered, but did not stand up. Only the armor made Orlando certain it was his friend, since her face was a mask of blood.

"It's me!" Orlando screamed. "You want *me,* you bastard!"

The man turned. For a moment, seeing the stranger's thick black hair and powerful muscles, Orlando thought he was looking at his own Thargor sim. "Glaucus?" the man called. "Why do you shout at me, noble Lycian? Is your house not bound by love and blood to that of my father Priam?"

For the first time, and with a sinking heart, Orlando knew who he faced. He had heard enough stories in the last two days about Hector to know he could not have picked a worse enemy, but things were too far gone to stop now. He reined up the horse and swung down. The ground felt strangely unsolid beneath his feet, as though he walked on clouds.

Oh, God, I don't think I'm strong enough.

The two tall men faced each other across the hummocky ground, each clutching a long spear. Other chariots had pulled up, but the occupants seemed to sense the momentous nature of what was happening and merely watched in gaping silence.

"I'm not Glaucus." Orlando pulled off his own helmet, letting the golden hair spill free. "And I'm not going to let you kill my friend either."

Hector did not react. Instead, a curious stillness seemed to flow through him, a stillness so complete that for a long moment Orlando wondered if the Trojan would ever move again.

"You are here, then," Hector said slowly. He picked up his helmet and pulled it on, so that his eyes were invisible in the blackness of the slot. "Raper of cities. Murderer of innocents. Great hero of the Greeks, more anxious to listen to songs of your own glory than to come out and fight. But finally . . . you are here." He clanged the shaft of his spear against his shield. "One of us will be carried from this field, his life smashed out of him. This the gods decree!"

"Gardiner, don't!" Fredericks shouted. "You're not strong enough. You're sick."

She was right, but a look around showed Orlando that although the largest part of the Greek force was now moving in their direction, the nearest Greek soldiers were still long minutes away. Much closer, a dozen Trojan soldiers and charioteers had formed a sort of gallery; they might be content simply to watch this exciting moment, but Orlando knew they wouldn't allow him to run away.

He walked with as much calm as he could muster to the wreckage of Fredericks' chariot. Achilles' shield lay on the ground beside it, wedged beneath the mutilated driver. Orlando rolled the man to one side, a little heartened to realize he had some strength after all, that even a sick Achilles was at least as strong as an ordinary mortal. He slid the shield over his forearm and curled his fist around the handle, then turned back to Hector, his heart beating so fast his head hurt.

I don't know enough about spear fighting. I've got to get him in close so I can use a sword, where all that Thargor experience might pay off. But he knew even as he thought about it that he could not trade blows long with this strapping, godlike figure. Just riding most of the way across the plain of Troy had left him exhausted, his muscles trembling.

"Gardiner! No!" Fredericks shouted again. Orlando did his best to ignore it.

"Right," he called to Hector. "Bring it, baby."

How well that antique Americanism translated to the world of Homer, Orlando could not know, but Hector seemed to understand it perfectly well. He took a few running steps, drawing his spear back, then sent it hissing toward Orlando. It was on top of him so quickly he barely had time to throw up his shield before it struck, a shocking impact that knocked him backward off his feet. As he tumbled, he felt a scalding pain in his ribs.

That's it. He's killed me.

He drew his knees under him and saw blood on his side, but although he felt like he had been struck by a car, a moment's inspection suggested the wound was more painful than it was mortal. His shield lay a short distance away, completely pierced, a full meter of Hector's spear sticking through it.

He climbed awkwardly to his feet. A larger crowd was beginning to form now as men hurried across the battlefield toward the showdown. Hector stood watching him, shield dangling at his side. Short of breath, Orlando did not waste any more energy on taunts. He didn't feel much like it, anyway. He found his own spear, which he had dropped, measured the distance with his eye, then ran forward and flung it as hard and straight as he could.

It flew fast and far enough, which was some relief—his virtual muscles were still strong and under his control—but it had been a long time since Thargor had fought with a spear: Orlando's skills were rusty. Hector did not even need the shield he had raised, but instead ducked to one side and let it buzz harmlessly past. He, too, seemed to think the time for shouting insults was over. He drew his bronze sword and sprinted toward Orlando.

I didn't even take out his shield, Orlando thought bitterly. *He's as big as I am, if not bigger, and he's got a big old scorching shield.* He drew his own sword, which came awkwardly to his hand, the balance strange and unfamiliar. Orland fought a feverish desire simply to drop it and lie down. *My sword—Thargor's sword—it's come through each simworld with me. It must be the one Fredericks took. It's probably still in the chariot.* He pulled a long dagger from his other sheath and stepped out to meet the charge of Priam's godlike son.

From the first moments, when he ducked Hector's brutal swipe, then retaliated with a chopping stroke of his own which sent a searing pain up his side but only bounced harmlessly off the rim of the other man's shield, Orlando knew he was in trouble. Whatever advantage he might have from Thargor's years of brawling in the taverns of Madrikhor was made useless by the curved shell of wood and metal which Hector had and he didn't. This was not the free-swinging combat Thargor knew—the Trojan fought as though he still held a spear, staying behind the shield and jabbing at Orlando's relatively unprotected limbs whenever he tried to carry the attack to Hector.

Within the first minute Orlando had already used the hilt of the long dagger to catch two different sword thrusts, and its crosspiece was nearly bent backward. Hector was incredibly strong—even if the other man had been without a shield, Orlando did not think he could survive trading blows with him for very long. Much of his own recovered strength, taxed by the long ride across the plain, had melted away in the first violent moments of the struggle, and every time he had to use his sword to push Hector's shield away he felt himself grow weaker. Nobody who had not practiced combat understood how fast strength could evaporate when the heart was beating fast and hard blows were being traded.

But if Hector was also feeling the effects of a long day on the battlefield, he was not showing it. He moved like a jungle cat, stalking, slashing. When the sun's rays caught them, his eyes glittered in the slot in his helmet, the brows drawn down into a permanent scowl.

By turning in a slow circle and giving ground in a calculated fashion—ground he would have been giving up anyway, since he could not hold against Hector's hammering assaults—Orlando managed to back some distance toward the spot where Fredericks stood watching in fright.

"Just run, Orlando!" she shouted miserably. "It's not worth it!"

He gritted his teeth. Fredericks seemed to think that this fight was like yesterday's battle, where both sides would back away from each other at sunset. But Orlando understood the look in Hector's eyes, knew the man's hatred would keep him in pursuit even if Orlando ran into the ocean and drowned himself. "Get my sword!" he shouted back at Fredericks. "The one you took— get it and throw it where I can reach it!"

"If Hephaestus himself forged your blade," Hector snarled, "it will not save your life, Achilles." He shoved his shield into Orlando's face and hacked at his legs. Orlando stumbled back, panting. He could feel his knees growing weak and wondered if he would be able to avoid the next such strike. Both men were breathing loudly, but it was Orlando's lungs that did not seem to be filling all the way.

Got to get that shield away, he told himself. *Got to . . .*

Something landed in the dirt behind him. Orlando barely had time to step over it without snagging his heels and tripping. He ducked a wicked stab that flicked out from behind Hector's shield like a serpent's tongue; then, forced into complete trust that Fredericks had done what he asked, he dropped his sword and reached down.

It was indeed his own blade—he knew it as it filled his hand, and did not waste time on the morbid thought of what he would have done if it had been something else, a rock thrown by a spectator, perhaps. Hector tried to take advantage of the changeover, and Orlando barely avoided another blow at his face. As he staggered back and lifted the sword, reveling in its familiar balance, he felt a moment of hope.

That hope did not last long. Even with the more familiar weapon, he was still outmanned. Hector kept coming, banging Orlando's arm and shoulder numb with his shield, hammering on Orlando's blade until his hand stung so badly he could hardly grip the hilt. Orlando kept giving ground, aware that he was being driven slowly toward the walls of Troy but helpless to do anything about it. The winds that scoured the plain turned the sweat chill on his skin. His strength seemed to be lifting away from him, rising like mist.

"The Greeks!" Fredericks shouted excitedly. "The Greeks are coming!"

Between dodged blows, Orlando could see a little of it from the corner of his eye, saw many of the Trojans who had been watching the duel turn to aid those of their countrymen who were being driven back by the Greek forces, but he knew it meant little as far as his own fate was concerned: even were the Greeks ultimately to win, it would be long after Hector had beaten him into bloody jelly.

The sun slid down into the arms of the sea, and for a moment fire spread across the waves. The sky was beginning to lose its color, but Orlando could still see Hector's bright eyes boring into his own. His arms were aching, and the curious sense of detachment had returned, as though his mind were about to abandon his doomed body. Orlando got his sword up in time to redirect a powerful backhand stroke by Hector, but his own dagger lunge failed to score before Hector swung his shield back. The blade struck hard against the shield's brass boss and the impact traveled up Orlando's arm like electricity; his dagger dropped from numbed fingers.

While Orlando was still trying to bring his sword up, Hector swung his shield and struck Orlando on the side of the helmet so hard that it flew off and Orlando was knocked off his feet. He dropped and rolled, correctly guessing that Hector would follow up with his sword, but although the attack did not find the crease in his body armor, he still felt the blade score the unprotected back of his leg, just missing slicing his hamstring. He tried to drag himself upright but he could not get his feet beneath him.

Orlando turned, still on his knees, and lifted his sword to protect his head. The hilt was slippery with blood and hard to grasp. Hector stood over him, staring down, then extended his blade until the point hovered just an inch from Orlando's face, all but blocking his view.

"Your body will not be ransomed," Hector said. "After the harm you have done to my father's people, you will feed the dogs. You will howl in the arid halls of Hades to see it."

Orlando tried again to get his legs set for one last spring, but they would not obey him. He crouched, trembling.

People were shouting all around now, cheering for the kill. Orlando took a ragged breath and felt it burn down his throat and into his lungs. *Nobody ever thinks much about breathing,* he told himself. *As long as they can do it . . .*

A deafening, grinding screech rose above the cries of men like the fingernails of God being drawn across a mile-wide blackboard. Startled, Hector turned and looked over his shoulder.

"The gates . . . ?" His voice was slow, devastated, as though he had been struck by lightning. "But what fool . . . ?"

Orlando knew he could not muster the strength to reach Hector's throat, so he grabbed the sword hilt with both hands and shoved it with his fading strength into the place where the man's legs met. When Hector dropped to his knees, gasping in helpless shock and fountaining blood from his groin, Orlando tugged the sword free and rammed it into the slit in his enemy's helmet.

Orlando did not realize that he had also fallen until the darkening sky was directly before his face, the first stars peering out of the dusk like shy children.

I lost. He beat me. Orlando struggled to keep the sky in front of him, but it was turning black. Somewhere, Fredericks was calling his name, but it was fading in a great roar of men's voices and the thunder of hooves. *He's dead now—but he beat me.*

"CODE *Delphi.* Start here.

"I do not know how long I have to record these thoughts, or even if they will be recoverable. I only know this might be my last chance. There is screaming all around me and the fires are everywhere. Just moments ago a spark caught Emily's hair, and if Florimel had not been right beside her, I think Emily might have been fatally burned.

"We are hiding in one of the deserted houses near the gate, but they are pulling women out into the street on all sides, raping and murdering them. The Greeks are almost insane with vengeance—they are slaughtering children, too, killing them even in the arms of their mothers. In only an hour great Troy has become Hell. I can hardly bear to think what I have done.

"T4b and !Xabbu made their way back into the city, claiming

to have an important message for King Priam. They found us in the women's quarters of the palace and breathlessly told us what happened since they left us. Florimel and I were astonished to learn that Orlando and Fredericks were still alive, but frightened to hear that Orlando had charged out into the battle. I could think of nothing to do about it—I was furious that we had not learned better how to manipulate the access device, which dangled in a pouch at my belt, useless as a stone—but we roused Emily and the five of us hurried across the city toward the walls. . . .

"My God. The roof of the house next door has just collapsed, and there is fire already in the window frame of this house where we are hiding. I do not know how much longer we can stay here, but there are too many Greek soldiers in the street—if we step outside, they will . . .

"No. Order, there must be order. I will record—I will save what I can.

"With !Xabbu and T4b, we ran to the city walls. T4b used his spear and shield to clear a space for our passage through the throng. All around us people were hurrying in fear and excitement, shouting bits of rumor—the Greeks were being destroyed, their ships burned . . . no, another screamed, great Hector had been killed and the Trojan forces were routed. People atop the walls tried to make sense of what they saw, and called down conflicting stories.

"We clambered up the steps onto one of the watchtowers. The action below was too distant for me to make out except as patterns of motion and heat, fractal swirls. The noise from those watching on the walls was louder to us than the sounds of battle, but the fighting was clearly moving closer. !Xabbu told me that the Greeks seemed to be pushing the Trojans back on the city, then he made a clicking sound of surprise. Orlando had charged out in front of all the others, he said, the gleaming bronze armor of Achilles impossible to miss. He was rushing toward the walls of Troy as though he intended to throw them down himself, stone by stone. Then his chariot turned, caught a wheel, and rolled over. Beside me, Florimel let out a muffled cry of anguish.

"The descriptions from the others were more confusing than my own strange senses—first that Orlando seemed to have been speared by Hector and had fallen, then that someone else in T4b's discarded armor had come to challenge Hector instead. I began to get an inkling of what might have happened—somehow the system is playing cruel tricks on us, forcing us to relive parts of the ancient poem, or else such things are just inevitabilities of the simulation. In any case, whichever was Orlando and whichever Fredericks, neither of them had the strength to stand for long against the powerful Hector.

"Beyond this combat the Greeks were pressing closer, pushing back the brave but outnumbered Trojans. It seemed only the death of the Greek champion Achilles might discourage them and save Troy—but that would mean the death of one of our friends. I curled my hands into fists so hard that my nails cut the skin of my palms.

"A desperate idea came to me. I led Florimel and the others down from the watchtower, to the half-dozen Trojan soldiers who stood just inside the massive Skaian Gate. As we had done, they were struggling to make sense of the conflicting information coming down from the wall.

"I shouted at the one who seemed to be their leader, 'King Priam orders you to open the gate!' I could not see his face, but I could guess his expression.

"'Are you mad?' he demanded, his voice angry but tight with fear—I think he recognized me.

"I shouted at him, 'I am the king's daughter—why do you think he sent me? So that you would know my face and trust my word. And here is the hero Glaucus of Lycia, too. Hector is driven back against the gate by Achilles. Priam wishes you to open the gate and let him in, or in moments the king's godlike son will be dead!'

"The other soldiers stirred, nervous and uncertain, but the leader was not so easily swayed. 'No woman can tell me to open the gate, king's daughter or not!'

"I looked at !Xabbu, then realized I did not trust him to act without question. To my shame, I did not even pause, but turned to T4b instead and said, 'Kill this man.'

"Even young Javier hesitated, but only for an instant—his blood was high with excitement and fear. As the soldiers looked on in stunned disbelief, T4b rammed his spear into the leader's stomach. The man fell to the ground, but did not die quickly. As he lay moaning, I knew I could not give the others time to think. 'There is no time—open the gate!'

"As if in a dream, the other soldiers began to heave on the ropes that would draw the mighty bolt, throwing frightened glances over their shoulders at their leader, who was still scrabbling in his own blood on the dusty ground. When the bolt had slid away, we all dragged back the gate, which swung open on screeching hinges.

" 'Now go and rescue Hector!' I said, thus adding five less direct but just as certain murders onto my conscience as the soldiers stumbled out into the teeth of the Greek attack.

"My friends and I had only moments to get away. Together we managed to drag over a large stone and shove it under the bottom edge of the gate to make sure no one could close it again easily, then we sprinted toward shelter. Behind us we could hear the shrieks of the Trojans on the walls and in the street as the first Greeks plunged through the open gates.

"I can talk no longer, even if this is my last journal. The fire is weakening the wall of our hiding place. The air is so hot our clothes are smoking. We must take our chances in the streets. We will try to find the others, but if we do not, we will try to make our way through to the Temple of Demeter. It is a slim hope, but there is no other.

"I can hear the Greeks baying like wolves outside, laughing, drunk already on murder and revenge. And I have done this. To save my friends, I have set the fall of Troy in motion—men, women, and children being slaughtered all across the city, as though by my own hand.

"I could think of nothing else to do. Oh, but the cries are terrible! Florimel is weeping too, I can hear it, but I cannot bear to look at her, even shielded by blindness. In any case, I can almost feel her thoughts, her horror at what I have done.

"The Greeks are inside the walls. Troy is burning, dying.

"And, God help me, I am the Trojan Horse.

"*Code Delphi.* End here."

CHAPTER 33

A Piece of the Mirror

NETFEED/ENTERTAINMENT: Obolos Troubles Deepen (visual: Obolos Headquarters, New York)

VO: It's been a tough year for Obolos Entertainment, with sagging ratings on some of their best-known shows, and their own decision to file a large intellectual property lawsuit against a Third World competitor, but the worst of all may be yet to come. Allegations have been made in a French courtroom that two Obolos executives participated in a so-called "snipe hunt"—the rounding up and murdering of street children—while attending a conference in Marseille last year. (visual: company spokesperson Sigurd Fallinger)

FALLINGER: "These are terrible allegations, but it must be stressed that the men in question are innocent until proved otherwise. Obviously, we here at Obolos are very concerned, since the happiness and well-being of children—all children—is our business. . . ."

VO: Obolos, a children's entertainment giant, has weathered storms in the past to remain a leader in its category, but many observers are privately wondering whether the ship can stay afloat through a storm of this magnitude. . . .

PAUL and Renie found Fredericks crouched over Orlando's body, weeping.

The Achilles sim had collapsed facedown across the legs of dead Hector, whose head was a bloody ruin that Paul could not look at for long. Instead, he tipped Orlando's face to the side, then bent over and held the polished surface of one of his arm-guards to the mouth of the fallen hero. "He's still breathing," Paul told Renie. "So what do we do?"

"Do? We have to get inside, find the others. I guess we carry him." Only a few hundred meters away the Greeks had already forced their way into the city via the gaping Skaian Gate. Paul could hear howls of anguish above the shouting of the victors, and the first flames were beginning to rise from the houses just inside the walls.

As Renie kneeled to take a grip on Orlando's feet, Fredericks seemed to notice the newcomers for the first time. She slapped at Renie's hands. "Who are you? Leave him alone."

"It's me, Fredericks—Renie Sulaweyo."

"But you're a man now . . ." Fredericks' eyes widened; a moment later, Renie had been dragged into a desperate embrace. "Oh, Renie, it's my fault! He came out after me, but I did it so they'd leave him alone, because . . . because . . ." As Fredericks began to cry again, Renie took a fold of Fredericks' own garment and began cleaning blood from the tear-swollen face.

"You've got a head wound, but it's shallow," Renie said gently. "They just bleed a lot."

"Orlando's still alive, but we need to get him inside the city." Paul made his voice harsh, trying to shock Fredericks into attention. "We need your help—he's going to be too heavy to carry otherwise. Pull yourself together. He needs you."

Fredericks paused, sniffling, then crawled back to Orlando's side and touched the handsome face. "He's dying."

"We know," Renie said.

"But he could have lasted longer, if I hadn't been so stupid! I was . . . I thought it was my time. To . . . to do something."

"You did the best you could," Paul said. "You're a good man."

Fredericks' sudden shriek of laughter caught Paul and Renie by surprise. "That's perfect! That's so . . . this is all so scanny! I'm not even a boy, not really. I'm a girl."

Renie seemed startled, but it made little difference to Paul. "That doesn't change what we need to do," he said. "Now come on—let's get rid of this bloody armor, then you can help us get him up."

Laughing and weeping in quiet alternation, Fredericks peeled away the gold-plated greaves while Paul and Renie unfastened the armor on his upper body. As they got ready to lift him, Fredericks paused. "He'll want his sword," she said softly. She uncurled Orlando's fist from the hilt, then slid the blade through her own belt. Paul and Renie got under Orlando's arms and lifted; Fredericks took his feet. The unconscious boy groaned once as they staggered toward the gates. Paul felt it rather than heard it, because the death cries of Troy were growing very loud now.

It was bad, even worse than Paul could have imagined. Children and old people were being chased out of their houses and speared like animals, or burned to death in their homes by laughing Greeks. It was hard for Paul to understand how in only a matter of moments the grave, honor-bound soldiers of Agamemnon could turn into demons like these.

"Try not to look," he told Fredericks, whose pale, shocked expression grew ever more alarming, as though she were slipping away from them, headed for some other place. "And if anyone stops us—Greeks, anyway—just let me talk. They all know who I am."

One group of new conquerors had formed a taunting circle around an old man, throwing the corpse of a small child back and forth above his head while he staggered from one to another, beseeching them to stop. The ghastly spectacle was blocking the street. Paul and Renie backed against a shadowed wall to catch their breath and wait for the Greeks to get bored and clear the way.

"Where are we going?" he asked Renie. He was struggling to remind himself that none of this was real, but it was not helping much. "Any idea?"

She looked like she was close to collapse herself. "When we first came through, we wound up in one of the palace courtyards. I suppose we should head for the palace."

Paul grunted. "Yes, along with every other Greek here."

"I killed him," Fredericks said mournfully.

Paul checked Orlando's breathing. "You didn't kill him—he's still alive. And you just tried to do your best." He winced. "God, I'm running out of ideas."

A figure suddenly leaped out of an alley behind them and clutched Renie's arm. She screeched; Paul's heart thudded to what seemed like a permanent stop, then sped on. He fumbled for his sword.

"!Xabbu!" Renie threw her arms around the ash-smeared apparition. "Oh, it's . . . it's so wonderful to see you."

"Like the Short-Nosed Mouse looking for Beetle, I will always find you, Renie." The man was smiling, but his face showed much strain. "Like the honey-guide looking for his friend the honey-badger, I will call out to you as I come." He quickly looked at Orlando, then turned his attention to Fredericks. "And is this Fredericks, after all this time? I am guessing only because you are slightly the smaller of the two, as you were before."

Fredericks looked up at him with red-rimmed eyes, a line of dried blood that Renie had not managed to clean surrounding her features like the edge of a mask. "It's me, !Xabbu. But you used to be a monkey."

He took a step forward and threw his arms around her. "It is such a goodness to see you, young fellow. How is Orlando?"

"He's dying, !Xabbu. He came after me—but I was trying to save him! And he killed that guy Hector!" She fought to hold back more tears. "And I'm not a fellow . . . I'm a girl!" This appeared to shatter the dam. She covered her eyes with her arm, chest heaving.

"You can be whatever you want, Fredericks," !Xabbu said softly. "A fellow or a girl. It is a happy thing just to see you again." He turned to Renie and put a hand on her arm. Paul could not help admiring how neatly he moved from one emotional situation to another. Paul knew almost nothing about Bushmen, but it was fascinating to see how the man's resilient calm translated through the Trojan soldier sim.

He wouldn't have made a very good Greek hero, Paul thought absently. *Not enough love of drama. Not enough self-obsession, perhaps.*

"Martine and the others are waiting for us," !Xabbu reported, "or were when I left, but this city is a very dangerous place now. Martine thinks she may know a way out."

Renie nodded wearily. "Then let's hurry."

!Xabbu led them off the main street and up the hill at an angle. They did not go quickly—Orlando's limp body was too awkward—but the Greek invaders were largely following the path of the main roads and were encountering many tempting distractions as they spiraled up toward the palace. Although the wind had already brought the fires to much of the city, and some streets were blocked by burning debris, Paul and his companions met Greek plunderers only in small groups; these took one look at him in his guise as King of Ithaca, waved merrily, and continued on about their business.

Orlando began to wake as they struggled up a hillside. He fought against his friends' grip in a detached, dreamy way, muttering and moaning.

"We can't carry him like this," Paul said after a dozen clumsy paces. He and Renie lowered Orlando to the ground. "The hill's too steep."

!Xabbu came and kneeled at Orlando's side. He put one hand on his chest, the other on Orlando's forehead. "What is his full name?" !Xabbu asked Fredericks. "I have forgotten."

"Orlando G-Gardiner."

"Can you hear me, Orlando Gardiner?" !Xabbu leaned close, so that his lips almost touched the restless youth's ear. "Orlando Gardiner, your friends need you. We cannot carry you, and we are fleeing for our lives. Come back to us, Orlando. We need you. Come back to us."

A chill ran up Paul's spine. It was so much like what the bird-woman had said to him, like the time-honed words to some magical spell. "Do you think he can . . . ?"

!Xabbu raised a hand, asking for silence. "Come back to us, Orlando Gardiner," he said, slowly and distinctly. "Your friends are here."

Orlando's eyelids flickered. He groaned. !Xabbu stood up.

"We will have to support him, but I think he will walk now. It is not his legs that are hurt, I think—his spirit is exhausted."

"Don't make him walk," said Fredericks miserably. "He's sick!"

!Xabbu spoke gently. "I think he would rather walk, no matter how sick his body is."

"Lean on us, Orlando." Renie got under his arm again, this time facing him forward. Paul took the other side. After a moment Orlando straightened his legs, and with their support took a few stumbling steps. Just below, a figure rippling with fire rushed shrieking down a narrow street, chased by laughing Greeks with torches. "Right," Renie said tightly. "Just go and try not to think about it."

Moving at Orlando's staggering pace, they made their way slowly up through the city until they had almost reached the palace of Priam, which was streaming with smoke and flames all along its roof. !Xabbu turned them to one side, through a carefully tended grove of trees surrounded by a low stone wall. In the depths of the tiny pine forest, with their vision of the catastrophe blocked for a moment and the noises of Troy's painful demise deadened by needles and branches, it almost seemed they had escaped the horror. Then they stumbled across the garden's caretaker, ribboned with bloody wounds, staring up sightlessly at the distant stars.

!Xabbu hurried them down a succession of narrow alleys behind the palace. All the houses here were abandoned, or the denizens had extinguished their lights in the futile hope of escaping the attention of the victorious Greeks. As they moved past these tight-packed dwellings into a street of large low buildings adorned by twin rows of cypresses, Paul saw a small knot of people waiting in the shadows.

"There's someone ahead," he whispered.

"It is the others," !Xabbu assured him. "Martine!" he called softly. "We are here."

The four figures moved out into the narrow, cobbled road. The largest held an unlit torch; Paul had no trouble recognizing T4b. The other three were women, two of them struggling with the third, who seemed to be having some kind of fit. Of these first two, one wore the body of a young, well-dressed Trojan woman, the other that of a crone, with much of her head and face swathed in bandages.

The younger of the two turned at their approach, but maintained a tight grip on the third woman, who continued to weep and struggle. "Renie?" she said. "And are these truly Orlando and Fredericks?"

"Orlando's sick, Martine," Renie said. "He's barely conscious."

"And Emily's pitching a fit," the older woman said shortly. "She hates this place." She turned her one good eye on Paul. "So this is Jonas?"

"We don't have time for long introductions," Renie said. "The city is falling apart out there—they're killing and raping and looting. Yes, this is Paul Jonas." She gestured to the two women. "That's Martine, and the one with the bandages is Florimel." She frowned. "The one crying and carrying on is Emily."

"It hurts! Take me away from here!" the girl wailed, and for a moment twisted free of Florimel's grasp. She lurched a step toward the newcomers, and for the first time Paul saw her face.

"Good Lord, don't you know who this is?" Paul took a step forward, half-certain that he would find himself in another dream. He seized the girl by her slender shoulders, astonished to be once more looking into that hauntingly familiar face. Something in her panicky expression pushed at his memory and he felt a name suddenly rise to the surface, something long hidden in shadows, but now flashing like a bird's wing in a beam of sunlight. *"Ava?"*

The girl they had called Emily froze, tearstains glinting on her cheeks. "I don't . . ." she said slowly, then her eyes rolled up until only the whites showed and she collapsed onto the road before any of her stunned companions could catch her.

"Ava . . ." Paul said wonderingly, and as he said it again, something inside him broke free. . . .

"You're perfect," Niles had told him, laughing. "No grudges, no skeletons in the closet, no strong political views. And, lucky you, apparently you went to the right public school, too."

It had been Niles, of course, who had found him the job— Niles, whose family loaned its summer cottages to net stars and foreign royalty, who had grown up calling the Archbishop of Canterbury "Cousin Freddy." If Niles or his family didn't know someone, it was likely no one else knew them either. "It's a strange little setup, mate, but you said you wanted some time to think about things—getting a bit bored of the routine, and all that . . ."

This was what happened when you made idle chitchat about

changing your life in front of Niles—you wound up with an embassy job in Brazil, or owning a nightclub in Soho, or doing something even stranger. The younger sister of one of Niles' other friends had just decided that although she'd love to work in the U.S., she didn't want to be quite so isolated, so Niles had put in a good word for his friend Paul instead. Thus Paul had found himself at the far end of a six-month security clearance and an eight-hour jet flight, being shuttled across the New Orleans international airport tarmac toward a helicopter as shiny and sleek as a black dragonfly.

When Paul had fastened his webbing, the helicopter suddenly surged into the air. He was its only passenger.

"You're a bit younger and a bit more male than what they wanted," Niles had said, "but I had Uncle Sebastian put in a good word for you." The uncle in question was a former Treasury Minister, presumably the kind of person that even global business magnates might listen to when it came to references. "So don't do anything stupid, will you, laddie?" Niles had added.

As the helicopter rose, Paul wondered what stupid thing even he could possibly do to bollocks this up. He was going to live on the estate, so it wasn't likely he would oversleep and miss work. And he liked children, so it seemed equally unlikely he would forget he was dealing with some of the world's most powerful people and give one of his charges a brutal thrashing.

The black helicopter swung out over Lake Borgne. A ragged flock of seagulls broke apart before them, wheeling and scattering. Birds. Paul had never been to Louisiana, had not known how much like a tropical jungle the place was. There were so many birds here, in so many shapes and colors. . . .

Despite the spyflick precautions, the net-star luxuries, all of the evidence that he was far, far out of his league, Paul had almost convinced himself that everything was going to be fine until he saw the tower jutting up from Lake Borgne like a vast black fang.

Oh, my God, he thought—it's huge. He had seen net footage, but that had been nothing like the experience of the real thing. It's like something out of a fairy tale—an ogre's castle. Or one of the watchtowers of Hell . . .

The helicopter did not land on top of the massive spike, but

*instead settled slowly toward a domed structure a few kilometer.
away across the island, whose roof plates slid open like the aper.
ture of a camera to reveal the landing spot. Feeling more than
ever as though he had entered some kind of dream, Paul was hus.
tled from the helicopter by several conspicuously well-armed, ef.
ficient men in military-style uniforms. After a curt formal greeting.
one of them accompanied him on a quarter-hour shuttle bus jour.
ney to the black skyscraper, through street after street of low build.
ings and cultivated parks, an entire small town that seemed to
have grown like a patch of mushrooms in the tower's shadow.*

*The armed man delivered him to the gold-plated doors of the
tower and watched with professional patience as Paul walked in
beneath the vast, stylized "J" above the entrance and into the
lobby, a huge space full of low lighting, spotlit sculpture, trick.
ling water, and clusters of well-cushioned seats. The entire British
Army, Paul could not help thinking, could have waited for an ap.
pointment in that lobby.*

*Almost two more hours of security clearance—fingerprints and
retinal scans being among the less intrusive methods—dragged by
before he was at last ushered into one of the several banks of el.
evators and puffed silently up to the 51st floor to meet a man
named Finney.*

*The huge office had the most fabulous view Paul had ever
seen—almost half the tower's circumference of glassed wraparound
panorama—but Finney himself did not seem the type to enjoy it.
He was several years short of middle age but as sexless as a
harem eunuch, a slender man with long surgeon's hands, small
eyes that appeared grotesquely large behind thick, old-fashioned
lenses, and the smile of a bored sadist.*

*"Right, then." Finney watched Paul trying to make himself
comfortable in the too-large chair on the other side of the desk.
"You come with good references—yes, truly excellent references—
which we have decided compensates for your lack of a great deal
of experience as a tutor. You understand our security concerns.
I'm sure—I hope everyone treated you well, nevertheless?" His
smile flicked on then off, an implement used only for political pur.
poses. "Mr. Jongleur is one of the world's most powerful men,
and you are being given a position of great responsibility. He was*

most insistent on a traditional education—a 'good old British public school education,' as he puts it."

Presumably without the beatings, the sodomy, and the cold food, Paul thought but did not say—he could no more imagine making a joke to this pale, affectless man than swearing in front of his grandmother. He opted instead for the safely polite. "I'm sure Mr. Jongleur will be happy with my work. And I'm looking forward to meeting the children."

One thin eyebrow crept up Finney's forehead. "Children? No, I'm afraid you've jumped the gun a bit. For the moment there is only one child." He leaned forward, fixing Paul with a stare that seemed oddly intrusive, peering through the bottleglass lenses as though he had Paul under a microscope. Paul could not hold the man's eyes for more than a moment, and looked down guiltily. "I'm sure there are things you will find surprising here, Mr. Jonas. We are a family-owned company, and we have our idiosyncratic ways. The last tutor . . . well, she made herself very difficult and disagreeable. I think it is safe to say she will not work again in that profession." He sat up. "But that was largely due to misunderstanding, so let me make something perfectly, perfectly clear. Mr. Jongleur will do whatever is necessary to make sure no harm comes to any of his family or intimates, Mr. Jonas. That includes unwanted publicity. If you are a loyal employee, you will come to value this, as I do. But you do not ever want to be on the wrong side of the equation. Not ever."

"I . . . I beg your pardon?"

"Rich men are particularly susceptible to kidnapping and extortion, Mr. Jonas, and the richer they are, the more attractive to criminal minds. It goes without saying that we have taken careful precaution against such things—as you have no doubt noticed, Mr. Jongleur has gone to great lengths to ensure the security of his home and business . . . and your pupil. But just as he firmly defends his assets against overt threats, he also considers unwanted attention from the media to be a form of assault as well. Your contract was very explicit about the Jongleur family's privacy, both during and after your employment. I hope you read it carefully. The penalties for breach are . . . severe."

He knew what was expected, and said it. "I take my responsibilities very seriously, Mr. Finney."

"Good, good. Of course." Although Finney neither moved his hand nor made any other telltale sign, the door at the back of the office opened and a huge shape appeared there. *"Mr. Mudd will take you up and introduce you."*

"To . . . to Mr. Jongleur?" Paul was reluctant to look away from Finney, but from the corner of his eye, the newcomer seemed to be as large as a bus.

Finney laughed, a most disconcerting sound. *"Oh, no! No, Mr. Jongleur is a very, very busy man. I doubt you will ever meet him. No, my associate is going to take you to your charge."* He shook his head, still amused.

There was barely room for Paul to fit in the same elevator with Mudd, a vast pink man whose shaved head seemed to have grown directly out of his massive shoulders.

"Jonas . . ." Mudd grinned, showing a row of perfect, large white teeth. His voice was surprisingly high. *"Is that Greek?"*

"No, I don't think so. Might have been French at one point."

"French." Mudd grinned again. He seemed to find the whole thing very funny.

The elevator stopped so smoothly that it was only when the door opened that Paul knew they had arrived. Outside the elevator was a little enclosed bay which ended in a door that might have come from a bank vault. Mudd applied his thick fingers to the code pad, then blew into a grille. The door hissed open.

"What . . . what is this?" Paul asked, startled. They seemed to have entered some kind of indoor garden, a massive place as wide as a football field, if Paul could judge from what he could see of the distant ceiling and walls. A path led away from the door, snaking through tall trees rooted in actual soil.

"Conservatory." Mudd took him by the arm, giving him the impression that he could shatter Paul's elbow with a light squeeze. *"She's always in here."*

She was kneeling beside the path, partially hidden by a tree—he saw the hem of her skirt before he saw the rest of her, a fold of pale blue cotton with a froth of white petticoat peeping from beneath. *"He's here, Princess."* Mudd spoke with the cheerful familiarity of a sailor greeting a favorite whore. *"Your new tutor."*

As she rose and stepped out from behind the trunk like a dryad slipping its bark, a bright bird fluttered up from where she had *been crouching, flared its wings, and shot away into the upper branches. The girl's eyes were huge, her skin pale as cream silk. She looked Paul up and down, then gave him a strange, solemn smile and turned back to watch the spot where the bird had disappeared.*

Mudd extended his hand in mocking party manners. "Mr. Paul Jonas, this is Miss Avialle Jongleur."

"Ava," she said dreamily, still looking in the other direction. "Tell him to call me Ava."

". . . And . . . and that's all," Paul said after long moments had passed. "I can feel the rest of it just . . . just there. But I can't reach it." He shook his head. It had all come so quickly, so completely, like plaster sloughing off an old wall to reveal an intricate fresco hidden beneath, but the returned memories had ended just as suddenly. He looked down to where Emily lay in the darkened street, her head propped on crouching Florimel's knee, and wished he had time to give the others more than a sketchy summary of what had come back to him. Clearly this was the heart of the matter: even the smallest details might be important.

"You worked for . . . ?" Renie put her hands to her forehead as though it hurt. "And the woman who keeps appearing is Jongleur's daughter? But what's she doing here? And what did you do to make them so upset with you?"

"We can try to make sense of it later," Martine said quietly. "For now, we must get ourselves to some kind of safety—perhaps even out of this simulation."

"But it was the girl who told us to come here—or some other version of her did." Renie blinked slowly, as if trying to wake up. "What the hell is going on here? And how could it be Emily? I mean . . . Emily?"

A great shout echoed up from the street below them. A knot of armored men carrying torches swirled out from the shadows, two bands locked in deadly conflict.

"And here comes *The Aeneid,* right on schedule," Martine said. Paul looked at her, but if it was a joke, she wasn't smiling. "We cannot talk here—perhaps we cannot afford to talk at all, not until we have found some kind of sanctuary."

"We finally have some answers, or the beginning of some answers," Renie said stubbornly. "If we make a mistake now because we didn't think carefully, we might not live to try again."

"I'm impressed to hear you argue thought over action, Renie," said the bandaged woman called Florimel. "But Martine is right—if we stand here, we may lose our chance to do either."

Renie shrugged helplessly. "Where do you think we should go, Martine?"

"Pick up Emily—it's just as well she's passed out. She hated the place we are going." As !Xabbu and T4b lifted Emily's slender form at armpits and ankles, Martine turned back to Renie and Paul. "I cannot see that anything Paul Jonas has told us changes what I have learned. Emily is almost . . . allergic, you could call it, to a place I found called the Temple of Demeter—the same way as she reacted to the Lady of the Windows in the House simulation, which according to what we've heard seems to have been another version of herself loose in the system. Similarly, I think there is something in the temple to cause her reaction—a gateway perhaps, or some other part of the Otherland infrastructure—Kunohara told you that this was the first simulation they built—in any case, I believe there is a maze in the temple, which also jibes with what Kunohara said."

Renie sighed. "I can't make sense of it, Martine." The noise from below grew louder as some of the men who had been fighting broke away and tried to escape up the hillside. "We'll just have to trust your instincts."

"Now!" Florimel urged.

Orlando, who had been sitting dazed on the cobbled street during Paul's hurried explanation, now lurched upright and out of Fredericks' grip. "Where are we?" he said. His head wobbled as he looked up and down the dark street. "Where's Hector?"

"You killed him, Gardiner. You saved my life." Fredericks took Orlando's arm and tried to lead him after T4b and !Xabbu, who were already carrying Emily away, but he shook her off.

"No," he said slowly. "I didn't save anybody. I lost."

The noble face of Patroclus crumpled in misery, but as Paul watched, Fredericks lowered her head to hide it and shoved her friend after the others.

"He should have killed me," Orlando protested. "He beat me."

*   *   *

The Temple of Demeter crouched deep in shadow against the hillside, as though it waited for them half-asleep, but Paul paid it little attention—he was painfully fascinated by the slack face of the young woman he could only think of as Ava. The abrupt triggering of memories had at first promised a full, cathartic return, but they had stopped as suddenly as they had begun, a feeling even more sickeningly frustrating than the amnesia.

I worked for the man who built all this? He had—he could remember getting the job, arriving, those horrible men Finney and Mudd . . .

Finch and Mullet . . . the Twins . . .

There was a piece of the puzzle—or was it? If they were real people, Jongleur's right-hand men, then how had they come to be roaming the Otherland network in various incarnations, messing about in backwater places like the Oz Renie and !Xabbu had visited?

He pushed that speculation aside. There were more important questions, and perhaps the most vital of all was this young woman. He watched as the shadows from !Xabbu's torch slid across her pale features. Was there a real Ava out there somewhere, perhaps still in the real world, but manipulating the network to help him? But why should she want to do that? What was Paul to her? And if she was trying to assist him, then what explained the other versions—this one called Emily, Odysseus' wife Penelope, the bird-woman Vaala—all flitting through the network like lost souls?

Paul had followed the others into the temple without realizing it. It was a surprisingly low and narrow building, scarcely twenty meters from end to end; the torchlight revealed little furniture except for a small altar and a statue of a woman with a sheaf of grain cradled in her arms.

"There's nothing here . . ." Renie began, but her next words were drowned out by rising noise from the street outside—people shouting and screaming, pottery and other things smashing on the cobbles. The Greek pillagers had finally reached the quiet old temple district.

"There *is* something here," Martine said.

Paul tried to push away the obsessive thoughts about Ava. They might have only moments before the invaders came to see if

Demeter was hiding any treasure in her temple. "Look for stairs," he suggested, remembering the crypt in Venice.

"Over here." Florimel had found a recessed stairwell and door behind the altar, hidden under drapery in the far wall. Emily groaned as !Xabbu and T4b brought her near it, helpless as someone in a nightmare; Paul felt a swift twinge in his heart, a lost memory or a presentiment.

"Who is that?" Martine said abruptly, turning to look back at the temple's outer door. "Is someone there?"

Renie snatched the torch from T4b, but the small temple was empty except for their own numbers. "Nobody, but there are a lot of nasty people just down the street and they're getting closer. Let's see what's down the stairs."

Martine tugged at the stairwell door, but it did not budge. They could hear the shouts and laughter of drunken men just outside now, and the whooping sobs of some female captive. Renie kicked the heavy wood, cursing, but the door barely shuddered.

If only that big lad Ajax was here, Paul thought miserably. *He'd pull that bastard off its hinges in a second.*

"Wait," he said, hurrying forward. "I keep forgetting we're in a bloody simulation. Fredericks, come here. T4b, you, too." Paul waved his hand impatiently as T4b relinquished Emily's ankles to Florimel. "We're heroes, remember? Practically gods, stronger than ten men. You're Patroclus and Glaucus, stars of the Trojan War. If Orlando wasn't so woozy, he could probably kick it in by himself, but we'll have to do. Come on, give it some shoulder." He crouched as Fredericks and T4b crowded into the alcove at the base of the stairs beside him, then counted to three. They sprang forward. The door shattered beneath their combined force as though built of matchsticks and they tumbled through into the darkness on the far side.

"Chizz." T4b clambered back onto his feet. "Chizz the biz. Did you op that?"

"I wish you had left us a way to close it behind us," Renie said.

!Xabbu came forward with the torch, revealing walls much older than those of the temple above, so age-worn and slick with damp that they seemed organic, almost intestinal. Remnants of faint carvings held only vague hints of human and animal shapes.

"Follow me, now," said Martine, moving past !Xabbu. "If it is a maze, I will be best able to lead us through."

"What is she talking about?" Paul asked Renie. "Doesn't she want the torch . . . ?"

"It's hard to explain—I forget sometimes myself—but she's blind."

Paul stared at her, then at Martine's back, but no matter how he tried, he could not think her explanation into sensible shape. And it did not matter. There were too many questions; this was only one more.

The apparently blind woman had already disappeared around the first turning. !Xabbu hung back with the torch until the others were all in line, then strode off after her. Near the back, with only Renie behind him, Paul was walking in nearly total darkness, following the Florimel-shape in front of him rather than the dimly reflected gleam of the torch off the carved walls ahead. His feet splashed through puddles he could not see as they turned left, then turned left again, seemingly spiraling back onto their own path, but after several more leftward twists the corridors grew even narrower, so that it was all Paul could do to walk without bumping the walls.

People's voices floated to him, murmuring sounds that he first thought were the companions in front of him talking among themselves, but the bits he could make out did not seem to be voices he recognized, nor did the words make any sense. It was not madness, or not his alone, for the others heard it too.

"Martine, is it the same as the voices in the Place of the Lost?" Florimel called softly. She sounded frightened, but trying to keep it in check.

Martine's words drifted back, almost as faint as the ghost-voices. "It does not feel the same."

"I think there are people behind us," Renie said grimly. "Nothing tricky, just men with swords and spears. Keep going."

Paul was not so certain—why would men with a whole city to plunder risk a maze in a small temple?—but he kept his doubts to himself.

They quickened their pace, but it was not easy to navigate the dark, confined spaces with a long row of jostling people, especially with Emily being laboriously carried and Orlando still hobbling like a stroke victim. They passed through some places where the way seemed to widen and the torchlight revealed statues and bits of strange, crude furniture, slab tables topped with empty bowls, but Martine did not let them stop to examine any of them, nor did anyone argue that they should—the sense of being pursued, perhaps even driven into a corner, was very strong. Paul began to see something like flame glinting high on the walls, and at first thought they were reaching an area where the maze was lit, but after a while it became apparent that the light was either some strange multiple mirroring of their own torch through the complex underground warren or there were indeed others in the maze, and they were bearing fire. Whatever the case, the sounds still followed them, sometimes snatches of whispering speech, occasionally just the amplified patter of footfalls.

As they hurried on, Paul was astonished to see starlight appear for a moment high over their heads, a single clear window of midnight blue flecked with blazing white; when they turned another corner, it vanished. The fleeting vision made Paul realize how deceptively the slope had descended: the walls of the maze now stretched upward perhaps twenty meters or more above them.

Two more gaps to the star-riddled sky had passed overhead when Paul followed Florimel's almost invisible form through into a larger space, the wide, outward-curving walls only partially illuminated by !Xabbu's torch. The sides of the large circular room stretched up as though toward the sky, but only starless blackness was visible above. They might have been standing at the base of a huge well, but if so, someone had left the cover on.

In the middle stood the only thing on the bumpy stone floor beside themselves, a small, pyramid-shaped altar of stone blocks, a crude ziggurat of damp stone less than two meters high. Half a pomegranate sat on the top slab, as though it had been set down only a moment before. As !Xabbu leaned closer with the torch, they could all see a few seeds couched like rubies in the dry white pith.

A moment of almost reverent silence ended as a flurry of echoes drifted down the passageway behind them, louder and closer than before.

"What do we *do,* then?" Fredericks said desperately. "They're after us. It's probably Hector's friends—they'll kill us!"

The woman Paul could not help thinking of as Ava, whose head T4b was tenderly supporting where she lay on the stone floor, stirred and let out a murmur of pain. Paul felt curiously separate from her, but it did not seem like a healthy separation. He could sense that something had been set in train, and that no matter what he did, it would take its course, but past experience also told him that he should not allow himself to go numb.

"The lighter, Martine," Renie said. "Open a gate."

The woman took it from a pouch on her belt. Although Renie and the others had talked about the access device at length, this was the first time Paul had seen it. He was faintly disappointed by how much it looked like an ordinary lighter.

"Emily! Come back!" T4b said suddenly. The girl had twisted out from under his arm and was crawling across the stone floor, moaning. She threw herself at Martine's feet and pressed her face against the woman's ankles like a cat begging to be fed. But cats did not sob.

"Oh, please, take us away from here!" she whimpered. It stabbed at Paul's heart to see the familiar face in such pain, but he still felt curiously unable to act. "Make a gate, yes, make a gate! I have to get away!" She wrapped her arms around the blind woman's legs. "They want to take my baby! It hurts!"

Martine tottered, shaking her head in fear and frustration. "I cannot make anything happen if she knocks me over. Please, someone . . . !"

T4b hurried forward and gathered up the weeping girl. Martine held the lighter before her, frowning with such concentration that Paul half-expected a nimbus of sparks to form around her, but nothing so dramatic happened. Nothing happened at all.

"I . . . I can't make it work," Martine said shakily after a long minute had passed. "Even the simplest commands. The device won't respond."

Noises of pursuit were whispering all around them now, accompanied by the rippling smack and patter of echoing footfalls. Paul noted them, but only just: a cold certainty was growing inside him, stronger every second.

"How could it break *now?*" Renie said. "Just when we really need it the most? Someone must be doing this to us!"

"Maybe we aren't supposed to leave," Florimel said suddenly, heavily. "Have we done what we were meant to do here in Troy?"

"Meant to by *who?*" Renie almost shouted her frustration.

"Perhaps if I try the lighter . . ." !Xabbu offered.

"No."

They all turned. Paul felt their eyes on him, but he was looking only at the strange, sparse altar. "I know why we're here, down here in this place . . . or at least I think I do. I don't really understand everything, but . . ." He stepped forward. The others shrank back, as though he were carrying some extremely reactive explosive, but he held only a wisp of cloth, a scarf with an embroidered feather. When he reached the altar, he set it gently on the cold stone.

"Ava!" he called. The girl restrained by T4b stirred and whimpered, but Paul ignored her. "Ava . . . Avialle. You came to me on the beach, when I prayed to the Earthbound, but of all the places in this world, this is *your* place." He struggled to think of the simple, incantatory way !Xabbu had spoken earlier. "I need you to come back to me again, Ava, one more time. Come to me!"

He could feel the others holding their breath, waiting, wondering if he had some actual plan or had just snapped under the pressure, but although the room was tense with expectancy, nothing else was happening. A laugh floated in from the corridor, so close that several of the others flinched.

"God damn it, Ava! I've crossed world after world, looking for you. You told me to come, and I've come. Now I need you— we all need you. Come to us! Whatever you need me for, whatever it costs me, make it now! *Now!*"

The air began to thicken and bend above the ancient altar like heat shimmer over a desert road. For a moment it seemed that a female figure would appear there, unfolding like a butterfly—the torchlight revealed gleams of eye and shoulder and spread fingers—but some elementary circuit would not close. The shape remained amorphous, twisting in the air like smoke.

If the voices from the maze behind them had seemed almost at their elbows, this seemed to float to them down a million miles of hollow space.

"*. . . I . . . cannot . . . again . . . too late . . .*"

The one called Emily writhed on the floor at Martine's feet, her groans muffled by her own hands, feet drumming on the stone floor. T4b hurried to comfort her, but she was gripped by a kind of seizure.

"You must," Paul said. "We are trapped here. Whatever you wanted of us will not happen otherwise. Come to us, Ava. Come to me."

"Then . . . must take back . . . pieces . . . mirror . . ."

He could not imagine balking at anything at this crucial juncture. "Take it. Whatever you need, take it—or tell us how to get it. Do whatever you have to do, but hurry!"

Suddenly Emily's muffled scream jumped an octave, a shrill sound of terror and agony so fierce it cut through Paul's concentration like a jagged blade. The girl's jittering body suddenly went rigid. Her eyes widened and bulged as though they would burst from her head, and her face turned slowly, lurchingly toward Paul.

"You . . ." Emily choked out each word through purpling lips. ". . . My baby . . . !" And then the girl heaved once, like a hooked fish dragged into the smothering air, and a wave of distortion passed from her to the shimmering half-presence above the altar. A moment later she fell face-forward onto the stone, gray and limp.

"Emily!" T4b screeched, and jerked her up into his arms where she dangled lifelessly.

The shape above the altar took on dimension now, rounding into the dream-shape Paul had seen before, but he felt no joy. It was clear what he had unwittingly given her permission to take, and although there was much he could not grasp, what he did understand sickened him.

She was beautiful as a goddess, this Ava, a perfect angel. She raised her arms above her head and shimmering trails of light followed them through the air, like wings. *"It is late,"* she said— her voice now seemed intimately close. *"You were meant to climb—you were meant to find your own way . . ."*

Even as she spoke those cryptic words, the place above her head began to glow, a glaring red radiance framed between her uplifted arms. Slowly she brought them down and the glow spread outward, until it seemed that the chamber walls, the maze, even great Troy itself had dissolved away behind her, revealing a sky of ultimate black and stars that made even the bright constellations of the Age of Heroes seem guttering candles. As Paul and his companions stared, a shape coalesced, jutting up into the night, stretching beyond vision. It was a tortured shape surrounded by clouds, its twisted subsidiary peaks gleaming a glassy scarlet where lightning flickered around the heights, but the mass of it was black, black, black.

"The black mountain . . ." Paul whispered. Beside him, Orlando was also murmuring to himself.

"It is late." The angel's voice spoke with exhaustion and regret. *"Perhaps it is too late."* She raised her arms again. The view of the impossible black peak remained, but where her palely glittering hands moved, lines of molten gold throbbed in the air. In a moment, the woman herself was gone; where she had stood, a narrow oval of golden fire billowed in an unfelt wind.

Renie took a hesitant step toward the light. "It's . . . it's a gate."

"It is, but it is not." Martine sounded equally overwhelmed. "It does not feel like the other gateways, but it is clearly a passage."

"You must hurry." The voice came from everywhere now. *"This is all I have left here . . . but it will take you . . . to the heart of . . ."*

Her crystalline tones died away; Paul could not tell if the last word had been *"his"* or *"him"*.

He forced himself to take a step toward the pulsing light. The vision of the black mountain still lay beyond it, but it was growing noticeably dimmer. "We had better . . ." he began, then something struck him hard in the back and flung him into the golden fire.

Paul had passed through several gateways, both on land and water, but even without the suddenness of his entrance, this was the strangest. For the first moments it seemed as though he were in an endless corridor of shining amber flames, but at the same moment, he felt himself to *be* flame—the dance of unbridled energy passed right through him, threatening at any moment to dissolve him into some larger and completely mindless chaos of creation. As he struggled to maintain the pattern that was Paul Jonas, unaware of the nature of the binding force, but desperate to cling to it nevertheless, bits of thought whirled through him.

They might have been memories, scraps caught in some inner wind, but they were not quite familiar. . . .

Birds . . . bursting out like a cloud of smoke . . . wheeling against the sky.

Showers of sparkling ice, sun glinting, a shattered kaleidoscope . . .

A shadow in a cold, empty room, waiting . . . waiting . . . and singing . . .

More birds, shadow-birds flocking, calling to each other across the darkness with the voices of children, keening together in a desolate place . . .

And then, as though the flames had taken all of him they could consume and then begun to die, the endlessly seething glow began to lessen. Bits of darkness appeared, shapes with notional solidity, a sense of up and down. The golden flames licked at Paul and then withdrew, cool as melting snow, and for a moment he was conscious that he stood on something hard and flat, with a great black wall on his left side and a sense of open space to his right. Then something struck him again, smashed him down and clung to him, and he was rolling over and over with hands closing around his neck.

"Killed her!" someone was shouting at him. "Killed her all total!" Paul's face was pressed hard against smooth cold stone; he could not see his attacker. He tried desperately to get his legs under him and failed, but managed to shift his weight enough to pull one arm under his chest, making space to bring his other hand up to pry at the fingers on his throat.

His head was being pulled back, and his awkward position gave him little leverage to resist. Worse than the pain, though, was the view: he was crouching on the edge of a nearly vertical drop, swaying in place as his assailant straddled him like a hobbyhorse. Just beyond his bracing hand the sheer, glossy black side of the mountain fell away into nothingness, the bottom hidden either by distance or the midnight hue of the stone.

Paul tried to scrabble away from the rim, but his weeping attacker was either oblivious to the danger or did not care. The legs around his rib cage tightened—he braced himself for either a jerk backward to snap his neck or a shove forward that would take them both over the edge—but instead the weight on his back was suddenly partially lifted, and the legs still hooked around his torso even dragged him back a few inches from the precipice.

"Let him go!" someone was shouting from a long distance away.

"You're impacted!" someone else screamed faintly as his assailant was pulled completely off him. Paul turned and crawled a short distance back from that soul-freezing drop, then collapsed, struggling to get oxygen back into his lungs. He could hear nothing now except a single thin, continuous tone, nor did he care.

The first voice he could identify as his hearing came back was Renie's.

"He didn't kill her, you idiot! She wasn't really alive, not the way you're thinking."

"He gave her to that . . . that . . ." The voice was sullen, miserable.

"That angel thing was another version of Emily." This was another woman, perhaps the one called Florimel. "It just . . . took her back."

Paul sat up, rubbing his neck. They were crouched against a sheer face of shiny black rock, in the widest part of a path along the mountainside, but the drop and the limitless sky were still uncomfortably close. Paul, who had been so close to falling, could not look out at that gulf for more than a second without shuddering. The sky had the sullen gray-blue tone of an approaching storm, but it seemed to extend outward with limitless clarity, and although the sun was not visible, stars glimmered faintly in the firmament.

The young man was not fighting anymore, but several of the others crouched around him, touching him with their hands as though ready to restrain him again. "I don't blame him," Paul said hoarsely. "I know what it looked like." He tried to meet the youth's eyes but the other would not cooperate. "Javier . . . T4b . . . I didn't know what she meant when she said she needed something.

But I think the others are right—Emily was a part of her some-how. I think she had to take that part back before she had the strength to bring us through." He stopped and looked up, then down the featureless black trail. Because of the sheerness of the rock face, it was hard to tell how much of the mountain still lay above them, but it was clear a great deal lay below. "But . . ." Paul finished, suddenly overwhelmed, "but brought us *where?*"

"Orlando, don't," Fredericks said suddenly as her friend stag-gered to his feet. "Just rest. You need to save your strength!" She rose along with him, trying to pull him back, but the boy in the blond, heroic body of Achilles began trudging unsteadily up the trail.

"Well, there you go." Renie's voice was flat and weary. "Might as well follow him, I suppose. !Xabbu, what do you think? Mar-tine?" She looked to !Xabbu, but he had joined Florimel, crouch-ing at Martine's side. "Martine, are you all right?"

"She is shaking," !Xabbu reported.

"It's . . . it's much like it was . . . when I first came into the sys-tem." Martine's eyes were squeezed shut, her hands pushing at either side of her face as though to keep her skull from flying apart. "So much noise . . . so much . . ." She grimaced.

"Don't move." Florimel tried to find the pulse at the corner of her jaw, but Martine shook her off.

"No. Follow Orlando. I'll . . . I'll be moving in a moment. There's something at the top—something big. It feels like . . . like a volcano." She levered herself to her feet, eyes still closed. She stumbled, but !Xabbu caught her before she could veer toward the far side of the path and the endless nothing beyond. "It would be good . . . if someone walked with me," she conceded. "I am having trouble."

"Paul, can you go with Orlando and Fredericks while we get the rest moving?" Renie asked. Paul nodded and stood, swivel-ing his head to try to remove the unpleasant physical memory of T4b's fingers around his throat. The young man still watched him, dark hair sweat-curled across his forehead, his face a mask that revealed nothing.

Paul caught up with Orlando and Fredericks within moments, since Orlando's stride, though determined, was slow and awk-ward; he also seemed to be having trouble breathing. The others

soon caught up as well, and they made their deliberate way up
the curving mountain path together.

The trail was no natural feature, Paul realized, although it might
have been more surprising if it had been. Instead, it was simply
a crudely functional walkway etched in the side of the mountain,
a spiraling vertical slice that shaved the mountain's edge and a
perpendicular horizontal one on which to walk. The path was
rougher than the rest of the stone, scored as though the titan blade
which had carved it had a serrated edge, which was a very good
thing: Paul did not want to think what it would be like to climb
this precarious track if its surface had been the same glaze-smooth
black volcanic stone as the mountain itself. As it was, and especially when the way narrowed, he was pathetically grateful that
there was no wind: it was already hard enough just to keep Orlando and Martine to the middle of the path. Paradoxically for
someone who had been so cavalier about the edge while stran-
gling Paul, T4b seemed nervous about being in such a high place,
and insisted on walking as far to the inside as possible.

As it turned out, they did not have far to go. Before an hour
had passed, they made their slow way around the edge of an outcropping and found that the path now curved sharply inward toward the mountain itself, passing between the outcropping beside
them and another huge peak rather than continuing along the
perimeter.

Paul was glad to leave the limitless drop behind them, but it
was only when they finally reached safer ground, the path now
walled by stone on both sides, that he became aware of how hard
his heart had been beating, and for how long.

Although the farthest heights of the mountain still stretched
above them, they passed quickly between the two peaks to find
more crowded beyond, a forest of high pinnacles. Although they
could not see its source past the intervening spires, a soft ver-
milion light bathed the sides of these black peaks, as though somewhere ahead of them lay a lake of fire. Paul could not help
remembering Martine's comment about a volcano, and wondered
if she might have a clearer idea now about what was before them,
but the blind woman was spending all her energy on dogged forward motion; it seemed cruel to make her speak.

At last the path led them up a steeply rising slope between another pair of sentinel peaks. The warm light spread widely just beyond, as though the straggling company had discovered the ultimate source of sunrise, and the next set of peaks were very distant—on the far side of the glow, Paul guessed, since their facing slopes shimmered with its radiance. Orlando and Fredericks were in the lead, and thus were the first to be able to see what lay beyond the rise; Paul saw them stop at the top of the path, frozen in silhouette against the persimmon-colored light.

"What is it?" he called, but neither of them turned. When he had struggled up the last few meters to stand beside them, he understood why.

As the others jostled in behind, most asking the same question, Paul Jonas could only stand and gape. The rest of the company pushed their way up onto the rise one by one, and one by one they fell silent, too.

In the center of the crown of peaks, in a wide shallow valley as barren as the lunar surface but large enough to hold a small city, lay a body. It was human in shape, or seemed to be, but it was oddly out of focus—at moments it seemed about to become clearly visible, but it never quite did. It lay stretched on its back, arms tight to its sides as though bound there, and seemed to be the source of the glow that illuminated the mountaintop and flickered gently beneath the black skies. The titanic figure filled the entire valley.

"Jesus Mercy," Renie whispered at Paul's shoulder, the first one to speak in half a minute.

Tiny figures swarmed across the monstrous thing; the nearest of them, clambering across feet which were almost as tall as the surrounding peaks, seemed as oddly formless as the giant itself. They, too, had a vaguely human shape, but seemed to be wrapped in garments of fluttering white, like shrouds.

Or laboratory coats, Paul thought, his brain snatching at minuscule details in the midst of such overwhelming madness. The only comparable thing he had ever seen swam up from childhood memory, a picture in an old book of Gulliver made prisoner by the Lilliputians, but that had possessed nothing of the blasted, ultimate strangeness of this place, this spectacle. For a moment he felt again as he had on the Ithacan beach, as the sky had folded down close around him and every molecule of the air had seemed feverishly charged.

"Oh . . ." someone breathed—Paul dimly thought it might be Fredericks, but his mind could clutch at nothing so prosaic: the overwhelming vision that lay before him kept smashing his collecting thoughts back into pieces again. "Oh, they've killed God."

A sigh vast as a gale wind echoed around the great bowl, most of the sound so low that they could only feel it in their bones and in the reverberation of the mountain beneath their feet. It came again, but this time the portion they could hear had a distinct rhythm to it, mournful and completely, utterly strange.

"I don't think He's dead." Paul marveled to hear coherent words come out of his own mouth. "He's singing."

Martine suddenly let out a muffled little gasp and sank to her knees. Florimel bent to help her, slow as someone moving in hardening ice, never taking her eyes from the immense shape that lay before them.

"God help me," Martine murmured, her voice choked by tears. "I know that song."

CHAPTER 34

To Eternity

THEY had clearly come to the end of something, or reached some important moment, but once the shock of the nightmare vision had eased a little, Renie felt mostly frustration.

"Is this all supposed to *mean* something?" she demanded. "Martine, you said something about a song?" She looked down to where the French woman was kneeling, rocking back and forth as though overcome with grief. She spoke again, more softly. "Martine?"

"I . . . I know it. I taught it to someone, long ago. To . . . something. I think this is that something." Her head turned listlessly from side to side, as though complete blindness had overwhelmed her again. "It is hard to explain, and the forces moving here are very confusing to me. I lost my sight in an accident, long ago. I was a child, being tested . . ."

Renie looked up, startled by movement. T4b was heading down the slope toward the immense, glowing figure. "What is he doing? Javier!"

His laugh trailed back to them, faint and cracked. "Going to go ask God some questions, seen? Got a whole *lot* of questions . . ."

"Somebody stop him," Renie pleaded. "We don't have any idea what this is all about, and we certainly don't need a teenager with a spear starting the conversation."

!Xabbu and Florimel had already started down the slope after him. Paul Jonas made a move to accompany them, then hesitated. "Perhaps I'm not the best person," he said.

"Probably not." Renie turned back to Martine. "Quick—what were you saying?"

The blind woman groaned. "Forgive me. It is hard to hear, hard to think. There are so many . . . voices in my head . . . !" She raised her hands to her temples. "I was in an experiment. Something—perhaps a neural net, some kind of artificial intelligence— was in it with me, although I thought it another child. It was strange, it thought and spoke strangely. But it was lonely, or seemed to be. I taught it some games and songs." She smiled through what must have been great pain. "You see, I was lonely, too. That song you heard is an old song from my childhood." She furrowed her brow, and then sang in a croaking voice:

> *"An angel touched me, an angel touched me,*
> *The river washed me and now I am clean . . ."*

"There is more," she said. "It is only a . . . a children's nursery rhyme I knew, but I cannot believe it is coincidence that I should hear it again in this place."

"So you're saying that giant out there is an AI?" Renie asked.

"Is that . . . the operating system? For this whole crazy Otherland network?"

"The One who is Other," murmured Paul Jonas, as distantly as if he also heard some old, half-remembered song.

Martine nodded, grimacing, pressing her hands harder against her skull. "The One who is Other. That is what the voice of the Lost called it."

At the bottom of the rise T4b had shaken off Florimel and !Xabbu and continued marching toward the vast figure. Renie watched with growing despair. "He's going to ruin everything, that idiot. We're going to get ourselves killed because he's acting like an angry child."

"But it's all about children, isn't it?" Orlando was climbing shakily to his feet, supported by Fredericks. "Right?" he said. His eyes did not quite seem to be tracking. "You came here to save the children, right?" He drew his sword out of Fredericks' belt, then gently pushed her away and began to stumble down the side of the rim, extending the blade to steady himself.

"Now what are *you* doing?" Renie demanded.

He paused to get his footing. Already he was short of breath again. "The One who is Other. I know that name, too. And that must be what I'm . . . here for." He glowered briefly at Fredericks, who was slipping down the dusty wash toward him, but his friend would not be turned away. "See, I was almost gone before, but I . . . but I got sent back. No, I chose to come back." Orlando let his head droop for a moment, then lifted it. For the first time, he looked full at Renie. "But there has to be a reason. So if that's it, that's it. I don't know if I can kill the Dark Lord over there with a sword, but I can sure as hell try. If it doesn't work . . . well, maybe the rest of you will think of something." He turned and continued down the hill.

"Orlando!" Fredericks hurried awkwardly after him.

"That's not the Dark Lord of anything," Renie shouted. Their little group was now a scattered line along the slope. "It's a damned VR simulation! This is just another simworld!"

If he heard her, he did not slow.

"I'm not sure that it is," said Paul Jonas; at Renie's startled glance, he hurried to add, "I'm not saying that *is* God, or Orlando's Dark Lord, but I don't think this is a normal simworld."

He was frowning, distracted, only a little less overwhelmed than Martine. "Ava, or whatever she is, brought us here for a reason. It took an awful lot out of her, too—that's why she had to absorb Emily. I think we're in the heart of the system now, even if this—" he waved his hand, "—is all just some kind of metaphor. As far as that giant thing, I don't know if we're actually supposed to kill it, but I'm pretty sure it's the reason we're here."

"If that's the operating system," Renie said grimly, "then it murdered our friend Singh. It turned my brother into a vegetable, and Florimel's daughter, too. If there's a way to kill it, I think I might be on Orlando's side after all. But we'd better catch up to them before someone does something unforgivably stupid." She turned to help Martine up. "Can you walk?"

The blind woman nodded weakly. "I believe so. But there is . . . a tremendous amount of information going in and out of this . . . place."

"So you definitely think that's the thing that runs this network?"

Martine flapped her hand. "I do not know anything definitely, except that my head feels like it's going to explode."

"We'd better hurry." Renie saw that the rest of the company had already reached the bottom of the slope, and T4b, the farthest in advance, was astonishingly close to the base of a skyscraper-tall foot. She swore. "How did the others get so far ahead of us?"

Before they could take a step, something rippled out from the great figure, a wave of distorting energy that blurred everything. For half an instant Renie thought it was the thing's sighing, earth-rattling voice again, but then she was gripped and frozen and broken into component pieces and scattered across a suddenly empty universe. She had time only to think *It's happening again* . . . and then she lost track of herself entirely.

There was little conscious thought this time; Renie could not even consider the nature of the fugue state until it had begun to recede, but the effect seemed to take a very long time to wear off. At last things began drifting back together, accumulating as slowly as droplets of water in zero-gravity—first bits of consciousness assembling themselves, followed by sequences of thought. Body awareness and sound grudgingly began to function, then a sense of color—the possibility of color to begin with, but not color itself—collected out of the blackness. The surrounding void began to have meaning and identifiable shape, then at last the desolate mountaintop scene reassembled itself, smearing together like footage of a melted oil painting run in achingly slow reverse.

Renie straightened from the bent-legged crouch she found herself in, and saw that several of the others had actually fallen.

"That was . . . bad, this time," Paul Jonas muttered. They helped Martine up, but she seemed stunned and could barely walk, let alone speak.

"The breakdowns in the system are getting worse somehow," Renie said as they forced themselves forward once more. "Longer and darker. Maybe we won't have to kill that thing. Maybe it's dying."

Paul said nothing but his expression was bleakly dubious.

Within moments they found themselves much closer to the giant shape than they should have been, and Renie began to understand why the others had moved so quickly. Some strange effect was compressing the distance, so that with each step the landscape flowed dizzyingly past them; a journey that should have taken them hours was going to be much shorter.

As they drew nearer to the immense body, Renie had a better view of the tiny white shapes clambering over it like fleas on a sleeping dog. They were humanoid, as they had appeared from a distance, and seemed almost the same size as Renie and her friends, but even under much closer inspection they had no obvious form—faceless, almost shapeless phantoms which seemed oblivious to the presence of the human company.

Renie felt a sudden catch in her throat. *Could those somehow be . . . the children? Stephen and the others?*

!Xabbu and the rest had stopped near the titan's foot. Hoping that he and the other adults had hammered some kind of sense into Orlando and T4b, Renie urged Paul on, and together they nearly lifted Martine off the ground to increase the pace.

"Look," !Xabbu called as they approached. He pointed.

Almost a mile distant, the hand of the supine giant, which had been curled in a loose fist on the ground at its side, had begun to open.

As they watched in stunned silence, the great fingers slowly rose and separated, as if performing the finale of some aeons-long magical trick. It took minutes, but when at last the hand was spread in a monstrous star shape, nothing was revealed but the huge, empty palm.

"Is it reaching for us?" wondered Renie.

"Summoning us," suggested !Xabbu.

"Or warning us to go away," Florimel added quietly.

They began to walk toward it; again the distance telescoped, so that before they had taken a hundred paces it loomed above them, a massive shape that could have enfolded a stadium as though it were a teacup. Close up, the hand was even more disturbing, inconstant in outline, shimmering and blurring along its edges and across its surface so that it hurt to look at it too long or too closely.

"It's like mine," said T4b, hoarse with wonderment. The anger had dropped from his face, replaced by pure amazement. "Like mine." He held up the hand that had been damaged in the patchwork country. It did look something like a tiny version of the unspeakably large thing spread above them.

"What does it mean?" Fredericks asked helplessly. "It's so . . . scanny!" Even Orlando, faced with the astounding size of the thing, had lowered his sword.

"We can't just . . ." Renie began, then stopped to stare as a glow began to spread in midair at the center of the spread fingers. "Jesus Mercy." The magic trick had been even slower than they had guessed, and it was not over yet.

At first, as golden light shimmered, she thought that a gateway was forming, but the gleam flattened and extended until it became clear that they were looking not at something, but *through* it—an irregular window forming in the naked air between the giant's fingertips and the ground: the yellow gleam was something on the far side. The hole in the air grew sharper and deeper, until Renie could clearly see a vast chamber all of beaten, reflecting gold, and the animal-headed figures who sat within it, still and majestic as statues. Beside each throne lay a huge sarcophagus, red and shiny as a gigantic drop of blood.

"Who are they?" Paul whispered.

Renie shook her head in nervous wonder. "I don't know, but I don't think they can hear us. It feels like we're looking at them through a one-way mirror."

"I know who they are," Orlando said wearily. "We met one of them already, in that Egypt place. That's Osiris. We're looking at the Grail Brotherhood."

The crowned figure at the center of the golden room rose and extended long arms wrapped in white bandages, then spoke to its silent companions on their thrones.

"The hour has come." The voice of Osiris floated faintly to Renie and her companions as though down a long dusty corridor, a breath out of the tomb. *"Now the Ceremony begins . . ."*

FELIX Jongleur paused to collect himself. The violent spasm that had passed through the system only minutes before had shaken him as well as the other masters of the Grail: he could hear the Ennead still whispering among themselves, not even bothering to shield their communications.

"Now the Ceremony begins," he announced again. "We have all waited long for this moment. My servant will bring you your cups."

The jackal-headed god Anubis appeared from the shadows, holding a large golden goblet in his black fingers. Jongleur forced down his irritation—this should have been Dread, acting his assigned role in the simulation, but he had dropped out of contact, forcing Jongleur to concoct this soulless Puppet version of the Messenger of Death. Jongleur comforted himself with the thought of what punishments he would inflict on his wayward servant when he found him again. "Take what he offers you," he instructed the others. "There is one for all." And indeed, as ibis-headed Jiun Bhao took the goblet, another appeared in Anubis' hands, which the jackal then obediently presented to the next in line, yellow-faced Ptah. When Robert Wells had received his goblet, and Anubis had moved on to Daniel Yacoubian wearing the falcon-beaked head of Horus, Wells turned and lifted his cup toward Jongleur in a mocking salute.

I suppose that is acceptable, Jongleur thought, although he was annoyed with the American. *Barely. But I will see him suffer forever if he does anything to give our game away.*

When one of the ever-multiplying goblets was in the hands of each of the Ennead, the jackal servant dutifully vanished into the shadows once more. *I suppose it's actually better Dread is not here,* Jongleur thought. *I couldn't have trusted that young fool not to do something flippantly stupid and spoil the gravity of the moment. . . .*

The slightly awkward pause was broken by Sekhmet. The lion-headed goddess peered into her goblet, then said, "What is the need for this? Can we not simply push a button, or . . . or whatever people do? Why all this nonsense?"

Jongleur paused. *It is close now, so close. Be patient.* "Because we do what no one has ever done, Madame. This is a moment unlike any other in history—is it not worth a little ceremony?" He tried to smile, but the Osiris face was not really made for such things.

Ymona Dedoblanco was not so easily pacified. "It all seems strange to me. We are . . . we are to drink poison?"

"Only symbolically, my fierce Sekhmet. In reality, you have each of you chosen the methods you deem best to . . . to effect your passage. Whatever is in keeping with your other arrangements." Meaning of course that some of the Brotherhood could not let their physical deaths be known for some time, either to help preserve their power or simply to prevent the world noticing that a surprising number of famous and powerful people had all died at the same time. "But if you are asking is the death of your physical body necessary, the answer is yes. Come, Madame—surely this has all been explained to you."

The African president-for-life with the crocodile head was also restive. "Why can I not save my real body?"

Jongleur was losing the battle with his own anger. "I cannot believe you are asking such things at this late moment, Ambodulu. The reason is, not only will you not be able to reenter your physical body, you would effectively be creating two versions of yourself—the physical version you now are, and a separate but immortal version living inside the network. You would be creating the fiercest rival for yourself imaginable—a twin who knows all your sources of power, who has the right to all your resources."

He shook his head. "Wells, you created this system—please explain it to him. I am losing patience."

The lemon-hued face of Ptah remained solemn, but Jongleur thought he detected a hint of amusement as Wells rose. That was the problem with Americans, Jongleur reflected sourly—they loved chaos for its own sake.

"Most of you have long understood and come to terms with this," Wells said smoothly, "but I will explain one more time, just to insure there are no doubts. I know it's a frightening step." He looked briefly to his falcon-headed confidant—less asking for help, Jongleur guessed, than silently requesting that the volatile Yacoubian keep his mouth shut. "The problem is that mind-transference is not truly possible . . ."

"What?" Sekhmet almost rose from her chair as she showed her fangs. "Then what are we doing here . . . ?"

"Please, show some courtesy. You were not required to study the Grail process, Ms. Dedoblanco, but I would have thought it worth your while." Wells frowned. "I was trying to say that mind-transference of the type so often used in science-fiction entertainments is not possible. The mind isn't a thing, or even a collection of things—you can't simply make an electronic copy of everything that exists in the mind, then . . . turn it on." He mimed the button-pushing she had suggested earlier.

"The mind is an ecology, a combination of neurochemical elements and the relationship between those elements. Some of how it works is so complex even the people who have perfected our Grail process still do not fully understand it, but they—we—have learned how to do what we need. We cannot simply move the mind from a physical location to a computer system, no matter how powerful and complex the system. Instead, we have created a mirror version—a virtual mind, as it were—for each of us, and then allowed our own brains to make it identical to the original. Once the initial matrix was created—the raw system in which an artificial mind could exist—you will remember that you were all fitted with what we call a *thalamic splitter,* an engineered biological device that creates a doubling effect of all brain activity. From then on, the process of simply using your brain began to create the duplicate here in the Grail system.

"Certain elements built into the splitter stimulated your actual

physical minds to duplicate themselves into the online minds—
creating mirrored storage of memories, among other things—until
both versions existed in parallel. Your nonphysical duplicates have
been kept effectively unconscious through this process, of course,
in a sort of dreamless sleep, waiting for today. That's a gross over-
simplification, but all the literature has been available to you. You
can look up anything you want, any time." Now he did smile. "It
seems a bit late for it, though.

"Now the time has come to finish the process—but it is *not* a
transfer. Even as we speak, even as we sit in this virtual room,
you are updating the waiting online minds. But if we simply woke
those online minds, you yourself would perceive no change—you
would still be inside your dying, mortal bodies. Instead, an identical version of you would suddenly exist, one with every memory of yours right up until the moment it was awakened, a version
of you which could live entirely in the network. But it would not
stay you for long—from the moment it gained consciousness it
would begin to diverge, to become something separate—a thing
with your memories, anxious to lead its own life. But although it
would be immortal, you—and by that I mean the you listening to
me now—would still grow older and more ill, and eventually die."

Wells leaned forward, apparently enjoying the lecturer's role,
as though he spoke before a group of new Telemorphix engineers
instead of the most powerful cabal on Earth. "That's why you
must abandon your physical bodies. If you do, in the moment
your body dies, your virtual duplicate will live. And it won't be
a duplicate then—it will be the only version of you, every memory intact right up to the moment the cup touched your lips." He
looked at the circle of largely impassive beast-faces. "When you
go to sleep each night, are you afraid you won't be the same person when you wake up? This won't even be like sleeping—less
than a second, then you'll be alive in the network, unlimited by
physicality, by age or injury or death."

"But if we truly die," the crocodile-headed god asked, "and it
is only another version of ourselves that survives, what of our
souls?"

Wells laughed. "If you really believe in such things, you should
have found a different way to spend your money."

A silence fell over the room. "Enough," said Jongleur, rising.

"This is not the time for discussion. Everyone has had a chance to make his or her decision long ago. If some wish to bow out at this late moment, we will not miss them—they have already paid their portion of constructing the eternal life the rest of us will share. Raise your cups!" More than a few followed him, although others among the Ennead still seemed troubled. "If you do not drink—if you do not trigger whatever form of physical death you have prepared for your old body, you will not step through. You will not join the rest of us as gods."

Still no one moved. Jongleur considered starting the procedure himself, but since he was not actually abandoning his physical body just yet, but only pretending to, he was not certain he wanted himself, Wells, or the other two forced to endure a too-close scrutiny.

The moment was saved by Ricardo Klement, who lifted his goblet and declared, "I believe. I believe in Senor Jongleur and I believe in the Grail. *Ad Aeternum!* To Eternity!" He tipped the goblet to his strange beetle-mouth and downed the contents. Somewhere in the physical world, his life-support systems disengaged.

Even Jongleur found himself staring in fascination. For a moment the scarab-faced Khepera only sat, looking mildly from side to side, then the sim abruptly stiffened as the body that animated it began to die. The waving, segmented antennae hardened into petrified branches, then Klement slid off the huge stone chair and clattered onto the golden floor.

A heartstoppingly long moment passed. All eyes turned from Klement's beetle sim, which lay on the gleaming floor like a dead cockroach in the middle of St. Peter's Basilica, to the sarcophagus beside his vacated throne. The polished scarlet lid began to lift, at first revealing only shadows. A figure slowly sat up, rising into the reflected sunlight of the golden walls. It was human, an idealized version of Ricardo Klement's younger self, sveltely naked and handsome, but the eyes were unfocused. The murmuring of the Ennead grew louder each moment that the figure sat in unmoving silence.

"Who are you?" Jongleur called. He stood for dramatic effect, and stretched out his arms. "What is your name, O resurrected soul, O newborn god?"

"I . . . I am Klement," the naked youth said. It turned to look at the others with slow curiosity. "I am Ricardo Klement."

A gasp circled the room. There were a few cries of joy and relief. "And how do you feel?" Jongleur asked, amazed to find even his own distant, ragged heart pumping with excitement. They had done it! The oldest punishment of all had been overthrown, and soon he, too, would be immortal. The Brotherhood had killed death—put the terrible, cold-eyed Mr. Jingo to final flight.

"I feel . . . well." The attractive face did not move much, but the eyes blinked as though in surprise. "It is good . . . to have a body."

Others called questions. The new Klement answered them slowly, but the answers were the right ones. Soon the rest of the Brotherhood were raising their cups, shouting *"Ad Aeternum!"* and drinking deeply, greedily, some laughing and calling to each other as they murderered their time-bound physical bodies. One by one, some immediately, some only after a space of minutes due to the method of real-life suicide they had chosen, the animal-headed sims of the Ennead stiffened upon their thrones. Some of the gods tottered and crashed to the floor, some simply hardened like statues where they sat.

Jongleur, Wells, Yacoubian, and Jiun Bhao drained their own cups without even the slight trepidation some of the others showed, since for the present the four of them were only miming suicide.

Within a minute four sarcophagi opened like chrysalises and four handsome new bodies sat up, one each for Jongleur, Wells, Jiun Bhao, and Yacoubian—the false revivifications Jongleur had prepared to keep the other members of the Brotherhood convinced that he and his companions had joined them. The empty sims sat up, blinked their eyes, and looked around in imitation wonderment, performing a programmed charade for an audience that was no longer present.

None of the other sarcophagi had opened.

Confusion turning rapidly to alarm, Jongleur shut off the four false rebirths and levitated himself to the nearest of the Brotherhood, a Portuguese industrialist named Figueira. His ram-headed incarnation as the god Khnum, which had slid halfway to the floor, was as rigid as marble.

"Is there a problem here?" Jiun Bhao asked with deceptive mildness.

"If you're pulling some kind of trick, old man . . ." growled Yacoubian.

"They're dead." It was like listening to someone speak in a dream. Jongleur could not make sense of it—had the Other finally malfunctioned for good? But everything else seemed as normal. "They're all dead, they've all killed their real bodies. It's no trick—but they were supposed to wake up here . . ." He turned to Ricardo Klement. The handsome youth still sat in his sarcophagus, unquestionably alive but apparently content simply to exist in his new body, paying no attention to what went on around him. "But it worked for Klement! How can all the rest of them be . . . be . . . ?"

Wells was examining the contorted, solidified sim-corpse of Ymona Dedoblanco. "It seems you were right to hold back on our own rebirth, Jongleur." He stood up. The yellow smile was back, although it was a bit strained around the edges. "I suppose that once we iron out this little problem, it just means there'll be more birthday cake for the rest of us."

"I DON'T understand," Renie said breathlessly. "What's happening? Are all those Grail people really dead?"

Orlando scarcely heard her. The voices in his head were back, filling his skull with whispering confusion—a thousand velvet-winged birds trapped in an abandoned cathedral, swishing and fluttering and murmuring. He clung to one thought with the last of his fading strength.

"That's it," he said. It was hard to speak—every word wasted precious breath. Somewhere far away his body was failing, and this time there would be no recovery. "That's why I'm still here."

Fredericks pulled at his arm, questioning, but Orlando shook off his friend. He had been prepared to throw his exhausted body against the gigantic shape on the mountaintop, but had not done so. He had known before he started down into the valley that the monster would not feel even his most murderous assault, but something far different from the certainty of failure had kept him from attacking: as he drew nearer, the titan figure, though terrifying because of its sheer, incredible size, began also to seem oddly pitiful—trapped, tormented, and helpless. The realization had left Orlando bewildered, a fading hero with no quest. But now he thought he understood why he was still alive and still breathing, however laboredly.

He reached out a hand to the shimmering vision of the Grail chamber. The others were arguing among themselves and scarcely noticed, but Fredericks saw.

"Orlando? What are you doing?"

He felt a certain unphysical resistance, but the surface of the image was no more substantial than the tension on a pool of mercury. As his fingers passed through, a shudder coursed along the enormous hand that framed the window, which in turn made the golden chamber ripple, and distorted the already grotesque forms of the Grail Brotherhood. Orlando took another painful breath, then stepped through.

The room of gold now stretched on all sides. There was no sign of a gateway behind him, only the gleaming walls incised with faint carvings. Orlando lifted his sword and took a few steps toward the circle of thrones and the four Grail masters still alive and moving. The god with the yellow face saw him first; his eyes widened, and the two gods with bird heads turned to see what had surprised their comrade. A moment later Fredericks spilled out of nowhere behind Orlando and flopped to the floor.

"Don't do this," his friend said, struggling up. "Don't do it, Gardiner."

Orlando ignored Fredericks and pointed his sword at the one called Osiris, whose mummified body showed he was startled even if his stiff, masklike face did not. "You," Orlando shouted. "Yeah, you, Napkin Boy. I'm going to kill you."

The god with the falcon's head turned first to Osiris, then to the yellow-faced god. "Damn it, Bob, what the hell is going on around here?" he demanded.

"You scanny old bastards have hurt a lot of people." Orlando was trying desperately to keep his voice strong. "Now I'm going give you some of it back."

The god Osiris stared at him. "Who are you?" he snapped. "One of those sobbing ninnies from the Circle? I am too busy to dally with the likes of you." He raised a bandaged arm, index finger outstretched and beginning to smolder. Orlando pushed Fredericks behind him.

"*Stop!*"

Osiris paused, nonplussed by the midair entrance of yet another stranger.

Renie held something shiny in front of her as she stumbled forward, thrusting it toward the Grail people like a suicide terrorist with a hand grenade. Even as he struggled to make one breath follow another, Orlando could see that she was scared rigid. "I've got one of your access devices and I know how to use it," she shouted. "If you try anything, I'll make sure that what happened to the others happens to you. And if you think you're faster than me, go ahead, try—we'll all go together."

But she doesn't know how to use it, Orlando thought dreamily, *and we didn't have anything to do with those people dying. It's a good idea, but it won't work.* "It's all right, Renie," he said aloud. "I know what I'm doing."

Before she could reply, the falcon-headed god was shoving his way past the others. "That's my lighter!" he bellowed. "So *you're* the little thieving scum who took it."

"Don't be stupid," Osiris snapped, but the falcon god was not listening to him. With each stride Horus grew larger, swelling until he was almost three times Orlando's size, his eyes glowing like blue coals. Orlando lifted the sword again and stepped in front of Renie.

"Daniel!" the god with the yellow face called. "We don't need to . . ."

Orlando felt a deeper shudder run through not just the room, but through him, the air, everything. The voices in his head rose to an abrupt screeching peak, so shrill with terror that he felt himself growing faint. Spots flickered before his eyes. For a timeless instant everything hung, gold and black and echoing, then reality folded in on itself.

A second later light and sound rushed back like clouds before a storm, carried ahead of a terrible thunderous groan that seemed to turn Orlando's bones to water.

The light fragmented. The golden chamber suddenly became a thousand chambers which spread out in tesseract profusion, as though Orlando, Fredericks, and the others were prisoners in a giant kaleidoscope. Countless ghostly versions of the chamber stretched away in each direction like the concatenating reflections of facing mirrors, but at the same time, as though some boundary between worlds had broken down, the black mountaintop and its writhing giant prisoner loomed above it all.

Not just the room, but the people as well had been endlessly multiplied.

"Orlando!" Fredericks screamed—a million Frederickses screamed. "Look out!"

In the midst of unspeakable confusion, Orlando turned as slowly as if he waded in a nightmare. The falcon-headed god was still bearing down on him, radiating transparent ghost versions of itself. A massive multiple hand snatched at him; as he tumbled to the side, he felt its powerful talons scrape along his back like the blade of a steam shovel, ripping cloth and skin.

The temple and the mountain had not just multiplied but merged: the black peaks showed through every version of the temple walls and the valley floor glimmered like the temple's polished gold. Fredericks, crouching stunned on the chamber floor that was simultaneously black dust beneath mountain sky, Renie, the gods of the Grail Brotherhood, and all the rest of the companions Orlando had left behind on the mountaintop—everyone was now folded in on the same spot and simultaneously replicated out into infinity, reeling in the madness of endless refraction. The only thing that had remained singular was the giant figure stretched across the mountaintop—the Other—which now seemed to be the suffering heart of a universe that was both collapsing and expanding at the same time. Even the stars seemed to have multiplied upon themselves, so that each distant sun was part of a fractal cloud of light.

Ignoring the chaos, the stubborn falcon god turned and lurched toward Orlando once more, roaring with mindless rage. As its actions rippled out through its shadows, and Orlando's exhausted, stumbling mind tried to decide which of the countless versions was real, the blurry, titan shape of the Other began to struggle even harder, bending at the middle as though trying to burst its bonds and sit up.

The giant screamed. Its cataclysmic howl seemed the noise of a universe beginning or ending, and for a moment reality threatened to dissolve completely.

Far above them, the blurred gigantic face suddenly began to take on a more definite shape, as though something inside the amorphous figure was struggling to get out. As Orlando and the others watched in stunned surprise, it stretched and darkened into something snarling and bestial, looming a mile over the plain. The distortions subsided a little.

"Hello, Grandfather." The beast's yellow eye was bright and big as the moon, its voice loud enough to shake down the stars. *"Fancy meeting you here. Oh, and look at who else has joined the party, too!"*

The god Osiris stared upward, frozen at the center of his own galaxy of reflections. "Dread . . . ?" he croaked.

At the sound of the name, Orlando heard a few of his companions cry out.

The jackal-thing laughed. *"I've found your secret, old man. And soon your system will do what I tell it to do. I think I'm going to like being the master of an entire universe."*

Another terrible shudder passed through the body of the giant, and for a moment the beast's features were subsumed by the blurry face it had worn before. *"It's still fighting me,"* the voice said, a little less thunderingly present, but still echoing in Orlando's mind and all across the mountain. *"But I've found how to hurt it, you see."* The giant shape howled and spasmed; again the mountaintop vibrated on the edge of dissolution. *"Just give me a few moments and I'll have it behaving again. . . ."*

The field of distortion pulsed. The giant continued to fight against something invisible, but its struggle was weakening. Through the storm of insanity Orlando heard a distant cry and turned to see that the falcon god had seized Fredericks and had lifted her up to its deranged, beaked face.

"What are you bastards doing to our system?" the falcon-thing bellowed. "What the hell have you done?"

Orlando staggered toward them, trying to ignore both the panicky voices in his head and the shadow Orlandos radiating away from him in all directions. Compelled by reflexes developed over half his young life, he had clung to his sword through everything; when he reached the Grail monster, he hacked at the back of its knee with all his failing strength. It dropped Fredericks in a heap and turned on him.

"Get away from it!" Renie screamed somewhere behind him, but Orlando paid no attention. The huge falcon-thing stooped, hands flexing, so angry it could think of no strategy but grab and crush. Orlando ducked under a flailing arm, then tried to stab at its unprotected side, but the other great hand flashed in and caught his blade and snapped the sword in half. Orlando tried to leap away, but he had little strength left. The creature lashed out and struck him like the front bumper of a truck; the impact was so great that he only knew he had been flung through the air when he smashed to the ground.

Darkness came down around him, and this time he almost did not find his way out again. He could barely see. His breathing was no longer just difficult but almost impossible. Even his inner voices seemed to have been shocked into silence.

Worst of all, he had lost his sword. He could see the hilt with its broken blade lying what seemed only a few meters away, but the distortion was still so fierce it was hard to judge—hard even to be sure it was really the sword and not one of its countless mirror-copies. Orlando began to crawl toward it, conscious through the pain only that his business was somehow unfinished. Things inside him were no longer connected the way they should be— he could feel things rubbing together—and a tiny, remote part of him marveled that he could feel so much damage to an imaginary body. Waves of blackness, red at the edges, rolled across him. He crawled on, trying to blink away the spots before his eyes, hoping that he was moving in the right direction.

Just as his hand closed on the hilt, something caught him by the foot and jerked him into the air. He hung upside down before a pair of massive legs. As blood rushed to his head, he lunged at the nearest one, hoping at least to scratch the god's skin with his broken sword, but the distance was too great. People were shouting his name, but they were also shouting Fredericks' name, even T4b's name. None of it mattered. The thing dangled him by his heel, swinging him like a clock's pendulum.

"You saboteurs have guts, I'll give you that," the falcon god rumbled. "But I'm still going to kill you, you little shit."

Fredericks desperately struck at the thing's legs, again and again, her hands bloodied, but the monster didn't even seem to notice her. Orlando hung, helpless in the Grail monster's grip, and waited to die.

PAUL shouted in fear as the universe fragmented, but there was too much noise even to hear himself. Everything was coming apart and nothing made any sense.

It had all happened so quickly—Orlando walking right into the image where they watched the Grail Brotherhood, Fredericks shoving through after him. Renie had screamed for Martine to give her the lighter, then she, too, had leaped through, but even as she vanished, the scene of the golden chamber had started to dim, and the giant shape stretched across the valley had begun tossing and moaning like a man in a nightmare, making the very stone of the mountain shake. Then everything had turned inside out, and Renie and all the others had reappeared, along with the Grail people, while reality broke down around them all.

For a moment something possessed the giant entity—some wolfish presence the Grail people seemed to recognize, and whose very voice made Martine begin to shriek and hold her hands to her ears—then that apparition had flickered out again, sending the giant into convulsions once more. Now the whole of the mountaintop seemed shattered into a thousand reflecting pieces . . .

The thought bounced through his head like an echo: *Shattered . . . glass falling . . . shattered . . .*

. . . And Orlando was fighting for his life against one of the Grail masters, who had grown to huge proportions, although still only ant-sized in comparison to the giant Other spread across the mountaintop, whose spasms of anguish washed across them all in waves of distortion. People were screaming, Renie and !Xabbu were chasing the one called T4b as he ran toward Orlando and the falcon-headed ogre, and . . . and . . .

Paul took a step to follow them, but a thousand Pauls moved at the same time in all directions, and he stopped, dizzy and confused.

"Jonas, help me!" The woman called Florimel raised the ghosts of a thousand hands toward him, her terror multiplied across an equal number of scarred, one-eyed faces. "It is Martine—I think

she is dying!" The blind woman lay rigid at her feet, eyes rolled
back beneath the lids.

Paul tried to go to them, but it was like trying to find someone in a hall of mirrors. As Florimel shouted again, he closed his
eyes and staggered toward the sound of her voice, stopping only
when he and Florimel collided.

"Give her air," Florimel directed, then dropped to her knees
and began pushing on the blind woman's chest. Paul had no idea
what she meant, and was still staring a few seconds later when
Florimel looked up. "Air, you fool!" she shouted. "Mouth to
mouth!"

Paul closed his eyes again to shut out the dizzying, kaleidoscopic view. He found Martine's face by touch, then clamped his
mouth on hers and blew. He could not help wondering what good
it would do to try to resuscitate an unreal body, but none of it
bore thinking about much—such mundane remedies in the middle of such chaos seemed like using a whisk broom to clean up
a sandstorm.

Florimel gasped. Paul opened his eyes and saw her looking
not at her patient but at something above them. The giant figure
of the Other had lifted one arm toward the sky; impossibly massive, it stretched above their heads and over much of the valley,
like a planet coming into view. As the giant groaned, still racked
with nightmares, the ground shook and the visual distortions
danced like windblown flames.

His stupefied attention fixed on the massive shape of the Other,
Paul only half-heard Martine's gasp. Her hand, as if in imitation
of the giant shape above them, rose and clutched at him.

"Martine, don't move!" Florimel reached to check her pulse.
"You've had a bad . . ."

The blind woman struggled to sit up even as her friend tried
to hold her down. "No!" Martine choked. "The children . . . they
are terrified! They are all alone! We have to go to them!"

"What are you talking about?" Florimel said harshly. "You
aren't going anywhere. The whole world is going mad, and you
almost died."

Martine began to weep. "But you don't understand—I can hear
them! I can feel them! The birds are so frightened. Something has
got in with them, something hungry, and they can't escape!" She

grabbed at her hair as though she would pull it out. "Make it stop! I can't stand to hear them screaming!"

As Paul crouched beside them, helpless, Florimel wrapped her arms around Martine. "We are here with you," she told the blind woman. "We are here with you." Her eyes too had filled with tears.

"But they are so f-f-frightened," Martine sobbed.

An even stronger distortion rippled across Paul's vision, so that for a moment the two women seemed to recede from him down a long corridor. He staggered to his feet, flailing for balance. The giant's arm still hung poised above their heads, but no one else seemed to notice it. The falcon-headed Grail monster had lifted the boy Orlando into the air where he hung without moving, dead or as good as dead. Paul thought he could see Fredericks at the thing's feet, and another figure running toward them, but simply trying to focus on anything for more than an instant made him vertiginously ill. A couple of other shapes that might have been Renie and !Xabbu were running toward the monster and its captive, but they were still far away, tripping and stumbling through the shifting, inconstant landscape. Everything was falling apart. Everything was going hopelessly wrong.

"Ava!" Paul shouted into the air. "Why did you bring us here? What have you done to us . . . ?"

As if he had summoned her with his desperate cry, the angel appeared out of nowhere, flickering, inconstant, replicated a millionfold on all sides, and all her hopeless voices screamed in unison.

"Stop! You are killing him!"

Paul had no idea who she was pleading with, and whether the one for whom she feared was Orlando, the giant stretched across the mountaintop, or even Paul himself.

The multiplied angel cried out once more, and her cry was echoed in the ground-shaking, hollow voice of the Other. The great arm looming above them trembled for a long moment, then the massive hand plunged downward like a moon falling from orbit and crashed into the dust on top of Renie, !Xabbu, Orlando, and the rest. The ground jumped as though a bomb had exploded, and Paul was knocked off his feet. A moment of comparative stillness followed. The angel and all her phantoms hung in the air, mouths open, eyes wide. The dust drifted down across the huge hand.

Orlando, Renie—they're . . . gone . . . was all Paul had time to think, then everything hardened and shattered, a thousand angels flying apart, a stained-glass window smashed, shards flying, glittering, and he . . .

Shattered . . . glass falling . . . shattered . . .

He was in the black tower, and it was all happening again, too late to stop it . . .

. . . The glass flying and the thousand thousand versions of Ava all crying out, and then the birds, swirling up like plumes of multicolored smoke, the birds and the glass and the voices of children crying . . .

The glass shattered and Paul shattered with it, broken and scattering, then and now, scattering until the fragments became too small and his thoughts no longer held together.

ONE moment Renie and !Xabbu had been in the great golden tomb-chamber of the Grail Brotherhood. An instant later, the world had fallen in upon itself.

!Xabbu snatched at her as countless identical shadows of themselves sprang out in all directions. The tomb and the mountain-top had folded together, somehow—the Grail survivors, Orlando, Paul, even the mysterious, giant Other, all inhabited the same accordioned, rippling space.

"It's all falling apart!" Renie shouted.

A huge creature with a falcon's head and mad blue eyes was bearing down on Orlando. Somewhere nearby Martine was screaming. Everywhere Renie looked, friends and enemies had been replicated like infinite strings of paper dolls.

There was no way even to grasp what was happening, let alone try to stop it, but Orlando was in immediate danger from the Grail monster—that was something Renie could understand. Even as she pulled !Xabbu toward their embattled friend, the vast shape of the Other, large as a row of hills, began to convulse. Its seismic roar of pain knocked her and !Xabbu to their knees.

Something was forming in the shadowy regions of the thing's face—a beast shape, dark, contorted, and sinister. A great yellow eye opened.

"Hello, Grandfather," it rumbled. Renie recognized the voice, and let out a shriek of despair.

"It's him! The murderer!"

Each word the thing spoke made the ground tremble. Renie reached for !Xabbu, but her friend lay stretched on the ground, face rammed against the black dust that was also somehow the golden chamber floor.

"Get up," she shouted, so close herself to the edge of despair that she almost could not remain standing. "Get up! We have to help Orlando."

"It is the All-Devourer," !Xabbu moaned. He clung to the ground as though it were the deck of a storm-wracked ship. "He has come to take us all. This is the end of things!"

Renie wanted to weep. "Get up! It's not your All-Devourer, it's the Quan Li thing—it's trying to take over the system!" She bent and grabbed at his arm to pull him upright, struggling to remember the story he had once told her. "You said Porcupine beat the All-Devourer, remember? That's what you told me. You said *I* was the Porcupine, didn't you? Well then, get up, damn it! I need you!" She leaned close to his ear, still tugging hard on his arm. "!Xabbu! Even Porcupine couldn't do it by herself!"

Whatever the murderous Quan Li thing had done to the Other, it had not completely overwhelmed the giant's resistance. As the immense shape struggled against its possessor, the beastlike head blurred and vanished, but reality still remained fragmented.

!Xabbu allowed himself to be drawn up into a crouch. After a moment in which he would not meet her eyes, he stood. His sim had gone deathly pale, but when he turned his face to her, a certain miserable resolution had returned.

"You shame me, Renie," he said.

"I'm sorry, but we have to . . ."

"No!" He angrily waved his hand. "What you did was right. Let us hurry to help Orlando."

A rippling, distorted figure lurched past them toward the spot where Orlando and the falcon god had closed on each other.

"Javier!" Renie shouted after the dwindling shape. "T4b! What are you *doing*?"

He dug on, ignoring them, hurrying toward the unfair combat between Orlando and the huge Grail monster.

"Jesus Mercy!" Renie shrieked as she began to run after him. "I am never, never, never, *never* going anywhere with teenage boys again!"

With !Xabbu following her, they raced across the distorted landscape, fighting waves of dizziness and confusion. Somewhere that might have been ten meters ahead or a thousand, Orlando was flung sideways by a horrendous blow from his enemy's gargantuan hand. Renie cried out, certain he had been killed. To her astonishment, Orlando and his army of phantom duplicates struggled up onto hands and knees and began to crawl, but the multiplied forms of the Grail monster snatched him up a moment later. Orlando's bleeding, broken form swayed upside down in the creature's grasp like a gutted animal. Renie was sprinting now, but even through the distortions she could tell that she and !Xabbu were still too far away. They would be too late.

A ripple of angel-shapes suddenly filled the sky and a thousand terrified female voices cried out at the same moment, *"Stop! You are killing him!"*

The sound was so desolate, so full of despair and the certainty of failure that Renie stumbled and almost fell. When she regained her balance, she saw that something was now climbing the falcon monster's back. For a moment, she thought it was Fredericks making a suicidal bid to save her friend.

"No—it's T4b!" Renie gasped. !Xabbu said nothing, but pelted on beside her.

The Grail creature had become aware of the thing on its back: it snapped its vast, clacking beak at the interloper, then brought up its free hand to swat T4b away like a fly, but the teenager ducked under the blow and scrambled up onto the huge head. T4b raised his altered hand—for a brief, hallucinatory instant, Renie saw it glowing a cool blue-gray—then jammed it into the falcon-god's head just behind the nictitating eye. It entered the giant skull without resistance, but the effect was startling: the Grail-thing abruptly stiffened and straightened, as though a powerful electric current ran down its spine. As it lifted trembling hands to its head, Orlando managed to grab at the creature's body and drag himself closer, then thrust the jagged remains of his sword into the falcon god's chest.

The Grail monster suddenly found its voice, roaring and choking. It knocked T4b flying, then lifted Orlando up to its staring eye as though wondering what sort of creature could cause it so much pain. The brute fell silent, swayed in place, then let Orlando drop. A moment later it collapsed on top of him like a razed building.

"Orlando!" Fredericks screamed and beat at the massive, inert form of the Grail monster. "Orlando!"

Renie and !Xabbu stumbled to a halt beside the leveled god. The falcon-thing had fallen so hard it had cratered the ground. Only one of Orlando's feet could be seen protruding from beneath the monster's chest; Fredericks was struggling uselessly to shove the massive creature aside so she could reach her friend's body.

Renie had only a shocked moment to survey the scene, then she became aware of something moving above her head—a shadow, a change of air pressure. She looked up to see the titan hand of the Other dropping toward them, a shape so vast that it swallowed the sky and even the light as it fell.

"Oh, no . . ." was all she had time to say before the roof of the world collapsed on top of them.

ORLANDO did not fight the darkness this time.

He could feel himself dissolving, slipping away, but there was nothing to be done about it. All that made him what he was seemed to be growing diffuse, like the scant substance of a cloud melting into hot sunlight—but it was darkness, not light, that refined and absorbed him.

For a moment he thought he saw again the hospital room and his parents. He tried to speak to them, to touch them, but he had already made that decision, and now had no more substance than an idle thought: he could only skim past them into the growing dark.

I'm just a memory now. The realization should have been terrible and sad, but it felt different than that, somehow. Still, though he had left them behind, he badly wanted to let them know he had not forgotten them. He could only hope some unimaginable wind might carry his voice back to them through the empty spaces.

I love you, Mom. I love you, Dad.

It wasn't your fault . . .

He rushed on. The voices were back, whether real or not, but now they were calling to him in welcome. He was disappearing even as he simultaneously grew wider, grew deeper, until there was almost nothing left of him, but still he could encompass whole universes.

And after all that he had done to fight it, to flee from it, to deaden his fear of it, when he was finally ushered through into that ultimate moment, Orlando Gardiner found he did not fear the darkness after all.

CHAPTER 35

The White Ocean

NETFEED/NEWS: Ambodulu's Absence Sparks West African Chaos
(visual: President-for-life Edouard Ambodulu meeting dignitaries)
VO: ... The apparent disappearance of President Ambodulu has sent this West African nation into even greater instability. As rumors of illness, abdication, and death fly in the marketplace, his lieutenants seem to be scrambling for power. Despite repeated demands by both national political figures and international media, there has been no public statement from the presidential palace in 48 hours, fueling speculation that some kind of power seizure within Ambodulu's own tribal group may have left the nation with no ruler. ...

SOMEONE was tugging at her hand. Stephen, of course—he always managed to beat her pad's alarm by five minutes, always dragged her up out of those desperately-needed last few minutes of sleep. Renie groaned and tried to roll over. Let him make his own breakfast for once. After all, he was eight years old ...

But no, he wasn't anymore, he was . . . how old now? Ten? Eleven? Nearly a teenager, and old enough that he had become the hard one to wake, burying himself deeper in the pillow, ignoring her warnings that he would be late for school . . . lost in sleep, sleep, deep down where she could not reach him . . .

Stephen. The memory abruptly became clear, like a card turned over. *Stephen is in a coma.* She had to do something. But if it wasn't Stephen pulling at her, then who . . . ?

She opened her eyes, struggling to focus. For a split instant, the face hovering over her was almost unfamiliar, but then she suddenly realized who it was, the pale brown skin and peppercorn hair . . .

"!Xabbu . . . !" She sat up and was almost dropped again by a swirl of dizziness. "!Xabbu, it's you! I mean, the real you!"

He smiled, but there was something strange about it, something held in reserve. "It is me, Renie. Are you well?"

"But . . . but you're in your own body!" In fact, he was in his own body and nothing else, crouching beside her completely naked. "Are we . . . are we back? Home?" She sat up again, more slowly this time. The strange black mountaintop still surrounded them but its lines were different—even the texture of the rocks was different, oddly smooth and strangely angular. But the greatest difference of all was that the giant humanoid shape which had dominated the valley had disappeared, leaving only an empty crater between the peaks—a crater that had collapsed along one side, so that half the mountaintop was now open to the sky.

There was no visible sun, but a kind of morning seemed to have come to the place, the sky a strangely familiar gray. Confused, Renie looked away from the broken mountainside to examine herself, and saw that like her friend, she too was naked. She was also a woman again. "Jesus Mercy, what's going on here?" Despite !Xabbu's own careless nudity, she folded her arms over her breasts. "Am I . . . ?"

"Yes." His sad smile returned. "You appear to be the Renie I first met."

"Except with fewer clothes. What's happened? Where are the others?"

"Most are gone, I do not know where. Only . . ." He pointed. Renie twisted around. Behind her, a few meters distant, sharing the shadow from the same rocky outcrop but somehow as separated as if they were behind glass, lay two still figures. One of them was the golden-haired Achilles sim of Orlando Gardiner, still wearing its tattered Greek clothes. The other, lying curled across his chest as though she were a castaway and he were the piece of flotsam that had saved her life, was a naked girl Renie had never seen before.

"Oh, my God." Renie levered herself upright, ignoring the wash of vertigo, and hurried to them. She kneeled and touched Orlando's arm, then his face; both were cold and hard as stone. Renie's eyes filled with tears, but she wiped them away, forcing herself to focus on what would come next. The girl was still alive, clinging to the empty sim and sobbing almost noiselessly, a quiet hitch of sound that Renie could tell had been going on for a long time. Renie reached out to her. "Are you . . . are you Fredericks?"

The girl only clutched the deserted sim tighter. Tears spilled from her tight-shut eyes and rolled down her cheeks onto Orlando's chest. Seeing this, something Renie had held tightly inside finally slipped from her grasp and she began to cry as well, deeply and helplessly. She felt !Xabbu's hand come to rest on her shoulder, but he did not try in any other way to console her. Renie cried for a long, long time.

When she had some control of herself again she sat up, drained and exhausted. Fredericks would not be pulled from Orlando's empty sim, and Renie could see no reason to force the issue. They were in an empty place and seemed to be the only people there. The giant shape of the Other, the surviving Grail Brotherhood, and their other companions had all vanished.

"What happened?" she asked !Xabbu. "At the end, everything . . . everything went completely mad."

"I do not know. I am full of shame that I was so frightened." His look was dark, troubled. "I thought I was afraid when I first saw the giant here on this mountain, but what came after was worse. I am embarrassed for my fear at a time when you needed me, but that does not change what I believe. I think we have truly met the All-Devourer."

"Don't say things like that." Renie shuddered. "We can't think that way. Everything has an explanation, even if it's an unpleasant one. That giant was the operating system—Martine said it was—and the Quan Li thing was trying to take it over."

"I understand," !Xabbu said. "And I agree. But I also know what I know."

"It's so frightening, to think of a monster like him with so much power. What did Martine say his name was? Dread." She shook her head, feeling like she wanted to cry again. "I wish Martine was with us."

!Xabbu sat back on his heels. "Perhaps I should build a fire. It is not too cold here, but it might bring some warmth to our hearts, at least."

"Do you think you can?"

He shrugged. "I did in that other place—the one you called the Patchwork World. And this seems much like it."

"It does, doesn't it?" Renie flicked a glance over to Fredericks. The girl had slid off Orlando's unresponsive form and now lay curled against him on the ground. Renie turned her attention back to the strange crumbled mountaintop. "This place has changed, somehow. It looks a lot like that unfinished place now—like nothing's quite ready. I wonder what that means. More important, how do we get out of here so we can find the others?" A sudden thought ran through her like a lightning strike. "My God! The lighter!" She had actually run her hands down her own skin before she realized that without clothes she would have no pockets. "It's gone."

!Xabbu shook his head. "I found it beside you." He opened his palm. The shiny object looked quite out of place in their desolate surroundings.

"Does it work?" Renie asked eagerly. "Did you try it?"

"I did. I could make nothing happen."

"Let me see what I can do." She reached out and took it from him. She weighed it briefly in her hand, reassured by its familiar heft, then let her fingers travel over one of the sequences she and Martine had discovered. The object remained inert. No gateway shimmered into existence. Renie cursed quietly and tried a different sequence.

"What you are doing is useless," a new voice said.

Renie was so startled that she dropped the lighter. The stranger who had appeared from behind the outcropping of stone and now stood only a few meters away was a tall slender Caucasian, muscular in a sinuous way, stamped as at least middle-aged only by his white hair and the wrinkles on his long, sharp-nosed face. Renie tried to imagine which of her companions this could be, but failed. She snatched the lighter from the ground. "Who . . . who the hell are you?"

The man blinked slowly. His stare had a cold, almost reptilian quality. "I suppose I could make up something, but I see no reason to lie." His speech was careful, precise, and as emotionless as his gaze, with just the faint hint of some accent Renie could not place. "My name is Felix Jongleur. To save you your second and third questions—yes, I am the leader of the Grail Brotherhood, and no, I have no idea where we are." He allowed himself a tight, mirthless smile. "I am not ungrateful to have been given a healthy body—I have not been this young in over a century—but I would have preferred to remain a god."

Renie stared at him, aghast. This was one of the men she had been hunting for so long that she almost could not remember the beginning of it—one of the bastards who had destroyed Stephen's life, who had ordered Susan Van Bleeck beaten to death. She found her fingers curling into fists as she drew her legs beneath her.

He raised an eyebrow, coolly amused. "You can attack me, but it will do you no good—presuming that you could actually overpower me, which might be more difficult than you think. If you wish, you may ease your conscience with the knowledge that I find you just as unpleasant as you find me. But it seems we will need each other, at least for a while."

"Need each other?" she asked. "!Xabbu?" She turned, keeping Jongleur in the corner of her vision, although the man had not made even the smallest movement toward them. "Is there any reason we shouldn't just throw this evil bastard off the mountain?"

Her friend was also tense—she could feel him like a coiled spring beside her. "What do you mean, we need each other?" he demanded of the stranger.

"Because we are trapped here together. Your stolen access device—I take it you pilfered it from that idiot Yacoubian—will not function. Neither will any of my own codes or commands. I have my own reasons to need your help, but my value to you should be obvious."

"Because you built the whole network."

"More or less, yes. Come—I want to show you something." He gestured to the place where the peaks had fallen and only a naked rim of black stone remained. "If you still distrust me, I will step away." He backed off, looking briefly and without curiosity at Fredericks, who still huddled beside Orlando's vacated body. "Go on, look."

She and !Xabbu walked forward, moving with increasing caution as they reached the sheer edge of the mountain. Renie guessed they were standing where the giant's shoulder had once lain. Something as smoothly effective as a hot knife had sliced the shiny black stone away, but that was not what caught her eye. She and !Xabbu took another few steps forward until they had a good angle to look down.

The great black mountain dropped away beneath them for a long distance. It would have been hard enough to judge their height even if they could have seen the ground, but there was no ground to see. Instead, the mountain was entirely surrounded by what Renie at first thought was a blank of fog, a sea of flat white cloud that stretched away in all directions until it disappeared into the gray horizon. As she stared, she saw odd glints of light in the formless stuff, sparkles that gave the endless cloud bank a faintly silvery sheen, but somehow did not detract from its white uniformity.

It's like being in that old story, "Jack and the Beanstalk," she thought. *Like we've climbed up into the sky.* Another thought came to her, one that was far less pleasant. *We're going to have to climb down from here. That's why he needs us. Nobody sane would try to climb down that far on his own.*

"Do you see it?" Jongleur called, an edge of impatience in his voice.

"Yes. What is all this white stuff?"

"I don't know." He watched them as they returned. He seemed even less bothered by nakedness than !Xabbu, if such a thing were possible. "I thought I knew everything I needed to know, but clearly I was wrong. I mistrusted one servant, but it was another one who betrayed me."

"Dread . . . he works for you." Renie again found herself nauseated even to be talking to this man."

"Worked." Jongleur flicked his hand—it was not important. "I knew he was ambitious, but I admit he surprised me."

"Surprised you?" Renie fought hard against the rising, molten surge of anger. "Surprised you? He killed our friends! He tortured people! *You* killed friends of ours, too, you bastard! You're a selfish, vicious old man, and you want us to help you get away from here?"

Jongleur watched as !Xabbu put an arm around her. Renie fell silent, shivering with fury and revulsion.

"Yes, the world is indeed full of sad things," Jongleur said flatly. "I don't care if you wish to murder me—the fact is, you do not dare. I built this system, and if you want to get out of here, you'll need me. As far as I know, there may only be five of us alive in this entire world, whatever it is."

"Four," Renie said bitterly. She gestured at the spot where Fredericks lay curled against the body of her friend. "Your friend with the falcon's head murdered Orlando."

"I was not referring to your fallen comrade." Jongleur smirked. "I was referring to *my* companion."

Renie looked up to see a newcomer standing beside the rock, handsome face blank, staring out at nothing. "That's . . . that's the first one who went through your ceremony."

"Yes," Jongleur said as the empty-eyed man turned and wandered away again. "Ricardo is our only success story so far—a limited success, of course, since he seems to have suffered a bit of brain damage during the transition. That and the larger failure of the Grail Ceremony are all thanks to my unfaithful servant, I would guess." He shook his head. "I imagine now that young Dread has gotten at least partial control of the network, he's busy enjoying his newfound godhood, handing out plagues and destroying cities. I imagine it's going to be rather like the Old Testament—except with no Chosen People." He chuckled, a quiet dry scrape like a lizard's belly on stone. "You think *I'm* vicious? You haven't seen anything yet."

Renie struggled to calm herself. "Then if this Dread's got control of the network and he hates you so much, why are you still alive? Why . . ." she waved her hands, ". . . why doesn't the sky just open up and a bolt of lightning come down and burn you to ashes?"

Jongleur surveyed her for a silent, impassive moment. "I'll answer your question, and give you the only piece of information you will receive from me for nothing. Little Johnny Dread may be god of the network now, but I constructed much of the thing myself, and nothing was done without my approval. This place where we stand now?" He lifted his hand to indicate the colorless sky, the curiously textured stone. "This is not part of what the Grail Brotherhood built. I have no idea where we are or what is happening to us—but this isn't part of the network."

The white-haired man's smile returned, twisting the thin lips while his eyes remained cold and dead. "So . . . do we have a bargain?"

Afterword

HER rap on the spare tire compartment had been hard and sudden enough to startle him badly. What she had said had been worse. "Some MPs just came and took Mike and my little girl." She had kept her voice so quiet that he could barely hear her through the metal compartment lid and the carpeting, but she was clearly frightened. "I don't know what to do. I'm going to drive." He had tried to call her back, but a moment later the back door of the van had thumped shut.

Sellars was accustomed to darkness, to waiting. He did not mind confined spaces. Still, this was torture. The van was still moving—he could feel every small bump of the road through the shock absorbers and the undercarriage—so that was something, but after two hours, it was very little solace.

He had already tried the Sorensens' private line several times, which should have connected him to the inside of the van, but Kaylene Sorensen was not answering. She was the wife of a security officer; she was probably worried about calls being monitored. Sellars had also tried to contact Ramsey, but he wasn't taking calls either. The answer to what was going on must only be a few meters from the dark hole in which he was prisoned, but he could not reach the bolts holding down the compartment lid, and until he was certain who was in the van—Mrs. Sorensen's message to him might have been the product of a moment's free-

dom before she was joined by an armed escort—he dared not
make his presence known by banging to be let out. The answers
might be inches away, but they might as well have been on the
other side of the universe.

Sellars dropped back into his system and called up his
metaphorical Garden for the third time since Christabel's mother
had made her cryptic announcement. His information model remained in complete and shocking disarray, and although several
of the new patterns had continued to change and to grow, he still
could make little sense of any of it. A strange blight had over-
taken the Garden. Whole plants were gone, entire sections of stored
information corrupted or interdicted. Other information sources
had taken on strange new shapes. The saprophytic growth that
represented the mysterious operating system had mutated out of
all recognition, as though it had received some murderous dose
of radiation, contorting its points of connection with the rest of
the Otherland model and changing the exposed areas of its contact with the metaphorical air of the Garden—those few places in
which his information about the operating system had been sufficient that he could actually study its actions—into unrecognizable, nightmarish growths, eruptions of discolored tendrils, smears
of escaping spores.

It was enormously frustrating. Something crucial had happened—was *happening right now*—that he could not understand.
The terrifying vitality of the Otherland ecology, which had come
to dominate everything else, had in the space of a few hours been
turned into something even more disturbing . . . something that
would not just dominate his information Garden, but would poison it. Already growths representing his various interests, the people he had sent into the system and those he was tracking outside
of it, were beginning either to wither away or to be absorbed into
the accelerating rot at the Garden's center.

Sellars had to look squarely at the likelihood that he had failed.
He had done all that he could—in the last few days, as his ap-
prehension had mounted, he had even reached out to several new
sources, hoping to strengthen the frail web of resistance—but it
appeared now that even in his deepest despair he had underestimated the extent of the danger.

There was nothing else he could do but wait. Wait for the van to stop, wait for someone to tell him what was happening, wait for the nightmare changes in his Garden to present some kind of sense, some answers that would allow him to go forward.

It was almost certainly too late, of course. He knew that, but it did not really matter; he had no other options.

Sellars watched his blighted garden. Sellars waited.

A continent away, for two people in a hospital room in California, the waiting had finally ended.

The equipment in the white room had been disconnected. Machines which had purred or ticked or gently pinged were now silent. In a few minutes, after the two people who still remained in the room had left, orderlies would come to take the expensive machines away and put them to use again somewhere else.

Two people who had no tears left leaned over a silent form in a hospital bed, side by side but not touching each other, together in silence like lost explorers. Their waiting had ended. Tomorrow was unimaginable. They stood in the still, arid center of time, dry-eyed and desolated.

For the woman on the Louisiana motel balcony, the waiting had just begun.

She leaned on the railing and looked out across a flat, fog-shrouded expanse of water. In the middle of the vast lake a vertical black line floated above the mist like the mast of a ghostly ship.

She had come far to find this place, this tower. The voices in her head had led her through nights and days, across pine-forested mountains and a rain-battered coast where the orange lights of oil derricks gleamed out beyond the tide flats like spaceships searching for a dry spot to land. The voices had led her to this spot. Then, without warning, they had deserted her.

They were gone now, all those voices, utterly gone. The nights were suddenly empty. In all the years of her mostly solitary life, the woman had never felt so alone.

She leaned on the balcony railing, waiting for the end of the world.

SEA OF
SILVER LIGHT

THE FINAL VOLUME OF
OTHERLAND

A DAW BOOKS HARDCOVER
SPRING 2001

TAD WILLIAMS

Tailchaser's Song

Fifteenth Anniversary Edition

With a New Introduction by the Author

Available December 2000
in Stores Everywhere